The Treasure

In Silver-Lake

Cover image: Old Firehand gallops past Winnetou
in the fog to cross Smoky Hill River.
Cover design, pencil drawings, traditional and digital art: Marlies Bugmann.
Outline and cross section of Old Shatterhand's 'magic' rifle: Philip Colston.
(See footnote after 'The Realisation Of The Magic Rifle').
Karl May book cover scans for collage of earliest Indonesian language
publications courtesy of Pandu Ganesa; Karl May portrait courtesy of
Hans Grunert, KMG, Germany; Karl May costume photo courtesy of
KMG, Germany.
Photography: David Irwin; Editing: Marlies Bugmann
Proof reading: David Irwin; Text Review: Philip Colston

~~~

~~~

First independently published
© 2012 Marlies Bugmann
© 2019 Verlag Reinhard Marheinecke

Verlag Reinhard **M**arheinecke
www.Marheinecke-verlag.de

The Treasure In Silver-Lake

Translated by

Marlies Bugmann

2012

The Treasure In Silver-Lake

From Karl May's classic adventure novel:
Der Schatz im Silbersee
Written 1889 for serialized publication 1890/91; published 1894 in book version. This translation is based on the earlier edition with an eight-chapter structure; the book edition published later was divided into sixteen chapters.

An Adventure With Winnetou

2012

Contents

Acknowledgments

I thank my husband, David, for his unwavering support and encouragement in my endeavours to create a worthy series of English Karl May translations; as of the date of this publication it is almost eight years since I began translating the first novel. David has proofread more than fifteen novel-length works, and is an enthusiastic Karl May fan; I couldn't have done it without him.

Once again, Karl May friend Philip has assisted me with countless technical details in various aspects of this text. My thanks to him for giving Gunstick-Uncle, the intrepid prairie sage, such a splendid rhyming voice; for his assistance in finding the only possible historical gun that could have served Karl May as the model for the secret sphere of Old Shatterhand's 'magic rifle'; for solving the conundrum with the locomotive tender and the design of the passenger cars of American trains; for many small, or not so small, yet important details about life in the Wild West of the first half of the nineteenth century; and I most sincerely thank him for both, designing a functional 'magic rifle' for Old Shatterhand, the story of which is told in 'The Realisation Of The Magic Rifle', and joining me in the adventure of finding Silver-Lake.

Thank you to Rolf Dernen and Rene Griessbach for their assistance with the Lewis & Clark journal research, which was integral to the subsequent discovery of the important and relevant passage in Josiah Gregg's *Commerce Of The Prairies*, where Gregg documented his reliance upon 'Colt's invention', which was perhaps Karl May's inspiration for Shatterhand's 'Henry rifle'—a Henry by name only, because the famous 'magic rifle' has a rotating (but spherical) magazine (see special article 'Old Shatterhand's Magic Rifle' in the introductory section to *The Treasure In Silver-Lake*, as well as the free PDF on my website.)

I would also like to express my sincere gratitude to Friedrich, Walter-Joerg, Pandu, Reiner, and Philip, Karl May friends from America, Europe and South-East Asia, for their contributions to the segment *Karl May Today*.

Marlies Bugmann

Translator's Notes

No attempt has been made to verify the meaning or correct spelling of foreign terms (fictional and factual); readers may research them for their own amusement. Foreign words or phrases within the tales have been rendered in italics at their first use only. Some German expressions and words have been retained in passages where appropriate and where indicated that dialogue within the plot occurs in the German language, and are rendered in italics. The names and descriptions of some regions and natural features are fictitious but have not been indicated as such, except those detailed in 'Research'. The German 'sch' has been replaced with 'sh' or 'ch' or 'j' where appropriate and according to phonetic preference. For technical reasons foreign language special characters cannot be accommodated and the normal English equivalent letter has been used instead and as appropriate, and for the same reasons the internationally accepted alternatives of oe, ae, and ue have been applied to replace the German umlaut, except where they are an integral part of a book title, or part of an author's name of a book quoted. Measurements are expressed in metric system terms, where measurements are expressed in imperial terms within dialogue they have been maintained as such. German syntax may at times be evident; May's excessive use of punctuation marks, especially the comma, semicolon and exclamation mark, has been preserved as far as practicable. Commentary by Karl May, as well as notes or references by the translator, are placed in footnotes.

The following criteria apply to all of my Karl May translations: a) verbatim, rarely possible; b) conventional (interpretational), bulk of text; c) substitution where German terms do not have the equivalent in English; d) use of correct English terms when clearly evident technical mistakes, slips and errors are encountered in the German text; e) adjustments to passages that contain: grave (and oftentimes obscure) errors that break plot continuity; direct contradictions to earlier passages; wrong counts of people and animals; impossible measurements of distances or time. (e.g. the beginning of an event after midday, the conclusion of the same event before midday of the same day); other intrusive inconsistencies; all such adjustments are documented.

At one stage, Hobble-Frank declaims a poem that he says had been penned by Heinrich Heine. Fat Jemmy points out to him that, first of all, the six-line poem is by Gottfried Buerger, and secondly, that two lines have been substituted by Hobble-Frank himself. Fat Jemmy is correct indeed: the first four lines are by Buerger from his poem *Der Wilde Jaeger*, 1777[1], the last two lines ad-libbed by Hobble-Frank, with the English version by Philip Colston.

Karl May gave a stretch of prairie in Kansas, with a peculiar appearance, the name 'Rolling Prairie', an English term within his German narration. Although there are prairies of similarly 'wavy' appearance in various locations, and 'rolling prairie' can be applied to any number of them, the term as given by Karl May, both words with upper case initials, is maintained as such.

The various dialects of the characters Aunty Droll, Hobble-Frank and Fat Jemmy have been approximated as far as practicable, to indicate an accent; similarly, their idiosyncratic expressions have been translated as far as practicable and approximated where intent of content was required; the text is as true as possible to May's own, however, it has been adjusted to accommodate the impossibility of straightforward translation.

---

[1] The English translation for the four lines of the poem applied to *The Treasure In Silver-Lake* is by Charles J Lukens, ca 1885.

The author and translator wishes to advise that May's narrative is of historic value and that the text has been translated as published during May's lifetime, and does not endorse or confirm any of the views, terms, interpretations, representations, opinions, cultural sentiments, religious expressions, or conjectures of the original author, Karl May, 1842-1912, or those attributed to his fictional characters, antagonists and protagonists alike, within the translation. Terms for ethnic groups commonly used by the culture of his era were acceptable in those times and, where appropriate, have been maintained within the narrative translations, because the use of contemporary, twenty-first century politically correct, and racially or culturally sensitive terms would seem out of place. We ask the reader not to judge.

Where an inaccuracy of fact, or of continuity, has been identified, minor adjustments for ease of reading have been effected; but it was not intended to correct or edit May's own (German) text, nor to censor or enhance Karl May's work per se (see previous page). Guest writers' styles have been preserved.

Last but not least, these are the 'vital statistics' of the anniversary edition of *The Treasure In Silver-Lake*, a translation of Karl May's famous *Der Schatz im Silbersee*:

-beginning of work on the ninth of October 2010;

-more than fifty points of research are discussed, including but not limited to errors of fact, inconsistencies, historical facts woven into the story (some referenced in German language secondary literature, others mentioned for the first time), geographical features and their locations, a few peculiar passages, pin-pointing the possible time-span and year of the fictional events, as well as comparisons to works of May's contemporaries, or those of earlier explorers and novelists;

-six contributions to 'Karl May Today' from Karl May friends in Europe, Indonesia, USA, and Australia (my own musings on May's victory in Vienna);

-twenty-three illustrations, pencil drawings, photos, digital work;

-first faithful graphical realization of Old Shatterhand's special rifle in pencil drawing, digital image, as well as colour image on the back cover;

-the story of the seven-month-long journey, from February to September 2011, searching for and creating Old Shatterhand's 'magic' rifle—after all, chapter six of this novel deals almost exclusively with Karl May's famous 'Henry' rifle.

And thus I hope to have demonstrated how involved a Karl May translation is. Karl May, the author, was often forced to write vast amounts of text at an extraordinary rate, and convincingly at that, since he was seeking to persuade his readers to accept that he and Old Shatterhand were one and the same persona. Such time pressure did not allow for extensive editing and proofing; all manuscripts were hand-written. But does a translator have to invent 'slips' and 'errors' to mirror those in the native German text? I think not, hence, not only the textual correctness such as spelling or grammar must be taken into account, but also a whole-of-text rendering acceptable to modern, discerning readers, including but not limited to the intent of content, era-specific idiosyncrasy, avoidance of anachronisms, as well as the correction of original errors of fact or plot-related continuity, which ought to have been caught by May's editors in the nineteenth century, but weren't (errors are errors, and not peculiarities attributable to a writer's style; the minimal, and documented, corrections are deemed necessary to produce an English text that is as flawless as possible with the resources available to me). There are other, but insignificant peculiarities in the text, but they neither impact the story line, nor are they a distraction to the reader.

URLs last accessed February, 2012; URLs within *The Treasure In Silverlake* are listed on my website (no responsibility is assumed for content of external websites):

http://australianfriendsofkarlmay.yolasite.com.

Marlies Bugmann

Adventure Novels

Travel Fiction Novels

Explanation of the difference between Karl May's Adventure Novels and his Travel Fiction Novels.

Adventure Novels:
Karl May wrote eight novels in a genre that differs from all of his other work; they were written in third person for a particular target readership: teenage boys, or male students, during a decade between 1887 and 1897. In Karl May's day, most of the young people who read adventure stories were boys. Thus, such books and stories were often known as 'boys' adventures'. Although I endeavour to use era-specific terms and expressions within the narrations, I also understand the need for something that is less discriminatory to label the genre! To this day, I haven't come by a sufficiently concise, one-word translation for what May called 'Jugenderzaehlungen', but have regarded the term 'adventure novels' as a compromise to distinguish the eight

special books from all other works. Besides, these eight books are not only for 'boys' but the young at heart of any age—boys or girls.

Travel Fiction Novels:

May termed the majority of his body of work '*Reiseromane*' (travel novels) at first, and later '*Reiseerzaehlungen*' (travel stories). These 'tales' of his fictional travels are best termed 'Travel Fiction Novels' (sometimes also shortened to 'Travel Fiction'); they are anything but accounts of the author's travels— May was not merely describing the exotic places he visited: he was telling of great adventures, and doing vastly more of the latter than the former. The settings may have been real places, but he had never been to those locales, and the adventures are invented, as all of May's work is fiction.

Today, of course, May's work could be classed as 'nostalgia', but they weren't written as such, although one could say, they were 'memoirs' of Old Shatterhand/Kara ben Nemsi's travels; yet, while May's works had been written in the guise of travel narratives, they are really adventures. A true travel narrative would consist of a description of the author's travels. Most people, and thus the majority of travellers, experience little adventure in life. And very few people in history ever experienced anything near the amount of adventure Old Shatterhand, aka Kara ben Nemsi, aka Karl May, enjoyed in his fictional life!

In addition, May wrote works in several other genres, notably his early works including colportage, or 'pulp fiction' romance novels, his autobiographical writings, musical compositions, the script for a play, as well as his important late works, which leaned increasingly towards the philosophical the older he grew.

Marlies Bugmann

Karl May ca. 1906

Karl May Today

Karl May's works have long since travelled the globe, where they have found friends in more than forty languages; their creator was only permitted to dream of globetrotting. By putting his imagined travels to paper, he left behind a rich and colourful legacy for his readers.

Since my first Karl May translation in 2004, I've become very interested in how Karl May is received in other parts of the world; for this anniversary edition of *The Treasure In Silver-Lake*, I have invited Karl May friends from different continents to give their impressions.

The contributions contained in this segment are thoughts about the personal relationship between Karl May fans and his works; the influence Karl May had on an individual or even national level within their culture; and how his many heroes continue to step out of his beautiful alternative reality to become an enduring part of their lives. The contributions clearly show that Karl May built bridges, and that his works continue to build bridges between people and cultures—TODAY.

A Modern
Old Shatterhand Story

By
Friedrich Abel

Friedrich was born in Graz, Austria, studied at Stanford University (Master of Arts), became a journalist, is now a retired border protection officer, and lives in Rio Rico, Arizona, USA since 1978. He is the author of *Die zehn Lehren der indianischen Medizinmaenner*, ('*The Ten Lessons Of The [American] Indian Medicinemen*'), ISBN 3-451-04405-6.

Friedrich has jotted down a few thoughts about the German relationship with the Native American Indian ideal and idea for *The Treasure In Silver-Lake*.

*   *   *

There is a light-hearted saying, in one form or another, among Germans living in America that goes something like this: 'Germans have always been the more orthodox Indians.' This refers to Karl May's portrayal of the American native peoples, and the fact that a Karl-May-inspired visitor to a reservation oftentimes feels more traditionally Indian than today's American native people appear.

American friends of mine, immigration officers at the airport, shake their heads when they tell me stories about German tourists who state as their 'reason for the trip' when completing the questionnaire: 'visiting reservations'. Then the Germans ask: 'Where is the nearest Indian reservation?' White Americans are baffled: 'Who in the world wants to go out there? No American would voluntarily visit a reservation...'.

In post-World-War-II Europe, many young Germans and Austrians felt the urge to shed their identity, because of the Nazi stories of their parents. And so I encountered a number of them on the roads of the American West, seeking Indian culture and Indian friends. Two German friends each married an Indian woman, and my own girlfriend was Navajo—we had found Nsho-Chi [the fictional sister of Karl May's most famous creation, Winnetou]. I lived with a medicine man for two years, in the role of his fire chief as well as his sidekick, to study ritual ceremonies; there were other Germans who chose similar experiences. I accompanied my medicine man until he died, and then was invited to bury him: 'You were like a son to him and he called you *son*.' My relationship with him was more intense than with my biological father.

Nevertheless, the Indians were sceptical and puzzled about the positive attitude of the Germans and their efforts to befriend them almost to the point of ingratiating themselves with the native inhabitants. 'What do they want? Why are they doing this?' But once Karl May was explained to them, they understood that it was a kind of 'Lone Ranger and sidekick Tonto' story, with the Indian being the Lone Ranger. Almost all of them took it in their stride, and from there developed life-long, meaningful friendships. Those were not simply imaginary, romanticized, casual contacts, but rather genuine relationships that sprung from a Karl-May-literature origin. Of course, Karl May is almost genetically anchored within the German and Austrian culture, the people do not even have to read his works anymore; the love for the Native American Indians is a fixed part of the German way of life, often ridiculed by others, and many times not confessed by the individual because he/she is embarrassed to admit it; but it is there, it exists just like the proverbial German loyalty, diligence, quality and punctuality. I know from experience that German friends are for life, American friendships are much more fleeting.

In the meantime, several books have been written about the era of communist East Germany after the Second World War, during which the Karl-May-inspired enthusiasm for the Native American Indians helped thousands of Germans to survive until the fall of the wall. During my work as a journalist for STERN, a German high-profile magazine, I visited one such Indian club and witnessed how the members lived in teepees on the weekend, learnt to speak Lakota, and sat around the powwow drum dressed in their buckskin outfits. They survived intact because of Karl May; communism left them almost untouched because they had built a cultural wall around themselves by pretending to be Indians. Consequently, the American West and the Indian reservations are the primary travel destinations for many former East Germans.

I sense within myself that 'being American Indian' is as much a part of my identity, as my Austrian origin and the German language are. This is neither an artificial construct, nor a whim, it is real, it feels genetic, and of course the root of it lies with Karl May and his fantastic idea that Whites and Indians could live together in brotherhood. (It is a shame that this sentiment didn't carry over to the German attitude towards the Jewish people, and that it didn't create more tolerance in that respect.) While an American might have feelings of guilt, and negative impulses towards a Native American, a German approaches him completely uninhibited: 'He's a brother, I've known him since childhood.' Germans want to relive the Shatterhand-Winnetou experience; and why not? This unique approach has in reality created many good relationships... and endless wonderment among the Indians: 'What is it with these Germans? Why do they like us?'

A small story to conclude: I have regular contact with a Hopi woman who holds a well-paid position within a government department. Her first marriage was to a Karl-May-inspired German; but he was a scoundrel. After the divorce, she married his best friend, Peter, also a German. Peter suffered a stroke eight years ago and is permanently incapacitated as a consequence. The Indian woman is caring for him, as well as the two children; she sticks with him, and attends to the finances because he doesn't have a penny, never had insurance—what a story! Nsho-Chi is taking care of stroke victim Old Shatterhand. The real tales are even better than the fictional ones.

Friedrich Abel, USA, February 2011

Karl May And The Treasure In Silver-Lake

By

Walter-Joerg Langbein

Walter-Joerg studied Protestant theology in Erlangen and Muenster, Germany, before he became a freelance writer. To date around thirty non-fiction works from his pen have been published, in the field of frontier science. Langbein's works have been translated into various languages. In the year 2000 he was awarded the *Prize for Exopsychology of the Dr.-Andreas-Hedri-Foundation* at the University of Berne, Switzerland. His latest work is *2012—Endzeit und Neuanfang. Die Botschaft der Mayas*, (*2012—Endtime and New Beginning. The Message Of The Maya*) Muenchen 2009; ISBN 978-3-7766-2618-6.

Walter-Joerg is drawing parallels between his own and Karl May's philosophy on life for *The Treasure In Silver-Lake.*

*   *   *

In 1842, Karl May was born as the fifth of fourteen children, nine of which died within several months of birth. He was facing a life of privation. Yet the boy Karl received extra tuition, as well as private composition and music lessons.

It appeared as though Karl was going to do well; although a teacher's life would have been a rather modest one, it would nevertheless have been one without hunger and hardship. But fate cruelly intervened. Through intrigues he was accused of criminal offences and he strayed onto the wrong path.

Many of his judges were of the opinion that he would end his life as a lawbreaker. Harmless pranks, deemed crimes at the time, earned him harsh prison sentences. But gaol was unable to break Karl May's spirit: he fled into a world of fantasy. During his childhood, his grandmother introduced him to the realm of fairytales. As an adult, Karl May created his own world of fables.

Karl May could have ended up as an impoverished weaver. Or he could have become an insignificant teacher, and no one would remember him today. Or Karl May could have been pulled increasingly deeper into the world of crime and died in prison as an aged convict. Ironically put: he was given the choice of several paths into misery.

However, Karl May fled into his world of fantasy. He made astonishingly precise plans about the works he was going to create as a writer. And that's the road he took—the poet from Saxony. He created—for himself as much as for us, his readers—his own world of the Orient and of the Wild West. He penned exciting adventures, expansive, complex colportage, as well as a set of philosophical late works.

Within his travel tales and novels he turned from a man persecuted by the law to one who brought criminals to justice. He, who found himself falsely written off as a wrongdoer, fought for law and order in his fiction works. More often than not it was his alter ego, the fictional hero, who brought about victory for justice, while the law played an ineffective role, if any.

In his later years May insisted that his novels were merely something akin to 'finger exercises'—preliminary studies for his real work: his philosophical writings. Nevertheless, it is an indisputable fact that Karl May owes his international fame to his novels. Had May restricted himself to philosophical matters, he would certainly not have become one of the most successful fiction writers of all time.

The Treasure In Silver-Lake is one of Karl May's most exciting works, indeed one of his best. It has been captivating readers for one hundred and twenty years: in the form of successful adventure literature, unusually harsh in some parts, but also full of humour in others.

And yet, *The Treasure In Silver-Lake*, which is available in an excellent English translation at last, also explores profound matters. This work, published first in 1890/91, already deals with the contest between the most diverse interests—or the most diverse worlds.

On one hand there is the search for material gains without consideration for morals and ethics; the toughest competitor wins, the most unscrupulous will hold the gold in his hands in the end. Really? In opposition, there is the righteous element, the powers of the good. The honest human being strives for wealth of a different kind: for the treasures of virtue...for spiritual value, not material wealth.

Evil is greedy for the silver treasure, lies, steals and kills—just like the European scum that destroyed ancient civilizations in Central and South America in order to accumulate as much material wealth as possible. Evil perishes—in the novel, in the moral fairytale. The good element wins.

The righteous element in *The Treasure In Silver-Lake* by no means spurns all material prosperity. One is content with the necessities and abstains from exploitation. If silver stands for worldly possessions, then it is the gold of the human soul that symbolizes the true treasure for Karl May.

Karl May's *The Treasure In Silver-Lake* is a fairytale in a Wild West costume. Like it does in every fairytale, the good wins over evil: and that gives us hope—subliminally or consciously; good can be victorious! The noble element stands above the mundane.

Karl May's novels are accounts of journeys into the human soul; but in contrast to most theological or philosophical works, they are anything but dreary and boring—on the contrary, they are rather captivating and exciting! They touch our hearts, just like beautiful fairytales do. Fairytales, however, are so much more 'real' than any other 'documentary'.

In my opinion, Karl May is the last of the great tellers of fairytales. I cannot possibly pay a greater compliment to an author. With admiration and gratitude I bow to the great Saxon who gave us so many great gifts.

I wish the splendid translation of May's *The Treasure In Silver-Lake* the deserved great success. I'm sure Karl May would have grown very fond of Marlies Bugmann.

Walter-Joerg Langbein, Germany, March 2011
Translated: Marlies Bugmann

Karl May In Indonesia

By
Pandu Ganesa

P andu Ganesa has always been enthusiastic about Karl May's works, and since 2000 is the driving force behind Paguyuban Karl May Indonesia (PKMI), the Karl May Society of Indonesia, a large, and growing group of Karl May enthusiasts on the world's largest archipelago. Pandu was born in Kediri, East Java, has studied at the University of Santo Tomas, in Manila, lives in Jakarta, Indonesia, knows various languages (Kromo Inggil, Ngoko Alus, Ngoko Kasar, Indonesian, English, and Filipino) and has recently travelled along the 'trails of Karl May' when he visited the US. His book *Menjelajah Negeri Karl May* is the only book about Karl May in the Indonesian language, the publication of which was financed by the Ford Foundation. The title literally means: *Across The Land Of Karl May*, which is an apt title for this book; it contains more than fifty photographs, and was published in 2004 by Pustaka Primatama, ISBN 979973763X. It is available from http://tokowinnetou.com, numbers are limited.

Pandu sheds light on how Karl May came to Indonesia for *The Treasure In Silver-Lake*.

*   *   *

Karl May's books had probably already landed in Indonesia while the author was still alive, but no later than when the Dutch versions, published in The Netherlands, became popular in the early nineteen hundreds. I personally have a 1915 edition of the first Dutch edition of *Satan and Ischariot*. The first Indonesian vice president, Mohammad Hatta, writes in his biography that Karl May's books in those days were extremely popular among the teenagers in Batavia[1]. The books were not only read by the Dutch people living in Indonesia, but also by the Indonesians who spoke Dutch. This was also mentioned by Theodor Baltrusch, (Dipl.-Ing.) in the article titled: *Wie denkt man in Indien[2] ueber Karl May* 'What is Indonesia's opinion about Karl May?', an article written for the 1926 Karl-May yearbook in Germany (translated by Marlies Bugmann, 2010), when he wrote: "In Indonesia, Karl May has had a loyal readership for approximately fifteen years. Unaffected by the Karl May turmoil [in Germany/Europe], they won't let anything spoil their enjoyment of his works." A former Indonesian general, Brigadier General Suhario, a hero during the war of independence in November 1945), who had read May's novels during the 1930s, and who was interviewed for our film *100 Years of Karl May In Indonesia*, (2010) confirmed it. The film was screened at the Goethe Institute, Jakarta, on 22 December 2010, to commemorate 60 years of Karl May's work in the Indonesian language (1950-2010); the film has no English subtitles at this point.

---

[1] Old name of Jakarta.

[2] The geographical reference in German language to 'Indien' (India) is misleading. In earlier times, Indonesia was referred to as 'Niederlaendisch Indien' in German language, which means 'Dutch East Indies', or 'Netherlands' East Indies'. In German language there was no distinction made between 'India' and 'Indies' in spelling. Both were referred to as 'Indien', with Indonesia having been prefixed with the extra word 'Niederlaendisch'.

Prof John David Legge, AO, in his book, published in 1988, *Intellectuals and Nationalism in Indonesia: A Study of the Following Recruited by Sutan Sjahrir in Occupation Jakarta (Cornell Modern Indonesia Project)*[3] wrote that the youth of the Indonesian elite involved in the movement towards Indonesian independence in the 1930s, under the guidance of Sutan Sjahrir (the first Indonesian Prime Minister) were also avid readers of Karl May, which may have fuelled their aspirations towards independence. The government of the time supplied the schools with Dutch books, including works by Jules Verne, Mark Twain, and Karl May, among others, for the students to learn the language because of the ethnic policy of the Dutch colonialists during the early 20th Century. This led to the drawing of parallels between the struggle of the Indonesian people against colonialist powers, and the Red Indians' struggle against the palefaces. Sjahrir himself read Karl May, which was confirmed by Rudolf Mrázek, Professor of History at the University of Michigan, in his book *Sjahrir: politics and exile in Indonesia*, 1994[4].

During the 1930s, in an attempt at promoting local literature for the general education of the indigenous people, the colonial government, through the Balai Pustaka publisher, distributed either local literature in Malay and Indonesian languages, or works that were translated into those languages. Among them, so the story goes, were May's works. But Old Shatterhand was cancelled because the rumours of Karl May's bad character as a 'swindler' had seeped through to Indonesia—believe it or not. Frits Roest from The Netherlands has researched especially that chapter in the history of Karl May in Indonesia; he says: "In the early 1900s, the Dutch colonial administration of the Netherlands' East Indies had reformed their educational policy and needed to provide reading material for the new students. To this end, a Committee was created (Commissie voor de Volkslectuur or Balai Pustaka) charged with the task of identifying suitable books to be translated into the local languages (Malay, Javanese, Sundanese, Madurese). In the first instance, they published traditional literature, popular folk stories and classical tales like the Mahabharata.

---

[3] Indonesian language edition quoted: John D Legge : *Kaum Intelektual dan Perjuangan Kemerdekaan : Peranan Kelompok Syahrir*, Grafiti Press, Jakarta, 1993.
[4] Indonesian language edition quoted: Rudolf Mrázek: *Syahrir: Politik dan Pengasingan di Indonesia*, Yayasan Obor Indonesia, Jakarta, 1996.

The translated modern books were either educational (e.g. addressing hygiene, health, agriculture, industry, radio, sports) or popular adventure books with a romantic mixture of adventures, fighting and love (e.g. Marryat, Malot, Curwood, Jules Verne, Mark Twain, Dickens, Cervantes, Sven Hedin etc).

Frits Roest writes: "Although Karl May was by far the most popular author in the Netherlands in the 1910s-1930s, his work was not translated because of the negative opinion about May and his work from the leading educationalists of the time.

"This did not mean that the leaders of the future independence movement had no access to Karl May's work. The well-educated elite were fluent in Dutch, and May's work was immensely popular among the Dutch in the East Indies as well, so they could easily get hold of it. One of the first batches of 'rebels' admitted later that reading May's work had contributed to his awareness of the need for freedom for his people.

"Where can this information be found? This is the result of my own research on 19th century adventure stories including May and Jules Verne, mostly derived from newspaper articles from the 1920s-1930s now available in digitized form. [...]"5

During the Japanese occupation of Indonesia there were no Karl May publications at all.

After Indonesia's freedom from colonialization in 1945, the war of independence ravaged the country until 1949. After Indonesia claimed sovereignty in December 1949, the Dutch publisher, Noordhoff-Kolff NV, invested in Karl May works and published several novels for students in Jakarta in the national language, or Bahasa6 Indonesia. Some of the titles translated and published were: *Raja Minyak* (*Oil Prince*) (1950), *Disudut-sudut Balkan* (*In the Gorges of the Balkans*) (1951), *Winnetou Gugur* (*Winnetou's Death*) (1952), and *Wasiat Winnetou* (*Winnetou's Testament*) (1954). Of course the publisher used Dutch editions, such as those of former Dutch publisher H.J.W. Becht.

By the late 1950s, the Dutch companies were 'nationalized', and with that Noordhoff-Kolff NV publishers were renamed to Pradnyaparamita and became a government-owned company.

---

5 Private message from Frits Roest, The Netherlands, 17 September 2011, to clarify the circumstances of how the gossip about 'Karl May's bad character as a swindler' came to infiltrate Indonesian society. Thank you Frits.
6 Bahasa means 'language'

They published twenty-five titles between 1961 and 1980 (including the four titles mentioned above during the 1950s, but in the new, modern Indonesian writing). In addition to the Dutch editions of H.J.W. Becht, they also used those of Schoonderbeek, as well as others, which were abridged versions. An interesting note to that period is the fact that the Indonesian publisher also translated the introductions to the Dutch editions, probably those of the Schoonderbeek books, in which it was said that the journeys of Karl May were real, that he visited America three times, and that the original rifles (the silver rifle, the Henry rifle and the bear killer) were held in Radebeul, among other things. For forty years, right up to 2000, the readers were so impressed with the statement of his travels that they disregarded magazine articles translated from German language publications that stated Karl May was a swindler, had been to prison, and had never set foot on American soil. The confusion lasted until the beginning of the Internet era.

In 2000, the Indonesian Karl May Society began to untangle the matter, with the help of the Internet, and started a self-financed program to publish Karl May's works from the texts made available through the Karl May Gesellschaft's website[7], and were lucky enough to find a big publisher, Kepustakaan Populer Gramedia (KPG), Jakarta, who produced *Dan Damai di Bumi!*, *And Peace on Earth!*, in 2002. There have been very few German-to-Bahasa Indonesia translators; some books were translated by one translator, others by six or seven translators over a lengthy period of time, as it is a huge task. People have even called it the 'trials and tribulations' project. There are also several editors involved: one to edit and polish the meaning of the text, the other to ensure the book is written in Karl May's style. But one important link in the chain is the cooperation between so many like-minded Karl May enthusiasts from around the world.

The books produced during the 1960s experienced a third or fourth reprint within a two-decade period. This means between nine and twelve thousand copies per title. Moreover, during the 1970s, the minister for education ordered the publisher to print a special edition, counting forty thousand copies, of *Winnetou I*, for the education department in Indonesia. It's been said that *In The Gorges of the Balkans* experienced a similar treatment, although I personally have no copy, and can therefore neither elaborate nor confirm it.

---

[7] http://www.karl-may-gesellschaft.de

At the beginning of the twenty-first century, *Winnetou I* has already experienced a six-fold reprint, totalling eighteen thousand copies, *Winnetou II* five thousand, *Winnetou III* nine thousand, and *Winnetou IV* two thousand copies.

Maybe Indonesian Winnetou fans do not want to find out that their hero dies in *Winnetou III*.

As of the publishing of this translation of *The Treasure In Silver-Lake*, the Karl May Society in Indonesia has published twenty-one original texts, among them Karl May's autobiography *My Life And My Aspirations, And Peace On Earth!*, a volume of short stories, a series of comics, and many others; the journey is still continuing. We do not know whether we will ever accomplish the translation and publishing of all of Karl May's works. Let Manitou decide.^{endnote}

Why do Indonesians like Karl May? There is an epic in Indonesia, which originated in India and is called *Wayang*[8]; it is performed in the form of a puppet shadow play; there is one master player on stage who performs the story during the night from nine o'clock in the evening to five o'clock in the morning (even without a rest room break). The story or stories are derived from the ancient epics Mahabharata and Ramayana. Everyone in Indonesia knows the *Wayang* stories (at least the members of the more mature generation, the young people nowadays seem more familiar with *Manga* stories). The *Wayang* epic is talking about the never-ending battle between good and evil. This, again, draws parallels with May's stories, as well as with his 'Hakawati style' of narration, therefore his novels have an air of familiarity about them for the Indonesian readership.

When Gramedia, the largest publisher in Indonesia, asked around twenty-two Indonesian authors, who contributed works for a new book, what kind of works had inspired them to follow a writing career, ten or so mentioned the Dutch Karl May books, the 1950s translations, and the younger among them the 1960s Karl May books.

Aside from that, the archipelago that is today known as Indonesia had been colonialized, in turn, by the Portuguese, the Spanish, the Dutch, and the British for hundreds of years; the fighting spirit against a colonizing power is almost genetic, and a

---

[8] To see *Wayang* performed, you may wish to watch the movie *The Year of Living Dangerously*, which won an Oscar, with Mel Gibson in the male lead, based on the novel by Australian author Christopher John Koch.

similar fighting spirit clearly also emanates from May's stories. As oppressed people, the Indonesians have understood the sorrow of the American Indian very well.

But the story of Karl May in Indonesia continues. Here is a short snippet of trivia from the present time: Although Indonesians are not wealthy people, and travelling abroad is far too costly, and equates to a luxury that is out of reach, we are nevertheless able to follow Karl May's trails—as he described them in *And Peace On Earth!* One Karl May enthusiast visited Dschebel Mukattam, and one of the hotels in which May stayed near the pyramids in Egypt; another visited Point de Galle, in Ceylon. I visited the hotel where May took lodgings in Penang, Malaysia; and someone else travelled to Ulhelee (Aceh) Port, and of course visited the hotel where May lived during his stay in Padang.

The history of the first Bahasa Indonesia Karl May books:
The three images in the collage on the previous page are the first Karl May hard cover books in Bahasa Indonesia, *The Oil Prince*, or *Radja Minjak*. Volume one is in the background, volume two on the bottom left; they are of identical art and design, only the colours differ. The image on the bottom right is that of the first volume (*Djilid I*) imprint page. The second volume (*Behagian Kedua*) imprint page is not pictured. These are valuable historical documents, especially when considering under what kind of circumstances these books came into existence.

In 1950, two Dutch publishing companies, Noordfhoff and Kolff, merged into Noordhoff-Kolff NV. They published *The Oil Prince* in Bahasa Indonesia, in 2 volumes. Those books were in hard cover, and so were three more titles, eight volumes in total, including *Radja Minjak*, as each of the titles was published in two volumes. Hard cover books were a rare commodity in Indonesia, given the fact that the country was extremely poor; hence the two volumes, to make them more affordable.

The imprint page pictured for *Radja Minjak* reveals a translator's name: R.M. Soedibio Soewardipoetro. R.M. stands for 'Raden Mas', or 'Earl'. Soewardipoetro was a member of the Indonesian royal family, and thus educated and fluent enough in Dutch to translate a Karl May novel.

However, the most remarkable name of a Karl May translator appears on the imprint page of *In the Gorges of the Balkans*, or *Disudut-sudut Balkan* (see collage opposite). It was translated by W.J.S. Poerwodarminta; the gentleman was the first Indonesian to write an Indonesian dictionary, therefore the readers knew him well. In short, the Indonesian Karl May books received very special, even royal treatment.

Not only do most of the two-volume hard covers have identical covers in colour as well as title (you'll have to open a book and start reading to find out which of the two volumes it is), but the manner in which other Karl May novels were translated is also mind-boggling.

In the endnote the reader will find the following listing: Published by *Pustaka Dua Tiga* in the 1960s, *Winnetou I* (in 6 volumes of very small trim sizes), and *Winnetou II* (in 5 volumes of very small trim sizes). Why? So that the selling price would be similar, and no higher than, the price of one kilogram of rice. In those days, the Indonesian economy was so bad, it was better to eat rice, than to buy a book, unless the price of a book was kept low.

Pustaka Dua Tiga was a small family venture. A seventeen-year-old teenage boy, Ludwig Suparmo, translated *Winnetou I* and his twenty-one-year-old brother, Wally, translated *Winnetou II*, both young men also created cover art and illustrations. Their fifteen-year-old sister did the typewriting. The father, who was the manager of erstwhile Dutch Printing Mill, van Dorp in Semarang, Central Java, published the books. I met the three siblings in 2000; they had no idea at the time that the publisher Pradnyaparamita in Jakarta was publishing the same Karl May novels.

After the hard cover editions by Noordhoff-Kolff NV no other Karl May books were published by a commercial publisher for several years, until, at the beginning of the 1960s, a chance find in a flea market reignited interest in Karl May books, so the rumour goes.

An employee of the publishing house Pradnyaparamita (formerly Noordhoff-Kolff NV), who spoke Dutch, strolled around the flea market and found a Dutch book. It was a Karl May novel. He took it back to his employer and enthusiastically proclaimed that it was a wonderful book. The publisher agreed, and so Karl May's novels were again translated into Bahasa Indonesia and published.

But not everything went smoothly. Pradnyaparamita started to release their version of *Through The Desert*, a three-volume edition; the first and second volumes were indeed published in the 1960s, however, the third volume never made it, the manuscript was lost. It wasn't until the beginning of the twenty-first century, when the Society re-translated the novel and published it in its entirety, that the readers were able to find out the conclusion to the story—they had to wait for forty years. The rest, as they say, is history.

Pandu Ganesa, Indonesia, September 2011

The Adventures of Winnetou, Old Shatterhand & Co

By
Reiner Boller

R einer Boller has a degree in business economics, and is working as a financial accountant in the public sector. He is actively documenting the careers of Hollywood actors, and has dedicated the past few years to establishing countless international contacts with professionals in the movie industry. He interviews the stars of the 'golden years of the cinema'—and especially those actors and actresses who played in the Karl May movies, one of the most successful cinematographic achievements in Germany, to document their careers. He has written a number of biographies, including that of Martin Boettcher, the composer of the Karl May film scores, *Winnetou-Melodie – Martin Böttcher – Die Biographie*, ISBN 3-896-024-442; of Gustavo Rojo, an actor who portrayed several of Karl May's characters, including Winnetou (Berliner Deutschlandhalle, stage play: *Der Schatz Im Silbersee*, 1968), *Gustavo Rojo, Abenteuer von Tarzan bis Winnetou*, ISBN 978-3-932053-67-2, and (together with co-author Christina Böhme) that of Lex Barker, the Hollywood star who became Old Shatterhand, *Lex Barker - Die illustrierte Biografie*, ISBN 978-3-8960-2908-9.

For this translation of *The Treasure In Silver-Lake* Reiner is telling the rather adventurous tale of how Germans suddenly started making Western movies in former Yugoslavia.

*   *   *

After film producer Horst Wendlandt was successful in bringing a crime drama series, based on the novels by Edgar Wallace (1875-1935), into the cinemas, he went on the lookout for new avenues to success. The movies were going to be Westerns; the idea was to film the works of Karl May (1842-1912), an author who wrote a multitude of fictional adventures during the last quarter of the nineteenth century, which are exceedingly popular in Germany, and are set against the backdrop of diverse scenes and events world-wide. People in the movie industry displayed a very sceptical attitude towards the plan, and secretly rejoiced in anticipation of the failure of the successful producer. But it was to turn out differently; a new, brilliant wave was going to capture the European cinema. Years later, when the continental Western had become an institution, Horst Wendlandt's opposition would pay him a great tribute.

None other than Sergio Leone emphasized that he wouldn't have dared to shoot Westerns without the work of the German producer. But while the makers of the first Italo Westerns did not yet have the courage to put their names into the credits, the creators of the 'Westerns made in Germany' never put that consideration up for discussion. From the beginning, the American media took notice of the 'German Kraut Western'. The *Hollywood Reporter* informed its readers as early as November 1962 of the German Western, with the headline: "Lex Barker stars in Western Abroad."

Instead of Kansas, the producers relatively swiftly agreed on the former Yugoslavia as the location for the Westerns (because of economic reasons), where landscapes reasonably similar to the original setting were available. Then, they set about to film one of Karl May's most successful novels—the story of a treasure hunt.

At great expense, Harald Reinl directed *Der Schatz im Silbersee (The Treasure in Silver Lake) / The Treasure of Silver Lake* (1962). The production team was able to contract Lex Barker, an erstwhile *Tarzan* actor, who was shooting successful movies in Italy and Germany at the time, for the lead role of the good-natured frontiersman Old Shatterhand. It was only some time into the filming work when the casting for the role of his Indian blood brother, Winnetou, the noble Apache chief, was finalized. The contracting of hitherto fairly unknown Frenchman Pierre Brice was soon going to prove the ideal selection. Lex Barker and Pierre Brice formed the dream-pair of the German cinema for years to come. For other roles, too, the filmmakers engaged experienced performers, like the comedian Ralf Wolter as the peculiar 'Westerner' Sam Hawkens, or the athletic young thespian Goetz George as Fred Engel, or Herbert Lom, who delivered a truly masterful depiction of a villain with his Colonel Brinkley. The movie subsequently presented countless highlights. The attack of the 'tramps' [outlaws] on Butler's farm, wherein the Indians provide the salvation in the last minute, has become legendary.

Special tribute must be paid to director Harald Reinl, who was successful in bringing Karl May's fairytale-style narrative to the silver screen, and yet managed to create a captivating Western at the same time. Hence *Treasure of Silver Lake* swiftly advanced to become a huge success in Europe and prepared the ground for the series. One must not fail to mention the musical score. Composer Martin Boettcher created a milestone for the German film, or rather Western, with the romantic 'Old-Shatterhand Melody'. It has become an evergreen that enjoys constant popularity.

Even in the homeland of the Western, America, the movie *The Treasure of Silver Lake* won recognition as a pacey B-movie.

After the success of the first Karl May Western, the team immediately embarked upon the realization of the next adventure—the first part of the well-known Winnetou trilogy: *Winnetou 1. Teil (Winnetou Part 1) / Apache Gold*, again directed by Harald Reinl. And once more they succeeded in creating an extraordinarily good movie that contains everything the heart of a Western buff desires. The filming was once more done in the Yugoslav 'prairie' landscape, as it was for all other subsequent cinema movies in the Karl May series. The dramatic love story between the frontiersman Old Shatterhand and the Indian woman Nscho-tschi [Nsho-Chi], played by Marie Versini, which doesn't have the usual happy ending, and which includes the villainous deeds of Santer, played with especial nastiness by Mario Adorf, undoubtedly counts among the classics of the German, if not European, cinema. A Western locomotive that flattens a saloon in which *Santer* and his accomplices are holed-up creates one mighty explosive action scene. And again Martin Boettcher's music underscores the events in splendid fashion. American actor Walter Barnes experienced his first Karl May appearance in this movie; in a total of four roles he became a well-liked face as a simpatico 'Westerner' in the Karl May movies.

Of course, the huge success of the Winnetou movies inspired other producers in Germany to also shoot Westerns based on the novels by Karl May. Producer Horst Wendlandt, however, had taken precautions and secured the rights to May's Wild West stories, as well as Winnetou-actor Pierre Brice, with an exclusive contract. Nevertheless, the resourceful producer from Berlin, Artur Brauner, wasn't one to give up; he kept working on a story written especially, and after tough negotiations was even able to obtain Pierre Brice on loan for one movie. Brauner's plans were for an 'American Western' right from the start, and thus he hired Hugo Fregonese, an experienced Western movie director, and presented two additional international names with popular appeal: Guy Madison and Daliah Lavi. The resulting monumental Western titled *Old Shatterhand / Apaches Last Battle* (1963) held its own on the international stage. Italian Riz Ortolani composed the score, after a contract with Western legend Dimitri Tiomkin proved unrealizable.

After the intermezzo by producer Artur Brauner, Horst Wendlandt continued the Winnetou movie series unchallenged. Part two of the Winnetou trilogy became his next project, *Winnetou 2. Teil / Last of the Renegades* (1964). Winnetou, Pierre Brice, is permitted to fall in love with squaw Ribanna. But in the end he sacrifices his love for the sake of peace. Action-packed scenes in a romantic landscape, including a shoot-out in a cave labyrinth, create a continuous visual delight.

Brit Anthony Steel plays the villain in this motion picture. His Bud Forrester, as well as Klaus Kinski's outlaw, make life difficult for the blood brothers. Mario Girotti, who later became world-famous as Terence Hill, made his Western debut in *Last of the Renegades*. And Martin Boettcher contributed the newly composed *Winnetou Melodie* for the grand entrances of the Apache chief.

Lex Barker, meanwhile, became the most popular actor in Germany, as well as the rest of Western Europe, even ahead of Clint Eastwood or John Wayne; for Barker, the film work came thick and fast. In order to supply the audience with regular Karl May Westerns, Horst Wendlandt also made broader plans and created a huge sensation. He was able to win none other than Stewart Granger for the role of Old Surehand. Being also one of Karl May's heroes, a noble-minded hunter, Old Surehand never misses the target with his gun. In contrast to Lex Barker, Granger plays his character with a fair amount of self-irony, and thus creates many laughs for the audience.

But he did not win the hearts of the loyal Karl May readership with that. Yet there was no negative impact on the movie *Unter Geiern (Amongst Vultures) / Frontier Hellcat* (1964), directed by Alfred Vohrer; on the contrary, as a seasoned actor, Granger fitted the bill perfectly.

Pierre Brice rides at his side as Winnetou; and actors Terence Hill, Goetz George, and Elke Sommer join them. The movie tells the story of the 'vultures', a gang of outlaws that lures a trek of unsuspecting pioneers into the hot Llano Estacado to ambush them. But in this adventure also, the friends Winnetou and Old Surehand, together with the Red Indians, come to the rescue.

The movie magazines in the USA reported about this motion picture as well. But the interest was centred more on Elke Sommer, a German actress who was working in Hollywood at the time, hence she was featured as the title character for the US audience. Aside from that, several movie critics had no idea how to interpret Granger's depiction of a 'Westerner'.

The next adventure was titled *Der Oelprinz (The Oil Prince) / Rampage At Apache Wells* (1965), directed by Harald Philipp. Horst Wendlandt sent Stewart Granger and Pierre Brice once more into the Wild West.

They are to hunt down the oil magnate, played by Harald Leipnitz, who sells fake oil wells to gullible buyers, and foil the villain's plans. The dramatic rafting scene on a river torrent, as well as diverse fist fights, provide the high points of this Western.

A good portion of routine had become a part of the Winnetou movie productions, recognizable in the well-coordinated team. But the international success was already waning with *Rampage At Apache Wells*. The series had become too much of a routine.

The series created one last sensation in the final part of the Winnetou trilogy, *Winnetou 3. Teil / The Desperado Trail* (1965), directed by Harald Reinl, and with Lex Barker again as Old Shatterhand.

It depicts the last battle of the Apache chief. Winnetou is still struggling against the displacement of the 'Red Nation', but in the end he doesn't have a chance. A bullet from Rollins, played by Rik Battaglia, kills Winnetou.

There will never again be as many tears shed in German cinemas as during Winnetou's death scene. The American critics took note of the German Western wave one more time. One of them reported that Lex Barker had never before been so sad on the silver screen.

Nevertheless, the money fount in the German market hadn't dried up yet. In order to exploit the Winnetou fever, *Old Surehand / Flaming Frontier* (1965), directed by Alfred Vohrer, was shot directly after the conclusion to the trilogy.

The Apache chief rides again. Of course, the adventure is set prior to the chief's death. A nasty former army general, played by Larry Pennell, attempts to make shady deals to the detriment of the settlers, but he doesn't figure on Old Surehand and Winnetou. The film is well crafted, and offers a fair story with the usual ingredients.

However, the Karl May wave was by then beginning to ebb even in the German cinemas. There had already been too many motion pictures centring on the Apache in the past; the really big success stayed away. Having said that: Columbia Pictures acquired the rights to the Karl May movies; they were shown in US cinemas with mixed reviews.

Subsequently, the producers tried a different, but not necessarily better, approach with *Winnetou und das Halbblut Apantschi (Winnetou and the Half-Blood Apanatschi) / Half-Breed* (1966). The style of narration had became monotonous, the focal points shifted exclusively onto action scenes. The beginning of the end! After the respectable *Rampage At Apache Wells*, director Harald Philipp failed in his attempt at recapturing the artistic merits of his first Western. The audience smelt a rat, which became obvious at the box office.

But that didn't deter Horst Wendlandt, and he strove even more to emulate the Italo Westerns, which had become very popular in the meantime. Columbia Film also became involved as a co-producer for the next project, *Winnetou und sein Freund Old Firehand (Winnetou and his Friend Old Firehand) / Thunder at the Border* (1966), which was evidence enough that the Karl May movies were still being observed. A superficial story, which had not much in common with Karl May's novels, but was punctuated with many explosions, was supposed to rekindle the success on a fresh basis. The producers went looking for, and found, a new companion for Winnetou. The casting of Rod Cameron as Old Firehand, another strong frontiersman character from Karl May's pen, was a stroke of luck. Cameron delivered a believable performance of popular 'Westerner' number three. His misfortune, however, was the fact that the time of the Karl May movies had come to an end. The stringing together of explosions and cliches in the story drove away even the most loyal viewers of the series. Wendlandt finally cancelled the exclusive contract with Pierre Brice and declared the series concluded.

Enter Artur Brauner one more time. With his idea to bring another Winnetou movie in the style of *Treasure of Silver Lake* to the cinemas, he hoped to mobilize the Karl May fans again. Unfortunately it didn't work out, although *Winnetou und Shatterhand im Tal der Toten (Winnetou and Shatterhand in the Valley of the Dead) / In the Valley of Death* (1968) became a Karl May Western from the old mould. Winnetou and Old Shatterhand are (almost) as good as in bygone times, with countless parallels to earlier works of success. But the time of the Karl May Western had gone for good; the brutal Italo Western had won.

What remains, however, is a series of the most successful contributions to the European motion picture industry. Without exaggeration, one can say that movies like *Treasure of Silver Lake* and *Apache Gold* belong to the classics of the Western genre, and that Lex Barker and Pierre Brice have secured their place in the Western movies' history.

Last, but by no means least, not only the Winnetou series, but also other movies based on novels by Karl May became successes. More adventure stories by Karl May, which were set either in the Orient, Mexico, or South America, also lured the masses into the cinemas. Except for one film, Lex Barker played the lead roles. He rode through the Orient as Kara ben Nemsi in *Der Schut / The Shoot* (1964), directed by Robert Siodmak, *Durchs wilde Kurdistan (Across Wild Kurdistan) / Wild Men of Kurdistan (U.S. TV)* (1965), as well as *Im Reiche des silbernen Loewen (In the Realm of the Silver Lion) / Attack of the Kurds / Fury of the Sabers (U.S. TV)* (1965), directed by Franz Josef Gottlieb. *Der Schatz der Azteken / Treasure of the Aztecs* and *Die Pyramide des Sonnengottes /*

Pyramid of the Sun God (1965), directed by Robert Siodmak, was a two-part adventure in Mexico, with Lex Barker as Dr Karl Sternau, and a very effective folkloristic musical score by Erwin Halletz. The action packed hunt for an Inca treasure, *Das Vermaechtnis des Inka / Legacy of the Incas* (1966), directed by Georg Marischka, with Guy Madison in the lead role, was partially filmed on location in Peru.

Actor Kelo Henderson, known from the TV series *26 Men* plays the revolver-toting Westerner Frank Wilson. Spanish actor Gustavo Rojo cuts an excellent figure in the role of the Aztec *Lieutenant Potoca*. Otherwise the script of the story is too convoluted.

The movies of the two Mexico adventures were indeed shown in the USA, and travelled as far as Mexico. The tale of the Inca treasure presents an enjoyable performance by Guy Madison as the hero, and a great characterisation of the villain Gambusino by actor Francisco Rabal.

But of all of these movies shot outside the Western genre, *The Shoot* remains in the audience's memory above all. The story, mainly filmed on location in Kosovo, tells of cruel crimes perpetrated by the 'Schut' against the people. The 'Schut' is played by Rik Battaglia, and his crimes are only brought to a halt when Kara ben Nemsi intervenes. Martin Boettcher wrote the heroic as well as romantic music, which remained the only one of his Karl May movie scores outside the Western genre.

However, the chapter of the Winnetou movies hadn't quite come to its conclusion yet with *In the Valley of Death*. Eight years after the last Karl May cinema movie, Pierre Brice began to ride across the open-air stages in Germany as Winnetou again. He continued to delight hundreds of thousands of spectators each season with the role of his life. That did not go unnoticed by the German television producers.

In 1979 the time had finally come. The seven-part television series *Winnetou Le Mescalero (Winnetou the Mescalero) / My Friend Winnetou* came into existence in Mexico. Directed by Marcel Camus, it starred Pierre Brice as the Apache chief, and Siegfried Rauch as Old Shatterhand. Ralf Wolter from the original cinema cast played his customary role of Sam Hawkens. The stories had undergone a significant change: the life of the American Indians was highlighted in an authentic manner. But the television episodes had no resemblance to the earlier cinema movies, and thus big success remained unattainable. Besides,

Siegfried Rauch, a well-known German TV performer, was unable to replace Lex Barker. In hindsight, however, the authentic landscape shoots in the surroundings of the Mexican township of Durango turned out a splendid new interpretation of the Indian Winnetou.

In 1997 another new Winnetou project caused headlines. The two-part project *Winnetous Rueckkehr / Winnetou's Return*, directed by Marijan D. Vajada, was filmed in Spain. Once again, living legend Pierre Brice played the role of Winnetou; he had turned sixty-eight years young by then. But the result was of only mediocre quality; the venture didn't fail because of the 'old' Winnetou, but because of the ineffective script, a director without talents for Westerns, and a half-hearted production model. But particularly questionable were the explanation that Winnetou hadn't actually been killed, the Indian's romance with a young settler woman, and the pale villains. Not even Martin Boettcher's accomplished score was able to alleviate that; a score that rekindled old memories—memories of movies and actors that refuse to fade.

In the meantime, plans for the anniversary year of 2012 are afoot, which encompass a remake of the Winnetou material. American author Michael Blake (*Dances with Wolves*) is working on a new script for the German Constantin-Film, the company that had started the legendary movie series in the 1960s. According to a press release, the new film is supposed to tell "of the times back then in an authentic manner". Let's wait in anticipation for how Karl May will influence the cinema world this time. Howgh!

Reiner Boller, Germany, October 2011
Translated: Marlies Bugmann

Another Special Karl May Anniversary

By
Philip Colston

The Western unfolded on the screen, in expansive wide-
format colour, to the strains of grand, yet bittersweet
melodies. The blood-brother heroes, an American Indian and a
white frontiersman, rode across a spectacular Old West vista with
confidence born of integrity and virtue, undimmed by the shadow
of changing times—in past or present. After all, there were a few
good years yet to go, before the golden age of Western films came
to an unheralded end.

It was soon apparent that something was different. It wasn't
just the strangely exotic landscape, or the presence of an Indian
hero, or the unabashedly positive portrayal of Indians in general.
There was something about the blood-brothers' bond that

seemed absolutely genuine, and not the charade of actors going through familiar motions. The uncompromising goodness of these heroes seemed to radiate from a pure and kind heart at the centre of the film. An extraordinary person had given life to the world that bloomed on the cinema screen, and the credits disclosed that his name was Karl May.

In some parts of the world, Karl May is a household name. In others, including those where English is the spoken language, he remains essentially unknown. Yet in the 1960s, new audiences made his acquaintance, usually without realising it. A few of those who filled the cinema seats sensed that they were seeing something special. They could not read the books behind the films, for the only English-language translation was a two-volume abridged and grossly altered edition of May's *Winnetou* trilogy, published in 1898 and by the 1960s in the category of antiquarian books.

The year 2012 is not only the centenary of Karl May's passing, and of his triumphant lecture in Vienna. It is also fifty years since the film *Der Schatz im Silbersee (The Treasure of Silver Lake)* premiered in Germany on 12 December of 1962. This was the first film based on May's Winnetou stories, and it was a record-breaking success. It led to ten more films through 1968, as well as two television mini-series in 1979 and 1998. In all of them, Winnetou was played by French actor Pierre Brice, who remains famous and beloved for his sublime portrayal. These beautiful German Westerns inspired the very different Italian Western genre, and inaugurated for Karl May a new and enduring era of popularity.

The films also introduced May to new audiences throughout the world, including America, where the stories and films took place. Most Americans did not know what to make of these films, with their unusual sensibility and utopian ideals. It did not help that the films were poorly presented, with often ridiculous titles, and poor dubbing for Winnetou; though Lex Barker and Stewart Granger, as Old Shatterhand and Old Surehand, respectively, voiced their own lines in English in all but one each of their films. But even under the best of circumstances, the films would be a hard sell to Americans, whose pragmatic inclinations and frontier heritage engendered a preference for hard-edged, even cynical Westerns. The Winnetou films did not do very well in the English-speaking world. Yet, a fortunate few found in them a passage to a different, more beautiful, and higher reality: Karl May's world.

Novelists create worlds of the imagination to serve their artistic aims. But May's world was created out of necessity: born of despair, wrought by a quest to find good in a bad world, and culminating in a belief in the perfectibility of Man. It would be facile to say that May replaced an inadequate reality with a better one, and chose to live in it. His spirit so infused that world—and vice-versa—that he could not live fully outside of it. He was no crank or idle dreamer; he knew the difference between his world and external reality. He simply had no choice in the matter, with the felicitous result that he could with sincere honesty conquer both the iniquity of the every-day world, and his own internal and external limitations as well.

In Karl May's world, the best of men were incorruptible, and the vilest of men always had a chance at redemption—even if they did not always accept it. In his world, May could have the adventures that fate had denied him, and which could never otherwise have reached the standard of his dreams. By introducing his readers to this higher world—and so baring his innermost spirit—he hoped that he could inspire and elevate them as he had assiduously elevated himself in a life-or-death struggle to save his own soul.

May travelled to America once, in 1908, but although he stayed for over a month, he did not venture farther West than Niagara Falls. Perhaps he initially had some idea of visiting the West of his adventures; but the reality of it could never live up to his beautiful dreams. He can hardly be faulted for avoiding such profound heartbreak, especially considering how grievously he had lately been made to suffer for the conflict between his world and the world at large. But the stay in America provided some material and inspiration for his final novel—one of his greatest works—which was published in 1910.

In *Winnetou IV* (translated by Marlies Bugmann under the title *Winnetou Book 4*), Old Shatterhand, who is May himself, returns to the American West in the early 1900s; and one of his concerns is the publication of English-language editions of his works. Yet until the films of the 1960s, the defective and unauthorised 1898 books remained May's only artistic communication with a country he would have loved to reach with his message of peace and a shining future for American Indians; and by the time the films arrived, it was too late....

....Or was it? On 3 December, 1939, the New York Times published the story *Reite Ihn, Cowboy*, an account of a moment on the set of the classic Western film *Destry Rides Again*. Star

Marlene Dietrich started things off by asking, 'Did you ever hear of Karl May?' A discussion ensued, in which producer Joe Pasternak, a Hungarian, speaks lovingly of May's Western stories, which had made a powerful impression on him as a child. He reads aloud to the group, including actors James Stewart, Brian Donlevy, and Una Merkel, from a book Dietrich had purchased for her daughter Maria, during a trip to Salzburg:

> The Apache's nervous hand drew the tomahawk. Then, suddenly, he stopped.
> 'Has Winnetou forgotten his brother?' I cried.
> The Indian's eyes sparkled with joy. 'Scharlih!' he murmured.

Hollywood was a highly international place. The studios were loaded with Europeans, many of whom had grown up reading Karl May. Although Hollywood never produced a film based on May's works, his powerful influence on some of the creative talents in all areas of production almost certainly affected—likely more in sensibility than in specific detail—some elements of Westerns, particularly those films that dealt with the interaction of Indians and Whites. On occasion, a fascinating clue will appear. In *Broken Arrow*, 1950, Jeff Chandler as Apache chief Cochise (the historical personage who most closely parallels Winnetou) carries an elaborately silver-mounted Stevens Tip-Up rifle that is uncannily reminiscent of Winnetou's Silver Rifle. The entire film is suffused with a May-like spirit.

But it was the 1960s films that finally made a direct connexion between Karl May and English-speaking audiences. One result is the present volume. Had it not been for the films, my contributions to it would not exist. Yet, because of them, an entire chain of connexions has extended through the world, returning home to May—for example, by at last giving him his beloved Magic Rifle.

First through the films, and then through his literary works, Karl May showed me a beautiful world that I had not before perceived. It is acquaintance with this world that enriches May's fans for life. Mine has been a life of the mind; and although I had very early on arrived at virtue through reason, it was May who showed me how virtue could come from the heart, with equally indomitable sincerity and integrity.

My contributions to translations and scholarship, and the creation of Scharlih's Magic Rifle, are my way of saying 'thank you' to Karl May for the transcendent gift he has bestowed upon the world.

This anniversary edition of *The Treasure in Silver-Lake* was created not only to please fans, but also to forge new connexions for Karl May and his message of virtue, tolerance, and peace.

Philip Colston, USA, November 2011

Victory In Vienna

By
Marlies Bugmann

The year 2012 is not only a year to reflect on Karl May's passing, the persecution he had to endure for his humanitarian ideologies, and for his visions about peace among nations—so poignantly relevant at this particular turning point in our culture's history—but also a year to rejoice in the fact that immediately before he passed on he experienced his, and his work's greatest triumph: his victory in Vienna. In 2012 several Karl May anniversaries are marked by fans world-wide: on the twenty-fifth of February 1842 he was born in Hohenstein-Ernstthal, a small town in the Ore Mountains of Saxony, in Germany; 2012 marks his 170th birthday. On the twenty-second of March 1912 he was invited by the Academic Association for Literature and Music in Vienna to give a speech where he received a standing ovation from a packed audience; and on thirtieth of March 1912, he died.

2012 marks the centennial of both latter dates. This anniversary edition, a new translation of *The Treasure In Silver-Lake*, a quintessential, if not the most successful single-volume Karl-May work, likely sharing that distinction only with the three volumes of the Winnetou trilogy, celebrates May's literary victory in Vienna.

Der Schatz im Silbersee—the novel—was penned in 1890/91, which makes it already more than one hundred and twenty years old; however, on the twelfth of December 2012, the movie *Der Schatz im Silbersee* celebrates the fiftieth anniversary of its premiere in Stuttgart, Germany. It was Horst Wendlandt's first instalment of one of the most successful film series in German motion picture history, which began with *Der Schatz im Silbersee* in 1962. The venture was announced to the public at the end of March, 1962, on the fiftieth anniversary of Karl May's death.

With the translation of his adventure novel, *The Treasure In Silver-Lake*, I pay homage to a writer who has given me many happy hours during my childhood and teenage years. When I immigrated to New Zealand in my early twenties, I lost touch with Winnetou and Old Shatterhand; in 2000, however, the two blood brothers, together with their creator, Karl May, came back into my life, and my fascination with the works of one of the most-loved European fiction writers of all time was re-kindled so much that in 2004 I decided to translate his novels.

In 2008 I published the first English biography of Karl May, endeavouring to bring him closer to English speaking readers by tracing his life and the most crucial aspects of his career. *Savage To Saint, The Karl May Story* is available from www.karl-may-friends.net. The following excerpts of his final victory, a speech he gave in Vienna eight days before he passed on, are taken from *Savage To Saint*; his victory in Vienna was the turning point in his works' fortune as he advanced from a much-embattled, persecuted writer of what his enemies termed 'trash novels' to a respected member of the literary community. The success of his works is to date unequalled, and Encyclopaedia Britannica lists him as one of the most successful fiction writers of all time.

My translation of his best-known adventure novel, *The Treasure In Silver-Lake* is dedicated to a man who has shaped the lives of millions of readers since he published his first adventure tale in 1875. His fans have taken his values into their own lives and careers, and around the world with his books, and still do, today. Karl May was, in many ways, a hundred years ahead of his time, with his principles even more valid today than they were in the culture of his era, though rarely heeded and mostly ridiculed as he advocated humanitarian sentiments and peace among nations, as well as respect for the environment and all creatures that inhabit our planet.

I have read James Fenimore Cooper, Mark Twain, Robert Louis Stevenson, and many others, but have always come back to Karl May for adventure tales that reverberate with my own sense of being. Karl May might have departed into another state of existence, but his works, liberated by his speech in Vienna, have since circled the globe, have been translated into forty-four languages at last count in 2009, and will continue to travel, giving their creator life with every new edition.

2012 marks the one hundredth anniversary of Karl May's victory over adversity, and the beginning of the setting free of his works for them to enjoy a life of their own, which they have without interruption since that time, as not even two world wars were able to halt their advance.

The following are some of the note fragments from May's handwritten outline of the two-hour talk that he gave in Vienna on the twenty-second of March 1912. He talked extemporaneously most of the time and no complete record of this famous presentation was ever made.

What is the fable?
The earthly truths are brought to us by science. The heavenly truths come from above. They descend along the light beams of the stars.

The greatest, most content-rich, and my most favourite form of poetry is the fable. I love the fable so much that I have dedicated my entire life and my entire work to it. I am Hakawati. This oriental word means *Storyteller*. Those who don't know that I am Hakawati will judge me wrongly, because they cannot possibly comprehend me. I will tell you how I became Hakawati...

"Grandmother, I want to be Hakawati. I want to tell of Jinnistan; that's why I have to leave Ardistan!"

And I became Hakawati, nothing else...what for?

*   *   *

Item 5.

My Self: but who am I that I may dare to regard my thoughts as so important that I must broadcast them? I will tell you honestly. I herewith introduce myself: like every human being, I have an external and an internal life. Both are to be developed to become a personality. Many, very many [people] never achieve an inner personality, indeed, unfortunately, many [achieve] not even an external personality.

My external personality is called Karl May and is occupied with writing. My inner personality has no name. But you will make its acquaintance. Because it is especially [the inner personality] who today speaks to you. My external personality can't claim to be of great importance. It would disappear very, very quickly, if I weren't forced to make a few remarks about it from another viewpoint. There exist two fundamentally different Karl May's, you see, a genuine and a fake one, a real and an invented one, a serious one and a caricature who is being sketched in newspapers as a slipshod and a clown. The genuine [Karl May] was born in Hohenstein-Ernstthal, a small town in the Ore Mountains [Saxony], but the caricature [was born] in Dresden, in a colportage and trash novel publishing house, where the honest Karl May was shaped into a fraudulent grimace for legal reasons, and then sent out into the newspapers. But because the Academic Association for Literature and Music invited the true, unadulterated Karl May to give a talk, and doesn't want to hear from the caricature, that affair will remain solely in the court of law, where it belongs in any case.

*   *   *

Item 6

Therefore not my external, but my internal personality, my heart shall speak to you! That's the right thing! From soul to soul, mind to mind, heart to heart. *Then* we will understand each other! But as such I am obligated to show you my soul, my mind, my heart openly and honestly, so that you get to know me, not as I am depicted by misinformed sources, but *as I truly am*! But who and what am I?"[1]

*   *   *

May's works have been available to the public since 1963; they are in the 'public domain'. Many volunteers spent countless hours, days, weeks, months, even years digitizing May's works published during his lifetime, making them available online for researchers, fans and Karl May aficionados—it is a labour of love, you'll find them at karl-may-gesellschaft.de. I translate Karl May because I enjoy his adventure stories, and because I see the role of a translator, in this case, as that of an important link in the continuation of his life's work. It is a labour of love for me, whereas Karl May's only means of earning a living, and surviving a dreadful time in Europe's history, was to write adventure stories. They gave me some of my happiest, and most memorable times growing up, and almost half a century later I still enjoy them; and each time I head into a translation of one of his adventures, I'm transported back in time not only to my childhood memories, but also to his time, to experience the adventures, in my mind, together with Winnetou and Old Shatterhand. Karl May had a wonderful gift as a storyteller—yet at the same time he was much more than that; but one has to read a Karl May novel to find out why—and he instilled within his readers an enduring empathy and respect for other peoples and cultures. It comes as no surprise, then, that Europeans of Germanic background display a curiously brotherly attitude towards especially the native people of the Americas, with his monument to Winnetou, in the form of the famous three-volume saga, *Winnetou I, II and III*, as well as his most-loved adventure novel *The Treasure In Silver-Lake*, having become a part of the European culture and psyche like no other work before or after.

Marlies Bugmann, Australia, November 2011

---

[1] Ekkehard Bartsch carefully documented all fragments of May's notes in 1970: Ekkehard Bartsch, *Karl Mays Wiener Rede. Eine Dokumentation:* http://www.karl-may-gesellschaft.de/kmg/seklit/jbkmg/1970/47.htm.

Old Shatterhand's Magic Rifle

Old Shatterhand's magic rifle, with its peculiar, spherical bullet magazine, is described in detail, as well as demonstrated, in this adventure novel. I had in the past not found a sufficiently satisfactory explanation of the origin of this idea of a repeating weapon. The rifle on display at the Karl May Museum in Germany is a Winchester Model 1866 that still bears the stamp 'Henry's Patent'. However, it is nowhere near the design so clearly described in *The Treasure In Silver-Lake* or *Winnetou I*. The story of how I became interested in researching this particular firearm can be read in the free PDF available from my website.

In their journals, Meriwether Lewis and William Clark, who led the first U.S. expedition to the Pacific Coast, mention their repeating air gun thirty-nine times, and each time in the capacity of a 'magic gun' to forestall possible hostilities by natives. The first mention of the gun is in an entry by Lewis on the thirtieth August, 1803, which has an uncanny resemblance to an incident between Old Shatterhand and the Utah in this adventure novel. One of the more detailed entries is that of the thirtieth August, 1804, by Joseph Whitehouse; and again, how Lewis uses his air gun is very similar to how Old Shatterhand uses his rifle.[1]

Had these journals ever been translated into German? When I asked another Karl May friend, Rolf Dernen, the reply came: *Tagebuch einer Entdeckungsreise durch Nordamerika : von der Muendung des Missouri an bis zum Einfluss des Columbia in den Stillen Ozean, gemacht in den Jahren 1804, 1805 und 1806 auf Befehl der Regierung der Vereinigten Staaten / von den beiden Captains Lewis und Clarke.* Uebers. von Ph. Ch. Weyland; Person(en): Lewis, Meriwether; Ausgabe: Nachdr. der Orig.-Ausg. Weimar 1814; Verleger: Wyk auf Foehr : Verl. fuer Amerikanistik; Erscheinungsjahr: 1998; Umfang/Format: 198 S. ; 21 cm + Kt.-Beil. (1 Bl.); ISBN: 3-89510-054-4; however, this particular translation was from the book that Patrick Gass published in 1807. Gass was one of the men under the command of the captains Lewis & Clark who maintained their own diaries. Thanks to Rene Griessbach, a third Karl May friend who helped to research the 'magic rifle' mystery by emailing me further information on the above German translation, I have been able to determine that the 1814 translation of Gass' 1807 publication did not mention the air rifle at all; the 1958 (English) copy of a re-issue of a later (1810) edition of Gass' book clearly indicates this.

Further enquiries as to whether or not the 1814 German translation is or was contained in Karl May's private library, yielded a negative answer. However, the fact that a book is not, and perhaps never was, in May's personal library does not mean that he did not read it. It is certain that he made use of external libraries, especially earlier in his career, before he became wealthy. To consider the Lewis & Clark expedition journals, in which a gun was used in the way Old Shatterhand used his, results in a very interesting juxtaposition, even if one account did not lead to the other.

Early encounters with other repeating firearms, such as Colt's revolving pistols and rifles that first came on the market in 1836, had similar effects on Indians.

---

[1] The Lewis & Clark journals can be read via the link in the free PDF, downloadable from my website, see Appendix.

Josiah Gregg's *Commerce of the Prairies* was most definitely among May's sources. See 'Karl May & Josiah Gregg', free PDF from my website. When the research into the 1814 German translation of Sergeant Patrick Gass' journal of the Lewis & Clark expedition furnished no mention of Lewis' 'magic rifle' whatsoever, I suggested looking towards Josiah Gregg again; and a long-term Karl May friend, Philip Colston, pointed out an obscure but very important passage where Josiah Gregg extols the virtues of Colt's repeating rifle: "All I had to depend upon were my fire-arms, which could hardly fail to produce an impression in my favour; for, thanks to Mr. Colt's invention, I carried thirty-six charges ready loaded, which I could easily fire at the rate of a dozen per minute. I do not believe that any band of those timorous savages of the western prairies would venture to approach even a single man, under such circumstances. According to an old story of the frontier, an Indian supposed that a white man fired both with his tomahawk and scalping knife, to account for the execution done by a brace of pistols, fifty-six shots discharged in quick succession would certainly overawe them as being the effect of some great medicine."[2]

Considering the shape of the Colt's revolving cartridge chamber (round), and the fancy design of the mechanisms of some of the 'revolving pistols', and considering further that the term 'revolver', in the sense it is used today, was not in use at the time of Gregg's adventures, the Colt 1839 Paterson carbine is the most likely model for Karl May's fanciful 25-shot rifle designed by Mr Henry in St. Louis (Karl May calls his 'Henry' a *Stutzen*, which means carbine).

Some of the passages in Karl May's Wild West stories are very reminiscent indeed of Gregg's own remark: "...thanks to Mr. Colt's invention, I carried thirty-six charges ready loaded..."

It is not a big step from seeing a revolving cylinder shape to envisaging a revolving ball shape, and since Old Shatterhand was bound to have the 'most famous' rifle in the West, it could not have been named after Colt, because Colt's Patent Firearms Manufacturing Company were far more famous for their pistols; however, Henry was by then the name that attracted all the attention in rifles. Nevertheless, this does not mean that Karl May did not know about Meriwether Lewis' air rifle, which the

---

[2] Text on pages 56 (Depart to Santa Fe) to 57 (Distances and Directions) of Ch 3, Vol 2 of *Commerce of the Prairies* , see Appendix.

American explorer used on his expedition just as Old Shatterhand
used his own 'magic' rifle—to enforce peace by demonstration of
superior firepower. It is also possible that May had seen a
picture of a Colt revolving rifle since it has certain undeniable
commonalities with his magic rifle; however, his inspiration to
create a rifle with spherical magazine may have come from images
of the Colt pistols or the many other revolvers manufactured in
the U.S. as well as Europe in emulation of the Colt.

Karl May experimented with a few 'identities' of his own 'Henry'
rifle, so in *The Shatters* (refer *Old Shatterhand, Genesis*), for
example, he wrote that 'Jake Hawkins' from St. Louis had built
his 'Henry' rifle; or in *Old Firehand*, he wrote that his 'Henry'
rifle held 'twenty-five shots in the butt', that being a design detail
of the Spencer, as well as the Evans rifles, of which the latter held
twenty-eight or thirty-four cartridges. Karl May also repeatedly
mentioned soft covers that he folded over the rifle, or wrapped
the rifle into, in addition to scabbard-like holders. In the short
story he initially wrote as the conclusion to the Winnetou trilogy,
but which subsequently was too long and became inserted into an
Oriental multi-volume saga, he wrote that he folded a cover he
himself had fashioned over the rifle. In the same story, two
frontiersmen noticed that there was a silver plaque on the rifle
with 'Old Shatterhand' engraved on it. See *Savage To Saint, The
Karl May Story*, 'The Rose Of Shiraz'. Because the name 'Henry'
created an immediate association with the historical firearm of
the same name, he also played on the reputation of it, and in a
short story called *A Devil's Prank*, he says that: "...the Henry rifle
caused trepidation through the mere mention of the name,"
which mirrors the anecdotal expression attributed to the
Confederates who used to call it: "that damned Yankee rifle that
they load on Sunday and shoot all week!"

But all the while he describes his 'Henry' rifle as a firearm with
'a peculiar-looking magazine and/or firing mechanism'; in
1880/1, his 'Henry' rifle (as well as his revolvers) still had
safety mechanisms that others could not fathom or operate,
as described in what later became known as *Through Wild
Kurdistan*: "I meant the 'Henry' rifle. It, as well as the revolvers,
were fitted with a safety mechanism that the man was unable to
operate [...]" He requested a knife from the antagonist: "...so that
I can open the hammer." [...] "I took [the knife], pushed the
safety mechanism back with the aid of its tip, although I could
have done so with the slightest pressure of my finger [...]"—it is

also in this story where the cartridges are described as 'small things' by the antagonist; and by 1885/86 at the latest, in the story *The Last Ride*, Karl May's own image of Old Shatterhand's unique, famous 'magic' rifle began to solidify when he made one of the antagonists belittle the 'toy' rifle and say: "That stranger must have had rats in his head. This rifle is nothing but a toy for boys who are learning to parade. One cannot load it; one cannot shoot with it at all. Here is the barrel and there the butt; in between sits a steel sphere with many holes. What is the sphere for? To take the cartridges by chance? One cannot turn it! Where is the hammer? The trigger won't move. If the person were still alive I would invite him to fire a shot. He would be unable to do so, and would have to be ashamed!" By the time he wrote *The Treasure In Silver-Lake*, in 1891, he had refined the spherical magazine, lock, and firing mechanism, or rather, he had done so one year earlier already, in a story called *Krueger Bei*, where he gives a shooting demonstration and turns the sphere continually with his thumb, to advance it and line up the holes that contain the cartridges with the barrel—he repeats the demonstration in the *Silver-Lake* novel; but Mr Henry, the one who built Shatterhand's famous 'magic rifle' only made an appearance in 1893 for the first time, in *Winnetou I*. Although the magic rifle carries a famous name, its design is unique and special, as befits so famous and accomplished a frontiersman as Old Shatterhand; and the rifle is the spiritual brother of Winnetou's silver rifle, just as the two men are blood brothers.

More information about *The Story Of Old Shatterhand's 'Magic' Rifle* is contained in the PDF on my website.

There appears to be a definite connection between Shatterhand's 'Henry' rifle, and the famed Hawken muzzle-loading rifle of the Western plains and mountains. Jacob and Samuel Hawken were rifle smiths who operated a shop on Laurel Street, in St Louis, producing what became known as the 'Hawken rifle', or what they called the 'Rocky Mountain rifle'. The Hawkens produced small quantities of well-made, reliable firearms, with their greatest period of production during the 1840s and 50s. They did not mass-produce their rifles, but rather made each one by hand, one at a time, like fictional Mr Henry the gunsmith, Old Shatterhand's friend, who had a rifle shop in Front Street, St. Louis, and only ever made twelve of the famous 'Henry' rifles with the spherical magazine. Remember *Winnetou I*, when the greenhorn was given his farewell dinner in St. Louis and: 'Mr Henry and two other gentlemen had also been invited, and that one of them was a famous frontiersman by the name of Sam Hawkens'? And then there's the German adventurer's remark in Karl May's very early Wild West tale *The Shatters* (see *Old Shatterhand: Genesis*) "Don't worry, Mr Sam! Have you ever heard of a certain Jake Hawkins in St. Louis?" "I should think so! He's the best gunsmith in the States!" "Alright, he made this firearm, this Henry rifle, which shoots twenty-five rounds before it has to be reloaded, as well as these two revolvers [...]" Famous Westerners said to have owned a 'Hawken rifle' were Kit Carson, Daniel Boone, Buffalo Bill, explorers like John C Fremont and other people of note like Theodore Roosevelt[3].

As an aside: The Hawken family of Miller County (to which Jacob and Samuel Hawken of St. Louis belong) traces the roots of its origin to Rueggisberg of Bern, Switzerland. Three brothers, Niklaus, Christian and Wolfgang Hachen came to America in 1750 on the ship *Sandwich*, and landed in Philadelphia. All three were gunsmiths; the famous Hawken gunsmiths of St. Louis were their descendants.

Maybe Sam Hawkens and his shooting iron, Liddy, (refer especially *Winnetou I, II*, and the earliest mention of Liddy in the 1875 story *Old Firehand*, part of *Old Shatterhand—Genesis*) are Karl May's way of acknowledging the renown of the Hawken brothers' plains rifle, because Liddy, Sam Hawkens' old, notched, rusty rifle, was a solid, reliable firearm, the likes of which only a genuine Westerner could appreciate; for it is solely the fame of these particular plains rifles that would have appealed to May for him to place Mr Henry, his special friend, the famous maker of high-quality 'Henry' rifles, in St. Louis. (The fact that the gunsmiths Jacob and Samuel Hawken had a cousin by the name of Henry Hawken, who had a grandson also called Henry Hawken, and both were also gunsmiths, but of Springfield, Ohio, not of St. Louis, makes this short sojourn into a distantly peripheral connection to Old Shatterhand's magic rifle all the more intriguing, although it is most likely only coincidental; we'll ultimately never know all of the source material May had at the time he created his characters.)

Karl May kept the mechanics of his 'Henry' rifle secret; there are two preserved texts where Karl May expresses this: One reply

---

3 http://www.varsityrendezvous.com/pdf/HawkenRifle.pdf   and http://en.wikipedia.org/wiki/Hawken_rifle

published in March 1892, in response to a query by a reader of the magazine *Der Hausschatz* reads: "[...] The famous engineer Henry in St. Louis has constructed a repeating rifle the lock of which consists of a sphere that moves eccentrically; twenty-five bullets find room in its holes. May was tasked with testing it, declared it a unique rifle, but pointed out that, should it be produced and sold in large numbers, the extermination of the Indians and the wildlife would be the inevitable consequence. Subsequently, Henry, an old, but decent eccentric, decided to build only twelve, which he sold, but indeed at very high prices, to twelve famous Westerners. Eleven of them were 'extinguished' in the course of time; they disappeared in the Wild West, and their rifles with them. May is the only one [of the famous Westerners with a 'Henry' rifle] who is still alive, and his rifle the only one still in existence. He has been offered very high sums for it, but he doesn't sell it, and also won't allow anyone to examine its construction. Unfortunately, your wish can therefore not be fulfilled. Besides, this 'Henry' rifle has nothing in common with other rifles that carry similar names."

And in a letter dated the second of November 1894, to one of his fans, Karl May states: "The bear killer is a double muzzle-loader with balls weighing two lot [old unit of weight varying between sixteen and fifty grams], accuracy to eighteen hundred metres, weight twenty old pounds; it therefore requires a strong man. Built by the famous company M. Flirr, San Francisco. It is the only gun of its type." And: "The Henry Carbine is rifled; the barrel does not get warm, which is its greatest advantage. Accuracy to fifteen hundred metres. The cartridges are contained in a sphere that turns eccentrically. [...] The thirty-four-shot rifle by Evans is a fable. No other rifle surpasses my carbine. Henry only ever built twelve at the time; eleven have vanished; only mine is still in existence."

Repeating rifles were extremely popular in the West, for obvious reasons, and they sold in vast quantities. Thus, this aspect of the Old West differs greatly from May's West, where his repeating magic rifle was essentially unique. After 1874, a great many designs and models of repeating rifles appeared; some of the most famous, in existence prior to that year, were: Spencer, Henry, Winchester, and Evans, with capacity varying, depending on the make and model, between seven and thirty-four shots.

It is obvious that Karl May had a certain amount of 'Baron Muenchhausen' in him, which is an essential ingredient for any teller of fairytales and fiction (so, for example, does he purport to understand one thousand and two hundred languages and dialects); he also had a heightened need to be respected, and never again be downtrodden, especially in the years following the decade of going in and out of prison. His first posting as an editor after that unfortunate period of his life gave him the opportunity and the means to set the parameters for, and then gradually create, his persona in the Wild West, as well as the Orient—he had been globetrotting, not rotting in prison: special weapons, special horse, Winnetou as a special friend, respect of the famous heroes, and so forth, and he kept it going, almost at all cost—he wiped the slate clean, prison time vanished, and he had been a hero and adventurer, admired by the greats and the famous far and wide; and his readers admired him. Karl May was in a unique position as an editor; he not only had the gift of storytelling, but also access to international 'news'. It sometimes took more than a decade for information about country and culture from America, South America, Africa, etc. to filter through to a general audience in Europe. The readers of May's stories wouldn't even have known that the new repeating firearms were making such an impact in the Wild West; they were busy surviving and avoiding starvation. Who was to know in Germany? Did he know? In *The Shatters* he wrote that Jake Hawkins (Jacob Hawken) made him a 'Henry' rifle with twenty-five shots. The Hawken brothers' heyday was in the 1840s and 50s, and they never built repeating rifles. May himself was most likely not even aware that 'things' had changed so drastically from the 'plains rifle' days. However, both played into May's hands—he could weave anything around what was known about the Wild West at the time—savage natives, noble savages, and Europeans *en masse* finding El Dorado, or at least exotic, heroic adventures, as was the going cliche during a century that saw some of the greatest waves of migration out of Europe and into the new world.

In years to come he became aware of his 'error', and by keeping the magazine a secret, refusing to detail it, not showing it, he protected himself from being found out, which happened a few years later regardless. Thus, Mr Henry made only twelve of those 'magic rifles'; no other could ever be found and compared. As an aside, it was in 1902 when Karl May purchased the Winchester 1866, with the imprint 'Henry's Patent', which is now on display at the Museum in Germany; he was maintaining his Old Shatterhand legend to the very end.

Marlies Bugmann, August, 2011

Old Shatterhand's Famous Magic Rifle

Sights shown in both positions.

Old Shatterhand's famous Henry Rifle with the spherical magazine and 'secret' machanism. Mr Henry of St. Louis invented it and made the very first piece a gift to Old Shatterhand. Mr Henry only ever built twelve. This illustration has been created from Mr Colston's technical drawings, which were based on Karl May's descriptions. It could be built as a functional firearm.

Henry

The real Henry rifle provided the name for Karl May's fictional magic gun. This is the rifle depicted on The Winnetou Trilogy, *with a magazine holding twenty-five charges by artistic license. (Digitally created image.)*

Colt

The notion of the revolutionary rotating chamber invented by Colt, as applied to the Colt Paterson 1839 Carbine, inspired Karl May to let his fictional Mr Henry of St. Louis craft a special rifle with a spherical rotating bullet magazine. (Drawing of Colt rifle as used by J Gregg.)

Hawken

Last but not least, 'the' plains rifle of the 1840s and 1850s, preceding the era of the repeating firearms; it was made in St. Louis and created unparalleled fame for its maker because of its quality and reliability. Its prestige was a welcome attribute for the craftsman Mr Henry of St. Louis, the gunsmith who invented Old Shatterhand's famous magic gun. It was the Hawken Rifle.

***

The name was Henry, the mechanism was based on Colt's repeating rifle with a rotating magazine, but the maker's prestige, which gave the seal of quality to Old Shatterhand's magic rifle, was that of Jacob and Samuel Hawken, riflesmiths of St. Louis. (Digitally created image.)

ℭℬ

See Appendix for more information.

The Realisation Of
The Magic Rifle

When this special edition of *The Treasure in Silver-Lake* was under preparation, Marlies Bugmann enquired if there was any possibility that a graphical representation of Old Shatterhand's "Magic Rifle", as Karl May had imagined and described it, could be included. Thus commenced a challenging project that culminated in the rifle depicted in several illustrations herein, and on the rear cover. These are not fanciful renditions; they are accurate depictions of a rifle that has been designed to be as faithful as possible to May's descriptions, and also to be a real, functional rifle that could actually be manufactured.

Old Shatterhand had two special rifles: a heavy, large calibre percussion double-barrel rifle, called *Bärentöter (Bear Killer)*; and a unique repeating rifle of small calibre and large capacity, called *Henrystutzen (Henry Carbine)*. The name Henry evokes Benjamin Tyler Henry, the firearm designer who re-engineered the Volcanic Rocket Ball repeater into the famous lever-action repeating rifle that was placed on the market in 1860 as the *Henry rifle*, inaugurating a species of rifle that remains vigorous to this day. But May's "Mr Henry" was an entirely different person, a highly creative gunsmith of St. Louis, Missouri. It is this Mr Henry who provided Shatterhand with his Bear Killer and Henry Carbine, the latter being Henry's own invention: a 25-shot repeater with a magazine in the form of a sphere.

Other than the 25-shot capacity and the spherical magazine, May mentioned only that the sphere is advanced to successive chambers manually, by turning with the thumb. Old Shatterhand received this rifle in 1860. Exhaustive analysis showed that the rifle would have to be of the percussion type, with separate caps and paper cartridges. The principal reason for this is that it is impossible to devise a practical spherical magazine that can breech metallic cartridges and permit a mechanism to fire the cartridges, while also making possible the motions of the sphere required to bring each chamber in line with the barrel.

Geometrical analysis finally determined that a six-inch spherical magazine, with three courses of chambers radiating from a hollow centre, was the most practical implementation of May's concept. The chambers of the middle course radiate in a plane at the equator, whereas the upper and lower courses are arranged in crown patterns, so that their chambers can be put in line with the barrel by rocking the sphere forward or backward.

It turned out that this layout permitted sixteen chambers per course, for forty-eight shots altogether. Because it is impossible to reduce the size of the sphere and still enable it to carry chambers of reasonable calibre, and accommodate a firing mechanism, it was impossible to create a functional spherical magazine that would be constrained to a capacity of only twenty-five shots. Certainly, the six-inch sphere could be bored with fewer than forty-eight chambers, but no gun maker worthy of the profession in 1860 would have chosen to unnecessarily reduce the capacity of a gun, the principal merit of which was its repeating function.

We assume that May, who was Old Shatterhand, kept the true capacity of the rifle a secret, for strategic reasons.

Because it is not possible to provide the sphere with more than three courses of chambers; because the sphere must have a large hollow at the centre for the rear faces of the chambers, with their percussion caps, to be accessible to the firing mechanism; and because there must be an opening at the bottom of the sphere for the firing pin to enter, and for placing of the percussion caps when loading the gun; the sphere is truncated at the top and bottom. This, combined with the machined-out hollow, and the bored chambers, greatly reduces the weight of the magazine.

The Magic Rifle is of .38 calibre, and is provided with an adjustable aperture rear sight, and a globe type front sight, both of which can be folded down when the gun is not in use.

Next will be presented a transcript of the bi-fold instruction pamphlet that Mr Henry provided with each of his repeating rifles.

Philip Colston,[1] August, 2011

---

[1] Note: Marlies Bugmann had the idea of researching the origins of the Henrystutzen, and the idea of creating—for the first time—a faithful graphical realisation of it.

I developed the design of the rifle, and contributed the unshaded line drawing of the side view, as well as the section view of the spherical magazine that was used as an overlay.

All further art within the rifle theme was created by Marlies, including the extensive finish work on the side view, all variations, the woodcut style illustrations, and the splendid and quite challenging angled perspective drawing of the Magic Rifle that appears on the rear cover.

THE HENRY "MAGIC" REPEATING RIFLE

INSTRUCTIONS FOR USE

INTRODUCTORY

The new Henry Patent "Magic" Rifle introduces an entirely new principle in repeating rifles. Heretofore, such rifles have been of revolving or turret type, or have involved a needless and cumbersome multiplicity of barrels and locks. Although they have represented an undoubted advance, in comparison to the old single-shot weapons, even the best of them require reloading after but a few shots.

The Henry "Magic" Rifle has a magazine in the form of a Sphere, which is capable of containing 48 charges. The possessor of a Henry Rifle is thus unmatched in any conflict. He carries the equivalent of eight of Colt's revolving rifles, yet in a single compact weapon of great accuracy and reliability. He is ready to face any enemy, or to collect an abundance of game, without the necessity of reloading.

ACCESSORIES

Each Henry "Magic" Rifle is furnished with a fitted case, complete with all implements required for its use and maintenance:

Henry's Patented Cap Magazine, specially shaped
Henry's Patented Hard Grease Injector with 2 Nozzles
Henry's Patented Loading Implement
Henry's Patented Cone Wrench with Universal Joint
4 Screw-Drivers to fit all screws
4-Part Cleaning Rod
1 Chamber Brush
1 Sphere Brush
1 Tin, Henry's Improved Bullet Lubricant and Cap Seal
1 Tin, Henry's Ideal Sphere Grease
1 Oil-Bottle, Best Quality Whale Oil
1 Box, 48 38/100 Calibre Combustible Paper Cartridges
     Made Up Especially for the Henry "Magic" Rifle
1 Tin, 100 Waterproof Pistol Caps
1 Bullet Mould

USE OF THE HENRY "MAGIC" RIFLE

To load the Rifle, first make certain that the Axle Knob is in the central position, and draw the Hammer to the half-cock position. Unscrew the Thumb-Nut in the upper recess of the Magazine Sphere, and lift the latter out of the Rifle.

Using the Cap Magazine, *firmly* mount a cap on each Cone within the Sphere. *Do not use ill-fitting caps.* Install the small Nozzle of the Grease Injector, place it over each cap in turn, and turn the screw until grease is visibly exuded.

If caps are installed properly, and greased as just described, the liability of fire progressing from chamber to chamber is greatly reduced. Should greater safety be desired, or should it be impossible to grease the caps, twelve or fifteen chambers at one region of the Sphere may be left unloaded, and the Sphere so manipulated in shooting that the unloaded chambers face in the direction of the shooter.

Place a Cartridge in each chamber in turn, and seat it fully, using the Loading Implement.

Put the Sphere back into the Rifle, and then replace and tighten the Thumb-Nut. Rotate the Sphere until it locks into one of the sixteen positions.

Place the Sights in their upright positions, and draw the Hammer to the full-cock position. The Rifle can now be aimed and fired by pulling the Trigger.

To fire the next shot, draw the Hammer to either half- or full-cock, and rotate the Sphere to the next chamber, whereupon it will lock into position. The Sphere can be turned in either direction, as suits the shooter.

When all of the chambers in the first course have been fired, draw the Hammer to half- or full-cock, and unscrew the Axle Knob sufficiently to free it. Slide the Axle Knob in its slot, to either the foremost or rearmost position, and tighten it. Make certain that the Sphere is locked in one position. The next course of chambers may then be fired.

The same procedure will make available the final course of chambers.

When Cartridges are not available, bullets may be cast in the Mould provided, and the chambers loaded with separate powder and bullet. The bullets must be lubricated with Henry's Improved Bullet Lubricant, or a suitable substitute. For this purpose, the Grease Injector should be fitted with the large Nozzle.

After shooting, the gun must be cleansed in thorough manner, as customary, using water as hot as is available. Afterward, dry and lubricate all parts as appropriate. It is recommended that Henry's Ideal Sphere Grease be liberally applied to the inner surface of the hemispherical receptacle wherein the Sphere resides. This will help to prevent binding due to fouling.

ALSO AVAILABLE FROM
JOSEPHUS HENRY, GUNMAKER
428 FRONT STREET, St. LOUIS

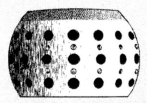

Extra Magazine Spheres for the Henry "Magic" Rifle...............$ 12 each

Henry's Improved Bullet Lubricant and Cap Seal
A hard lubricant that will not melt in hot weather..........25 c. per tin

Henry's Ideal Sphere Grease
A soft grease, suitable for lubricating the Magazine Sphere, and
other purposes. (An excellent ointment for dry skin).......25 c. per tin

38 / 100 Calibre Combustible Paper Cartridges
Specially made up for the Henry "Magic" Repeating Rifle, put up in
boxes of 48 cartridges...$ 2.50 per box

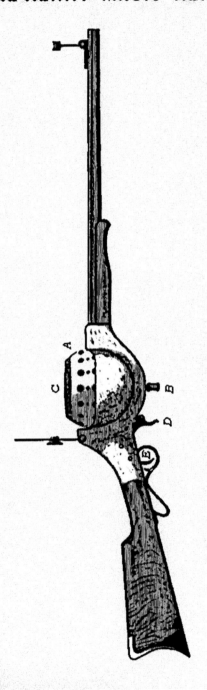

THE HENRY "MAGIC" REPEATING RIFLE

A   Magazine Sphere   D   Hammer
B   Axle Knob   E   Trigger
C   Thumb-Nut

RESEARCH BY MARLIES BUGMANN, WITH CONTRIBUTIONS BY PHILIP COLSTON, FOR *THE 2012 ANNIVERSARY EDITION OF THE TREASURE IN SILVER-LAKE*, A NOVEL TRANSLATED INTO ENGLISH BY MARLIES BUGMANN FROM A GERMAN NOVEL BY KARL MAY (1842-1912), *DER SCHATZ IM SILBERSEE* (1891).

Research

While Karl May is writing *Der Schatz im Silbersee* (*The Treasure In Silver-Lake*), he is working on several other projects more or less concurrently. During that time (the year is 1889) he hand-writes around three thousand seven hundred and seventy manuscript pages, or between seventy-five and one hundred pages per week—an incredible amount of work[1]. He begins the year writing the conclusion to *Kong-Kheou* during January, as well as the bulk of *Die Sklavenkarawane* between January and March. From April through to July he works on *El Sendador* (*From The Rio De La Plata To The Cordilleras*), and writes the conclusion to *Die Sklavenkarawane* from July to August. Between September and December he pens the bulk of *Der Schatz im Silbersee*, and then in December the conclusion to *El Sendador* ahead of the conclusion to *Der Schatz im Silbersee*. While he is working on those stories, no less than four novels, some written the year before, are being published as sequels in periodical magazines by two different publishers.

---

[1] http://www.karl-may-gesellschaft.de/kmg/seklit/biographie/747.htm (p759/year 1889)

*   *   *

Spoiler warning: some passages may reveal crucial parts of the plot, although I have endeavoured to prevent this by isolating the items discussed; readers may wish to read the research to the text after reading the adventure. Also see Appendix.

*   *   *

The first chapter of *The Treasure In Silver-Lake* consists, in part, of a scene that Karl May had used twice before in short stories, and involves a peculiar gadget: the lion, or, in this case, panther tamer's whip-cum-life-preserver. Yet only in *The Treasure In Silver-Lake* does the handle of the whip contain a propellant charge, and an explosive bullet.

The amount of invention in firearms design, during the nineteenth century, would be difficult to overstate. That century saw vastly more innovation in firearms than any other time in history, including the modern era. It is probably safe to say that, among all of the trap guns, novelty guns, and countless bizarre atypical guns of the nineteenth century, there must have been some that were activated by pressure against the muzzle. In any event, the concept is so simple that any gunsmith could have built such a gun—from scratch. Karl May might have heard of a gun such as he described, or he was sufficiently mechanically inclined to conceive the idea independently. Moreover, May does not specifically state that the gun is triggered by contact. His description would also be consistent with the user pressing a trigger button while slamming the gun into an animal.

The explosive bullet is another matter. The confusion between bullets containing an explosive substance, and hollow-point expanding bullets, exists in English as well as German. Hollow-point, expanding bullets are common today, and were reasonably common in calibres for sporting rifles in the Victorian era—though mostly after 1874 (when the Winnetou adventures came to an end; in 1874 the fictional death of the Apache chief occurred). However, *exploding* bullets have never been common. In order to be effective, they must be loaded with a *high explosive*, for the small amount of ordinary gunpowder that would fit in a bullet would have little effect on game. The explosive must then be ignited upon contact. If it is a secondary explosive, it requires a detonator made of primary explosive, and preferably a primary explosive that is also a contact explosive, such as mercuric fulminate. Alternatively, the entire charge can consist of a primary contact high explosive. The reader can imagine that there is some danger attendant to these bullets, depending upon the design. It could be disastrous for such a bullet to explode while still in the gun barrel (or the handle of the whip, for that matter). And for all of the complication and danger involved, explosive bullets are not always significantly more effective than other types.

However, explosive bullets did exist in the time the novel is set, though they were very uncommon. During that era, cartridge type guns were replacing muzzle-loaders; yet a custom-made gun for the handle of a whip would more likely than not have been a percussion type, either muzzle loading or with a screw-on barrel. This would mean loading with separate bullet, powder, and cap; and it would make handling of an explosive bullet even more hazardous. It may be impossible to know for sure which kind of bullet May had in mind, and since the text in question is integral to the localized plot on the steamer, the text has been left intact, with minor adjustments for ease of reading.

Two Indians, father and son, Nintropan-Hauey and Nintropan-Homosh are central to the story of *The Treasure In Silver-Lake*, and are introduced at the beginning of the steamboat journey up the Arkansas River. However, as the secondary literature about Karl May on the website of the Karl May Society reveals, 'Little Bear' (Nintropan-Homosch) should really be Nintropan-Komosch according to 'Gatschet', one of Karl May's language resources[2]. It is suggested that, because the word 'komosch' was too close to the German word for 'funny' (komisch), May deliberately changed it to prevent misunderstandings. Note: for this translation, the German 'sch' is being represented by the English 'sh' by phonetic preference of the translator.

And still on the paddle steamer on the Arkansas River: during a dangerous incident on the boat, a girl's life, that of Ellen Butler, is saved by Nintropan-Homosh's quick and courageous action. While both her father and mother, Mr and Mrs Butler, are present during the Arkansas trip, the mother suddenly receives no further mention as the story progresses, although the entire family travels to their destination, the farm of Mr Butler's brother. As the missing mother might interrupt the flow of the story for an

---

[2] *Twelve Languages from south-western North America (Pueblo- und Apache-Dialect; Tonto, Tonkawa, Digger, Utah)*: a Dictionary by Albert S Gatschet, published in 1876.

attentive reader, I have given Ellen's mother a couple of short mentions in an appropriate passage to correct that oversight, which does not impact the narration at all.

At the beginning of chapter two, 'The Outlaws', May describes the desperate economic times in the USA that form the backdrop of the novel. The manner in which he weaves the factual situation of the depression, which followed the Panic of 1873, and which was certainly felt in Europe, into the novel, to give the outlaws their reason for existence, is a perfect example of Karl May's weaving fact into his fiction. Although the story of *The Treasure In Silver-Lake* plays a few years prior to those events (see closing paragraph of 'Research'), it is nevertheless true that the economic downturn, combined with sociological factors from before, during, and following the American civil war, led to much outlaw activity, and to the 'gun fighter culture' that was most prevalent in the 1870s and early 1880s. However, Karl May used factual events as and when needed, and not necessarily in chronological order; the economic woes that began in 1873 were a perfect element for the plot of this novel.

While conducting his criminal activities, Red Brinkley climbs below deck on the *Dogfish*; he has to touch his way forwards in the dark (despite one hand that is severely injured by the three bullets Old Firehand had fired into it) and has to strike several matches to move along in the bowels of the paddle steamer. He then goes about drilling two holes by operating an 1800s hand drill. I can't imagine him doing that as smoothly as it is described, in complete darkness. As this volume of Karl May's novels is as much about translating one of his most beautiful Wild West adventure stories as it is about demonstrating the not-so-straightforward task of doing so, and the research required in the process, I am also documenting the slight adjustment of Red Brinkley lighting a nearby lamp, and then extinguishing it when he's done.

He also has to knock the drill through the metal cladding on the outside of the ship's hull by hammering the drill haft through it with one of the ballast rocks on the floor of the hull. Karl May writes that 'the noise of the engine had drowned out the sound of his knocking', which directly contradicts the remark in Brinkley's earlier order to his accomplices on deck: "If you need to warn me, then cough loudly. I will certainly hear it." Although I've documented this disparity, I have refrained from adjusting it because the meaning of his order could be taken to mean:

"...while I climb down." The reader's imagination will likely complete the scene.

During the skirmish between the twenty outlaws and the twenty rafters along Black-Bear River, the rafters capture the outlaws' horses, and are thus able to ride away with Old Firehand towards their next adventure at Butler's farm. May points this out several times. Old Firehand also carries a large sum of money that he is to deliver to the farm. In the meantime, Red Brinkley and the three outlaws, the only ones in the group of villains to have escaped the skirmish at the Black-Bear River, arrive at the great outlaw meeting. Red Brinkley is detailing his plans to attack Butler's farm; when asked whether or not the money, which they want to get their hands on, could already be at the farm, Brinkley says: "Not yet. The rafters didn't immediately obtain horses, while I found a few good nags early the next morning." Why would Brinkley lie to his fellow outlaws since the money is the carrot that he dangles in front of their noses to entice them to ride to Butler's farm with him? Given Karl May's penchant to occasionally miscount his horses, I'll err on the side of precedents and say that it is an oversight on the author's part. But the question remains: did May intend that Brinkley lie to the outlaws, or is the appearance of this merely the felicitous outcome of an error? In most cases, May would at least give the reader a small hint at the reason for the lie. However, as there is no indication that he intended Brinkley to lie, as part of the villain's scheming, we'll ultimately never know; and since the thought of Brinkley lying to his fellow outlaws adds just a pinch of spice to the scene (which in turn mirrors his later conduct), I'll leave it to the reader to decide and will not adjust the passage.

Old Firehand, observing through Castlepool's large telescope the direction from which he expects Red Brinkley and his gang of outlaws to approach Butler's farm, at last sees the villains arrive at a distant point. He also observes three of the men separate from the group and approach the farm, on foot. There is no mention that they have arrived on the other side of the river, and would have to cross the water first to get to Butler's farm; yet this becomes clear a short time later, when Red Brinkley and his men ride along the water at a gallop, and attempt to cross the river when they get to the ford (they are on the far bank of the river, and the three sham workers are still on the farm side). I have adjusted one sentence, when Old Firehand observes the three men separate from the main host of outlaws, to read: 'Not long after, three of them separated from the bunch, crossed the river at a shallow section, and then moved in the direction of the farm on foot, not on horseback.'

At one stage, two hundred Indians on foot join Old Firehand, the hunters, rafters and farmhands on Butler's farm to repel the attack of the outlaws. Firehand divides them into two groups; one of them is to stay on the farm to assist with repelling the outlaws' attack; there is no further mention of that particular group of Indians. After successfully beating back the attackers twice, he and all Whites mount up and charge out to assist the Indians guarding Butler's cattle, because the outlaws are headed in that direction. At that point it becomes clear that May has simply overlooked the existence of the one hundred Indians inside the farm. However, during their two failed attacks, the outlaws lose a number of horses, around thirty in the first attack alone, as their riders are shot out of the saddles; those horses run towards the farm, where they are herded inside. Of course, now the one hundred Indians have horses to ride, and can join Old Firehand and his friends to ride counter-attack with them, and to rejoin their fellow warriors afterwards. I have taken the liberty to add one short part-sentence to account for the one hundred forgotten Indians on foot: "...the Indians who had stayed on the farm took possession of the captured horses and rode, mostly double, to join the other riders."

Karl May quite frequently slips up with continuity in time (I have already documented such time errors in *Winnetou II*), and creates quite a conundrum when he lets the abovementioned two hundred Indians arrive when 'midday had already passed', repel two major attacks, deal with the lengthy interlude of three outlaw scouts, and after the second attack has refreshments served to the defenders of the farm since 'in the meantime midday had arrived'. This being a plain error of fact and continuity, I have adjusted the Indians to arrive 'close to midday', and the refreshments served after the second skirmish when midday had well and truly 'been and gone'.

At the end of chapter four, 'On Butler's Farm', they take stock of the fallen adversaries and those that got away. May writes: 'There were two fallen outlaws for every man on the victorious side'. Considering that the victorious side consists of two hundred Indians and around fifty hunters, rafters, and farmhands, and that the outlaws counted four hundred men, that would mean there would have been five hundred dead outlaws; yet a significant number of them got away, and then later combined with more gangs at Osage-Nook, to head for Sheridan, where two hundred of them descend upon the railway. Even if May only counted the Whites, about fifty of them, there would only have been one hundred dead outlaws, with three hundred getting away, which wouldn't have tallied with the two hundred arriving in Sheridan; as May writes, they combined with more outlaws later. The passage has been adjusted to read: '...there were more fallen adversaries than there were men on the victorious side', which assures continuity of the plot.

As an aside, Butler's farm lies up to sixty kilometres south-east of Fort Dodge, which lies near modern-day Dodge City, Kansas. (The city was founded in 1872, two years after the setting of *The Treasure In Silver-Lake*; it began as a tent city with the intent of becoming a cattle town upon the arrival of the rail line that was progressing westward). The Butler brothers and young Ellen ride to Fort Dodge for purchases and the length of the ride can be assumed to take one day (they arrive back at the farm towards evening, which indicates a day's ride, assuming they left Fort Dodge early in the morning, as would be the case in a frontier situation); a horse can cover around sixty kilometres per day without it being an endurance ride. They return to the farm from a north-westerly direction.

It is peculiar to note that when the Butler brothers and young Ellen return from Fort Dodge, the young lady wears a riding outfit complete with veil, as was fashion at the time. This, and the fact that she had ridden to Fort Dodge and back, points to her being an accomplished rider, since she would have ridden side-saddle as was the custom during that era; however, the story from Butler's farm onwards continues with her travelling in a sedan chair, or litter, carried by two Indian ponies, up to Silver-Lake, and when she does get to sit on a horse later on, Old Firehand is 'holding and supporting the girl' while walking at the horse's side. I've not tried to explain that discrepancy, nor have I adjusted anything.

At one point, Old Firehand outwits an outlaw and gets to read a letter with a secret message; however, in the subsequent passages, Karl May seems to have forgotten about it and has Old Firehand say that he hadn't read the note yet, which is repeated a few sentences later when the famous frontiersman asks someone else to finally read the content and make it known. As Old Firehand is not known for fibbing, I've adjusted a couple of sentences within that passage slightly for continuity; it does not impact the overall plot.

The red-haired colonel, or Red Brinkley, is described as wearing a wig in one passage, and at a later point in time with reference to the plot, as having his hair dyed with Hackberry bark. To avoid confusion, a slight adjustment has been effected for the logical continuity of the villain wearing a wig during his earlier misdeeds, and afterwards having taken to dying his hair because a wig could come off easily and reveal his real hair colour. There is also confusion as to whether Brinkley has short-cropped hair, or wears his hair long enough, so that someone is able to grab a solid hold of it, as is the case when Great Bear slices his ears off; I've omitted 'short-cropped' hair twice: first when he is described on board the paddle steamer, and the second time when Fred recognizes him at the rafters' camp. Other researchers attribute that oddity to the fact that Brinkley had various predecessors in other works that served May as template for Brinkley[3].

After the same villain has three bullets shot through his hand, and has his outer ears sliced off by an Indian—both severe injuries—Karl May does not pay any further mind to the potentially debilitating wounds, as a matter of fact, Red Brinkley carries on as if nothing had happened, and a reader might be left wondering what became of the injuries; I've been bold enough to give them a couple of mentions where appropriate.

Lord Castlepool is described as having two rifles mounted on either side of his saddle, with their butts resting on the shoe-like stirrups, next to the rider's feet. This is most likely an error of fact, not author's intention, which I have corrected. There were two desiderata in packing a rifle on a horse in the Old West: (1) The position of the rifle should not cause harm or discomfort to either the horse or the rider; and (2) The rifle should be readily accessible to the rider while mounted. Lord Castlepool might be a quirky adventurer, but he is quite adept at being a frontiersman. As he explains, he is riding a Kurdish Husahn, in other words a Kurdish stallion; the Kurdish horses are also known as Akhal Teke. One might say May intended Castlepool to appear crazy, however, having the guns sit on the stirrups, as well as the telescope case lie across the front of the saddle are uncharacteristic for an accomplished horseman like Castlepool. I beg that the correction,

---

[3] See, for example: http://www.karl-may-gesellschaft.de/kmg/seklit/jbkmg/1997/292.htm

if it seems too much of an intrusion, be accepted; Karl May is alive after all: in the year 2010, during the open air performance of *Der Schatz Im Silbersee* in Austria, Old Shatterhand and Old Firehand were joined by Old Surehand, who belongs in a different novel, and does not make an appearance in *The Treasure In Silver-Lake*[4].

This, of course, also opens the door for one other person, Old Shatterhand's Mr Henry of St. Louis, to attain an identity—and first name—of his own; his address is in the bi-fold pamphlet titled: *The Henry "Magic" Repeating Rifle Instructions For Use*.

During the defence preparations to repel the expected attack on a railway station by a gang of outlaws, Old Firehand suggests sending a security locomotive ahead of the real money train as a feint to trick the villains. However, Firehand subsequently changes his mind and does not send it; but because the outlaws are expecting a security engine ahead of the money train, yet are not aware that Old Firehand has changed his plans, it is odd that the villains do not become suspicious at its absence—Karl May does not account for that detail. A small adjustment to that effect has been made by way of the engineer loudly proclaiming (while he sees off an earlier 'special train' to Fort Wallace) the fact that the security train is superfluous, so that the spying villains can hear it.

Just ahead of the railroad skirmish between numerous parties, Karl May describes the train involved: "The passenger cars were built according to American construction. One had to climb aboard at the back of the last one, in order to get to those ahead; [...]" This is, of course, wrong. I have corrected this error of fact by simply deleting the half sentence: "One had to climb aboard at the back of the last one, in order to get to those ahead;" and have adjusted subsequent references accordingly and minimally if and where required.

There is some confusion about the kind of locomotive that pulled the train. May uses the German term *Tendermaschine*, which means 'tank locomotive' in English. A tank locomotive carried its own water and fuel, the former in tanks usually located on the sides, and the latter in a bunker usually located at the rear. However, most locomotives in the 'Wild West', during or after the

---

[4] http://www.wild-west-reporter.com/wp-content/uploads/2010/03/A5 -Flyer-KMSG-2010.pdf - Winnetou: Okitay Doganay / Old Shatterhand: Friedrich Grud / Old Surehand: Michael Allmer / Old Firehand: Kurt Allmer.

construction of the transcontinental railroad lines, were 'tender locomotives', which were supplied with water and fuel by a separate tender car. This is the kind of locomotive that would have hauled excavated rock, heavy machinery, sleepers, rails, coal, wood, and other necessities through Kansas in that era on a daily basis. An American style tank locomotive of the Winnetou era would have had the wood or coal bunker behind the cab, and since this bunker was smaller than a tender car, it would tend to be taller, or stacked higher with wood. Sometimes, the water tank was located there, too, making for still more bulk. Such tank locomotives were normally used on short lines or for utility work in rail yards. Hence the locomotive that pulled Old Firehand's train was very probably a simple tender locomotive, with a low tender to give Woodward the line of sight into the cab to recognize Old Firehand. A possible reason for the discrepancy is that May could have read about American railroad practice, taken the term 'tender locomotive' to mean the same as *Tendermaschine*, and then simply envisioned the tank locomotives with which he was familiar, since they were extremely common in Germany. The term 'tender locomotive' properly translates as *Schlepptendermaschine*, but the confusion between the English and German terms remains common today. I have slightly adjusted two passages to account for the existence of the tender.

On the subject of the fireman on the locomotive: Karl May was likely unaware that there are not just two people required to operate a train of that era, but three—a driver, a fireman, and a brakeman. In this particular case, the fireman is doubling as brakeman, courtesy of a small adjustment in the appropriate passage.

Karl May has six passenger cars hitched to the locomotive; the tunnel where he traps the outlaws in the train is only seventy metres long. Six passenger cars will not quite fit into such a short tunnel. As May has the number of outlaws down to less than one hundred and eighty or so inside the tunnel, the train actually only requires four passenger carriages, and will thus fit into the tunnel, just as Old Firehand had planned; the text has been adjusted accordingly.

The plot around the skirmish in the railway tunnel plays on a factual railway line that headed west from Kansas City to unite with the one that was constructed heading east from Denver. There are three railway construction stations involved in the plot: Carlyle, Sheridan, and Wallace. Carlyle was renamed to Cleveland

first, and then Oakley in 1885[5]; Sheridan (officially 'Phil Sheridan')
is a ghost town, and a patch of pasture today with one lot of stone
foundations located by the owner of the land as of 2008[6],
presumably belonging to the stage-coach building as this was
most likely the only stone building; the wild boomtown existed
between 1868 and 1871 and its remnants are located near the two
buttes close to McAllaster in Logan County, Kansas[7]. Karl May
was right when he wrote about the disreputable make-up of the
railroad construction workforce at the time, because 'Sheridan
was home to every sort of seedy character and misdeed imaginable
during its hectic lifespan'[8]. Wallace still exists today; and so does
the fourth station on a different, more southerly railway line,
Kinsley, as well as the fifth mentioned in this narration: Kit Carson.

Karl May's 'Eagle-tail', or Eagle Tail, was later renamed to
Sharon Springs.

When Aunty Droll tells Fred's story to the men assembled
around the campfire, ready to defend the railroad, it is in part
inconsistent with a remark Fred made at an earlier stage. Fred
then stated that when Brinkley had kicked him to the ground, he
had driven a knife through the villain's lower leg, the calf muscle,
in one end, and out the other, so that it remained stuck. However,
this is not possible because Fred and Brinkley have no chance for
such a clash, according to Aunty Droll's account. There is also no
opportunity for such an incident to have taken place either before
or after the event in question (which I shall not reveal so as not to
spoil the reader's enjoyment). I have slightly adjusted two passages
for continuation purposes: a) Fred has witnessed the only possible
person stab Brinkley in his leg; and b) Aunty Droll's account of
the incident has been augmented accordingly, and very minimally
to account for this, and also to correct May's obvious slip of
having Droll say that Fred's father had told him, Aunty Droll, the
story of the adventure near Silver-Lake, which is also impossible
since he clearly states that only after the father's death did he
become acquainted with the only survivor, Fred Engel, and the

---

[5] http://www.discoveroakley.com/city-of-oakley/history-oakley.
[6] http://forums.ghosttowns.com/showthread.php?16740-Sheridan-Kansas
[7] The region today known as Logan County was one half of Wallace
County at the time of the story; Logan County came into being in
February of 1887, effectively cutting Wallace county in half, which
created two counties of similar size to most others in Kansas, refer
Wikipedia and http://www.kansasmemory.org/item/214196/page/1
[8] http://www.kans.com/bfrahm/sheridan.htm.

story of Fred's family. Neither adjustment impacts the overall plot, or the continuity of the story immediately surrounding those two adjustments.

After the events conclude at the Border between Kansas and Colorado, there is a large scene break between the end of chapter five and the beginning of chapter six, located in the Rocky Mountains somewhere west of South Park. That, and other locations, are discussed a few pages further on.

When two strangers join Old Shatterhand and his four friends, Karl May clearly counts those two as the only surviving members of a raiding party that had attacked a camp of Utah Indians. The Indians hunt all of them down, six get away temporarily, but the Indians catch up to them a day before the last two meet Old Shatterhand, and thus: '[...]four of them were killed the previous day and only the two leaders [...] had been lucky enough to have escaped the avenging missiles of the Indians'. Yet, when the Utah chief observes Old Shatterhand's group of four, sitting together with the two strangers, he says: "Those are probably the six men who escaped yesterday." I thought it advisable to add: 'He therefore didn't know that another party had killed four more of the horse thieves', because it is somewhat pivotal to the immediate continuity.

After the foot race in chapter six, Hobble-Frank has a lengthy talk to the Utah chief—in English, since he doesn't speak the Utah language, but the chief understands and speaks English. However, a few minutes later, when Old Shatterhand issues a few instructions to Hobble-Frank in German language, and the Utah chief demands to know what he said and why he was speaking in a language the Indians couldn't understand, Old Shatterhand says: "Because that's the only language [Hobble-Frank] understands." The error in continuity has been adjusted by Old Shatterhand saying: "Because that's the language we customarily speak." The Utah chief is depicted as a smart and cunning (though superstitious) fellow, and thus would become suspicious with Old Shatterhand's excuse that Hobble-Frank only understands German, after just having had a lengthy discourse with him in English.

Old Shatterhand lights his calumet several times during the story in order to seal an agreement with the Utah chief; although the treacherous chief makes his promises, he breaks them each time. He argues that he wasn't required to keep his promise because it was not his calumet that had been used, but that of a paleface. When it comes to smoking the calumet over an agreement yet again, and another chief suggests they use Old Shatterhand's peace pipe (obviously also not intending to honour his promise), the hunter responds: "We had better take yours." The enemy chief asks: "Why? Is your pipe not as good as ours? Or is yours only capable of creating clouds of untruth?" to which Old Shatterhand responds: "The other way round would be correct. My calumet always speaks the truth; but the pipe of the red men is untrustworthy[...] The pipe of Great Wolf has repeatedly lied to us[...]" Great Wolf lied when he smoked Old Shatterhand's calumet—not his own. Hence, saying 'the pipe of the red men is untrustworthy', as well as 'the pipe of Great Wolf has repeatedly lied to us', while at the same time requesting that the Indian chief's calumet be used, is a direct contradiction. Why does he say that? It could be that Karl May simply made a mistake and didn't realize that he gave ownership of the calumet dishonoured by the Indian's lies to Great Wolf instead of Old Shatterhand. Then again: the German word for 'pipe' is '*Pfeiffe*'; that for 'whistle' (noun) is '*Pfeiffe*', and for 'whistle' (verb) is '*pfeiffen*'. There are numerous negative phrases that incorporate 'whistle' (the verb), but the most commonly known is: 'I don't give a damn' (*ich pfeiff drauf*). Thus Karl May could have intended this to be a play on words, meaning that the enemy Indian 'did not give a damn' about his promises, and intended to fool the palefaces all along. Since 'whistle' (the noun) and 'pipe' are not interchangeable in the English language, this play on words cannot be replicated in English, or adequately conveyed in as short a dialogue as the original German. There is also another possibility for the contradiction: by pointing out the broken promises of the enemy chief after having smoked Old Shatterhand's calumet, the hunter indicates that he does not wish for his own calumet to be dishonoured in this manner again. Minor adjustments to that part of their dialogue have been made.

The group of hunters, rafters, and other adventurers, led by Winnetou, Old Firehand and Old Shatterhand, head towards, and ultimately cross, a river that Karl May refers to as 'Grand River'. From 1836 to 1921, this was the name applied to the Colorado River from its headwaters in the Rocky Mountains to its confluence with the Green River in Utah. May gives a description of the 'Valley of the Grand River' that is reminiscent of that of sections of the Colorado River as it passes through Grand Canyon in Arizona. It is well known that Karl May read the published accounts of Heinrich Balduin Moellhausen's adventures, and that

Moellhausen, in turn, didn't look favourably upon May taking inspiration from his published diaries[9]. A short excursion away from *The Treasure In Silver-Lake*, and into Moellhausen's own experiences during several expeditions he accompanied, and the subsequent publications of his diaries, is appropriate at this point.

Moellhausen had travelled along and around the Colorado River with two expeditions: one in 1853 under Lieutenant Amiel Weeks Whipple along the 35th parallel, and one in 1857 under Lieutenant Joseph Christmas Ives, exploring parts of the Rocky Mountains. [10] The similarity between individual descriptions of the landscape is striking at times (without being of plagiaristic nature) and indicates that May imagined the Valley of the Grand River in his fictional tale to be as majestic as that of the actual Grand Canyon area. (The Grand Canyon received its name much later.)

There are many passages within Karl May's body of work that remind the reader of the accounts of travellers, explorers and adventurers of the early nineteenth century. Works by Lewis & Clark, Gass, Fremont, Carvalho, Moellhausen, Gerstaecker, Gregg, Cooper and others are literature of historic importance. Some certainly became Karl May's references, if available in German translation; alas, time, two world wars, as well as his widow, who cleansed his library of works of adventure literature in particular, have wiped away many trails that could otherwise furnish valuable connections. Some clues can still be found within May's texts, like those that led to Josiah Gregg's *Commerce Of The Prairies*, but others will be lost forever. Balduin Moellhausen's published journals of his expeditions into the Wild West are still in May's library, and many passages within *The Treasure In Silver-Lake* were inspired by Moellhausen's accounts. Passages that seem to mirror the texts of others cannot be attributed to

---

[9] http://www.karl-may-gesellschaft.de/kmg/seklit/jbkmg/1991/324.htm (page 355)
[10] His account of it was published as: *Tagebuch einer Reise vom Mississippi nach den Kuesten der Suedsee*, 'Diary of a trip along the Mississippi to the Gulf'; Leipzig, 1858); and another in 1857 under Lieutenant Joseph Christmas Ives (published as: *Reisen in die Felsengebirge Nordamerikas bis zum Hochplateau von Neu-Mexiko* 'Travelling in the Rocky Mountains of North America up to the high plateau of New Mexico'; 2 vols., Leipzig, 1861); (see also Andreas Graf's detailed study comparing Moellhausen's texts to Karl May's on the Karl May Gesellschaft's website http://www.karl-may-gesellschaft.de/kmg /seklit/jbkmg/1991/324.htm.)

them with certainty, and their resemblance to other reference works will remain shrouded in mystery; even a comparison to Moellhausen's text must necessarily remain slightly speculative, but interesting nevertheless.

Moellhausen's way of constructing his diary of the Whipple expedition in 1853 (by interspersing his observations of the landscape, native people, plants and animals with tales unrelated to the experience of their monumental journey, as told by his comrades around the campfires in the evening), points to Karl May's Old Surehand trilogy, where May dedicates the entire second volume to the patrons in a Jefferson City pub telling story after story, completely unrelated to the Old Surehand thread. However, many other writers employed that concept within their novels as well.

Then there is the unnamed German naturalist in Moellhausen's account of the Whipple expedition, who tells the story about how he, as a young man, fell in love with a beautiful half-breed girl, Amalie Papin, somewhere along the shores of the Missouri, a disguised re-telling of Moellhausen's first excursion into the Wild West with Duke Paul of Wuerttemberg, which was ill-fated and nearly cost his life[11]. Karl May's own fictional narration about how he, as a young man, fell in love in the Wild West with Ellen, Old Firehand's half-breed daughter in the short story titled *Old Firehand*[12] (see *Old Shatterhand—Genesis*) becomes even more interesting when one considers that Old Firehand asks him: "And you're supposed to have only come to the Wild West to get to know rocks and plants?" *Old Firehand* is set along the Mankizita River, not far from the Missouri River. While Moellhausen's

----

[11] See http://www.kancoll.org/khq/1948/48_3_mollhaus.htm; most 'tales' told around the campfires in Moellhausen's account of the Whipple expedition are episodes of his own first journey into the Wild West.

[12] Karl May created two different versions of the character Old Firehand; the travel fiction version in the short story, which was later incorporated into *Winnetou II*, is older, grey, and a father of several children; the adventure novel version in *The Treasure In Silver-Lake* is younger, blond and unattached. Karl May's travel fiction works are written in first person; his adventure novels (eight in total) are written in third person. *The Treasure In Silver-Lake* is an adventure novel. Karl May sometimes cross-referenced earlier 'events' between individual travel fiction works, for reasons of verisimilitude; however, there was no cross-linking from his travel fiction works to his adventure novels and vice versa, with the exception of a very short list of major characters, notably Winnetou and Old Shatterhand, who appear in both genres.

characters were stiff and stylized, which may explain why he has slipped into the obscurity of history, May's heroes and villains, as well as the staffage surrounding them, were portrayed in the most life-like, colourful and engaging fashion, giving them the immortal qualities that are likely one reason why his works have remained alive today.

At times Karl May utilized several resource works concurrently, as in the case of *Winnetou III*: Winnetou, Old Shatterhand and friends lasso a cow from a group of wild cattle, to obtain provisions when, in the first instance, May writes: 'Every traveller—according to custom—is permitted to kill one for his use but has to deliver the skin to the owner', which is almost a verbatim quote of Leroux's 1854 account of the custom: '...that when he travelled there in earlier times, everyone was permitted to kill as many steers as he wished, to obtain meat for provisions, but it was common practice to deliver the hide of the slaughtered beast to the owner.' Joaquin Antoine Leroux was the guide of Whipple's expedition along the 35th parallel; when the expedition arrived in California in 1854, Leroux reminisced about earlier times; Moellhausen re-told Leroux's accounts in his German publication.

In the second instance, only a couple of pages later, May quite clearly utilizes Josiah Gregg's *Commerce Of The Prairies*, 1844: Old Shatterhand and his friends have an encounter with Mexican vaqueros and May details at length the vaqueros' outfits, their weapons, as well as the horses' saddles and tack, from the original sombrero: '...low crowned hat with wide brim...', down to the *cola de pato*: '...duck's tail'. (See PDF on my website.)

Regardless of whether or not Karl May drew inspiration and details from the works of other writers, real adventurers and fiction novelists alike, it is a fact that only his works have remained alive for more than a century, enthralling legions of readers to the extent that they have become an integral aspect of an entire culture, being re-worked, re-designed, re-invented, filmed, continuously published, translated, and performed on a regular basis. The works of the others have long since slipped into the static slot of 'historical literature', to be dusted off every now and then for research purposes (on Karl May's life and work, for example).

Returning to *The Treasure In Silver-Lake*
At one point, Winnetou, Old Shatterhand and Old Firehand leave their hiding place and go scouting in the dark; they move

along the left side of the valley, although they had turned right. The left and right side of a valley are determined by its inclination, or the direction in which the water flows—if there is a watercourse—looking downhill/stream. The party turned right to move along the left side of the valley, which means, as observed by Winnetou a few scenes beforehand, that the valley slopes away towards their left.

Fred Engel, the sixteen-year old heir to the map of the secret treasures that his uncle had received a couple of years earlier at the shores of Silver-Lake, is an integral part of the story of *The Treasure In Silver-Lake*. He rides with Aunty Droll. From about the centre of the novel Fred Engel simply vanishes from the pages of this book—inexplicably—in the middle of a long ride from one event to the next. Or does he? He receives no further mention by Karl May after chapter five, 'At Eagle Tail'. However, at the end of that chapter, Aunty Droll unites the boy with the only other person to whom he still has a connection, by introducing him: "...Look here! This boy's name is Fred Engel; he is the nephew of your friend from Silver-Lake..."; and when Karl May reconnects with these men in chapter seven, 'An Indian Battle', he writes: "...the troop consisted of all the Whites who had experienced the adventure at Eagle Tail...". It includes Fred Engel, of course, and this is the inspiration for the illustration to the last chapter—a way to give a neglected character a spot in the limelight.

One more point on the subject of who speaks which language: since Lord Castlepool of Castlepool Castle has travelled the globe widely, one can safely assume that he has also extensively travelled in Saxony, and is, of course, fully conversant with Hobble-Frank's idiosyncratic Saxon dialect, and able to hold a conversation with him in that language.

At the end of chapter seven, 'An Indian Battle', Old Firehand unexpectedly seems to have forgotten about Great Bear and Little Bear. During the story of *The Treasure In Silver-Lake* he meets up with them twice, experiences two adventures in their company (and on the first occasion explains their names and other details about the Tonkawa to Butler, the engineer); at one point he even completes details of a story about them that is being told to him by Watson, the overseer in Sheridan while they prepare for the outlaws' attack. Then, after the 'Indian Battle', Old Firehand is reminded of the fact that the grandson and great-grandson of the old Indian who had owned the treasure map, the 'two bears', live at Silver-Lake, whereupon the hunter asks: "The two bears? Is that what they were called?" Watson confirms: "Of course, yes! Great Bear and Little Bear." And Old Firehand exclaims: "Tarnation! How could I have overlooked that? Indeed, I remember that those were their names. How is it possible that I didn't immediately think of the two Tonkawa, who were on the paddle steamer with us! Nintropan-Hauey and Nintropan-Homosh, Great Bear and Little Bear, those were their names indeed!" Would famous Old Firehand be so forgetful? Not a month earlier he was fighting at their side, and explaining the meaning and origin of their names to others. The interpretation of the peculiarity is quite simple: Karl May suddenly realized that he had forgotten about the connection between the lake and the two bears (Old Firehand knew from Watson's story, and probably also from Aunty Droll and Fred Engel, that the Nintropans were the owners of the original map, handed down to them by the old Indian) and that he hadn't taken that into consideration when he let Old Firehand be so adamant about taking the map off the outlaws, as otherwise the treasure was going to be lost. It is possible that Old Firehand might not immediately have thought of Nintropan father and son, but it is peculiar that he is unsure of their names all of a sudden; the passage received a minor adjustment.

During the meeting in the dry canyon below Silver-Lake, between Winnetou, Old Shatterhand, Old Firehand, and four chiefs of the Utah, in an attempt at settling the hostilities in a peaceful manner, one of the Utah elders says: "Didn't you knock down the old chief in the Forest of the Water, and then take him as well as other chiefs and warriors with you?" As this is a clear continuity problem—because Winnetou jumped at the old chief, Nanap Neav, toppled him over, and then kicked him to death—I have amended the passage to read: "Didn't Winnetou knock down and kill the old chief in the Forest of the Water, and didn't you take the other chiefs and a number of warriors with you?"

At Silver-Lake, Watson, one of the two men who spent the winter a couple of years prior to the setting of *The Treasure In Silver-Lake* at the lake in the company of an old Indian, and then received the treasure map from him, asks Nintropan-Hauey whether he remembers him, and the Indian confirms. It is of course entirely possible that Nintropan-Hauey and Watson have met at another time prior to, or after the winter at Silver-Lake, however, the dialogue centres on that particular winter, during which the Indian and his son had been away, 'across the Wasatch

Mountains'. That means Nintropan-Hauey remembers Watson from another meeting, and he may have learnt then, or from someone else on another occasion, that Watson was one of the two men who had received the treasure map (especially the period waiting for the enemies to arrive at Silver-Lake would have given the men enough time to exchange information). I have given the dialogue a slant in that direction with one or two words because May's own text alludes to Watson and Nintropan-Hauey having met during that fateful winter at Silver-Lake (or is at the very least abstruse), which can be seen as a break in continuity and would thus also be a direct contradiction to the earlier plot outline.

When Great Bear asks Old Shatterhand what he knows about the treasure, just before the trap shuts behind the treacherous Utah in the tunnel under the lake, the hunter replies: "Nothing; but I can guess well." Yet when he and his friends meet Winnetou and Old Firehand as they flee from the Utah camp, after the various duels a couple of chapters earlier, Old Shatterhand answers Old Firehand's similar question with: "More than you think." I have left the possible contradiction in place; Old Shatterhand might withhold what he knows from Great Bear in consideration of the Indian's already compromised status as a keeper of secrets.

And in the end there remains a mystery: When asked about the map and the treasure, Nintropan-Hauey states that he moved the objects; and when the enemies enter the submerged chambers, they only ever unwrap one of the parcels down there; it contains a golden idol, indeed, but they never take a look at the other covered objects—were there more treasures? Or was the one object a decoy? Did Nintropan-Hauey tell the truth when he said he moved the objects? Were they hidden somewhere else? Did he move them to the secret tunnel? Or did he move them from the tunnel to a new, secret location?

One last, and odd, discrepancy shall be discussed, but not corrected. As the group of friends arrive below Silver-Lake, in the canyon, there are two access routes to reach the lake: the first one is the secret path along a winding ravine that takes three hours (one hour to the silver and gold veins that Old Firehand wants to exploit, and two hours from there to the lake), and the second one is the well-known, but much more narrow continuation of the canyon (which, from the description, could also be termed 'gorge' as it once carried a stream, and thus, to prevent misinterpretation, I have taken the liberty to call the narrow extension of, and connection between the main canyon and Silver-Lake 'gorge'). A rider, charging down said gorge from the lake at a helter-skelter gallop, can cover its length in about fifteen minutes. Firehand's group subsequently covers that distance, riding up the gorge back to the lake, in one hour. In the lead-up to the skirmish below Silver-Lake, as both parties are nearing their destination, and are making their way up the canyon, the enemy Indians are close behind our friends, yet the latter decide to take the much longer route to the lake. The matter is made even more confusing because of a small remark a few days (or two pages) earlier. At the departure from Elk Valley, Old Firehand says: "...the Utah will be between us and the lake...", whereby Winnetou assures him that he knows a secret path to bypass the enemy. Yet at the approach to the lake, where the secret path begins, the Utah are already behind them. Firehand's group of riders therefore overtook the enemy even before they arrived in the canyon. Maybe Winnetou knew yet another secret path? With the three-hour detour along the secret path from the canyon to Silver-Lake they are actually giving the enemy an opportunity to close the gap. During the later skirmish, the traitor says to the enemy chief when he betrays the secret path as they're lying in ambush at the bottom of the narrow gorge: "A stretch further back from here there is a narrow gap between two rock pillars through which one reaches an elevation, and then a deep mountain basin; from there a hollow ravine leads to the lake." The bottom of the narrow gorge and the entrance to the secret path along the winding ravine are therefore not far apart, because the traitor gives the time needed to reach the lake from where they are positioned at that point (where the canyon becomes the narrow gorge) as three hours. The enemy chief is also surprised, because he says: "That's a long time!" Uff, uff!

Ellen Butler, the thirteen-year-old daughter of engineer Butler, who accompanies her father to Silver-Lake in Old Firehand's troupe, is 'taking care of the meal preparations' in the mining operation set up by Old Firehand; Karl May also writes: "[her] presence was a genuine comfort for the tough men". There are in excess of fifty hunters, rafters, and other frontiersmen, who make up the mining population, yet a thirteen-year-old girl is in charge of their meal preparations? While being a 'genuine comfort for the tough men' can justifiably be interpreted as a positive idea, putting a thirteen-year-old girl to work in the wilderness of the Rocky Mountains as a cook for fifty rough mine workers conjures up the negative notion of 'child labour'. Old Firehand's mining operation is a private venture, not a situation in a wild mining town; the yields are substantial enough to hire several cooks with the stamina to deal with such a task on a daily basis. Having said that, of course Ellen is always at liberty to show an interest in the preparations of the meals.

Karl May was well known for his love of children; in autumn of 1891, while the last instalments of *Der Schatz im Silbersee* are being published—the final one in September—May invites his nine-year-old niece Clara, the daughter of his sister Karoline Wilhelmina Selbmann to live with him and his wife Emma. They even consider adoption as they have no children. Ellen Butler, the girl who loves her father so much she accompanies him into the wilderness of the Rocky Mountains might well be interpreted as being a reflection of May's yearning for a child of his own.

There is another twist to the girl Ellen: Karl May's alleged, illegitimate daughter, Helene, was thirteen years old when thirteen-year old Ellen made her appearance on the paddle steamer on the Arkansas in 1889, at the time of writing the novel.

Where is Silver-Lake?

Karl May was a fiction writer, a writer of fables, not an explorer writing a scientific report on landscapes with factual topography. The landscape needed to fit his story, which was not always possible by placing the fictional events into an actual place; but lands that had not yet been completely explored, mapped and named, such as parts of the Colorado and Utah Rockies during the time frame of Karl May's adventures—between 1860, the time he met Winnetou, and 1874, the time Winnetou died—were ideal.

Atlases, maps, explorers' accounts of the wilderness, newspaper articles, and other sources of information were tools that he used to furnish his fiction with factual features and events, in order to give his tales verisimilitude. He was careful to conceal the sources of his knowledge, and to make sure that although many actual geographical features were cited, not enough information was provided to enable his stories to be 'disproved'. And he did a marvellous job, too, for one hundred and twenty years later, we're still looking for the location of Silver-Lake. The exploration into 'his' wilderness, trying to join the dots to find 'X' on the map, has become the true adventure.

The Treasure In Silver-Lake offers several mysterious locations that researchers and editors on several occasions have placed in the actual topography of the region between the Colorado headwaters and the Wasatch Mountains. They are: the Orfork of Grand River, the Cumison River, Night Canyon, Elk Valley, and the mysterious lake with the submerged treasure, Silver-Lake itself. Given the period of the plot in the novel, that being the summer and autumn of 1870 (see the concluding paragraph of 'Research'), that area would still have contained mysterious, unknown pockets of landscape: blank spaces on maps that were ideal to create a secret, mystical landscape from early explorer's reports about the topography, but fictional with regard to its location in, as well as connection to, the surrounding factual areas.

The Orfork of Grand River
The events around the Orfork take place two years before the actual Silver-Lake plot. After a hard winter, when Engel and Watson had left Silver-Lake on foot to get back east to civilization, heading for Pueblo, they are attacked by a band of Utah Indians; the two men then meet Brinkley, who attempts to kill them to get his hands on the treasure map. Brinkley stabs Watson and leaves him for dead; he shoots and wounds Engel. Winnetou subsequently finds Watson, takes him to the Timbabachi Indians who nurse him back to health, and then takes him to the nearest settlement. Engel, fleeing from Brinkley, manages to hide in the 'Orfork of Grand River', and then reaches people who help him and take him to Las Animas. The term 'Orfork' may be a misinterpreted, or misread contraction of 'North Fork', or 'Northfork', and could be attributable to a number of rivers or creeks having once been called 'North Fork'. Engel's 'Orfork of Grand River', therefore, is a conundrum.

One modern edition of *Der Schatz Im Silbersee* has 'Orfork of Grand River' corrected to 'North Fork of the Gunnison River'. If Old Shatterhand did indeed travel into the Book Mountains and up to the lake (the destination he gives when he mentions the Book Mountains for the second time), then the 'Orfork' might have been the 'North Fork of Grand River', today's upper Colorado east of Grand Junction, that Engel and Watson encountered first, if indeed they were travelling east, or south-east (around numerous canyons, mesas and other mountain formations) from Silver-Lake towards Pueblo on the Santa Fe trail.

May most likely used 'Stieler's Hand-Atlas' of 1888-91[13] (among others) to establish his Silver-Lake region. And that map was

---

[13] Plate 1: http://www.maproom.org/00/09/present.php?m=0083, plate 4: http://www.maproom.org/00/09/present.php?m=0086.
Also see http://australianfriendsofkarlmay.yolasite.com/silver-lake-ma ps.php for more information.

published just a year before Karl May wrote the adventure *The Treasure In Silver-Lake*. (Footnotes within the narrative also refer to Stieler's Hand-Atlas with regard to other locations.) The region of the upper Colorado is shown in two parts on two separate sheets, number one and number four. In essence: the Colorado River forked into two Grand Rivers at 'Grand Junction', with each map sheet showing only one of them. On the bottom right hand side, sheet one names as 'Grand R' the fork of the Grand that will later become the true upper Colorado; on the top right hand corner of sheet four, the southern fork of the Grand, from Grand Junction south-eastwards, which is actually the Gunnison River, is inscribed with 'Grand River', and further upstream with 'Grand Canyon of the Gunnison'. When Captain John Williams Gunnison explored the area of that canyon and river system, in 1855, he took exception to the fact that even the more correct maps of his time didn't mark the river as 'the Grand'[14]; but Stieler's Atlas did, more than three decades later.

Because of Karl May's own deep interest in the exploration of the Old West, he would have examined maps in great detail, but there are many factors to consider: multiple and changing place names, changing understanding of geographical and geological features, errors and variations in survey data, as well as the whims of map makers. And then of course there are the directions given within the narration, and the difference between overall and 'instantaneous' direction. What a traveller can see at any point along a canyon or river is an instantaneous direction—in other words, the direction of a very small section. A river (for example) could have an overall direction north to south, yet a short section may be aligned east to west. The reader cannot always tell whether May is referring to an overall, or to an 'instantaneous' direction during his narration. We will never know all the details, and much of it will remain speculation.

Coming 'down' from Silver-Lake, Watson and Engel would have encountered the river at the bottom edge of sheet one, today's upper Colorado, a river that had names like Grand River, Nah

---

[14] Page 50 of: *Report of Explorations for a Route for the Pacific Railroad by Captain J W Gunnison, Topographical Engineers, near the 38th and 39th Parallels of North Latitude, from the Mouth of the Kansas River, Mo., to the Sevier Lake in the Great Basin; Report by Lieut. E G Beckwith, Third Artillery* (1855))
http://quod.lib.umich.edu/m/moa/AFK4383.0002.001?rgn=main;view=fulltext.

oon Kara, North Fork, North Fork of Grand River[15], Nah-Un-Kah-Rea (Gunnison report, others), Blue (Gunnison report, others), Bunkara (1864 Johnson map), Nahoom Kara, Avonkarea[16], Rio Colorado, and possibly others on the various maps of the early or middle decades of the nineteenth century. Since the Orfork as such has no bearing whatsoever on the actual Silver-Lake plot, it will have to remain a mystery; and although the 'North Fork of Grand River' may well have been misinterpreted as 'Orfork of Grand River', I have yet to find a map to show such an inscription. I see it as a fair assumption that if a document is found with a name or term May used, then he didn't simply invent it, but probably had access to information that provided him with the name or term.

The Cumison River

At the beginning of chapter six, Old Shatterhand and his three friends are riding 'where the Elk Mountains rise on the far side of the Cumison River'. There is no 'Cumison River', but there is a famous 'Gunnison River'—more recent editions of Karl May's German *Der Schatz im Silbersee* have the term 'Cumison' replaced by the (probably) correct name of 'Gunnison'. As this is a translation of the early, serialized version, I have opted to retain the name 'Cumison River'. The transcription error 'Cumison' might be due to how it is presented on an old 1864 map by Johnson & Ward, which will play an even more important role shortly. On that map, the name of the river in question is 'Gunnison River', and it flows around the Elk Mountains in a semi circle. (The Elk Mountains on Stieler's map are in a slightly more north-easterly location, and there it is the West Elk Mountains that are bounded on almost three sides by the Gunnison.) On the map in the Johnson atlas, the word 'Gunnison' is printed along the wavy line that depicts the watercourse; however, there is a double line through it, and that double line indicates the route Captain Gunnison took in 1855. The double line crosses the capital letter 'G' right where the small cross bar of the upwards curve sits, and further along the word also cuts diagonally through the double 'n' of Gunnison. May could either have misread Gunnison as Cumison

---

[15] Renaming of the Grand River, Colo. Hearing before the Committee on Interstate and Foreign Commerce of the House of Representatives, Sixty-sixth Congress, third session on H.J. Res. 460, February 8, 1921–page 19
[16] http://www.gregmetcalf.com/stallions.html – chapter 24

(it is well known that he had eye trouble throughout his life[17]), or his handwriting may have been misinterpreted upon typesetting at the publisher's printing press; he may even have changed the name on purpose. Either way, Karl May's Cumison River is almost certainly the Gunnison River.

Shatterhand's location, when he and his party first appear, would likely be somewhere north-east of the West Elk Mountains, near the western foothills of the Elk Mountains. The direction in which he is heading has these points of orientation: He and his friends are travelling towards the Gunnison (Cumison) River from Leadville (a town that didn't exist at the time the plot plays; it was founded in 1877 as a mining town, so it is shown in Stieler's Hand-Atlas, but not on the Johnson & Ward map of 1864). The group then travels towards the Elk Mountains, and the riders intend to get across to the Book Mountains. The Utah capture the four friends; when they escape, they encounter Winnetou, who directs Old Shatterhand to ride across the Elk Mountains, into Night Canyon. After the skirmish on the other side of Night Canyon (which is a very narrow, but deep and endlessly long cut into the mountain rock, and which permits only two riders abreast), the combined group of all the people involved in the various adventures since the beginning of the novel then ride on towards the Grand River. They cross the Grand, ride up a narrow gulch with a small creek, into Elk Valley, which is most likely a fictional valley, with a secret path and a hidden rock gap that is large enough to accommodate the riders, as well as their horses, for a night. After the great Indian battle, and another 'arduous' ride of several days, Old Shatterhand and friends then arrive in the canyon below Silver-Lake, where they find another secret track to Silver-Lake, while the canyon continues on and also connects with Silver-Lake at almost the same point as the hidden path, but from a slightly different direction. At the very end of the novel, the men ride to Fillmore City to finalize various business matters.

Night Canyon
If Old Shatterhand was riding towards the Elk Mountains, was then captured by the Utah, who dragged him and his friends into the foothills of the mountain range, and upon escaping then rode

---

[17] http://www.karl-may-gesellschaft.de/kmg/seklit/biographie/747.htm, year 1893; Karl May had been to a specialist in Leipzig twice that year because of his eyes.

across the Elk Mountains down into Night Canyon away from the
Utah, in a westerly direction, then where is Night Canyon situated?
There are Elk Mountains, West Elk Mountains, and also an Elk
Ridge—on Stieler's Atlas. If Shatterhand crossed Elk Mountains
(near modern-day Aspen, coming from Leadville) in a westerly
direction, he would have encountered the upper, narrow portions
of the Black Canyon of the Gunnison; and he would have done so,
too, if he was somewhere east or north-east of the West Elk Mountains—May didn't say at which angle they entered Night Canyon.
Did May take his description of Night Canyon from Moellhausen's
Black Canyon? Moellhausen's published adventures along the
Colorado were among May's sources for his landscape descriptions;
however, Moellhausen, in turn, was forced to rely upon Ives' over-
romantic description of the canyon on the Colorado[18] (near
Hoover Dam) to create his image of the Black Canyon, because Ives
didn't take him along as he went inside to explore it. There were a
number of descriptions of the real Black Canyon of the Gunnison
available during the nineteenth century, but most were published
relatively late; Moellhausen's 'Black Canyon' remains the most likely
candidate for May's 'Night Canyon', but because there were other
publications describing the canyon during the mid-1880s this
cannot be fully asserted.

Only after traversing another plateau and a ride through a couple
of other canyons, do Winnetou, Old Firehand, Old Shatterhand
and their friends arrive at the Grand (or Blue, or Nah-Un-Kah-Rea,
whichever name one wishes to apply to the upper Colorado), from
where they head up into Elk Valley immediately after crossing the
Grand. At this stage, the landscape becomes even more mysterious.
Where are they really?

Elk Valley and Silver-Lake
Fillmore City, south of Salt Lake City, and the region called
'Silver Lake Desert', west of Fillmore City, are on the west side of
the Wasatch Mountain range—too far for just a few days' riding.
Old Shatterhand and friends do not cross the Wasatch Mountains;
but father and son Bear did, two years earlier, during that severe
winter in the Rockies, when the two Indians were unable to get
back to Silver-Lake before spring. Very few maps of the era would
have had printed 'Silver Lake Desert' instead of 'Sevier Desert' on
the area of Sevier Lake. I have only been able to find one copy:

[18] http://go.owu.edu/~jbkrygie/krygier_html/envision.html

Johnson's New Illustrated Family Atlas, (1864) Johnson & Ward Edition[19]. Did May have one of these maps with 'Silver Lake Desert' emblazoned near Sevier Lake? Did he make use of the fact that later maps no longer referred to it? What better treasure hunt than for one buried in a mythical lake that made only a brief appearance on one or two maps, but thus had become part of history. However, if Engel was to make it to the 'Orfork of Grand River' on foot, from Silver-Lake, then May couldn't possibly leave 'Silver Lake' on the west side of the Wasatch Mountains (Engel would then have been better off with seeking help from the Latter Day Saints at Salt Lake City, or indeed, from people in Fillmore City).

Some researchers suggest, though with a hint of doubt, that the small lake in Big Cottonwood Canyon, south east of Salt Lake City was Karl May's inspiration for the lake in his novel *The Treasure In Silver-Lake*[20]; however, this lake is a very small body of water, not shown on such large-scale maps as May is known or suspected to have used, so doubt is justified. (There are also several other small 'Silver Lakes' in an adjacent area called Uinta National Forest, Silver Glance Lake, Silver Lake, and Silver Lake Flat). This was not a true 'wilderness' region, even in the Winnetou era. Had May known of the Silver Lake at Brighton, he would have needed to give his special lake a different name, in order to make it fit the requirements of the story. The fact is that there was a hotel a the lake from very early on. This, combined with the lake's location in a well-travelled region very near to Salt Lake City, would have made the lake a poor choice for his mystical body of water. The Silver Lake Desert, on the other hand, is prominent on one widely distributed map that May likely often used, yet is otherwise rather obscure.

There were (and still are) many small place names around the area that contained 'silver' in their name, as the region was rich in silver and therefore saw much mining activity. The small lake in Big Cottonwood Canyon was first simply called 'Big Cottonwood

---

[19] http://www.geographicus-archive.com/P/AntiqueMap/Southwest-johnson-1864. There were a number of atlases available to Karl May in Europe, http://www.atlassen.info/atlassen/atlassen.html, but perusing them online brought no other inscription of 'Silver Lake Desert' to light. Also see http://australianfriendsofkarlmay.yolasite.com/silver-lake-maps.php for more information.
[20] http://www.karl-may-gesellschaft.de/kmg/seklit/jbkmg/1997/361.htm#a34

Lake'. In the early 1870s William Stuart Brighton recorded mining claims near Big Cottonwood Lake, and also built a cabin there. Around 1874, when the Brightons built their first hotel on the meadow near the lake, his wife Catherine began to refer to it as 'Silver Lake'[21]. Other local historians also confirm a change in the name of the lake: 'Silver Lake used to be called "Trout Lake" but Mrs. Catherine Brighton changed the name to "Silver Lake" because according to her, when you see it in the morning sun, it gleams like silver spangles'.[22] This substantiates the notion that such places frequently had varying names. At the time that Silver Lake was still referred to as Big Cottonwood Lake, it was the scene of one of Utah's lesser-documented events: Apparently, two thousand people listened to Brigham Young's 'declaration of independence' on the twenty-fourth of July 1857, during the tenth anniversary celebrations of the pioneers entering Salt Lake Valley. In *The Rocky Mountain Saints: A Full and Complete History of the Mormons* (1873), the writer, T B H Stenhouse claims Young delivered his prophecy that twelve years hence, 'he himself should be President of the United States, or would dictate who should be.'[23]

It is indeed doubtful that Karl May would have known of the small lake in Big Cottonwood Canyon, called Silver Lake. But he knew of 'a' Silver Lake, and makes one more mention of the location of 'his' Silver-Lake in another adventure novel titled *Der Oelprinz*. Someone asks Hobble-Frank: "You found a large amount of gold back then, up there, near Fillmore City, at Silver-Lake, I believe. Isn't it so, sir?" 'Near Fillmore City'—that points directly to the rare map inscription of 'Silver Lake Desert', and could be said to have been a 'spoiler'. Silver-Lake was thus a lake that once existed on a map, if only by a possible error on the map-maker's part; therefore it can be said to be 'real', but is no longer found on any later maps.

May had to move Silver-Lake somewhere east of the Wasatch Mountains, accessible by riding through the fictional Elk Valley— perhaps somewhere north, north-west, or west of the Book Plateau (remember Shatterhand and his friends were travelling towards the Book Mountains, and according to Old Shatterhand,

21 Email correspondence with Rod Morris of Balsam Hill Cabin, and website http://balsam-hill-cabin.com/php/book/ch1.php; thank you, Rod.
22 http://americantalesandtrails.com/history/brighton-jewel-of-the-wasatch-mountains-of-utah
23 http://www.nevadaobserver.com/Reading%20Room%20Documents/stenhouse_2.htm

into those mountains, and 'up' to Silver-Lake), and possibly even west of the Green River. Why west of Green River? When the men in the group led by Winnetou, Old Shatterhand, and Old Firehand ride up the dry, gravel-filled canyon towards Silver-Lake, May (or rather: Old Shatterhand) notes that the canyon shows signs of being a turbulent river at certain times, carrying its raging water into the Colorado. On most maps available at the time, the Colorado was named 'Colorado River' only from the Green and Grand Rivers junction downwards, as it was on the map in Stieler's Hand-Atlas. From that confluence upwards, the river was named 'Grand River', with a plethora of confusing names to the various forks and tributaries further up. Despite that, the Green River location allusion must remain speculative, if not doubtful; but May's mentioning of a canyon discharging flash flood, or seasonal torrents, directly into the Colorado deserves attention, because of the implied location—and that location would likely be south of the confluence of the Green and Grand Rivers, not north in the Book Mountains, or west of the Colorado River. But Stieler's Atlas also has 'Colorado Vall[ey]' inscribed just inside the Utah border, while at the same time the name 'Grand River' is still written next to the actual watercourse.

The first clue that points in a southerly direction comes in the form of a group of cavalry. When Old Shatterhand and his friends arrive 'where the Elk Mountains rise on the far side of the Cumison River', the hunters have an encounter with a lieutenant and his twelve soldiers. The lieutenant informs Old Shatterhand that the cavalry at Fort Mormon and Fort Indian are forced to ride patrol from both forts because the Utah have raised their war hatchets. Then, there are two outlaws, Knox and Hilton, who lie when they say they had just come from San Juan River, because, as we know, they crossed the mountains at Breckenridge, and then travelled south from there.

As May tells us, Old Shatterhand, Hobble-Frank, Fat Jemmy and Long Davy are riding towards 'Cumison (Gunnison) River', or at least within its vicinity. There are two other directional statements, prior to the Whites being taken captive by the Utah. The first is about the direction and destination of the soldiers either on patrol or simply on their way to Fort Mormon; they were coming from a south-westerly direction, and were headed north-east, and ultimately towards Fort Mormon—this statement could be seen to mean that Fort Mormon lies north, or north-east of the Elk Mountains. They also call Old Shatterhand a liar when he informs them that he came from Leadville. The lieutenant insists that Shatterhand and his friends have come 'up from Indian Fort'—this statement, too, implies that Fort Indian is located somewhere south of the Elk Mountains. When he has cleared the matter up, Old Shatterhand has to decline the lieutenant's invitation to visit Fort Mormon, as his route takes him in the 'opposite' direction, towards the Elk Mountains, and then onwards to the Book Mountains, which would more or less be correct if Fort Mormon were situated north, or north-east of the Elk Mountains. If May means the Elk Mountains that stretch around Aspen from west to south, then Shatterhand's encounter with the soldiers takes place somewhere around Aspen (which didn't exist in 1870, of course), if he means West Elk Mountains, he would be situated somewhere north-east of them, on the western slopes of the Elk Mountains.

The lieutenant also makes an entirely baffling comment, when Old Shatterhand informs him that he knows nothing of trouble with the Utah Indians. The soldier says: "I can believe it because you've come from Colorado, where the news hasn't reached yet."

The lieutenant's statement implies that the location of their meeting is in Utah (both Utah and Colorado were still territories during the time of the story, not states yet, though this is inconsequential to the story). Yet Leadville, both Elk mountain formations, and the Gunnison (Cumison) River are located in Colorado. Did Karl May mistake Elk Ridge, which is located south, across the border in Utah territory, for the Elk Mountains further north-east in the Colorado Rockies? Johnson's map referred to the mountain range that comprises Elk Ridge and the Abajo Mountains as 'Sierra Abajo'. On Stieler's Atlas that range is divided into 'Elk Ridge' and 'Abajo Mts', and the Colorado-Utah border is clearly marked in two colours; if May mistook 'Elk Ridge' on sheet four of that atlas as 'his' Elk Mountains, which were clearly marked as such in the Johnson map, but obscured and abbreviated on the Stieler map, close to the top right hand side edge of that sheet, then he would have mistakenly (or purposely) placed Mormon Fort, as well as Indian Fort relative to the meeting between Old Shatterhand and the soldiers in the Elk Mountains. Old Shatterhand's reason for declining the invitation of the Lieutenant to visit Mormon Fort, because he is riding in the opposite direction towards Book Mountains, would only be correct if the location of their meeting were in the Elk Mountains or West Elk Mountains, with Mormon Fort north, or north-east of the Elk Mountain location—which it isn't. The lieutenant appears to give their location as Utah, and approximately south-west of Fort Mormon, since he is heading in a north-easterly direction towards it.

I'm inclined to think that, in his rush to get things done (at the same time as he wrote the latter parts of *Der Schatz im Silbersee* he was also doing likewise for his South American novel *From The Rio De La Plata To The Cordilleras*), May could have been distracted enough to mistake Elk Ridge for the Elk Mountains, or the West Elk Mountains. This would be an explanation for the peculiar statement of the lieutenant, implying they're in Utah, and the mention of the forts in the 'wrong' location—in Colorado, because Shatterhand had just arrived 'where the Elk Mountains rise on the far side of the Cumison River', travelling from Leadville; both forts are situated in Utah territory.

The Book Mountains receive no further mention after Old Shatterhand's second statement that these mountains are his destination, which occurs in the vicinity of Night Canyon just before the group departs for the Grand River to cross it, and to head into fictional Elk Valley. Did May intend the Book Mountains to be the location for his fictional Silver-Lake initially, but subsequently change his mind and fail to correct Old Shatterhand's statements, as well as the mysterious 'Orfork of Grand River'?

There is another remark from the lieutenant, which attains significance when compared to text in the Gunnison report: *"...Your route leads you right through the middle of Utah terri-tory..."* (German: *"...Euer Weg fuehrt euch mitten durch das Gebiet der Utahindianer..."*). The location where Old Shatterhand and the soldiers meet is somewhere approximately north-east of May's Night Canyon, or the Black Canyon of the Gunnison (if one assumes that both canyons are one and the same). The following incident, which occurred in 1855, as the Gunnison party travelled towards the middle of said canyon, is worth noting: After they left one of their camps, they could see a "large smoke ascending from our last camp, from the grass taking fire after we left it" because they hadn't extinguished the campfire. Ahead of them they could see another large smoke rising, ... "made doubtless by *the Utah Indians, in the heart of whose country we have been travelling* for several weeks..." so says the Gunnison report only one page after the image of the rock formation along 'Grand River' on page fifty-five.

The Gunnison report refers to today's Gunnison River as the Grand River without exception. The 'real' Grand, so marked by other maps, is consistently referred to as the Nah-Un-Kah-Rea, or Blue River[24].

Beginning Ch 8 descr. canyon below Silver-Lake (1889)

View of ordinary Lateral Ravines on Grand River (1855)

[24] http://quod.lib.umich.edu/m/moa/AFK4383.0002.001/72
This picture is part of the Gunnison Report and depicts a section of what's today known as the Black Canyon of the Gunnison. Compare with the image that was featured on this page of the early, serialized publishing *Der Schatz Im Silbersee* in 1891: http://www.karl-may-gesellschaft.de/kmg/primlit/jugend/silbers/reprint/zeitung/288.gif - it is accompanied by the caption that opens chapter eight, when the Firehand/Shatterhand party arrive in the canyon below Silver-Lake "Colossal rock pyramids, one standing next to the other, or forming a staggered backdrop, were reaching skywards in individually coloured layers and storeys." The image is placed with the text that still refers to events in the fictional Elk Valley right at the conclusion of chapter seven. The reply on 6 January 2012 from the Deutsche Forschungsgemeinschaft to my email query about a German translation of the Gunnison Report said: "Unfortunately we have not been able to locate a German translation of the title." However, that does not mean there never was a German translation of it—and it appears there was. The text comparison, but more so the comparison between the two images, which bear a striking resemblance, is compelling evidence that the Gunnison report had made its way to Germany.

Is this the reason Gunnison River became 'Cumison River'? To mask the region somewhat (although it is most likely a transcription error)? Is this the reason that Black Canyon became 'Night Canyon'? Perhaps Karl May didn't want to be seen to be following a known explorer's trail; but this must remain speculation, of course.

The third directional statement, made only hours after that of the lieutenant, consists of Knox and Hilton's lie, that they've just ridden all the way to the Elk Mountain region from the San Juan River—that's a very long way to ride in four days from the New Mexico border, could it be that May looked at Elk Ridge on Stieler's Hand-Atlas, and saw San Juan River just to the south of it? San Juan River winds its way west, along the Colorado-New Mexico border, with a north-westerly turn into Utah at its border with Colorado, to empty into the Colorado River. In addition, Knox and Hilton say they bought the horses they were riding in Fort Dodge, Kansas, which would mean they were supposed to have come from an easterly direction, indeed from a long distance away. Did Karl May not realize that he had just misidentified the Elk Ridge location, including the two forts in the previous passage, as being the Elk Mountain location further north east?

When Old Shatterhand and his friends flee from the Utah, they do so in an overall westerly direction. They are in the Elk Mountains, held captive by the Utah in their camp along a lake. Winnetou arrives there at the same time Old Shatterhand is riding out of the Utah camp, and with his troop rides along the northern ridge around the lake, from east to west; the general direction of travel for all parties is roughly west, upstream, and along the watercourse that feeds the small lake of the Utah camp from a westerly direction, coming down from a mountain massif. After traversing a high plateau, they then arrive in Night Canyon, where another skirmish takes place. May's depictions of Night Canyon, like this one, for example: "And the canyon was long— endlessly long! Occasionally it widened somewhat, so that it afforded room for five or six riders across; then the walls closed in again so tightly that some would have liked to scream out for fear of being crushed..." perfectly describe stretches of the Black Canyon of the Gunnison at its narrow sections. Night Canyon, as well as the parallel 'Forest of the Water', where the large Utah camp is situated, run roughly north to south. When Droll and Frank flee from the Utah, they initially run 'downstream', south, and then jump across the watercourse, turn right, up a narrow gorge west, while the main canyon takes a turn east, and the watercourse with it; when the combined group leaves the 'Forest of the Water', they travel along the continuation of said narrow gorge—west. Upon their departure, Winnetou says: "If we want to travel to Silver-Lake from here, then our route takes us first across the Grand River and into the *Teywipah* [the Elk Valley]." They are still in the vicinity of the West Elk Mountains that 'rise on the far side of Cumison River' (both the Elk Mountains, and the West Elk Mountains can be said to rise on the far side of Gunnison River, the former more to the north-east, the latter to the north). The crossing of the Grand River (as mentioned earlier, that part of the Gunnison River was also called 'Grand River' on Stieler's map), could take place in several directions, south, south-west, or west—but according to the directions of Old Shatterhand, the group has to get across to the Book Mountains, and they lie north-west of the Black Canyon of the Gunnison. After they leave the 'Forest of the Water' in a westerly direction through a steadily climbing narrow gorge, the landscape remains fictional; May does not give any further directions. They then ride at a gallop across a high plateau in an area of which Gunnison's report on page fifty-three says: "The agreeable and exhilarating effect of the pure mountain air of these elevated regions, ever a fruitful theme of eloquence among trappers and voyagers, exhibits itself among our men in almost constant boisterous myrth. But violent physical exertion soon puts the men out of breath; and our animals, in climbing the hills, unless often halted to breathe, soon become exhausted, and stop from the weight of their loads, but after a few moments' rest move on with renewed vigor and strength." In other words, the thinner, high-altitude air would have been troublesome for the galloping animals and riders alike. Towards noon, after a speedy ride, Old Shatterhand and friends arrive at, and descend into, a narrow, dark, moist canyon with a peculiar feature: it had been sliced into the rock as if by a giant plane—it didn't show the slightest bend. At the other end of the straight canyon they see the light through the gap: they have arrived at the Valley of the Grand River, which runs north to south, and for which May offers a description reminiscent of the Colorado along its lower sections: "It was perhaps eight hundred metres wide. The river streamed along the middle and left a strip of grass on either side, which was bounded by vertically ascending canyon walls. The valley ran north to south, as straight as if drawn by a ruler, and neither side showed even the narrowest crack or the smallest protrusion. Above it stood the glowing sun, which caused the grass to almost wither despite the depth of the canyon."

Where would one find such a junction of a canyon and a valley both as straight as if drawn with a ruler? Anywhere, and nowhere at the same time. The only factual features are Leadville, the Elk Mountains, the Book Mountains, and Grand River at a north-south running section; everything else is left up to the imagination of the reader.

If they follow the Gunnison valley (or what is inscribed as Grand Canyon of the Gunnison on the map in Stieler's atlas) west, and later Gunnison's 1855 route (Gunnison didn't travel through the canyon, he descended into the valley through the Uncompahgre River canyon), they will arrive at the same crossing the explorer used, and cross the 'real' Grand River on the southern reaches of the Book Mountains, where Elk Valley is supposed to begin at the opposite bank of Grand River. If one takes the striking images on page [cxii] as evidence that May had at least knowledge of the Gunnison report, and the artist's rendering of the cliffs in the Gunnison Valley, then he would have been able to deduce that there is a maze of canyons that criss-crosses the landscape, and that he could weave any combination of twists and turns, canyons following high plateaus, or meeting at unusual angles, into the 'factual' landscape around the Elk Mountains—after all, Winnetou knew all the secret paths.

Grand River, today's upper Colorado, has a roughly north-to-south direction just before the bend west into Grand Junction— when looking at Stieler's Hand-Atlas, slightly further east of where Gunnison crossed. Directly opposite the spot where Old Shatterhand, Winnetou, Old Firehand and the others enter the Grand River Valley, in the 'vertically ascending canyon wall', there is a gap, a crack in the rock, where a small stream emerges. This is the access to Elk Valley. The group crosses the Grand—the last factual point of orientation—and heads into the rest of the adventure, in an entirely fictional landscape, fitted out with descriptions inspired from various sources.

Karl May might perhaps have left a small clue, maybe alluding to the fact that it would be very difficult to unearth all of the sources he utilized to create this tale, when the Utah, who have pursued Old Shatterhand, Winnetou, Old Firehand and their friends, arrive at Elk Valley, expecting to find the Whites sandwiched between them and those Utah camped in the valley, only to find they had simply vanished into nothing: "The Yampa didn't want to believe that the group, whose trail they had followed, hadn't arrived. Questions were asked back and forth; a hundred speculations were voiced, but the truth remained a riddle."

From Elk Valley, everyone then arrives in a dry canyon at the beginning of chapter eight 'after an arduous ride of several days', and another sizeable scene break. The reader knows only the direction Old Shatterhand has given a couple of times—into the Book Mountains and up to Silver-Lake. The map in Johnson's Atlas of 1864 depicts a long mountain range named Roan-Or-Book-Mountains, which reaches from Utah across the border into Colorado, from where Old Shatterhand is travelling. However, Stieler's Atlas shows a Book Plateau in Colorado, and a mountain range called Book Cliffs, as well as one called Roan Cliffs hugging the former, which are in Utah. Later on, engineer Butler says: "What a find! And indeed, in Utah one finds chiefly horn silver. Where is the vein in question?" The Book Mountains have disappeared from Stieler's Hand-Atlas, or rather, have undergone a name change since they had last been called Book Mountains on an older map.

What about Fillmore City, the remnants of an ancient civilization, a dry canyon that empties its flash-flood into the Colorado River, the tales of the lost silver mines, the Timbabachi territory[25] (which other sources place around the Great Salt Lake, Utah, and therefore in close proximity to Silver Lake Desert on the map in the 1864 Johnson Family Atlas, as well as to Fillmore City)? All of this points to a southerly location, or even a location around Sevier Lake. The description of the grandeur that they encountered when they arrived in the dry canyon below Silver-Lake is inspired by Moellhausen's Grand Canyon depiction. The details surrounding

---

[25] *The Indian Tribes of North America* by John R. Swanton, 1953; http://americanindian.net/StatesUV.html: places "Tumpanogots or Timpaiavats, about Utah Lake, Utah." (Karl May's German spelling *Timbabatschen* is translated as Timbabachi; alternative names as listed in: *Handbook of American Indians North of Mexico, Volume 4*, by Frederick Webb Hodge, 1912, (one of Karl May's many sources - http://www.karl-may-gesellschaft.de/kmg/seklit/jbkmg/1997/361.htm#8) include: Timbabachis, Timbachis, Timpaiavats. The *Personal narrative of explorations and incidents in Texas, New Mexico, California, Sonora, and Chihuahua, volume 2: Connected with the United States and Mexican Boundary Commission, during the years 1850, '51, '52 and '53* by Bartlett, John Russell, 1805-1886 (Also one of May's sources - http://www.karl-may-gesellschaft.de/kmg/seklit/m-kmg/093/bilder/m093s026.gif)
http://scholarship.rice.edu/jsp/xml/1911/27279/1/aa00374.tei.html notes the following: "On the old maps there are found west of the Colorado the *Genigueh*, the *Chemeguabas*, the *Jumbuicrariri*, and the *Timbabachi*, tribes of whose existence in our day we know nothing. The missionaries who mention them, are correct in all their statements, as far as we are now able to judge, and it is therefore probable that there were small tribes bearing the above names."

the Silver-Lake location are situated south of the Green and Grand Rivers confluence, on Stieler's map.

Elk Ridge, mentioned earlier, is quite some distance further south-west, around 'fifty miles' due south of the Book Mountains, according to one account in the Gunnison exploration report. On page 62, the writer tells us that... "Fifty miles apparently below us on the river, the high snow-peaks of the Sierra Abajo are visible." Those are the mountains that, in other atlases, are called Elk Ridge, and on the map in Stieler's Atlas, are separated into Elk Ridge and Abajo Mountains.

Old Firehand asks Great Bear who owns the land around Silver-Lake, and the desolate valley basin he wants to mine. Silver-Lake used to belong to the Timbabachi, and Great Bear had bought it from them; the area Firehand wishes to buy still belongs to the Timbabachi at the time of the fictional events in this plot. They will sell it to him, and for that purpose will travel to Fillmore City to sign the contracts.

How many maps and atlases did Karl May utilize? If we look at another map[26] in the German Sohr-Berghaus Handatlas of 1855 (most likely readily viewable in some libraries—May lived near Dresden, which was a well-known centre of education in Europe at that time[27]), we find the Timbabachi territory inscribed not too far south from the confluence of the Green and Grand Rivers (on a 1863 Johnson Map[28] as well). The cataract canyon area just south of the confluence is home to White Canyon, a canyon that has become famous through the tale of Cass Hite, a prospector who was called 'Silver Hunter' by the Navajo; he came to the Colorado River via White Canyon in 1883. White Canyon rises in the Abajo Mountains, just like the dry canyon below Silver-Lake rises in the mountains that surround the artificial Silver-Lake.

The Timbabachi Indians are first mentioned in chapter five, by Watson. But already in chapter two, Old Firehand explains to engineer Butler that Great Bear and Little Bear, two Tonkawa Indians, are allies of those Indians (unnamed at that point) into

---

[26] http://www.davidrumsey.com/luna/servlet/detail/RUMSEY~8~1~33 527~1171013:Vereinigte-Staaten-von-Nord-America?sort=Pub_List_No _InitialSort%2CPub_Date%2CPub_List_No%2CSeries_No&qvq=q:Soh r;sort:Pub_List_No_InitialSort%2CPub_Date%2CPub_List_No%2Cseri es_No;lc:RUMSEY~8~1&mi=82&trs=134
[27] see 'Translator's Notes' in *The Inca's Legacy* about Dresden University of Technology
[28] http://www.geographicus.com/P/AntiqueMap/CaliforniaUtahNew MexicoArizona-johnson-1863

whose territory he and his associates were planning to travel…up to Silver-Lake.

But if Silver-Lake were situated in that southerly location, then Old Firehand's party, including engineer Butler and his daughter Ellen, would have been better off taking a more southerly route, not the arduous one across the parks from Denver.

There is no directional information given for Elk Valley, or for the continuation of the group's ride, nor are any distinguishing landscape features mentioned; likewise, a blank scene break remains between the departure from Elk Valley and the arrival in the dry canyon.

The bottom of the unnamed canyon below Silver-Lake is covered with river gravel that makes riding along it difficult. That, and the description of the grandeur that presents itself to the adventurers, is most likely inspired by Moellhausen's own account of the Colorado River canyons published in his diaries, as was the description of the Grand River valley earlier on. The dry canyon walls, however, show signs of water running, and quite turbulently, at certain times of the year; it flows into the Colorado. As mentioned before, on maps at that time, the Colorado River was only named thus from its confluence with the Green downwards—but there is the name 'Colorado Vall[ey]' inscribed along the stretch of river above that confluence that also bears the name Grand River, on Stieler's map.

May had given his mystical lake the name Silver-Lake, and that term is found only on one old map in the 1864 Johnson atlas, south of the Great Salt Lake, on the great salt plain west of the Wasatch Mountains; but that area was too far removed from the high reaches of the Rocky Mountains, and too populated. Up to the point when Old Shatterhand arrives in the region 'where the Elk Mountains rise on the far side of Cumison River', all place names can be verified, and thus followed along most maps of the era (whether strictly consistent with the year 1870 or not). On the western side of the Rocky Mountains watershed, however, things became problematic. He (most likely) used a map—Stieler's Hand-Atlas—which, by then, already showed advanced settlement in the area, including railroad lines through the valley of Grand River; blank stretches of landscape were increasingly difficult to find. Yet he still had the 'old, unexplored' mountains of the West in mind for his adventure tales. He knew where the various old Indian tribes had once been situated: the Navajos come to the Timbabachi's aid from the south, for example, which is correct when looking at the German atlas of 1855.

After the troop departs from the dry canyon, up a narrow and winding gulch, which represents another secret path known only to Winnetou (and Old Firehand, by coincidence), they arrive at the desolate valley basin where Old Firehand shows his companions the silver and gold that he had discovered, and which he intends to mine, an hour's ride uphill, above the dry canyon. After that, they head south, towards Silver-Lake, through Timbabachi territory.

Silver-Lake once belonged to inhabitants that had long since disappeared; they vanished in ancient times, as mentioned several times within this work. The Fremont culture was only identified as such in 1928, but there could have been tales of 'ancient' civilizations in earlier times; the term Anasazi was only assigned in 1888-89 to the ancient civilization that once inhabited the more southern region; and as with the one further north, tales of or about them would have been told, and artefacts or ruins found, as noted on Stieler's map: the area south and east of Elk Ridge and the Abajo Mountains bears the following German inscriptions: *Ruinen* (ruins) twice, *Begraebnisplatz* (burial place) once. There are no such inscriptions between the Fremont and Green rivers, where the ruins of the people belonging to the Fremont culture are situated. There are other historic sites in that region of the Rocky Mountains, but they are not indicated on the maps of Stieler's Atlas. When Great Bear challenges Old Shatterhand to guess the purpose of the dam, which was built to hold the water of Silver-Lake, he says: "The conquerors of the southern regions all came from the north. This large gorge was a preferred route of the conquerors." He is referring to the dry canyon as seen from the Silver-Lake position, where the canyon has become a narrow gorge. The waters of the Silver-Lake valley had once emptied north, into the dry canyon; by building a dam, the ancient inhabitants caused the water to stop flowing north, and to rise; it subsequently found an exit south. The valley of Silver-Lake runs north-to-south.

The old German map of 1855 distinctly places the Timbabachi (at least the word pointing to their territory) in the region west of the of the Colorado River, at around the latitude of the San Juan and Colorado Rivers confluence; as mentioned, other sources place them around the Great Salt Lake, Utah—either way, May was stretching their range quite a bit when he placed Silver-Lake into the Book Mountains.

Karl May's fictional Silver-Lake, which once belonged to an ancient civilization, can be reached by leaving the Elk Mountains in a westerly direction, galloping across an unnamed plateau, riding along a canyon that leads to the Grand River, crossing it, entering a narrow gorge on the other side, following a creek that leads up to Elk Valley, riding through Elk Valley—and then after another few days of riding (and a scene break), by travelling up a dry canyon to Old Firehand's silver mine, as well as climbing up a secret, winding path south. Although this description is consistent with Shatterhand's stated location of Silver-Lake in or around the Book Cliffs (Mountains) on the Utah side of the border, many details also point considerably farther south, to the region of Elk Ridge, which places the lake within reach of the Timbabachi territory as shown on the 1855 map by Sohr. Elk Ridge may exist on the map in Stieler's Hand-Atlas, but not in Karl May's tale of *The Treasure In Silver-Lake*. By incorporating details from the area around Elk Ridge, like the two forts, artefacts of an ancient civilization, a dry canyon (perhaps White Canyon, with Moellhausen's description of a *Giessbach*, a seasonal torrent), the close proximity of the Timbabachi territory (west or south), he had effectively created a mysterious location for his Silver-Lake. There is one additional, and peculiar, inscription next to a watercourse along Elk Ridge on Stieler's map: 'Butler Wash'. Engineer Butler had accompanied Old Firehand to Silver-Lake to establish whether or not a pipeline could be built from Silver-Lake to the proposed mining operation.

Old Firehand, Winnetou and the entire group reach Silver-Lake after at most two weeks' riding from the beginning of chapter six: Old Shatterhand and his four friends are taken captive by the Utah the same day they encounter the soldiers. They spend one night at the Utah camp in the Elk Mountains; after they escape, they spend another night in the Utah camp not far from Night Canyon at the beginning of chapter seven. When they head off towards Elk Valley, they spend the third night in a hidden canyon at Elk Valley, and then travel on, to Silver-Lake. Chapter eight begins 'a few days of arduous riding' later. 'A few days' may mean as many as six days, or a week. This would mean that they reached Silver-Lake in just under two weeks after Old Shatterhand met the soldiers on his approach to Elk Mountains. Would it be possible to ride from the place of that encounter to Elk Ridge in two weeks, if the 'few days' were stretched to ten or more? May was known for covering great distances in impossibly short (fictional) times. They are also in a hurry. Captain Gunnison may have taken six weeks to cover the distance between Coochetopa Pass and the Wasatch Mountains (admittedly they were surveying the region, and thus travelling slowly), but Old Shatterhand and his friends must reach Silver-Lake in a much shorter time. However, they have a child in their group, who is travelling in a sedan, carried by two Indian ponies, and can therefore not travel too fast.

The southern location fulfils many requirements: it is close to the old Spanish trail to take them to Fillmore City (so is a location in the vicinity of Book Cliffs, in Utah); it is close to the Timbabachi territory (the Book Cliffs marginally fulfil that requirement), has clear evidence of ancient inhabitants (the Book Cliffs just might; they are within reach of the ancient people's range). There is a 'Butler Wash' along Elk Ridge, although that might be coincidental (however, it is notable that the man whose daughter was threatened by a large cat on board the paddle steamer had a different name in the previous version of the story that was used as the basis for chapter one; Karl May wrote *Der Schatz im Silbersee* during September to December 1889, one year after Stieler's Hand-Atlas had been published, so he had enough time to adjust such details to fit the map). The dry canyon empties its seasonal waters into the Colorado, which it could do in a location north of the Green and Grand River confluence if the Colorado Vall[ey] is meant by 'the Colorado'. Old legends of lost silver mines in the more southern region, as well as the Wasatch ranges to the west, would also have circulated in certain circles in Germany at a time Europe experienced some of the largest waves of emigration to the new world, which would have made the invention of a southern location very attractive.

May might have desired elements from the southern location around Elk Ridge, to populate his fictional region around fictional Silver-Lake. Just as he had seemingly placed the Mormon and Indian Forts around the Elk Mountains, and relocated the name of Silver-Lake from the Sevier region south of the Great Salt Lake, by the sleight-of-hand that fiction permits—and often requires— so did he describe a region within, or behind the Book Cliffs, east of the Green River, as if it possessed elements of the region further south, around the Elk Cliffs and Abajo Mountains. As mentioned earlier, he did a marvellous job, because today we're still looking for the 'X' that marks the spot.

Can the story of *The Treasure In Silver-Lake* be dated?

The events take place no earlier than June 1870, and no later than August 1870 by the end of chapter five at least; the only date indicator for chapters six through to the end is the fact that there is no snow at that particular time in the plot, which means it may be autumn of the same year, but not winter yet. How can the time and date of the adventure be determined? Because Sheridan is already connected to Kit Carson, but the eastward construction from Denver, and the westward construction from Sheridan, which are to meet to complete the Kansas Pacific Railway, have not met yet, the line is still under construction. October 1869: Westward construction resumed from Sheridan[29], Kansas; March 1870: Eastward construction started from a connection with Denver Pacific in Denver (DP completed between Cheyenne and Denver in June 1870); August 15, 1870: Westward construction and eastward construction met at Comanche Crossing[30], Kansas Territory[31]; September 1, 1870: Formal operation began between Kansas City and Denver[32]. As we read right at the beginning of *The Treasure In Silver-Lake*: 'It was around noon on a very hot June day...'.

Marlies Bugmann, Tasmania, 2012
With contributions by Philip Colston.

---

[29] Thank you to Don Strack, of utahrails.net for this historic snippet about Sheridan. From the work of James L. Ehernberger and Francis G. Gschwind, published as "Smoke Above The Plains" in 1965, and compiled as part of "Union Pacific Steam, Eastern District" in 1975: Numerous legendary figures of the Great American West have left their indelible imprints in the annals of Kansas Division territory. At the long-vanished town of Sheridan, Kansas, near present-day Wallace, the dynamic William F. Cody won his immortal soubriquet of "Buffalo Bill"—probably the most glamorous name of the western saga. Sheridan was then the terminus of the [Kansas Pacific] and Cody had been employed by the road to provide buffalo meat for the construction gangs. However it remained for a buffalo shooting match with another skilled hunter, Billy Comstock, to provide Cody with his deathless epithet. Cody won impressively and the legend of Buffalo Bill was born.
[30] http://www.cchscolorado.com/
[31] Kansas Territory was only known as such until 1861, when, on 28 February, 1861, the eastern portion of modern-day Colorado was named Colorado Territory, to govern the western region of the former Kansas Territory - http://en.wikipedia.org/wiki/Kansas_Territory.
[32] Courtesy of http://utahrails.net/up/kansas-pacific.php, copyright 2000-2011 by Don Strack.

The Treasure In Silver-Lake

Marlies Bugmann

Nintropan-Homosh   *Nintropan-Hauey*

Marlies Bugmann

1

On The Arkansas

It was around noon on a very hot June day when the *Dogfish*, one of the largest passenger and cargo steamers on the Arkansas, churned the waves of the river with its mighty paddle wheels. It had departed from Little Rock early in the morning and was soon to arrive in Lewisburg, where it was to dock in case there were new passengers to board and goods to be loaded.

The oppressive heat had driven the more well-to-do travellers into their cabins, and most of the deck passengers were lying behind barrels, crates and other pieces of luggage that afforded them a little shade. The captain had installed a 'bed-and-board' facility under a canvas awning for those travellers. Under it, all manner of glasses and bottles were standing on the table; their contents were undoubtedly not meant for sensitive gums and tongues. The barman was sitting behind the makeshift bar with his eyes closed, tired from the heat, nodding off. When he did lift his lids occasionally, a faint swear word or other strong expression came over his lips. His bad mood was directed at a group of perhaps twenty men who were sitting on the deck in front of the table, handing the dice shaker around. They were playing for drinks; at the end of each game the losing participant had to pay a round of whiskey. Consequently, the barman was deprived of his nap, which he dearly would have liked to have.

Those men had obviously not just met there and then on the steamer, because they were addressing each other in familiar terms, and each one also seemed to know the personal circumstances of his fellow group members, as the occasional casual remark indicated. Set apart from the general familiarity was one among them who seemed to be shown a certain amount of respect. They called him 'colonel'.

The man was tall and gaunt; his cleanly shaven, sharply delineated face was framed by a stroppy, red throat beard; the hair was also ginger coloured, which was even more obvious since he had pushed the worn-out old felt hat far down the back of his neck. His outfit consisted of heavy leather hobnail boots, Nankeen trousers and a short jacket of the same fabric. He wasn't wearing a waistcoat; in its stead a dirty, creased shirt was evident, the broad collar of which was wide open, not held in place by a bandana, so that it revealed the naked, sunburnt chest. Around his waist he had wound a red, fringed cloth from which the grips of a knife and two pistols protruded. Behind him lay a fairly new rifle, and a linen knapsack that was fitted with two straps, so that he could carry it on his back.

The other men were similarly dressed in a careless and dirty manner but very well armed in contrast. There was not one among them who would have been trustworthy. They conducted their game of dice with veritable fervour and conversed in such an uncouth language that no halfway decent human being would have paused near them for more than a minute. In any case, they had already played for countless drinks because their faces were heated not only from the sun, but also the alcoholic spirit, which had gained control of them.

The captain left the wheelhouse and went aft to the helmsman in order to give him a number of necessary instructions. When that had been taken care of, the latter asked:

"What do you think of the boys who are playing their dice up front there, captain? They don't seem to be the kind of gents one likes to see come aboard."

"I agree," the captain replied. "They may have pretended to be harvesters on their way west to get work on farms, but I wouldn't want to be the man they asked for work."

"Alright, sir. I personally think they're real outlaws. Hopefully they'll keep the peace here on board at least!"

"I wouldn't advise them to become more bothersome than we'd tolerate. We've got enough hands on board to toss them into the old, blessed Arkansas. Aside from that, prepare to dock because Lewisburg will be in sight in ten minutes!"

The captain returned to his bridge to issue the necessary orders upon docking. Soon the houses of the town came into view, which the ship greeted with a long-drawn roar of the steam whistle. Someone on the pier gave the signal for the steamer to take on freight and fare. Passengers who had been below deck up to that point came up to enjoy the short interruption to the monotonous trip.

Of course they weren't offered a very entertaining spectacle. The place back then wasn't of the same significance as it is now. Only a few idle people stood around the landing; there were some crates and packets to load, and three new passengers came on board. The officer who issued the tickets didn't treat them like gentlemen at all.

One of them was a tall White with a very strong physique. His dark beard was so dense that only the eyes, nose and the top part of his cheeks were visible. On his head sat an old beaver cap that had become almost bald over the years. It was impossible to determine its original shape; it most likely had all manner of modifications. The suit of the man consisted of trousers and jacket made from strong, grey linen. The broad leather belt contained two revolvers, one knife and several small implements that were indispensable for a Westerner. In addition he carried a heavy double-barrelled rifle, to the stock of which was tied a long axe, in order to carry both implements more comfortably.

After the man had paid for his passage he threw a searching glance across the deck. The well-dressed cabin guests didn't seem to interest him. Then his gaze fell upon the others who had risen from their dice game to look at those who were boarding the ship. He saw the colonel and immediately looked away, as if he hadn't noticed him; but while he pulled the long shafts of his boots up his powerful thighs, he quietly murmured to himself:

"Behold! If that isn't Red Brinkley, they can smoke me and eat me, skin and all! He cannot possibly have a good reason for gathering such a horde of boys. I hope he hasn't recognized me."

The one he was referring to had seen him as well and was taken aback. He quietly addressed his companions:

"Have a look at the black-haired fellow! Do any of you know him?"

His question was answered in the negative.

"I must have seen him some place else once, and under circumstances that weren't actually very pleasing for me. I seem to have a dark memory of it."

"In that case he ought to know you as well," one of the others remarked. "He looked at us but didn't even notice you."

"Hm! Maybe I will remember in due course. Or better still, I'll ask him for his name. When I hear it I'll know immediately where I stand. I might forget faces, but not names. Let's have a drink with him!"

"If he goes along with it!"

"It would be a despicable insult if he declined, as you all know. The one who has a drink invitation turned down has the right to reply with a knife or a pistol in this country, and if he kills the one who insulted him, nobody cares two hoots about it."

"But he doesn't look like someone who can be forced to do something he doesn't want to do."

"Pshaw! Will you bet on that?"

"Yes, let's have a bet, a bet!" those in the group piped up. "The loser buys three drinks for every one."

"That's alright with me," the colonel agreed.

"And with me," the other one remarked. "But there must be an opportunity to reciprocate. Three bets and three drinks."

"With whom?"

"Alright, first with the black-haired fellow, the one you claim to know without remembering who he is. Afterwards with one of the gentlemen who are standing over there still gawking at the bank, the tall fellow who looks like a giant among dwarfs. And lastly the Red Indian who came aboard with his boy. Or are you afraid of him?"

The answer to his question was general laughter, and the leader of the group of louts contemptuously remarked:

"Do you think I'm afraid of the red face? Pshaw! More likely of the giant you want me to tackle. All devils that fellow must be strong! But giants like him have the least courage, and he's dressed all neat and smart, which means he only knows how to conduct himself in a salon, but not how to deal with people like us. Alright, I'll match the bet. Three drinks for each of the three bets. Let's get to work!"

He had shouted the last three sentences loud enough for all passengers to hear. Every American, and especially every Westerner, knows the significance of the word 'drink', especially when it's being spoken in such a menacing manner, as was the case then. Hence everyone looked at the colonel. It was obvious that he and the men in his gang were already half inebriated, yet no one left, since everyone expected an interesting scene and wanted to see which of the passengers were going to be the ones to be offered a drink.

The colonel had someone fill the glasses, took his and walked over to the dark-haired passenger, who was still nearby, looking for a comfortable seat. He then said:

"Good afternoon, sir! I'd like to offer you this drink. I'm of the opinion that you're a gentleman because I only drink with truly noble people and hope that you'll empty it with a toast to my wellbeing!"

The beard of the man addressed by the colonel attained a broad shape, and then contracted again, which was indicative of a merry smile that had crossed his face.

"Alright," he replied. "I'm not disinclined to do you the favour, but would like to know beforehand who affords me such an honour."

"Quite right, sir! One has to know whom one is drinking with. My name is Brinkley, Colonel Brinkley, if you don't mind. And you?"

"My name is Grosser, Thomas Grosser, if you don't mind. Alright, to your health, colonel!"

He emptied the glass, whereby the others also drank up, and handed it back to Brinkley. The man saw himself as the victor, scrutinized Grosser in an almost insulting manner from head to toe, and then asked:

"Methinks that's a German name. You must be a damned Dutchman, eh?"

"No, I'm German, sir," the man said in the friendliest tone without letting the rudeness of the other ruffle him. "You'll have to deliver your Dutchman somewhere else. It cuts no ice with me. Thank you for the drink and good bye!"

He turned sharply on his heels, and while he quickly walked away he quietly muttered to himself:

"It is indeed Brinkley! And he calls himself colonel! The fellow is up to no good. Who knows how long we'll have to be on board together. I'll keep my eyes open."

Although Brinkley had won the first part of the bet, he didn't look very victorious. His expression had changed; it evidenced that he was annoyed. He had hoped that Grosser was going to refuse, and thus give cause to be forced to drink; but the dark-haired had been the smarter of the two, had accepted the drink first, and then made clear that he was too smart to give cause for a brawl. That irked the colonel. Hence he approached his second victim, the Indian, after he had refilled the glass.

At the same time as Grosser, the two Indians had come aboard, an older and a younger one, who was perhaps fifteen years old. The unmistakable similarity in their features led to the assumption that they were father and son. They were also dressed and armed alike, so that the son seemed to be the younger mirror of his father.

Their outfits consisted of leather leggings with fringes down the sides, and yellow moccasins. There was neither a hunting shirt nor coat visible because they had wrapped colourful Zuni blankets, which can often cost more than sixty dollars apiece, around their bodies from the shoulders down. Their black hair was plainly combed away from the face to fall straight down the back; it gave them a woman-like appearance. Their faces were round and full, and had an exceedingly good-natured expression, which was emphasized by the fact that they had coloured their cheeks a bright vermilion-red. The rifles they held in their hands didn't seem worth half a dollar combined. On the whole, the two Indians looked completely harmless and so peculiar on top of it that they had prompted the drinking buddies to break out in laughter, as mentioned earlier. They had bashfully moved aside, as if they were afraid of other people, and were leaning against a crate made from strong timber. It measured as much in height as a man and was as wide as it was long. They didn't seem to pay attention to anything at all, and even when the colonel approached, they only lifted their gaze when he stood right in front of them and addressed them:

"Hot weather today! Don't you think so, you red fellows? That's when a drink does you good. Here, take it old man and pour it onto your tongue!"

The Indian didn't move a muscle and replied in broken English: "Not drinking."

"What, you don't want to?" the owner of the ginger throat beard snapped at him. "I'm offering you a drink, understood, a drink! To have it refused is a bloody insult for a real gentleman like me, and that can only be paid back with the knife. Now then, will you drink or not? But I'll have to know who you are first. What's your name?"

"Nintropan-Hauey," the older Indian calmly and modestly replied.

"To what tribe do you belong?"

"Tonkawa."

"Therefore to the tame Indians, who are afraid of every cat, understood, every cat, even the littlest kitten! I'll make short work of you. Alright, will you drink?"

"I don't drink firewater."

Despite the threat Brinkley had issued, the Indian replied as calmly as before. However, the former swung back and gave him a resounding smack in the face.

"Here's your reward, you red coward!" he shouted. "I won't take any further revenge because a dog like you is too far beneath me."

No sooner had the strike been issued, than the Indian boy pulled his hand under the Zuni blanket, no doubt to reach for a weapon, and at the same time he looked at his father's face to glean what he was going to do and say.

The face of the older Indian had attained a completely different expression, and had become almost unrecognizable. His figure seemed to have grown taller, his eyes were aglow, and a distinct energy had suddenly come to life and flashed across his face. But he lowered his eyelids just as swiftly again; his figure slumped, and his face resumed the earlier demure expression.

"Well, what do you have to say to that?" the colonel mocked him.

"Nintropan-Hauey thanks you."

"Did you like the smack to your face so much that you're thanking me for it? Alright, here you have another one!"

He swung back again; but because the Indian moved his head away as fast as lightning, Brinkley's hand struck the wooden crate against which Nintropan-Hauey was leaning, so that it created a loud, hollow sound. At that moment a short, sharp growling and hissing resounded from inside the box and fast swelled to a wild, horrible scream followed by a thunder-like roar, so that everyone thought the entire ship was trembling under the terrible sounds.

Red Brinkley jumped back with a mighty start, dropped the glass and yelled at the top of his lungs:

"Heavens! What's that? What kind of beast is inside this box? Is that allowed? I could have died of shock or at least contracted epilepsy!"

The fright had affected not only him, but also the other passengers. Most of those on deck had called out loudly just like Brinkley. Only four of them did not bat an eyelid, namely the dark-haired passenger who was sitting right up front at the bow at that point, the tall gentleman who was going to be the third to be invited to a drink by the colonel, and the two Indians. Just like everyone else, those four people were unaware that a wild animal was on board, and inside the crate in question, to be precise; but they had years of practice in self-control, so it wasn't difficult for them to conceal their surprise.

The animal's roar had been heard even down below in the berths. Several loudly screeching ladies came rushing up on deck to enquire about the danger they were exposed to.

"It's nothing, ladies and messieurs," a very elegantly dressed gentleman, who had just then come out of his cabin, replied. "It's only a wee black panther, nothing more! A very cute *Felis panthera*, but a black one, messieurs!"

"What? A black panther!" a short, spectacle-wearing man squawked with trepidation. It was evident that he was more acquainted with the contents of zoological books than with actual wild animals. "The black panther is simply the most dangerous beast there is! It is larger and longer than the lion or the tiger! It murders its prey out of sheer bloodlust, and not out of hunger. How old is it?"

"Only three years, sir, no older."

"Only? You call this 'only'? It means that the animal has fully matured! My God! And such a beast is here on board! Who could possibly take responsibility for that?"

"I can, sir," the elegant stranger replied while he bowed to the crowd. "Allow me to introduce myself, ladies and gentlemen! I'm the famous menagerie owner Jonathan Boyler, and have been stationed in Van Buren for some time with my troop. When the black panther arrived in New Orleans for me, I went there with my most experienced animal tamer to fetch it. Upon my payment of an expensive fare, the captain of this good ship gave me permission to load the panther here. One of his conditions was that, if at all possible, the passengers weren't to know about the company in which they were travelling. Hence I feed the panther only at night and have, by God, always dished out a whole calf, so that the cat would eat enough to sleep during the day, and hardly be able to move. Of course, if one punches the crate with one's fists, it'll wake up and give voice. I hope that the ladies and gentlemen will no longer take notice of the wee panther's presence, which isn't causing any disturbance at all, really."

"What?" the one with the glasses replied, whereby his voice almost cracked. "Doesn't cause any disturbance? Don't take any notice? By all the devils, I really have to say that no one has ever made such demands on me! I am to inhabit the ship together with a black panther? I'll be lynched if I can do that! Either the cat goes or I'll go. Throw the beast into the water! Or take the crate back to shore!"

"But, sir, there's absolutely no danger," the menagerie owner reassured him. "Have a look at the crate, and..."

"Crate be damned," the short fellow cut him off. "I can bust that crate; how much easier will it be for a panther?"

"Please, let me finish what I was going to say, namely that inside the crate there is the actual steel cage; not even as many as ten lions or panthers together would be able to smash it."

"Is that true? Show us the cage! I must satisfy myself of it."

"Yes, show the cage, the cage! We must know where we stand," ten, twenty, thirty or more voices demanded.

The menagerie owner was a Yankee and thus grabbed the opportunity to turn the general request to his benefit.

"With pleasure, with pleasure!" he replied. "But, ladies and gentlemen, you can easily appreciate that one cannot view the cage without seeing the panther. However, I cannot allow that without a certain something in return. In order to enhance the attraction of the rare spectacle, I'll order the animal to be fed. We'll arrange for three seat categories, the first sells for one dollar, the second for half a dollar, and the third for a quarter dollar. But since there are only ladies and veritable gentlemen here, I'm convinced we can leave out the second and third class seats altogether right from the start. Or would anyone here want to pay only half or a quarter dollar?"

Of course no one answered.

"Alright then, only first class seats in that case. Please, ladies and gentlemen, one dollar per person."

He took off his hat and collected the money while his animal tamer, whom he had called on deck for that purpose, made the necessary preparations for the show.

Most of the passengers were Yankees, and as such they agreed wholeheartedly with the new turn of events. While most of them had initially been outraged about the fact that the captain had made his steamer available for the transport of such a dangerous predator, for the moment they felt assuaged by the prospect of a welcome change in the monotony of life on board. Even the short scholar had overcome his fear and was looking forward to the show with great interest.

Brinkley used the opportunity to put the following to his companions:

"Listen, boys, I've won one bet and lost the other, because the red scoundrel didn't want to drink. That evens things out. We'll change the third bet from three glasses of whiskey to the one-dollar entry fee we have to pay. Do you agree?"

Of course his chums agreed to the suggestion because the tall man didn't look like he was going to let someone instil fear into him.

"Good," said their leader, who was feeling cocksure because of the large quantity of alcohol he had already consumed. "Pay attention to how gladly and readily the Goliath will drink with me!"

Brinkley had the glass filled again, and then he approached the passenger in question. The physique of the man was of towering proportions indeed. He was even taller and more broad-shouldered than the dark-haired passenger who had given his name as Grosser. He was definitely no house mouse because his face was sun-tanned; his handsome features were boldly cut, and his blue eyes had that certain indescribable gaze by which people who live in open spaces, where the horizon is unrestricted, stand apart, in other words sailors, desert dwellers and prairie men. It was noteworthy that his face was cleanly shaven, that he was perhaps forty years of age, and that he wore an elegant travelling suit. There were no weapons apparent. He was standing in the company of several gentlemen with whom he held a lively conversation about the panther. The captain was also among them. He had come down from the bridge to see the panther presentation.

At that point the colonel walked up to them, stood in front of his intended third victim and said:

"Sir, I'm offering you a drink. I hope you won't refuse to tell me, a veritable gentleman, who you are."

The so-addressed gave him an astonished look and turned away again to continue the conversation that the impertinent interloper had so rudely interrupted.

"Pooh!" Brinkley said. "Are you deaf, or do you intentionally refuse to hear me? I wouldn't advise the latter because I have no sense of humour when it comes to offering a drink. I'll give you the good advice to take the Indian as an example!"

The harassed man shrugged his shoulder lightly and asked the captain:

"Did you hear what this fellow said to me?"

"Yes, sir, every word," the man replied.

"Alright, in that case you're a witness to the fact that I didn't call him to come here."

"What?" The colonel's temper flared up. "You're calling me a fellow? And you're rejecting the drink? Do you want the same thing happening to you that happened to the Indian, whom I..."

Brinkley didn't get any further because at that moment the tall man boxed his ears so mightily that he crashed onto the deck, slid along it for quite a stretch, and then even rolled over. He lay motionless for a moment, but then hastily struggled to his feet, pulled out the knife, lifted it for a thrust while he rushed at the tall man.

The latter had put both of his hands into his trouser pockets and was standing there as casually as if he weren't in the slightest danger, as if Brinkley didn't even exist. The attacker, however, furiously hollered:

"Dog, you boxed my ear! That costs blood, and it will be yours!"

Several men, including the captain, wanted to step in, but the tall gentleman prevented them with an emphatic shake of his head. When the assailant had approached to within two paces, the man lifted his right leg and gave the colonel a kick to the stomach with such force that he crashed to the ground and rolled away once more.

"That'll do now, or else..." the tall man warned.

But the colonel jumped up again, pushed the knife back into his belt, all the while growling with wrath, and then pulled out one of his pistols to aim at his opponent. The tall man withdrew his right hand from the pocket in which he had kept a revolver.

"Away with the pistol!" he ordered while he aimed at the right hand of the colonel with his small, but good weapon.

One, two, three flat, sharp cracks—the colonel screamed and dropped the pistol.

"Alright, my dear fellow!" the tall man said. "You won't be smacking anyone's face for a while, when they refuse to drink from the glass on which you've wiped your big mouth before. I've smashed your hand. And if you still want to know who I am, then..."

"Damned be your name!" The colonel was seething. "I don't want to hear it. But I must and will have you. Upon him, boys; go on!"

It became apparent that the men indeed formed a real gang in which all stood up for one. They pulled the knives from their belts and rushed at the tall man, who seemed to be lost before the captain was even able to call his crew to assist. But the daring man placed one foot out the front, lifted his arms, and called out:

"Keep coming if you dare to tackle Old Firehand!"

The sound of that name had an immediate effect. The colonel, who had again grabbed the knife, but with his left hand, stopped walking and exclaimed:

"Old Firehand! All devils, who would have thought! Why didn't you say so in the first place?"

"Is it only the name that protects a gentleman from your rudeness? Clear off, quietly sit down in a corner somewhere and don't let me see you again, or else I'll extinguish you all!"

"Alright, we'll talk again some time later!"

The colonel walked away with his bleeding hand and returned to the gang's seating. His cronies followed him like dogs that had received a beating. They sat down, bandaged their leader's hand, spoke quietly among themselves and in the process cast glances across to the famous hunter that weren't necessarily friendly, but nevertheless proved what great respect they had for him.

But the widely known name had had an effect on other people as well. There was probably no one among the passengers who had not already heard of the daring man whose entire life was assembled from dangerous deeds and adventures. The passengers reflexively stepped back out of respect for him and looked at the tall figure more closely, although the harmonic dimensions and proportions had already been conspicuous before.

The captain shook the man's hand and said in the friendliest tone a Yankee was capable of:

"But sir, I ought to have been informed of that! I would have assigned my own cabin to you. By God it is an honour to have your feet step onto the planks of the *Dogfish*. Why did you give a different name?"

"I gave you my real name. Old Firehand is the prairie name the Westerners gave me because the fire of my rifle, guided by my hand, always brings ruination."

"I heard that you never miss!"

"Pshaw! To miss is impossible! Every good Westerner can do just as well. But you can see what advantage such a nom de guerre has. If mine hadn't been so widely known, there would have been a brawl."

"Whereby you would have been beaten because they outnumbered you!"

"Do you think so?" Old Firehand asked while a self-conscious but not at all proud smile glided across his face. "I'm not worried as long as they come at me with knives only. I would certainly have stood my ground until your crew was at hand."

"There would have been no shortage of men, of course. But what am I going to do with the scoundrels? I'm the master, the ruler and the judge here. Shall I put them in chains, and then deliver them to the law?"

"No."

"Or shall I put them ashore?"

"Not that either."

"But there must be punishment!"

"I'd advise against it. I figure that this is not the last run you intend to make with your steamer, yes?"

"Wouldn't think of it! I plan on swimming up and down the Arkansas for many a long year yet."

"Alright, then beware of arousing the vengeance of those people! It would certainly lead to your ruination. They'd be capable of ambushing you from somewhere along the banks, and play a prank on you that would not only cost your ship, but also your life."

"They wouldn't dare!"

"They certainly would. Besides, it wouldn't be a great risk for them. They'd be acting in secrecy and work it so that no one could prove anything."

At that point Old Firehand spotted the dark-haired passenger. Grosser had approached and was standing nearby with an inquisitive gaze directed at the hunter. Firehand walked up to him and asked:

"You look like you wish to talk to me, sir. Can I do you a favour?"

"A very big favour," the German replied.

"Then tell me what it is!"

"Allow me to shake your hand once, sir! That's all I'm asking of you. After that I'll go away satisfied and won't bother you any further. But I'll be thinking back on this hour with joy for the rest of my life."

It was evident by his open gaze and the tone of his voice that the words truly came from the heart. Old Firehand extended his right hand and asked:

"How far do you intend to travel with this steamer?"

"With this one? Only to Fort Gibson."

"That's far enough, isn't it?"

"Oh, but then I'll continue on by another boat. I'm afraid that you, the famous man who's never been defeated, thinks I'm scared."

"Why?"

"Because I've accepted the colonel's offer of a drink before."

"Oh, no. I can only praise you for having been so circumspect. Of course, when he hit the Indian I decided to give him a strong lesson, which has happened now."

"It will hopefully serve him as a warning. Besides, if you've crippled his fingers, he'll be finished as a Westerner. However, I don't know what to think about the Indian."

"What do you mean?"

"He really behaved like a coward, and yet didn't as much as flinch when the panther growled. I can't reconcile one with the other."

"Alright, I'll make the rhyme for you. It won't be difficult for me to put it together."

"Do you know the Indian?"

"I have not seen him before, but have heard about him all the more."

"I heard the name he gave. It's a word that will not roll easily over one's tongue. It was impossible for me to memorize it."

"Because he used his mother tongue so as not to let the colonel know whom he was dealing with. His name is Nintropan-Hauey, and that of his son is Nintropan-Homosh; that means Great Bear and Little Bear."

"Is that possible? I've often heard of father and son Bear. The Tonkawa culture has become degenerate. Only the two Nintropan have inherited the warrior spirit of their ancestors and wander about the mountains and the prairie."

"Yes, they're two capable men. And you will probably no longer think that they neglected to give the colonel a more appropriate answer because of cowardice."

"Another Indian would have killed the fellow immediately!"

"Perhaps. But didn't you see that the son immediately reached for his knife or tomahawk under the blanket? Only when he saw the expressionless face of his father did he abstain from avenging the insult immediately. I tell you, a short glance suffices between those two Indians where we Whites would require a long speech. The colonel's death was a foregone conclusion since the moment he struck the Indian's face. Father and son Bear won't get off his trail until they've extinguished him. But say, you mentioned your name before, which I've recognized as that of a German. We're therefore compatriots."

"What? You're German as well?" Grosser was astonished.

"Indeed. My actual name is Winter. I will also travel a fairly long stretch with this steamer, which means we'll have enough opportunities to converse again."

"If you'll consent to that, it would be my very great honour, sir."

"No compliments. I'm no more than you—a Westerner, nothing else."

"Yes, but the general is also no more than the recruit, namely a soldier."

"Are you comparing yourself to a recruit? That would mean you've been in the West only for a short time."

"Well, it's actually been a little longer than that," the man with the dark beard humbly replied. "My name is Thomas Grosser. They leave out the family name in this country; Thomas is turned into Tom, and because I've got such a mighty black beard, they call me Black Tom."

"How? What?" Old Firehand exclaimed. "You're Black Tom, the famous rafter?"

"I am Tom, I am a rafter, but I doubt that I'm famous."

"You are, sir, you are. I'll assure you of that with a shake of hands!"

"Not too loudly, please, sir!" Tom warned. "The colonel mustn't hear my name."

"Why not?"

"Because he would recognize me by that name."

"Does that mean you've had dealings with him?"

"Some. I'll tell you in due course. Don't you know him?"

"I saw him for the first time today."

"Alright, look at his beard and his ginger hair and put the name Brinkley to it."

"You don't say! Does that mean he's Red Brinkley, who's committed a hundred shameful deeds without anyone having been able to prove that he was the perpetrator?"

"It is he, sir. I've recognized him."

"In that case, I'll keep an eye on him as long as he stays on board. At the same time I wish to get to know you more closely. You're a man who fits into my plans. If you're not already committed otherwise, I could use a man like you."

"Alright," Tom replied and pensively stared at the ground. "The honour to be in your company is worth much more than anything else. Although I've entered an agreement with other rafters, who have even elected me their leader, I can easily withdraw from it if you can give me some time to notify them."

"Splendid. You must move into a cabin, so that we can be together. I'll gladly pay the difference."

"Thank you, sir! Rafters like me also earn good money if they're diligent. And at the moment I've got my pockets full because I'm returning from Vicksburg where I've presented our bill and turned it into cash. I can therefore pay for a cabin myself. But look! It seems the show is about to begin."

Jonathan Boyler had turned boxes and packets into several rows of seats and was in the process of inviting the spectators with due pomp and ceremony to take their seats. They did. The deck hands were permitted to watch for free, if they weren't busy with their tasks. Neither the colonel nor his gang came to watch; he had lost his enthusiasm for it.

The two Indians hadn't been asked whether or not they wanted to join in. The owner of the animal didn't want to be accused of forcing two natives upon the ladies and gentlemen who paid a dollar per person. They therefore moved aside and seemed to pay no attention to either the cage or the spectators, while not the slightest detail of what was going on escaped their secret, but keen gazes.

The spectators were sitting in front of the closed crate. Most of them had no real idea of a black panther. The feline predators of the new world are significantly smaller and also less dangerous than those of the old world. The gaucho, for example, catches the jaguar, which is also called the American tiger, with the lasso and drags it along behind the horse. He wouldn't dare do that with the Bengal tiger. And the American lion, the puma, flees from human beings even if it is starving. People imagine that the panther may be significantly smaller than the lion or the tiger, and since the spectators were thinking of the puma and the jaguar when they heard the term 'panther', most of them expected to see a predator no more than half a metre tall and of corresponding length. Hence they were all the more shocked when the front of the crate was removed and they saw the panther.

The animal had been surrounded by darkness since New Orleans; its crate had only been opened during the night. At that point, it saw the first daylight in a long time, which temporarily blinded it. The cat closed its eyes and remained lying in the crate where it stretched out as long as the crate was. Then it squinted gingerly, whereby it noticed the people sitting in front of it. The cat immediately jumped to its feet and emitted a roar that caused the majority of spectators to jump up and retreat.

The panther was indeed a fully grown, magnificent specimen of at least one metre height and twice as long without the tail. It grabbed the bars of its iron prison with its front paws and shook them until the crate started to move. It revealed is terrible teeth. The coat's dark colour only enhanced the impression it made.

"Yes, ladies and gentlemen, the black variation is at home on the Sunda Islands," the menagerie owner explained. "But these animals are small. The true black panther, which is rare, of course, is found in North Africa, along the borders of the Sahara. It is just as strong as the lion, and far more dangerous, and is capable of carrying a grown ox away in its jaws. You'll see in a moment what its teeth are capable of because the feeding will begin in a moment."

The tamer brought one half of a sheep and placed it in front of the cage. When the panther saw the meat, it behaved like a mad creature. It jumped up and down, hissed and roared, so that the more fearful spectators retreated even further.

A Negro who had been busy near the engine had not been able to resist curiosity and had sneaked closer. The captain spotted him and ordered him to return to his work immediately. Because the black man didn't immediately obey, the captain grabbed a nearby hawser end and gave him a few whacks with it. The punished deck hand quickly withdrew but lingered in the hatch opening that led to the machine room, pulled a threatening grimace at the captain behind his back, and shook his fists at him. Because the spectators were paying attention only to the panther, they hadn't noticed the incident. But the colonel had observed it and said to his companions:

"That Nigger doesn't seem to like the captain. He might perhaps be of some use to us. Let's befriend him. A few dollars usually work wonders with a black man."

At that point the animal tamer pushed the meat through the bars into the cage, scrutinized the spectators with a searching look, and then said a few quiet words to his employer. Jonathan

Boyler shook his head with an expression of concern; the other continued to talk to him and seemed to be able to allay his fears, because at last the owner of the panther nodded and explained to those who were sitting and standing in front of the cage:

"Ladies and gentlemen, let me tell you that you're incredibly lucky. A tame black panther has never before been seen, at least not here in the States. During the three-week stay in New Orleans my tamer has trained the panther and explained just now that he intends to go inside the cage in public for the first time, and to sit down next to it if you promise him a corresponding reward."

The tamer was a strong, very muscular person with an unusually self-assured expression. There was no doubt that he was convinced of the successful outcome of his undertaking, which was obvious by his confident mien.

The panther had gotten into its meal, crushing the bones to pulp between its teeth. It seemed to pay attention only to the food, hence even a layman would have come by the opinion that there was no great danger involved in entering the cage at that point.

Someone replied enthusiastically:

"That would be marvellous, sir! And it's nothing short of a daring feat for which one wouldn't mind paying some money. How much does the man want?" It was none other than the previously so frightened, short, spectacled scholar.

"One hundred dollars!"

"Hm! Isn't that a bit much?"

"No, on the contrary, it's far too little, sir. The risk is not insignificant because he's not even half sure of the animal."

"Ah! I'm not wealthy. But I'll contribute five dollars. Gentlemen, who's going to pay some more?"

There were so many who put their hands up that the sum was bound to be raised. The show had begun, after all, and one wanted to enjoy the spectacle to its fullest. Even the captain became excited and offered bets.

"Sir," Old Firehand warned him. "Don't make a mistake! I'm asking you not to risk it. You have the responsibility to raise objections to it, especially since the man is not yet completely sure of the animal."

"Objections?" the captain laughed. "Pshaw! Am I the tamer's father or mother, perchance? Do I have to give him orders? Here in this blessed country everyone has the right to risk his neck as he desires. If the panther eats him, then the affair is entirely his and the cat's, but not mine. Alright, gentlemen, I claim that the man doesn't come back out of the cage as hale as he goes in, and put up one hundred dollars. Who will match that? And the tamer shall receive an extra ten percent."

Everyone was electrified by his example. Several bets of significant amounts were placed, which were going to earn the tamer almost three hundred dollars if his daring stunt succeeded.

It hadn't been mentioned that the tamer ought to be armed. He fetched his killer, a whip that carried an explosive projectile in the pommel. Should the animal attack him, one powerful strike with the handle was sufficient to kill the panther immediately.

"I don't even trust such a weapon," Old Firehand said to Black Tom. "An impact firecracker would be more practical since the animal would be scared away without being killed. But each to his own. I shall praise the undertaking if it concludes successfully."

At that point the tamer delivered a short speech to the spectators, and then turned towards the cage. He opened the heavy bolts and pushed the narrow grate, which formed the door, and which was less than one and a half metres tall, to the side. In order to walk inside the cage he had to duck. He needed both hands to hold the door and held the whip between his teeth, so that he could close it again once he was inside the cage, and was therefore defenceless for that brief moment. Although he had often been inside the cage with the animal, the circumstances had always been entirely different. The panther had not been in the dark for days on end, there had been no such crowd nearby, and there had neither been the noise of the steam engine stomping nor the churning of the paddle wheels. Neither the menagerie owner nor the tamer had taken such conditions into consideration, and the consequences became apparent immediately.

When the panther heard the sound of the iron grate it quickly turned around. The tamer poked his lowered head inside; the predator moved as quick as a flash, and with a lightning-fast jerk it had the man's head—from the mouth of which fell the whip—between its jaws and crushed it to mush with a single bite.

There was no describing the commotion that arose in front of the cage. Everyone jumped up and ran away. Only three people remained on the scene: the menagerie owner, Old Firehand and Black Tom. The former attempted to push the steel grate door closed, but that was impossible because the corpse was lying halfway in the opening. He then tried to grab it by the legs and pull it out.

"For God's sake, not that!" Old Firehand called out. "The panther would follow it. Push the corpse in all the way; he's dead after all. The door will then close!"

The panther was lying in front of the headless corpse. It kept a glinting eye on its master with the mouth full of bone splinters and bloody slaver dribbling from it. It seemed to guess the man's intentions because it roared angrily and crawled forwards over the corpse, holding it down with its weight. The cat's head was only a couple of hand widths from the door opening.

"Away, away! It's coming outside!" Old Firehand shouted. "Tom, your rifle! Your rifle! A revolver would only worsen the situation."

Black Tom ran to fetch his rifle.

Only ten seconds had elapsed since the tamer had entered the cage. No one had found the time to get to safety completely. The entire deck was a confusion of fleeing and fearfully screaming passengers. The doors to the cabins and lower decks were blocked. People ducked behind barrels and crates, but immediately jumped up again because they didn't feel safe behind them.

The captain ran towards his bridge and jumped up the stairs three and four steps at a time. Old Firehand followed him. The menagerie owner fled around the cage to the back of it. Black Tom ran for his rifle. Along the way he remembered that he had tied the axe to it, and that it was therefore not immediately ready to use. He stopped beside the two Indians, instead of running past them, and snatched the rifle out of Great Bear's hand.

"I shoot," the Indian said and stretched his hand out for the weapon.

"Let me!" Black Tom barked at him. "I'll most certainly shoot better than you!"

He turned around to the cage. The panther had just left it, lifted its head and roared. Black Tom aimed and pulled the trigger. The shot rang out, but the bullet didn't hit. Tom hastily took the rifle from Little Bear's grasp as well and fired its contents at the animal—with the same lack of success.

"Shoot bad. Don't know rifle," the old bear said as calmly as if he were sitting in his safe wigwam eating a roast.

The German ignored the remarks. He tossed the gun away and hurried forwards to where the firearms of the colonel's people were lying. The gentlemen had not been in the mood to tackle the animal, and instead had hastily hidden.

At that moment a ghastly scream came from the bridge. A lady attempted to flee up the stairs. The panther had spotted her after the first commotion had abated somewhat. It crouched, and then leapt in long, bouncing jumps towards her. She saw it and emitted that ghastly scream. She was still at the bottom of the stairs, while Old Firehand was already standing on the fifth or sixth step. He grabbed the woman immediately, pulled her up to his level, and then with powerful arms hoisted her higher up to where the captain took a hold of her. That had been the work of a mere two moments, and the panther had arrived below the bridge. It already put its front paws onto one of the lower steps and flexed its body in readiness to lunge up at Old Firehand. The man gave the cat a kick to the nose with all his might, and then fired the three remaining bullets from his revolver at the cat's head.

But, of course, that kind of deterrent was ridiculous. One does not repel a black panther with a kick and three pea-sized revolver bullets; but Old Firehand had no other, more effective means of defence. He was convinced that the animal was going to seize him; but it didn't happen, on the contrary, the panther slowly turned its head to the side while it remained in its upright position against the stairs. Had the three bullets, fired from such close proximity, only grazed its skull and stunned it for a moment? Or had the kick to its nose been too painful? In short, it averted its eyes from Old Firehand, and instead stared towards the fore deck where a girl, approximately thirteen years old, was standing motionless, as if paralysed from the shock, and holding both arms stretched out towards the bridge. She was the daughter of the lady whom Old Firehand had just a moment earlier saved from the panther. The girl had also been fleeing; but when she saw that her mother was in danger, she was gripped by horror and froze. She wore a light-coloured dress that was visible over a great distance, and it caught the panther's attention. The cat took its paws from the stairs, turned away from it and bounded towards the child in three-metre leaps. The girl saw the terrifying creature approach and was incapable of either moving or making a sound.

"My child, my child!" the mother cried.

Those who witnessed it screamed or hollered as well; but none lifted a hand or foot to save the girl. There would not have been time for it anyway. No time? And was there truly no one who moved? But there was someone; in fact, it was the one who would have seemed the least likely, namely the young Indian.

Together with his father, he had been standing about ten paces away from the girl. When he realized the danger she was in, his eyes flashed. He looked to his right and left, as if he were searching for a way out; then he dropped the Zuni blanket from his shoulders and in the Tonkawa language called to his father:

"*Tiakaitat; shai shoyana[1]!*"

He rushed up to the girl in two leaps, grabbed her by the belt around her waist, pulled her to the railing, and then hoisted her and himself onto it. He stopped for a moment to look back. The panther was behind him, and just then prepared to jump. As soon as the paws of the animal left the ground, the young Indian jumped from the railing into the water. So as not to land next to the animal, he had directed his leap sideways. The water closed above him and his burden. At the same time the panther sailed out over the railing and down into the river, since the animal had been unable to stop because of its momentum.

"Stop, engineer, stop immediately!" the captain had the presence of mind to issue his command through the speaking tube into the engine room.

The engineer immediately reversed the engine; the speed of the steamer slackened, with the wheels only churning enough to prevent drifting.

Since the danger to the passengers had disappeared, everyone hurried out from various hiding places and over to the railing. The mother of the girl had fainted; the father shouted:

"One thousand dollars for the rescue of my daughter, two thousand, three thousand, five thousand, and more, much more!"

No one took any notice of him. Everyone leaned over the railing to look down into the river. There the panther, as an excellent swimmer, was floating on the surface with its paws stretched out wide, looking for its prey—in vain. The daring boy and the girl were nowhere to be seen.

"They've drowned, they've drifted into the wheels!" the father lamented while he was tearing at his hair with both hands. At that moment the voice of the old Indian echoed across the deck from the other side:

"Nintropan-Homosh was smart. Swim away under ship, so that the panther doesn't see. They are down here!"

Everyone ran across to starboard, and the captain ordered heaving lines to be lowered. And indeed, in the water below, hard

---

[1] Stay here; I'll swim

against the hull of the steamer, the young bear slowly swam alongside it on his back, so as not to drift away. He had placed the unconscious girl across his body. The lines were quickly at hand; they were lowered. The boy fastened one of them under the arms of the girl, and while she was being pulled up on board he nimbly climbed up another.

Resounding cheers greeted him, but he proudly walked away without saying one word. However, when he passed the colonel, who had also been among the spectators, he stopped in front of him and loudly said, so that everyone could hear it:

"Well, does Tonkawa fear small, mangy cat? Colonel has run away with all of his twenty heroes; but Tonkawa has drawn big monster onto him to save girl and passengers. Colonel soon hear more about Tonkawa!"

The rescued girl was carried into the cabin. At that moment the helmsman, who had the best lookout position, pointed portside and called out:

"See the panther; see the raft!"

Everyone ran to the other side again where a new and no less exciting spectacle was on offer. Because of the events just mentioned, no one had noticed the small craft, which had been put together with tree branches and reeds, and which was carrying two people who were obviously attempting to reach the steamer from the right river bank. They were working with two makeshift paddles that had also been fashioned from branches. One of the people was a boy, the other seemed to be a woman wearing peculiar clothing. The passengers saw a head covering, akin to an old poke bonnet, and underneath it a full, red-cheeked face with small eyes. The rest of the body was clad in a wide sack or some such thing, the cut and style of which was undeterminable because the person was sitting down. Black Tom stood next to Old Firehand and asked him:

"Sir, do you know this woman?"

"No. Is she so famous that I ought to know her?"

"Indeed. To be precise, she is not a woman but a man, a prairie hunter and trapper. And there the panther is approaching. You're about to see what a woman, who's a man, is capable of."

He leaned over the railing and called down:

"*Hola*, Aunty Droll, pay attention! This animal here wants to eat you."

The raft was still approximately fifty metres from the steamer. The panther had been swimming up and down the side of the vessel, all the while looking for its prey. At that point it spotted the raft and headed for it. The person on it, who looked like a woman, gazed up at the deck, recognized the one who had called down, and then replied with a high-pitched falsetto voice:

"What good luck, is that you, Tom? I'm very pleased to see you if that's necessary! What kind of animal is it?"

"A black panther that's jumped overboard. Get away from here, quickly, quickly!"

"Oho! Aunty Droll doesn't run away from anyone, not even from a panther, may it be black, blue or green. Am I permitted to shoot the beast?"

"Of course! But you won't be able to do it. It belongs to a menagerie and is the most dangerous predator in the world. Flee to the other side of the steamer."

No one except Tom knew the peculiar figure, yet everyone shouted their warning in the direction of the raft. The person, however, seemed to derive some kind of pleasure from playing catch with the panther. She worked the paddle with astonishing precision, and with the same falsetto voice called the question:

"I'll certainly do it, old Tom. Where shall I shoot such a creature, if that's necessary?"

"Into the eye," Old Firehand replied.

"Alright! Then let the water rat come a little closer."

The person put the paddle aside and reached for the rifle, which had been lying next to her. Raft and panther quickly drew closer. The predator stared at the enemy with wide-open eyes; the person lifted the firearm, aimed swiftly and pulled the trigger twice. To put the gun down, grab the paddle and drive the raft back a stretch was the work of a single moment. The panther had disappeared. Where it had last been spotted a swirl marked its death struggle; then it surfaced again further downstream, motionless and dead; it drifted for a few seconds and was then pulled back into the deep water.

"A masterful shot!" Tom shouted down from the deck, and the other passengers enthusiastically agreed, except for the menagerie owner, who had lost his expensive panther as well as his tamer.

"There were two shots," the odd-looking person replied from down below. "One in each eye. Where is this steamer headed, if it's necessary?"

"It'll go as far as it finds enough water," the captain replied.

"We wish to board, and have built a raft on the bank for that purpose. Will you permit us to come up?"

"Can you pay your fare, Ma'am, or Sir? I truly don't know whether to haul you up as a man or a woman."

"As an aunt, sir. To be precise, I'm Aunty Droll, if that's necessary. And talking of the fare, I'm used to paying with real money, or even gold nuggets."

"In that case I'll send the rope ladder down to you. Come aboard! We'll have to see to it that we can get away from this unfortunate spot."

The rope ladder was lowered. First the boy, who was also armed with a gun, climbed up; then the other person hung the rifle across her back, grabbed the ladder, pushed the raft below away and, as agile as a squirrel climbed up on deck where she was greeted by the stares of the incredulous, astonished passengers.

Aunty Droll

2

The Outlaws

"Despite, or rather because, of their liberal institutions, the United States of America are the forge of entirely unique social scourges, which would be impossible in a European state."

Experts on the circumstances there will agree that the above claim by a contemporary geographer has its good points. One could divide the scourges of which he speaks into chronic and acute. With regard to the former, the runner, loafer and rowdy element, being smugglers, who prefer to target immigrants, as well as layabouts and ruffians, who seek to squabble and cause brawls, must be mentioned. This element has become stabilized, so it seems, and will survive for another few decades.

It is a different matter with the other kind of plague, which develops much faster and is of shorter duration. The lawless situation of the far West has resulted in the forming of organized gangs of robbers and murderers. Only by applying the strictest measures was Master Lynch able to destroy them. The Ku Kluxers, who were at work during, and for some time after, the civil war, must also be mentioned. However, the outlaws, representing the roughest and most brutal drifters, evolved into the worst and most dangerous scourge.

When great pressure weighed upon business and commerce during one particular period, and thousands of factories stood still, tens of thousands of workers became unemployed and joined the migration that headed in the preferred, westerly direction. The states along and on the far side of the Mississippi were literally swamped by the flood of migrants. Soon a separation process was in place whereby honest folk among them took work where they found it, even if the occupation was strenuous and brought little in the way of earnings. Most of them were hired on farms as harvesters to help with the crops.

The work-shy individuals among them, however, combined into gangs that eked out a miserable existence by robbery, murder and arson. Their members quickly descended to the lowest rung of moral depravity and were led by men who had to avoid civilization because the eager fist of the penal law stretched out for them.

Such outlaws usually made an appearance in large groups, and occasionally combined up to three hundred men or even more. They attacked not only individual farms, but also small towns to rob them completely. They even seized the railways, overpowered the employees and used the trains to quickly travel to other regions where they carried on committing their crimes. Their troublesome activities got out of hand, so that the governors of several states were forced to call in the militia in order to combat them.

As mentioned, the captain and the helmsman of the *Dogfish* were of the opinion that Colonel Brinkley and his men were such outlaws. That assumption, even if correct, was no reason for concern. The group was only about twenty men strong, and therefore far too weak to tackle the other passengers and the crew, but caution and attentiveness were never considered to be superfluous.

Of course, the colonel had also focussed his attention on the peculiar figure who had approached the steamer on the fragile raft, and who had killed the mighty predator in such a casual manner. He laughed when Tom spoke the strange name Aunty Droll. But when the stranger climbed on deck, and the colonel could clearly recognize the person's face, he frowned and directed his men to follow him. He led them to the very tip of the foredeck, and when they asked the reason for his retreat, he replied:

"This fellow isn't as ridiculous as he makes out; I'm telling you that we have to beware of him."

"Why? Do you know him? Is he a man or a woman?" one of the colonel's men asked.

"A man, of course."

"Why the masquerade?"

"It's no disguise. The man really is a unique character, and at the same time one of the most dangerous police spies there is."

"Pshaw! Aunty Droll and a police spy! The man may be anything you like, I'll believe it, except a detective!"

"And yet he is. I've heard of Aunty Droll; he's supposed to be a half crazy trapper who's on the best terms with all Indian tribes because of his funny demeanour. But now that I've seen him I know better. This fat person is a detective right out of the book. I've encountered him in Fort Sully along the Missouri where he alone extracted one of our comrades straight from our midst and delivered him to the rope, and we were more than forty men!"

"That's impossible. You could have punctured him at least forty times!"

"No, we couldn't. He works more with cunning than with force. Just have a look at the sly, mole-sized eyes! Not even an ant in thick grass will escape those. He applies a great, irresistible friendliness to sidle up to his victim, and then shuts the trap before it is even possible to recognize the deception."

"Does he know you?"

"I think that's impossible. He was unable to pay attention to me back then; it's been a long time since those events, and I've changed quite significantly in the meantime. Nevertheless, I'm of the opinion that we'd be well advised to keep quiet and act natural, so that we don't attract his attention. I think that we'll strike it lucky here and don't want him to be in our way. Old Firehand is the most famous hunter of the West, next to Old Shatterhand. Black Tom also proved that he's a man to be reckoned with, but Aunty Droll is even more dangerous than those two. Beware of him, and pretend you haven't even noticed him."

Of course, Droll didn't look as dangerous as the colonel had described him; instead, everyone had to make an effort not to burst into insulting laughter. Since he had climbed on deck, the clothing he was wearing could be scrutinized.

His head covering was neither hat nor cap nor bonnet, and yet one could describe it with each of those terms. It consisted of five pieces of leather each shaped differently. The one in the middle, which sat on his head, had the shape of an upturned pot; the one at the front shaded the forehead, and was definitely intended to be some sort of visor or brim; the third covered his neck, and the fourth and fifth were broad flaps that covered his ears.

His coat was very long and excessively wide. It was put together entirely from leather patches and splotches that had been stitched one upon the other. None of the pieces were of the same age; on the contrary, it was obvious that they had gradually been combined at different times. The edges at the front of the coat were fitted with short straps that were tied together to replace the missing buttons. Since the length and width of the unusual piece of clothing hampered walking, the man had cut it open at the back from the hem to the seat and had tied the two halves around his legs like knickerbockers, which gave Aunty Droll's movements a truly ridiculous appearance. The improvised breeches reached down to his ankles. Two leather shoes completed his lower attire. The sleeves of the coat were also unusually wide, and far too long for the man's arms. He had sewn the openings together and cut two holes further back, through which he poked his hands. That way, the sleeve ends formed two dangling pockets where he stashed all sorts of things.

Because of that particular piece of clothing, the figure of the man attained an unshapely appearance, and, together with the full, red-cheeked, incredibly friendly face, and eyes that wouldn't stop moving for even a moment, so that nothing escaped them, it literally provoked the desire to laugh.

Such apparitions aren't rare in the West by any means. Someone who spends years in the wilderness has neither time nor opportunity or money to replace his torn clothing with anything else than what his solitary life handed him, and one often meets famous people whose attire is such that, anywhere else, children would run laughing and screeching along behind them.

In one of his hands the man held a double-barrelled gun, which was definitely of a very honourable age. Whether or not he had other weapons on him remained a guess since the coat enclosed him like a tied up sack inside of which he was able to secrete all manner of objects.

The boy in his company was probably sixteen years of age. He was blond, strong-boned and had a serious, even defiant expression on his face like someone who already knows how to find his own path. His attire consisted of a hat, a hunting shirt, breeches, leggings and shoes, all made from leather. Apart from his rifle, he was also armed with a knife and a revolver.

When Aunty Droll stepped onto the deck, he extended his hand to Black Tom and exclaimed in his high-pitched falsetto voice:

"Hello, old Tom! What a surprise! It's been a veritable eternity since we've seen each other last! Where from and where to?"

They shook hands most cordially, whereby Tom replied:

"I've come up from the Mississippi, and am headed into Kansas where my rafters are stationed in the woods."

"Alright, everything's fine, then. We've got the same route. I'm also going there, and even further. We can therefore spend some time together. But let me attend to the matter of the fare first, sir. What do we have to pay, that's me and the young man, if it's necessary?"

He had directed the question at the captain.

"It depends rather a lot on how far you'll come along, and what accommodation you want."

"Accommodation? Aunty Droll always travels first class; a cabin, sir. And how far? Let's say to Fort Gibson for the moment. We can always extend the lasso later. Do you take nuggets?"

"Yes, gladly."

"But what about your gold scales? Are you honest?"

The question came out in such a droll manner, accompanied by a series of peculiar winks from his tiny eyes, that it wasn't taken serious. Nevertheless, the captain pretended to be vexed, and replied:

"Don't ever ask that again, or else I'll toss you overboard immediately!"

"Oho! Do you think Aunty Droll is easily expedited into the water? You would be mightily mistaken. Try it why don't you!"

"Well, one must be polite to ladies, and since you're an aunt, you sure belong to the fairer sex," the captain graciously declined. "I will therefore not take any offence at your question. Besides, there's no rush with making payment. See the purser when you can!"

"No, I won't consent to borrowing anything, not for one minute; that's my principle, if that's necessary."

"Alright! Come to the office with me."

The two men left, which gave the others the opportunity to exchange their opinions about the peculiar person. The captain returned earlier than Droll. He sounded quite astonished:

"Gentlemen, you should have seen the nuggets, the nuggets! He pulled one of his hands back into his sleeve, and when he stretched it out of the hole again, it was full of gold pieces the size of peas, hazelnuts and even larger. The man must have discovered a bonanza and has emptied it. I bet he's much wealthier than he looks."

In the meantime, Droll paid his fare, and then looked around the immediate vicinity of the purser's office. First he saw the colonel's people. Since he wasn't one to be on a ship without finding out what kinds of passengers were sharing his journey, he slowly ambled towards the fore deck and had a look at the men. His gaze rested on the colonel for a while before he asked him:

"Excuse me, sir, haven't we met some place before?"

"Not that I'm aware of," the man replied.

"Oh, I have a feeling we've bumped into each other already. Have you ever been up north along the Missouri?"

"No."

"Not in Fort Sully either?"

"Don't even know it."

"Hm! May I ask what your name is?"

"Why? What for?"

"Because I like you, sir. And as soon as I take pleasure in someone I won't be satisfied until I find out their name."

"Concerning that, I like you as well," the colonel replied in a cutting tone. "Nevertheless, I wouldn't be so rude and ask you for your name."

"Why? I don't think it's rude and would answer your question immediately. I don't have cause to keep quiet about my name. Only those with somewhat dishonest reasons will refuse to give theirs."

"Is that supposed to be an insult, sir?"

"Wouldn't think of it! I never insult another person, if it's necessary. *Adieu*, sir, and keep your name to yourself! I don't want to know it."

He turned around and left.

"That has to happen to me!" Red Brinkley hissed. "And I have to take it!"

"Why did you take it?" one of his men laughed. "I would have given this leather pouch an answer with my fist."

"And come off second best!"

"Pshaw! This toad didn't look like it had a lot of physical strength."

"Don't underestimate a man who lets a black panther approach to within arm's length, and then cold-bloodedly fires a couple of shots as if he had a prairie chicken in front of him. Besides it wasn't just a matter of him alone. I would immediately have had others against me, and we must avoid drawing attention to us."

Droll was walking towards aft and came past the two Indians, who sat on a bale of tobacco. When they saw him they rose like people who expected to be addressed. Droll slowed his pace when he spotted them, and then hurriedly approached them and said:

"*Mira, el oso viejo y el oso mozo*[1]!"

That was Spanish. He therefore knew that the two Indians spoke and understood Spanish better than English.

"*Que sorpresa, la tia Droll*[2]!" the older Indian replied, although he had already seen the short hunter while he was still sitting on the raft.

"What are you doing in the East, and on this ship?" Droll asked while he shook hands with both of them.

"We were in New Orleans with several red brothers, to purchase goods, and are on our way home while the others are transporting the merchandise. Many moons have passed since we last saw Aunty Droll."

"Yes, the young bear has grown twice as tall as he was back then. Are my brothers living in peace with their neighbours?"

"They have buried their war hatchets and don't wish to raise them again."

"When will you arrive home?"

"We don't know. We thought we were going to be away for two weeks, but now it will take longer."

"But now? What's the meaning of these two words?"

"They mean that the old bear cannot return home until he has plunged his knife into the blood of the offender."

"Who's that?"

"The white dog over there with the red hair. He struck Great Bear's face with his hand."

"All devils! The fellow has to be crazy! Surely he must know what it means to strike an Indian with his bare hand, particularly Great Bear."

"He doesn't seem to know that this is my name. I've given it in the language of my people and ask my white brother not to translate it into English."

"Should I ever translate anything for him, then it will be something completely different, not the name of my brother. Now

---

[1] Behold, the old bear and the young bear!
[2] What a surprise, Aunty Droll

I'll have to leave you because the others want to talk to me; I'll return to you often to hear your voices."

He continued his interrupted stroll and headed for the afterdeck. The father of the rescued girl had stepped out of the cabin to announce that his daughter had regained consciousness, that she felt relatively well but required rest to recuperate completely. Then he hurried to the two Indians to give the courageous boy his thanks for the daring deed. Droll heard what he said and enquired about the events. When Tom described them to him, Droll said:

"I believe indeed that he's capable of it; he no longer is a child, he's a grown man now."

"Do you know him and his father? We saw that you were talking to them."

"I've met them a few times."

"Met them? He called himself a Tonkawa, and people of that near-extinct tribe never roam about, they stay on their miserable reservation in the valley of the Rio Grande where they've settled."

"Great Bear has never settled down, and instead remained true to his forefathers' custom. He roams about just like the Apache chief, Winnetou. Although it is to be expected that the two Tonkawa have a fixed place where they rest from their exertions, they keep it a secret. Nintropan-Hauey speaks of his people occasionally, and as often as I meet him, I enquire about their wellbeing; but I've not been able to find out who they are and where they live. He's on his way to them now, but finds himself held up because of his revenge on the colonel."

"Did he say that?"

"Yes. He won't rest until the deed is done. In my eyes the colonel is therefore a lost man."

"That's what I said, too," Old Firehand remarked. "As far as I know Indians, he didn't submit to the blow to his face out of cowardice."

"Oh?" Droll asked while he scrutinized the tall man. "You've also made the acquaintance of Indians, if that's necessary? But you don't look like it to me, although you seem to be a veritable Goliath. Methinks you fit into a salon much better than into the prairie."

"Oh, my, Aunty Droll!" Tom laughed. "You've certainly put your foot in it now. Guess who this gentleman is!"

"Wouldn't think of it. You might want to be gracious enough to tell me instead."

"No, I won't make it that easy for you. At least strain your head somewhat. This gentleman belongs among our most famous Westerners."

"Oh! Not 'famous', but 'most famous' Westerners?"

"Yes."

"In my opinion there are only two of the sort, because no third deserves that superlative like they do."

He paused, squeezed one eye shut, winked at Old Firehand with the other, emitted a short laugh that wasn't unlike a high pitched clarinet tremolo, and then continued:

"And those two are Old Shatterhand and Old Firehand. Since I know the former, if that's necessary, this gentleman cannot be anyone else but Old Firehand. Did I guess correctly?"

"You did," Firehand replied.

"Egad?" Droll exclaimed and retreated a couple of steps, only to have another close look at him with the one open eye. "You really are the man who makes every scoundrel shake. Your figure is exactly how it's been described, but—perhaps you're only joking?"

"Well, is that also a joke?" Old Firehand asked while he grabbed Droll by the collar of his coat with his right hand, lifted him up, swung him three times around in a circle, and then placed him on a nearby crate.

The face of the Westerner, who had thus been put in his place, had become dark red. He was gasping for air and in short, disjointed sentences exclaimed:

"Zounds, sir, are you mistaking me for a pendulum, or a centrifuge? Have I been created only to dance around you in a circle through the air? How fortunate my sleeping-gown is made from strong hide, otherwise it would have been torn apart and you would have flung me into the river! But the test was good, sir; I can see that you really are Old Firehand. I must believe it for the simple reason that you would otherwise feel compelled to demonstrate to these gentlemen the lunar orbit around the Earth with me. I've often imagined what a pleasure it would be to shake your hand, should I ever meet you. I'm only a plain trapper, but know very well what a man of your calibre represents. Here's my hand, and if you don't wish to sadden me deeply, then don't reject it!"

"Reject it? That would be a great sin. I'll gladly shake hands with any decent man, and all the more so with one who has introduced himself in such a splendid manner."

"Introduced? How?"

"By shooting the panther."

"Ah, so! That wasn't a deed to brag much about. The animal didn't feel too comfortable in the water; it had no intentions of doing me harm, it simply wanted to save itself. Unfortunately I wasn't very hospitable in that respect."

"That was very smart of you because the panther had indeed set its sights on you. These animals aren't afraid of the water; they are excellent swimmers. The cat would have reached the shore without much effort. What a calamity if it had succeeded. By killing it you've undoubtedly saved the lives of many people. I'll shake your hand and wish to get to know you better."

"That's entirely my wish as well, sir. But may I now suggest that we have a drink to toast our acquaintance. I've not boarded this steamer to die of thirst. Let's go into the salon."

The men acquiesced to the request. Tom upgraded his fare in order to join them, but he gladly did so.

When the gentlemen had left the deck, the Negro, who hadn't been allowed to watch the panther, exited the boiler room. Another crew member had relieved him, and he was about to look for a shady spot to have his siesta. Slowly, and with a sullen mien he sauntered towards the front of the steamer while he made a face that clearly expressed his bad mood. The colonel noticed it; he addressed him and signalled him to approach.

"What is it, sir?" the Negro asked when he approached. "If you have a request, then turn to the steward. I'm not available for the passengers."

He had spoken English like a White.

"I can imagine that," the colonel replied. "I only wanted to ask you whether you'd like to drink a glass of whiskey with us."

"If that's the case then I'm your man. Both the throat and the liver dry out down there in the boiler room. But I don't see a single drop here!"

"Here you have a dollar; go fetch what you like over by the bar, and then sit down with us!"

The sullen expression disappeared immediately from the face of the Negro, and he became a lot more agile. He brought two full bottles and some glasses, and then sat down next to the colonel, who willingly moved to the side. After the contents of the glass he poured himself had flowed across his tongue, he filled it a second time, and emptied it again. Then, he asked:

"That's the kind of refreshment people like us can't afford very often. But what made you invite me? You Whites are usually not as accommodating towards us Blacks."

"My friends and I value a Negro just as much as a White. I've noticed that you're employed in the boiler room. That's hard and thirsty work, and since I don't think the captain pays you with hundred dollar bills, I told myself that a good drop would be very welcome."

"You've had a splendid thought. The captain does indeed not pay well; it's impossible to buy a decent drink, especially since he doesn't give advances, at least not to me, and only reaches into the money pouch at the end of the trip...damn!"

"Then he's got it in for you?"

"Yes, especially me."

"Why?"

"He says I'm too thirsty; he pays the others by the day, but not me. It's no surprise that the thirst gets bigger and bigger."

"Well, it depends entirely on you whether or not you'll be able to quench your thirst today."

"Why?"

"I'm prepared to give you a few dollars if you do me a favour in return."

"A few dollars? Heigh-day! I'd be able to get a few bottles full! Out with your wish, sir. I'll gladly do it, and well at that."

"The matter isn't that simple. I don't know whether you're the right man."

"Me? If I can earn a bottle of whiskey, I'm always the right man."

"That's possible. But it has to be done in a clever way."

"Clever? It won't be anything that'll damage my back, will it? The captain won't tolerate irregularities."

"Don't worry; it's nothing like that. You'll only have to listen to a conversation, do a little bit of eavesdropping."

"Where? On whom?"

"In the salon."

"Oh? Hm?" he pensively grunted. "Why, sir?"

"Because—well, I'll be honest with you." Brinkley pushed another full glass in front of the Negro, and then continued in a confidential tone: "There is a tall, strong gentleman by the name of Old Firehand, furthermore a dark-haired fellow with a beard called Tom, and lastly a clown in a long leather coat who answers to the name of Aunty Droll. Old Firehand is a wealthy farmer, and he's invited the other two to be his guests. Coincidentally, we also want to go to that farm in order to ask for work. Of course, this is a good opportunity to learn what kind of people we're dealing with. I think they'll talk of their affairs, and if you keep your ears open, it won't be too difficult to make us happy. You can see and hear that I ask nothing wrong and unlawful of you."

"Quite right, sir! No one forbade me to listen when others speak. The next six hours are mine; I'm off duty and can do as I please."

"But how will you do it?"

"That's a question I'm thinking about right at this moment."

"Are you allowed to go into the salon?"

"It's not exactly prohibited; but I've no business in there."

"Then invent an excuse!"

"But what kind? I could carry something inside, or fetch something. But that'll take so little time that I won't reach my objective."

"Is there no task that would keep you in there a little longer?"

"No—oh, but yes! Something just came to mind. The windows are dirty; I could clean them."

"Won't that be conspicuous?"

"No. Because the salon is always full, the job cannot be carried out at a time when no one is in there."

"But it's not your job."

"That won't do any harm. It's actually the steward's affair; but I'll be doing him a great favour if I relieve him of it."

"But he could become suspicious."

"No. He knows that I don't have any money and yet like to have a drink. I'll tell him that I'm thirsty and want to clean the windows for a glass of whiskey. He won't have any misgivings. Don't worry, sir; I'll certainly do it. How many dollars will you pay me?"

"I'll pay by the value of the news you'll bring me, but at least three."

"Alright; consider it done. Fill my glass up one more time; then I'll go."

After the Negro had left, the others asked the colonel about the purpose of the errand. He replied:

"We're poor outlaws and have to make every post a winner. We've had to pay for the fare here, and I will at least make an attempt at finding out whether there is a possibility of recouping that money somehow. The long march we've got planned requires preparations that cost a lot of money and you know that our purses have become fairly empty."

"But we'll fill them with the contents of the railroad coffers!"

"Do you know for sure that our plan will succeed? If we can make some money here already, then it would be the greatest stupidity to let the opportunity go by unused."

"I'll say it straight out, theft here on board? That's dangerous. We wouldn't be able to get away immediately and if the person in question discovers the loss, then there will be a horrid hullabaloo upon which will follow the search of all persons and corners on this ship. And we'll be the first ones to be under suspicion straight away."

"You're the biggest numbskull I've ever encountered. The matter is dangerous, and yet it's not, depending on how it's tackled. And I'm not the one to go about it the wrong way. If you follow my instructions, then everything, even the last coup, must succeed."

"The one up there at the Silver-Lake? Hm! If only you haven't been taken for a ride."

"Pshaw! I know what I know. I wouldn't think of giving you a detailed report already. Once we're there I'll inform you of everything. Until then you must trust me, and believe me when I say that there are treasures that would take care of each one of us for the rest of our lives. Let's avoid all unnecessary chitter-chatter now and instead calmly wait for what the stupid Nigger will report."

Brinkley leaned back against the cladding and closed his eyes, which was the signal that he didn't want to hear or say anything else. The others also made themselves as comfortable as possible. Some made an effort to sleep, but were unable to do so; the others whispered with each other about the great plan to which they were committed for life or death.

The 'stupid Nigger' seemed to be up to the task after all. Had he encountered an insurmountable obstacle, he would certainly have returned to report it. But as it was, he first went to the office to speak to the steward, and then he disappeared through the door of the salon, and didn't reappear. It was more than an hour before he returned to the deck. He had several rags in his hand, took them away, and immediately afterwards rejoined Brinkley and his men, who became animated again, without noticing the four eyes that sharply observed him and the outlaws. The eyes belonged to the two Indians, Great Bear and Little Bear.

"Well?" the colonel asked in anticipation. "How did you fare with your task?"

The Negro replied in a moody voice:

"I made a great effort, but I don't believe I'll receive more than the three agreed dollars for what I've espied."

"Why?"

"Because my eavesdropping was for naught. To be precise: you were mistaken, sir."

"Mistaken in what?"

"The tall man's name is indeed Old Firehand, but he's not a farmer at all, and could therefore not have invited Tom and the person called Aunty Droll to visit him."

"I'll be!" colonel exclaimed, whereby he feigned disappointment.

"Yes it is so," the Negro confirmed. "The tall man is a famous hunter and is headed deep into the mountains."

"Where to?"

"He didn't say. But I've heard everything and didn't miss a single word of their conversation. The three men and the father of the girl, whom the panther had wanted to eat, were sitting away from everyone else."

"Is Firehand travelling into the mountains on his own?"

"No. The girl's father is an engineer by the name of Butler; he want's to accompany him."

"An engineer? I wonder what those two want in the mountains!"

"Perhaps someone discovered a vein of ore and Butler is supposed to inspect it."

"No, because Old Firehand knows how to do that better than the smartest engineer."

"They first want to visit Butler's brother who's got a splendid farm in Kansas. The brother must be a very wealthy man. He's delivered cattle and grain to New Orleans and the engineer has received the payment for it to take it to his brother."

A gleam flickered in Brinkley's eyes, but neither he nor any of the outlaws revealed with as much as a movement or facial expression how important that information was.

"Yes, there are incredibly wealthy farmers in Kansas," the colonel answered in an indifferent tone of voice. "But the engineer is a careless person. Is it a large sum?"

"He whispered of nine thousand dollars in paper money; I understood it nevertheless."

"One doesn't carry such an amount of money around in one's pockets. What purpose would the banks otherwise have? If he falls into the hands of the outlaws, then the money will be lost."

"No; they wouldn't find it."

"Oh, they're cunning fellows."

"But they will certainly not look where he's got it."

"Then you know the hiding place?"

"Yes. He showed it to the others. In fact, he was being secretive, because I was present. I had my back turned towards them, and so they believed that I wasn't going to see their fingers pointing; but they didn't think of the mirror. I looked into it and observed everything."

"Hm, a mirror is treacherous. It's common knowledge that someone standing in front if it sees their right side left, and the left side right."

"I haven't observed that yet and don't know anything about it; but I know what I've seen. The engineer has an old bowie knife with a hollow grip in which the banknotes are secreted. If he does fall into the hands of the outlaws they may well rob him of everything. But even the worst thief won't take such an old, useless knife because he has no use for it and has to leave his victim with at least one weapon, a tool without which he would be lost in the West."

"That makes sense, of course. But where is the knife? He's not wearing a hunter's outfit, or a belt."

"He wears the belt under his waistcoat, and the leather sheath that holds the knife is attached to the belt on the left side, and is covered by the coat."

"Oh! That's not of interest to us, of course. We're honest harvesters, not outlaws. I'm sorry I've been mistaken in the tall man. The likeness to the farmer I was talking about is striking, and he's got the same name."

"Perhaps they're brothers. Besides, it's not only the engineer who has such a lot of money on him. The dark-haired gentleman with the beard also spoke of a significant sum, which he received to divide among his comrades who are rafters."

"Where are they?"

"They're cutting their trees along the Black-Bear River, which I don't know, of course."

"I know it. It joins the Arkansas below Tuloi[3]. Is it a large company?"

"Around twenty men, all capable boys, so he said. And the funny fellow in the leather nightgown has a whole lot of nuggets on him. He's also headed for the West. I'd like to know why he's

---

[3] Although there is a Black Bear Creek that flows into the Arkansas River north-west of Tulsa, OK (near Pawnee), which, according to description, is May's *Blackbear Fluss*, I have been unable to locate a place named 'Tuloi'.

taking the gold along. Dragging it through the wilderness is not the thing to do!"

"Why not? People also have needs in the West. There are forts, seasonal stores and pedlars where one can get rid of enough money and nuggets. Alright, I have not the slightest interest in these people now. What I can't understand, though, is the fact that the engineer is heading into the mountains and yet he's accompanied by a young girl."

"She's his only child. The daughter loves him very much and didn't want to separate from him. And since he intends to stay in the mountains for an unusually lengthy period, whereby it will be necessary to build log cabins, he finally decided to take her and her mother along."

"Log cabins? Did he say that?"

"Yes."

"One log cabin would suffice for him, his wife and daughter. One must therefore assume that they will be joining a larger group. I'd like to know what purpose they're pursuing."

"The dark-haired fellow with the beard wanted to know that as well; but Old Firehand told him that he'd find out later."

"They're keeping it a secret in that case. It will probably be about a bonanza, a rich ore vein, which they want to secretly investigate and exploit, if at all possible. I wouldn't mind finding out where their destination is located."

"Unfortunately they didn't name it. It seems they also want to invite the one with the dark beard and Aunty Droll to accompany them. They seem to enjoy each other's company; and so much, in fact, that they'll be sleeping in adjoining cabins here on the steamer."

"In which ones? Do you know?"

"Yes, because they discussed it loudly. The engineer sleeps in number one; number two has been allocated to Old Firehand, number three to Tom, number four to Aunty Droll, and number five to young Fred."

"Who's that?"

"The boy Aunty Droll brought along."

"Is he Droll's son?"

"No, I've guessed that much."

"What's his family name and why is he with Droll?"

"They didn't speak about it."

"Are the cabins one to five on the right or left side?"

"On starboard side, which means they're to the left from here. The engineer's daughter and her mother sleep in their ladies' chambers, of course. But I don't have to talk about that because that's not of interest to you."

"That is indeed correct. And since I've been mistaken in the identity of these people, I'm indifferent to where they're resting and sleeping. Besides, I don't envy them for their confined cabins in which they're bound to almost suffocate, while we on the open deck have as much fresh air as we could possibly ask for."

"Well said! But the gentlemen in the cabins have also fresh air because the windows have been taken out and replaced by sheets of gauze. Of course the crew fared the worst. We actually ought to sleep down there when we're not on duty at night." The Negro pointed to a hatch not far from them, which led below deck. "The officer allows us to sleep up here, where the passengers are, only as a special favour. The tight opening prevents fresh air from getting down, and from below rises the musty smell. It's stifling on hot days."

"Are your sleeping quarters connected to the bilge?" the colonel casually asked.

"Yes. There's a staircase leading down into it."

"Couldn't you close it?"

"No, because that would be too awkward."

"In that case I have to feel sorry for you. But enough of these stories; we still have whiskey in the bottle."

"You're right, sir! Talking dries out the throat. I'll have one more drink, and then I'll find some shade to take a nap. When my six hours are over, I must return to the boiler. What about my dollars?"

"I keep my word, although I'm paying them for naught. But since that's to be blamed on my own error, you won't have to bear the consequences. Here are the three dollars. You can't ask for more since your favour hasn't brought us any benefits."

"I don't want more, either, sir. I'll get enough whiskey for these three dollars to drink myself to death. You're a noble gentleman. If you have any other wishes, come and see me, no one else. You can count on me."

He drank another full glass, and then retreated to the side and stretched out in the shade behind a large bale of merchandise.

The outlaws gave their leader inquisitive glances. They understood the gist of the matter, but could not make the right connections between several of his questions and enquiries.

"Now you are looking at me and want answers," he said while he gave a superior, smug smile. "Nine thousand dollars in banknotes, therefore cash and not cheques or bank drafts with which one would risk getting arrested! That's a decent sum and very welcome to us."

"If we had it!" said the one who seemed to be the speaker for all the others.

"We have it!"

"Not by a long shot!"

"Oho! If I say so, then it is so."

"Alright, and how will we get it? How shall we get the old knife?"

"I'll fetch it."

"From the cabin?"

"Yes."

"You? In person?"

"Naturally. I wouldn't leave such important work to anyone else."

"What if they catch you?"

"That's impossible. My plan is complete and will succeed."

"If that's true, then I'd appreciate it. But the engineer will miss his knife when he wakes up. And then all hell will break loose!"

"Indeed, it will; but we'll be gone."

"Where?"

"What a question! Ashore, of course."

"Are we to swim across?"

"No. I wouldn't expect that from either you or myself. I'm not a bad swimmer, but I wouldn't want to entrust myself to this broad river, the banks of which are hardly visible."

"Are you thinking of seizing one of the two tenders?"

"Not that either. It would not be impossible to do this, without being seen, but I prefer to figure on circumstances I'm familiar with, rather than unforeseen ones that could thwart my plans."

"In that case I can't envisage how we'd get on land before the theft is discovered."

"Which just goes to show that you're a numbskull. Why do you think I've so casually enquired about the bilge?"

"I can't know that!"

"Perhaps not, but you could guess it. Look around! What's that there next to the rolled up anchor hawser?"

"That seems to be a toolbox."

"Well done! I've seen that it contains hammers, files, pliers and several drills of which one has a diameter of one and a half inch. Now combine both, the bilge and the drill!"

"Tarnation! Do you perchance intend on drilling a hole in the hull?" the other exclaimed.

"I do indeed."

"So that we'll all drown!"

"Pshaw! Don't be ridiculous! There's no question about drowning. I only want to force the captain to put to shore."

"Ah, so! Do you think you'll succeed in doing that?"

"Most definitely. If the ship takes water, there must be a leak, and when there is a leak, one puts to shore to escape danger and inspect the ship at leisure."

"What if they discover it too late?"

"No need to be so scared. When the ship begins to sink, which will happen very slowly, then the water on the outside will rise correspondingly. The helmsman is bound to notice that, if he isn't blind. There will be such a noise and fright that the engineer won't even think about his knife initially. When he discovers the loss we'll be long gone."

"And what if he does think about the knife and the ship is put to shore but no one is allowed to leave the ship? We have to think of everything."

"In that case they'll also find nothing. We'll tie the knife to one end of a rope, lower it into the water and tie the other end to the outside of the ship's hull. If someone discovers it there, then he must be all-knowing."

"That idea isn't bad at all. But what will happen once we're off the ship? We actually wanted to travel as far as possible with it."

"One doesn't mind walking a stretch for nine thousand dollars. When we divide the shares, there will be a sum in excess of four hundred dollars for each one of us. Besides, we won't have to rely upon our own feet for too long. I think that we'll soon find a farm or an Indian camp where we can buy horses without having to pay."

"I'll accept that. And then we'll ride where?"

"To the Black-Bear River first."

"To the rafters, perchance, of whom the Negro spoke?"

"Yes. It will be easy to spy on their camp. Of course we won't show ourselves there, but ambush the bearded fellow to take the money off him as well. Once that's done we've got enough to equip ourselves for the continuation of our ride."

"Therefore we'll forego the railroad coffers?"

"Not at all. They'll contain many, many thousands of dollars, and we'll go and get that money. However, we'd be fools if we didn't collect what we can along the way. And now you know where you stand. There's much to do tonight and no time to sleep. Hence you had better stretch out now, so that you'll be rested and will be able to walk well!"

The men obeyed his orders. There was unusual peace and quiet on the boat in general as a consequence of the heat. The landscape to either side of the boat didn't offer anything that would have drawn the attention of the passengers, so they spent the time either sleeping or at least dozing, which is somewhere between being asleep and awake, and offers neither body nor spirit true respite.

Movement only returned on deck when the sun neared the horizon. The heat had subsided and a reasonably fresh breeze had come up. The ladies and gentlemen came out of their cabins to savour the refreshing change. The engineer was also among them. His wife and daughter accompanied him; the latter had completely recovered from her shock and the involuntary bath. The three went to visit the two Indians because the women hadn't extended their gratitude yet.

With genuine Indian poise both the old and the young bear had spent the entire afternoon on the same crate. They had moved there even before Aunty Droll had come to greet them, and were still sitting on the same spot when the engineer approached with his wife and daughter.

"*He—el bakh shai—bakh matelu makik*[4]," Great Bear said to his son in their Tonkawa language when he saw them walk up.

His face turned dark because the kind of gratitude he had indicated was an insult for Indians. The son held out his hand, palm down, and swiftly lowered it, which meant as much as disagreement with his father. His eyes expressed pleasure when he looked at the girl he had rescued. She approached him swiftly, took his hands between hers, and squeezed them heartily while she said:

"You are a fine and courageous boy. It is a pity that we don't live close to each other; I would be very fond of you."

He looked into her pink face and replied:

"My life would be yours. The Great Spirit may hear my words; he knows that they are true."

"In that case I shall give you a memento at least, so that you'll remember me. May I?"

---

[4] Now they'll give us money

He only nodded. She pulled a small gold ring from her finger and placed it on the little finger of his left hand, where it fitted. First he looked at the ring, and then at her, before he reached under his Zuni blanket, where he fumbled to untie something from his neck. He gave her a small, strong, square piece of leather, tanned white and pressed flat, with several embossed marks.

"I will also give you a memento," he said. "It is a totem from Nintropan-Homosh, only leather, no gold. But should you ever be in danger among Indians, and show this totem to them, the danger will immediately vanish. All Indians know and love Nintropan-Homosh and obey his totem."

The girl had no idea what a totem was, and what great value it could have under certain circumstances. She only knew that he returned her gift of a ring with a piece of leather; but she didn't show any disappointment. She was too kind-hearted and would not permit herself to offend him by rejecting his seemingly poor gift. Hence she tied the totem around her neck, whereby the eyes of the young Indian shone with delight, and then replied:

"Thank you! Now I have something from you and you have something from me. We will both be pleased by it, although we would not have forgotten each other without these gifts, either."

Then the girl's mother expressed her gratitude with a simple handshake. Afterwards, her father said:

"How shall I reward Little Bear's deed? I'm not poor; but everything I own would be too little for what he has preserved for me. I must therefore remain his debtor, but at the same time also be his friend. I can only give him a memento with which he can protect himself against his enemies, like he has kept my daughter safe from the panther. Will he accept these weapons from me? I ask him to take them."

He pulled two new, and expertly crafted revolvers, the grips of which were inlaid with mother-of-pearl, out of his pocket and held them up to him. The young Indian did not need even a moment to contemplate what he had to do. He took a step back, rose up proud and said:

"The white man is offering me weapons; that's a great, great honour for me because only men receive weapons. I accept them and will only use them to defend innocent people and shoot the evil ones. Howgh!"

He took the revolvers and placed them into his belt under the blanket. At that point his father could no longer contain himself.

It was evident in his face that he was fighting with his emotions. He said to Butler:

"I also thank the white man that he didn't give money to us like to a slave or to people who have no honour. This is a great reward that we will never forget. We will always be friends of the white man, his squaw and his daughter. You must keep the totem of Little Bear safe; it is also mine. May the Great Spirit always send you sun and joy!"

The thanks-giving visit had come to its conclusion; the Butlers and the two Indians shook hands once more, and then parted. Father and son Nintropan sat back down on their crate.

"*Tua enokh*[5]!" the father said.

"*Tua—tua enokh*[6]!" his son agreed. Those comments were the only emotional outbursts their Indian taciturnity allowed for after all. The father felt especially honoured because the white people had only given gifts to his son, of whom he was especially proud, and not to him as well.

The reason for the engineer's tactful expression of gratitude, according to Indian concept, wasn't to be found with Butler. He was not familiar enough with the opinions and traditions of the Indians to know how to conduct himself in such a case. Hence he had asked Old Firehand for advice and had received the necessary information. Butler returned to the hunter, who was sitting in front of his cabin together with Tom and Droll, and let him know how the gifts had been received. When he mentioned the totem, it was evident from the tone of his voice that he was unable to appreciate its true value.

"Do you know what a totem is, sir?"

"Yes. It's an Indian's sign, similar to a seal as we know it, and may consist of the most varied objects or materials."

"That explanation is correct, but not adequate. Not every Indian is allowed to use a totem; only famous Indians have them. The fact that the boy already uses one, regardless of whether it is his father's at the same time, is proof that he's already accomplished deeds that are considered exceptional even among the red men. Moreover, the totems differ according to their purpose. But one type of totem will indeed only be used for the purpose of identification and endorsement, and is akin to our seal or signature. The kind that's most important for us palefaces,

---

[5] Good people
[6] Very good people

however, is the one that is considered to be a recommendation of the one who has received it. The endorsement can differ according to its method of execution, that being the grade of its warmth. Let me see the leather!"

The girl handed it to him, and he had a close look at it.

"Can you decipher these signs, sir?" Butler asked.

"Yes," Old Firehand nodded. "I have dwelt often and long enough among the most diverse tribes, so that I not only speak their dialects, but also understand their written signs. This totem is very valuable, and of the kind that are rarely given away. It has been written in the Tonkawa language and reads: '*Shakhe-i-kauvan-ehlatan henshon-shakin, henshon-shakin shakhe-i-kauvan-ehlatan, he-el ni-ya.*' Accurately translated, these words mean: 'His shadow is my shadow, and his blood is my blood; he is my older brother.' And underneath there's the name sign of Little Bear. The adage of 'older brother' is even more honourable than simply 'brother'. The totem contains a recommendation that couldn't be any more sincere. Anyone who harms the owner has to expect the harshest revenge from Great Bear and Little Bear and all of their friends. Wrap the totem up well, sir, so that the red colour will be preserved. There is no way of knowing what great service it might render to you because we're travelling into the region in which the allies of the Tonkawa dwell. Many peoples' lives could depend on that small piece of leather."

During the afternoon, the steamer had passed Ozark, Fort Smith and Van Buren, and was nearing the bend in the Arkansas where the river bed described a significant change of direction due north. The captain announced that they were going to reach Fort Gibson approximately two hours past midnight, where the boat had to remain anchored until the morning because he had to first enquire about the water level further upriver. In order to be up and about upon arrival, most of the travellers retired very early, because they expected to stay awake until the morning in Fort Gibson. The deck became almost completely devoid of cabin passengers, and even the salon only contained a few passengers who were playing chess and other games. In the adjoining smoking room sat only three people, namely Old Firehand, Tom and Droll, who conversed about their experiences, undisturbed by others. Tom and Droll afforded Old Firehand an almost reverential respect, which didn't mean that Firehand had been able to learn anything about the circumstances or immediate intentions of Aunty Droll. At that point he enquired about how the droll Westerner had attained the peculiar title of aunt. Droll replied:

"You know the habits of frontiersmen, to give everyone a nickname or nom de guerre that relates to some outstanding and unique characteristic of the person in question. I do indeed resemble a female, dressed in my sleeping gown, and my high-pitched voice fits that circumstance. When I was younger I had a bass voice, but a severe cold robbed me of the lower tones. And since I have the additional tendency to take any decent fellow under my wings like a good mother or aunt, they gave me the name Aunty Droll."

"But Droll isn't your family name by chance, is it?"

"No. But I like being funny, perhaps even a little droll. Hence the name."

"May we perhaps hear your real one? My name is Winter, and Tom's is Grosser; you've no doubt heard that we're German. But you seem to want to cloak your origin in deepest darkness."

"I've indeed got reasons not to speak of it, but not because I would have to be ashamed of anything. These reasons have more to do with...business."

"Business? How am I to understand that?"

"About that later, perhaps. I know full well that you'd like to know what I'm up to in the West, and why I am dragging a sixteen-year-old boy around with me. There will be a suitable time for me to tell you. The matter with my name now, well, that would make a poet cringe, because it is incredibly un-poetic."

"That won't hurt. No one is to blame for their name. Alright, out with it!"

Droll closed one eye, gulped and gagged as if he were choking on something, and then uttered the words:

"My name—is Pampel."

"What, Pampel?" Old Firehand laughed. "The word is indeed not poetic, and if I laugh, then it is not because of the name, but because of the face you're pulling. It seemed as though a steam engine would be required to get the word out of you. Besides, the name isn't that rare. I've known a privy councillor by that name, and he wore it with great dignity. But the name is German; are you also of German extraction?"

"Yes."

"And born in the United States?"

That's when Droll's face changed to his wiliest and funniest expression, and he replied in German:

"Nee, det wouldn't have occurred to me at det time; I chose German parents."

"What? German-born, a fellow countryman?" Old Firehand exclaimed. "Who would have thought?"

"Didn't ye catch on to it? And I thought it was immediately obvious that I was born as a descendant of the old Germans. Can ye perhaps guess where I've put on and scuffed my first toddler boots?"

"Of course! Your dialect tells me so."

"Is det still audible? I'm extremely pleased because I've always been madly keen on our beautiful dialect, which later ruined my entire career, if that's necessary. Well, then, tell me: where was I born?"

"In the beautiful dukedom of Altenburg, where the best curd cheese is made."

"Correct, in Altenburgia; ye've guessed it immediately! And det thing with the cheese is also very true; we used to call them *Quaercher*, and there's nothing like it in all of Germany. Ye know, I wanted to surprise ye and det's why I haven't immediately told ye det I'm a fellow countryman. But now det we're so nicely sitting alone together, it finally slipped out, and now let's chat about our nice homeland, which won't leave my mind, although I've been in this country for such a long time."

By all appearances, a very animated chat was about to develop; but unfortunately it couldn't because some of the gentlemen from the salon had become tired of playing cards and entered the smokers' room to partake of a decent puff. They engaged those present in their conversation, so that the Germans had to relinquish the pursuit of their topic. When they retired some time later, to get some sleep, Droll took his leave from Old Firehand with the comment:

"It was a real pity det we couldn't keep chatting; but tomorrow is another day and we can continue where we left off. Good night fellow countryman; sleep ye well and a little fast because we'll have to get up after midnight already!"

The cabins filled and the lamps in the salons were extinguished. The only lanterns that were burning on deck were those at the bow and the one aft. The former illuminated the river so brightly that the sailor on lookout was able to see possible obstacles in the water early enough to sound the alarm. The sailor, the helmsman and the officer, who was strolling up and down the decking, were seemingly the only people still awake, apart from the crew who operated the machines.

The outlaws were also lying on the boards as if they were asleep, at a fair distance from the sailors, who were sleeping on deck because of the prevailing heat below. The colonel had been cunning enough to place his men around the hatch that led downstairs, so that no one was able to get to it unnoticed. Of course, none of Brinkley's gang was asleep.

"That's a bedevilled turn of events!" he whispered to his neighbour. "It didn't occur to me that there would be a man stationed up front to observe the waterway. The fellow is in our way."

"It's not as bad as you think. He can't see right up to the hatch. It is pitch black; there's not a single star in the sky. Besides he's got to look into the lantern light and will therefore be temporarily blinded when he turns around. When will we begin?"

"Immediately. We can't lose any time because we must be finished well ahead of Fort Gibson."

"You'll fetch the money first, of course."

"No. That would be stupid. If the engineer wakes up and notices the theft before the ship has to put to shore, everything could go wrong. But, on the other hand, if we have to head for the banks before I've got the money, then nothing will be lost because it will be very easy to snatch the knife from him in the turmoil, and then to disappear with it. I've already got a hold of the drill; I'll climb down now. If you need to warn me, then cough loudly. I will certainly hear it."

Brinkley, aided by the dense darkness, pushed forwards up to the hatch and placed his feet on the top of the narrow stairs that led down. He quickly descended the ten steps and inspected the floor below by touch. When he found the opening that led even further below deck he climbed down the second staircase, which had more steps than the one above. When he arrived at the bottom he lit a match to look around. In order to find his bearings precisely he had to move along while striking several more matches.

The room in which he stood was just high enough for him to stand upright, and extended to almost the middle of the ship. Having no divider at all, it spanned the entire width of the hull from one side to the other. There were several small luggage pieces strewn about; he also found a small lantern, which he lit.

The colonel went portside and placed the drill against the wall, below the water line, of course. Under the strong pressure of his hand the tool quickly ate into the timber. But then it hit something hard that resisted it—the metal with which the submerged part of the ship's hull was clad. Brinkley needed to puncture it with the drill. But in order to swiftly fill the bilge at least two holes were required. The colonel first went as far back as possible and drilled a second hole, also until it stopped at the metal cladding. Then he picked up one of the rocks that were lying there, serving as ballast, and hammered the drill's haft until the tool broke through the sheet. The water immediately seeped in and wet his hand; but when he pulled the drill back with some effort, a strong, powerful jet of water hit him, so that he hastily jumped aside. The noise of the engine had drowned out the sound of his knocking, so that it was impossible for anyone to hear it. After that, he knocked out the metal sheet on the outside of the first hole, which was closer to the stairs, extinguished the lantern, and then returned upstairs. He had kept the drill and only discarded it when he arrived at the bottom of the upper staircase. Why would he want to bother taking it upstairs?

When he returned to his gang, they quietly asked him whether everything had worked out. He answered in the affirmative and explained that he'd immediately sneak to cabin one.

The salon and the adjoining smoking room were situated on the afterdeck, and on either side of them were the cabins, each of which had its own door that led to the salon. The thin, wooden, external walls were fitted with fairly large windows covered only with fine gauze. Between the external cabin walls and the bulwarks on either side there were narrow corridors to allow for easy passage.

The colonel headed for the corridor along the starboard side, which was to his left. Cabin number one was the first one, and therefore situated on the corner. He lay down on the floor and cautiously crawled along, hard up against the railing, so as not to be discovered by the officer who was strolling back and forth. He safely reached his destination. Dim light shone out of the window. A lantern was burning in the cabin. Was Butler still awake, reading a book perhaps?

The colonel was reassured after he had satisfied himself that all cabins were lit. Perhaps that circumstance was going to aid the execution of his plan, which was quite difficult in the dark. He pulled out his knife and cut the gauze from the top to the bottom without making a noise. A curtain prevented him from seeing into the cabin; he gingerly pushed it aside, and could have rejoiced loudly about what he saw.

On the left cabin wall hung a night lamp; it was shielded at the bottom, so as not to disturb the sleeping person. Beneath it lay the engineer. He slept soundly with his face turned towards the wall. His clothing lay on the chair. On the wall opposite was a fold-down table on which Butler had placed his watch, his wallet and—his knife, within easy reach from the outside. The colonel reached inside and took the knife, but left watch and wallet behind. He pulled the blade from its sheath and tested the grip. It readily swivelled to open like a pencil or needle box. That sufficed.

"Devil, that was easy!" the thief breathed. "I would have had to climb inside otherwise and possibly even strangle him!"

No one had seen what had transpired; the window faced the water at starboard side. The colonel tossed the sheath overboard, placed the knife into his belt and lay down on the decking again to return to his men. He safely sneaked past the officer. A couple of metres further on he happened to glance to his left; he thought he could see a couple of faint phosphorescent dots, which immediately disappeared. They were eyes; he knew it. He flung himself forwards with a powerful, yet silent movement, and then just as quietly rolled to the side, to get off his original route. Indeed! From where he had spotted the eyes came a sound as if someone had attempted to jump at someone else. The officer heard it and approached.

"Who is there?" he asked.

"Nintropan-Hauey," the answer came.

"Oh, the Indian! Go to sleep!"

"A man sneaked here; he did something bad; I saw him; but he quickly left."

"Where?"

"To the front of the ship, where the colonel lies; perhaps it was him."

"Pshaw! Why would he or anyone else sneak around here! Go back to sleep and don't disturb the others!"

"I'll sleep, but won't be blamed if something nasty happens."

The officer listened in the direction of the bow, and when he couldn't hear anything, he relaxed. He was convinced that the Indian had been mistaken.

A long, long time went by; then the sailor on outlook duty called him to the bow.

"Sir," the man said. "I don't know what the reason for it is, but the water is rising fast; the ship is sinking!"

"Nonsense!" the officer laughed.

"Come and see!"

He looked down, said nothing, and hurried away to the captain's cabin. After two minutes he returned with him. They had a lantern and shone it over board. Someone fetched a second lantern. The officer descended down the hatch on the after deck, and the captain down the opening on the fore deck to inspect the bilge. The outlaws had moved away from it in the meantime. After only a short time the captain climbed back up and hastily went to the helmsman.

"He doesn't want to sound the alarm," the colonel whispered to his people. "But pay attention, the steamer will head towards the bank!"

He was correct. The sailors and other crew were quietly being woken, and the ship changed direction. It was impossible to do that without a certain amount of noise; the deck passengers woke up and several cabin passengers came outside.

"It's nothing, gentlemen; there's no danger," the captain called to them. "We've got a little water in the bilge and have to pump it out. We'll tie up on the bank and those of you who are afraid can go ashore."

It was intended to reassure the passengers, but had the opposite effect. People started to holler, some called for lifebelts; the cabins emptied. Chaos ensued as people started running everywhere. That's when the light of the bow lantern fell onto the tall river bank. The steamer turned, so that it came to sit parallel to it, and then dropped anchor. The two gangplanks proved long enough; they were lowered and the fearful passengers pushed their way across and onto land. The outlaws left the ship ahead of all the others, of course, and then quickly disappeared in the dark of the night.

Aside from the crew, the only other people who had remained on board were Old Firehand, Tom, Droll and the old bear. Firehand had climbed below deck to inspect the water ingress. He climbed back out of the hatch with the lantern in his right hand and the drill in his left, and asked the captain, who was supervising the installation of the bilge pumps:

"Sir, where's the rightful place of this drill?"

"There in the tool box," one of the sailors replied. "It was still in there this afternoon."

"It was lying on the 'tween deck just then. The point has been blunted, most likely on the metal cladding. I'd bet that the hull has been drilled."

It's not hard to imagine the impression his remarks made. Someone else joined them. Butler had brought his wife and daughter ashore as a matter of priority; then he had returned to the ship to finish getting dressed. At that point he came out of his cabin and shouted, so that everyone could hear it:

"I've been robbed! Nine thousand dollars. Someone cut the gauze window and took it from the table!"

That's when the old bear shouted even louder:

"I know, the colonel has stolen it, and he drilled a hole in the ship. I saw him; but the officer didn't believe me. Ask the black man from the boiler room! He was drinking with the colonel; he went into the salon to clean windows; he came back out and drank some more; he must tell everything."

At once the captain, the officer, the helmsman, as well as the Germans crowded around the Indian and the engineer to question them in even more detail. But they were interrupted by a cry that came from downstream of the ship's anchoring place.

"That's Little Bear," the Indian exclaimed. "I've sent him after the colonel, who rushed ashore; he'll tell us where the colonel went."

The young bear rushed up the gang plank, and then pointed into the river, which by that time was illuminated by the many lanterns that had been lit aboard the ship, while he said:

"They are paddling out there! I couldn't find the colonel at first, but then I saw the large boat, which they have cut from the rope at the back; I watched them get in to row to the other river bank."

The situation became clearer, but not in every detail. The people watched the large tender get away. The outlaws on it rejoiced and sent sneers across to the steamer; the crew and a large number of the passengers angrily retorted. In the heat of the general agitation no one was paying attention to the two Indians; they slipped away. At last Old Firehand's mighty voice was successful in restoring calm, and then there was also another voice that came from the water:

"The old bear has borrowed the small boat. He is going after the colonel to take revenge. He will tie the small boat to the bank on the other side; the captain will find it. The chief of the Tonkawa won't let the colonel escape. Great Bear and Little Bear must have his blood. Howgh!"

The two Indians had taken the small tender and were paddling after the fugitives. The captain was cussing and cursing mightily, but it was for naught.

While the crew were busy pumping the water from the ship's hull, the others interrogated the black deck hand from the boiler room. Old Firehand cornered him with his keen questions, so that he confessed everything and recounted every word that had been spoken. From that, the men were able to explain the entire incident. The colonel was the thief and had drilled holes in the ship, which had preoccupied the crew. During the ensuing turmoil he had been able to escape ashore before anyone had discovered the theft. The Negro was not going to get away unpunished for his betrayal. The deck hands tied him up, so that he couldn't flee, to administer the beating to which the captain had sentenced him. Of course, he couldn't be held accountable in a court of law.

It soon became evident that the pumps made light work of the water. The ship was in no danger and able to continue the journey within a very short time. The passengers therefore came back aboard from the inhospitable river bank and made themselves comfortable. The loss of time didn't worry them, after all; indeed, many were pleased about the interesting interlude in the dull journey.

The engineer, however, was unable to find anything enjoyable about the interruption. He had lost a significant amount of money, which he needed to replace. Old Firehand calmed him down by saying:

"There's still hope that the money can be recovered. Continue on your trip with your wife and your daughter, in God's name. I'll meet you again at your brother's place."

"What? You want to leave me?"

"Yes, because I'm going after the colonel to recover the loot."

"But that's dangerous!"

"Pshaw! Old Firehand is not a man to be afraid of such outlaws, as that's what they are."

"Nevertheless, I'm asking you to leave it be. I'd rather lose that sum of money."

"Sir, it's not just a matter of your nine thousand dollars, but much more. The outlaws had learnt from the Negro that Tom also has money on him, and that his companions are waiting for it by the Black-Bear River. I'm certainly not mistaken when I say that's where they're headed to commit a new crime, whereby human lives could be at stake. The two Tonkawa are behind the colonel like good bloodhounds and we'll follow their trail at the break of day; that's to say, Tom, Droll, his boy Fred and I. Won't we, gentlemen?"

"Yes," Tom replied simply and earnestly.

"Indeed," Droll also agreed. "The colonel must become ours, for the sake of others, as well. If we catch him, then woe to him, if that's necessary!"

Black Tom

3

The Rafters

A large campfire was burning on the high bank of the Black-Bear River. Although the moon was shining, its light wasn't able to penetrate the dense crowns of the trees, beneath which there would have been deep darkness without the fire. The flames illuminated a cabin that had been built in an unconventional manner, not by stacking the logs horizontally. Someone had cut the crowns off four trees, which had grown in positions that marked the corners of an ordinary square, and had then placed horizontal beams on top of the cut trunks to support the roof. The latter as well as the walls consisted of so-called clapboards split green from branchless cypress or red oak trunks. The front wall contained three openings: the large one served as the door, and the small ones to either side of it as the windows. The fire was burning in front of that building; about twenty wild figures were sitting around it. It was evident that they hadn't had any contact with so-called civilization for quite some time. Their outfits were tattered and their faces had not only been bronzed, but also literally turned into tanned hide by the sun, the wind and the weather. The men carried only knives; all other weapons were probably stored inside the timber cabin.

Over the fire, suspended from a strong tree branch, hung a large iron pot in which enormous pieces of meat were being cooked. Next to the fire stood two giant hollow gourds that contained fermented honey water, or mead. Those who felt like it helped themselves to a drink of the beverage, or a beaker full of meat broth from the pot.

The company entertained a lively conversation. The men seemed to feel secure because none made an effort to speak quietly. Had they even suspected the presence of an enemy nearby, they would have maintained the fire Indian fashion, with small flames, not visible at a great distance. Tools such as axes, adzes, and large saws, which were leaning against the house wall, gave an indication that the people were a group of lumberjacks and rafters.

Rafters are a unique type of backwoodsmen. They are classed somewhere between the farmers and the trappers. While the farmers are closely associated with civilization, and belong to the settled people, the trappers lead an almost primitive life, not unlike that of Indians. The rafters are not tied to one particular clod of earth, either, and have a free and independent existence. A rafter roams from one state or county to the next. He doesn't readily visit people or settlements because his occupation is actually illegal. The land on which he cuts the lumber is not his. He only rarely has the inclination to ask who owns it. Once he finds a suitable forest, and a convenient watercourse nearby, he begins his work without bothering about whether the place he's at belongs to the government or is already private property. He fells, trims and cuts the lumber, after having chosen only the best trees, ties the logs into rafts, and then floats down river on them to sell the seized goods somewhere else.

The rafter is not a welcome guest. It is true that the dense forest encountered by many a new settler causes him much trouble, and that he would be glad to find it cleared; but the rafter doesn't clear. As mentioned, he only takes the best trunks, cuts the crowns and leaves them lying where they fall. Under and between those canopies new vegetation shoots will sprout, which will combine to an impenetrable whole, together with wild grapevines and other climbers; the axe, and often even fire, achieve little against it.

Nevertheless, the rafter remains mostly unchallenged because he's a strong and bold fellow, and tackling him, in the wilderness, far from any assistance, isn't something anyone would be careless enough to do. Of course, one rafter cannot work alone; there are usually several, mostly about four to eight, who form a group. Occasionally such a company might consist of even more men; rafters in such groups will feel safer because no farmer or other land owner will instigate a fight with such a large number of people who are willing to risk their lives for the ownership of a tree trunk.

Of course they lead a very hard and strenuous life full of privations, but their reward in the end is quite substantial. The rafter earns a decent amount of money because the material doesn't cost him anything. While most of the men in a company of rafters are at work, one or two, or more, depending on the size of the group, see to the provisioning of it. Those are hunters who spend the day, and oftentimes the night, traipsing around the region to 'make meat' as they say: to shoot game. That isn't difficult in areas where there are plenty of wild animals. However, if there isn't enough game, then the hunters don't have much spare time to search for honey and other delicacies, and the rafters have to also eat those cuts of meat a backwoodsman usually turns down, even the entrails.

The company that was at work there, at the Black-Bear River, didn't seem to suffer, as the full pot over the fire evidenced. Hence the men were in a good mood, and there was much merry-making and joshing after the day's work. They were telling each other witty or otherwise interesting experiences; some were describing people they had met who had some kind of quirk that gave reason to have a laugh.

"You should have been there when I met that one fellow up north in Fort Niobrara," said an old, grey-bearded rafter. "The man was a man, and yet they called him 'Aunty'."

"Are you talking of Aunty Droll, perchance?" someone asked.

"Yes. I'm talking about him and no one else. Have you met him, too?"

"Yes, once. That was in Des Moines, in a guesthouse where his visit drew great attention and everyone made fun of him. There was one particular patron who didn't let up, until Droll grabbed him by the hips and tossed him out of the window. The man didn't come back in again."

"I'll readily believe that he is capable of that. Droll loves to have his fun and doesn't object to being laughed at; but one mustn't overstep the mark, otherwise he'll bare his teeth. Besides, I'd knock down anyone, who intended to insult him in earnest, immediately."

"You, Blenter? Why?"

"Because I owe my life to him. The Sioux had captured both him and me. I'm telling you that they would have sent me into the Eternal Hunting Grounds for sure and truly. I'm not a man who's afraid of three or five Indians; I'm also not in the habit of whimpering if things go wrong for once; but I didn't have a glimmer of hope and really saw no way out. However, Droll is a crafty devil without equal; he pulled the wool over the Indians' eyes until they couldn't see anything. We escaped."

"How did that happen? What went on? Tell us, go on, tell us!"

"If you don't mind I'd rather keep my mouth shut. There's no joy in recounting an event wherein one has played a less-than praiseworthy role, and has been hoodwinked by the redskins. Suffice it to tell you that it is thanks to Aunty Droll, not my own capabilities, that I'm sitting here today enjoying my deer roast."

"In that case the mire you were stuck in must have been very deep and very muddy. The old Missouri-Blenter is otherwise known as a Westerner who'll find the door if there is one at all."

"I didn't find it back then. I was almost standing at the stake already."

"Truly? That, of course, is a situation with little chance of escape. The stake is a diabolical invention! I doubly hate the rogues when I think of that word."

"Then you don't know what you're doing and what you're saying. Those who hate the Indians judge them wrongly, and haven't thought about the hardships they endured. If someone came here now, to chase us away, what would you do?"

"Defend myself, even if it costs either his or my life."

"And is this place your property perchance?"

"Don't know at all who owns it; I certainly haven't paid for it."

"All the land belonged to the Indians; we have taken it from them, and if they put up resistance, to which they have a greater entitlement than you, then you condemn them?"

"Hm! What you say is correct; however, the red man must disappear, must become extinct; that's his destiny."

"Yes, he's dying out, because we're murdering him. They say he's incapable of attaining culture and thus has to disappear. Culture, however, cannot be discharged like a bullet from a barrel; much time is required for it, much time. I don't understand it, but I'd imagine it would take several centuries for that. Are we affording the Indians the necessary time? Would you send a six-year-old boy to school, and then hit him over the head if he hasn't turned into a professor within a quarter of an hour? That's precisely what's being done to the Indians. I'm not about to defend them, because I won't benefit from it; but I've met just as many decent people among them, if not more, as among the Whites. Whom do you think I have to thank for being forced to roam around the Wild West as an old, grey fellow, instead of owning a pretty home and having a family: the Indians or the Whites?"

"I wouldn't know. You've not spoken about it."

"Because a real man would rather bury such things deep inside of him, than talk about them. I have only one more to find. He's the last of them and has escaped me thus far; he was their leader, the worst of them!"

The old man had spoken between clenched teeth, slowly, as if he wanted to place great emphasis onto each word. That only increased the attention of the others; they moved closer together and looked at him expectantly, but didn't say anything. He stared at the fire for a while, kicked the burning logs with his boot, and then continued as if he were talking only to himself:

"I didn't shoot or stab them; I whipped them to death, one after the other. I had to have them alive, so that they would die exactly like my family had to die, my wife and my two sons. There were six of them; I extinguished five within a short period of time; but the sixth got away. I've chased him across the entire United States, until he managed to make his trail invisible. I've not yet crossed it again; but he's still alive because he was younger than I am, much younger, and that's why I think that my old eyes will see him again before I shut them forever."

There was silence. They all sensed that they were about to hear something unusual. Only after a long time did one of the men dare to ask:

"Blenter, who was the man?"

The old man roused from his thoughts and replied:

"Who was he? He wasn't an Indian, he was a White, a monstrous beast the likes of which does not exist among Red Indians. Yes, men, I will even tell you that he was what you all are, and what I also am at present, namely a rafter."

"What? Rafters killed your family?"

"Yes, rafters! You don't have any reason for being proud of your occupation, and especially not for thinking you're better than the Indians. We are effectively sitting here as thieves and scoundrels."

That assertion met with lively objections, of course. But Blenter continued, unperturbed by them:

"This river, this forest, and the trees that we're felling and selling, they're not our property. We're here illegally and are misappropriating what belongs to the state or even a private person. We would shoot anyone, even the lawful owner, if he attempted to chase us away from here. Isn't that theft? Isn't that robbery?"

He looked around the circle, and when he didn't immediately receive an answer, he continued:

"And that's the sort of robbers I was dealing with at that time. I had come across the Missouri with the proper land deed in my hands. My wife and my sons were with me. We had a few head of cattle, several horses, pigs and a large cart full of household implements, because I was fairly well off, I tell you. There was no other settler nearby; but we didn't need anyone else because we had eight arms that were strong, and we were diligent enough to do everything ourselves and even finish the tasks quickly. The log cabin was built within a short time; we burned and cleared a stretch of arable land and began to sow. One beautiful day a cow was missing and I went into the forest to look for it. I heard the sound of axe blows and followed them. I found six rafters who were cutting down my trees. The cow was lying next to them on the ground; they had shot it to eat. Tell me, mesh'shurs, what would you have done in my stead?"

"Shot the fellows!" one of them replied. "And with every right to do so. According to the law of the West, a horse or cattle thief has forfeited his life."

"That's correct; yet I still didn't do it. I spoke to the people politely, and only requested that they leave my land and pay for the cow. Was that too much, perchance?"

"No, no!" the men around him replied. "Didn't they do that?"

"No. They laughed at me. I didn't immediately go home, though, because I wanted to shoot game for supper. When I returned home, the second cow was missing as well. In the meantime the rafters had taken it, too, to spite me, and to demonstrate that I meant nothing to them. When I went back to their camp the next day, they had already cut it into pieces, and hung them up to dry to make pemmican. I repeated my demand and raised it, of course, but it was ridiculed just like the day before. I therefore threatened to assert my rights and demanded money; at the same time I aimed my gun at them. Their leader also lifted his gun immediately. I could see that he was serious, and smashed his weapon with my bullet. I didn't want to injure him and had aimed at his gun. Afterwards I rushed back home to get my sons. The three of us were by no means afraid of the six of them, but when we got back, they had left. Of course, caution was a priority at that point and we didn't venture past the periphery of the log cabin for several days. On the fourth day our rations were depleted. Together with one of my sons I went to shoot some game. We were cautious, naturally, but there was no trace of the rafters. When we were stalking game through the forest, perhaps twenty paces apart from each other, I suddenly spotted the rafters' leader standing behind a tree. He saw my son and aimed his gun at him; he was unaware of my presence. If I had shot the fellow on the spot, as was my right and my duty, then I would certainly not have become a childless widower. But it has never been my passion to kill a human being without being in dire straits, and so I merely ran up to him, wrenched the gun from his hands, the knife and pistol from his belt, and struck him across the face, so that he fell over. He didn't lose his presence of mind for one moment; on the contrary, he was too fast for me to catch. In no time at all he had jumped up and was running away before I could even stretch a hand out for him."

"Tarnation! You were bound to pay for that stupidity afterwards!" one of the men called out. "It's a foregone conclusion that the man would have avenged that blow later."

"Yes, he took revenge," the old man nodded while he rose to pace up and down a few times. The memory tormented him. Then he sat down again and continued: "We were lucky and had a good hunt. When we returned home I went to the back of the house to deposit the game there for the time being. I thought I heard a shout of fear from my son, but unfortunately I didn't pay attention to it. When I went inside the house, I saw my family bound and lying by the hearth. At the same time, someone grabbed me and pulled me to the ground. During our absence the rafters had gone to the farm and overpowered my wife and my younger son. They then waited for us. When my older son entered ahead of me, they grabbed him so swiftly that he had hardly time for the shout. I didn't fare any worse or better than the others. It came as such a surprise and happened so quickly that I was bound before I could even think of resistance; then they stuffed some piece of fabric into my mouth, so that I couldn't scream."

"That's your own fault! Why weren't you more careful? Someone who alienates rafters, and has even hit one of them, must be vigilant."

"Very true. But I was still inexperienced at that time. If rafters killed one of my cows nowadays, then I'd shoot them individually without showing myself to them. But on with it! I'll make a long story short, because what followed then cannot be described in words. They held court; the fact that I had discharged a bullet was deemed to be a crime punishable by death. Besides, they also got into my liquor; they had become so drunk that they were no longer human, not even animals; they had turned into beasts. They decided to kill us. Their leader demanded that we be flogged; in other words, beaten to death as an added punishment for the strike I had served him. Two of them agreed with him, three were against it; he still got his way. They moved us outside to the fence. My wife was first. They tied her up and beat her with clubs. One of them must have felt a kind of pity for her because he put a bullet through her head. My sons fared worse than their mother; they were literally bludgeoned to death. I was lying next to them and was forced to watch it, because I was going to be the last. People, I tell you: that quarter of an hour turned into eternity for me. I won't even attempt to describe to you my thoughts and feelings. The terms fury and wrath are meaningless, there is no suitable word for it. I felt I was losing my mind, going mad, yet couldn't even move or shift around. At last it was my turn. They put me upright and tied me to the fence. I didn't feel the blows. My soul was in a state in which it was unable to focus on the physical pain at all. I only heard a shout from the corn field, and that someone fired a shot when the rafters ignored the shout. Then, I fell unconscious."

"Ah, chance had brought people who saved you!"

"People? No, because it was only one. Of course he was unaware of the circumstances and thought that a thief or other criminal was being punished. By the position of my head he realized from afar that my life wasn't worth a penny if he didn't stop the beating from that distance already. Hence his shout and his shot. He had only fired a warning shot in the air, because he didn't believe that he was dealing with murderers. When he rushed closer, one of the rogues recognized him, got a shock and called his name. They were capable of cowardly murder, but the six of them together didn't have the guts to face him alone. They ran off; by using the house as cover they escaped to the forest."

"In that case the stranger had to be a famous and feared frontiersman."

"Frontiersman? Pshaw! He was an Indian. Yes, folks, I tell you, a redskin saved me!"

"A redskin? Feared enough for six rafters to run from him? Impossible!"

"You had better believe it! If you had cause to have a guilty conscience, you'd abandon everything to get away from him, because he was none other than Winnetou."

"Winnetou, the Apache? What luck! Yes, that makes sense. But was he already as famous then as he is now?"

"He was still young[1], of course, but the one rafter who had called his name, and had then run away, had obviously made his acquaintance in a way that didn't make him wish for another encounter. Besides, anyone who's seen Winnetou even once knows what impression his appearance alone creates."

"But did he let the fellows get away?"

"For the time being, yes. Or would you have acted differently? Although he deduced from their hasty retreat that they had a guilty conscience, he still didn't know the situation. Then he saw me hanging there, tied to the fence, and on the ground the bodies of the others, which he hadn't noticed before.

"That's when he realized that a crime had been committed; yet he couldn't go after the perpetrators because he had to take care of me, above all. It didn't matter, because Winnetou knows how to find such people with near certainty. I had lost consciousness and when I came to, he knelt beside me just like the Samaritan in the Holy Scriptures. He had freed me from my ties, as well as the gag, and forbade me to speak. I didn't take any notice of it, because I really didn't feel the pain, and wanted to go on to get my revenge.

"He wouldn't let me, and instead moved me, as well as the bodies, into the house where I could easily defend myself should

---

[1] Karl May gave Winnetou's birth year as 1840; he doesn't mention the silver rifle in Missour-Blenter's tale (because that still belonged to the young Apache's father, Inshu-Chuna when the young adventurer, Karl May, met Winnetou at twenty years of age for the first time, see *Winnetou I* by the same translator), hence Winnetou could have been as young as fifteen or sixteen years of age when he saved Missouri-Blenter. As *The Treasure In Silver-Lake* plays during the summer of 1870, Blenter's tale might go back into the past as much as fifteen years.

the rafters return. After that he rode to the nearest neighbour to fetch help. I tell you that the people lived more than thirty miles away, and that Winnetou had never before been in that area. He still found them, although he only arrived there in the evening, and brought the neighbour, together with a farm hand, back to me the next morning.

"Then he left to follow the tracks of the murderers. I had to promise him not to do anything on my own because that would have been pointless. He stayed away for longer than a week. In the meantime, I buried my dead and entrusted my neighbour with the sale of my property. My broken limbs hadn't quite healed yet but I waited with great anticipation for the return of the Apache.

"He had followed the rafters, and had then spied on them during the night whereby he had found out that they were headed for Smoky Hill Fort. He didn't approach them; neither did he do anything to them, because the revenge was mine entirely. After he departed I took my gun, climbed into the saddle and rode off. You know the rest, or can guess it."

"No, we don't know it and won't guess it, either. Tell us more, go on! Why did Winnetou not go with you?"

"Most likely because he had other and better business to attend. Or do you think he hadn't done enough yet? And I won't continue with my story, either. Surely you can imagine that it cannot be a pleasure for me. I've extinguished five of them, one after the other; the sixth, being the worst of them, has escaped me. He was a rafter and might still be active in that business; hence I became a rafter as well, because I figure it's the surest way to come across him one day. And now—behold! Who's that over there?"

He jumped up, and so did the others, because two figures, clothed in colourful blankets, had stepped out of the dark of the forest into the light of the fire. They were Indians; one was older, the other young. The former reassuringly lifted his hand and said:

"Don't be afraid, we are not enemies! Do rafters work here, who know Black Tom?"

"Yes, we know him," old Blenter replied.

"He left to get money for you?"

"Yes, he's to collect it, and then return here a week from now."

"He will return earlier. We have found the right people, the rafters we were looking for. Reduce the fire, it will otherwise be visible into the distance. And speak softly, too, otherwise your voices will be heard far away."

He threw off his blanket, walked up to the fire, pulled the burning logs apart, extinguished them and left only a few to continue flickering. The young Indian assisted him. When that was done, he cast a glance into the pot, sat down and said:

"Give us a piece of meat, because we rode far and didn't eat; we're very hungry."

His confident entrance astonished the rafters. The old Missouri man voiced it by asking:

"What are you thinking? You're taking a risk by entering our camp, at night no less, although you're an Indian! You behave as if this place belongs only to you!"

"We take no risk," the old Indian replied. "The red man doesn't have to be a bad man. This red man is a good man. The paleface will find out."

"But who are you? You certainly don't belong to a river-country or prairie tribe. By your appearance I'm inclined to assume you're from New Mexico and are perhaps a Pueblo Indian."

"I come from New Mexico but am not a Pueblo Indian. I'm a Tonkawa chief; my name is Great Bear, and this is my son."

"What? Great Bear?" several rafters exclaimed in surprise, and the man from Missouri added: "In that case the boy is Little Bear?"

"That's correct!" the older Indian nodded.

"Alright, that's a different matter! The two Tonkawa Bears are welcome everywhere. Take as much meat and mead as you like, and stay with us as long as you please. But what leads you into this region?"

"We come to warn the rafters."

"Why? Are we in danger?"

"Great danger."

"What kind? Speak!"

"Tonkawa first eat and fetch horses, then speak."

He gave his son a signal, whereby Little Bear left, and then he pulled a piece of meat from the pot, which he began to eat as calmly as if he were at home in his secure wigwam.

"You have horses along?" the old Missouri man asked. "At night, here in the dark forest? While you were searching for us? The fact that you found us is a veritable masterpiece!"

"Tonkawa has eyes and ears. He knows that rafters always live near water, along a river. You talk very loudly and burn a large fire, which we could see from afar and smell even further. Rafters very careless, because enemies easily find you."

"There are no enemies here. We're alone in this region and are strong enough to deal with possible enemies at any rate."

"Missouri-Blenter is mistaken!"

"What? You know my name?"

"Tonkawa was standing behind the tree over there for a long time and hear what palefaces spoke; also heard your name. Even if the enemies are not here yet, they'll come. And when the rafters are careless, then they will be overpowered by even a small group of enemies."

At that point they heard hoof beats. Little Bear brought two horses, tied them to a tree, took a piece of meat from the pot and sat next to his father to eat. Great Bear had eaten his portion, pushed the knife back into his belt, and then said:

"Now Tonkawa will speak, and the rafters will then probably smoke the peace pipe with him. Black Tom has much money. Outlaws are coming to ambush him and take it from him."

"Outlaws? Here on the Black-Bear River? You must be mistaken."

"Tonkawa is not mistaken, but knows precisely and will tell you."

He reported the events on the steamer in his broken English, but was too proud to mention his son's heroic deed with even one word. The men listened to him with great tension, of course. He also recounted what happened after the escape of the outlaws. Great Bear and his son had reached the banks of the Arkansas River a short while after the villains, and had remained there until dawn because they couldn't follow the outlaws' tracks during the night. Their trail had remained very clear and pointed west, avoided Fort Gibson, and led the two Indians between the Canadian and Red Fork[2] rivers, after which it turned north again. During one of the following nights the outlaws had attacked a village of Cree Indians to obtain horses. At midday of the following day the two Tonkawa had met a group of roving Choctaw warriors and bought a couple of horses from them. However, because the ceremony, which was traditional during a horse deal, had taken such a long time, the outlaws had gained an entire day. They had then ridden across the Red Fork and across the open prairies towards the Black-Bear River. The Tonkawa, however, had managed to close the gap. The outlaws were camped on a small clearing at the river bank, and the Tonkawa regarded it as imperative to contact the rafters first, to notify them.

The effect of the report was immediate. The men conversed only by whispering and extinguished the fire entirely.

---

[2] Cimarron River

"How far is it from here to the camp of the outlaws?" the old Missouri man asked.

"As far as the palefaces call half an hour maybe."

"Tarnation! This means they might not have seen our fire but still smelt the smoke. We did indeed feel too secure. And since when are they camped there?"

"A whole hour before evening."

"In that case they've certainly been looking for us. Do you know anything about it?"

"Tonkawa did not spy on outlaws because it was still daylight. Moved on immediately to warn rafters, then..."

He stopped and listened. Then he continued in an even more hushed tone:

"Great Bear saw something, a movement at the corner of the house. Sit still and don't speak! Tonkawa will crawl away and find out."

He lay on the ground and crawled towards the log cabin, leaving his gun behind. The rafters strained their hearing. After maybe ten minutes a short, shrill scream pierced the night, a scream known to every Westerner—the death scream of a human being. A short while later the Tonkawa chief returned.

"A scout of the outlaws," he said. "Tonkawa gave him the knife, hit the heart from behind. He won't be able to say what he's seen and heard here. But perhaps there is a second one. He will return and report. Therefore hurry if white men want to spy on the outlaws perhaps."

"That's true," the old Missouri man whispered his agreement. "I'll come along, and you'll lead me, because you know their campsite. For the moment they have no idea that we know of their presence. They will therefore feel secure and will talk about their plans. If we depart immediately we might learn of their intentions."

"Yes, but do it very quietly and secretly, in case there is a second spy, so that he can't see that we leave. And don't take rifle along, only knife. The gun will be a hindrance."

"And what shall the others do here in the meantime?"

"Go inside the house and wait until we're back."

The men followed the advice. The rafters went inside the log cabin where they couldn't be observed; Missouri-Blenter and the chief crawled away a stretch before they rose and started their walk downriver, to possibly spy on the outlaws.

The Black-Bear River might be termed the border of the peculiarly shaped hills of a landscape that's known as the Rolling

Prairie. Hill after hill rises, one almost like the other, separated
by valleys that are just as similar. It stretches right through the
entire eastern part of Kansas. The Rolling Prairie has a rich
supply of water, and is well forested. Seen from a bird's eye
perspective, one could compare the endless succession of hills
and valleys with the rolling surge of a green-coloured ocean.
Hence the name, which makes one realize that the term prairie
does not always denote flat grassland. The waters of the Black-
Bear River had eaten deep into the soft, humus-rich ground, so
that the banks up to where the river left the Rolling Prairie were
mostly steep and yet covered with dense stands of trees. That is,
or rather was, genuine, true wilderness, because in more recent
times, the Rolling Prairie has become relatively heavily populated
and robbed of its wildlife by the Sunday hunters.

Where the rafters had established their patch for logging, the
banks fell away steeply to the water. That was very convenient
because, not far from their log cabin, it had enabled the
construction of a slip on which the rafters were able to move the
logs into the water without great effort. Fortunately the bank was
devoid of undergrowth; yet it was still difficult to walk along it in
the darkness. Missouri-Blenter was an old, agile and much-
experienced Westerner; nevertheless, he was still astonished
when the chief took him by the hand and silently walked between
the trees. He knew how to evade the trunks as confidently as if it
were broad daylight. The rushing of the river below was audible,
which was a fortuitous circumstance because it masked any
noises made by their feet.

Blenter had been in the region for some time. He didn't work as
a rafter, but as a hunter for the company, supplying the men with
meat. He knew the area very well, yet was all the more
appreciative of the confidence with which Great Bear moved,
although the Indian had never been there before, and in addition
had arrived at night.

After a long quarter of an hour, the two men descended into a
valley, between the green wave-like hills, that cut across the river.
That, too, was heavily studded with trees; a quietly murmuring
brook irrigated it. Near the spot where it emptied into the river
there was a clearing on which only a few bushes grew. That's
where the outlaws had made camp and lit a fire, the sheen of
which the two men already saw when they were still under the
closed canopy of the forest.

"Outlaws just as careless as rafters," the Tonkawa chief whispered
to his companion. "Burn large fire as if roasting a whole, big

buffalo. Red warriors only ever make a small fire. The flame cannot be seen, and there is little smoke. We easily get there and arrange it so that they can't see us."

"Yes, we'll get there," the old man remarked. "But I doubt that we will get close enough to hear what they're saying."

"We get very close; we will hear. But help each other if outlaws discover us. Stab attacker, and then quickly run into the forest."

The two men moved forwards to the last trees and gained a good view of the fire as well as the people sitting around it. In the lower location there were more mosquitoes present than in the elevated location of the rafters' camp; the insects were the usual plague along the watercourses in that region. That might have been the reason for the outlaws to maintain such a huge fire. The horses were standing to one side. The two men were unable to see them, but they could hear them. The animals were tormented by the mosquitoes so much that they moved about continuously to fend them off. Missouri-Blenter heard the stomping of their hooves; indeed, the chief even heard the swishing of their tails.

Both men lay on the ground and crawled towards the fire while using the bushes that were growing on the clearing as cover. The outlaws sat close by the brook, the banks of which were covered in dense reeds; the latter reached right up to the camp.

The Indian, who crept ahead, turned towards the reeds, which offered the best opportunity to hide. In the process of it he revealed his masterful skills in the art of sneaking up. It was a matter of getting through the tall, dry blades without causing the reeds to rustle, which was almost unavoidable. At the same time, the tips weren't permitted to move, because the two men could then easily have been discovered. The old bear avoided that danger by simply cutting himself a path. With his sharp knife he snipped the reeds in front of him and laid them down, and could still devote attention to the old Missouri man, to afford him easier passage behind him. The scything of the reeds happened so silently that even the old man couldn't detect the falling of the blades.

Thus they moved closer to the fire and lay still only when they were so close to the outlaws that they could hear their conversation, which wasn't carried on quietly. Blenter hadn't stayed behind the Indian but moved level with the chief. He scanned the figures sitting in front of him and quietly asked:

"Which one is the colonel you mentioned?"

"Colonel is not here; he's away," the Indian whispered.

"Most likely to search for us?"

"Yes; can't be for anything else."

"Is he the one you've stabbed?"

"No, that wasn't him."

"You wouldn't have been able to see that!"

"Palefaces only look with eyes; but Indians also see with hands. My fingers would have recognized the colonel for sure."

"That means the one you've stabbed was the one who had accompanied him."

"That's correct. Now we'll wait here until the colonel returns."

The outlaws conversed very lively; they chatted about anything and everything, except about something of interest to the two eavesdroppers, until one of them said:

"I wonder if the colonel guessed right. It would be vexing if the rafters weren't here any longer."

"They're still here, and quite close at that," someone else replied. "The axe chips that got washed up here are fresh; they were made yesterday or the day before at the most."

"If that's correct, then we must turn back because we're so close to the fellows here that they'll detect us. And they mustn't see us yet. We actually have nothing to do with them since we only want to catch Black Tom with his money."

"And won't get it," a third one interjected.

"Why not?"

"Because we've tackled it so stupidly that we will almost certainly fail. Do you think, perchance, that the rafters won't notice our being here if we double back a stretch? They would have to be blind. We'll be leaving tracks behind that are impossible to wipe. And once our presence is betrayed our plan is ruined."

"Not at all! We'll shoot the fellows!"

"Will they stand still for us and calmly submit to being shot? I gave the colonel the best advice, but unfortunately he rejected it. In the large cities of the East, someone who has been robbed goes to the police and leaves the catching of the thief to them; but here in the West, everyone takes matters into their own hands. I'm convinced that someone came after us at least for a stretch. And who would have followed our tracks? Most certainly only those among the passengers who know how to do that, namely Old Firehand, Black Tom, and perhaps that peculiar Aunty Droll. We should have waited for them, and then it would have been easy for us to take the money off Black Tom. Instead, we've undertaken such a long ride and are now sitting by the Black-Bear River without knowing whether or not we'll get it. And the fact that the colonel is traipsing around the forest during the night to look for the rafters is just as stupid. He could have waited until the morning and..."

He interrupted his tirade because the person in question came out from under the trees at that moment and walked up to the fire. He saw the curious gazes his people directed at him, took the hat off, tossed it on the ground, and then said:

"I'm not bringing good news, people; I've had a mishap."

"What kind of mishap? How?" the men in the circle asked. "Where's Bruns? Why isn't he with you?"

"Bruns?" the colonel replied while he sat down. "He's not coming back at all; he's dead."

"Dead? Are you bedevilled? How did the accident happen? There's no one around to kill him."

"How smart you are!" the colonel replied. "Of course the poor devil had only an accident, but because of a knife that was thrust into his heart."

The news was very disconcerting. Everyone asked about the how and where, so that the colonel was unable to give an answer because of the flood of questions. Hence he ordered them to be quiet. When the men were silent he reported:

"I took Bruns along because he's the best tracker, or rather he was. He proved his worth because his nose led us straight to the rafters."

"His nose?" asked the man who seemed to have the habit of acting as the spokesman for the entire gang.

"Yes, his nose. We assumed that the company was further upriver and therefore took that direction. We had to be careful, of course, because we could easily have been spotted. For this reason we only made slow progress and it grew dark. I wanted to turn back, but Bruns didn't want to know about it. We had seen several tracks, from which he deduced that we were getting close to the slipway. He thought that we'd be able to smell the rafters since they'd have to have a fire for the mosquitoes alone. He was correct because at last we were able to smell smoke, and on the crest of the river bank there was a faint shimmer, like that of a fire when it penetrates the bushes and trees. We climbed up and saw the fire ahead of us. It was burning in front of the log cabin, and the rafters were sitting around it. There were twenty of them, just as many as we are. We crawled closer to spy on them. I remained lying under a tree, and Bruns moved behind the house.

We hadn't even found time to listen to their conversation when two fellows arrived. They were not rafters. And who do you reckon they were? But no, you'd never guess it. They were the two Indians from aboard the *Dogfish*, namely Great Bear and Little Bear."

The outlaws were astonished about that news; they found it hard to believe. They were shocked when the colonel informed them about what the chief had said to the rafters. Then, Brinkley continued:

"I watched as the Indian extinguished the fire, and then they all spoke so quietly that I couldn't understand anything else. I would have liked to get away at that point, but had to wait for Bruns, of course. Suddenly I heard a scream, so terrible, so horrible that it went right through me. It came from behind the log cabin, where Bruns was. I was afraid for him and sneaked around the camp towards the hut. It was so dark that I had to feel my way forwards. While doing so I touched a human body with my hand. The corpse was lying in a pool of blood. By the clothing I could tell that it was Bruns and got a mighty shock. He had a stab wound in his back, which had obviously gone through to his heart; he was dead. What was I to do? I emptied his pockets, took his knife and revolver and left him lying there. When I sneaked to the front of the building I noticed that the rafters had all gone inside the log cabin, and then I quickly skedaddled."

The outlaws poured forth raw expressions of pity about the death of their companion, but their leader put an end to it by saying:

"Leave that be! We don't have the time for it because we've got to get away."

"Why?" the others asked.

"Why? Didn't you hear what I said? The Indians know the whereabouts of our campsite! The rafters will want to attack us, of course, and will probably do so in the morning. However, they'll undoubtedly realize that we'll become suspicious when our spy doesn't return. It is therefore possible that they'll come here even earlier. If we let them surprise us, then we'll be lost. We must head off immediately."

"But where?"

"To Eagle Tail."

"Ah, to fetch the railroad coffers! Will we have to forego the rafters' money?"

"Unfortunately! That's the smartest thing to do, and…"

He cut himself short with a hand gesture of surprise, which the others didn't understand.

"What is it? What's the matter with you?" one of them asked. "Keep talking!"

The colonel rose without giving an answer. He had been sitting close to the spot where the two spies were lying. Great Bear and Blenter were no longer side by side.

As soon as Missouri-Blenter had spotted the colonel, he had become gripped by an agitation that only increased when he heard the sound of the man's voice. He didn't remain lying still, but pushed increasingly further forwards through the reeds. His eyes were aglow and it seemed as if they wanted to pop out of their sockets. In his state he forgot the necessary caution; he didn't pay attention to the fact that his head protruded from the reeds almost entirely.

"Don't let them see you!" the chief whispered and grabbed him to pull him back.

But it was too late, because the colonel had already spotted Blenter's head. That's why he interrupted his report and rose swiftly to render the spy harmless. He acted very cleverly in the process, by saying:

"I just remembered that, over by the horses, I've—but, you two, come along with me!" He signalled the two men who were sitting to either side of him. They immediately got up as well, and the colonel whispered:

"I'm only pretending because there's a fellow lying in the reeds behind us, a rafter no doubt. If he sees that I'm on to him, he'll run away. As soon as I jump at him, you also grab him at once. That way we'll have a solid hold on him right from the beginning, so that he cannot resist and injure me. Let's go!"

At that command, which he called out loudly, he turned around as quick as lightning and jumped towards the spot where he had seen the head.

The Tonkawa chief was an exceedingly cautious, experienced and astute man. He saw the colonel rise and whisper something to the other two; he saw that one of them had made a reflexive move backwards. Although it was a small and insignificant movement, it nevertheless revealed to Great Bear what it was all about. He touched the old man with his hand and whispered:

"Get away, quickly! Colonel saw you and catch you. Quickly, quickly!"

At the same time he turned around and catapulted himself away and behind the next bush, without rising from the ground. That had taken a mere two seconds before the command "let's go!" came from the colonel, and when the Indian looked back he saw that the man threw himself onto Missouri-Blenter with the other two following immediately.

Despite Blenter's praiseworthy presence of mind he was taken by complete surprise. The three outlaws were lying or kneeling on top of him and pinned him down by his arms and his legs. The others near the fire jumped up and rushed over. The Indian had pulled out his knife to assist Blenter; but he realized that he couldn't achieve anything against such a superior number. He couldn't do any more than to wait and see what was going to happen to Missouri-Blenter, and then to notify the rafters. To avoid also being discovered, he crawled away a stretch from the path he had cut into the reeds, and then hid behind a bush.

The outlaws wanted to raise a noise when they saw their prisoner, but the colonel ordered them to be silent:

"Quiet! We don't know whether or not others are here as well. Hold him down. I'll look around."

He investigated the surroundings of the fire, but was relieved when he couldn't see anyone else. Then he ordered the man to be brought to the fire. The latter had applied all his strength to get away, but for naught. He conceded defeat and submitted to his fate. There was a possibility it wouldn't be too dire since he hadn't done anything to the outlaws. Besides, the thought of the Indian was bound to reassure him. Great Bear was undoubtedly rushing away to fetch help.

While the four men held Blenter down, the colonel bent over him to have a look at his face. He did so with a long, sharply searching gaze. Then he said:

"I ought to know you! Where have I seen you before?"

The old man guarded himself from telling him, because he would have been lost in that case. The hatred was boiling in his chest, but he made an effort to show the most indifferent expression possible.

"Indeed I must have seen you," the colonel repeated. "Who are you? Do you belong to the rafters who are working further upriver?"

"Yes," Blenter replied.

"Why are you sneaking around here? Why are you spying on us?"

"That's a peculiar question! Is it forbidden to have a look at a group of men here in the West, perchance? On the contrary, I think common sense demands one does so. There are enough fellows about one has to be wary of."

"Are you counting us among them?"

"It remains to be seen what kind of people you are. I don't know you."

"That's a lie. You've heard what we've been talking about and will therefore know who and what we are."

"I didn't hear anything at all. I was downriver and was heading back to our camp; that's when I saw your fire, and of course sneaked up to see who's camped here. I didn't even find time to listen to what was said because I was too careless. You saw me as soon as I prepared to eavesdrop on you."

He was hoping that only the dead outlaw behind the log cabin had seen him, since he had had his face turned towards him; but he was mistaken, because the red-haired outlaw replied:

"That's a fabrication. I not only saw you sitting with the rafters before, but also heard you speak and recognize you. Will you admit to that?"

"Wouldn't think of it! What I've said is true; you're therefore mistaking me with someone else."

"Were you really here alone?"

"Yes."

"And you claim not to have heard anything of our conversation?"

"Not a word."

"What's your name?"

"Adams," Missouri-Blenter lied. He thought he had every reason not to mention his real name.

"Adams," the colonel repeated pensively. "Adams! I've never known anyone by the name of Adams and with your face. And yet I feel as if we've met before. Do you know me? Do you know my name?"

"No," the old man again told an untruth. "Now let me go! I've not done anything to you, and hope that you're honest Westerners who leave other honest people in peace."

"Yes, we are honest men indeed, very honest," Brinkley laughed. "But you've stabbed one of us, and according to the laws of the West, such a deed screams for revenge. Blood for blood, life for life. No matter who you are, you're done for!"

"What? You want to murder me?"

"Yes, just like you've murdered our companion. It's a matter of deciding whether you'll die by the knife, just like he did, or we'll drown you in the river. But we certainly won't stand on ceremony.

We've got no time to lose. Let's decide quickly. Gag him, so that he can't scream. Those of you in favour of tossing him into the water raise your arms."

That request was directed at the outlaws, the majority of whom gave the indicated signal immediately.

"Drowning in that case!" the colonel remarked. "Tie his arms and legs solidly, so that he can't swim; then quickly into the water with him. Afterwards we'll get going before his people get here!"

Several outlaws held down Missouri-Blenter while they carried out the interrogation. The men were about to apply the gag. He knew that the Indian could not possibly have returned to the rafters already; there was no counting on help. Nevertheless, he did what anyone else in his situation would have done: he resisted with all of his strength and screamed for help. The shout echoed far into the stillness of the night.

"Tarnation!" Brinkley angrily snapped. "Don't let him scream like this. If you can't deal with him, then I'll shut him up myself. Watch!"

He grabbed his gun and swung back to hit the old man over the head with the butt, but didn't get to make good on his intention, because...

A short time before evening broke, four riders were following the river bank upstream, keeping a sharp eye on the outlaws' tracks, namely Old Firehand, Black Tom, and Aunty Droll with his boy. The trail led along under the trees; although it was easily recognizable, its age was difficult to determine. Only when it led across a grass-covered clearing did Old Firehand dismount to inspect it, because the blades of grass gave a better indication than the low forest mosses. When he had examined it closely, he said:

"The fellows are about a mile ahead of us because the tracks were made half an hour ago. We must let our horses lengthen their strides."

"Why?" Tom asked.

"In order to get close enough to the outlaws, so that we'll find out the site of their camp."

"Won't that be dangerous for us?"

"Not that I'd know of."

"Oh, but yes! They'll be making camp before it gets dark, and if we rush we must expect to ride straight into their arms."

"I don't expect we will. And even if your assumption is correct, then we still can't get to them before dusk. Various indications make me think that we are close to the rafters, whom we have to warn about the outlaws first. In order to do that, it would be beneficial for us to know the location of the scoundrels' campsite. Hence making haste is advisable. Otherwise the night will surprise us, during which much can happen that we cannot prevent. What do you think, Aunty Droll?"

The two men had spoken German. Hence Droll replied in his own dialect:

"Ye've spoken entirely my own opinion. If we ride briskly, then we'll have them sooner; but if we ride slower, then we'll catch them later, whereby we could easily get ourselves into an unfortunate predicament much sooner and more deeply than those we wish to save. Hence, dear gents, let's trot, so that the trees shake!"

Since the trees weren't growing in dense formation, the men were able to follow that suggestion even in the forest. But the outlaws had also utilized the remaining daylight, and had only stopped when darkness had forced them to it. Had Old Firehand held a little closer to the river bank, and not ridden on the trail of Brinkley and his men, he would have come across the tracks of the two Tonkawa Indians, who were only a short distance ahead.

When it became so dark that the hoof prints were no longer recognizable while sitting in the saddle, he dismounted again to inspect the tracks. The result was:

"We've made up half a mile; but unfortunately the outlaws rode fast as well. Nevertheless, we'll try and catch up to them. Dismount; we must continue on foot and lead the horses!"

Unfortunately the stretch they were still able to cover wasn't significant because it became so dark that the trail was no longer visible. The four riders therefore stopped.

"What now?" Black Tom asked. "We're almost forced to camp here."

"*Nee*[3]," Aunty Droll replied. "I'll not be camping here; we'll keep on traipsing until we find them."

"They'll hear us approach!"

"Then we'll proceed gingerly. They'll not be hearing me, and they'll not be catching me. Don't ye agree, *Herr*[4] Firehand?"

"Yes, I share your opinion," Firehand replied. "But caution forbids us to adhere to the direction of the trail. If we did this,

---

[3] No
[4] Mr

then Tom's prediction would come true; the outlaws would have to hear our approach. Let's keep more to our right, away from the river; we'll then have them between us and the river and must see their fire without them noticing us."

"And what if they don't have a fire?" Tom asked.

"Then we'll smell their horses," Droll replied. "It's easier to sniff out horses in a forest than it is out on the open paddock. My nose has not ever left me in the lurch in det regard. Let's march on, over to the right!"

Leading his horse by the reins, Old Firehand walked ahead; the others followed in single file. Unfortunately, the river described a large bend to the left in that particular spot. Subsequently, the group moved too far away from it. Old Firehand realized it by the increasingly dry ground, as well as the surroundings, and hence headed more to the left. However, the detour could not be undone, especially since they could only walk very slowly in the dark forest. The foursome came to the conclusion that they had made a mistake and thought it was advisable to return to the river as a matter of priority. They didn't know that they had walked around the outlaws' camp and at that point were situated between it and that of the rafters. Fortunately, Old Firehand detected the smoke and stood still to ascertain from which direction it came. Behind him, Droll sniffed the air, and then remarked:

"Det's smoke; thence it comes; hence we must head whence it rose. But let's pay attention; methinks it's getting lighter there. Det can only be caused by the fire."

He wanted to stride out, but stopped because his keen hearing had detected the sound of footsteps approaching. Old Firehand had also heard them, as well as the racing breath of the person rushing towards the men. He let go of his horse's reins and walked ahead several paces. He was able to hear that the man was going to move past that spot. In the dark of the night and the forest, a figure, hardly discernible even for the sharp eyes of the famous hunter, emerged in front of him and was about to flit past. Old Firehand grabbed the person with both hands.

"Stop!" he gave the order with a suppressed voice so as not to be heard too far away. "Who are you?"

"*Shai nek-enokh, shai kopeia*[5]," the man replied while he tried to pull free.

Even the most fearless man will get a shock when he's suddenly seized by a couple of strong fists while he thinks he's alone in a

[5] I don't know, no one

forest at night. During such a moment of surprise, anyone will use his mother tongue reflexively. And so did the man Old Firehand held. The latter was surprised when he understood the words of the stranger, and said:

"That's Tonkawa! Great Bear and his son are ahead of us. Are you perchance—say: who are you?"

At that point the stranger ceased to resist; he had recognized the voice of the great hunter and hastily replied in his broken English:

"Me Nintropan-Hauey; you Old Firehand. That's very good, very good! Are any other men with you?"

"You are Great Bear after all! What a lucky coincidence. Yes, I'm Old Firehand. There are three other people with me and we have horses. What are you doing here? The outlaws are nearby. Be careful."

"I've seen them already. They took old Missouri-Blenter prisoner. Will probably kill him. I was running to the rafters when Old Firehand grabbed me."

"They want to kill a rafter? We must prevent that. Where are they?"

"There, behind me where it is lighter between the trees."

"Is the red-haired colonel with them?"

"Yes, he's there."

"Where are their horses?"

"If Old Firehand walks straight towards the outlaws' camp from here, then the horses are standing to the right, before you reach the fire."

"And where are the rafters?"

"Up on the hill. The old bear already visited them and spoke to them."

In greatest haste he recounted what had transpired, whereupon Old Firehand replied:

"An outlaw has been killed; now they'll want to murder the old Missouri man, and will do so at once, for they must flee because their presence has been betrayed. The four of us will tie up our horses here and rush to the fire to prevent the murder. You run to the rafters and lead them here! We might not be scared of these outlaws, but it is better to have the lumberjacks join us as soon as they can."

The Indian ran off. The four riders tied their horses to the nearest trees, and then walked as fast as possible towards the camp of the outlaws. After only a short while the sheen grew brighter, and soon they were able to see the fire glow between the trunks of the trees. They spotted the horses to their right.

Thus far they hadn't made any effort to move quietly or take cover. But at that point they crouched low and crawled towards the fire. Old Firehand was about to turn to Fred, the boy. He wanted to direct him to head over to the horses and shoot any outlaw who wanted to mount up and escape; but he had hardly said the first word when a loud, piercing scream arose in front of them. That was the already mentioned cry for help by the old Missouri man.

"They're murdering him!" Old Firehand said, still with a hushed voice. "Upon them, quickly, right into their midst. Don't spare those who resist!"

He rose, ran towards the fire and in the process tossed three, four outlaws to the side to get to Brinkley, who was swinging back right at that moment to strike. Firehand was just in time to knock the colonel down with the butt of his rifle. The three outlaws, who had been busy tying up and gagging the old Missouri-Blenter, in preparation to toss him into the river, fell under Firehand's subsequent blows. Afterwards, the hunter threw the still-loaded gun to the ground, pulled out his revolvers and fired upon the rest of the enemies. He didn't say a word. To be silent during a battle was his way, except when he was forced to issue orders.

The other three, however, were all the more vocal. Black Tom had charged into the outlaws like a thunderstorm and worked them to the ground with the butt of his rifle, while he threw the nastiest insults and a volley of abuse at them. Sixteen-year-old Fred had first fired his rifle at them, then he tossed it to the ground and pulled out his revolver. He discharged shot after shot and yelled at the top of his lungs to increase their panic.

The loudest of them all, however, was Aunty Droll's screeching, high-pitched falsetto voice. The peculiar hunter screamed and raged for virtually a hundred people. His movements were so incredibly swift that none of the enemies was able to shoot at him. There was no one among the outlaws who even dared to entertain such a thought. They were so completely bewildered from the shock of the unexpected attack that at first they didn't even think of resistance. When those who hadn't been injured regained their composure, they saw the large number of their comrades lying on the ground dead or wounded and thought the smartest thing to do was to take flight. They ran away without having taken the time to count the attackers, whom they assumed to be in great numbers on account of Aunty Droll's incessant shrieking. Not even a minute had elapsed from Old Firehand's first strike to when the uninjured outlaws fled.

"After them!" Old Firehand shouted. "I'll secure the camp. Don't let them get to the horses!"

Amid great hollering Black Tom, Droll and Fred ran towards the spot where they had seen the animals. The outlaws who had fled in that direction to find safety in the saddle abandoned their intentions out of fear; they fled further into the forest.

Meanwhile, the rafters in their log cabin had been waiting for the return of the two scouts, Missouri-Blenter and Tonkawa chief Great Bear. When they heard the shots being fired further downriver, they believed the two men were in danger. In order to possibly rescue them, they grabbed their weapons, left the cabin and ran as fast as the darkness allowed in the direction from which the sound of the gunfire had originated. They were hollering as loudly as they could in an attempt at scaring the outlaws away from their victims. The young bear ran ahead of them since he knew precisely where the camp of the outlaws was situated. From time to time he called out to keep the rafters going in the right direction. They had hardly gone half way when they heard someone else's voice right in front of them, namely that of Great Bear.

"Come quickly!" he called out. "Old Firehand is here and is shooting at outlaws. He only has three men along; help him."

The rafters moved downriver with increased speed. The shooting stopped, and therefore the men didn't know what the situation was. The consequence of the rafters' hollering was that the fleeing outlaws didn't stop running and endeavoured to get away as far as possible. The former were in a similar hurry. Many collided with tree trunks and got hurt, without taking notice. By the time they arrived at the outlaws' fire, Old Firehand, Black Tom, Aunty Droll, Missouri-Blenter and Fred were sitting around it as calmly as if it had been lit for them, and as if nothing out of the ordinary had happened. On one side lay the corpses, on the other the tied-up, injured outlaws, the colonel among them.

"Tarnation!" the rafters who arrived first called to the old Missouri man. "We thought you were in danger, and now you're sitting here as calmly as in Abraham's fold!"

"That's how it was, too!" the old man replied. "I was going to be transported into Abraham's fold. The butt of the colonel's rifle was already above me; and then these four gentlemen came along and got me out. Fast and excellent work! You could learn much from them, boys!"

"And...is Old Firehand really here?"

"Yes, there he sits. Have a look at him and shake his hand! He's deserved it. Just think: only four men take on twenty, kill nine and make six prisoners without suffering as much as a scratch; not to mention the bullets and punches they've undoubtedly served those who have escaped! Or more accurately: three men and a boy. Can you imagine that?"

He rose from the fire while he spoke. The others also got to their feet. The rafters remained standing at a respectful distance with their gazes on Old Firehand. He invited them to move closer and shook each one's hand. He welcomed the two Tonkawa with a special compliment by saying:

"My red brothers have delivered a masterpiece with the pursuit of the outlaws, which made it easy for me to follow. We have also bought horses from Indians in an effort to possibly catch up with you before encountering the outlaws."

"The praise of my white brother honours me more than I deserve," the old bear humbly replied. "The outlaws created a trail as deep and wide as that of a buffalo herd. One has to be blind not to see it. But where is the colonel? Is he also dead?"

"No, he lives. My blow with the rifle butt only rendered him unconscious. He came to and we tied him up. There he lies."

He pointed to the spot where Brinkley lay. The Tonkawa Indian walked over to him, pulled out the knife and said:

"He might not have died from the knock, but he'll die through my knife. He struck me; now I'll take his blood!

"Stop!" the old Missouri man exclaimed and grabbed the Indian's raised arm. "This man doesn't belong to you, he's mine."

The old bear turned around, looked into Blenter's face with a stern expression, and then asked:

"You, too, seek revenge upon him?"

"Yes, and then some!"

"Blood?"

"Blood and life."

"Since when?"

"Since many, many years. He had my wife and my two sons whipped to death."

"You're not mistaken?" the Indian asked. He found it difficult to give up his revenge, which the laws of the prairie forced him to do.

"No, there's no error possible. I've recognized him immediately. One cannot forget such a face."

"You will kill him?"

"Yes, without mercy or compassion."

"Then I'll step back, but not entirely. He will give his blood to me, and to you his life. Great Bear won't entirely release him from punishment; he'll cut off his ears. Do you agree?"

"Hm! What if I don't agree?"

"Then I'll immediately kill him!"

"Alright, take his ears! It may not be entirely Christian that I agree with it; but anyone who has experienced the kind of torture he has continued to inflict on me to this day will hold with the laws of the prairie, not mercy, which would even spare evil like him."

"Who else wants to speak to the Tonkawa?" the chief asked while he looked around the circle to see whether someone else had any objections. But when no one said a word against it he continued:

"Alright, the ears are mine, and I'll take them immediately."

He knelt beside the colonel to make good on his intentions. When Brinkley saw that the deed was about to be carried out, he cried out:

"What are you thinking, gents! Is that Christian? What did I do to you that you allow this red heathen to mutilate my head?"

"We'll talk about what you did to me a little later," Missouri-Blenter replied cold and severely.

"And I'll show you right now what the rest of us are going to accuse you of," Old Firehand added. "We still haven't inspected his pockets; let's see what's in them!"

He gave Droll a signal and the man emptied the prisoner's pockets. Next to many other items there was also the outlaw's wallet. When they opened it they found the entire roll of banknotes that had been stolen from the engineer.

"Ah, you haven't shared it among your people yet!" Old Firehand smiled. "It just goes to show that they had more trust in you than you in them. You're a thief and probably even more than that. You don't deserve any mercy. Great Bear may please himself."

The colonel screamed in horror; but the chief didn't bother about the yelling, grabbed him by the hair and with two fast, well-directed cuts sliced the two ears off, which he then tossed into the river.

"There!" he said. "Tonkawa has taken revenge, and will now ride away."

"Now?" Old Firehand asked. "Won't you ride with me, or at least spend the night with us?"

"It doesn't matter to Tonkawa whether it is day or night. His eyes are good, but his time very short. He wasted many days to follow the colonel; now he'll have to ride day and night to reach his wigwam. Great Bear is a friend of the white men; he is a good friend and a brother to Old Firehand. May the Great Spirit always give much powder and much meat to the palefaces who have been friendly to the Tonkawa. Howgh!"

He shouldered his gun and walked away. His son also hoisted his rifle onto his shoulder and followed him into the night-time forest.

"Where are their horses?" Old Firehand enquired.

"Uphill where our log cabin is," Missouri-Blenter replied. "Of course they'll go up there to fetch them. But whether they'll find their way out through the forest at night is another..."

"Don't worry," the hunter interjected. "They know the way, otherwise they would have stayed. The old bear has made many purchases, as he said. The merchandise is on its way; he must join the wagon train, yet has lost much time. That easily explains why he's in a hurry. Let's turn our attention to our own affairs and let them ride. What shall happen to the dead and imprisoned outlaws?"

"We will toss the former into the water tomorrow, and will now hold court over the others according to established tradition. But let's first satisfy ourselves that those who have escaped aren't posing a threat to us."

"Oh, there are so few that we don't have to fear them; they'll have run as far as possible. Besides, we can post a few guards; that's more than enough."

The colonel was lying between his captured outlaws and the corpses, and was whimpering in pain; but no one took any notice of it, at least not yet. There was no danger expected from the river side, and a few guards were placed towards the land side. Old Firehand sent one of the rafters to fetch his horse as well as that of his three companions, and then the prairie court could begin.

First the ordinary outlaws were processed. There was no proof that they had caused harm to any of the other men present. The injuries they sustained, as well as the loss of their horses and weapons were counted as the punishment for what they had planned. They were permitted to bandage each other's wounds.

Then it was the colonel's turn, the main culprit. He had been lying in the dark thus far and was brought near the fire. As soon as the glow of the flames fell onto his face, Fred, the boy, emitted a scream, ran up to him, bent down, looked at him as if he wanted to devour him with his eyes, and then called back to Aunty Droll:

"It's him, it's him, the murderer! I recognize him. We've got him!"

Electrified, Droll rushed over immediately and asked:

"Are you sure? It can't be him at all; it's impossible."

"Oh, yes, it's him; it sure is!" the boy insisted. "Look at his eyes! Don't they have the fear of death in them? He realizes that he's been revealed and has relinquished all hope of rescue."

"But if it were him, then you ought to have recognized him on the steamer already."

"I didn't get a look at him. I saw the outlaws alright, but not him. He must have been sitting in a place where the others always obscured him."

"That was indeed the case. But one more thing: you've described the culprit with black, curly hair, the colonel here has straight red hair."

The boy didn't immediately reply. He clutched his hand to his forehead, shook his head, took a step back, and then said with evident doubt in his voice:

"That of course is true! It is entirely his face; but the hair is completely different."

"This is most likely a case of mistaken identity, Fred. People can resemble one another; but black hair cannot become red."

"Maybe not that," Missouri-Blenter cut in. "But one can shave dark hair off, and then wear a wig."

"Ah! Would that be...?" Droll asked but didn't finish his question.

"Naturally! I didn't let the red hair confuse me. The man I've been searching for so long, the murderer of my wife and my children, also had black, curly hair; this fellow here has a red head, but I still claim that he's the one I was after. He's wearing a wig."

"Impossible!" Droll said. "Didn't you see how the Indian grabbed him by his mop before when he cut his ears off? If the fellow were wearing false hair, then it would have been pulled off his head at that moment."

"Pshaw! It is well made and solidly attached. I'll prove it to you immediately."

The colonel was lying stretched-out on the ground, bound on arms and legs. Blood was still streaming from his ears; they were undoubtedly causing him great pain; but he ignored it. His entire attention was focussed on what Droll and Blenter were saying. He may have presented a fairly dismal picture initially, but the expression on his face had completely changed. Fear had given way to hope, dread to mockery, and despair to arrogance. Old Missouri-Blenter was convinced that the colonel was wearing false hair. He pulled him up into a seated position, grabbed him by the hair and pulled it to tear the wig from his head. To his great astonishment, however, he was unsuccessful because the hair held; it really was the man's own hair.

"All devils, the scoundrel really has hair on his skull!" he was astonished and made such a shocked face that the others would have laughed had the situation not been so serious.

The face of the colonel distorted to a sneer, and with a tone of unrestrained hatred he shouted:

"Well then, you liar and slanderer, where is the wig? To accuse someone wrongly because of his resemblance to another person is easy. Prove that I'm the one you say I am!"

Missouri-Blenter looked at him, then at Old Firehand, back and forth, and being at a loss said to the latter:

"Tell me what you think of it! The one I'm thinking of really had black, curly hair; the man here has straight, red hair. And yet I would swear a thousand oaths that it is him. My eyes cannot possibly fool me."

"You may still be mistaken after all," the hunter replied. "It seems there is a similarity here that fools you."

"Which means I can no longer trust my good, old eyes!"

"Open them a little better!" the colonel mocked. "The devil shall get me if I know anything about a mother and her two sons who have been murdered, or, as you say, beaten to death no less!"

"But you know me, regardless! You've said so yourself before."

"Must I be the one you're referring to simply because I've seen you somewhere? The boy is also completely wrong about me. The man he was talking about is undoubtedly the same you were referring to; but I don't know the young boy and..." He suddenly interrupted himself, seemingly startled or astonished about something, but immediately recovered and continued in the same tone of voice: "...and have never seen him before. You can accuse me as far as I'm concerned; but bring evidence. If you want to sentence and execute me because of a coincidental likeness with someone else, then you simply are murderers, and I believe that at least Old Firehand, in whose protection I am placing myself herewith, is incapable of that."

There was a good reason he had cut himself short in the middle of a sentence. He was sitting with his back towards the corpses, and had propped his head up on one of them. When Missouri-Blenter pulled him away into a seated position, the seemingly lifeless, stiff body rolled ever so slightly, which wasn't conspicuous to anyone, because it had lost its support. At that point the corpse was lying close to Brinkley in the shadow behind him, away from the fire. But the outlaw wasn't dead, he wasn't even wounded. He belonged to those whom Old Firehand had knocked down with the butt of his rifle. The blood of his dead comrades had splashed on him and given him the appearance of also having been hit. When he came to he found himself lying among the dead when their pockets were being emptied and the weapons removed. He would have liked to jump up and flee, since he only counted four enemies, but he didn't want to jump into the river, and the noise of the approaching rafters came from the other side. Hence he decided to wait for a favourable moment. He succeeded in pulling out his knife while unobserved and stash it in his sleeve; then Missouri-Blenter stepped over to him, turned him back and forth, believed him to be dead, took what was in his belt and his pockets, and then pulled him towards the spot where the corpses were placed.

From that point onwards the outlaw was observing everything from under his lowered lids. He hadn't been tied up and was therefore able to jump up at the most suitable moment and run away. But then the rafters laid the colonel across him and he immediately got the idea to free him as well. When Brinkley was pulled up, the seemingly dead outlaw rolled ever so slightly towards him, so that he came to lie behind him, close to his tied hands. While the colonel spoke, and everyone's attention was directed at him, the outlaw behind him pulled the knife from his sleeve and carefully cut the strap, and then put the grip of the knife into Brinkley's right hand, which would enable him to swiftly cut his leg ties as well, jump up and flee. Of course, Brinkley felt the clandestine freeing of his hands; he felt the knife handle, which he gripped immediately, and was so astonished about it that he lost his composure for a moment and interrupted his speech, but only for a short moment; then he continued talking and no one noticed what had taken place behind the back of the accused. Since he had been referring to Old Firehand's sense of justice, the hunter replied:

"Where I'm involved there won't be any murder; you can rely on that. But it is just as certain that your red hair won't fool me. It might be coloured."

"Hah! Is it possible to colour hair, which is still growing on someone's head, red?"

"Indeed," the hunter nodded knowingly.

"Perhaps with ruddle?" the colonel asked with a forced laugh. "That would nicely stain everything!"

"You may laugh; but you won't be doing so for long," Old Firehand replied in a calm, superior tone of voice. "Perhaps you can fool others, but not me."

He walked over to the weapons and things that had been taken off the prisoners and the dead outlaws, bent down, picked up the leather pouch that had hung on the colonel's belt, and then continued talking while he opened it:

"I've already inspected this pouch before, and have found several items, the purpose and application of which were unclear to me; but now I'm beginning to get a hunch, and it might perhaps be correct."

He pulled out a small, plugged bottle, a small rasp and a finger-long piece of twig that still had its bark, held the three objects in front of Brinkley's face and asked him:

"Why are you carrying these items around with you?"

The outlaw's face turned a few shades paler, yet he replied immediately and confidently:

"What a surprise that the great Firehand bothers about such bagatelles! Who would have thought! The bottle contained some medicine; the rasp is an essential instrument for any Westerner, and the piece of wood got into the pouch by mere coincidence, without it having a particular purpose. Are you satisfied now, sir?"

"Indeed, I'm satisfied—but with my own conclusions, and not with what you said. An outlaw doesn't need a rasp, at least not such a small one; a file would be of much better use to him. This little bottle contains wood shavings in alcohol, and this piece of wood is, judging by its bark, a piece of twig from a Hackberry tree[6]. As it so happens, I know precisely that even the darkest hair can be dyed red using Hackberry wood shavings that have been steeped in alcohol; ergo...well, what do you say to that?"

"That I don't understand a single word of the entire deliberation," the colonel replied angrily. "I'd like to see the person who would

---

[6] *Celtis occidentalis L.*

want to dye his beautiful black hair ginger red. The fellow would have to have impeccable taste!"

"Taste is immaterial in this case; the purpose matters. Someone who's wanted for a serious crime gladly dyes his hair red if he can save his life by it. I'm convinced that you're the wanted man and will inspect your head and hair thoroughly tomorrow morning as soon as there's daylight."

"We don't have to wait that long," Fred cut in. "There's a distinguishing feature. I saw how someone stabbed him through the calf, in one side and out the other, so that the knife got stuck. He'll have to uncover his leg. If he's the right person, which I don't doubt he is, then the two scars must still be visible."

Nothing could have been more welcome to the red-haired outlaw than that suggestion. If they untied his legs, then he wouldn't have to cut the straps himself. Hence he quickly replied:

"Alright, my smart boy. In that case you can satisfy yourself that you're all mistaken. But I'm surprised that you with your great astuteness are expecting me to pull up the trouser leg. That's obviously impossible for someone who's got his arms and legs tied up."

"I know that. Hence I'll do it myself."

The boy's zeal drove him to approach the prisoner. He knelt beside him and fumbled around with the strap, which had been tied around the prisoner's legs about mid-calf. After he had opened the knot he wanted to pull up one leg of the Nankeen trouser; but he received a kick from Brinkley with both feet, so that he was catapulted far away. The next moment the colonel leapt to his feet.

"Good bye, mesh'shurs! We'll see each other again!" he shouted and lunged into the gap between two rafters to get out and across the clearing to the trees.

The man's escape came so unexpectedly to everyone present—except two—that they stood as if they were bolted to the ground. The two exceptions were Old Firehand and Aunty Droll. The former possessed a presence of mind that was reliable even in the most unusual situations, and the latter was almost equal to him in that regard, despite his other peculiarities, which didn't even allow for a comparison between him and the famous hunter.

As soon as Brinkley leapt up from his seated position and lifted the knife, Old Firehand was also ready to jump, grab him and hold him down; but he met an entirely unexpected obstacle. The seemingly dead outlaw had decided that his time had come, too.

Since everyone's attention was directed at the colonel, he believed he could easily flee at that point. He jumped up as well and charged past the fire to break through the circle of rafters. At that moment Old Firehand bounded over the flames and collided with the outlaw. To seize him, lift him, and then throw him on the ground with a crashing thud was the work of a mere two seconds for Firehand.

"Bind this fellow, who wasn't dead!" he called out, turned around towards the colonel, snatched the rifle to his cheek, and aimed at the fugitive to drop him with a bullet, for the two men's collision had given Brinkley the time to get out of the camp area.

Firehand recognized the impossibility of executing his intention because Droll was hard behind Brinkley and covered him with his body in such a way that the bullet would have hit him.

The red-haired outlaw ran like a man fleeing to save his life. Droll stormed after him with all he had. He would undoubtedly have caught him had he not been wearing his famous leather sleeping gown. The garment was simply too heavy and cumbersome for such a pursuit. Hence Old Firehand dropped his gun and ran after them with panther-like leaps.

"Stand still, Droll!" he called out.

But Droll ignored the shout and kept running although Firehand repeated it several times. At that point Brinkley left the reaches of the light thrown from the fire, and disappeared in the darkness under the trees.

"Stand still, for Heaven's sake, Droll, stand still!" Firehand shouted angrily for the fifth time. He was only three or four paces behind him.

"I must have him, must have him!" the excited Droll retorted in his usual falsetto, and also dashed between the trees.

That's when Old Firehand stopped short amid-sprint, like a well-trained horse that obeys the reins even at a stretched gallop, turned around and slowly returned to the fire as if nothing had happened. Those that had stayed back were standing together in individual groups, nervously gazing towards the forest in anticipation of the chase's outcome.

"You're returning on your own!" the old Missouri man exclaimed.

"As you can see," Firehand calmly said and shrugged his shoulders.

"Was he impossible to catch?"

"On the contrary, it would have been very easy had not that bedevilled outlaw gotten in my way and collided with me."

"The fact that none other than the chief villain has to escape us is a lamentable affair!"

"Well, you have the least cause to complain about it, old Blenter."

"Why?"

"Because only you are to blame for it."

"Me?" the old man was astonished. "I don't understand. With all due respect, sir, you need to explain that to me!"

"That's easily done. Which one of you inspected the outlaw, who came back to life again?"

"I did, of course."

"And believed he was dead! How could that have happened to the experienced rafter and hunter that you are? And who emptied his pockets and took the weapons from him?"

"I did that, too."

"And left him with the knife!"

"He had none."

"He had it hidden. Then he came to lie behind the colonel, and while he was playing dead he not only cut his ties, but also gave him the knife."

"Do you think that's how it was, sir?" the old man was embarrassed.

"Ask him yourself! There he lies."

Blenter gave the tied-up outlaw a kick and through all manner of threats forced him to give answers. He found out that the incident had occurred the way Old Firehand had guessed. The old man grabbed bunches of his long, grey hair, ruffled it indignantly, and then angrily said:

"I could box my own ears. A stupidity like this has never happened in all the states. It's my fault, entirely my fault! And I'd bet my life that he was the one I have been after."

"Of course he was, otherwise he would have calmly submitted to the inspection of his leg. If the two scars were non-existent, then nothing would have happened to him because we couldn't punish him for the theft of the engineer's money, according to the laws of the prairie, since Butler isn't present."

At that point Droll slowly and hesitantly returned across the clearing. It was obvious from afar already that he had also failed. He had followed the fugitive for quite a stretch through the forest, or so he believed, had met a number of trees head-on, at last stood still to listen, and when he couldn't hear the slightest noise around him, turned back.

Old Firehand had become fond of the peculiar man, and therefore didn't want to embarrass him in front of the rafters. Hence he asked in German:

"But, Droll, didn't you hear what I shouted to you several times?"

"I sure heard what ye called out," Droll replied.

"And why didn't you act accordingly?"

"Because I wanted to catch det fellow."

"And to do that you run after him into the forest?"

"How else should I have done it? Was he supposed to run after me perchance?"

"Of course not," Old Firehand laughed. "However, in order to catch someone in a forest, one has to see him, or at least hear him if it's during the night. If you're running as well, then the sound of his steps will become inaudible for you. Understood?"

"Det's easily comprehensible. I should therefore have stood still?"

"Yes."

"Oh, goodness gracious me! Who's going to make sense of that? If I stand still, then he runs away and I can wait on that spot until the day of reckoning! Or do ye think perhaps that he'll come back of his own accord and throw himself into my arms?"

"Not quite, but almost. I'd bet he was smart enough not to run too far. He only went a short stretch into the forest, and then stood behind a tree to casually let you tear past him."

"What? How? Past him? If det's true, then I've embarrassed myself like never before!"

"It certainly is so. That's why I called out for you to stop. Once inside the dark woods, we would have been able to lie down on the ground and listen. We would undoubtedly have been able to hear his steps, and determine their direction by putting our ears to the ground. Had he stood still we would have snuck up on him. And I know that you do extraordinarily well at spying."

"I can believe det!" Droll replied, flattered by the praise. "If I think about it, methinks ye're completely correct. I was stupid, somewhat very stupid. But we can perhaps correct it a little. Don't ye think so? What do ye say to det?"

"It certainly is possible to correct the mistake, but it won't be easy for us. We must wait until tomorrow morning to find his tracks. We can then follow his trail and will most likely catch him."

He also informed the rafters of his opinion, whereby Missouri-Blenter said:

"Sir, I'll ride with you. We've captured enough horses for me to get one. The red-haired colonel is the one I've been seeking for

many long years. I'll now get on his trail and my comrades won't
take offence at me leaving them. It won't be a loss for me at all
because we've only begun work here a short while back."

"I'd like that," Old Firehand replied. "I've already on the way
here decided to put a proposal to you all, which I hope you'll
accept."

"Which one?"

"About that later. We've got more pressing matters to attend.
We must get to the cabin."

"Why not stay here until the morning, sir?"

"Because your property is in danger. The colonel is capable of
anything. He knows that we're down here and can easily come by
the idea to visit your cabin a second time."

"Zounds! That would be dire! We've got our tools and spare
weapons in there, as well as powder and cartridges. Quickly, we
must leave!"

"Indeed! You might as well go ahead, Blenter, and take another
couple of men with you. We'll follow with the horses and the
prisoners. We'll light the way with burning logs from the fire
here."

The astute hunter had judged the red-haired colonel correctly.
As soon as Brinkley was inside the forest, he stood behind a tree.
He heard Droll run past him and saw Firehand return to the fire.
Since Droll was headed away from the cabin, Brinkley would
certainly move quietly towards it. So as not to hit his face on the
trunks of the trees, he held out his uninjured hand and headed up
the incline.

Along the way he realized what a boon the cabin was. He had
already been there once and couldn't possibly miss it. It would
undoubtedly contain most of the rafters' property; he was able to
take revenge on them. Hence he hastened his steps as much as
the darkness allowed.

When he arrived at the top of the incline he first stopped and
listened. It was possible, after all, that one or several rafters had
stayed back at the hut. Since everything was quiet, he approached
the cabin, listened again, and then groped along the wall towards
the door. He was in the process of inspecting the mechanism with
which it was shut, when someone suddenly grabbed him by the
throat and pulled him to the ground. Several men knelt on top of
him.

"At least we've got one of them, and he'll pay!" one of them said.

Brinkley recognized the voice; it was that of one of his outlaws. He made a supreme effort to free his throat enough to squeeze the words out:

"Woodward, are you crazy? Let go of me!"

The gang's second-in-command was called Woodward. He recognized the leader's voice and let go, pushed the others away and replied:

"The colonel! It truly is the colonel! Where did you come from? We thought you were captured."

"I was, too," Brinkley wheezed and rose to his feet. "But I've escaped. Couldn't you be a little more careful? You've nearly killed me with your fists!"

"We mistook you for a rafter."

"Ah! And what are you doing here?"

"We three found each other down there by chance, but don't know where the others are. We saw that the rafters stayed at the fire and came by the idea to come here and play a prank on them."

"That's very good! Exactly the same idea has led me here, too. I'd like to burn this shack for them."

"That's what we've got planned, too, but not without having had a look at the hut's contents first. We might find much that could be of use to us."

"That requires light. These scoundrels have taken everything off me, even my fire lighter; we could be searching forever in here and not find one."

"You forget that we still have ours because we've not been robbed."

"That's true. Do you still have your weapons?"

"Yes, everything."

"And you've satisfied yourself that there's no ambush prepared here?"

"There's no one; the door is easily unlocked. We were in the process of getting in when you arrived."

"Then let's hurry before the fellows get the idea of coming back up here!"

"May we learn what took place down there after we had left?"

"Not now, later, when we've got the time for it."

Woodward pushed back the bolt and the men entered. After he pulled the door shut behind him, he made a light and shone it around the room. Shelves had been mounted on the wall above the beds, and on them were deer tallow candles of the sort that every Westerner fashioned for himself. The four outlaws lit one each, and then hurriedly searched for useful items.

There were several guns, full powder horns, axes, hatchets, saws, knives, powder, cartons with cartridges, meat and other provisions. Each took what he needed and what he liked; and then they put the burning candles into the reed mats of the bedding. They were alight in no time, and the arsonists rushed outside. The men left the door open to create even more draft than the windows, and then stood still outside to listen. There was no other sound except the crackling of the fire and the whooshing of the air in the treetops above.

"They're not coming yet," Woodward said. "What now?"

"Away, of course," the colonel replied.

"But where? We don't know the region."

"They'll find our trail tomorrow and follow it. We therefore mustn't create tracks."

"That's impossible, except in water."

"In that case, we'll take to the water."

"How, or in what?"

"In a boat, of course. Don't you know that rafters must build one or several boats because they need them for their business? I'd bet the canoes are lying on the bank below, somewhere near the raft anchorage."

"We didn't know that."

"Let's find it. There, look, the slipway leads down there. Let's see if we can get to the bottom."

At that point the flames broke through the roof and illuminated the entire campsite. At the edge of the forest, in the direction of the river, the outlaws noticed a gap in the vegetation. They rushed towards it and realized that their leader had guessed correctly. There was a straight, steep, narrow slide next to which a rope was fastened to hold onto. The four outlaws descended along it.

When they reached the river bank they heard distant hollering; those were the voices of Missouri-Blenter and his two companions who had gone ahead to the cabin.

"They're coming," the colonel said. "Let's hurry and find a boat!"

It didn't take them long, because there were three canoes tied up where the men were standing. They had been built Indian fashion from tree bark and sealed with resin, each large enough to take four people.

"Tie the other two to the back of this one," the red-haired outlaw ordered. "We must take them with us and later destroy them, so that they cannot pursue us."

The others obeyed him. Then the four men climbed into the first canoe, grabbed the paddles that were lying in it and pushed off the bank. The colonel sat aft and steered it. One of his men began paddling as if he wanted to head upriver.

"Wrong!" Brinkley said. "We're going downriver."

"But we want to get further into Kansas, to the great outlaw meeting!" the man replied.

"Indeed. But Old Firehand will find that out, because he'll no doubt squeeze it out of his prisoners. He'll be looking for us upriver tomorrow; we must therefore head downriver to lead him astray."

"That's a mighty detour!"

"Not at all. We'll paddle down to the next prairie, which we'll reach in the morning. There we'll scuttle the canoes and steal horses from the nearest Indians. After that we'll quickly head north and make up the detour within a single day, while the rafters will be hampered by the tedious and futile search for our trail."

The outlaws steered the canoes along the shadows of the river bank, so that they wouldn't be in the sheen of the fire glow from above. Then, when they had left its reaches, the colonel steered the canoes towards the middle of the river at the same time as the rest of the rafters arrived at the burning cabin with the horses and prisoners.

The rafters broke out in noisy laments when they saw their property going up in flames. There were a hundred curses and emphatic wishes that were meant for the arsonists. However, Old Firehand assuaged them by saying:

"I suspected that the colonel was going to hatch a plan like this. Unfortunately we've returned too late. But don't take it too much to heart. If you accept the offer I'm going to put to you, you'll soon receive more than full recompense for the loss."

"How?" Missouri-Blenter asked.

"I'll tell you more in a little while. For the moment we have to ensure above all that there aren't any more of these scoundrels nearby."

The entire surroundings were searched thoroughly, but nothing suspicious was found. Then everyone gathered around Old

Firehand in the light of the fire. The prisoners had been placed to the side, so that they couldn't hear what was being spoken.

"First, gentlemen, you will give me your solemn promise that you will not reveal to anyone what I'm about to tell you, even if you reject my proposal!" the hunter began. "I know that you're are all men of honour, and that I can rely on your word."

   He received the required promise, and then continued:

"Does anyone know the large body of water between the cliffs up there in the mountains, the one they call Silver-Lake?"

"I do," one person replied, namely Aunty Droll. "Everyone knows the name, but no one has been up there except me, as I might be permitted to glean from the silence of these gentlemen."

"Alright! I know that rich, very rich mines are up there. They date back to the people from pre-Columbian cultures, who didn't exploit those riches. There are also ore deposits and veins that have never been quarried. I know several of those tunnels and deposits and plan on heading up there with a capable geological engineer to inspect the matter and ascertain whether or not it is possible to start a large-scale operation, and whether the necessary hydraulic energy can be drawn from the lake. That undertaking is not without risks, of course, hence I have need of a group of capable Westerners who'll be working for us. Let your tasks rest here for the time being and ride up to the lake with me, gentlemen! I will pay you very well!"

"That's a word, indeed that's a beautiful word!" the old Missouri man exclaimed amid utter excitement. "There's no doubt that Old Firehand pays well and fair, and it is just as certain that those who participate will experience a hundred, nay a thousand true adventures. I would immediately and at once join you, but I cannot, I must not, because I have to catch the colonel."

"Me, too; me, too," Droll chimed in. "I would dearly love to go along, not because of the payment, but because of the adventures, and because I deem it a great honour to ride with Sir Firehand. But it cannot be, because I can also not afford to get off the red-haired colonel's trail."

A faint, superior smile crossed Old Firehand's face when he replied:

"Both of you have a wish that will most assuredly be fulfilled if you stay with me. We all know why Mr Blenter strives for revenge. But Droll hasn't told us yet why he is after Brinkley, together with his brave boy Fred. I have no intentions of prying into his secrets; he'll open up when he's good and ready. However, there is something I mustn't keep from you. When we left the fire below to climb up here, we needed to lead the fettered outlaws. I took the youngest of them by the hand. He plucked up the courage to address me, and tell me that he actually doesn't belong among them, and that he's sorry for having been part of them, and that he only joined them out of consideration for his brother, who's lying down there among the dead. He actually had intentions of becoming a capable, decent Westerner, and he told me that ever since he's heard my name he's wished for the permission to join me, even as the lowliest of my people, he said. He promised to enlighten me about the intentions of the colonel, and I don't wish to reject him, partly for humanitarian reasons, and partly because it makes good sense. May I bring the man here?"

The others all agreed and Old Firehand rose to fetch the outlaw. The man wasn't much older than twenty years, and had an intelligent expression and a strong physique. Old Firehand took the fetters off the young man and directed him to sit down at his side. The hunter had previously separated him from the other outlaws. The gang members couldn't see the fellow from where they were lying. Hence, they were later unable to say what had happened to him, let alone that he had betrayed them and the colonel.

"Alright," Old Firehand turned to him. "You can see that I'm not disinclined to fulfil your wish. Your brother led you astray. If you promise me with a handshake to live as a decent human being henceforth, I'll free you this very moment, and you shall turn into a capable Westerner in my company. What's your name?"

"Nolley, sir," the young man replied while he shook hands with the hunter amid tears welling up in his eyes. "I won't bother you with my life story, you'll hear that later some time; and you're going to be satisfied with me. I would be grateful to you for as long as I shall live if you were to permit me two additional wishes."

"Which ones?"

"Forgive me not only on the surface, but also in reality, for having found me in such bad company; and give me permission to bury my brother, who was shot. He mustn't rot in the water and be torn apart by the fishes."

"Those wishes tell me that I wasn't mistaken in you; consider them fulfilled. From now on you belong to us and must not let your erstwhile comrades see you, because they're not to know that you're one of us now. You've spoken of the intentions of the colonel. Do you know them?"

"Yes. He held back for a long time, but then told us everything yesterday. First, he wants to head over to the great outlaw meeting, which is to be held in a short while."

"Heigh-day!" Droll exclaimed. "In that case I wasn't misinformed when I heard that these vagrants want to gather in their hundreds somewhere behind Harper[7] to carry out a few pranks en masse. Do you know the place?"

"Yes," Nolley replied. "It lies indeed behind Harper from here, and is called Osage-Nook."

"I've not heard of that nook until now. Peculiar! I wanted to visit that meeting to perhaps find the one I am after; yet I had no idea that I was travelling on the steamer with him. I could have apprehended him on board! Alright, the colonel wants to go to Osage-Nook; well then, we'll ride after him, won't we, Mr Blenter?"

"Yes," the old man nodded. "Of course we'll have to separate from Old Firehand."

"That's not the case at all," the hunter replied. "My next destination lies nearby, namely Butler's farm, which belongs to the brother of the engineer who'll be waiting for me there. We shall at least be together until we get to the farm. Does the colonel have any further plans?"

"Indeed," the converted outlaw replied. "After the meeting he wants to travel to Eagle Tail and attack the railway camp to take the coffers, which are said to be full."

"It's just as well that we're learning of it. If we fail to catch him at the meeting, we'll surely get him at Eagle Tail."

"And should he escape you there, then you can apprehend him later at Silver-Lake," Nolley continued.

----

[7] The county of Harper, Kansas, was not legally settled until 1877; http://www. kancoll.org/books/cutler/harper/harper-co-p1.html, after having fraudulently been 'organized' in 1873.
The township of Harper was founded in 1877 http://skyways.lib.ks.us/kansas/counties/HP/index.html.
The settlement of Harper in McPherson county (closer to Smoky Hill River) was a farming and stock raising place and not of enough significance to be placed on a map. http://www. kancoll.org/books/ cutler/mcpherson/mcpherson-co-p7.html#HARPER_TOWNSHIP.
Stieler's Hand Atlas shows the township of Harper, in Harper County, close to the Oklahoma border, which lies 'within a (fictional) few days' riding distance' of Black-Bear River (where the foregoing events took place in what was then known as the Indian Territory, on Stieler's Atlas), and which was situated en route to Butler's farm.

His remarks caused general surprise; they even made enough of an impression on Old Firehand, for him to quickly ask:

"At Silver-Lake? What does the colonel know about that place and what does he want there?"

"He wants to lift a treasure."

"A treasure? Is there supposed to be one?"

"Yes, the people of ancient cultures are supposed to have buried or submerged immense riches up there a long time ago. He's got a precise map of the spot one has to search."

"Did you see the map?"

"No. He doesn't show it to any one."

"But we've searched him and taken everything from him, yet we've not found anything like that on him!"

"He must have hidden it well enough. I even believe that he hasn't got it on him at all. I deduced from one of his remarks that he might have it buried somewhere."

The attention of the rafters was directed at the young man, hence no one took any notice of Droll and Fred; both had become very excited. Droll stared at the erstwhile outlaw as if he not only wanted to hear the words, but also swallow them with his wide-open eyes. When Nolley had finished talking, Fred exclaimed:

"The colonel, it's him, it's him! That map belonged to my father!"

Everyone looked at the boy, and assailed him with questions. But Droll fended them off energetically and said:

"Not now, mesh'shurs! You'll hear the facts later. The main thing for the moment is that I can say I'll definitely be at Old Firehand's service, together with Fred."

"Me, too!" Missouri-Blenter declared with an elated tone of voice. "We've become involved in a whole bunch of secrets that make me curious how we're going to unravel them. You'll all come along, won't you, comrades?"

"Yes, yes, of course, yes!" came the rafters' unanimous agreement.

"Alright!" Old Firehand said. "We'll be on our way early tomorrow morning. We don't have to bother about the colonel's trail since we know the place he's to be found. We'll hunt him down through the forests and across the prairies, over hill and down dale, and if need be even up to Silver-Lake. Exciting times are awaiting us. Let us be good comrades, gentlemen!"

Lord Castlepool

Gunstick-Uncle   Humply-Bill

4

On Butler's Farm

The Rolling Prairie lay in the shimmering glaze of the midday sun. Hill upon hill, covered in dense grass, the blades of which gently moved in the breeze, it resembled an emerald sea with its waves frozen solid at an instant. Each of the rigid waves resembled the next in length, shape and height, and if a rider moved from one of the dales between them into the next, he could have become confused and mistaken the next with the previous. There was nothing, absolutely nothing else all around except wavy hills, as far as the horizon went. Someone not taking guidance from the compass or the position of the sun was going to lose his way, just as the novice in a small boat would be lost on the high seas.

There seemed to be no living being in the green desert; only up above, high in the air, two black turkey buzzards drew their circles, seemingly without moving their wings. Were they really the only creatures in that area? No, because at that point a strong snort became audible and a rider appeared from behind one of those wave hills, and he was wearing a very peculiar outfit at that.

The man was of average figure, not too tall, not too short, neither too fat nor too skinny, but he seemed to be strong. He wore long trousers, a waistcoat and a short jacket all fashioned from waterproof rubber fabric. On his head sat a pith helmet with fabric nape shield, like the English officers wear in the East Indies and other hot countries. He wore moccasins on his feet.

His posture was that of an experienced rider; his face—indeed, that face was actually quite peculiar. The expression on it might have been described as 'awkward', and not only because of the nose, which had two completely different sides. On its left side it was white and had a lightly curved aquiline shape; on the right half of the face it was distended, as if it were swollen, and of a colour that was somewhere between red, green and blue. The thin hair of a throat beard bristled forwards from the neck past his chin, and framed the face. The two gigantic wings of a Gladstone collar, the bluish-white sheen of which revealed that the rider preferred to wear rubberized clothing on the prairie, supported the beard.

Two guns were mounted to the left and right side of the saddle. The bottom of the scabbards reached to the shoe-like stirrups. Fastened across the back of the saddle was a metal tube, or capsule, the purpose of which was impossible to guess. The man wore a box-type leather knapsack of medium size on his back with several tin containers and oddly shaped wires attached to it. His belt was broad, also made of leather, and resembled a money pouch. Several satchels hung from it; the grips or handles of a knife and several revolvers poked out from it at the front, and at the back it held two bags that undoubtedly contained ammunition.

His horse looked like an ordinary nag, and it seemed equal to the exertions of the West; there was nothing special to be noticed about it except that it wore a saddle blanket that would have cost a pretty penny.

The rider seemed to assume that his horse had more prairie sense than he; at least one didn't notice that he gave it any directions; he let it run as it pleased. It walked through a few wave valleys, climbed up onto one of the hills, ambled down the other side, fell into a trot of its own volition, slowed down again; in short, the man with the pith helmet and the awkward face didn't seem to have a particular destination, but much time and leisure at his disposal.

Suddenly the horse stopped; it pricked up its ears, and the rider was slightly startled because ahead of him, though not visible anywhere, someone with a sharp, commanding voice called out:

"Stop, not one step further, or I'll shoot! Who are you, mister?"

The rider looked up, ahead, behind, to the left and right; there was no one to be seen. He didn't as much as bat an eyelid, took the lid off the long tin tube that was hanging across the back of his saddle, pulled a telescope out and extended its segments, so that it reached more than one metre of length. Then he squeezed the left eye shut, held the lens to his right and aimed the instrument at the sky, which he scrutinized in earnest and with enthusiasm, until he heard the same voice again, but with a laugh:

"Push your star pipe back into its case! I'm not sitting on the moon, which is not visible anyway, but on Mother Earth. And now tell me where you've come from!"

The rider collapsed the telescope and placed it back into the tube, carefully and slowly replaced the lid, as if he weren't in any hurry at all, and then pointed behind him with his hand and said:

"From there!"

"I can see that, ol' boy! And where are you going?"

"There!" the rider said while he pointed ahead.

"You really are a delightful chap!" the still invisible inquisitor said. "But since you are on this blessed prairie now, I'm assuming that you know the conventions that apply on it. There's so much questionable rabble about that an honest man is forced to look sharply at every movement. You may ride back to where you came from, in God's name, if you like. However, if you want to continue on, which seems to be the case, then you'll have to answer a few questions, and truthfully at that. Alright, out with it! Where are you from?"

"From Castlepool Castle," the man replied with a voice that sounded like that of a school boy who's afraid of the teacher's stern face.

"I don't know it. Where would that place be found?"

"On the map of Scotland," the rider explained, whereby his face attained an even more awkward expression.

"God bless your senses, sir! Scotland is none of my business! And where are you riding?"

"To Calcutta."

"Don't know it, either. Where is that nice place situated?"

"In the East Indies."

"Lackaday! Do you mean to ride from Scotland, across the United States to the East Indies during this sunny afternoon?"

"Not entirely today."

"Ah! You wouldn't be able to easily accomplish that anyway. Are you perhaps an Englishman?"

"Yes."

"And what's your profession?"

"Lord."

"Tarnation! An English lord with a round hatbox on his head! I'll have to have a closer look at you. Come, Uncle, the man won't bite us. I've a good mind to believe what he says. He's either crazy or a genuine English lord with a five metre quirk and ten hectolitres of liver problems."

At that point the figures of two men, who had been lying in the grass on the nearest hill-wave, came into view: a tall one, and a very short one. Both were clothed identically, and entirely in leather, like genuine, true Westerners: even their broad-brimmed hats were made from leather. The tall chap stood on the hill as rigid as a pole; the short one was hunch-backed and had a beak-like nose that was almost as sharp as a knife's blade. Their guns, too, were of the same size and construction; they were old, very long rifles. The short hunchback held his with the butt resting on the ground, yet its barrel still extended almost ten centimetres above his hat. He seemed to speak for both of them, because the tall chap hadn't spoken a word thus far, and continued:

"Stay where you are for the moment, mister, or else we'll shoot! We're not quite finished with each other."

"Shall we bet?" the Englishman asked the two men on the hill.

"What?"

"Ten dollars or fifty or a hundred dollars, whatever you like."

"On what?"

"That I'd shoot you before you shoot me."

"Then you'd lose!"

"Do you think so? Alright, let's bet one hundred dollars!"

He reached for one of the cartridge pockets at the back, pulled it to the front, opened it and pulled out several banknotes. The two men on the hill looked at each other in astonishment.

"Mister, I believe you're serious!" the short chap exclaimed.

"What else?" the Englishman was surprised. "Betting is my passion, that is, I like to place a bet at every opportunity."

"And carry a bag full of banknotes through the prairie!"

"Would I be able to place a bet if I didn't have money on me? Alright then, one hundred dollars you said? Or do you want to place more?"

"We have no money."

"No matter; I'll lend it to you in the meantime, until you can pay me."

He said it in all seriousness, so that the tall chap took a deep breath of surprise and the hunchback called out truly flabbergasted:

"Lend it to us—until we can pay? In that case you're sure to win?"

"Very!"

"But, mister, in order to win the bet, you would have to shoot us before we shoot you; but, as corpses, we would be unable to repay you!"

"That's all the same to me! I would have won anyway and have so much that I don't need your money."

"Uncle, I've never seen or heard of such a squire before," the short fellow said to the tall one and shook his head. "We must get down and take a close look at him."

He swiftly walked down from their wave-hill, and the tall chap followed him with a stiff and bolt upright bearing as if he had a beanpole inside his body. When they arrived in the wave-valley, the hunchback said:

"Put your money back; nothing's going to come of the bet. And take some advice from me: don't let anyone see this banknote pouch; you could come to regret it or even pay with your life for it. I really don't know what I should think or make of you. You don't seem to be quite right in the head. Let's sound you out for a bit. Come with us, only a few more steps!"

He stretched his hand out to grab the Englishman's horse by its reins; at that moment the metal of revolvers glinted in both hands of the rider and he gave the short, stern shout:

"Hands off, or I'll shoot!"

The short chap recoiled with a start and wanted to lift his gun.

"Leave it where it is! Don't move, or I'll pull the trigger!"

The bearing and the face of the Englishman had undergone a sudden change. They weren't the previously stupid features, and from his eyes glinted an intelligence, an energy that rendered the others speechless.

"Do you really think I'm crazy?" he continued. "And do you really take me for a person who'll be intimidated if you behave as if the prairie were entirely your property? You're mistaken. You've asked the questions thus far, and I've answered them. But right now I am the one who wants to know with whom he's dealing. What are your names, and what are you?"

He had directed the questions at the short fellow, who looked into the sharply searching eyes of the stranger. They made an entirely peculiar impression on him, and he therefore replied half vexed, half embarrassed:

"You're new around here; that's why you don't know. But we're known as honest hunters and trappers from the Mississippi across to Frisco. We're presently on our way into the mountains to find a company of beaver men, to join them."

"Alright! And your names?"

"Our real names won't be of any use to you. I'm called Humply-Bill because I am hunch-backed, unfortunately, but have not the slightest inclination of dying from sorrow over it, and my comrade here is only known as Gunstick-Uncle because he walks around as stiff as if he had swallowed a ramrod. Well, now you know us and will hopefully tell us the truth about you, too, without making stupid jokes."

The Englishman scrutinized them with a penetrating gaze, as if he wished to see right into their hearts; and then his features took on a friendlier expression. He took a piece of paper from the banknote pocket, unfolded it and held it out for the two men to read, and then replied:

"I wasn't jesting. Since I deem you to be decent and honest people, you shall see this passport."

The two hunters and trappers read it, and then looked at each other. Then Gunstick-Uncle opened his mouth and his eyes as wide as he could, and Humply-Bill said in a very polite tone of voice:

"You really are a lord! Lord Castlepool! But, milord, what do you want in the prairie? Life for you..."

"Pshaw!" the lord cut him short. "And what do I want? To get to know the prairies and the Rocky Mountains, and then to go to Frisco. I've been everywhere in the world, except the United States. But we've introduced each other now and needn't be reserved any longer. Come to your horses! I do think you have horses, although I've not seen them yet."

"Of course we've got them; they're behind the hill, where we've stopped to rest."

"Then follow me there!"

Judging by his tone, he was the one giving them instructions at that point, instead of them ordering him about. He dismounted and walked ahead along the wave-valley and around the wave-hill behind which two horses were grazing. They were of the kind that could ordinarily be termed 'hacks', 'billy goats', or even 'nags'. All the while, his own horse had followed him like a dog. The two nags approached it; but it angrily neighed and kicked out against them, to chase them away.

"A nasty beast!" Humply-Bill remarked. "Seems to be unsociable."

"Oh, no," the lord replied. "It knows precisely that I'm not yet closely related to you and wishes to remain distant to your mounts as well."

"Would it really be so smart? It's not obvious. It seems to have been a plough horse."

"Oho! He's a purebred Kurdish *husahn*, or stallion, with your kind permission."

"Ah! Where is that country?"

"Between Persia and Turkey. I bought him there myself and took him home."

He mentioned it as casually as if to transport a horse from Kurdistan to England and from there to the United States were as simple as taking a canary from the Harz Mountains to the Thuringian Forest. The two hunters threw each other clandestine glances. Lord Castlepool, however, sat down in the grass completely uninhibited, on the spot where the other two had been sitting earlier. There was a leg of venison they had roasted the day before. He pulled out his knife, cut a decent piece off and began to eat as if the meat belonged to him, and not the others.

"That's the way!" the hunch-backed fellow said. "Don't make a fuss in the prairie."

"I won't, either," the lord replied. "If you've shot game yesterday, then I'll shoot some today or tomorrow, for you as well, of course."

"Oh? Do you think, milord, that we'll still be together tomorrow?"

"Tomorrow and much longer. Shall we bet? I'll put up ten dollars, or even more if you wish."

He reached for his money pouch.

"Leave your banknotes in the back of your belt," Humply-Bill replied. "We won't bet with you."

"Then sit down with me! I'll explain it to you."

They made themselves comfortable opposite him. He once again scrutinized them with a keen gaze, and then said:

"I have travelled up the Arkansas and disembarked in Mulvane[1]. There, I intended to hire one or two guides; but I couldn't find a

---

[1] Mulvane was founded in 1879, and named for Joab R. Mulvane, who came to Kansas in 1876; the town is on Stieler's Atlas.

single one I liked. They were utter trash, the fellows. I therefore rode on because I told myself that I would likely find genuine prairie men only in the prairie. Now I've come across you, and I like you. Will you come along?"

"Where to?"

"Across to Frisco."

"You're saying this as calmly as if it were only a day's ride!"

"It is a ride. Whether it is going to be of a day's or a year's duration is all the same to me."

"Hm, yes. But do you have any idea what we could encounter along the way?"

"I haven't thought about it, but hope to experience it."

"Don't wish for too much. Besides, we won't be able to come along. We aren't as rich as you seem to be; we live off hunting and can't afford a detour to Frisco that'll last for several months."

"I'll pay you!"

"Ah? Well, in that case we could talk about the matter."

"Can you shoot?"

Humply-Bill gave the lord an almost pitiful look when he replied:

"Asking a prairie hunter whether he can shoot! That's almost worse than asking a bear whether he can eat. Both are as obvious as my hump."

"I would still like to see a demonstration. Can you get the vultures down from up there?"

Humply-Bill measured the height of the two birds with his eyes, and then replied:

"Why not? Of course you wouldn't be able to replicate the shot with your Sunday rifles."

He pointed to the Englishman's horse. The rifles were still hanging on the saddle; they were polished, so that they looked like new, which is a horrible thought for any Westerner.

"Then shoot!" the lord ordered while he ignored Humply-Bill's jibe.

The hunter rose, lifted his rifle and put it to his cheek, aimed swiftly, and then pulled the trigger. The men saw that one of the vultures received a jolt; it fluttered its wings and attempted to stay in the air, but in vain; it was forced down, slowly at first, and then increasingly faster; in the end it folded its wings to its body and fell vertically to the ground as a heavy clump.

"Well, milord, what do you say to that?" the short marksman asked.

"Not bad," came the cold answer.

"What? Not bad? Is that all? Consider the height, and that the bullet hit the bird straight into the core of its life, its heart, because it was dead in mid-air already! Any expert would have called that a masterful shot."

"Alright, next!" the lord nodded in the direction of the tall hunter, not paying heed to the short fellow's reproach. Gunstick-Uncle stiffly rose from the ground, supported himself on his long rifle with his left hand, raised his right like someone about to declaim, looked up to the second vulture in the sky, and with a dramatic tone of voice spoke:

"The buzzard glides sky fields of blue; Crypt and crevasse lie in its view; For carrion's stench it yearns anew; But dead I'll shoot it, through and through!"

During the improvised rhymes he posed as stiffly and squarely as a jointed puppet. He hadn't spoken a single word thus far, and the magnificent poem was bound to impress all the more. That's what he thought. Hence he slowly lowered his arm, turned towards the lord and looked at him with proud expectation. The Englishman had long since attained his awkward face again; at that moment there were twitches evident on it as if laughing was doing battle with crying.

"Did you pay attention to what he said, milord?" Humply-Bill asked. "Indeed, Gunstick-Uncle is an elegant chap. He was an actor once, and still is a poet. He says precious little, but when he does open his mouth, he only speaks honeyed words, that's to say, in rhymes."

"Fine!" the Englishman nodded. "Whether he speaks in rhymes or cucumber salad is his problem, not mine; but can he shoot?"

The tall poet skewed his mouth all the way to his right ear and flung his hand out in a wide sweep, which was supposed to be a gesture of disdain. Then he lifted his rifle to aim, but put it down again. He had missed the opportune moment because during his poetic outpouring, the vulture female, shocked at the death of her male, had decided to clear off. The bird had already flown quite a distance.

"It's impossible to hit," Humply-Bill said. "Don't you think so, Uncle?"

The tall man lifted both hands heavenward, in the direction of the spot where the vulture was still visible, and then replied in a tone of voice as if he wanted to resurrect the dead:

"By its wings does it sail; Over far hill and dale; With delight all aflame; Has evaded my aim; And who would still catch; May fly with despatch!"

"Nonsense!" the lord exclaimed. "Do you really think the bird can no longer be shot?"

"Yes, sir," Humply-Bill replied. "Not even Old Firehand, Winnetou or Old Shatterhand would be capable of bringing it down now, and those are the three best shots in the far West."

"So!"

While Lord Castlepool muttered, rather than clearly spoke the utterance, a bright twitch flashed over his face. He rushed to his horse, took one of the rifles from the saddle, undid the safety catch, put the firearm to his cheek, aimed, pulled the trigger—all of it within one short moment, lowered the rifle again, sat down, reached for the leg of venison to cut himself another piece, and then said:

"Well? Was it still within shooting distance or not?"

An expression of greatest astonishment lay on the faces of the two hunters; indeed, it was admiration. The bird was hit, and well at that, because it fell with increasing speed in an ever-tightening spiral down to Earth.

"Wonderful!" Humply-Bill exclaimed full of excitement. "Milord, if that wasn't a coincidence..."

He cut himself short. He had turned around towards the Englishman and saw him sitting on the ground, chewing food, with his back towards the direction of the masterful shot. That was almost unbelievable!

"But, milord," he continued. "Turn around! You have not only hit the vulture, but actually also killed it!"

"I know that," the Englishman replied without turning around while he put another piece of meat in his mouth.

"But you haven't even looked at it!"

"That's not necessary; I know it anyway. My bullet never fails."

"In which case you're a fellow who can safely take on the three famous men I mentioned before, as far as shooting is concerned! Don't you think so, Uncle?"

The illustrious ramrod uncle posed again and, gesticulating with both hands, replied:

"The vulture is struck; The shot more than luck; My fame's out of time..."

"And I'll cease to rhyme!" the Englishman cut him short. "Why such rhymes and hullabaloo? I wanted to know what sort of marksmen you are. Now sit down again and let's continue to negotiate. Right then, you'll come with me and I'll pay your way. Agreed?"

Humply-Bill and Gunstick-Uncle looked at each other, nodded and emphatically replied in the affirmative.

"Alright! And how much do you charge?"

"Well, milord, you're embarrassing me with this question. We've never been employed by a gentleman, and we cannot possibly be talking about a so-called payment for scouts like us."

"Alright! You've got your pride, and I like that. It will thus be a question of an honorarium to which I will add an extra gratuity if I'm satisfied with you. I've come here to have experiences, to see famous hunters, and therefore make you the following offer: I'll pay you fifty dollars for each adventure we'll have."

"Sir," Humply laughed. "We'll turn into wealthy people because there's no shortage of adventures here; we'll experience them, indeed, but whether or not we'll also survive them is a different matter altogether. We'll do what we can; but the best advice for a stranger would be to avoid adventures, rather than seek them out."

"But I want to have them! Understood? I also want to meet famous hunters. You've earlier mentioned three names I've already heard a number of times. Are those three men in the West at present?"

"Now you're asking a question I can't answer. Those famous people are everywhere and nowhere. It's only by coincidence that one gets to meet them, and even if one encounters them, one needs to ask whether such kings among Westerners stoop to notice one."

"They shall and will notice me! I'm Lord Castlepool and I know what I want! I will pay you one hundred dollars for each of the three hunters we meet."

"Tarnation! Do you have that much money on you, milord?"

"I carry enough for my needs along the way. You'll get the money from my banker in Frisco. Are you satisfied with that?"

"Yes, very much. We'll shake on that. We couldn't possibly do any better than agreeing to your suggestions."

Both shook hands with him. Then he pulled the second pouch from the back to the front, opened it and pulled out a book.

"This is my notebook where I will enter everything," he explained. "I will open an account for each of you and put his head and name above it."

"His head?" Humply-Bill was astonished.

"Yes, his head. Remain seated like that and don't move for a while!"

He opened the book and took the pencil between his fingers. They saw how he looked at them, and then into the book, repeatedly, wherein he moved the pencil. After a few minutes he showed them what he had drawn; they recognized their well-sketched heads, as well as their names underneath them.

"On these pages will be entered the debt I'll accumulate as time progresses," he explained to them. "If I meet with misfortune, then you'll take this book to Frisco and show it to the banker, whose name I'll tell you later; he will pay you the relevant sum immediately and uncontested."

"That's a very splendid arrangement, milord," Humply replied. "Although we shall not wish...behold, Uncle, have a look at our horses! They're wiggling their ears and flaring their nostrils. There must be something untoward nearby. The Rolling Prairie is dangerous. If one climbs onto the hills, one will be spotted, and if one stays down below, one is unable to notice the approach of an enemy and can easily be surprised. I might just climb up."

"I'll climb up with you," Castlepool said.

"Stay down here, sir! You could spoil the matter for me."

"Pshaw! I won't spoil anything."

The two men climbed from the wave-valley up to the tip of the wave-hill. When they had almost reached it, they lay down and carefully crawled up the rest of the way. The grass covered their bodies, and they lifted their heads only far enough to look around.

"Hm, you're handling things rather well for a newcomer, sir," Humply praised him. "I truly could not do it much better myself. However, can you see the man over yonder two hills away straight ahead of us?"

"Yes! An Indian, is it not?"

"Yes, he is an Indian. Had I only...ah, sir, please hurry back down and fetch your telescope, so that I can make out the face of the man."

The lord obeyed the request.

The Indian was lying on the hill in the grass and attentively looked east, where nothing was evident. Several times he lifted his upper body, to enlarge his field of vision, but quickly dropped down again. If he was expecting someone, then it could only be a hostile being.

Lord Castlepool brought the telescope, pulled it long and handed it to Humply. Just when the hunter aimed the lens onto the Indian, he looked back for a moment, so that his face was completely recognizable. Humply immediately laid the scope aside, jumped to his feet in order for his entire figure to be visible from the Indian's spot, cupped his hands around his mouth and shouted:

"Menaka Shecha, Menaka Shecha! My brother, come across to your white friend!"

The Indian spun around, recognized the figure of Humply-Bill and immediately slithered down from the tip of the hill, so that he disappeared in the wave-valley.

"Now, milord, you'll soon have to pay your first fifty dollars," Humply said to the Englishman while he crouched down again.

"Will there be an adventure?"

"Most likely, because the chief was definitely on the lookout for enemies."

"He's a chief, is he?"

"Yes, a capable fellow, a chief of the Osage."

"And do you know him?"

"We not only know him, but have also smoked the pipe of peace and brotherhood with him and are obligated to support him in any situation, as he is obligated to assist us, too."

"Alright, in that case I hope that he's expecting not one, but as many foes as possible!"

"Don't tempt fate! Such wishes are dangerous since they're only too easily fulfilled. Come back down! Uncle will be pleased but also astonished to see the chief in this region."

"What did you call the Indian?"

"Menaka Shecha; in the language of the Osage that means Good Sun, or Great Sun. He is a very courageous and experienced warrior and at the same time not an actual enemy of the Whites, although the Osage are a tribe of the still uncivilized Sioux."

When they returned to the bottom they found Gunstick-Uncle in his rigid theatrical stance. He had overheard everything and struck the pose to greet his red friend with as much dignity as possible.

After a short while the horses gave a snort, and immediately afterwards the men saw the Indian approach. He was in his prime and wore the traditional Indian leather garb, which was torn in some places and in others stained with fresh blood. He didn't have any weapons. There was a sun tattooed on each of his cheeks; the skin on his wrists showed deep score marks. It was obvious that he had been tied up, but broken his fetters. He was undoubtedly on the run and being followed.

Despite the danger the Indian was in, and which was likely very near, he approached very slowly, extended his hand to both hunters without paying attention to the Englishman initially, and then calmly, and in very good English, said:

"I recognized the voice and the figure of my brother and friend immediately and am glad to be able to greet you both."

"We're equally glad; you can believe us," Humply replied.

The tall uncle stretched both hands out over the head of the Indian, as if he wanted to bless him, and exclaimed:

"Greetings in this Earthly vale; A thousand times, without curtail; Great chief and noble treasure; Sit by your friends with pleasure; And with haste do please partake; Of venison, and your hunger slake!"

With the last words he pointed into the grass and at the lord's leftovers, namely the bone with a few tough meat fibres that hadn't wanted to yield to his knife.

"Quiet, Uncle!" Humply ordered. "Now is truly not the time for poems. Can't you see what state the chief is in?"

"Though tightly bound, he did yet flee; And also very luckily; 'Twas here he came when he was free!" the just reprimanded uncle declaimed his retort.

The hunch-backed hunter turned away from him, pointed to the lord, and then said to the Osage:

"This paleface is a master marksman and our new friend. I sincerely recommend him to you and your tribe."

At that point the Indian shook hands with the Englishman as well, and replied:

"I am the friend of every decent and honest White; the thieves, murderers and scoundrels who desecrate corpses, however, shall be eaten by the tomahawk!"

"Have you encountered people as bad as that?" Humply enquired.

"Yes. My brothers may keep their weapons ready because those who are chasing after me could be here at any moment, although I haven't spotted them yet. They'll be on horseback, and I had to walk; but the feet of Great Sun are fast and tireless like the legs of the stag that cannot be caught by a horse. I've walked in many bends and circles and have often moved backwards, heel fist, to delay and confuse them. They intend to kill me."

"They shall leave that be! Are there many?"

"I don't know because I had already left by the time they would have discovered my escape."

"Who are they? What kinds of Whites would dare to capture Great Sun to kill him?"

"There are many, many people, several hundred, bad people, which the palefaces call outlaws."

"Outlaws? How do they get here and what do they want in this remote region? Where are they?"

"They are camped in the corner of the forest that you call Osage-Nook; we named it Murder Corner because our most famous chief and his bravest warriors have treacherously been murdered there. Every year after the moon has filled thirteen times, a number of people from our tribe are delegated to visit that place to perform the dance of death beside the graves of the fallen heroes. And so I left our grazing grounds this year with twelve of our warriors to travel to Osage-Nook. We arrived the day before yesterday, searched the area and satisfied ourselves that there were no enemies about. We therefore felt safe and made camp beside the graves. We went hunting yesterday, to have meat to eat, and performed the rites today. I had been circumspect enough to place two guards, and yet the white men had been successful in sneaking close to us unnoticed. They had seen the tracks that both we and our horses had created during the hunt, and attacked us so suddenly during the dance that we only had a few moments to resist. The outlaws were several hundred men strong; we killed a few of them; they shot eight of us and overpowered the remaining four warriors and me, and then tied us up. Then, they held court over us and we learnt that we were going to be tortured at the fire tonight, and then burned to death. They camped near the tombs and separated me from my warriors, so that I couldn't speak to them. I was tied to a tree and received one white guard; but the strap that held me was too weak; I tore it apart. Although it cut deep into my flesh I freed myself, and when the guard left for a moment, I used the opportunity to sneak away."

"And your four companions?" Bill asked.

"They're still there, of course. Or do you think I should have searched for them?"

"No; you would only have been captured again."

"My brother speaks true. I wouldn't have been able to rescue them, and would instead have died with them. I decided to hurry to Butler's farm and fetch help from there. The owner is my friend."

Humply-Bill shook his head and said:

"That's nearly impossible! It takes almost six hours to ride from Osage-Nook to Butler's farm; even longer with a bad horse. How would you have been able to return by the evening during which your companions are supposed to die?"

"Oh, the feet of Great Sun are just as fast as those of a horse," the chief confidently replied. "As a consequence of my escape the execution will be postponed and the outlaws will first endeavour to recapture me. Help would therefore arrive in time."

"That calculation may be correct, and then again it may not. It is good that you've met us, because now it is not necessary to run to Butler's farm; we will go with you to free your companions."

"Will my white brother really do this?" the Indian asked with a glad tone of voice.

"Naturally! What else? The Osage are our friends, while the outlaws are the adversaries of any honest man."

"But there are so very many, and together we've only got eight arms and hands!"

"Pshaw! You know me! Do you think I've got intentions of charging openly right into the middle of them? Four cunning heads can certainly risk sneaking up on a horde of outlaws to pluck a few prisoners out of their camp. What do you say to that old Uncle?"

The stiff-necked poet spread his arms out wide, closed his eyes gleefully and exclaimed:

"With pleasure I at once do ride; To where the foul white scoundrels hide; And with no fear or dread shall see; That all red brothers be set free!"

"Splendid! And what about you, milord?"

The Englishman had pulled out his notebook to write down the name of the chief; he slipped it back into the bag and replied:

"Of course I'll ride along; it's an adventure after all!"

"But a very dangerous one, sir!"

"All the better! In that case I'll pay ten dollars more, namely sixty. But if we are to ride, then we'll have to find a horse for Great Sun!"

"Hm, yes!" Humply-Bill replied while he gave the Englishman a surprised look. "But where would you take one from, eh?"

"From his pursuers, of course, who'll probably be near enough behind him."

"Quite right, quite right! You're not a bad sort, sir, and I think that we'll work fairly well together. Now it would also be desirable for our red friend to have a weapon."

"I'll lend him one of my two rifles. Here it is already; I'll explain to him how it works. And now we mustn't waste any time. My suggestion is to take up positions, so that those chasing the Indian will be surrounded on all sides."

The expression of astonishment on the short hunter's face grew gradually more intense. He scrutinized the Englishman with a sceptical gaze and replied:

"You're talking like an experienced hunter, sir! How do you think we ought to go about doing that?"

"Very simple. One of us stays here on the hill where you and I climbed up just before. He'll welcome the fellows the same way you two have greeted me. The other three walk out and around the area at an arc, so that their tracks are not evident, and climb up on the three neighbouring elevations. When the chaps get here, they'll be between the four occupied hills and we've got them fast because we're covered up top and can clean them up at our leisure, while they'll only see the smoke of our gun fire."

"You truly talk like a book, milord! Tell me honestly, are you really in the prairie for the first time?"

"Indeed I am. However, I've earlier travelled in places where one must apply no less caution than here. We've already spoken about it."

"Alright! I can see that we won't have too much trouble with you, and that's just to my liking. I must admit that I intended to make the exact same suggestion. Do you agree old Uncle?"

The rigid man executed a theatrical arm movement and replied:

"Yes, indeed, surrounded they'll be; Shot dead in their own company!"

"Splendid, in that case I'll stay here to address them as soon as they arrive. Milord heads off to the right; you'll turn left, and the chief will take up his post on the protruding hill. That way we'll get them between us, and whether or not we'll kill them will depend entirely on how they conduct themselves."

"Not kill!" the lord remarked.

"Quite right, sir! I'm also against that; but these scoundrels don't actually deserve any leniency, and if we spare them, what are we going to do with them? Can we drag them along with us? Impossible! And if we let them go, then they'll betray us. I'll talk to them so loudly that you'll hear every word; you will thus know what to do. If I shoot one of them, then it'll be a sure signal for you to shoot the others. None must escape. Remember that they have killed eight Osage without prior hostile treatment from them! And now let's go, mesh'shurs; I think we can no longer hesitate."

He climbed up the nearest wave-hill and lay down in the grass on the same spot where he was lying when he and the lord had observed the Osage chief. The other three disappeared along either side of the wave-valleys. The horses were left where they were. The English lord had taken his telescope along.

Nearly a quarter of an hour passed in which not a trace of an approaching person was evident. The guard, from whom the chief had slipped away, must have been very negligent and was late in discovering the escape. Then came the call from the hill on which the Englishman was posted:

"Attention, they're coming!"

"Quiet!" warned Humply-Bill a little less loud.

"Pshaw! They can't hear it, they're still almost a mile away."

"Where?"

"Straight east. I've seen two fellows through the scope; they were standing on a hill and looked in our direction, probably trying to spot the chief. They've left the horses down below, no doubt."

"Then pay twice as much attention and spare the horses, we need them!"

Some more time went by; then they heard the hoof beat of the approaching animals. Two riders came into view in the wave-valley right in front of the hunch-backed hunter: they were very well armed and mounted, and kept a sharp eye on the trail of the chief as they followed it. Immediately behind them appeared two more and then another one; therefore there were five adversaries. When they had reached the middle of the vale, and were between the four hidden posts, Bill called to them:

"Stop, mesh'shurs! Not one step further or you'll hear my gun speak!"

The men stopped the horses in surprise and looked up the incline but couldn't see anyone since the hunter was still lying in the tall grass. Yet they obeyed his order, and the one in the lead replied:

"All devils! What kind of hidden highwayman is this then? Show yourself and say what right you've got to stop us!"

"The right of any hunter when strangers cross his path."

"We're hunters, too. If you're an honest fellow, then let's see you!"

The five outlaws held their guns ready in their hands; although they did not look at all peaceable, the short hunter still replied:

"I'm an honest man and can always show myself. There you have me!"

He jumped up, so that the men were able to see his entire figure; but he kept them under keen observation, so that not the slightest movement would escape him.

"Zounds!" one of them exclaimed. "That's Humply-Bill, if I'm not mistaken!

"That's indeed what I'm called."

"That means Gunstick-Uncle is also nearby because these two never separate!"

"Do you know us?"

"I do indeed; I've got unfinished business with you from earlier!"

"But I don't know you!"

"Possibly, because you've only seen me from afar. Boys, this fellow is in our way; I also believe that he's made common cause with the Indian. Let's get him down from up there!"

He aimed at Humply and pulled the trigger. Bill fell into the grass as quick as lightning, as if the bullet had hit him.

"Heigh-day, that was well aimed!" the man called out. "Now there's only Gun..."

He didn't get to finish the sentence. Bill had dropped on purpose, so as not to be hit. At that point the flashes of two shots from his double-barrelled gun came in quick succession, and not one second later the men at the other posts also fired their rifles. The five outlaws fell from their horses and the four victors came down from their hills into the vale to prevent the horses from running away. The outlaws were inspected.

"We didn't do too badly," Bill remarked. "Not a single miss. Death was immediate."

The Osage chief looked at the two men at whose forehead he had aimed. He saw the small bullet holes right above the bridge of their noses and turned to Castlepool:

"The rifle of my brother is of a very small calibre, but it is an excellent, reliable weapon."

"Indeed it is," the Englishman nodded. "I've had both rifles made especially for the prairie."

"I wish to buy this one from my brother. I'll give him one hundred beaver skins for it."

"It's not for sale."

"Then I'll give him one hundred and fifty!"

"Not even then!"

"What about two hundred?"

"No, not even if the beaver skins were ten times as large as elephant skins."

"In that case I'll offer him the highest price there is; I'll exchange the best riding horse of the Osage for this gun!"

It was evident on his face that he believed to have made an offer that had never been made before, but the Englishman shook his head and replied:

"Lord Castlepool never swaps or sells. What would I do with the horse, since mine is at least as excellent as the one you've mentioned?"

"No horse on the entire prairie can match mine. But since I cannot force my brother to sell his gun to me, I'll return it to him. The dead outlaws have more weapons than I have need of."

He returned Castlepool's gun but made a face that clearly expressed greatest regret. Any useful items were taken off the corpses. When their pockets were searched, Bill said:

"The fellow knew me; yet I can't remember ever having seen him. That may be so! From his remarks I can deduce that I had nothing positive to expect from him or the others. Hence we won't mourn the demise of these people. Who knows how many dirty deeds we may have prevented by giving them our bullets? Now the chief has a mount, and there are four horses left, which are just enough for the Osage we want to free."

"Will we now ride to the outlaws immediately?" the Englishman asked.

"Of course! I know the region and know that we cannot arrive at Osage-Nook before nightfall since we cannot take the straight route, but have to ride in an arc to reach the forest behind them."

"What about these corpses?"

"We'll simply leave them lying here. Or do you feel like building a tomb or a mausoleum for these scoundrels? May they be buried in the stomachs of the vultures and coyotes; they're not deserving of more!"

That may have been a hard and not very Christian speech, but the Wild West has its own kind of sensitivities; in a region where death and destruction threatens all around, a person is forced to consider only himself first and avoid anything that could endanger his own safety. Had the four men decided to stay with the corpses to bury them and speak a prayer over their graves, it would have been a waste of time, and they might easily have paid for it with their lives; but the imprisoned Osage would certainly have lost theirs. The men tied the riderless horses together, mounted up and rode away, due north initially, and then to turn east later.

The chief led them because he knew the camp of the outlaws. They rode across the Rolling Prairie all afternoon and saw neither a trail nor another person. When the sun dipped towards the horizon, the men saw a dark strip of forest in the distance, and the Osage explained:

"That's the side of the forest that faces away from the camp. The other side has a recess that forms the angle we call Murder Corner, and that's where the graves of our dead are."

"What's the distance from this side of the forest straight through it to the corner in question?" Lord Castlepool asked.

"Once we've entered the forest we must walk a quarter of an hour to reach the camp of the outlaws," the Indian explained.

That's when Bill stopped his horse, dismounted and sat down in the grass without saying a word. Uncle and the Indian followed suit matter-of-factly. Consequently, the Englishman dismounted as well, but enquired:

"I thought we mustn't lose any time. How can we free the Osage if we sit down here and twiddle our thumbs?"

"That's the wrong question, sir," the hunch-backed hunter replied. "You had better ask: 'How can we free the Osage if we've been shot dead?'"

"Shot dead? Why?"

"Do you think the outlaws are calmly sitting in their camp?"

"Hardly!"

"Definitely not! They must eat and will therefore hunt. They'll swarm around in the forest, which is only a quarter of an hour broad where we have to enter it. We can most certainly expect people there who'd see us approach. We must therefore wait until it has become dark; by then all the men will have congregated at the camp and we can reach the forest unnoticed. Can you understand that?"

"Alright," Castlepool nodded while he also sat down. "I didn't think I could still be so ignorant!"

"Indeed, you would have ridden straight into the arms of those good people, and I would have had to take your diary to Frisco without receiving a single dollar."

"Not receive anything? Why not?"

"Because we've not quite had our adventure yet."

"Have so! It is already over and even noted. Encounter with chief and shooting of five white outlaws was a complete adventure for fifty dollars. It's already in the book. Freeing of the Osage will be a new adventure."

"Also for fifty dollars?"

"Yes!" Castlepool nodded.

"Alright, then keep making notes, sir," Bill laughed. "If you divide each adventure into so and so many sub-adventures, then you'll have to pay us so much money in Frisco that you won't know where to take it from!"

The lord quietly chuckled to himself and replied:

"It'll stretch that far. I'll be able to pay you without having to sell Castlepool Castle. Shall we bet? I'll put up ten dollars. Who else?"

"I won't, sir. If I were to bet with you at this rate, then I'd gamble away everything I'm earning in your employ, and that won't happen to the nephew of my uncle."

The sun disappeared and the shadow of dusk skulked through the wave-valleys, climbed higher and higher, flooded even the wave-hills and at last cloaked the entire Earth in its dark raiment. Even the sky was starless.

The four men went on their way; but they didn't ride up to the forest entirely. Caution dictated they leave the horses out in the open. Every Westerner carries wooden pegs, so that he can tie his horse to the ground by its reins. That's how they secured their animals, and then approached the forest in single file.

The Indian went ahead. He walked so quietly that the others were unable to hear his footsteps. Castlepool behind him made every effort to walk just as quietly. There was no other sound all around apart from the soft breeze that moved the tree canopies.

At that point the Osage grabbed the right hand of the Englishman and whispered to him:

"My white brother, take the hand of the next man, so that the palefaces form a chain, which I will lead to ensure none walks into a tree."

While he touched his way forwards with the one outstretched hand, he pulled the Whites along behind him. Castlepool almost got bored, because in such situations the minutes seem to stretch to hours. At last the Indian stopped and whispered:

"My brothers may listen. I've heard the voices of the outlaws."

The men listened and soon found that the Indian was correct. They heard voices, even though they came from a fair distance, so that the words weren't discernible. After a few more steps they saw the faint glow of a fire, which made it possible to distinguish the tree trunks.

"My brothers wait here until I return," the Osage said.

The Indian had no sooner given his directive, than he had vanished into the dark. He stayed away for longer than half an hour before he returned. The Whites had neither seen nor heard his approach; he suddenly appeared before them, as if he had risen out of the Earth.

"Well?" Bill asked. "What have you got to tell us?"

"That more outlaws have arrived, many more."

"Tarnation! Are these fellows intending to hold a meeting? Then woe to the farmers and anyone else who lives in this region. Did you hear what was spoken?"

"There are several fires and the entire site is illuminated. The outlaws had formed a circle in which a paleface with red hair was standing and making a long speech."

"What did he talk about? Did you understand him?"

"I understood him very well, because he almost shouted; but I focussed my attention on finding my red brothers, and so I've only memorized little of what he said."

"Alright, and that little, what's that?"

"He said that wealth was theft from the poor and that one had to take everything from the rich people. He claimed that the state wasn't allowed to tax its subjects and one must therefore take all the money in its coffers away again. He said that all outlaws are brothers and would become rich quickly if they follow his suggestions."

"Go on! What else?"

"I didn't pay any attention to anything else he said. He also spoke of the large, full coffers of a railway, which have to be emptied. But then I didn't listen to him any further because I saw the place where my red brothers are."

"Where is that?"

"Near a smaller fire where no one was sitting. They were standing against tree trunks to which they were tied, and they were guarded by one outlaw each sitting next to them."

"Does that mean it is not easy to sneak up on them?"

"We can sneak up. I would have been able to cut them free; but I thought it was better not to do it and came to fetch my white brothers to help me because together we would be much faster. However, I've sneaked up to one of my red brothers first and whispered to him that they'll be rescued."

"That's very good, because now they're prepared and won't reveal us with a gesture of joy or surprise when we get near them. These outlaws are no Westerners. It is an immense stupidity on their part not to guard the prisoners by placing them in the middle of the camp, in which case we would not be able to free them by clandestine means. Although we're only four people we would be forced to jump into the circle of the fellows to cut the Osage free during the moment of surprise. Take us to where they are!"

The chief in the lead, the four flitted from tree to tree, while making every effort to remain in the shadows of the trunks as much as possible. They quickly came near the camp and were able to count eight fires. The smallest of them was burning on the innermost area of the angled forest indentation, very close to the trees, and that's where the chief was headed. He stopped once for a few moments and whispered to the three Whites:

"Now several palefaces are sitting around that fire. There was no one before. The man with the red hair is among them. These people seem to be the leaders, the chiefs. Can you see my Osage on the trees a few paces away?"

"Yes," hunch-backed Bill said. "He finished his speech, and now the fellows are sitting away from the rest to hold counsel. It could be very important to find out what their intentions are. There wouldn't be so many outlaws gathered here for just a minor issue. Fortunately there are several bushes between the trees. I'll sneak up to hear what they're talking about."

"My brother had better not do this," the chief warned.

"Why? Do you think I'll let myself be caught?"

"No. I know my brother understands how to sneak up; but he could still be spotted."

"Spotted but not caught!"

"Yes, my brother has fast feet and would quickly escape, but then it would be impossible for us to free the Osage."

"No. We would kill their guards and cut the prisoners' ties in a few moments; then make off quickly through the forest and to the horses. I'd like to see the outlaw who'd prevent it! Alright, I'll sneak there. If they spot me, you'll run to the prisoners. Nothing will happen to us. Here's my gun, Uncle."

So as not to be encumbered by the weapon, he handed it to his companion, lay down on the ground and crawled towards the fire. His task was easier than he had believed. The outlaws were talking so loudly that he was able to lie still when he had only gone halfway, and yet he understood every word.

The chief had been correct in his opinion that the four men, who sat around the small fire, were the leaders. The one with the red hair was Colonel Brinkley, who had escaped the rafters with a few of his cronies and had arrived at the camp that evening. He was talking, and Humply-Bill heard him say:

"I can promise you great success because that's where the main cash box is. Do you agree?"

"Yes, yes, yes," the other three replied.

"And what about Butler's farm? Do you want to take it as well? Or shall I do that on my own and hire a score and ten of your men?"

"Of course we'll participate!" one of them declared. "I don't see why we should let the money fall into your pockets! The only question is whether or not it is at the farm already."

"Not yet. The rafters didn't immediately obtain horses, while I found a few good nags early the next morning. They cannot be on the farm already. But Butler is wealthy enough anyway. We'll attack the farm, rob it, and then calmly wait for the rafters and the scoundrels who command them to arrive."

"Do you know for sure that they'll go there?"

"I do. Old Firehand is forced to visit there because of an engineer, who's waiting for him."

"What engineer? What's the story with him?"

"Nothing. It's a matter that ought to leave you indifferent. Perhaps I'll tell you about it some other time. Perhaps I'll also hire you for a completely different coup, where there's a pile of money to be had."

"You're talking in riddles! To be quite honest, I'd rather not have anything to do with Old Firehand. I've often heard about him."

"Are you scared?" the red-haired outlaw sneered.

"Not scared, but I have a compelling aversion to that type of person."

"Nonsense! What would he be able to do against us? Consider that we've got four hundred fellows together, who'd tackle the devil himself!"

"Are all of them supposed to come to Butler's farm?"

"Of course! The way there coincides with our own route. We wouldn't want to return here, would we?"

"No, that's correct. And when will we break camp?"

"Tomorrow afternoon, so that we'll arrive at the farm by the evening. It is large and will provide a nice fire over which we can cook many roasts."

Humply-Bill had heard enough; he retreated and crawled back to his companions and requested that they make themselves busy with the freeing of the Osage. According to his opinion each of the men ought to have sneaked behind one of them; but the chief cut him short and said:

"I've only come to fetch my white brothers to swiftly assist me in case I wouldn't be successful in freeing my red brothers on my own. What follows now is a matter for the red men, not the Whites. I'll go alone, and my brothers may only come to my aid if my activities are being noticed."

He sneaked away on the ground like a snake.

"What's he got in mind?" the Englishman quietly asked.

"A masterpiece," Bill replied. "Lie down, if you don't mind, and keep a sharp eye on the spot where the prisoners are standing. If things go bad we'll rush up and help. We only need to cut their straps, and then run to our horses."

The lord obeyed Bill's directive. The outlaws were sitting around a fire that was perhaps ten paces away from the edge of the forest, where stood the trees to which the prisoners were tied upright by their hands and feet. Beside each prisoner sat or lay an armed guard. The Englishman strained his eyes, in order to see the chief, but in vain. He only saw that one guard, who had been sitting, lay down with a swift movement as if he had collapsed. The other three guards moved as well, one after the other and in a way, oddly enough, so that their heads came to lie in the shadows of the trees. There was no sound, not the slightest noise evident.

After a short while the lord suddenly saw the chief lying between him and Bill on the ground.

"Well? Finished?" Humply asked.

"Yes," the Indian replied.

"But your Osage are still fettered!" Castlepool whispered to the chief.

"No; they're only standing still until I've spoken to you. My knife struck the guards right in the heart, and then I took their scalps. Now I'll sneak back to go to the horses with my red brothers because ours are still there. Since everything went so well, we won't leave without taking our horses."

"Why take that risk?" Bill warned.

"My brother is mistaken. There's no more danger now. As soon as you see the Osage disappear from their trees, you can leave. Soon you'll hear the stomping of the horses and the screams of the outlaws who are guarding them. After that we'll come to the place where we've dismounted before; howgh!"

With the last word he meant to indicate that any objection was futile; then he suddenly vanished again. The English lord focussed on the prisoners; they were leaning bolt upright against their trees, and then they were gone in an instant, as if they had disappeared into the Earth.

"Wonderful!" he excitedly whispered to Humply-Bill. "Just like reading it in a novel!"

"Hm!" the short hunter replied. "You're yet to experience many more novels with us; reading, of course, is easier than taking part."

"Shall we leave?"

"Not yet. I'd like to see the faces the fellows are going to make when the hullabaloo breaks loose. Wait another few moments."

It didn't take long before a scream of fear resounded from the other side of the camp; a second one replied, followed by several piercing yells, which undoubtedly emanated from Indian vocal cords—and then came a snorting and stomping, a neighing and thundering under which the Earth seemed to shake.

The outlaws leapt up. Each one shouted, screamed and asked what had happened. Then the red-haired colonel hollered:

"The Osage are gone. All devils, who's got them..."

Stunned he stopped mid-sentence. While he had been speaking, he had been running across to the guards, and had then grabbed the nearest one to pull him up. He saw the glazed-over eyes and the hairless, bloody skull. He pulled the second, third and fourth into the light of the fire, and then cried out in horror:

"Dead! Scalped, all four of them! And the redskins are gone! Where to?"

"Indians! Indians!" came a voice from the side where the horses had been.

"Get your weapons, to the horses!" the colonel barked. "We're being attacked. They're stealing our horses!"

There was a scene of indescribable confusion as the outlaws were running every which way. But there was no enemy to be seen and only when they had restored some semblance of calm did it become obvious that only the captured Indian horses were missing. At last, but too late since the mishap had already occurred, the outlaws posted guards. They searched the surroundings of the camp, but for naught. They concluded that there had been other Osage in the forest, apart from the imprisoned ones, and that they had sneaked up and freed their comrades. In the process they had stabbed the guards from behind, scalped them, and then taken the Indian horses. The outlaws were at a loss to explain how the murder of the guards could have occurred so silently. They would have been astonished had they known that only one man had accomplished that Indian masterpiece.

When the leaders had gathered around the fire again, the colonel said:

"Although the incident is no great calamity for us, it nevertheless forces us to change our plans for tomorrow. We must head off very early."

"Why?" they asked him.

"Because the Osage heard everything we discussed. Fortunately they know nothing of our intentions concerning Eagle Tail, because we only spoke about it over at the other fire. But they know what we aim to do with Butler's farm."

"And you think they'll reveal it?"

"Of course!"

"Could these savage scoundrels be friends with Butler?"

"Friends or not; they will alert him to take revenge on us, and to give us a warm welcome."

"That, of course, is easily imaginable, and thus it is advisable indeed that we make as much haste as possible. I'd rather like to know where those five fellows are, who went after the chief!"

"Incomprehensible to me, too. Had he fled into the forest, then it would have been difficult or even impossible to find him; however, his trail led out into the open prairie, and he had no horse. They ought to have caught him!"

"No doubt about it. But they might have been late returning, and were surprised by the night and got lost. Or camped so as not to get lost, and will join us tomorrow morning. We'll definitely come across their tracks because they went in the direction we have to take."

However, the outlaw, who had voiced his opinion, was wrong in that respect. The sky, or rather, the clouds were going to ensure that the trail in question would be wiped away because light rain lasting several hours was about to fall, which would erase any and all hoof and footprints.

As soon as the noise near the horses had arisen, it was time for Bill, Uncle and the Englishman to get to safety. As fast as the darkness permitted, they rushed through the forest, back to their horses. The acute senses of the hunters alone ensured that they found their mounts again. The Englishman wouldn't have found his bearings as easily as that, since one wave-hill and wave-valley resembled the other all the more so during the night. They untied the horses, mounted up and took the riderless animals by their reins.

As soon as that was done, they heard the Indians approach. The chief had found his way to the exact same spot in the darkness as confidently as in broad daylight.

"The outlaws were blind and deaf," he said. "We were unable to kill more of them. We couldn't waste time with people since we wanted to have our horses back; but there will be many of them wandering into the Eternal Hunting grounds to serve the spirits of the Osage."

"Are you going to take revenge?" Bill asked.

"Why is my white brother saying that? Didn't eight Osage die today? Their deaths must be avenged! Did the outlaws not plan to torture and murder us, whom they captured, as well? We will ride to the wigwams of the Osage to fetch many warriors. Then we'll follow the trail of these palefaces to kill as many as Manitou will give into our hands."

"In which direction are the herds of the Osage grazing at present?"

"Due west."

"In that case you have to travel past Butler's farm?"

"Yes."

"And how long will you ride from the farm to reach your people?"

"We will encounter the first groups after half a day's ride; if one has a good horse and makes haste."

"That's very good. We will have to make haste to save Butler's farm."

"What's that my brother is saying? Butler is the friend and protector of the Osage. Is he in danger?"

"Yes. But let's not speak of it here and now. We must get away and out of reach of the outlaws above all. They want to attack the farm tomorrow morning, and we must go there to warn the owner."

"Uff! My red brothers may lead the riderless horses, so that my white brothers can follow me more easily!"

His warriors obeyed and took over the captured horses in addition to their own; and then the group charged away at a gallop between the low hills, not on the trail they had ridden earlier, which would have been a detour north, but on the trail the chief and his pursuers had travelled in the afternoon. It led in a straight line towards the region in which Butler's farm was situated.

At a gallop! And in such darkness at that! And yet it was so. Only someone with a good knowledge of the Rolling Prairie would have been able to find his way around without getting lost; but not getting lost during the night could almost count as a miracle. When the Englishman remarked about it to Bill, who rode next to him, the short hunter replied:

"Yes, sir, although I've noticed that you weren't born yesterday, you'll nevertheless see, hear and experience many more things you wouldn't have thought possible otherwise."

"Then you wouldn't become lost here, either?"

"Me? Hm! I'll have to tell you honestly that I wouldn't dream of charging into these wavy hills like that. I would ride nice and slow and precisely study the bend of every vale I have to follow. Yet I would still end up in a completely different place to the one I had wanted to reach."

"In that case it could happen to the chief as well?"

"No. An Indian like him virtually smells the direction. And he's got his own horse again, which is the main thing. This animal will certainly not divert by even a step from the trail its master walked today. You can rely on that. The sky is as black as a sack full of pitch, and of the ground below I can't see as much as I can place on a fingernail; nonetheless, we're galloping along as if we were on a level road in broad daylight and I'd bet that our horses will stop right outside Butler's front door before the six hours are up."

"What? What?" the Englishman rejoiced. "You want to bet? That's marvellous! So, that's what you claim? In that case I'll claim the opposite and wager five dollars, or even ten. Or would you like to go higher? Count me in!"

"Thank you, milord! The remark about the bet was only a phrase. I repeat that I never bet. Keep your money! You'll need it somewhere else. Just think what you already have to pay me and Uncle for today!"

"One hundred dollars. Fifty for the outlaws we shot, and fifty for the liberated Osage."

"And soon there will be more."

"Indeed, because the attack on the farm, which we'll repel, is another adventure that will cost fifty dollars."

"Whether or not we will be able to successfully repel the attack is still uncertain; if we are unable to do so, then it will also be an adventure that is going to cost you fifty dollars, should we survive it. But what about Old Shatterhand, Winnetou and Old Firehand? How much did you say you would pay if you laid eyes on one of those three men?"

"One hundred dollars, if you don't mind."

"Don't mind at all, because it is very possible that we'll meet Old Firehand either tomorrow or the day after."

"Truly? Truly?"

"Yes. Because he's also headed for Butler's farm."

The chief, who was riding in the lead, had heard the remark. Without slowing the speed of his horse he turned around and asked:

"What was that my white brother said? Old Firehand, the famous paleface, will be coming?"

"Yes. The red-haired colonel said it."

"The red-haired man who held the long speech? How does he know that? Has he seen the great hunter, or even spoken to him?"

While they were chasing along Bill recounted what he had heard.

"Uff!" the chief exclaimed. "In that case the farm is saved, because the mind of that paleface is worth more than the weapons of a thousand outlaws. I'm overjoyed to be able to greet him!"

"Do you know him?"

"All the chiefs in the West have met him and smoked the calumet with him. Why should I alone not know him? Can you feel that it is beginning to rain? That is good because the rain will give the trodden grass the strength to stand up soon. The outlaws will therefore no longer be able to see our tracks in the morning."

That's where the conversation ended. The speed of the ride, and the attention required, made talking difficult; besides, rain always causes one to be less talkative.

The ground didn't pose any difficulties; no rock, no ditch, or similar obstacles delayed the ride, and the wave-valleys were so broad that several horses were comfortably able to walk, trot, or gallop side by side. The ground consisted exclusively of soft grassland. Only the darkness required conquering.

Occasionally, the riders let their horses slow down to a walk, so as not to tire them unduly; afterwards the ride continued in trot or gallop again. When several hours had passed, Bill's earlier confidence seemed to wane after all, because he asked the chief:

"Is my brother convinced that we're still riding in the intended direction?"

"My white brother ought not worry," the Indian replied. "We made great haste and will soon reach the spot where I met you and Uncle earlier today."

Was it experience or inborn instinct for the Indian to make the claim in such a determined voice? Bill found it hard to believe that they had already covered such a great distance. However, together with the rain, a sharp wind had also come up at the riders' backs, which made running easier for the horses.

A short while after the last remark, the chief's horse suddenly slowed from gallop to a walk, and then even stopped without the rider giving the command, and snorted quietly.

"Uff!" the Indian whispered. "There must be people ahead. My brothers listen; don't move, and sniff the air!"

The troop stood quietly, and the men were able to hear the chief sample the smell of the air.

"A fire!" he whispered.

"I can't see a trace of it!" Bill said.

"But I can smell smoke, which seems to come from around the nearest hill. My brother; dismount and climb the hill with me, so that we can see what's behind it."

The two left their horses, and side by side sneaked towards the wave-hill. However, they hadn't gone ten paces when two hands clutched the Indian's neck with great force. He was pulled to the ground, and thrashed about with arms and legs, but was unable to make a sound. At the same time two other hands grabbed Humply-Bill by the throat and also pulled him to the ground.

"Have you got him?" the one who had seized the Osage asked the other at a whisper, and he did so in German.

"*Ja*[2], I'm holding him tight enough, so det he cannot talk at all," came the answer just as quietly.

"Then let's get away from here, behind the hill! We must know whom we're dealing with. Or is he too heavy for you?"

"Wouldn't occur to me! The fellow is lighter than a fly det hasn't eaten for three weeks. Oh my! He seems to have a hump on his back, what we'd call a crooked spine! It wouldn't by chance be..."

"What?"

"Be my good friend Humply-Bill!"

"We'll find that out at the fire. For the moment we're sure that no one will follow us. I'm inclined to guess the troop to be at least a dozen men strong. They won't move from the spot because they must wait for the return of these two."

All of it had happened so lightning fast and noiselessly that the companions of the two captured men had no idea of their plight

---

[2] Yes

despite the close vicinity in which it had taken place. Old Firehand—that's who it was—lifted his prisoner up, and Droll pulled his behind him along on the turf, around the hill. On the other side, tired horses were lying on the ground; a small fire was burning, the sheen of it illuminated more than twenty figures who had taken up positions with their weapons aimed, ready to greet a possible enemy with just as many bullets.

When the two men brought their prisoners to the fire, each of them gave a shout of surprise.

"Tarnation!" Old Firehand exclaimed. "That's Menaka Shecha, the chief of the Osage! We don't have to be afraid of him."

"*Sapperlot!*[3]" Droll chimed in. "It truly is Bill, Humply-Bill! Dear fellow, friend, beloved soul, couldn't ye tell me det when I grabbed ye by the throat! Now ye're lying here and can neither breathe nor talk! Stand up and come into my arms, dearest brother! Ah, so, he can't understand German. He won't die on me, will he? Jump up already, treasured heart! I really didn't mean to throttle ye, if it's halfway possible!"

The thoughtful man from Altenburg suffered more anguish at that moment than the one he had choked into unconsciousness, and who lay there with his eyes closed. Humply-Bill was greedily gasping for air, and then finally lifted his eyelids to cast a gradually more conscious gaze at Droll, who was bending over him. He hoarsely asked:

"Is it possible? Aunty Droll!"

"The Lord be thanked, I've not murdered you!" Droll rejoiced, in English at that point. "Of course it is I. Why didn't you tell me that it was you?"

"Was I able to speak? Someone I was unable to see grabbed me so swiftly that I...Heavens, Old Firehand!"

He saw the hunter standing near him, and that restored his mobility completely. The pressure of Firehand's stranglehold had been far more intense than Aunty Droll's. The chief still lay on the ground with his eyes closed, motionless.

"Is he dead?" Bill asked.

"No," the tall hunter replied as he reached out and shook hands with Humply-Bill. "He's only unconscious and will soon come to. Welcome, Bill! What a friendly surprise. How come you're in the Osage chief's company?"

"I've known him for years."

---

[3] Upon my soul!

"Ah! Who else is with you? Probably Indians from his tribe?"

"Yes, four men."

"Only four? Have you taken riderless horses along?"

"Indeed. Besides, Gunstick-Uncle, whom you know as well, and an English lord are with us."

"A lord? Noble encounter in that case. Go and lead them here. They've nothing to fear from us, and vice versa."

Bill hurried away; but he only went half the way, and then joyfully called out:

"Uncle, keep riding ahead! We're with friends. Old Firehand and Aunty Droll are here."

Gunstick obeyed Humply's call. The rafters rose from their firing positions in the grass to welcome the arrivals. They were astonished to see the chief unconscious, but then learnt what had happened. After the Osage had dismounted they stood aside and respectfully looked at the famous hunter from afar. Wide-eyed Lord Castlepool stared at the tall man and approached him with hesitant steps; the expression on his face was so awkward that one might have been forgiven for laughing about it. Old Firehand noticed it, as well as the thickly swollen nose on one side. He shook hands with him and said:

"Welcome, sir! You have been to Turkey, India, or perhaps even Africa, yes?"

"How do you know that, sir?" the Englishman asked.

"I'm guessing it, since you're still wearing the rest of a *Bouton d'Alep*[4] on your nose. Someone who's undertaken such journeys will find his way around here as well, although..."

He cut himself short and with a smile cast a glance at the Englishman's equipment, especially the frying apparatus that was strapped to his backpack. At that moment the chief came to. To open his eyes, draw a deep breath, jump up and pull out his knife was the work of one moment. But then he saw the hunter; he lowered his arm and exclaimed:

"Old Firehand! Was it you who grabbed me?"

"Yes. It was so dark that I couldn't recognize my red brother."

"That makes me glad. To have been overpowered by Old Firehand is no shame. Had it been someone else, the shame of it would have weighed me down until I had killed him. My white brother is headed for Butler's farm?"

"Yes. Who told you that?"

---

[4] Leishmaniasis

"Palefaces said it."

"I want to go to the farm later. My present destination is Osage-Nook."

"Whom are you looking for there?"

"A White by the name of Colonel Brinkley, and his cronies, all outlaws."

"In that case my brother can safely ride to Butler's farm with us because the red-haired man will go there tomorrow morning to attack it."

"How do you know?"

"He himself said it, and Bill heard it. The outlaws ambushed me and my Osage earlier today, killed eight of us and took me captive together with the four surviving warriors. I escaped, came upon Bill and Uncle and led them to the outlaws' camp where they and the white Englishman helped me to free my red brothers."

"Were you followed by five outlaws to here?"

"Yes."

"Bill and Uncle were camped here?"

"It is so."

"And the Englishman came upon them only a short while earlier?"

"You said it; but how do you know?"

"We rode upstream along the Black-Bear River and left it early this morning to get to Osage-Nook. We found the corpses of five outlaws here, and..."

"Sir," Humply-Bill interrupted him. "What makes you say that those men were outlaws? There was no one around who could have told you that!"

"This piece of paper revealed it to me," Firehand replied. "You searched the fellows but left the paper in the pocket of one of them."

He pulled out a piece of newspaper, held it up to the fire and read:

"An omission due to oversight, which is hard to believe, has been revealed by the inspector of the land offices of the United States. The officer brought to the attention of the government the astonishing fact that there is a strip of land within the United States, larger than many a nation, which enjoys the distinction of being entirely un-governed. That peculiar piece of land is an immense rectangle of forty miles width and one hundred and fifty miles length and contains nearly four million acres of land. It is situated between the Indian Territories and New Mexico, north of

Texas and south of Kansas and Colorado. As has been pointed out, this land has been overlooked during the official surveying and owes its mentioned advantage to a mistake in the fixing of adjoining territories' boundary lines. Consequently, it is not apportioned to any state or territory in any way, nor is it under the jurisdiction of a court. Law and order, as well as taxes, are unknown there. In the report of the investigator, the land in question is depicted as one of the most beautiful and fertile regions of the entire West, superbly suited for stock farming as well as agriculture. The few thousand 'free Americans' who inhabit it, however, are not peaceful farmers or herders, but form gangs of rag-tag rabble, scoundrels, horse thieves, desperadoes and fugitive criminals who have converged there from all directions of the compass. They are the horrors of the neighbouring territories in which the cattle ranchers in particular are suffering the most from the depredations of these people. The terrorized neighbours urgently request that an end be put to the free state of highwaymen, so that the lawless activity might cease with the instalment of government authority."5

The Indians who had listened to Firehand's words remained indifferent; the Whites, however, looked at each other in astonishment.

"Is that true? Is this possible?" Castlepool asked.

"I think it is true," Firehand replied. "But whether the article is true or not is immaterial in this case. The main thing is that only an outlaw would drag such a newspaper clipping around for so long and so far. This piece of paper is the reason I identified those five as outlaws. When we arrived here and saw the corpses, we knew at once that a fight had taken place. We inspected the bodies and tracks and concluded the following: Two Whites camped here, a tall one and someone who was shorter. Then came a third White who joined them and ate the rest of the meal. They conducted a shooting contest whereby two vultures were killed. The third White proved that he was a good marksman and

---

5 This was an actual newspaper article, discovered by Wilhelm Brauneder, which had been published on 11 February 1881 in the German-American paper, *Germania*, in Lawrence, Kansas. http://www.karl-may-gesell schaft.de/kmg/seklit/jbkmg/1997/361.htm#a4.
The first issue of *Germania* appeared on 1 September, 1877 and was printed by Gottlieb Oehrle.
http://history.lawrence.com/project/community/thesis/chap4.html

was accepted into the others' company. Then an Indian approached in great haste. He was fleeing from the direction of Osage-Nook and was pursued by five outlaws. It turned out that he was a friend of the Whites; they assisted him and shot the five pursuers. Then the three Whites and the Indian mounted up to ride to Osage-Nook along a detour; they wanted to attack the outlaws. I decided to help them. However, since night had fallen in the meantime, I was forced to wait until morning because I was unable to follow their tracks in the night."

"Why did my brother overpower us?" the chief asked.

"Because I had to assume you were outlaws."

"For what reason?"

"I knew that a great number of outlaws were at Osage-Nook. Five of them had ridden away, to follow an Indian. They were shot here, therefore didn't return. That was bound to worry the others, and it was entirely possible that they would send help after them. Hence I posted guards who reported that a troop of riders was approaching. Since the wind was blowing from the direction of Osage-Nook, we would detect your approach quite early. I instructed my people to ready their weapons, and sneaked towards you, together with Droll. Two of the riders dismounted to sneak up on us, and we grabbed them to see their faces in the light of the fire. You know the rest."

"My brother has once again proved why he's the most famous among the palefaces. What do you intend to do? Are the outlaws your personal enemies?"

"Yes. I'm going after the red-haired fellow to apprehend him. But I can only decide what to do once I've learnt what the situation is at Osage-Nook, and what's happened there. Won't you tell me, Bill?"

Humply-Bill fulfilled the request and gave a detailed report. He concluded by saying:

"You'll realize that we'll have to act fast, sir. You'll gladly mount up and immediately ride with us to the farm."

"No. I won't do that."

"Why? Do you want to engage the outlaws in a battle along the way?"

"Wouldn't think of it. But I'll stay here, although I know that the danger is much greater than you think."

"Greater? Why?"

"You are of the opinion that the fellows will break camp as late as the afternoon?"

"Yes."

"And I'm telling you that they'll commence their ride early in the morning already!"

"But the colonel said so!"

"He's changed his mind in the meantime, Bill."

"What makes you think that, sir?"

"Where were the Osage tied up?"

"Near the fire where Brinkley sat."

"Did they hear what was spoken?"

"Yes."

"Also that Butler's farm was going to be attacked?"

"That, too."

"Alright, and now they've escaped. Wouldn't the colonel necessarily think that they'd rush to Butler to notify him?"

"Devil, that's right! That goes without saying!"

"Indeed. In order to minimize the loss they could suffer through that, they'll break camp earlier. I'll bet they're already prepared to mount up at dawn."

"Bet?" Castlepool exclaimed. "Alright, you're my man, sir! You're betting that they're departing so early? Good, and I'll claim they'll leave Osage-Nook only in the evening. I'll put up ten dollars, twenty even or thirty. Or would you prefer fifty?"

He pulled one of the pouches to the front and opened it to take out money. A faint signal from Humply-Bill, unnoticed by the Englishman, sufficed for Old Firehand to realize that he was dealing with a passionate gambler. Hence he replied:

"You can safely close your satchel again, sir, I wouldn't think of taking the phrase 'I'll bet' seriously. Such important matters are not at all suited for betting purposes anyway."

"But I like betting, after all!" Castlepool insisted.

"I don't!"

"That's a pity; what a shame! I've heard many splendid things about you. Every true gentleman bets. The fact that you don't almost forces me to change my good opinion of you."

"You can do that, if it pleases you! The time will come all too soon when you'll restore your earlier views. But now we've got other and better things to do than place bets. The lives of many people, as well as their property, are at stake, and it is our duty to avert that disaster. One does not achieve that by betting."

"Quite right, sir. I only bet on the side. When it comes to deeds, you will certainly find me standing squarely on my spot, perhaps just as solidly and calmly as you stand on yours. Physical strength alone doesn't do it. Mark my words!"

He had worked himself into a state of exasperation and looked the Herculean figure of the hunter up and down with an almost offensive stare. Firehand didn't seem to know how to take the Englishman; his face threatened to darken, but then it quickly lit up again because he had guessed Castlepool's thinking. Hence he replied:

"Take it easy, sir! Let's not be rude before we've gotten to know each other. You're still new in this country."

The word 'new' didn't fail to have the intended effect, because Castlepool became even angrier:

"Who told you that? Do I perhaps look like new? At least I'm equipped according to the demands of the prairies; but you sit there as if you had just come from a club or even a ladies' gathering!"

So that's what it was! Old Firehand was still wearing the same elegant travel suit he had worn on the steamer. He had not been able to change clothes, since his trapper outfit was at Butler's farm. The suit had suffered along the ride to the rafters and beyond, but still seemed fresh in the sheen of the small fire that was being kept low by the rain. He smiled, nodded and said:

"I can't say you're wrong there, sir. Perhaps I might yet make myself at home in the old West; but we shall be friends in any case."

"If you're serious about that, then don't argue about betting again, because the stake reveals the genuine gentleman. By the way, I don't understand why you want to stay here and not immediately ride to the farm. That's what initially confused me about you."

"I've got a good reason for it."

"Will my white brother tell me that reason?" the Osage asked.

"Yes. It suffices if you ride to the farm and alert Butler. He's the right man to arrange the necessary preparations. I'll stay here with my rafters and keep the outlaws so well in check that they will only make slow progress and won't arrive at the farm until the people there are ready to receive them."

"My brother always has the best thoughts, and it would be the case this time as well; but Butler is not in his wigwam."

"He's not?" Firehand was surprised.

"No. When I rode to Osage-Nook, I came past the farm and visited to smoke the calumet with my white brother Butler. I didn't find him at home. His brother had come from far away with his family to visit him. They had ridden to Fort Dodge to buy clothes for the white daughter."

"Ah, his brother has already arrived! Do you know how long Butler intends to stay at Fort Dodge?"

"Several days."

"And when were you on the farm?"

"In the morning of the day before yesterday."

"In that case I must go there at all costs," Old Firehand exclaimed and leapt up. "How long will it take until you can bring help with your Osage?"

"If I ride now, we'll be on the farm by midnight tomorrow."

"That will be much, much too late. Are the Osage friends with the Cheyenne and Arapahoe?"

"Yes. The war hatchet is buried."

"Those two tribes live on the other side of the river about four hours away. Will my brother ride off right now and take a message to them from me?"

The chief didn't say a word; he walked to his horse and climbed into the saddle.

Old Firehand continued:

"Ride to them and convey to both chiefs that I am asking them to come to Butler's farm with one hundred warriors each!"

"Is that the whole message?"

"Yes."

The Osage clicked his tongue, tapped the horse's sides with his heels and a moment later disappeared into the darkness of the night. Castlepool looked baffled. Would such a warrior truly obey the man with the salon jacket so unconditionally and without question? But the latter was already sitting in the saddle as well.

"Gentlemen, we mustn't lose another minute," he said. "Our horses might be tired, but they must hold out until we're on the farm. Let's go!"

In no time at all, the entire group was ready. The men put out the fire, and then the troop moved out. Old Firehand rode in the lead with his closest friends and fellow hunters, followed by the rafters and the few Osage, who brought up the rear with the horses.

Initially they rode slowly, then at a trot; and when everyone's eyes had grown used to the dark, away from the fire, they moved at a gallop. Castlepool turned to Bill and asked:

"Say, won't Old Firehand lose his way?"

"Oh, even less than the Osage chief. They say Firehand can see like a cat at night."

"And he's wearing a formal suit. Queer fish!"

"Just wait until you see him in the buffalo leather coat! He'll cut a different figure then."

"Well, he's got enough of a figure now. But who on Earth is the woman who manhandled you?"

"Woman? Oh, that lady is a man."

"I can't believe that!"

"You can trust me on that!"

"But they called her 'Aunty'!"

"That's his nickname because he talks in a high-pitched falsetto voice and dresses himself in such peculiar garb. His name's Droll and he's a very capable hunter. He's even got a special reputation as a trapper. Beaver and otter virtually jostle for position in his traps. He seems to have a secret, a lure, like no other. But let's leave the chatting be. One has to focus one's available wit for this kind of riding."

He was right. Old Firehand was riding ahead like the devil personified, and the others chased after him at the same speed regardless. Castlepool was a passionate endurance rider and had often risked his neck; but he had never experienced a ride like the one on which he found himself that night. They were in such dense darkness that it was like being in a tunnel without a light; none of the wave-hills were recognizable, and neither was the ground the horses were running on. It was as if the animals were moving through an endless, lightless chasm; and yet, not one lost its footing or stumbled! One horse followed the other precisely and everything hinged solely on Old Firehand's skills. His horse had never been in that area and was an ordinary nag at that. The hunter had had no choice but to take it when the men had acquired their mounts, because no better horse was available. Castlepool's respect for the man began to rise again.

And on it went, for half an hour, then a whole hour and a second one, with only short interruptions during which the horses were afforded a breather. The rain was still falling, but so thinly and lightly that it was not at all annoying for the men. Then, they heard Old Firehand call out from the front:

"Pay attention, gentlemen! The ground will drop away, and then we'll move across a ford. But the water will reach no higher than to the horses' bellies."

The riders slowed down. They heard the rushing of a river, and despite the Egyptian darkness, saw the phosphorescent surface of the water. The feet of the riders dipped into the water; then the group reached the other bank. After another short ride of perhaps a minute, they stopped, and Castlepool heard the sharp ringing of a bell. It was still as dark before him as it had been during the ride.

"What's that? Who's ringing a bell, and where are we?" he asked Humply-Bill.

"At the gate of Butler's farm," Bill replied.

"Can you see anything of the farm?"

"No. But ride along a few more paces and you'll be touching the wall."

Dogs were barking. Their deep, coarse voices revealed their size. Then there was a voice asking:

"Who's ringing, who wants to enter?"

"Is Mr Butler back yet?" the hunter asked.

"No."

"Then go and fetch the key from the lady of the house and tell her that Old Firehand is here!"

"Old Firehand? Alright, sir, shall do immediately. Mrs Butler isn't asleep, and no one else has their eyes shut, either. The Osage stopped in on his way past and announced your coming."

"What kinds of people are there around here?" Castlepool thought. "The chief rode even faster than we did!"

After a short while orders emanated from within, by which the dogs were chased back; then a key rattled in a lock, wooden bolts squealed, hinges squeaked, and at last Castlepool saw several lanterns, the light of which seemed to make the blackness of the endless yard even more impenetrable. Farm hands rushed up and took the horses from the riders, who had dismounted, and then the guests were led into a tall, stygian-looking house. A maid asked Old Firehand to follow her upstairs to see Mrs Butler, the farmer's wife; she was in the company of the engineer's wife, her sister-in-law, who had not gone to Fort Dodge because she was too exhausted and felt poorly from the long journey.

Old Firehand's companions were led into a large, smoke-stained room that had been prepared for them on the ground floor. A heavy petroleum lamp hung from its ceiling. There were several tables with benches and chairs for the men to sit down. An array of food and drink had been arranged as a consequence of the Osage chief's announcement of the troop. The rafters and the Osage sat down at two long tables and immediately tucked in. A frontiersman dislikes airs and graces. By an almost natural process, the elite of the company had come to sit at a table removed from the others. Castlepool was first to sit down, then came Humply-Bill who signalled Gunstick-Uncle to sit beside him; Aunty Droll and Fred Engel sat down next to them, and then Black Tom, together with old Missouri-Blenter, joined them.

At that point, food and drink received undivided attention. Castlepool seemed to have reminded himself that running with wolves meant howling like them, because he had discarded all of his status decorum and conducted himself no better or worse than his table mates.

Later, Old Firehand accompanied the lady of the house into the room. She welcomed her guests most cordially, and then went on to explain to the Englishman that she had prepared a separate chamber for him. But he declined it, and any other preferential treatment above that of his comrades, since he was henceforth nothing more than a Westerner, so he explained. That conduct pleased the others so much that they loudly voiced their heartfelt commendations. Old Firehand informed his companions that they weren't required during the night and that they ought to rest in order to be fresh and ready in the morning; there were enough farmhands and herders present to assist him with the necessary preparations.

Castlepool was unable to avert his eyes from the hunter because the famous man had taken off his 'civilized' suit and donned his hunter's outfit. He wore fringed leggings that were richly embroidered on both sides and reached to his knees, with the cuffs tucked into tall boots, a vest of soft, white-tanned buckskin, a short buckskin hunting shirt and a strong coat of buffalo belly over the top. He had strapped a broad leather belt around his powerful loins and placed the short weapons in it, and he wore a beaver hat with a very broad brim. A beaver tail was hanging down from the back of it, which was less intended to give the tall man a daredevil look, than to protect his neck from the effects of a blow by a treacherous enemy. He wore a long necklace, made from the teeth of the grey bear, and on it hung the peace pipe with a bowl masterfully carved from the sacred clay. All seams of the coat were decorated with grizzly claws, and since a man such as Old Firehand certainly wouldn't wear other people's trophies, it was evident from those trimmings, as well as the pipe necklace, how many of those terrible animals had fallen victim to his accurate bullets and his mighty fists. After Firehand had left the room with Mrs Butler, the Englishman said to the others:

"Now I readily believe everything that's being said about him. The man is a veritable giant!"

"Pshaw!" Droll replied. "A Westerner doesn't fancy being judged by his figure; his spirit has far greater value. Old Shatterhand isn't as tall and broad, and Winnetou, the Apache, is built less tall again; but both are his equal in every respect."

"Even with regard to physical strength?"

"Yes. I've seen Old Shatterhand throw, and then pull up, a mustang three times with one arm. Who knows whether Old Firehand is capable of matching that? The muscles of a Westerner will gradually become like iron and the tendons like steel, even if he doesn't have the stature of a giant."

"In that case you'd also be made of iron and steel, Mr Droll?"

It sounded almost like there was a trace of mockery in his tone of voice, but the short hunter replied with a friendly smile:

"Would you like to find out, sir?"

"Yes, very much so."

"But it seems you're doubtful!"

"Indeed! An aunt with muscles and tendons of steel! Want a bet?"

"What and how?"

"Who's stronger, you or I."

"Why not?"

At last the Englishman had found someone who didn't reject him. He joyfully jumped off his seat and exclaimed:

"But, Aunty Droll, I've overpowered many a chap who had to bend down to even see you! Will you really risk it?"

"Of course!"

"For five dollars?

"Alright!"

"I'll lend them to you."

"Thanks! Droll never borrows."

"You have money?"

"It will certainly be enough for what you could win, sir."

"Even ten dollars?"

"Even that."

"Or twenty?"

"Why not?"

"Perhaps even fifty?" Castlepool blissfully exclaimed.

"Agreed! But not more, because I don't want to take all your money from you, sir."

"What? Take money from Castlepool! Are you mad, Aunty? Out with the money! Here are fifty dollars."

He pulled one of the pockets attached to the strong belt forwards, took out ten five dollar notes, and then placed them on the table.

Droll reached into the dangling sleeve corner of his sleeping gown and brought up a pouch. When he pulled it open it became evident that it was filled with hazelnut-sized nuggets. He placed five of them on the table, slipped the pouch back into the sleeve and said:

"You have paper, milord? Fie! Aunty Droll only deals in real gold. These nuggets are worth more than fifty dollars. And now we can get started, but how?"

"Give me a demonstration and I'll copy it; then we'll do it the other way around."

"No. I'm only an aunt; you, however, are a lord. Therefore you go first."

"Alright! Stand squarely and resist; I'll lift you onto the table!"

"Try it!"

The others cleared the table of dishes, of course; Droll spread his legs, and Castlepool grabbed him by the hips to lift him; but the feet of Aunty Droll didn't leave the floor at all. It was as if Droll were made of lead. The Englishman struggled for naught and in the end had to concede that he was incapable of making good on his intentions, yet he consoled himself with the loud remark:

"If I was unable to lift you, then you'll have even less success with me."

"Let's see," Droll laughed while he looked up to the ceiling, where a strong hook had been installed right above the table to hang a second lamp. The others, who saw Droll's gaze and knew the man possessed unusual physical strength, furtively nudged each other.

"Let's get on with it!" Castlepool urged.

"Only onto the table?" Droll asked.

"Do you intend to lift me higher?"

"As high as is possible here. Pay attention, sir!"

Despite the clumsiness of his clothing, Droll came to stand on the table in one single leap, and then grabbed Castlepool by his shoulders. The Englishman felt that he was being flung up in the air so fast that he didn't even realize how it was being accomplished; he flew past the table and hung on said hook by his belt one moment later. Droll, however, jumped off the table and laughed:

"Well, sir, are you up there?"

The Englishman thrashed about with arms and legs and cried:

"Good Heavens, where am I? Woe to me, on the ceiling! Take me down, take me down! If the hook lets go I'll break my neck!"

"Tell me first who's won the bet!"

"You have, of course."

"And what about the second part of the bet where I was to give you a demonstration first?"

"I'll give you dispensation from it. Just take me down! Quickly, quickly!"

Droll climbed up onto the table again, grabbed the Englishman with both hands by the hips, lifted him, so that the hook disengaged from the belt, and then swung him down onto the table first before he placed him back on the floor. After he had jumped down as well, he put his hand on Castlepool's shoulder and asked:

"Well, sir, how do you like Aunty?"

"Much, very much, too much!" the Englishman said while he was still looking at the spot where he had been hanging just before.

"Into the pocket with the old paper, in that case!"

He stashed the notes and nuggets in the pouch, and then continued with a grin:

"And please, milord, if you ever feel like making a bet again, then you can safely turn to me! I'll always participate."

He returned the plates, bottles and glasses to the table whereby he received nods of approval from everyone around. Castlepool sat down again and palpated his arms, legs and hips to ascertain whether or not anything had worked itself loose, and when he was satisfied that he was still intact, he shook hands with Aunty Droll and said with a merry smile:

"Splendid bet! Wasn't it? Aren't those Westerners magnificent fellows? One only has to treat them properly!"

"Methinks that, on the contrary, it was I who treated you, sir!"

"That's correct, too! You're truly strong. But that has its good reasons, because you're undoubtedly from merry old England, yes?"

"Oh, no, sir. I'm German," Aunty Droll modestly replied.

"German? In that case you must surely be from Pomerania, yes?"

"You've guessed wrong! Plants there grow taller and broader than I am. Altenburg is where I'm from."

"Hm! Small nest!"

"German dukedom, sir! That's where the best goat cheeses are made."

"Don't know them."

"That's a great shame!"

"Which won't reduce me to tears. You're a capable fellow, Aunty. I'm interested in you. Surely you've not always been a Westerner, have you? Or are there trappers in Altenburg?"

"Not in my time. Some might have made themselves at home there by now."

"What did your father do, and why have you come to the United States?"

"My father was no lord, he was much, much more."

"Pshaw! That's not possible!"

"Indeed it is! You're only a lord, most likely nothing else. My father, however, was many a thing."

"Alright, what was he?" Castlepool pushed because he expected to hear an interesting life story.

"He was a wedding-, christening-, and funeral crier, bell ringer, verger, waiter, and gravedigger, scythe grinder, orchard guard and at the same time sergeant of the civilian guards. Is that enough?"

"Alright, more than enough!"

"Correct, because if I'm to make it short, then I'd have to say he was a decent man."

"Is he dead?"

"A long time already. I have no more family."

"And you've crossed the Atlantic because of grief?"

"Not grief. My dialect has driven me across."

"Your dialect? How is that possible?"

"In order to understand that, you'd have to be German, or at least speak German. It is said that every person has an invisible angel and an invisible devil at their side; well, my devil was the Altenburg dialect. It's driven me from house to house in the old country, from one street into the other, from one place to the next and finally even across the sea. At last I've been able to shake that demon because they speak English here. I'm longing for my homeland, and would have the means to retire over there, but unfortunately I can't go because the demon is waiting to join me again as soon as I land in either Hamburg or Bremerhaven."

"I don't understand that."

"But I do," Black Tom interjected. "Droll speaks such a dreadful German, you see, that it's thoroughly embarrassing for him to even utter a word over there."

"Well, then he must learn to speak it better!"

"That's not possible! He's been put through all manner of remedial drills that resulted in one and the same thing: he became even more confused. Let's talk about something else; he's not fond of this topic."

At that moment Old Firehand returned to point out again that it would be advisable to get some rest because everyone had to be up again very early. The men obeyed his request with commendable readiness and went to a room where hides stretched over wooden frames were hanging. They served the farm hands as hammocks and beds at the same time. Padding and soft blankets provided the comfort. The defenders of the farm slept splendidly on those genuine western beds until they were woken fairly early in the morning.

The day ahead seemed to want to turn hot and sunny. In the friendly morning light the building looked completely different than the foreboding appearance it had made the night before. It was fitted out for many inhabitants, built of brick, very long and broad, and consisted of the ground floor and one upper storey with a flat roof. The windows were quite tall, yet so narrow that a person could not get through. Such precautionary measures were necessary in a region crisscrossed by gangs of thieving Indians. It quite often happened, in such an area, that an isolated homestead or a farm had to be defended against that kind of rabble for several days.

Just as practical was the large, roomy yard, which was surrounded by a tall adobe wall with embrasures, or crenelles, for the same defensive purposes. Between them were installed broad wall ledges to climb up behind the merlons, the raised portions, if shooting across the wall was required.

Not far from the house, the river rushed past the ford through which the riders had arrived the night before. The crossing could easily be covered by gunfire from the wall; and on the behest of Old Firehand, barricades had been installed during the night to make the ford inaccessible.

The second and very necessary precautionary measure he had directed was the moving of Butler's herds to the pastures of the nearest neighbour, also accomplished during the night. Then, a messenger was sent towards Fort Dodge to warn the two brothers, should they already be on their way home, to prevent the outlaws from capturing them.

Old Firehand led the comrades onto the roof of the house, from which they had sweeping views east and west onto the Rolling Prairie, as well as south and west across extensive corn and other crop fields.

"When will the expected Indians arrive?" Droll asked.

"According to the calculations the chief made yesterday, they could get here soon," Firehand replied.

"I'm not counting on it. The Indians must first be called together, perhaps even from far afield, and they never embark upon a war expedition without doing justice to their old rituals. We will have to be content with them getting here by midday. But by then the outlaws could also be nearby already. I don't credit the Cheyenne and Arapaho with much."

"Me neither," Bill agreed. "Both tribes are very small and their warriors haven't held a war hatchet in a long, long time. We cannot rely on them; there are no strong neighbours, either, and we must therefore be prepared for a long siege."

"That's nothing to worry about, because the cellars hold large stores," Old Firehand informed them.

"What about water, which is the main thing!" Droll remarked. "Once the outlaws are outside, we can't go to the river to fetch water!"

"That's not necessary, either. There's a well in one of the cellars, which supplies potable drinking water for the people, and the canal provides for the animals."

"Is there a canal?"

"Yes. Everything here has been constructed and fitted out in preparation for a war. You'll find a wooden trapdoor behind the house. If you open it, you'll see steps that lead down to the vaulted canal, which is connected to the river."

"Is it deep?"

"The vault is as tall as a man, the water reaches almost to one's chest."

"And its mouth to the river is open?"

"Oh, no. The enemy mustn't see it; hence the place in question has been planted densely with bushes and climbing plants."

Droll had no particular purpose for enquiring so specifically about the canal, but his knowledge about it proved useful for him later on.

Mrs Butler wasn't available yet; she was worried and had stayed awake all night with Old Firehand, and had only retired to her chambers at dawn; nevertheless, the guests weren't missing out on anything, because all of their wishes were seen to. The tables, chairs and benches had been moved out into the yard, so that breakfast could be eaten outdoors. Afterwards, all weapons and ammunition stores in the house were collected and inspected for their usefulness.

Later, Old Firehand sat on the roof platform, together with Mrs Butler, and looked longingly out towards the south, from whence the Indians would come. At last, close to midday, a long row of Indians walking single file approached; they were the expected ones. Great Sun was on horseback, leading them.

When they moved through the gate, Old Firehand counted more than two hundred men. Unfortunately, only a few of them were well armed. Most of them owned no horses, and those who did had refused to take them along; they preferred to risk their own lives, rather than have their horses wounded or even shot. Besides, riders were not at all required for the defence of the well-fortified homestead.

Old Firehand divided the once so proud, but increasingly down-at-the-heels Indians into two groups; one was to remain on the farm, and the other, under the Osage chief's command, was to take up position along the border to the neighbour, where Butler's herds had been moved. Those people were given the task of repelling any of the outlaws' attempts to attack there. To spur them into being attentive and courageous, a reward was set for dead outlaws. Then the chief moved out with that group.

Inside the wall at that point were more than a hundred Indians, twenty rafters and the Westerners. It certainly wasn't much against the large number of outlaws; but one hunter or rafter undoubtedly made up for several outlaws. The wall, as well as the house, also offered quite significant protection. It was too early to give specific orders, since the manner of the outlaws' attack was still unknown.

There was nothing left to do but calmly wait for their arrival. Fortunately, Mrs Butler remained calm in the face of the looming danger. She didn't entertain the notion of confusing her people with laments; on the contrary, she invited them in and held out the prospect of appropriate rewards for loyal and courageous conduct. There were around twenty farm hands, who knew how to use their weapons. Old Firehand was certainly able to count on them.

After all the preparations had been made, Old Firehand, Mrs Butler and the Englishman went back up to the platform. The hunter held Castlepool's gigantic telescope and diligently searched the horizon where the outlaws would approach. After a lengthy period of futile effort, he finally discovered a large number of people and horses that could not possibly be discerned with the naked eye. They were definitely the outlaws. Not long after, three of them separated from the bunch, crossed the river at a shallow section, and then moved in the direction of the farm on foot, not on horseback.

"Ah, they're sending scouts!" Old Firehand said. "Perhaps they'll be audacious enough to demand entry."

"I can't believe they'd be capable of such temerity," Castlepool remarked.

"Why not? They send three fellows, who are not known here, to gain entry with some excuse; why would they be treated with animosity? Let's get back down, so that they can't see us on the roof. We can still observe them with the telescope through the window."

The captured outlaw horses were behind the house, so that the three scouts couldn't see them. Everyone assigned to the defence of the property had to hide as well. As soon as the three outlaws came into the yard, they were left with the opinion that the house was insufficiently guarded.

They slowly approached. Old Firehand observed how one lifted the other, so that he could look through one of the embrasures into the enclosure. The hunter hastily issued another few orders before he hurried down to the yard. The arrivals rang the bell; Firehand went to the gate and enquired about their wishes.

"Is the farmer home?" someone asked.

"No, he's away," Firehand replied.

"We're looking for work. Do you require a herder or a farm hand?"

"No."

"Then we'd like to ask you to give us some food, please. We've come from far away and are hungry. Please let us in!"

The man spoke in a very pitiful voice. There's no farmer in the entire West who would refuse someone who is hungry. Among all indigenous people, and in regions where there are no hotels or guest houses, that shortcoming is made up for by the beautiful custom of hospitality; and so, too, in the far West. It would not only be cruel towards the needy, but also a disgrace to the farm, or rather to the owner, to withhold it from a stranger who asks to be taken in.

The men were therefore granted entry, and after the gate was bolted again, they were directed to the seats alongside the house. But the latter didn't seem to agree with their intentions. Although they assumed an appearance of nonchalance, it was inevitable that the interest with which they scrutinized the house and its surroundings, as well as the meaningful gazes they gave each other, would be noticed. One of them said:

"We're only poor, humble people, who don't wish to be an inconvenience. Allow us to remain near the gate, where we'll have more shade than there! We'll fetch a table."

Their wish was fulfilled, although it was a treacherous one, because they wanted to remain near the gate in order to open it to their comrades. They carried the table and chairs there, and then the maid served them plentiful food. Afterwards there was no one in view on that side of the yard, since everyone, including the maid, had retreated.

The fake workers were very satisfied about that circumstance, as Old Firehand, with his keen eyesight, was able to read from their expressions and gestures, which accompanied their quiet conversation. They had become convinced that the farmhouse had so few defenders that they needn't be taken into consideration at all. After some time one of them got up and took what looked like an innocent stroll to the nearest crenelle to look outside. He repeated it several times. It was a sure sign that the fellows were expecting the outlaws to arrive soon.

Old Firehand stood at the windows on the upper floor and through the telescope again surveyed the direction from which the villains were expected to approach. They had retreated after the dispatch of the scouts, so that they couldn't be spotted; at that point they came into view again. They were moving at a gallop in order to cover as fast as possible the stretch on which they could be observed from the farm.

It was obvious that there were some among them who knew the locality, because they rode towards the ford in a straight line. When they reached it, and found it obscured by the barricades, they stopped to inspect the spot. The time had come for Old Firehand to act. He went down to the gate. Just then one of the three fellows was standing at an embrasure to again take a peek outside at his comrades. He was obviously startled when he realized he had been caught out, and quickly stepped away.

"What are you doing? What business of yours is that embrasure?" Old Firehand harshly asked.

Embarrassed, the fellow looked up at the tall man and replied:

"I...I wanted...I wanted to see where we are headed from here."

"Don't lie! You already know your way. It leads outside to the river and the men who are down there."

"What men are you talking about, sir?" the outlaw scout asked with feigned surprise. "I've not noticed anyone."

"If that were so, then you'd have to be blind. You're bound to have seen the riders."

"Not one of them! Who are they?"

"Stop trying to pretend; it's of no use. You belong to the outlaws of Osage-Nook who intend to attack us, and have been sent out to reconnoitre."

The fellow put on an expression of being deeply insulted and called out in a tone of indignation:

"What? We're supposed to be outlaws? Sir, we're honest and diligent workers and have nothing to do with any vagrants, if indeed there are such people around here. We're looking for employment, and since you're not hiring, we'll move on to enquire elsewhere. You're insulting us by saying we count among such rabble. Just think about it! If it were true that we belong to outlaws planning to attack you, then what would be the purpose of visiting you first? It would be a risk with a bad outcome for us."

"Your visit has a very specific purpose. Our walls are tall; hence you were sent to open the gate from the inside, and gain entry for that purpose with the excuse of looking for work. That's the reason you sat so close to the wall."

"Sir!" the man angrily snapped, and reached into his pocket.

But Old Firehand had his revolver in his hand immediately and warned:

"Leave your concealed weapons where they are! As soon as I see one, I'll pull the trigger. Yes, you took a risk by coming here, because I could apprehend you and call you to account; but I fear you so little that I'll let you go. Get outside and tell the rabble that we'll give a bullet to anyone who crosses the river. Now we're finished and you had better be on your way."

He opened the gate. The three men looked like they wanted to say something else, but kept their mouths shut at the sight of the revolvers aimed at them. However, when they were outside, and the gate was bolted again, they sneered, and Old Firehand heard the following remarks:

"Numbskull! Why are you letting us go if we're outlaws? Count us, why don't you! We'll give your few people short shrift. You'll all be hanged within a short quarter of an hour."

"And you'll be the first to receive bullets from our guns!" he called after them. Then he gave the agreed upon signal and the hitherto hidden defenders of the farm came out from behind the house and took up their posts along the crenelles. Firehand stood at one of them to observe the movements of the enemy.

The ejected scouts reached the near bank of the river and shouted something across to the rest of the gang; it was unintelligible from the distance of the wall. Subsequently the outlaws galloped a short stretch along the water, in order to swim across. They rode their horses into the river.

"You'll aim at the scouts immediately, like I've warned them we would," Old Firehand ordered Droll and Black Tom, who were near him. "I'll aim at the first two who land. Bill, Uncle, Blenter, Castlepool and the rest, one after the other, as you're standing now, will shoot after me. That way each gets his own man, there won't be two aiming at the same outlaw, and we'll avoid wasting ammunition as well."

"Good!" Humply-Bill replied. "I'll keep to that sequence."

And his sidekick, Gunstick-Uncle agreed:

"As soon as they cross to this side; From the sights of our guns they can't hide; To be shot one by one; And to Hell they'll be run!"

At that point the first rider arrived on the near bank; the second followed him. The three fake workers were standing where the others were coming ashore. Old Firehand gave the signal. His two shots rang out almost at the same time as those of Tom and Droll; the two riders were thrown from their horses, and the scouts were lying on the ground. When the outlaws saw that, they raised a furious howling and pushed forwards to reach dry ground. One pushed the other towards ruination because as soon as a horse climbed up the bank, fire from the farm shot its rider out of the saddle. Within not quite two minutes, twenty to thirty riderless horses ran about aimlessly on the farm side of the river.

The outlaws hadn't expected that kind of reception. The remarks the scouts had shouted across the water had undoubtedly conveyed the message that the farm was ridiculously short of defenders. Shot upon shot was fired from the embrasures. None of the bullets missed; each hit the man it had been aimed at! The howls of fury turned into fearful cries; a voice shouting orders prompted the riders in the water to turn their horses and return to the far bank.

"Repelled!" Missouri-Blenter remarked. "I'm curious to find out what they'll do next."

"There's no doubt about it," Old Firehand replied. "They'll swim across in a spot that lies outside the range of our guns."

"And then?"

"Then? That's impossible to say at present. If they're smart we'll have a difficult stand."

"And what do you think is smart?"

"They mustn't advance in a combined bunch, but have to spread out. If they leave their horses behind, and run at all four sides of the wall at the same time, then we'll be too weak to fend them off. We would be forced to divide into four fronts. Should the outlaws then suddenly regroup in one spot, it will be possible for them to get across the wall."

"That's true, but many of them would be picked off. Of course we would also be forced to face them without much cover."

"Pshaw! We'd retreat into the house, and would then be numerous enough to chase them back across the wall. Fortunately the yard is large and unobscured, and the house stands right in the middle of it. I'm not worried; let's wait and see what they'll do. They seem to be holding counsel."

The outlaws had gathered in a bunch from which four had separated, most likely their leaders. The faces were unrecognizable; but it was evident from their gesticulations that they were talking about something important. Afterwards they all moved upriver, in a northerly direction, until they were outside the firing range of the farm, where they crossed the river. When all had gathered again they formed a closed bunch with the front pointing at the gate in the wall. Until that moment the defenders had manned the eastern side of the wall; but Old Firehand called out:

"Quickly, get across to the north side! They want to storm the gate."

"They cannot possibly run it down!" Blenter replied.

"No; but if they reach it, they can clear the gate and the wall from their saddles, which might make it possible for them to overwhelm us here in the yard."

"But many will fall beforehand!"

"And even more left over! Don't shoot before I give the order; but then everyone at the same time, two salvos from the double-barrelled rifles, into the middle of the bunch!"

The men quickly occupied the northern wall. Some of the defenders were standing by the openings, others behind the merlons, the raised portions between the crenelles, from where they could shoot over the top of the wall. The latter were ducking down behind them, so as not to be seen too early by the attackers.

It became obvious that Old Firehand had come to the correct conclusion. The troop began to move, at a gallop, straight towards the gate. Only when they were at the most eighty paces away from it, did the hunter give the order to open fire; two salvos came in quick succession, fired so precisely that they sounded like two individual shots. The result was according to Firehand's expectations. It looked as though a rope spanned across the outlaws' path had stopped them. They formed a confused heap and were unable to unravel it quickly enough. Castlepool, who owned two guns, fired another two shots. The confusion among the outlaws gave the others time to quickly reload, if only one barrel, and then to fire into the melee at liberty; their gunfire came without interruption. The outlaws were unable to deal with it; they scattered and left their dead and wounded behind since it was dangerous to stay with them. The riderless horses instinctively ran towards the farmhouse where the gate was opened to let them inside to join the first lot. When the outlaws made an effort to attend to their wounded, they were not prevented, as an act of humanity. They were observed moving their casualties under a distant group of trees to bandage them as well as was possible under the circumstances.

In the meantime midday had been and gone, and the brave defenders of Butler's farm received food and drink. Soon after, they observed how the outlaws departed, yet left their wounded behind under the trees; they rode west.

"Are they withdrawing?" Humply-Bill asked. "They've received a decent lesson and it would be smart of them to take it to heart."

"They wouldn't think of it," Aunty Droll replied. "If they really had intentions of giving up, then they would take their wounded with them. I think they're going to pay attention to the herds that belong to the farm. That's where their present attention is directed. There, look up to the top of the house! Old Firehand is standing up there with the telescope in his hands. He's observing the fellows, and I think we'll soon receive an order."

"What order?"

"To render assistance to the herders and Indians."

Aunty Droll's guess turned out to be correct. Although the outlaws had moved sufficiently far away that they couldn't be observed from the wall, Firehand was still able to see them; he shouted down:

"Saddle the horses, quickly! The rogues are turning south and will encounter Great Sun and his warriors."

In less than five minutes the horses were ready, and everyone mounted up, except a few farm hands who were to stay back in the yard in case the gate required opening in a hurry; the Indians who had stayed on the farm took possession of the captured horses and rode, mostly double, to join the other riders. With Old

Firehand in the lead they rode out of the gate, and around the nearest corner of the wall, to head south. Behind a few cultivated fields the green grazing pasture of the prairie began. Bushes came into view every now and then.

The outlaws were still not visible with the naked eye; but Old Firehand was observing them through his telescope. That made it possible for him and his troop to follow the outlaws in parallel fashion without being seen. After a quarter of an hour, Firehand stopped because the outlaws had also stopped. They had arrived at the neighbour's boundary and saw not only the grazing animals, but also their armed guards.

Old Firehand studied the various bush islands on the grassland and chose those that gave him cover. Concealed behind them he led his men to approach a spot where the clash was expected to occur. They left the horses behind when they had advanced sufficiently, and sneaked along on foot, crouched low until they reached a broad patch of scrub to which they assumed the outlaws were going to head during the skirmish. Firehand and his men took up positions, so that the outlaws couldn't see them, and held their guns ready. From their location, they were able to see the attackers, as well as the ones who were going to be attacked, with the unaided eye.

The former seemed to be taken aback by having encountered such a great number of Indians protecting the animals. Why had red men been hired to do that, and in such numbers at that? The outlaws hesitated. But soon they noticed that the Indians were armed only poorly because they had no rifles, and that reassured them. The leaders held a short discussion, and then gave the order to attack. The immediate manner in which it took place revealed that the outlaws intended to simply overrun the Indians. The riders charged straight towards them in closed formation amid intimidating howling.

At that point it became evident that Great Sun was equal to the task. He gave a loud order whereupon the densely grouped warriors scattered, so that it was impossible to ride them down. The outlaws realized it; they veered off to get around the right flank of the Indians in order to drive them towards their left flank. The Osage chief saw through their intentions. Again his loud voice resounded. His men swarmed into what for a moment seemed a confused bunch only to scatter once more. They had completely changed their formation. While it had been aligned in an east-to-west direction first, it had then changed into a north-to-south line-up. The Osage chief had arranged that change not because he knew his allies were nearby, but to show the enemy the strong, horned forehead like a cornered bison, instead of the vulnerable side. While that was a masterpiece in itself, it had one additional advantage of which he was unaware, of course—the gang of highwaymen was suddenly situated between the Osage's Indian troop and Old Firehand's group concealed behind the scrub. The outlaws saw their plans foiled and halted, which was a carelessness they would pay for immediately. They seemed to have miscalculated the range of the Indian weapons and felt safe from them. One of their leaders spoke to them, most likely to convey a new plan. The Osage utilized the interruption. He emitted a shout upon which the warriors swiftly leapt forwards, suddenly stood still, shot their arrows, and then retreated just as quickly. The missiles reached their targets; they resulted in dead outlaws and even more wounded ones, not only among the riders but also the horses. The animals reared; they wanted to bolt and were difficult to control. There was confusion, which Old Firehand needed to exploit.

"Now, let's go!" he commanded. "But only shoot the men, not the horses!"

The men of his troop came out from behind the trees; they were behind the enemy, who didn't see them. When the shots rang out and the bullets flew into the bunched outlaws, they turned around just when the second salvo was being fired at them, and cried out in panic.

"Away!" yelled someone among them. "We're surrounded. Break through the line of Indians!"

The men immediately obeyed the order. Abandoning their dead and wounded, the outlaws raced towards the Indians who were only too ready to open the way out for them, and then raise a triumphant howling behind them.

"There they run!" old Missouri-Blenter laughed. "They won't come back. Do you know who told them to flee?"

"Of course!" Black Tom replied. "That voice is unmistakable. It was Red Brinkley; Satan seems to protect him from our bullets. Won't we go after the scoundrels, sir?"

Tom had directed the question at Old Firehand, and the hunter replied:

"No. We don't have the numbers to match them in hand-to-hand combat. Besides, they might just guess that we've ridden here from the farm to assist the Indians. In that case it is very likely that they'll return there to force entry during our absence. We must return immediately."

"And what happens with the wounded outlaws and the riderless horses?"

"We must leave them to the Indians. But let's not lose time, to our horses, quickly!"

The men waved their hats and shouted a 'hooray' at the Indians to which they replied with shrill victory cries; then they returned to their horses, mounted up and headed back to the farm, while the two Indian groups reunited. No outlaws were spotted near the farm, except the wounded who had been left by the stand of trees. Old Firehand went up to the roof of the house immediately to survey the surroundings.

Mrs Butler, the farmer's wife, was sitting on the platform. She had been very anxious and was pleased to hear that the attack had been repelled so gloriously.

"That means we're safe, doesn't it?" she heaved a sigh of relief. "Since the outlaws have suffered such heavy losses, it is safe to assume that they've lost their nerve to continue the animosities."

"Perhaps," the hunter pensively replied.

"Only perhaps?"

"Unfortunately! They won't dare to approach the herds again because they have to assume that they are guarded by a sufficient number of Whites, and not only by Indians. But the house here is another matter. The outlaws will have realized that they cannot undertake anything against it during the day, but they could come by the idea that gaining entry at night might be possible. We must definitely be prepared for a night-time attack."

"But they'd surely not show themselves in broad daylight again, would they?"

"Oh, yes! They have to attend to their wounded, who are lying outside by the trees. I'm convinced we'll shortly see them there. They fled in a westerly direction, and they'll return from there."

He looked through his telescope in the indicated direction and after a short while continued:

"Quite right, there they are! They've ridden in an arc and are returning to their injured fellow outlaws. I'm assuming that..."

He hesitated. While he kept gazing through his telescope he moved it to point situated in a more northerly direction.

"What is it?" the woman asked. "Why won't you keep talking, sir? Why do you suddenly have such a serious expression on your face?"

He kept looking through the lenses for another short while before he put it down and replied:

"Because something is probably going to happen that isn't likely to improve our situation."

"What do you mean? What's supposed to happen?" she fearfully asked.

He contemplated whether or not he ought to tell her the truth. Fortunately his quandary came to an end when Castlepool climbed onto the roof platform to enquire about the whereabouts of the outlaws. Old Firehand used that opportunity to say to the woman:

"It's nothing we need to be too afraid of, Mrs Butler. You can safely go downstairs to let the thirsty men have a drink."

She obeyed his suggestion, but after she had left, the hunter said to Castlepool, who had brought up his giant telescope:

"I had good reasons to persuade the lady to leave. Take your scope, sir, and look straight west. Who do you see?"

The Englishman followed Firehand's prompt, and then replied:

"The outlaws. I can see them clearly. They're coming."

"Are they really coming?"

"Of course! What else would they do?"

"In that case my telescope seems to be better than yours, although it is much smaller. Can you see the outlaws moving?"

"No, they're standing still."

"With their faces turned in what direction?"

"Due north."

"Then follow that direction with your scope! You might perhaps see why the fellows have stopped."

"Alright, I'll have a look!" And after a few moments he continued: "There are three riders approaching, without noticing the outlaws."

"Riders? Really?"

"Yes! But no, one of them seems to be a lady. Right, it is a female. I can see the long riding outfit and flowing veil."

"And do you know who these three people are?"

"No. How could I know—heigh-ho, they wouldn't perchance be...?"

"Indeed," Old Firehand nodded with a serious expression on his face. "It's them; the Butler brothers and Ellen. The messenger we sent to warn them has missed them."

Castlepool collapsed his telescope and exclaimed:

"Then we must get on our horses and ride out there, otherwise they'll fall into the hands of the outlaws!"

He wanted to leave. The hunter held him back by his arm and said:

"Stay, sir, and don't make a noise! Mrs Butler and her sister-in-law mustn't know anything at this point. We can neither warn nor help, because it is already too late. Look, look!"

Castlepool extended his telescope and looked through again. He saw that the outlaws had begun to move and were approaching the three riders at a gallop.

"All devils!" he exclaimed. "They'll kill them!"

"They wouldn't think of it! Those fellows know the advantage they'll gain and will make good use of it. What would they gain by killing the three people? Nothing at all. On the contrary, they'd only make our conduct more aggressive. But if they let them live, and use them as hostages, they'd be able to extort concessions from us, to which we would not ordinarily submit. Pay attention! It's about to happen. The three are surrounded. We wouldn't have been able to prevent it. Firstly, we did not have enough time, and secondly, we're even now too weak in the open field against such a large number of outlaws."

"Well, that's correct, sir," Castlepool said. "But woe to the scoundrels if they don't treat the prisoners decently! And—will we really admit to being forced into any old concessions? We would actually have to be ashamed for even dealing with such people!"

Old Firehand shrugged his shoulders in his own peculiar manner, and a confident, almost disdainful smile played around his lips when he replied:

"Let me handle it, sir! I've never done anything I'd have to be ashamed of. Old Firehand won't take orders from outlaws, even if there were a thousand. If I tell you that the three people who've been taken prisoner out there are in no danger whatsoever, then you can believe me. Nevertheless, I'm asking you not to let the two women know what has transpired. I nearly revealed it during the moment of surprise, but it won't be of any use and will only be detrimental to our cause if they learn of it."

"Is no one else to know of it, either?"

"We'll tell the men closest to us, so that at least they know where we stand. If you'd like to do that, then you ought to go downstairs now; but they're not to chat about it. I'll keep observing the outlaws and will make my decisions according to their conduct."

Castlepool went back down into the yard to inform the men in question about the occurrence. Old Firehand returned his focus to the outlaws who were riding towards the stand of trees with their prisoners in the middle. They stopped, dismounted and sat down. Firehand saw that there was a very animated conversation or discussion among them. He was sure of its outcome, and was reflecting about how to act in response to it. Droll interrupted the hunter's contemplations when he came rushing up and asked in German:

"Is det really true, sir, what the Englishman came to tell us? The two gentlemen Butler have been taken captive, and the young miss as well?"

"Indeed," Old Firehand nodded.

"Who'd have thought det something like det is possible? Now the outlaws will think they are sitting on the high horse; they'll come to make grand demands. And what about us? What will we say to that?"

"What do you suggest?" Old Firehand asked while he cast a bemused, quizzical gaze at the short man.

"Must ye ask?" Droll returned. "Nothing, absolutely nothing will be conceded. Or are ye perchance contemplating paying a ransom?"

"Aren't we forced to do that?"

"Nee, nee, and for the third time, nee! These scoundrels are unable to do anything. What do they want to do? Kill the prisoners perchance? They wouldn't want to, or else they'd have to fear our retribution. They might threaten us with it, but we won't believe it and will simply laugh at them."

"But we have to consider the prisoners, even if your assumptions are correct, because their situation is undoubtedly very uncomfortable. Even if they're not harmed physically, they'll be subjected to all manner of abuse and threats that will distress them."

"Det won't do them any harm; they'll have to submit to det for crawling into the goose pen so carelessly! Let it be a warning to them for the future, and besides, the misery won't last too much longer. We're here as well, and the cuckoo would have to be in league with the devil to prevent us from finding ways and means to extract them from det mire."

"How would we go about it? Do you have a plan?"

"Nee, not yet; det's not necessary at this point. We must first wait and see what happens next; only then can we act. I'm not worried in the least, not for me anyway, because I know myself. Once the right moment announces itself, then I'll come by the correct presence of mind. Let's calmly wait for the night and pay attention to where they'll pitch their camp. I'll then gradually sneak up to extract the prisoners."

"I believe you're quite capable of taking that risk; but it is very dangerous!"

"*Papperlapapp!*[6] You and I, we've been through a lot worse. Neither of us are fools. There's an old proverb in Altenburg that says: 'we can do it, 'cos we've got it.' And so it is here. Someone who's got his head full of grey matter, that being the inborn intelligence, cannot possibly go wrong. Surely we're not afraid of such hayduks like these outlaws, who have not exactly been endowed with too much nous! I think det—stop!" he cut himself short. "Watch out! There they come. Two fellows, straight towards the house. They're flapping some cloth between their fingers for us to see that their parliamentary roles are to be respected. Will ye speak to them?"

"Of course! I have to know what their demands are for the sake of the prisoners. Come!"

The two men returned to the yard, where the crew were standing along the battlement, to observe the two negotiators. They stopped out of range and waved the rags. Old Firehand opened the gate, stepped outside and gave them a signal to approach. They obeyed. When they had joined him they greeted him politely, but made every effort to show confidence.

"Sir, we've come as envoys to make our demands," one of them said.

"Ah! Since when do prairie rabbits dare to approach a grizzly bear to give him orders?" the hunter replied with an ironic tone of voice.

The analogy he used wasn't bad at all. He stood in front of them so tall, broad and mighty; and out of his eyes shot a gaze at them that caused them to reflexively retreat a step.

"We're no rabbits, sir!" said the one who spoke before.

"No? Then you must be cowardly prairie wolves that are satisfied with cadaver? You're pretending to be negotiators. You're robbers, thieves and murderers, who have stepped outside the law, for any honest man to shoot at will!"

"Sir," the outlaw remonstrated to him. "I must reject such insults..."

---

[6] An English equivalent to this expression might be: *Poopadee-pooh-pooh!*—from *pooh-pooh!* to dismiss something.

"Shut up, scoundrel!" Old Firehand thundered at him. "You're villains, nothing more! It is actually a disgrace for me to talk to you. I've only permitted you to approach to find out how much cheek such riff-raff has. You will listen to what I'm going to tell you, and not bat an eyelid. Say one more word that I don't like and I'll immediately knock you to the ground. Do you know who I am?"

"No," the intimidated man meekly replied.

"They call me Old Firehand. Tell that to those who sent you; perhaps they'll know that I'm not a man to be fooled with. They've already had that experience today. And now make it quick: what's your message?"

"We're to inform you that the farmer, his brother and his niece have fallen into our hands."

"I know it already!"

"Those three people have to die..."

"Pshaw!" the hunter interrupted him.

"...if you don't agree to our conditions," the envoy continued.

"Old Firehand never agrees to conditions, least of all those made by people of your ilk. Besides you're the vanquished, and if anyone were entitled to make demands, I would be the one to do so."

"But, sir, if you don't listen to me, then the prisoners will be hanged on the trees over there right in front of your eyes!"

"Do that, why don't you! There are more than enough ropes on the farm for you."

The outlaw hadn't expected that. He knew very well that they weren't going to make good on their threat. He stared at the ground in his embarrassment, and then said:

"Consider, three human lives!"

"I am considering it very well—only three human lives for which we will extinguish you all! The advantage clearly lies on our side."

"But you could easily prevent the death of your friends!"

"How?"

"By moving out and handing the farm to us."

That's when Old Firehand placed his fist on the outlaws shoulder so heavily that he flinched, and then replied:

"Are you crazy? Have you got anything else to say to me?"

"No."

"Then you had best get away from here at once, otherwise I'll regard you as a madman who has to be rendered harmless."

"Are you serious, sir?"

"Completely serious. Away with you or else you're done for!"

He pulled out his revolver. The two outlaws hastily retreated; nevertheless, the one who spoke before dared to stand still at a safe distance and ask:

"May we return if we receive another message?"

"No."

"In that case you're rejecting all negotiations?"

"Yes. I'm only available to speak to the red-haired colonel, and for no longer than a moment."

"Do you promise him free return to us?"

"Yes, if he doesn't insult me."

"We'll tell him."

They ran away so fast that it was evident they were glad to have escaped the vicinity of the famous man. The latter didn't return inside the yard, but instead started walking away from the gate in the direction of the outlaws until he had gone half way. There, he sat on a rock to wait for the colonel. He was confident that the man was going to join him.

Those unfamiliar with Old Firehand would have considered it an extraordinary risk for him to move away from his men without at least carrying a rifle; Firehand, however, knew very well what he was able to risk.

It soon became evident that he hadn't been mistaken in his notion. The circle of outlaws opened and the colonel came walking slowly towards him. He executed a bow that was supposed to be elegant but turned out rather clumsy. His hand was still bandaged, and the long hair concealed the fact that his ears were missing. He said:

"Good afternoon, sir! You demanded to talk to me?"

"I know nothing of the sort," the Westerner replied. "I only said that I wouldn't talk to any one but you; I would have preferred it if *you* hadn't appeared, either."

"Mister, you're using mighty proud language!"

"I have cause for it. I wouldn't suggest, however, that you apply the same tone."

They stared at each other, eye to eye. The colonel lowered his gaze first and with barely concealed anger he said:

"We're likely standing face to face as equals!"

"The outlaw in front of the honest frontiersman, the vanquished in front of the victor—do you call that 'equal'?"

"I'm not vanquished yet. We will prove to you that your victories thus far are only transitory. We have the power to turn the tables."

"Try it, why don't you!" Old Firehand laughed disdainfully.

That vexed the outlaw and he snapped:

"We only had to use your carelessness!"

"Ah! Why? What carelessness have I committed?"

"Moving so far away from the farm. Had we wanted it, you would have fallen into our hands. And without you those behind the wall would have been no match for us."

A merry smile crossed Old Firehand's face, similar to the smile of a good-natured adult hearing a child's silly remarks.

"You don't actually believe what you're saying," he replied. "You, catch Old Firehand! Then why haven't you done so? The fact that you didn't even attempt it is the best evidence that you yourself don't believe in that possibility."

"Oho! Although you're known as a good frontiersman, you're nevertheless not as invincible as everyone believes. You're right in the middle between us and the farm. If only a few of us had mounted up to cut your retreat off, then you would have become our prisoner."

"Do you really think so?"

"Yes. And even if you were the fastest runner, a horse would be even faster; you must admit that. You would have been surrounded before you would have been able to reach the house."

"Your calculation is correct except for two points. Firstly, would I not have defended myself? I'm not afraid of a few of you. And secondly, you didn't consider that those who were going to catch me would have come within range of my men's rifles; they would have simply been potted off. But that's not what we ought to discuss."

"No, it is not, sir. I've come here to give you the opportunity to save the lives of our three prisoners."

"In that case you made the effort in vain, because these people are not in danger."

"No?" the colonel replied with a smug grin. "You're mightily mistaken, sir. If you don't accept our demands, sir, they'll be hanged."

"I've already informed you that you'll all be hanged, too, in that case."

"Ridiculous! Have you counted how many men are in our group?"

"Indeed; but do you perhaps also know how many I can set against you?"

"Precisely."

"Pshaw! You have not been able to count us."

"That's not necessary. We know how many farmhands there ordinarily are on Butler's farm; there won't be any more at present, either. One could at most add the rafters you brought along from the Black-Bear River."

Brinkley looked at Old Firehand from the side, expectantly, because he really was in the dark about the number of people Firehand had at his disposal. He wanted to observe the hunter's expression to get a clue as to whether or not his voiced guess was correct. Old Firehand knew that. He made a dismissive gesture and replied:

"Count your dead and wounded, and then tell me that the few rafters would have been capable of achieving this. Besides, you've seen my Indians and also the Whites who took you from behind."

"The other Whites?" the outlaw laughed. "They were the rafters, no one else. I'll admit that you out-foxed us there. You came to the aid of the Indians from the farm; unfortunately I considered that far too late. No, sir, you cannot impress us with your numbers. If we kill the prisoners, then it will be impossible for you to avenge them."

And again it was an overtly scheming gaze the colonel threw at Old Firehand. The latter disdainfully shrugged his shoulder and said:

"Let's not argue. Even if we only count as few as you seem to erroneously assume, we would be far superior to you. Outlaws, outlaws, what kind of people are they? Lazy workers, vagrants, drifters! Inside that wall, however, stand the most famous hunters and scouts of the Wild West. Each one of them will single-handedly take on at least ten outlaws. Even if we were only a group of twenty Westerners, and you dared to kill the prisoners, we would remain on your heels for weeks and months to annihilate you to the last man. You know that very well, hence you'll beware of even touching a hair on those three people."

He had spoken in a threatening and confident tone of voice, so that the colonel lowered his gaze and stared at the ground. The latter knew that the hunter was precisely the man to put his words into action. There had often been occasions when a single, brave man pursued an entire gang to exact retribution from them, and that, gradually, one after the other fell victim to his reliable rifle. If anyone, it would be Old Firehand who could repeat such a daring feat. Yet the outlaw was careful not to acknowledge that; he lifted his gaze, stared at the hunter with a sneer, and then said:

"Let's wait and see! If you were so sure of yourself you wouldn't be here. Only worry could have driven you out here to meet with me."

"Don't talk such nonsense. I've agreed to speak with you, especially with you, to memorize your face and your voice one more time, not out of fear, but to be sure of my future course of action. That's the reason. Now you're so indelibly imprinted on my memory that we can part. We're finished with each other."

"Not yet, sir! I must first know your answer."

"You've already got it."

"No, because I've got a new suggestion to make. We've decided to refrain from occupying the farm."

"Ah, very gracious of you! And what else?"

"You'll give us back the horses you captured; in addition you'll surrender all of your weapons and ammunition; and then you'll deliver the necessary cattle to us for provisions, and finally, you'll pay twenty thousand dollars; there will be that much on the farm."

"Is that all? Nothing else? Splendid! And what are you offering in return?"

"We'll deliver the prisoners to you and move out, after you've given us your word of honour that you'll cease and desist with any and all hostilities towards us henceforth. Now you know what I want, and I expect your decision. We've already been chatting unnecessarily for far too long."

He said that in a tone of voice that implied he had the greatest moral right to his demands. Old Firehand pulled out his revolver and replied very calmly, not angrily, and with an indescribably disdainful smile:

"Yes, you've chatted long enough, and nothing but mad, crazy babble to which I can only say: get away from here immediately, or else you'll get a bullet through your head!"

"What? Is that..."

"Away! Right now!" the hunter cut him short with a raised voice, while he pointed the barrel of the weapon at him. "One...two..."

The outlaw chose not to wait for 'three'; he turned around, uttered a threatening curse, and walked away hastily. He had realized that Old Firehand would truly have pulled the trigger after the count. The hunter watched him walk until he was certain not to be shot in the back by him; then he returned to the farm, where the others had watched the meeting with great attention.

When asked about the outcome of it, he gave a brief report, which was received with approval.

"You've acted correctly, sir," Castlepool declared. "One mustn't give even the slightest concessions to such scoundrels. They're scared and will not lay their hands on the prisoners. What do you think they'll do now?"

"Hm!" Firehand replied. "The sun is setting. My guess is that they'll wait until it has become dark, and then try to get over the wall. If that fails, they'll still have the prisoners for a second extortion attempt."

"Do you think they'll really attempt an attack?"

"I think it is probable. They know that they're still far superior to us in numbers. We must prepare for defence. Caution dictates that we observe them closely. As soon as it is dark, a few men must go outside to sneak up on them and inform me of every one of their moves. Who is going to volunteer for this dangerous mission?"

To a man they all came forward, and Old Firehand chose three whom he regarded to be best suited for the task; namely, Aunty Droll, Humply-Bill and Gunstick-Uncle; they were delighted at the mark of respect they received from him.

The sun was touching the horizon and its rays, which flooded the wide plain in liquid gold, were shining upon the outlaws, so that each one was clearly recognizable from the farm. They made not the slightest preparation, neither for departure, nor for a night camp. That led to the conclusion that they neither intended to leave the region, nor planned on staying on the spot they occupied at present.

Old Firehand had firewood moved to all four corners of the yard, as well as coal, which was found in great quantities in Kansas, and therefore very cheap, and in addition several barrels of coal oil. When it was completely dark the scouts were let outside. Against the possibility they would be pursued upon their return, and risk capture waiting for the gate to open, strong lassos were tied on several spots along the wall and lowered down the outside. The men could then quickly climb up and into the yard. Others doused the pieces of firewood in coal oil, lit them and tossed them out through the crenelles in each corner. After more wood, and then coals, had been heaped onto them, four fires were burning outside the four corners, as a result of which the walls on all sides, as well as the outlying terrain, were so brightly lit that the approach of the outlaws, not only as a group, but also individually, would be easily detected. The flames were fed as required through the embrasures, because that was the only way to avoid the enemy bullets.

More than an hour went by, and nothing seemed to stir outside. But then Gunstick-Uncle climbed over the wall on one of the lassos. He went straight to Old Firehand and in his own original way reported:

"The outlaws have gone from the wood; To an entirely new neighbourhood."

"I thought so. But where?" the hunter asked, and smiled about the rhyme.

Gunstick-Uncle pointed at the corner to the right of the gate and replied in unshakeable earnest:

"In the riverside vegetation; Is where we must start exploration."

"They've dared to come so close! But we ought to have heard their horses?"

"They wisely were sent to rest; On the prairie, the grass to ingest; But the spot I don't know; I'd no lamplight to show."

"And where are Bill and Droll?"

"They ardently wished to pursue; The scoundrels, the better to view!"

"Splendid! I must know precisely where the outlaws are. Please join the other two again, if you would be so kind. Ask Droll to come and inform me as soon as the scoundrels have settled down; they probably think they've been very smart, but have instead walked into a trap we have only to shut."

Gunstick-Uncle left, and Castlepool, who had heard the conversation, asked what trap Old Firehand was referring to. The hunter replied:

"The scoundrels are down by the river. The outlaws have the water behind them and the wall in front of them; if we block the two sides, we've got them locked in."

"Quite right! But how do you propose to execute that blockade?"

"By sending for the Indians; they'll have to take the outlaws from the south; we, however, will sneak out of the gate and will attack from the north."

"Then you want to leave the wall without cover?"

"No, the farmhands will stay behind; they'll suffice. But we would indeed fare badly if the outlaws come by the smart idea to storm the wall; however, I don't give them credit for being clever enough to assume we would be so bold as to expose the main defence position. I will also send someone to scout out the whereabouts of their horses. If we find that out, then the guards won't be difficult to subdue. Once we have possession of the horses, the outlaws will be lost because we can chase those who will escape tonight by daylight tomorrow, catch them and annihilate them."

"Alright, it's a daring but splendid plan. It is true, you are a capable fellow!"

At that point Black Tom and Missouri-Blenter were sent out to search for the horses. Then two farmhands, who knew the locality well, were sent to the Osage chief, to give him detailed instructions. Nothing could be undertaken until everyone had returned.

A long time passed before the farmhands at last came back. They had found the Indians and led them to the farm; they were lying in wait along the river only a few hundred paces away from the outlaws, and were ready to pounce on them with the first shot they heard.

Then Aunty Droll, Humply-Bill and Gunstick-Uncle returned.

"All three?" Old Firehand asked disapprovingly. "At least one ought to have stayed out there."

"I wouldn't know why, if that's necessary," Droll replied in his idiosyncratic manner.

"To keep observing the outlaws, of course!"

"That would be superfluous! I know where I stand because I've sneaked so close to them that I was able to hear enough. They're mightily vexed about our fires, which will make an attack impossible, and want to wait and see how long our firewood and coal lasts. They're of the opinion that the supply will be at an end in a few hours' time, since farmers wouldn't be prepared for such large blazes. And then they'll begin their onslaught."

"That's very advantageous for us indeed, because we're gaining time to shut the trap."

"What trap?"

Old Firehand explained what he had planned.

"Det's magnificent, hee hee hee!" Droll laughed to himself semi-audibly, the way he used to laugh when something lifted his mood. "That will and must succeed. But, sir, there's only one thing to consider, which is of great significance."

"What's that?"

"The situation of the prisoners. I'm afraid that they'll kill them as soon as we begin the hostilities."

"Do you think I haven't thought about it already? Fortunately I don't share the concern you've just voiced. Of course I'm convinced that the prisoners would be the first to fall; but we can prevent that by ensuring that nothing will happen to them. We'll sneak up, and three of us will immediately protect the Butler brothers and the young lady when we attack. Are they tied up?"

"Yes, but not heavily."

"Alright, they'll have to be freed from their fetters quickly, and then..."

"And then into the water with them," Droll quickly cut in.

"Into the water?" Old Firehand was astonished.

"Of course."

"No doubt you're joshing, dear Aunty, yes?"

"Joshing? Wouldn't think of it!" And when Aunty Droll saw the flabbergasted looks he attracted from those around him, he cackled and continued:

"Yes, into the water with them: hee hee hee, that's the best prank imaginable. Just think of the outlaws' faces! And how they'll scratch their heads!"

"They won't have the time for that because we'll smash their heads."

"Not immediately, not immediately, but later."

"Later? Why? Shall we give them time to escape us?"

"Not that; but we'll snatch the prisoners from them even before the attack."

"Do you think that's possible?"

"Not only possible but very necessary. It is difficult to ensure the safety of the prisoners during the battle; we must therefore extract them before it becomes dangerous for them. And that's not very difficult."

"No? Alright, how do you envisage doing that? I know you're a wily fox. I also know that you've outwitted many otherwise clever fellows over the years, and that you've pulled your head out of the noose unscathed although everything seemed lost. Have you had a stroke of genius this time around, too, perchance?"

"And then some!"

"Alright, explain!"

"It won't need much cleverness. I'm surprised you haven't come by this idea yourself, yet. Remember the canal that runs from the yard behind the house to the river? It's subterranean, or rather, under cover, and the outlaws have no idea that it exists. I sneaked past them right down to the river. Despite the darkness, I recognized the spot where the canal enters the river by the large boulders that had been rolled into the water to form a small dam by which the water is diverted into the canal. And—just imagine this, gents—the outlaws have camped right by that convergence. They've formed a half circle along the banks, inside of which the prisoners are being kept. They believe that the three captives are thus completely secure, and yet precisely that circumstance will enable us to get them out."

"Ah, I'm beginning to understand!" Old Firehand said. "Do you want to get into the canal here in the yard and follow it down to the river?"

"Yes. Not alone, of course; two others must come along, so that there's one man for each of the prisoners."

"Hm! That idea is actually superb. Let's find out first whether or not the canal is really passable."

Old Firehand asked several farmhands and to his delight found out that the canal was free of mud and contained no stale air; one could easily walk along it and—what was an especially fortuitous detail—there was a small dinghy, which was able to take three men, secreted at the canal mouth; the small boat was always well hidden there to prevent Indians or other strangers from absconding with it.

The plan devised by the cunning Aunty Droll was discussed in detail, and everyone agreed that he, Humply-Bill and Gunstick-Uncle would carry it out. Just when they were ready, Missouri-Blenter and Black Tom returned; they had searched a fairly wide circle but unfortunately not found the horses. The outlaws had been smart enough to take them as far as possible away from the farm.

First, Old Firehand climbed over the wall with the farmhand who had delivered the message to the Osage chief, to satisfy himself that Great Sun had been instructed correctly. When that was done, and Firehand had returned, Droll, Bill and Gunstick-Uncle took off their outer clothing and climbed down into the canal with a lantern. The water reached only to chest-level. They hoisted the rifles onto their shoulders and hung the knives and revolvers around their necks. Tall Gunstick-Uncle went ahead with the lantern. When they had disappeared in the canal, Old Firehand departed with his men.

He asked the farmhand, who quietly opened the gate, not to bolt it again and to leave it slightly ajar after he and his companions had passed through it, so that they would find it open should they be forced to retreat hastily. However, one farmhand remained at the gate as a guard to bolt it shut immediately, should the outlaws approach. The other farmhands, and even the maids, stood ready on the riverside wall to fend off a possible attack as best they could.

The rafters, and especially the frontiersmen in their company, were skilled at sneaking up. Under the leadership of the famous hunter they first moved north in an arc, so as not to be illuminated by the sheen of the fires; then, when they reached the river, they turned south and crawled along its banks until they could assume that they had drawn level with the outlaws. Old Firehand sneaked ahead on his own until, with his keen eyesight that penetrated the darkness, he saw the semicircle of the outlaw camp. At that moment he realized where the attack should be directed, and returned to his men to inform them, and to wait for the signal that had been prearranged with the three men who were going to free the prisoners.

In the meantime, those men had already gone the length of the canal, the water of which wasn't cold enough to bother them. Not far from the mouth, still inside the canal, the small boat was tied to a steel hook. Two paddles were lying inside it. Gunstick-Uncle extinguished the lantern and hung it on the hook; then Droll bade the other two to wait there while he went reconnoitring out to the river on his own. It was more than a quarter of an hour before he returned.

"Well?" Humply-Bill tensely asked.

"It wasn't a simple task," Aunty Droll replied. "The water won't be a hindrance since it is no deeper out there than it is in here; but the darkness between the bushes and the trees gave me trouble. I couldn't see anything and had to literally touch my way along with my hands. But now that I've got my bearings, the darkness is our best ally."

"But when looking against the fires of the farm, one ought to see quite clearly!"

"Not from the water; only from the river bank, since the former is lying deeper. In addition, the outlaws are sitting in a half circle with the river forming the diameter, and inside of it, not far from the water, are the prisoners..."

"What carelessness! The outlaws cannot possibly guard their prisoners effectively in such darkness. What if they succeed in ridding themselves of their fetters? It would then be easy for them to escape into the water since at least the two men would be able to swim."

"Nonsense! They have a special guard, one of the outlaws, who's keeping a keen eye on them."

"Hm! He must be removed. But how?"

"He'll be extinguished. There's no other way; it won't be a shame about the miscreant."

"Do you have a plan?"

"Yes, the prisoners don't need to go into the water. We'll move the boat out to them."

"The outlaws will see it, since it will be silhouetted against the shimmering waves."

"There's no shimmering! The water is so murky from yesterday's rain that it is indistinguishable from the solid ground, especially under the trees along the bank. We'll move the boat there and tie it up; you'll stay in the water with it, and I'll go on land by myself to give the guard the knife and cut the ties of the prisoners. I'll bring them to you; they'll paddle into the canal, where they're safe, and we'll make ourselves comfortable where they've been sitting before. When we give the signal, the vulture cry, the dance will begin immediately. Agreed?"

"Alright, there's no better way to do it."

"What about you, Uncle?"

"In the splendid manner that you've planned; Will be completed the task at hand," Gunstick-Uncle replied in his poetic way.

"Excellent, let's go!"

They untied the boat and pushed it out of the canal into the river. Droll, who knew the terrain, went ahead. The men kept close to the bank and moved along slowly and cautiously until Droll stopped, and the others behind him noticed that he had tied up the vessel.

"We've arrived," he whispered to them. "You wait until I return!"

The bank wasn't high in that spot. He quietly sneaked up the incline. Against the sheen of the fires that were burning beside the two wall corners on the other side of the bushes, he could see the outlined objects fairly clearly. Four people were sitting at the most ten paces away from the river bank, the three prisoners and their guard. Further back Droll saw the outlaws resting in all kinds of positions. Without putting his rifle down he kept crawling until he was behind the guard. Only then did he lay it on the ground and reach for his knife. The outlaw had to die without being able to make a sound. Droll pulled his knees up under his body, lunged at the man, grabbed a tight hold with his left hand on the man's throat from behind, and then pushed the blade into his back with the right, so that it cut through the heart. He dropped back down just as swiftly and pulled the outlaw beside

him on the ground. That had happened as fast as lightning, so
that the prisoners hadn't noticed anything at all. Some time
passed before the girl said:

"Pa, our guard has gone!"

"Really? Ah, yes; I'm surprised; but remain seated and don't
move; I don't doubt that he wants to put us to the test."

"Quietly, quietly!" Droll whispered to them. "No one must hear
a sound. The guard is lying dead in the grass; I've come to save
you."

"Save? Heavens! Impossible! You are the guard!"

"No, sir; I'm your friend. You know me from the Arkansas
River. I'm Droll, the one they call Aunty."

"My God! Is this true?"

"Quiet, sir, quiet! Old Firehand is also here, so are Black Tom
and many others. The outlaws wanted to plunder the farm; but
we've repelled them. We watched as they took you prisoner; I've
sneaked here with two other capable boys to get you out first. And
should you still not trust me, because you can't see my face, I'll
prove to you that I'm speaking the truth by untying you. Let me
have your fetters!"

A few cuts with the knife sufficed and the three people were in
full command of their liberated limbs again.

"Now we'll believe you, sir," the farmer whispered. He had been
silent up to that point. "You will see how I express my gratitude.
But where to now?"

"Quietly down into the dinghy. We've come through the canal
and brought the boat out. You'll climb in there with the little miss
and retreat into the canal, which you'll no doubt know, to wait
until the dance is over."

"The dance? What dance?"

"The one that's about to begin. The outlaws have the river here
on one side, and on the opposite side the wall, which are two
obstacles they cannot remove. Old Firehand is stationed to the
right with a number of rafters and hunters, and to the left the
Osage chief Great Sun with a host of warriors; they're all waiting
for my signal to attack. As soon as I'll give it, our people will know
that you're safe and will pounce upon the outlaws from the right
and the left. Being locked in by the river and the wall, the
scoundrels will at least suffer sufficient losses to dissuade them
from continuing their hostilities."

"Ah, that's how it is! And we're supposed to move to safety in
the boat?"

"Yes. The concern was that the outlaws would give you short shrift as soon as we attack. That's why we've come to get you out above all."

"That's as decent as it is daring of you, and you're deserving of our utmost gratitude; but do you really believe that my brother and I are such cowards that we'll stand by idly while you fight on our behalf and risk your lives? No, sir, you're mistaken there!"

"Hm, splendid! I like hearing that! It means we've gained two more men. Do as you please, in that case. But the little miss must not stay where the bullets will fly; we must at least take her away."

"Indeed. Please be so kind and take her to the canal in the boat! But what about weapons? Ours were taken from us. Couldn't you spare a revolver at least, or a knife?"

"That's not necessary, sir. We require what we've got; but here lies the guard, and his arsenal should suffice for one of you. I'll provide weapons for the other by sneaking up on the nearest outlaw, to...sh, quiet, there's one approaching! One of their leaders, no doubt, who wants to satisfy himself that you're well guarded. Let me handle it!"

Looking towards the fires, they were able to observe a man approach and inspect the ranks of the outlaws, to ensure all was well. He slowly walked closer, stood still in front of the prisoners and asked:

"Well, Collins, has anything happened?"

"No," Droll replied. The outlaw mistook him for the guard.

"Alright! Keep your eyes open! Your head will roll if you don't pay attention. Understood?"

"Yes. But my head is definitely attached much firmer than yours. Beware!"

He used the threatening remarks on purpose, and spoke them just as intentionally with an undisguised voice; he wanted the man to bend down to him. He achieved his objective. The outlaw came one step closer, indeed bent down and said:

"What are you thinking? What do you mean? Whose voice is this? Aren't you Collins, who..."

He couldn't finish his sentence because Droll clasped his hands around his throat like iron clamps, pulled him down entirely and squeezed his windpipe, so that the outlaw was unable to produce another sound. There was a short struggle wherein he kicked his legs; then all went quiet, until Droll whispered:

"So, he's brought you his weapons; that was decent of him."

"Do you have him secure?" the farmer asked.

"How can you ask? He's extinguished. Take his gun and everything else he's got on him; I'll take the little miss to the boat in the meantime."

Droll rose halfway, took Ellen Butler by the hand and led her down to the water where he informed his waiting companions of the situation. Bill and Uncle took the boat with the girl back into the canal where they tied the vessel up, and then waded back to join Droll and the two brothers Butler. The two men had armed themselves with the weapons of the dead outlaws in the meantime, and at that point Aunty Droll said in all earnest:

"Now it can begin. The fellows will undoubtedly come here immediately to seize the prisoners, which could become dangerous for us. Let's therefore crawl away a stretch, up to the right, to escape that."

The five men carefully moved along the river bank until they had found a suitable spot. There they rose and each stood behind a tree for cover. They were in complete darkness and saw the outlaws clearly in front of them for accurate aiming. That's when Droll placed his hand in front of his mouth and produced a short, tired squawk, as if made by a raptor that has momentarily woken from its sleep. The sound, so frequent in the prairie, couldn't arouse suspicion among the outlaws; they didn't pay any attention to it anyway, even when it was repeated twice. There was deep silence for a few moments; then, suddenly, Old Firehand's order resounded across the distance:

"Fire!"

To the right, the shots from the rifles of the rafters cracked; they had sneaked so close that each of them was able to aim at an individual outlaw. A moment later the ear-piercing, shrill war cries of the Indians arose. They sent their rain of arrows down onto the outlaws before charging them with their tomahawks.

"And now us!" Droll said. "First the bullets, and then upon them with the butts!"

A genuine, savage Western scene erupted. The outlaws had felt so completely safe that the sudden attack deeply shocked them. Initially they ducked like rabbits under the whooshing talons of an eagle, horrified and without resistance; then, when the attackers began to work among them with rifle butts, tomahawks, revolvers and bowie knives, the momentary paralysis fell away from them and they started to defend themselves. They were unable to count their adversaries; the fires only inadequately penetrated the surrounding darkness and caused the number of attackers to appear twice or thrice as large as it really was. That increased the outlaws' fear and fleeing seemed the only way to save themselves.

"Away, away to the horses!" someone yelled.

"That's the colonel," Droll hollered. "Upon him; don't let him get away!"

He rushed in the direction from which the shout had emanated, and others followed, but for naught. The red-haired colonel had been smart enough to immediately hide in the bushes and observe the scene from there. He slithered from bush to bush like a snake and kept to the dark shadows, so that he remained out of sight. The victors made every effort to let as few outlaws as possible get away, but there were so many that it was easy for them to break out, especially since they were smart enough to remain in a tight bunch. They ran away in a northerly direction.

"Keep going after them!" Old Firehand ordered. "Don't let them catch their breath!"

He meant to get to the outlaws' horses at the same time as they did, but that soon proved impossible. The further away they moved the more the light of the fires diminished, and in the end they were surrounded by utter darkness, so that they couldn't distinguish between friend and foe any longer. The former collided with each other and that held up the pursuit of the latter. Old Firehand was forced to call his men back; it was several minutes before he was able to assemble everyone, which gave the fugitives a head start that was impossible to make up, especially since the pursuers couldn't see them. Although Firehand's men kept going in the same direction, they soon heard the mocking and howling of the outlaws, and the hoof beats of horses racing away informed them that all effort was going to be in vain.

"Turn around!" Old Firehand ordered. "All that's left to do is to prevent the wounded outlaws from hiding, and then escaping later."

That was a superfluous concern. The Indians had not taken part in the pursuit. Greedy for the Whites' scalps, they had stayed back and thoroughly searched the battleground and the adjoining scrub right down to the river in order to kill and scalp any outlaws that were still alive.

When the corpses were counted in the torch light it turned out that there were more fallen adversaries, including those outlaws who had been killed during the day, than there were men on the victorious side; it was a terrible amount! In spite of that, the remaining outlaws, who had fled, numbered so many that congratulations were due the defenders for having successfully repelled them.

The men immediately fetched Ellen Butler from her hiding spot. The young girl hadn't been fearful at all, and had generally remained astonishingly calm and level-headed from the moment of the capture. When Old Firehand learnt of it, he said to the girl's father:

"Up to this moment I thought taking Ellen along to Silver-Lake would be very risky, but now I've got no more objections because I'm convinced she won't cause us any worries."

Since no one expected the outlaws to return, the rest of the night was dedicated to the victory feast, at least as far as the Indians were concerned. They received two steers that were slaughtered and the meat shared out, and soon the strong aroma of roasts came from the fires. Later the booty was distributed. The weapons and everything else the fallen outlaws had on them was left to the Indians, which delighted them. They expressed their joy in their traditional ways. Long speeches were given, and war and other dances performed. Only when day broke did the noise gradually die down; the cheers fell silent and the warriors wrapped themselves into their blankets to sleep, at last.

Not so the rafters. Fortunately none of them had been killed, but several were wounded. Old Firehand intended to follow the trail of the outlaws by daybreak to find out what direction they had taken. Hence the rafters, who were going to accompany Firehand, had gone to sleep in order to be rested and refreshed by dawn. They found that the trail led back to Osage-Nook, and they followed it right into the clearing; but when they arrived the place was empty. Old Firehand inspected it thoroughly and saw that more gangs of outlaws had arrived in the meantime; the fugitives had joined them and the combined host had without delay ridden away in a northerly direction, probably guessing that the pursuers would follow them to Osage-Nook. They had therefore given up their intention to attack the farm and were unaware that Old Firehand knew precisely what plan they were going to follow next.

Magister Doktor Jefferson Hartley

m611
Winnetou

Old Firehand

m611

5

At Eagle Tail

A man was walking across the prairie at a slow and tired pace; to see someone on foot where even the poorest devil owned a horse, since its upkeep didn't cost anything, was rare. Also, it was difficult to ascertain to which social stratum he belonged. He wore a city suit, which was very worn; yet it gave him the appearance of a peaceable man, whereby the old, mightily long firearm he carried over his shoulder didn't quite fit. His face was pale and gaunt, most likely as a consequence of the inevitable privations of a long march.

Occasionally he paused, as if to rest, but each time the hope of meeting people drove him to quickly recommence the exertion of his tired feet. Again and again he scanned the horizon, but always in vain, until at last his eyes lit up—he had spotted a man, also on foot, who was approaching from his right, which meant their paths would cross. It gave his limbs new energy; he lengthened his stride and soon saw that the other had noticed him, too, because he stood still and waited.

The other man was dressed in peculiar fashion. He wore a blue tailcoat with a red stand-up collar and yellow buttons, red velvet knickerbockers and tall boots with yellow leather tops. He had a blue silk neckerchief slung around his neck and tied at the front into a large, broad double bow that covered his entire chest. His head was covered with a broad-brimmed straw hat. On a strap over one shoulder he carried a small chest made from polished wood. The man was tall and skinny, with a cleanly shaven, sharply defined, gaunt face. Someone gazing into the small, sly eyes knew immediately that they were dealing with a genuine Yankee, who were known for their proverbial cunning.

When the man in the suit had approached to within earshot, the one who carried the chest lightly lifted his hat to greet the other:

"Good afternoon, friend! Where from?"

"From down Kinsley way," the man in the suit replied while he pointed behind him. "And you?"

"From everywhere. Last from the farm that lies behind me."

"And where are you headed?"

"Initially to the farm that lies ahead of us."

"Is there one?"

"Yes. We won't have to walk more than half an hour."

"God be thanked! I couldn't have gone on much longer!" the man from Kinsley said with a deep sigh. After having joined the other he also stopped, whereupon he was unsteady and swayed.

"Not gone on? Why?"

"Because of hunger."

"All devils! Hunger? Is that possible? Wait, I can help you with that. Sit down here on my box. You'll immediately have something to eat."

He placed the case on the ground, pushed the other down onto it, pulled two giant pieces of buttered bread from the chest pocket of his tail coat, and from the lower pocket a large piece of ham, handed both the bread and the meat to the hungry man while he said:

"Here, eat, friend! These aren't delicacies, but they'll suffice to sate your hunger."

The other hastily grabbed the food. He was so hungry that he wanted to put the bread into his mouth immediately; but he reconsidered, hesitated to lift his hand and said:

"You're very kind, sir, but these things are meant for you; if I eat them, then you'll go hungry."

"Oh, no! I'll get as much to eat on the next farm as I like, I can assure you of that."

"Are you known there?"

"No. I've never been in this region. But don't talk now, eat!"

The hungry man accepted the invitation; the Yankee sat in the grass and watched with delight as the bread quickly disappeared in large mouthfuls behind the man's healthy teeth. When the food had been eaten, he asked:

"You might not be completely full yet, but satisfied for the time being, yes?"

"I feel like a newly born, sir. Just think, I've been travelling for three days without having a single bite to eat."

"That's unthinkable! You haven't eaten anything from Kinsley to here? Why? Couldn't you take provisions with you?"

"No. My departure was a rather hasty one."

"Or call in somewhere along the way?"

"I've had to avoid the farms."

"Ah, so! But you've got a gun; surely you could have shot some game!"

"Oh, sir, I'm not a marksman. I'd sooner hit the moon than a dog that sits right in front of me."

"Then why the gun?"

"In order to frighten away any red and white outlaws."

The Yankee gave the man a probing look, and then said:

"Listen, mister, something isn't quite right with you. You seem to be on the run, and at the same time look like a very harmless subject. Where are you headed anyway?"

"To Sheridan and the railway."

"That's still far to go, and you're without provisions or other necessities! You could easily come a cropper in the process. You don't know me, but if one is in dire straits, it's good to trust someone. So, tell me what the problem is. Perhaps I can help you."

"That's told quickly enough. You're not from Kinsley, otherwise I'd know you, and therefore you cannot belong among my enemies, either. My name is Haller; my parents were German. They came over from the old country to better themselves, but were unable to make good. My life was no bed of roses, either. I was a jack-of-all-trades, until I became a railway clerk two years ago. I was last employed in Kinsley. Sir, I'm a fellow who couldn't hurt a worm, but if one gets insulted too much, one's blood begins to boil. There was an argument between the newspaper editor in Kinsley and me, which resulted in a duel. Just think, a duel with rifles! And I'd never before in my life held such a killing tool in my hands! A duel with rifles at a distance of thirty paces! My vision turned yellow and blue when I heard it. I'll make it short: the moment came, and we took up our positions. Sir, you can think of me what you like, but I'm a peaceful man and don't want to be a murderer. The thought alone, that I might kill my opponent, gave me goose flesh as rough as a rasp. Hence I aimed several feet to the side when the signal was given. I pulled the trigger, and so did my opponent. The shots were fired—imagine, I wasn't hit, but my bullet had gone straight through his heart. I held onto the gun, which wasn't mine, and ran away horrified. I say that the barrel of the gun is bent; the bullet travelled three feet too far to the left. But the worst aspect of it is that the editor had a large number of influential connections, which is of great significance here in the West. I had to flee immediately and only took the time to say a brief farewell to my employer. In order for me to continue earning a living, he gave me the advice to go to Sheridan and also handed me a letter of recommendation addressed to the engineer in that place. You can read it to satisfy yourself that I've spoken the truth."

He pulled a letter out of his pocket, opened it and gave it to the Yankee. Hartley read:

Dear Charoy,
With this letter I'm sending Mr Joseph Haller, my erstwhile railway clerk, to you. He is of German origin, an honest, loyal and diligent fellow, but has had the misfortune to shoot around the corner and because of it caused his opponent to expire. He must therefore leave this place for a while, and you would do me a favour if you could employ him in your office until the affair has been forgotten.
Yours sincerely,
Bent Norton

A seal had been affixed below the name for additional authentication. The Yankee folded the letter again, returned it to the owner, and with a half ironic, half contemptuous smile playing around his lips he said:

"I really believe you, Mr Haller, without having to see the letter. Anyone who takes a look at you and hears you talk would know that he's dealing with an absolutely honest person who wouldn't harm a fly on purpose. I feel exactly the way you do; I'm also not a great hunter and marksman before the Lord. That's not a flaw, because man doesn't live by powder and lead alone. But in your stead I wouldn't have been as fearful as that. I believe you've let them give you the shakes."

"Oh, no; the matter was really dangerous."

"Then you're convinced that someone has followed you?"

"Indeed! That's why I've avoided all farms thus far, so that no one is able to find out where I'm headed."

"And you're convinced that you'll be welcome in Sheridan and receive a job?"

"Yes, because Mr Norton is a close friend of Mr Charoy, the engineer in Sheridan."

"Well then, what sort of wages do you expect to be paid there?"

"I've been receiving eight dollars a week in Kinsley and think I'll be paid the same amount in Sheridan."

"Ah! I know of a position that pays that much again, sixteen dollars, plus free board for you."

"What? Really?" Haller rejoiced and jumped up. "Sixteen dollars? That could almost make me rich!"

"Perhaps not; but you can get some savings together."

"Where is the position to be had? With whom?"

"With me."

"With—you?" Haller asked with the sound of disappointment in his voice.

"Indeed. You probably don't believe I'm capable of employing you, eh?"

"Hm! I don't know you."

"I can immediately remedy that. I'm Magister Doctor Jefferson Hartley, physician and farrier in my own right."

"So, you treat people and horses?"

"I'm a doctor for people and for animals," the Yankee nodded. "If you like, you can become my famulus, and I'll pay you the wages I mentioned."

"But I don't know anything about it," Haller modestly explained.

"I don't either," the magister admitted.

"You don't?" the other was astonished. "But you must have studied medicine?"

"Wouldn't think of it!"

"But if you're a magister and also a doctor...!"

"I am that, indeed! I'm entitled to wear those titles and honours; I'm the best judge of that because I have awarded them to myself."

"You—yourself?"

"Of course! I'll be honest with you, because I think that you'll accept my offer. I'm actually a tailor; then I became a barber, and a dancing instructor after that; later I established an educational institute for young ladies; when that came to a close I grabbed the accordion and became a travelling musician. Since then I've excelled admirably in ten to twenty other professions. I have acquired an education about life and people, and this knowledge culminates in the understanding that a smart fellow mustn't be a numbskull. People want to be cheated; indeed, the biggest favour one can do them, for which they are extraordinarily grateful, is to pull the wool over their eyes. One must pander especially to their flaws, their mental and physical shortcomings and ailments, and I have therefore specialized in the latter and have become a physician. Here, have a look at my pharmacy!"

He unlocked the chest and lifted its lid back. The inside looked very elegant; it consisted of fifty compartments that had been lined with velvet and decorated with golden lines and arabesques. Each chamber contained a vial filled with a beautifully coloured liquid. There were all possible shades and nuances.

"So that's your pharmacy!" Haller said. "Where do you obtain the medicines?"

"I make them myself."

"I thought you said you don't know anything about it!"

"Oh, I understand that part, alright! It's child's play, really. What you see here is nothing but a small quantity of colour and a little bit of water, called *Aqua*. This word represents the sum total of my Latin. I've fabricated the rest of the names; they had to sound as beautiful as possible. Therefore you can read labels like: *Aqua salamandra, Aqua peloponnesia, Aqua chimborassolaria, Aqua invocabulataria*, and others. You wouldn't believe the kinds of cures I've already effected with these waters, and I don't blame you because I don't believe it myself. The main thing is that one doesn't wait for the effect, but instead pockets the doctor's fee and skedaddles. The United States is large, and many, many years might go by before I travel all the way around it; in the meantime I'll have become a rich man. Life costs nothing because everywhere I go, they give me more food than I can eat, and even fill my pockets when I leave. I don't have to be afraid of the Indians because, as a medicine man, I'm regarded as untouchable and sacred. Shake on it! Do you want to be my famulus?"

"Hm!" Haller grunted while he scratched behind his ear. "The matter seems dubious to me. It's not honest."

"Don't be ridiculous! Faith does everything. My patients believe in the effects of my medicine and become healthy because of it. Is that fraud? At least try it out the once! You've regained your strength now, and since the farm I'm headed for is on your way, you'll have no harm from it."

"Alright, I'll give it a try, out of gratitude; but I've no talent for fooling people."

"That's not necessary at all; I'll do that myself. You're to remain respectfully quiet, and your only work will consist of handing me the vial that I indicate from the case. Of course you must agree that I address you by your first name in the process. Let's get going!"

He hung the strap of the chest over his shoulder again, and then together with Haller walked towards the farm. After not quite half an hour they saw it from afar already; it didn't seem to be large. From that point onwards Haller had to carry the wooden chest since that wasn't befitting the principal, doctor and magister.

The main building of the farm was constructed from timber; along one side and in the back there was a well-tended orchard and vegetable garden. The public buildings were situated at some distance from the homestead. There were three horses tied to the hitching post, a sure sign that strangers were present. They were sitting in the parlour, and drinking some of the farmer's home brew. The strangers were alone because the farmer's wife was the only one home, and she was busy in the small stable. They saw the quack and his famulus arrive.

"Tarnation!" one of them exclaimed. "Am I seeing correctly? I ought to know him! If I'm not mistaken, then this is Hartley, the musician with the accordion!"

"An acquaintance of yours?" one of the other two asked. "Did you have business with him?"

"Of course. The fellow made good money and had his pockets full of dollars. Naturally I made just as good a deal by emptying them during the night."

"Does he know it was you?"

"Hm, probably. How fortuitous that I coloured my red hair black yesterday! Don't you go calling me Brinkley or colonel! The fellow could ruin our plans!"

It was evident from those remarks that he was the red-haired colonel. The bullet wound on his hand had barely healed over; he kept his hair long down either side of his head.

The two arrivals had reached the house just when the farmer's wife came from the stable. She greeted them politely and asked about their wishes. When she found out that she was looking at a physician and his famulus, she was very pleased, and invited them into the parlour while she opened the door.

"Gentlemen," she called inside. "Here comes a highly educated physician with his apothecary. I don't think the company of these two gentlemen will be a bother to you."

"Highly educated physician?" the colonel muttered to himself. "Impertinent fellow! I'd like to show him what I think of him!"

Hartley and Haller greeted those present, and without any fuss sat down at the same table. To his satisfaction, the colonel realized that Hartley hadn't recognized him. He passed himself off as a trapper and said that he was headed into the mountains with his two companions. Then, a conversation ensued while the hostess was busy on the hearth. Above it hung a pot in which lunch was cooking. When it was ready she went outside to the front of the house to call her family home, as was customary in that region, by way of blowing into the large tin dinner-horn.[1]

The farmer, a son, a daughter and a farmhand returned from nearby fields. They shook hands with their guests, especially the doctor, amid sincere friendliness, and then sat down to eat the meal; they said prayers before and after it. The members of the farmer family were plain, forthright and devout people who weren't a match for the cunning of a genuine Yankee, of course.

During the meal the farmer was fairly monosyllabic; afterwards he lit his pipe, put his elbows onto the table and expectantly said to Hartley:

"We must get back to the field shortly, doctor; but at this moment we've got a little bit of time to talk to you. I might perhaps call on your skills. With which diseases are you well-versed?"

"What a question!" the quack said. "I'm a physician and farrier and therefore cure the illnesses of humans and animals alike."

---

[1] Although the traditional noise maker, an iron triangle suspended from a chain, struck by an iron rod circling inside, is more widely known, Heinrich Lienhard's real-life account *From St. Louis to Sutter's Fort, 1846*, translated in 1961, also features a 'large tin dinner horn' to call the people of a wagon train to the meals or general assemblies. Lienhard's accounts were not published during May's lifetime.

"Alright, in that case you're the man I need. I hope you're not one of those travelling swindlers who have been everything and make all kinds of promises, but haven't studied anything?"

"Do I perchance look like such a scoundrel?" Hartley puffed himself up. "Would I have passed my doctor's and magister's exam if I weren't a learned man? Here sits my famulus. Ask him, and he'll tell you that thousands and thousands of people, not counting the animals, owe their health and life to me."

"I believe it; I believe it, sir! You have come at the right time. I've got a cow in the stable. You ought to know what that means. In this country, a cow only gets to be in a stable if it's very ill. The animal hasn't eaten in two days and hangs its head down to the ground. I deem it lost."

"Pshaw! I only regard a patient as lost when he's dead! The farmhand may show it to me; then I'll give you my opinion."

Hartley was shown to the stable, to examine the cow. When he came back he looked very serious and said:

"It was just in the nick of time, because the cow would have been dead by the evening. It ate henbane. Fortunately I have a sure remedy; the animal will be as healthy as before, by tomorrow morning. Bring me a bucket of water, and you, famulus, hand me the *Aqua sylvestropolia!*"

Haller opened the chest and picked out the relevant small bottle from which Hartley gave a few drops into the water. He instructed the people to administer two litres of the liquid to the cow every three hours. Then it was the human patients' turn. The wife had the beginnings of goitre and received *Aqua sumatralia.* The farmer suffered from rheumatism and was given *Aqua sensationia.* The daughter was as fit as a fiddle but was easily coerced into taking *Aqua furonia* for some freckles. The farmhand was limping somewhat, ever since he was a boy, but took the opportunity to get rid of the condition with *Aqua ministerialia.* Lastly, Hartley also asked the three strangers whether or not he could be of service to them. The colonel shook his head and replied:

"Thank you, sir! We're extremely healthy. And should I ever feel unwell, I'll help myself in a Swedish manner."

"How?"

"With physiotherapy. I'll have someone play a lively reel on the accordion and dance until I've worked up a sweat. That remedy is tried and tested. Understood?"

He gave Hartley a meaningful nod. The medical artisan was too shocked to speak and turned away from him to ask the farmer about the nearest farms. According to the information he received, the nearest one lay about a dozen kilometres west, and then there was one about twice as far to the north. When the magister explained that he'd immediately depart for the former, the farmer enquired about his fees. Hartley demanded five dollars and the people gladly paid immediately. Then he departed with his famulus, who shouldered the wooden box again. When they had gone far enough away from the farm so that they couldn't be observed from there any longer, he said:

"We've been walking west, but will now turn north, because I wouldn't think of going to the first farm; we'll go to the second one. The cow is so frail, it will probably die within the hour. If the farmer then comes by the idea to ride after me, I could fare badly. But isn't a meal and five dollars for ten drops of coloured water inviting? I hope you recognize your advantage and enter my employ!"

"Your hopes will be dashed, sir," Haller replied. "You're offering me quite a lot of money; but I'd also have to lie a lot. I don't mean to offend you! I'm an honest man and will remain that. My conscience does not permit me to accept your offer."

He said it with such sincerity and determination it made the magister realize that all further coaxing would be in vain. Hence Hartley shook his head with an expression of pity and said:

"I meant well. What a shame your conscience is so delicate!"

"I thank God that He hasn't given me a different one. Here is your box back. I would like to show my appreciation for your generosity, but I cannot; it is impossible."

"Alright! A man's free will is sacred; hence I'll cease to push. But we need not part immediately because of it. Your journey will stretch for another fifteen miles to the farm in question, so will mine, and we can stay together until then, at least."

He took possession of his wooden chest again. The silence into which he henceforth fell gave rise to the assumption that the righteousness of the railway clerk had made an impression upon him. And so they wandered side by side, and directed their eyes only to the front, until they heard hoof beats behind them. When they turned around, they spotted the three men they had met on the farm.

"Woe is me!" Hartley let slip. "This seems to have something to do with me. Those fellows were headed into the mountains! Why are they not riding west in that case? I don't trust them; they seem to be scoundrels, rather than trappers."

He would soon realise, to his chagrin, that he had guessed correctly. The riders stopped when they had caught up with the two wanderers, and the colonel sneered at the quack:

"Mister, why did you change your direction? Now the farmer won't find you."

"Find me?" the Yankee asked.

"Yes. After you left, I told him the truth about you and your beautiful titles, and he hastily took off to follow you and retrieve his money."

"Nonsense, sir!"

"It's not nonsense, it's the truth. He went over to the farm that you wanted to bless with your presence. But we were smarter. We know how to read tracks and followed yours to make you an offer."

"I wouldn't know what kind that could be. I don't know you and won't have anything to do with you."

"But we have business with you all the more. We know you. Because we tolerate that you cheat these honest farm folks, we've become your accomplices, which means it's only right and proper that you'll pay us part of your honorary. You're two people and we're three; therefore we're demanding three fifth of the amount. You can see that our actions are very just and reasonable. And should you not agree, then...well, look at my comrades!"

He pointed to the other two, who aimed their guns at Hartley. The quack deemed all further disagreement futile. He was convinced that he was dealing with highwaymen, and secretly rejoiced for having got off so cheaply. Hence he pulled three dollars from his pocket, held them up to the colonel and said:

"You seem to confuse me with someone else, and are in need of a part of my well-earned income. I'll take your demands as a joke and agree to them. Here are the three dollars, which, according to your calculations, are your portion."

"Three dollars? Are you bedevilled?" the colonel laughed. "Do you think we'd be riding after you for such a measly sum of money? No, no! I didn't just refer to the money you've taken today. We demand our cut of what you've earned in total. I'm assuming that you're carrying a nice sum of money around with you."

"That's not at all the case," Hartley exclaimed with trepidation.

"We'll see! Since you are lying I'm forced to examine you. I think that you'll admit to it calmly because my friends aren't joking with their guns. The life of a miserable accordion player isn't worth a dime to us."

He climbed from the horse and walked over to the Yankee. Hartley gave voice to all manner of remonstrations, to avert the looming disaster, but for naught. The gun barrels were staring at him so ominously that he surrendered to his fate. At the same time he secretly hoped that the colonel wasn't going to find anything, since he believed his cash was hidden very well.

The colonel with the black-coloured red hair inspected all pockets, but found only a few dollars. Then he proceeded to inspect the suit, feeling every little bit of the fabric to ascertain whether or not anything had been sewn into it. That was unsuccessful. At that point Hartley believed he had escaped danger, but the colonel was smart. He opened the wooden box and had a close look at it.

"Hm!" he grunted. "The entire apothecary chest is deeper than the compartments; they don't reach to the base. Let's see if they are removable."

Hartley grew pale, because the scoundrel was on the right track. Brinkley grabbed the compartment dividers with both hands, pulled—and the entire pharmacy lifted out of the box. Under it were several envelopes stashed crisscross. When Brinkley opened some of them he saw that they were full of banknotes of diverse denominations.

"Ah, that's where the hidden treasure is to be had," he merrily laughed. "I thought so! A physician and farrier earns a pretty penny; there had to be a few somewhere."

He reached into the box to pocket the money. That caused the Yankee to erupt with the greatest fury. He threw himself onto Brinkley to snatch the money from him. That's when a shot rang out. The bullet would certainly have gone through him had he not moved so fast; because of it, the projectile hit his upper arm only and smashed the bone. Hartley collapsed with a scream.

"Right so, you rogue!" the colonel exclaimed. "Dare to stand up or say a wrong word and the second bullet will hit more accurately than the first! Now let's inspect your famulus."

He placed the envelopes into his pocket and walked over to Haller.

"I'm not his famulus; I've only met him a short stretch before we arrived at the farm," Haller timidly explained.

"Oh? Who or what are you in that case?"

Haller answered the question truthfully. He even gave the colonel the letter of recommendation to read, in order to prove the veracity of his statement. Brinkley took no notice of the letter's content, returned it to Haller, and then disdainfully said:

"I believe you. Anyone who looks at you must immediately see that you're an absolutely honest fellow, but one who hasn't invented the wheel, either. Run to Sheridan for all I care; I've got no business with you." And addressing the Yankee again, he continued: "I spoke of our share; but since you've lied to us, you can't blame us for taking the lot. Strive to keep up the good deals. When we meet again, we'll be able to divvy it up much more precisely."

Hartley recognized that resistance was futile. He gave excuses, in an attempt at recovering at least some of the money, but his attempt only resulted in being laughed at. The colonel mounted up and rode north with his companions and the loot, proving that he wasn't a trapper and it had never been his intention to turn west into the mountains.

Along the way Brinkley and the other two outlaws discussed the adventure, laughed about it, and agreed to share the money without telling their comrades. After a lengthy ride they found a suitable place from which they could overlook the entire region, and where they could therefore not be observed, and dismounted to count the booty. When each of them had pocketed their share, one of the two other outlaws said to the colonel:

"You should have searched the other fellow as well. I would be surprised if he had no money."

"Pshaw! What could possibly be found with a poor clerk! A few dollars at the most, and that's not even worth the trouble."

"The question is whether or not he told the truth and he really was a railway clerk. What did the letter that he showed you say?"

"It was a letter of recommendation to the engineer Charoy in Sheridan."

"What? Really?" the man exclaimed. "And you returned it to him!"

"Yes. What good would the scrap of paper have been to us?"

"Much, very much! Must you ask? It's obvious that the letter would have aided our plans tremendously. It's almost baffling that you haven't realized it. We've left the others behind to secretly reconnoitre the situation first. We must get to know the locality and also the circumstances with the coffers, which is difficult enough because we must avoid being observed. Had we taken the letter off the man, then one of us could have ridden to Sheridan and pass himself off as the clerk; he would certainly have found employment in the office, gained access to the ledgers and would have been able to give us the necessary information after a day or two already."

"Tarnation!" the colonel uttered. "That's true. Why didn't I think of it? You in particular know how to handle a quill and could have played that role."

"And I would have played it properly. All difficulties would have been removed with that. There's perhaps still time to make amends!"

"Certainly! Of course there's still time! We know where the two fellows are headed; the farmer has given them directions and their route leads past here. We only have to wait for them to get here."

"Quite right; let's do that! But it's not enough to simply take the letter of the clerk. He'd go to Sheridan and spoil everything. We must therefore prevent him and the quack from doing so."

"That goes without saying. We'll give both a bullet in the head and dig them into the ground. You'll then go to Sheridan, try to espy all the necessary details, and then inform us of it."

"But when and how?"

"The two of us will ride back to the others and fetch them. You'll find us where the railroad crosses Eagle Tail. I can't give you more precise details. I'll place posts towards Sheridan. You're bound to find them."

"Splendid! But what if my departure arouses suspicion?"

"Hm, we have to take that into consideration. But you can work something out. Take Faller with you and tell them that you've met him along the way, and that he said he was looking for work on the railroad."

"Excellent!" the other outlaw agreed. His name was Faller. "I'll get work immediately, and if not, then it'll be even better because I can take the message to Eagle Tail straight away."

They discussed the plan further and agreed to execute it. Then they waited for the arrival of Hartley and his companion. But hours went by and no one came. The outlaws assumed that the two men had changed direction, so as not to encounter the three riders again. They decided to double back and follow the new trail.

When the outlaws had left the two men, the Yankee had first asked the clerk to apply a makeshift bandage. He had sustained a severe injury to his upper arm and was forced to find a place where he could find the necessary care for at least a few days. The nearest place was the farm they had wanted to visit next. But since the outlaws had travelled in the same direction, the Yankee said:

"Don't you think we're bound to come across them again? We must beware of the fact that they regret not having rendered us harmless, and will make up for it later, when we encounter them again. They have my money; but I wouldn't want to let them have my life as well. Let's find another farm!"

"Who knows how long it will take to find one," Haller said. "Will you be able to hold out on such a long walk?"

"I think so. I'm a strong fellow and will get there before wound fever sets in. In any case, I hope that you won't leave me in the meantime."

"Certainly not. And if you should collapse along the way, I'll find people who'll help me fetch you. But let's not waste time now. Where will we go?"

"North, like before, only slightly more to the right where the horizon is dark. There seems to be forest or some scrub growing, and where there are trees, there is water, which I need to cool my wound."

Haller picked up the wooden chest, and the two men left the fateful spot. The Yankee's assumption proved correct. After a while they reached a place where some water flowed between green bushes and they changed the bandage for the first time. Hartley poured all of his coloured water out and filled the vials with pure water, so that he was able to moisten the bandage as required along the way. Then they continued their walk.

They travelled across a prairie with such short grass that their footprints were hardly recognizable. The trained eye of a frontiersman was required to determine whether one or two men had made the trail. After a longer period of time, Hartley and Haller saw another dark streak on the horizon, which was a sign that they were approaching another wooded area. When the Yankee turned around coincidentally, he spotted three moving dots behind him. He was immediately convinced that they were the outlaws who were coming after them for a second time; it meant that they were in danger. Anyone else would have pointed the riders out to the clerk; but Hartley didn't do that. He doubled his pace, and when Haller asked about the sudden haste, he gave the first plausible excuse that came to his mind.

Riders are visible from further away than people on foot, of course. The distance between the outlaws and the two men was such that Hartley could assume they hadn't spotted him and his companion yet. That was the basis of the plan he began to shape for his salvation. He realized that resistance was going to be of no use. If the riders caught up with them, both would be lost. Only one of them had an opportunity to get away; but then the other had to be sacrificed, and that other one was going to be the clerk, of course. And Haller couldn't be permitted to find out what kind of danger was looming. Hence the cunning Yankee kept his mouth shut. Delivering his companion to ruination, since he would have been lost in any case, didn't in the least encumber Hartley's conscience.

And so they kept walking fast, on and on, until they reached the woods, which consisted of dense undergrowth, above which spread the canopies of individual hickory, oak, water elm, and walnut trees. The forest wasn't deep, but it stretched away into the distance to their right. When they had walked through it, and reached the other side, the Yankee stood still and said:

"Mr Haller, I've considered how much of a burden I must be for you. Because of me, you've deviated from your straight route to Sheridan. Who knows if and when we'll find a farm by walking in the present direction; you might have to bother with me for days, while there would be a very simple solution to make your self-sacrifice unnecessary."

"Oh? What would that be?" Haller asked innocently.

"You keep going, in God's name; and I'll return to the farm from which I came before we met today."

"I can't let you do that; it's too far."

"Not at all. I walked west initially, and then turned north together with you, having described a right angle by doing so. If I cut across it diagonally, I won't have to walk for more than three hours, and I'll be able to cope well for that amount of time."

"Do you think so? Alright; but I'll accompany you. I've promised not to leave you."

"And I must release you from that promise because I must not expose you to danger."

"Danger?"

"Yes. The wife of the farmer, so she told me, is the sister of the sheriff in Kinsley. If you're being followed from there, chances are a hundred to one that the sheriff will visit that farm. You'd walk straight into his arms."

"Of course I'll leave that be," Haller was aghast. "Do you really want to go there?

"Yes; it's best for me and also for you."

He depicted the advantages of the decision in such an honest and urgent manner, that the poor clerk finally agreed with the separation. They shook hands, wished each other well, and then parted company. Haller continued across the open prairie. Hartley kept observing him, and mumbled to himself:

"I ought to feel sorry for him; but there's no other way. If we had stayed together, then he would have been lost anyway, and I would have to die with him. But it's time for me to get going. Once they catch up with him and ask about me, he'll tell them where I am, over yonder to the right. I'll therefore hurry away to my left and find a place where I can hide."

He was no hunter or trapper; but he knew that he couldn't leave any tracks behind. He had also occasionally heard others describe how tracks were wiped. As he pushed into the bushes, he chose spots on the ground that didn't take any footprints. Whenever there was one noticeable, he wiped it with his hand. His injury was a hindrance, of course, and so was his wooden chest, of which he had again taken possession. He made only slow progress, but fortunately came upon a group of bushes soon, which were too dense to look through. He worked himself inside, placed the box on the ground and sat on it. Not long after he had done so, he heard the voices of the three riders and the horses' hoof beats. They rode past without noticing that the trail had reduced to only one set of footprints on the other side of the woods.

The Yankee parted the branches in the relevant direction; he could see right out into the prairie. Haller was walking out there. The outlaws spotted him and drove their horses into a gallop. The clerk heard them, turned around and stopped in his tracks. Soon the outlaws reached him; they talked to him; he pointed east, no doubt to tell them that the Yankee had gone back to the farm in that direction. Then Hartley heard the cracking shot of a pistol and saw Haller collapse.

"It's done," Hartley mumbled. "Just you wait, you scoundrels! Perhaps we'll cross paths once again, and then you'll pay for that shot! I'm curious to see what they'll do next."

He observed that they dismounted and inspected the dead man. Then they stood there for a while, discussing something, until the colonel loaded the corpse across the front of his saddle, and they mounted their horses again. To the amazement of the Yankee, he was the only one who returned, while his two companions rode on. When the colonel reached the undergrowth, he forced his horse into it for a stretch, and then dropped the body. There it lay, so that it couldn't be seen from outside the bushes, not far from Hartley. After that, the rider pulled his horse back and rode away; Hartley couldn't see in which direction he went, but heard the hoof beats for a while longer, and then silence fell.

Hartley was seized with horror. He almost regretted not having warned Haller. He had become the witness to the terrible deed; the corpse lay almost next to him, and he would have liked to get away but didn't dare to move because he had to assume that the colonel was still looking for him. Half an hour passed before he decided to leave the horrible place. Before he did, he looked out onto the prairie one more time, and saw something that prompted him to remain in his hiding place for a while longer.

A rider, who was leading a second horse next to his, came across the prairie from the right. He encountered the trail of the two outlaws and dismounted to investigate it. After he had carefully looked in all directions he bent down to inspect the tracks. Then he walked back along the trail, while the horses followed him of their own accord, to the spot where the murder had taken place. He stopped there to have a close look at the ground. It took some time before he rose from his crouched position and continued walking towards the stand of trees. While he was focussing on the ground, he was following the colonel's single trail. He stopped about fifty paces away from the woods, produced a peculiar guttural sound and with his arm pointed to the bushes. That seemed to be meant for his horse, because it left him, approached the edge of the undergrowth in a wide curve, and then walked along it, while it drew the air into its flared nostrils. And since there was no sign of trouble, the rider felt satisfied and walked closer as well.

At that point the Yankee saw that he was facing an Indian. The latter wore fringed leggings, a hunting shirt decorated with fringes as well as embroidery along the seams, and moccasins on his feet. His long, black hair had been gathered up in a helmet-like shape, but was not adorned with eagle feathers. A triple necklace of bear claws hung from his neck, as well as the peace pipe and the medicine pouch. In his hand he held a double-barrelled rifle, the wooden stock of which was studded with many silver tacks. His near-Roman facial features were of a velvet light brown with a faint hue of bronze, and only the slightly raised cheekbones pointed to the Native American race.

The close proximity of an Indian was bound to fill the Yankee, who wasn't born to be a hero, with dread. But the longer he looked into the face of the Indian, the more he realized that he didn't have to be afraid of the man, who had approached to within perhaps twenty paces. The horse at the front had come even closer, while the other was behind the Indian. It lifted its dainty front leg to take the next step—and reared to back away with a loud, conspicuous snort. The animal had obviously detected the scent of either the Yankee or the corpse on a draft of air. The Indian at once executed a veritable panther leap to the side and disappeared from sight, and with him the second horse as well. Hartley couldn't see them any longer.

The Yankee remained motionless and quiet for a long, long time, until he heard a suppressed "Uff!" from a different direction. When he turned his head to that side, he saw that the Indian had knelt down beside the corpse of the clerk to inspect it visually, as well as with his hands. When he was finished, the Indian withdrew and remained out of sight for another quarter of an hour. Then, suddenly, Hartley was startled by a voice right next to him:

"Why is the paleface hiding here? Why are you not coming out to show yourself to the red warrior? Do you perhaps refuse to say where the three murderers of the other paleface have gone?"

When Hartley jerked his head around to that side, he saw the Indian crouch next to him with a shiny bowie knife in his hand. The man's remarks revealed that he had read the tracks correctly, and had astutely judged them. He didn't think Hartley was the murderer; that calmed the Yankee. He replied:

"I hid from them. Two went away, into the prairie; the third threw the corpse in here. And I stayed in here because I don't know whether he's gone or not."

"He's gone. His trail leads back through the scrub, and then eastwards."

"That means he's gone to the farm to chase after me. But is he really not around any longer?"

"He's left. My white brother and I are the only living human beings in this place. You can come outside now and tell me what happened."

The Indian spoke English very well. He won the Yankee's trust with what he said and how he said it; hence Hartley didn't hesitate to comply with the request. When he had crawled out of the thicket, he saw the horses tied up a fair stretch further away.

The Indian looked at the White with a gaze that seemed to be able to penetrate everything, and then said:

"Two men were walking here from the south; one hid here, and that's you; the other continued on, into the prairie. That's when three riders came, who followed the other; they shot a pistol bullet into his head. Two rode away. The third put the corpse onto his horse, rode here, threw it into the scrub, and then galloped away eastwards. Is it so?"

"Yes, just like that," Hartley nodded.

"Then tell me why they shot your white brother. Who are you, and why are you in this region? Did the three men also injure your arm?"

The friendly tone in which the Indian couched his query proved to the Yankee that the man was well disposed towards him. Hartley answered the questions that were put to him. The Indian didn't look at him while he spoke; but then, with an unexpectedly penetrating gaze, he asked:

"Then your comrade paid for your life with his?"

The Yankee lowered his eyes and almost stammered:

"No. I asked him to hide with me; but he didn't want to."

"Did you show him the murderers, who were approaching from behind?"

"Yes."

"And also told him that you wanted to hide here?"

"Yes."

"Why did he then point to the farm in the east when they asked him about you?"

"To fool them."

"In that case he wanted to save you and was a brave comrade. Were you worthy of him? Only Great Manitou knows everything; my gaze cannot enter your mind. If it could, you might have to be ashamed. I will be silent; your God may be your judge. Do you know me?"

"No," Hartley meekly said.

"I am Winnetou, the chief of the Apache. My hand is raised against the villainous, and my arm protects anyone who has a clear conscience. I'll see to your injury; but finding out why the murderers have turned around to follow you is of even greater importance. Do you know the reason why?"

Hartley had often heard of Winnetou. And since the Indian had just stated that he was the famous chief, the Yankee replied twice as politely:

"I have already told you. They wanted to do away with us, so that we couldn't reveal they had robbed me."

"No. If it had been for that reason alone, they would have killed you both immediately. There must have been something that occurred to them later. Did they search you thoroughly?"

"Yes."

"And have taken everything from you? From your friend also?"

"No. He told them that he was a poor fugitive, and proved it to them by showing them the letter."

"A letter? Did they keep it?"

"No; they gave it back to him."

"Where did he put it?"

"In the chest pocket of his coat."

"It's no longer there. I've searched all pockets of the dead man and have not found a letter; they have taken it from him here. It was therefore the letter that prompted them to turn around and catch up with you."

"Hardly!" the Yankee shook his head.

The Indian didn't reply to that. He pulled the corpse out of the scrub and inspected the pockets one more time. The dead man looked dreadful, not because of the bullet wound, but because the outlaws had cut his face crisscross, so that he had become unrecognizable. The pockets were empty. Of course the villains had also taken Haller's gun.

Winnetou gazed pensively into the distance; then he said with firm conviction:

"Your comrade wanted to go to Sheridan; two of the murderers rode north, towards that place; they wanted to go there, too. Why did they take the man's letter? Because they need it, they want to use it. Why did they disfigure the face of the dead man? So that he was not recognizable. No one is to know that Haller is dead; he must not be dead, because one of the murderers is going to pass himself off as Haller in Sheridan."

"But for what purpose?"

"I don't know, but will find out."

"Then you'll go there, as well, after them?"

"Yes. I was headed for Smoky Hill River, and Sheridan lies near it; if I ride to that place, then my way won't become any longer. The palefaces are planning to carry out something evil in Sheridan. Perhaps I will be able to foil their plans. Will my white brother accompany me?"

"I wanted to visit a close-by farm to treat my arm. Of course I would prefer to go to Sheridan. I might perhaps recover my money there."

"Then you'll ride with me."

"But my wound!"

"I'll examine it. Although you will find care on a farm, there will be no physician; in Sheridan, however, there will be one. Winnetou also knows how to treat injuries. I can set splintered bones and have an excellent remedy against wound fever. Show me your arm now!"

The railway clerk had already cut open the sleeve of the Yankee's tailcoat; hence it wasn't difficult for Hartley to bare his arm. Winnetou examined it and explained that the wound wasn't as bad as it seemed. Because the bullet had been fired at such a close range, it had not splintered the bone, but had gone straight through it. The Indian went to fetch a dried plant from his saddlebag, moistened it and placed it onto the wound. Then he cut two wooden splints and with their aid bandaged the arm more skilfully than even a surgeon would have been capable of, with the means at hand. Then he explained:

"My brother can safely ride with me. The fever won't come, or only once he's already in Sheridan."

"But won't we first try to find out what the third of the three murderers is doing?" Hartley asked.

"No. He's searching for you, and if he doesn't find your trail, he'll turn around and follow the other two. But perhaps he won't do that, for he might have other allies nearby, whom he'd visit before riding to Sheridan. I've just come from inhabited regions and have learnt that many palefaces, who are called outlaws, are gathering in Kansas. It is possible that the murderers belong to those people, and that the outlaws are planning an attack on Sheridan. We mustn't waste any time; we must go quickly and warn the palefaces who live there."

"But won't the third outlaw find our tracks when he returns here, and deduce from them that we've followed his friends? Won't he become suspicious then?"

"We won't follow them. Winnetou knows where they're going and doesn't need their trail. We'll ride a different route."

"And when will we get to Sheridan?"

"I don't know how well my brother can ride."

"Ah, I'm not a trick rider, of course. I've not been sitting in a saddle much; but I won't let a horse throw me."

"Then we mustn't ride at a stretched gallop; but we'll make up for it with constancy. We will ride through the night, and will be at our destination in the morning. Those we're pursuing will make camp during the night, and therefore arrive after us."

"And what will happen to poor Haller's corpse?"

"We'll bury it, and my brother may say a prayer."

The ground was soft, and although they only had knives to use, they had soon dug an acceptably deep hole. After they had laid the dead man into it, they covered him up with the excavated soil. Then the Yankee took his hat off and folded his hands. But it was doubtful that he was praying at all. The Apache solemnly looked into the sinking sun. It was as if his gaze was seeking the Eternal Hunting Grounds on the far side of west. He was a heathen, but he was most certainly praying. Then they went to the horses.

"My white brother will ride my animal," the Indian said. "It has a soft gait, even and level like a canoe in the water. I'll ride the spare horse."

They mounted up and rode away in a westerly direction initially, and then turned north. The two horses had probably already travelled a long way, but strode out as lively and fresh as if they had been out to pasture for a few days. The sun kept sinking lower, and then it disappeared behind the horizon at last; the short dusk passed swiftly, and soon it became dark as night descended. That unsettled the Yankee.

"Won't you get lost in this darkness?"

"Winnetou never loses his way, neither by day nor by night. He's like a star that's always in the right place, and he knows all the regions of the country as precisely as a paleface knows the rooms in his house."

"But there are so many obstacles that one cannot see!"

"Winnetou's eyes can see by night as well. And that which he cannot see will certainly not escape his horse. My brother will ride behind me, not beside me, so that his horse won't take a wrong step."

The confidence with which horse and rider were moving was truly miraculous. They were travelling at walking pace one moment, then at a trot or often even at a gallop the next, and thus kept going hour after hour, evading any and all obstacles. There were swampy places they had to avoid, and then wade through creeks. They went past farms. Winnetou always knew where he was and not one moment did he seem to be in doubt. The Yankee was greatly relieved by this. He had been especially worried about his injured arm; but the medicinal herb was of extraordinary efficacy. He almost felt no pain at all and had nothing to complain about except the discomfort of the unusual ride. They stopped a few times to let the horses drink, and to moisten the bandage with cool water. After midnight Winnetou unwrapped a piece of meat, which Hartley had to eat. There was no other interruption, and when the increasing chill announced the morning, the Yankee realized that he was quite capable of staying in the saddle for a bit longer.

Morning dawned in the east, yet the contours of the terrain were still not recognizable because a thick fog lay on the ground.

"This is the fog of the Smoky Hill River," the chief explained. "We will soon reach it."

It was evident by his voice that he had wanted to say something else, but he stopped his horse and listened towards his left hand side, from which the sound of rhythmical hoof beats approached. It had to be a rider travelling at a gallop. Correct! There he came and flew past, *ventre a terre*—lightning fast, like a phantom. The two had not been able to see him, or his horse; only his broad-brimmed hat had been visible for a moment above the dense drifts of fog that were crawling along the ground. A few seconds later the hoof beat was no longer audible.

"Uff!" Winnetou called out in surprise. "A paleface! There are only two white men who can ride like this man rode, namely Old Shatterhand, but he isn't here because I plan on meeting him at Silver-Lake; the second is Old Firehand. Could he perchance be in Kansas at this time? Could that have been him?"

"Old Firehand?" the Yankee remarked. "That's a very famous frontiersman."

"He and Old Shatterhand are the best, most courageous, and most experienced palefaces Winnetou knows. He is their friend."

"The man seemed to ride with some urgency. Where might he be headed?"

"To Sheridan, because his direction is also ours. Eagle Tail is to our left and the ford that leads across the river is right ahead of us. We will reach it in a few minutes. And in Sheridan we will find out who the rider was."

The fog began to separate; the shreds were driven apart by the morning wind, and soon the two men saw Smoky Hill River in front of them. Again the Apache's extraordinary sense of direction came to the fore. He reached the banks at exactly the position of the ford. The water hardly reached to the horses' bellies, so the crossing was easy and without danger.

When they arrived on the other side, the riders had to pass through some scrub that extended along the river bank; then they were able to ride across open grassland again, until they spotted their destination.

At that time, Sheridan was neither a city nor a settlement, but rather a temporary camp for the railway workers. There were a number of stone, earthen, and log cabins: very primitive buildings, some of them with the most ostentatious inscriptions above their door lintels. There were hotels and saloons in which not even the lowliest worker would have wanted to dwell, had they been located in Germany. There were also a number of more elegant timber constructions that could be dismantled at any time and reassembled somewhere else. The largest of them stood on an elevation and had affixed to it the very visible signage of 'Charles Charoy, Engineer'. The two riders went there; they dismounted outside the door where a horse with Indian saddle and tack was tied up.

"Uff!" Winnetou remarked as he looked at it with a glowing gaze. "This horse is worthy of carrying a good rider. It must surely belong to the paleface who rode past us."

They also tied their horses to the hitching post. There was no one nearby; and because of the early hour, when they looked over the encampment they could see only three or four people, who were checking the weather. But the door was open, and they entered. A young Negro welcomed them and asked what they wished. Even before they were able to give an answer, a door to their side opened and a young white man walked out of the room. He was the engineer, and he looked at the Apache with a friendly, surprised gaze. His name, brown skin tone and dark, wavy hair indicated that he was the descendant of a French family from the southern states.

"Whom are you looking for so early, gentlemen?" he asked while he bowed respectfully to the Indian.

"We're looking for the engineer, Mr Charoy," Winnetou replied in fluent English, whereby he even pronounced the French name correctly.

"I am Charoy. Please enter."

He returned to the room, and the two arrivals followed him. The room was small and furnished plainly. The writing utensils on the desk led to the assumption that it was the engineer's office. He moved two chairs towards the visitors and with visible curiosity waited for them to tell him what they had come to report. The

Yankee immediately sat down; the Indian remained standing politely, lightly bowed his beautiful head in a gesture of greeting, and said:

"Sir, I'm Winnetou, the chief of the Apache..."

"I know already, I know already!" the engineer cut in hastily.

"You already know, sir?" the Indian asked. "Have you seen me before?"

"No; but there's someone here who knows you, and saw you arrive when he looked through the window. I'm very pleased to make the acquaintance of the famous Winnetou. Sit down, and tell me what leads you to me; afterwards I'll ask you to be my guest."

The Indian sat down on the chair and replied:

"Do you know a paleface who lives in Kinsley and goes by the name of Bent Norton?"

"Yes, I know him very well. The man is one of my best friends," Charoy replied.

"And do you also know the paleface Haller, his clerk?"

"No. Since my friend has moved to Kinsley I haven't been to visit him."

"That clerk will visit you today with another White, to deliver a letter of recommendation to you from Norton. You are going to be asked to employ Haller in your office, and also give the other man a job. But if you do that, you will be in grave danger."

"What danger?"

"I don't know yet. The two palefaces are murderers. If you are a smart man, you will guess their intentions as soon as they have spoken to you."

"Perhaps to murder me?" Charoy smiled, but with scepticism.

"Perhaps!" Winnetou nodded with a serious expression. "And not only you, but also others. I think they are outlaws."

"Outlaws?" the engineer hastily asked. "Ah, that's another matter. I've just found out that a horde of outlaws is travelling to Eagle Tail and to this place, to rob us. Those fellows are after our coffers."

"Who told you that?"

"It was...but, maybe I had best introduce the man to you, and not just give you his name."

Charoy's face beamed from the delight of being able to give the Indian a pleasant surprise. He opened the door to a side room, and out came—Old Firehand. If the engineer had been under the impression that the Indian would break into expressions of delight, then he wasn't familiar with the habit of the Indians. No red warrior will conspicuously voice either his joy or his pain in the presence of others. Although the eyes of the Apache shone, he remained calm otherwise; he walked up to the hunter and extended his hand. Firehand pulled him to his chest, kissed him on both cheeks and with a tone of joyful emotion said:

"My friend, my dear, dear brother! I was tremendously surprised and delighted when I saw you arrive and dismount! It's been a very long time since we saw each other last!"

"I saw you at dawn today when you raced past us in the sea of fog on the other side of the river," the Indian replied.

"And you didn't call out to me?"

"The fog enveloped you, so that I was unable recognize you clearly, and you had gone past like a storm wind."

"I had to ride fast in order to get here ahead of the outlaws. Besides, I needed to undertake this ride myself, because the matter is so important that I didn't want to entrust it to someone else. There are more than two hundred outlaws on the advance."

"That means I wasn't mistaken. The murderers are their scouts."

"May I know what's behind the story with the two men?"

"The chief of the Apache is not a man of many words, but of action. Here is a paleface who will explain everything precisely."

He pointed to Hartley, who had risen from his chair upon Old Firehand's entrance, and was still staring at the tall man with astonishment. Indeed, they were heroes, Old Firehand and Winnetou! The Yankee felt utterly small and pathetic, and the engineer probably experienced a similar feeling; at least his face and his respectful bearing pointed to it.

Hartley recounted the events of the previous day, after everyone had sat down again. When he finished, Old Firehand reported, though as briefly as possible, about his encounter with the red-haired colonel on the steamer, among the rafters, and then on Butler's farm. Afterwards he asked Hartley to describe the leader of the three men, the one who had shot the clerk, and who had then separated from the other two. When the Yankee succeeded to deliver a fairly accurate image of the person, the hunter said:

"I'll bet that was the colonel. He dyed his hair dark. I hope I'll get my hands on him at last!"

"And then he'll hopefully lose his appetite for such pranks!" the engineer angrily said. "More than two hundred outlaws! That would have resulted in a dreadful killing and burning! Gentlemen, you're our saviours, and I don't know how to thank you! Somehow the colonel must have found out that I collect the money for a long stretch of railroad, and then distribute it among the colleagues for payment of wages and expenses. Now that I'm forewarned let him come here with his outlaws: we'll be prepared."

"Don't feel too secure!" Old Firehand warned. "Two hundred desperate fellows are a force to be reckoned with!"

"Maybe; but I can amass a thousand railroad workers within several hours."

"Who are well armed?"

"Each of them has some kind of firearm. And in the end the knives, spades and shovels will do as well."

"Spades and shovels against two hundred guns? That would result in a blood bath for which I wouldn't want to be responsible."

"Alright, in that case I will readily receive up to two hundred soldiers from Fort Wallace."

"With all due respect to your courage, sir; but cunning is always better in such a case than force. If I can render an enemy harmless by a ruse, why should I sacrifice so many human lives?"

"What ruse do you mean, sir? I'll gladly do what you suggest. You're a different kind of fellow than I am, and if you'd like, I'd be prepared to immediately hand over the command of this place and my people to you."

"Not so fast, sir! We must consider the matter. First of all, the outlaws mustn't suspect that you've been warned. Neither must they know that we're here, or see our horses. Is there a hiding place for the animals?"

"I can let them disappear immediately, sir."

"But so that we can easily get to them?"

"Yes. Fortunately you've arrived here so early that none of the workers has been able to see you. The outlaws could otherwise find out about your arrival here, from them. My Negro assistant, who's loyal and discrete, will hide the horses well and look after them."

"Alright, please instruct him to do so! And you must personally take care of Mr Hartley. Give him a bed to lie down. But no one must know of his presence, except you, the Negro and the physician; I gather there's a doctor here?"

"Indeed. I'll send for him immediately."

Charoy left with the Yankee, who gladly followed him since he was beginning to feel exhausted. When the engineer returned after a while, to report that the injured man and the horses were well taken care of, Old Firehand said:

"I wanted to avoid a discussion in the presence of the quack because I don't trust him. There's a dark point in his tale. I'm convinced that he sent the poor clerk to his death on purpose, to save himself. I want nothing to do with such people. Now we are among ourselves and know that each can trust the other."

"Does that mean you'll reveal a plan to us?" the engineer asked with keen interest.

"No. We can only develop a plan once we know that of the outlaws, and that won't happen until the scouts have arrived here and have spoken to you."

"You're right. We must therefore be patient for the time being."

At that point Winnetou lifted his hand to signal that he had a different opinion and said:

"Every warrior can fight in two different ways; he can attack or defend himself. If Winnetou doesn't know how he would be able to defend himself, if at all, then he'd rather attack. That's faster, safer and also braver."

"Then my red brother doesn't want to know anything about the plan of the outlaws?" Old Firehand asked.

"I will definitely learn of it; but why should the chief of the Apache be forced to act according to their plan if it is easy for him to force them to follow his?"

"Ah, you've already got a plan?"

"Yes. It came to me during the ride this past night, and became complete when I heard what crimes the outlaws had committed beforehand. These creatures are no warriors who fight honestly, but mangy dogs that must be bludgeoned to death with cudgels. Why should I wait for such a dog to bite me when I can kill it beforehand with one strike or strangle it in a trap?"

"Do you know such a trap for the outlaws?"

"I do, and we'll build it. These coyote are coming here to rob the money box. If that box is here, then they'll come here; if it is somewhere else, then they'll go there, and if the box is in the wagon of the iron horse, then they'll climb inside and drive to their ruination without having harmed the people here in the least."

"Ah, I'm beginning to understand!" Old Firehand exclaimed. "What a plan! Only Winnetou could think of something like that! Are you saying that we ought to lure the fellows onto a train?"

"Yes. Winnetou knows nothing of the iron horse or how it is driven. I gave you the thought, and my white brothers can think about it."

"Lure them onto a train?" Charoy asked. "But what for? We can wait for them here and destroy them out in the open!"

"Whereby many on our side would have to die!" Old Firehand replied. "But if they get on the train, then we can transport them to a place where they have to surrender without being able to cause us any harm."

"They wouldn't think of getting aboard!"

"They'll get in if we lure them in with the coffer."

"Do you want me to put the strongbox onto train?"

That was an unexpected question from the intelligent-looking engineer. Winnetou made a disparaging gesture with his hand, but Old Firehand said:

"Who would expect that of you? The outlaws only have to be convinced that the money is on the train. You'll hire the scout as your clerk and pretend to trust him. You'll inform him that a train will stop here that carries a great amount of money. The outlaws will certainly all come here and cram into the cars. Once they're inside, they'll be moved away from here."

"That doesn't sound bad at all, sir, but it won't be as easy as you think."

"Oh? What difficulties could there be? Don't you have a train at your disposal for this purpose?"

"Oh, as many cars as you like! And I'll also gladly shoulder the responsibility, if only I could vaguely believe in the success of the undertaking. But there are other questions. Who shall drive the train? The outlaws will most certainly shoot at least the engineer, if not the fireman and the brakeman as well."

"Pshaw! We'll find an engineer, and I'll be the fireman. I think that if I volunteer for it, then I'll prove that there's no danger. We'll discuss the details later; the main thing is that we won't have to wait for too long. I suspect that the outlaws will arrive at Eagle Tail today, because that's where they're headed first. Therefore we can determine the time of the attack as being tomorrow night. Furthermore it will be necessary to specify a place where we can drive the fellows. We'll have to find one in the morning, because the scouts will be arriving in the afternoon. Do you have a handcar available, sir?"

"Of course."

"Alright, in that case you and I will drive together. Winnetou cannot accompany us; he must remain hidden; otherwise his presence will reveal our intentions. I must not be recognizable as

Old Firehand, either; I've anticipated it and have therefore brought along the old linen suit, which I carry with me on all my travels just in case."

Charoy looked increasingly embarrassed and said:

"Sir, you're talking about the matter like a fish about swimming. But it doesn't look easy and straightforward to me at all. How do we notify the outlaws? How will we get them to do exactly what we want them to?"

"What a question! The new clerk will sound you out, and everything you tell him, he will secretly relay to them as being the truth."

"Alright then! But what if they get the idea not to board the train? What if they prefer to lift the rails somewhere along the track to derail it?"

"You can easily prevent this by telling the clerk that a security locomotive will travel ahead of any such important money transport. Then they'll put aside any thought of destroying the tracks. If you're smart, everything will go well. You must keep the clerk busy, and befriend him, so that he doesn't get the chance to leave the building and talk to anyone else until it's time to retire. Then you'll allocate him the chamber in the attic, which has only one window. The flat roof is about one foot above it; I'll climb up and will hear every word that's spoken."

"Do you think he'll be talking out of the open window?"

"Indeed. The one who's posing as Haller will sound you out, and the one who is accompanying him will be the messenger. There's no other possibility; you'll soon find out. The other outlaw will also ask for work in order to be able to stay around, but won't take it for some reason, so that he can leave the place at will. He'll attempt to talk to the clerk to receive news, but cannot get to him before bedtime. Then he'll sneak around the house; the clerk will open the window, and I'll be lying above it and hear everything that's spoken. Of course, all of this will still seem very difficult and adventurous to you, because you're no Westerner; but once you've tackled the matter you'll find out that it will become second nature to you."

"Howgh!" the Indian agreed. "My white brothers will now go and find a place where the trap can be shut. When you return I'll leave, so that I won't be seen here."

"Where will my brother go in the meantime?"

"Winnetou is at home everywhere, in the forest and on the prairie."

"No one knows that better than I; but the chief of the Apache can find company if he wishes. I've ordered my rafters, and the hunters in their company, to a place an hour's ride away from here, below Eagle Tail. They're to observe the outlaws there. Aunty Droll is among them."

"Uff!" the Apache exclaimed, while his otherwise serious face attained a bemused expression. "Aunty Droll is a good, courageous and smart paleface. Winnetou will visit him."

"Splendid! My red brother will find other capable men in that company: Black Tom, Humply-Bill, Gunstick-Uncle. These are names you've at least heard before. But in the meantime you'll come with me and will wait in my chamber until we get back."

The engineer had allocated a chamber to Old Firehand prior to the arrival of the Apache; that's where the hunter went, together with Winnetou, in order to exchange his conspicuous trapper outfit for the linen suit. The railway crew would thus take him for a newly hired fellow worker. They weren't to know immediately that something unusual was in the making. The handcar was ready within a short time. Old Firehand and Charoy sat on the seats up front, and two workers took up their positions over the wheels where they began to operate the hand-levers. The vehicle rolled through the place, where everyone was busy by that time, and then out onto the open track, which was already connected to Kit Carson[2].

The Apache made himself comfortable in the meantime; he had been riding all night and didn't waste the opportunity to get some sleep. After the two men returned they woke him and informed him that Firehand had found a very suitable place. Winnetou nodded with satisfaction when he heard the description, and then said:

"That's good! The dogs will quiver from fear and howl in panic. It will be a relief for them to fall into our hands. Winnetou will now ride to Aunty Droll and let him and the rafters know that they have to get ready."

So as not to be spotted he sneaked away from the house in secrecy, to where his horses were hidden.

The astute chief hadn't been mistaken with regard to the arrival of the two scouts. As soon as the lunch break was over, two riders came from the direction of the river. Thanks to Hartley's description there could be no doubt that they were the two expected men.

---

[2] Connection occurred some time after June, but before 15 August, 1870

Old Firehand hurriedly went to see the Yankee, who was sleeping but gladly rose to ascertain that the two riders were the men in question. After he had positively identified them, Old Firehand went to the room next to the office, so that he could be witness to the conversation. During the drive on the draisine, he had won the engineer over to his plan and had explained it so precisely that it was nearly impossible for the railroad officer to make a mistake.

Charoy was in his office when the two men entered. They politely extended their greeting, and then one of them handed the letter of recommendation to the engineer without stating the purpose of his presence. Charoy read it, and then said in a friendly tone of voice:

"You were in the employ of my friend Norton? How is he?"

What followed were the usual questions and answers in such circumstances, and then the engineer asked for the reason that had driven the clerk out of Kinsley. The outlaw posing as Haller told a sad story, which harmonized with the contents of the letter, but was one he had invented. The railroad officer listened attentively, and then said:

"This is so sad that I indeed feel for you, especially since I glean from this letter that you've enjoyed Norton's trust and favour. Hence his appeal, for me to employ you, won't be in vain. Although I already have a clerk, I have for some time been in need of someone to whom I can entrust confidential and other important correspondence. Would you agree to a probationary period?"

"Sir," the counterfeit Haller rejoiced. "Please put me to the test! I'm convinced that you'll be satisfied with me."

"Alright, let's try it. We won't talk about your wages at this point; I must first get to know you better, and that will take only a few days. The more proficient you are, the more you'll be paid. I'm very busy at the moment. Have a look around the place and come back here at five o'clock. I will have prepared work for you by then. You'll live here with me, eat at my table, and will have to comply with the house rules. I don't wish that you keep company with the ordinary workers. The door will be locked at ten o'clock."

"That's just to my liking, sir, because I've always kept to precisely that routine as well," the man claimed. He felt great satisfaction for having been hired at all. Then he added:

"I have just one more favour to ask, and that concerns my travel companion here. Would you have work for him perhaps?"

"What kind of work?"

"Anything," the other outlaw modestly replied. "I would be glad to have employment at all."

"What's your name?"

"Faller. I met Mr Haller along the way and joined him when I heard that there's a railway being built here."

"Haller and Faller. That's a peculiar similarity between the two names. I hope you'll also be akin in other aspects. What kind of work did you do beforehand, Mr Faller?"

"I was a cowboy for some time on a ranch over in Las Animas. It was a rough, unsettled life, which I could no longer stand and therefore left. On the last day I got into a fight with another cowboy because of it. He was a rude fellow and during the altercation his knife went through my hand. The injury hasn't quite healed up yet; but I hope that I can use the hand in two or three days, should you have any work for me."

"Alright, you can have a job at any time. Stay around; nurse your hand, and when it's healed up report to me. You can go now."

The fellows left the office. When they walked past the open window of the room in which Old Firehand had secreted himself, the hunter heard one of them say with a suppressed voice:

"All's well! Let's hope the ending is as good as the beginning!"

The engineer joined Old Firehand and said:

"You were right, sir! Faller made sure that he doesn't have to work, and instead has the time necessary to go to Eagle Tail. His hand was bandaged."

"It's completely healthy no doubt. Why have you ordered the clerk to return as late as five o'clock?"

"Because I'm supposed to keep him busy until bedtime. That would tire him as well as me, and be conspicuous to him if it took too long."

And with that the first part of the prelude was concluded. The second act of the drama would only get underway once Firehand had eavesdropped on the two scouts. There was still a long time until then, and he used it to catch up on some sleep. When he awoke it was almost completely dark; the Negro brought his evening meal. By about ten o'clock the engineer visited him to report that the clerk had eaten long ago and was going to retire to his room shortly.

Subsequently, Old Firehand climbed the stairs to the top floor from which a square trapdoor led onto the flat roof. After climbing out, he lay down and quietly crawled towards the edge, below which the window in question was situated. It was so dark that he was able to risk reaching down. He was close enough to touch it with his hand.

After he had been waiting quietly for a while, he heard a door open and shut in the room below. He also heard footsteps approach the window, and then saw the light of a lantern shine out of it into the night. The roof consisted of a thin layer of boards and zinc sheets nailed onto them. Just as Old Firehand could hear the steps made by the person in the room below, so the clerk would be able to hear him; greatest caution was required.

The hunter strained his eyes to penetrate the darkness, and not for naught. Close to the outer reaches of the sheen that came from the window there was a figure. Then Old Firehand could hear the window being opened.

"Stupid!" someone called with a suppressed voice. "Put the lantern away; the light is hitting me!"

"Stupid yourself!" the clerk retorted. "Why are you here already? They're still awake in the house. Come back in one hour."

"Alright! But at least tell me whether or not you've got some information!"

"Yes, and then some!"

"Is it good?"

"Splendid! Much, much better than we could have guessed. But go now; they could see you!"

The clerk closed the window, and the figure disappeared. Old Firehand was forced to wait for an hour or even longer, without moving. But that was no exertion for him, because a Westerner is used to much more difficult things. The time passed, slowly but surely. The lights were still on in the houses below. But the house of the engineer up on the hill was dark; the lamp was no longer burning. The clerk was expecting his companion. Around the indicated time, there was the faint noise of a shoe crunching something on the ground.

"Faller!" the clerk whispered down from the window.

"Yes," the fellow on the ground replied.

"Where are you? I can't see you."

"Close to the wall, right below your window."

"Is it dark everywhere in the house?"

"Yes, everywhere. I've sneaked around it twice. No one is awake. What do you have to tell me?"

"That there is not much in the local cash box. They pay the wages on a fortnightly basis here, and yesterday was payday. We would have to wait around for two weeks, and that's impossible. There aren't quite three hundred dollars in the box; it's not worth the trouble."

"And that's what you call splendid information? Numbskull!"

"Shut up! The cash box might be empty; but tomorrow night there's a train coming through here that is transporting almost half a million dollars."

"Nonsense!"

"It is true. I've seen the papers with my own two eyes. The train comes from Kansas City and goes to Kit Carson, where the money is supposed to be used for the new stretch of railway."

"Do you know that precisely?"

"Yes. I've read the letter and the telegraph messages. The addlebrained engineer trusts me almost like himself."

"What good is that to us? The train drives past!"

"You oaf! It stops here for a full five minutes."

"Tarnation!"

"What's more, you and I will get to be on the locomotive."

"Thunder and lightning! You're imagining things."

"Wouldn't think of it! From Carlyle a special officer must accompany the train. That man stays on the locomotive until the train arrives here, and then he'll even continue on to Wallace, in order to hand over the train to his successor there."

"And you're supposed to be the special officer?"

"Yes. And you're to come along, or rather, you're allowed to come along."

"Why?"

"The engineer gave me permission to choose a second man to accompany me, and when I asked him whom he had in mind, he replied that he wouldn't make any stipulations in that regard; he would accept my choice. It goes without saying that I'll pick you."

"Don't you think that such swift and extensive trust is conspicuous?"

"Ordinarily, yes. But I realize from all of this that the engineer is in need of someone he can trust and that he hasn't had anyone like that. The splendid letter of recommendation greatly helped, of course. And besides, such promptly displayed confidence ought not make me suspicious because there is a warning that comes with the job."

"Oh! What kind?"

"The task is not without danger."

"Ah! That completely reassures me. Are the tracks unsafe?"

"No, although it's actually only a temporary line, as I could see from the documents and diagrams. But you can easily imagine that there aren't enough certified employees to cover such a large, new railroad. There are new drivers with unknown backgrounds and firemen with worrisome histories or demeanours. Just imagine a train that transports almost half a million dollars is driven by such people. If they come to an agreement, then they can easily stop the train somewhere along the line and make off with the money. Hence there must be an officer present, and since there are several people on the locomotive, the officer has to have an assistant as well. Do you understand? It's a kind of police position. You and I will each have a loaded revolver in the pocket to shoot the fellows immediately should they reveal any criminal intentions."

"That's funny. We are to guard the money! We'll force the fellows to stop along the way, and then take the dollars."

"That's impossible; because there is also the conductor, as well as the cashier from Kansas City who is responsible for the money in the box. Both are well armed. Although we might be able to force the men on the locomotive to stop the train, the others would immediately become suspicious and defend their car if the train slows down. No, this has to be tackled in a different manner. We have to attack with superior might, and do so in a place where it is least expected, and that's here."

"And you think that we'll be successful?"

"Of course! There's nothing to be concerned about, and none of us will sustain even a scratch. I'm so convinced of it that I'm sending you to the colonel now to inform him."

"I cannot possibly undertake the ride in the dark because I don't know the region."

"In that case you'll wait until morning; but don't leave any later because I must have a reply by midday. Use the spurs on your horse, even if it means you'll flog it to death."

"And what shall I tell them?"

"What you've just heard from me. The train arrives here at three o'clock in the morning. The two of us will already be on the engine and as soon as it has stopped, we'll tackle the men driving it. We'll shoot them if need be. The colonel and his men must secretly be posted beside the tracks at that point, and then immediately board the cars. Any inhabitants of Sheridan who are awake at that hour will be so surprised by the superior number that they'll have no time for defensive measures."

"Hm, the plan isn't bad at all. That's a frightening amount of money! If everyone receives the same share, each of our men will end up with two thousand dollars. The colonel will hopefully agree to your suggestion!"

"He would be mad if he didn't. Tell him if he doesn't I'll wash my hands of him and carry the robbery out myself. The risk would of course be much greater for me alone, but if I succeed, then I'll also pocket the entire amount."

"Don't worry! I wouldn't think of letting that opportunity slip through my fingers. I'll speak in favour of the plan in a way that won't even permit the colonel to put forwards an objection. I'll certainly bring you a positive reply. But how can I relay it to you?"

"That's a difficult question. We must avoid anything that could arouse suspicion and give the people here the idea that we've got secrets. Hence we must stay clear of personal visits. Besides, I don't know whether or not we'll find the time, or a suitable and inconspicuous opportunity for it. You must contact me via a written note."

"Wouldn't that attract the most attention? If I send a messenger to you, then..."

"A messenger? Who's talking about that?" the clerk interrupted the man below the window. "That would be the greatest stupidity we could commit. I cannot say at this point whether I'll get the opportunity to leave the house; therefore you must write everything down and hide the note nearby."

"Where would that be?"

"Hm! I must choose a place I can get to without arousing suspicion or taking too much time. I already know that I'll have to do a lot of work in the morning; there are long wages lists to be completed, so the engineer said. I'll definitely find a moment to step out of the door. There is a rain barrel next to it. You can hide the piece of paper behind it. If you weigh it down with a rock, no one can accidentally find it."

"But how will you know that there is a note in that spot? You cannot visit the barrel too frequently to check."

"That's also easily accomplished. I will have to tell you, or send word to you, that you're to man the money train with me. I'll do that in the morning already. I'll send someone out to look for you, and you'll learn of it upon your return. You'll then come here to ask why I've sent for you. You'll hide the note on that occasion, which means I will know it's there. Do you agree?"

"Yes. Are we finished now or do you have any other information?"

"I've got nothing else to tell you, except that you urge the colonel to accept the plan without changes, since they'd necessitate preparations for which we wouldn't find the time. And make haste along the way. Good night!"

The other returned the greeting and slipped away. Old Firehand heard the window being quietly closed. He remained lying for a while longer, and then carefully sneaked back to the trapdoor to climb back inside. When he sneaked down the stairs, he heard someone whisper:

"Who's that? It's me, the engineer."

"Old Firehand. Come to my chamber, sir!"

When they arrived there, the officer asked whether it had been possible for the hunter to eavesdrop on the conversation. Firehand recounted what he had heard and expressed his confidence in the desired development and outcome of the matter. After a few minor remarks, the men separated to retire for the night.

Old Firehand woke early in the morning. As a man used to activity and moving about, he didn't easily take to quietly hiding away in his chamber; yet he was forced to do so. Around eleven o'clock the engineer visited him. He informed the hunter that the clerk was deeply engrossed in his task and was making a great effort to appear as a person of good repute. He had also sent for Faller, who couldn't be located, of course. Consequently the workers had received the instruction to send the man to the engineer as soon as he returned. Just when the latter had finished making his report, Old Firehand spotted a short, hunch-backed fellow climbing the rise to the house; he wore a leather hunting outfit and a long rifle on a strap over his shoulder.

"Humply-Bill!" Old Firehand was surprised. And he added the explanation: "The man belongs to my men. Something unexpected must have happened; otherwise he wouldn't come here. I hope it's nothing too dire. He knows that I'm here incognito, so to speak, and won't ask anyone else but you about me. Won't you show him in, sir?"

The engineer left the room, and Bill entered the house at the same moment.

"Excuse me, sir," he said. "I can read on the shingle that the engineer lives here. May I speak to the gentleman?"

"Yes; I am the engineer. Come inside," Charoy said and directed him to Old Firehand's room.

The hunter welcomed Bill with a question about his reason for visiting without prior arrangement.

"Don't worry, sir; nothing bad has happened," Bill replied. "It might even be something very good, but it is definitely something you ought to know. Hence they chose me to bring you the news. I rode very fast and have kept to the railway tracks because the outlaws certainly won't want to be seen near them. They've therefore not spotted me. I've hidden my horse out in the forest and made my way here unnoticed by the locals."

"Good," Old Firehand nodded. "Alright, what's happened?"

"As you know Winnetou came to us towards evening. He caused immense joy for Aunty, and the others were no less delighted to welcome the man among them..."

"Were you hidden so poorly that he was able to find you that easily?"

"Don't think that, sir! We weren't supposed to be discovered by the outlaws and therefore found us a place that they were unable to locate. But there's nothing that escapes Winnetou's eyes! He had also scouted out the camp of the outlaws beforehand, and when it was completely dark he went back to observe them and perhaps spy on them. When he hadn't returned by the time morning was already a few hours old, we were getting worried about him; but that was superfluous. Nothing had happened to him; on the contrary, he had once again accomplished one of his masterpieces. He had sneaked so close to the villains by morning that he could understand their conversation, which, by the way, consisted of loud hollering rather than normal talking. A messenger had arrived from here, and caused quite a stir among the company with the news he brought."

"Aha, Faller!"

"Yes, Faller; that was the fellow's name. He spoke of half a million dollars that they are supposed to get from the train."

"That's correct!"

"Ah! The Apache also spoke of it. It is therefore a trap you're luring the fellows into. Faller only told the outlaws what you've let him know. And you already know that he went to tell them."

"Yes. For him to tell the gang is part of our plan."

"But you must also find out what they've decided afterwards, yes?"

"Of course! We've made arrangements through which this will be revealed to us shortly after Faller's return."

"Alright, but you won't need that fellow because Winnetou has espied everything. The scoundrels were hollering so loudly during their rapture that it was audible for miles around. Faller has a bad horse; he'll only get here after midday. Hence it was perhaps very circumspect of Winnetou to send me to you."

"He decided correctly, because the sooner we know the outlaws' decision, the sooner we can act accordingly. I'll tell you the details of our plan."

Old Firehand explained all the circumstances they had to expect and be prepared for. Bill listened attentively, and then said:

"Splendid, sir! Methinks that everything will develop according to your calculations. The outlaws have immediately agreed to all of the messenger's suggestions, and nothing will be changed, except for one point."

"Which one?"

"The place where the attack will occur. Since a large number of railroad workers live in Sheridan, and such a money transport arouses attention, the outlaws are of the opinion that many of the inhabitants will get up to have a look at the train. That could result in unexpected resistance, and the fellows wish to have the money but not to shed their blood in the process of getting it. Hence the clerk is to calmly let the train depart from Sheridan, but then shortly afterwards force the driver and fireman to stop on the open rail line."

"Did they determine a place?"

"No; but the outlaws want to light a fire along the tracks where the locomotive is to stop. And if the driver and fireman won't obey, they'll be shot. Is this perhaps an undesirable change, sir?"

"No, not at all, because we'll evade the probable danger of a fight between the townspeople and the outlaws. And what's more, we're no longer required to travel to Carlyle with Haller and Faller. We no longer need to keep them fooled. Did Winnetou tell you where to take up your positions?"

"Yes, in front of the tunnel that opens up on the other side of the bridge."

"Correct! But you must stay hidden until the train has entered it completely. The rest will fall into place all by itself."

At that point everyone involved knew where they stood, and the preparations could begin. The telegraph message was sent to Carlyle to assemble the train in question, and also to Fort Wallace to request a cavalry detachment. In the meantime Humply-Bill received food and drink, and then left as inconspicuously as he had arrived.

Around noon came the replies from Carlyle and Fort Wallace that the requests were being granted. About two hours later, Faller arrived. Old Firehand and Charoy sat in the latter's private room. Both observed the outlaw, who busied himself at the rain barrel for a moment.

"Receive him in your office," Old Firehand said. "Talk with him until I join you. I'll read the note."

The engineer went to his office, and when Faller was inside, Firehand went outside. When he looked behind the barrel he saw a rock lying on the ground. He lifted it up and found the expected piece of paper; he unfolded and read the message written by the colonel. The contents of it corresponded to Humply-Bill's report. He placed the note back under the rock, and then went into the office where Faller was standing in front of the engineer with a respectful bearing. The outlaw didn't recognize the hunter, who was wearing his linen suit, and therefore received quite a shock when Firehand put his hand on his shoulder and menacingly asked:

"Do you know who I am, Mr Faller?"

"No," the man replied.

"In that case you didn't have your eyes open on Butler's farm. I am Old Firehand. Do you carry any weapons?"

He pulled the knife from the outlaw's belt and a revolver out of his pocket. The terrified man didn't make one move to prevent it. After that, Firehand said to the engineer:

"Please, sir, go upstairs to the clerk and tell him that Faller came to the office, but nothing else. And then return here."

Charoy left. Old Firehand pushed the outlaw onto a chair and tied him to it with a strong rope that was lying ready on the desk.

"Sir, why are you treating me like this?" the outlaw asked. He had only then recovered from his shock. "Why are you tying me up? I don't know you!"

"Shut up now!" the hunter ordered while he pulled out his revolver. "If you make a sound before I allow it, I'll put a bullet in your head!"

The outlaw turned as pale as a corpse and didn't dare to even move his lips. The engineer returned. Old Firehand signalled him to stand ready at the door; the hunter positioned himself beside the window, so that he couldn't be spotted from the outside. He was convinced that curiosity wouldn't leave the clerk in peace for very long. It didn't take two minutes before he observed someone's arm stretch behind the rain barrel outside; the owner of the limb was not in view as he was standing hard up against the door frame. Firehand nodded to Charoy, who quickly opened the door just as the clerk wanted to sneak past it.

"Mr Haller, won't you come inside?" he asked him.

The man still held the piece of paper in his hand. He hastily pocketed it and followed the engineer's request with visible embarrassment. But that was nothing compared to the face he made when he saw his companion tied to the chair! But he quickly regained his composure and actually succeeded in displaying a fairly relaxed expression.

"What kind of paper did you just put into your pocket?" Old Firehand asked.

"An old paper bag," the outlaw replied.

"Oh? Show it to me!"

The fake clerk gave Firehand an astonished look and replied:

"What gives you the right to give me such an outrageous order? Who are you anyway? I don't know you. Are my pockets your property perchance?"

"Yet you do know him," the engineer cut in. "He is Old Firehand."

"Old Fi...!" the outlaw cried out. The fright prevented him from getting the last two syllables out. His eyes bulged as he stared at the hunter.

"Yes, I am he," Firehand confirmed. "You didn't expect to meet me here, did you? And I probably have a greater right to the contents of your pockets than you. Let's have a look!"

Old Firehand took the knife from the outlaw, who didn't dare to resist; then he pulled a loaded revolver out of a pocket, which he put in his own belt, and he also extracted the piece of paper from the same pocket.

"Sir," the clerk said grimly. "What authority do you have to do this?"

"The authority of the truthful and the more powerful party in the first instance, and in the second, Mr Charoy, who represents the police power in this place, has tasked me with representing him in this affair."

"In what affair? What I carry on me is my property. I've not done anything illegal and insist on being informed of the reasons why you're treating me like a thief!"

"Thief? Pshaw! You'd be fortunate if that were so! We're not dealing with theft, but firstly with a murder and secondly with something that's even worse than a single murder, namely the ambush and robbery of a railroad train, whereby many more people would lose their lives."

"Sir, am I hearing correctly?" the man exclaimed with feigned astonishment. "Who told you the lie about such an atrocity?"

"No one. We know precisely that this atrocity will indeed be carried out."

"By whom?"

"By you!"

"By me?" the outlaw gave a laugh. "No offence, sir, but one would have to be crazy to claim that I, a poor clerk who is standing here on his own, and who would therefore have to carry out the deed without accomplices, am about to stop a train and rob it!"

"Quite right! But firstly you're no clerk, and secondly you're not on your own as you're trying to tell us. You belong to the outlaws who ambushed the Osage at Osage-Nook, then attacked Butler's farm, and are now planning to get half a million dollars off a railroad train."

It was evident that the two men were shocked, yet the fake clerk Haller pulled himself together and proclaimed with the voice of a completely innocent person:

"I know nothing of the sort!"

"And yet you've come here for this purpose, to reconnoitre the best opportunity and notify your accomplices!"

"Me? I've not been able to leave the house for a moment!"

"Quite right; but your comrade here played the messenger. What did you two talk about last night through the open window? I was on the roof above you and heard every word. The answer is written on this piece of paper and the colonel sent it to you. I already know its content and will tell you what it says. The outlaws are camped over at Eagle Tail. They want to come here tomorrow night, take up position along the railway line outside Sheridan, where they are going to light a fire. That is to indicate the place where you are to force the driver to stop the train. The gang will then take the money."

"Sir," the false clerk could no longer hide his fear. "If there really are people who want to do that, then it could only be the consequence of unknown circumstances that seem to connect me with that crime. I'm an honest man and..."

"Shut up!" Old Firehand ordered. "An honest man doesn't kill another."

"Are you saying that I've murdered someone?"

"Indeed! Both of you are murderers. Where are the physician and his aide, whom you and the colonel followed? Didn't you shoot the railroad clerk, because you required his letter of recommendation in order to introduce yourself here as Haller, and to make playing the spy easier for you? Didn't you take all the money from the physician?"

"Sir, I know...not...nothing of any of this!" the outlaw stammered.

"No? Then let me convince you immediately. But so that you don't get the idea of trying to escape, we will secure you. Mr Charoy, be so kind and tie the fellow's hands behind his back. I'll hold him."

When the outlaw heard those words, he quickly turned towards the door to get away. But Old Firehand was even faster. He grabbed him, pulled him back, and held him despite the man's greatest efforts to resist, so that the engineer was able to tie him up effortlessly. Then Faller was untied from the chair and, together with the clerk, led to the room where injured Hartley was lying. When the Yankee saw the two men, whom he recognized at once, he sat up and exclaimed:

"Hello, these are the men who robbed me and killed poor Haller! Where's the third?"

"He's still missing, but will fall into our hands as well," Old Firehand replied. "They're denying the deed."

"Denying? I recognize them, very clearly, and will swear a thousand oaths that it is them. Hopefully my word will have more weight than their excuses!"

"We won't require your assurances, Mr Hartley. We've got enough proof to know where we stand with them."

"Splendid! But what about my money?"

"That'll be found as well. For the moment I've only taken their weapons away, and this note, which we shall now read for all to hear."

He unfolded the note, quickly glanced over it one more time, and then handed it to the engineer to read out aloud. Written on the note was precisely what Winnetou had espied, and Old Firehand had recounted to the outlaws before. The latter said nothing; they recognized that continued lying would be ridiculous.

Then their pockets were emptied. Banknotes that represented their portions of the loot were found and handed back to Hartley. The two outlaws confessed that the red-haired colonel had the rest of it. The two men's feet were also tied together, and then both were laid on the floor. There was no cellar in the house, or another secure room to lock up the two villains. Hartley was so ill-disposed towards them that he made the best possible guard.

He received a loaded revolver and the instruction to shoot them immediately as soon as they made an attempt at ridding themselves of their fetters.

When the men were finished with the two outlaws, they were able to attend to the further preparations for the execution of their plan. There was no longer a need to place the two outlaws on the locomotive, and therefore Old Firehand was not required to travel to Carlyle to drive the train that was put together for their purpose. Instead, a telegraphic instruction was sent to let it depart at a certain time, and then stop it a stretch outside Sheridan, at a prearranged spot, so that the hunter could take it over from there.

During the course of the morning, the return wire from Fort Wallace informed the men in Sheridan that a detachment of cavalry was going to leave at dusk and arrive at the rendezvous point around midnight.

Until that point the workers in Sheridan had no idea of what was about to happen. They were mostly Irish and German. There was a possibility that the colonel would send one or more scouts to observe them, and the conduct of the inhabitants might have revealed to them that they were informed. But when the end of the working day had arrived, Old Firehand accompanied the engineer as he went to notify the overseer of the necessary details and to give him the instruction to familiarize his workmen as inconspicuously as possible with the situation and point out to them that they had to behave as normally as possible, so that possible scouts wouldn't become suspicious.

The overseer, a New Hampshire man by the name of Watson, had had an exciting life. He had initially planned to follow a profession in the building trade, and had also been working in that field, but hadn't succeeded in becoming independent and thus turned his hand to something else, which is no disgrace in the eyes of a Yankee. However, luck wasn't on his side, so he bid his farewell to the East and crossed the Mississippi to make his fortune in the West; unfortunately, that endeavour resulted in failure as well. At last he found employment in Sheridan where he could apply the skills he had attained earlier; but he didn't feel satisfied at all. Someone who has breathed the air of the prairie and the forests will find it difficult, if not impossible, to settle down in a regulated life.

The man was exceedingly pleased when he heard what was about to happen.

"Thank God for some interruption to the endless, daily monotony!" he said. "My old rifle has been lying in the corner long enough and is longing for the opportunity to have something decent to say. I guess it'll have the chance today. But what do I hear? The name you just mentioned sounds familiar to me, sir. The red-haired colonel? And his name is Brinkley? I've once come across a Brinkley with fake red hair; the natural colour of his scalp was of a dark colour. I almost paid with my life for that encounter."

"Where and when was that?" Old Firehand asked.

"Two years ago, up in the mountains along Grand River. I had spent time at Silver-Lake with a friend, a German by the name of Engel; we had planned to head for Pueblo, and then east via the Arkansas trail to obtain tools for a venture that would have made millionaires of us."

Old Firehand became attentive.

"Engel was his name?" he asked. "A venture that would have brought you millions? May I know more about it?"

"Why not? Engel and I swore to remain silent about it; but the millions turned to nothing because the plan didn't come to fruition, and that's why I figure I'm no longer bound to the oath of silence. It's about the lifting of an immense treasure that's been submerged in the waters of Silver-Lake."

The engineer gave a short, incredulous laugh; hence the overseer continued:

"It may sound adventurous, sir; but it is true nevertheless. You, Mr Firehand, are one of the most famous frontiersmen in the West and will have experienced much that no one would believe if you told about it. Perhaps at least you won't laugh about my story."

"Wouldn't think of it," the hunter said in a most sincere tone of voice. "I'll gladly and readily believe you, and have good reasons for it. I, too, have been assured that a treasure is supposed to lie on the bottom of the lake."

"Truly? Alright, in that case you won't mistake me for a gullible person or even a swindler. I figure I can attest to the veracity of the report about the treasure with a clear conscience. The one who told us about it certainly did not lie to us."

"Who was that?"

"He was an old Indian. I've never in my life seen such an ancient person. He was literally emaciated to a skeleton, and told us that he had experienced more than one hundred summers. He called himself *Hauey-Kolakakho*, but at one point revealed that his actual name was *Ikhatshi-Tatli*. I don't know what those two Indian names mean."

"But I know," Old Firehand cut in. "The former belongs to the Tonkawa language, the latter to the Aztec one, and both mean the same thing: 'Great Father'. Keep talking, Mr Watson! I am incredibly keen to know how you met the Indian."

"Well, there's actually nothing special or adventurous connected to it. I had miscalculated the timing of my stay in the mountains, so that the first snow surprised me. I had to stay up there and find a place where I could spend the winter without starving to death. I was on my own, and snowed in, which was nothing to be pleased about! Fortunately I reached Silver-Lake and spotted a stone hut from which smoke rose; I was saved. The owner of that hut was the Indian in question. He had a grandson and a great-grandson, and their names were Great Bear and Little Bear, who..."

"Ah! Nintropan-Hauey and Nintropan-Homosh?" Old Firehand interrupted Watson again.

"Yes, those were the Indian names. Do you perchance know those two, sir?"

"Yes. But go on, go on!"

"Father and son Nintropan had gone across to the Wasatch Mountains, where they had to stay until spring. Winter had come too early, and it was impossible for them to cross back through the massive snow cover to Silver-Lake. No doubt they harboured great concern for the old man. They knew he was on his own and probably expected him to succumb to the cold up there in that solitude. As I said, I was lucky to get there, and I also found someone else in his hut already, namely the German I mentioned before: Engel. He had found refuge there from the first snowstorm just like I did. I figure it's advisable that I make a long story short and will only say that the three of us lived through the entire winter together. We didn't have to go hungry because there was enough game; but the cold had affected the old man too much and when the first balmy breeze came up we had to bury him. He had grown fond of us and to show his gratitude he had divulged the secret of the treasure in Silver-Lake to us. He owned an old piece of leather with a precise map of the place in question and permitted us to make a drawing. As coincidence would have it, Engel had pencil and paper on him without which we wouldn't have been able to receive the drawing because the old man didn't want to give us the piece of leather, but instead wanted to keep it for Great Bear and Little Bear. He buried it somewhere, one day before his death, but we didn't find out where because we respected the old man's wishes and didn't search. Once he was lying under his burial mound we departed. Engel had the drawing sewn into his hunting coat."

"You didn't wait for the return of father and son Nintropan?" Old Firehand asked.

"No."

"That was a big mistake!"

"Maybe; but we had been snowed in for months and were longing for the company of people. We also came upon some very soon, but what kind! We were ambushed by a host of Utah Indians and completely robbed. They would have killed us, no doubt; but they knew the old Indian, whom they revered greatly, and when they found out that we had looked after him, and had then buried him after he had died, they spared us, returned our clothes at least and let us go. But they kept our weapons, for which we were not very grateful because we were exposed to all kinds of dangers, even death by starvation without them. Luckily, or perhaps unluckily, on the third day we met a hunter who gave us meat. When he heard that we were headed for Pueblo, he pretended to have the same destination and permitted us to join him."

"That was Red Brinkley?"

"Yes. He gave us a different name; but I later found out that his real name was Brinkley. He questioned us, and we told him everything; we kept only the story of the treasure in Silver-Lake, and the fact that Engel had a drawing, from him, because he didn't look trustworthy. I can't help it, but I've always had an aversion to red-haired people, although I figure that there aren't any more scoundrels among them than there are among people who wear scalps of other hair colour. Of course our silence was of no use. Since only he had weapons, he often went away to hunt, and then the two of us would sit together talking almost exclusively of the treasure. On one occasion he secretly returned, sneaked up behind us and eavesdropped on our conversation. When he later went hunting again he requested me to accompany him, since four eyes could see more than two. After about an hour, when we had gone far enough away from Engel, he told me that he had overheard everything and was going to take the drawing away from us as punishment for our mistrust. He pulled out his knife as he spoke and attacked me. I resisted with all my strength, but for naught; he stabbed me in the chest."

"Deplorable!" Old Firehand exclaimed. "He intended to also kill Engel afterwards, to become the sole owner of the secret."

"Undoubtedly. Fortunately he had missed my heart, yet he assumed that I was dead. When I came to, I lay beside a large pool of blood, in the lap of an Indian who had found me. It was Winnetou, the chief of the Apache."

"What luck! You were in the best hands. It seems that this man is omnipresent."

"It is true that I was in good hands. The Apache had already dressed my wounds. He gave me water and I had to tell him what had happened as best I could in my weakened state. Then he left me and followed Brinkley's tracks. When he returned after more than two hours, he told me the results of his search. The murderer had returned directly to the camp to kill Engel as well. My companion had become suspicious because Brinkley had taken me along, and he secretly followed us. What happened afterwards was clearly evident from the tracks. Engel had recognized Brinkley's intentions from a distance already, but he was too far away and the scoundrel had acted too swiftly for him to help me. He obviously knew that he was in grave danger as well and since he wasn't armed he thought it was advisable to flee as quickly as possible. When Brinkley left me for dead and returned to the camp, he found Engel's tracks and followed them. But I found out later that the German escaped."

"Yes, he did escape," Old Firehand nodded.

"What? You know that, sir?" the overseer asked.

"Yes. But about that later. Keep talking!"

"Winnetou was on a ride north. He had no time to look after me for weeks on end, and brought me to a camp of the Timbabachi Indians, with whom he was on friendly terms. They nursed me back to health, and then brought me to the nearest settlement where I was taken in and found plenty of support. I did all kinds of work for half a year, in order to save up enough money to return to the East."

"Where did you want to go?"

"To Engel. I assumed that he had escaped. I knew that he had a brother in Russelville, Kentucky. We had decided to visit him, in order to make preparations for our journey to Silver-Lake. When I arrived I learnt that Engel's brother had moved to the state of Arkansas; but no one could tell me exactly where. He had given the neighbour a letter for his brother, in case he'd visit and ask about him. The latter had indeed arrived and received the letter, which had obviously contained the brother's new address, and then he left immediately. The neighbour was no more, for he had died. Consequently I went to Arkansas and searched the entire state, but for naught. In Russelville, however, Engel had recounted our adventure and called the murderer Brinkley. I don't know how he came by that name. So, gentlemen, that's what I had to tell you. If the name Brinkley is correct, then I look forward with great pleasure to meet that scoundrel. I figure that I've got an account to square with him."

"There are others who have the same intentions," Old Firehand said. "One point is still unclear to me. You said before that Brinkley's red hair was false. How could you know that?"

"That's easily explained. When he attacked me, and I defended myself, I grabbed him by his head. I would certainly have pulled him down, and would have overpowered him if the scalp had been growing solidly on his head; but I was holding the detached wig in my hand, and during the moment of my astonishment, he gained time to thrust his knife into my chest. The last thing I could see was that his own hair was dark."

"Alright! There's no more doubt that you were dealing with Red Brinkley. He's using Hackberry bark to dye his hair nowadays. The entire life and work of this person seems to be made up of nothing but crimes. Hopefully we'll be successful in putting an end to it today."

"I also wish for that from the bottom of my heart. But you still haven't told me how we're supposed to fend off the expected attack."

"That's not necessary for you to know at this point. You'll be informed of it at the appropriate moment. For the time being the workers have to remain quiet; they should prepare for a night without sleep. Also, they have to ready their weapons. Shortly before midnight they'll board a train that will bring them to the spot in question."

"Alright, I'll have to be content with that information. Your orders will be followed."

On the way back to the engineer's house, Old Firehand asked Charoy whether there were two workers who resembled the two outlaws in both stature and facial features; they also ought to have enough courage to replace the two outlaws on the locomotive. Charoy reflected on it, and then sent his Negro assistant to fetch two men he considered suitable.

When they arrived, Old Firehand saw that the engineer's choice wasn't bad at all. The men's figures were almost identical, and as far as the faces were concerned, it was to be expected that the difference couldn't be detected in the dark of the night. It was then a matter of ensuring that the voices didn't sound too dissimilar. Hence Old Firehand led the two workers into Hartley's room and conducted another, sham interrogation of the two outlaws. The former heard the voices of the latter and were therefore capable of imitating them later.

Afterwards, the hunter decided to reconnoitre and ascertain whether Red Brinkley had perhaps sent scouts. He left the house and in Westerner fashion searched the surroundings. Of course he did so towards the direction of Eagle Tail, from where spies were likely to arrive.

When an experienced hunter wants to sneak up on someone, and doesn't know the person's position, then he won't simply search at random, but consider the possible spots that the person in question could have chosen according to the situation and the circumstances. Old Firehand did exactly that. If spies had arrived, then they were going to be in a place from which the settlement could be observed safely and at the same time sufficiently well at night. And there was such a place not far from the engineer's house. A cut in the terrain had been required, which resulted in an embankment that rose up close to the railway line. Some trees were growing at the top. That elevated spot offered the best view, and the trees gave the necessary cover. If anywhere, then that was the place to look for the spies.

Old Firehand ensured that he reached the bottom of the elevation from the other side, unnoticed, and then silently crawled up. When he arrived up top, he saw that his calculation had been correct. There were two figures sitting beneath the trees talking with each other, but so quietly that they weren't detectable from below. The daring hunter crept so close to them that he touched the trunk of the tree, beneath which they sat, with his head. He could have grabbed both with his hands. He had been able to sneak so close because the grey colour of his suit was indistinguishable from that of the ground even for the keenest eye. It was a matter of hearing what they were saying. Unfortunately there was a pause in their conversation, and some time went by before one of them said:

"Did you find out what is to happen once we're done here?"

"Nothing specific," the other replied.

"There's much talk; but there are probably only a handful of members who know details."

"Yes. The colonel is secretive and trusts only very few of the men. His actual plan is probably only known to those who have been with him before we joined him."

"Do you mean Woodward, who escaped from the rafters with him? Well, he seems to be quite chatty with you in particular. Has he said anything to you?"

"He gave nothing but hints."

"But one can draw conclusions from such clues."

"Certainly! In this case I deduce from his remarks that, for example, the colonel does not have the intention of keeping the entire host together. Such a number of men is only a hindrance to him for his future plans. And I agree with him on that. The more people we are the smaller the windfall for each of us will be. I think that he selects the best, and then suddenly disappears with them."

"All devils! Are the others supposed to be cheated?"

"Why cheated?"

"What if the colonel clears off tomorrow with those he wants to keep?"

"That wouldn't do any harm. I would only be pleased about it."

"Oh? And I'd have none of it!"

"You? Numbskull! I thought you were smarter."

"In what way?"

"It goes without saying that you would not be among those who will be cheated and lose out."

"Can you prove that? If not, I'll keep my eyes open and sound the alarm."

"The proof is not that difficult to furnish. Hasn't he sent you here with me?"

"So what?"

"Only useful and reliable men get assigned such tasks. By charging us with the observation of this place, he gave us his sincerest vote of confidence. What do we deduce from that? If he really intends to rid himself of the bulk of our men, then we won't be among them, and instead be with those he'll take along."

"Hm! That's what I like to hear; this argument is good and puts my mind completely at ease. But if you think that I'll be among the chosen, then why are you so cagey and won't tell me what Woodward told you about the colonel's plans?"

"Because I'm not yet clear about them myself. It's about a ride up into the mountains."

"Why into the mountains?"

"Hm! I don't know if it is advisable to talk about it; but I'll tell you nonetheless. There was a tribe, whose name has escaped me, that lived up there in ancient times. Those people have either moved south or have been wiped out, and have submerged huge treasures in a lake beforehand."

"Nonsense! Someone who owns treasures takes them along when they move away!"

"As I said, they might possibly have been wiped out!"

"What do these treasures consist of? Money?"

"I don't know. I'm not a scholar and can therefore not say whether ancient nations had coins or printed money. The latter would by now have lost all value. Woodward said the people were thought to have been heathens and have had immense temples with solid gold and silver statues of their gods, and innumerable vessels of the same material. That treasure is lying in Silver-Lake, which received its name from it."

"Are we supposed to drink the lake empty to see the things lying on the bottom?"

"Don't talk foolish! The colonel no doubt knows where he's at and what he has to do. He's supposed to be in the possession of a drawing with which he's able to accurately determine the precise spot in question."

"Ah! And where is that Silver-Lake?"

"I don't know. The colonel will definitely only talk about it when he has decided who'll accompany him. It goes without saying that he can't blab about it any sooner."

"Of course! But the matter is dangerous at any rate."

"Why?"

"Because of the Indians."

"Pshaw! Only two redskins live there, the grandson and great-grandson of the old Indian from whom the drawing originates. And those two are easily put away with a couple of shots."

"If that's how it is, then I'll praise it. I have never been up there in the mountains and must therefore rely on those who understand the matter. But for the moment I think we need to direct our entire attention towards our present undertaking. Do you think we'll be successful?"

"Definitely. Just look at how quiet everything is in the place! No one has any idea of our presence and our intentions. And two of our best and most cunning people are already here to make preparations. Why would anyone even think of failure?"

"Alright! If only the workers are going to be smart enough and not meddle in the affair; otherwise they'd force us to make use of our guns."

"They cannot and will not think of it because they know nothing of it. The train arrives here, stops for five minutes, and then continues on. Our fire will be burning a one-hour's ride further on. Our two comrades on the locomotive will point the revolver at the driver and force him to stop the train. We'll surround it, and the colonel will climb aboard and take..."

"Oho!" the other interrupted him. "Who's going to climb aboard? The colonel alone, perchance? Or with only those few he'll intend to casually steam away with? And later he'll stop the train to get off, take the half a million dollars and disappear? And the rest of us will sit here, have nothing and see nothing but each other's baffled faces? No, that's not part of the deal!"

"What are you thinking?" his accomplice sounded annoyed. "I've already told you: if the colonel really intended to do this, then the two of us would be among those who'd be allowed to climb onto the train."

"If you're certain about it, then I'll believe it, and will wait and see; but I've also heard what others have been saying. They don't trust the colonel, and I'm convinced that when the train stops everyone will push onto the train."

"Fair enough! I don't intend to cheat a comrade and will warn the colonel from doing so. If Silver-Lake offers us such immense treasures, then we don't need to be dishonest towards our present companions. We share, everyone receives his money, and then the colonel can select those he wants to take into the mountains. *Basta*! Let's not talk about it anymore! Right now I'd like to know the purpose of the locomotive that stands down there. The fire under the boiler is lit; the engine is therefore ready to depart. Where to?"

"Could it be the security locomotive, which is supposed to drive ahead of the money transport?"

"No. That would not be ready now. The train arrives at three o'clock in the morning. This machine worries me, and I'm keen to find out what they have in mind with it."

The man voiced a suspicion that was to be taken seriously. Old Firehand realized that the locomotive couldn't remain standing there. It was an ordinary small construction train engine used for the transportation of the cars that contained excavated material. The workers would be driven in those cars to where they were required. In order to allay the suspicion of the two scouts, the train had to leave immediately, and not at midnight. Hence Old Firehand crawled back down and sneaked to the engineer's house to tell him what he had heard.

"Alright!" Charoy said. "In that case we must get the people away from here immediately. But the spies will see them board the train!"

"No. Let's give the order for the men to sneak away unseen; they may walk about a quarter of an hour along the line, and then wait for the empty train to stop, so that they can climb in. Since the tracks follow a bend, and the sound won't carry far, the spies will neither hear nor see that the train has stopped there."

"And how many people do I retain here?"

"Twenty will be sufficient for the protection of your house and the guarding of the two prisoners. Your instructions can be executed within twenty minutes; then the train can depart. I'll sneak back up to the two spies to hear what they're saying."

Firehand was soon lying behind the two men again, who were quiet at that point. He could see the terrain in front of them as well as they could, and made every effort to detect movements caused by the inhabitants—but for naught. The workmen departed so clandestinely and cautiously that the two outlaw scouts discerned not the least clue of it. Besides, the lamps that were lit in the buildings were incapable of illuminating the open areas outside the windows sufficiently for human figures to be clearly visible.

After a while, someone carrying a brightly lit lantern walked from the engineer's house to the railroad tracks. The man called out loudly enough to be heard for quite a distance:

"Empty construction train departing to Wallace! The cars are needed there."

It was the engineer who had said that. He had been astute enough that off his own bat he thought of a means of averting the spies' suspicion, without having been prompted by Old Firehand. Charoy had prearranged the scene with the driver, so the man on the engine replied just as loudly:

"Alright, sir! I'd like to get away at last and not burn my wood for nothing. Do you have a message for Wallace?"

"Nothing but a good night to the engineer, who'll no doubt be playing a game of cards when you get there. Send us a telegraph if something is amiss with the line; we won't send the extra security engine through. *Bonne route!*"

"Good night, sir!"

A few piercing whistles, and the train moved out. When the sound of it had dissipated, one of the scouts said to the other:

"Do you now know where you're at with this locomotive?"

"Yes, it put my mind at ease. It'll take the empty cars to Fort Wallace; they are needed there. My suspicion was unfounded. Misgivings on the whole are nonsensical. The plan is so well thought out that it must succeed unconditionally. We could even leave now already."

"No. The colonel has ordered us to wait until midnight, and we have to obey him."

"Fair enough! But if I'm to hold out until then, I don't see why I have to strain my eyes unnecessarily. I'll lie down and sleep."

"Me, too; that's the smartest thing to do. We won't have the time or the inclination to rest later."

Old Firehand swiftly retreated because the two outlaws moved away from their posts to make themselves as comfortable as possible. The hunter returned to Charoy to commend him for the remarks he had called out. With wine and cigars the two men spent the time waiting for the moment when Old Firehand needed to leave. There were only twenty workers in the place, and that was entirely sufficient, since no hostilities were expected.

All the other men had sneaked away, according to the orders they had received. They gathered outside Sheridan, and then followed the railroad track until they reached the indicated spot some distance away, where they waited for the train to come along and pick them up. It took them to Eagle Tail, where it stopped. It was impossible for the host of outlaws to observe what was happening on that far section of the railroad because they had already departed. The river forced them a considerable distance away from the railroad line, so they were unaware of any train movements on that stretch as they rode towards the agreed spot, where they would light the fire next to the tracks.

Old Firehand with his experience and astuteness had chosen a splendidly suitable terrain. The railroad had to be built across the river, which was framed on both sides by tall banks. The tracks led across a temporary bridge, and then immediately into a tunnel that was about seventy metres long. The train, which didn't consist of empty cars, as the two scouts had been made to believe, but was instead loaded with wood and coal, as well as Sheridan's workforce, stopped a few paces ahead of the bridge. As soon as it had been brought to a halt, a short, rotund fellow, who had the appearance of a woman, emerged from the surrounding dark of the night and approached the locomotive. With a high-pitched falsetto voice he asked the driver:

"Sir, what are you doing here already? Are you bringing the workers perchance?"

"Yes," the driver replied while he gave the peculiar figure he saw in the light of the engine fire a baffled look. "And who are you?"

"Me?" the rotund fellow replied and laughed. "I'm Aunty Droll."

"An aunt? Tarnation and the deuce! What are we supposed to do with womenfolk and old aunts?"

"Well, don't work yourself up too much! It might be detrimental to your nerves. I'm only an aunt in the passing; you'll get an explanation later. Alright, why did you get here already?"

"That was done on the orders of Old Firehand, who's done some eavesdropping on two outlaw scouts. They would have become suspicious if we had departed later. Do you belong to the people of the famous gentleman?"

"Yes; but don't run away from fright; there are only uncles, and I'm the only aunt."

"Wouldn't think of being scared of you, miss or madam. Where are the outlaws?"

"Gone; they left three quarters of an hour ago already."

"Does that mean we can unload the coal and firewood?"

"Yes. Put your people back on board, and I'll climb up next to you to give you the necessary hints."

"You? Give hints? They haven't made you the general of this here army corps by chance, have they?"

"Indeed that I am, with your kind permission, of course. Here I am. And now let your iron horse run across the bridge nice and slow, and then stop, so that the firewood cars stand at the entrance to the tunnel."

Droll climbed onto the locomotive. The workers had left the cars when the train stopped, but were required to return to them. The driver gave the rotund fellow another look that clearly expressed how difficult he found it to obey the orders of the dubious aunt.

"Well then, shall we?" Droll asked.

"Are you really the man I'm supposed to take instructions from?"

"Sure am! And if you don't immediately do so, I'll help it along. I've got no mind to remain stuck on this bridge until the day of reckoning."

He pulled out his bowie knife and aimed the tip of it at the driver's stomach.

"Tarnation, you're a pointy and sharp aunt!" the man said. "But I must think that you're an outlaw, instead of an ally, because you're showing me your knife. Can you legitimize yourself?"

"Don't carry on the nonsense," the rotund fellow replied in a serious voice while he put the knife back into his belt. "We're camped on the other side of the tunnel. The fact that I came across the bridge to meet you ought to have indicated to you that I knew you were coming, and that I could therefore not belong to the outlaws."

"Alright, I'll believe you now. Let's drive across."

The train went across the bridge, and then drove far enough into the tunnel, so that the two last cars came to a halt just outside it. The workers jumped off again and poured the contents out of one of the tipping cars. Then the train moved forwards and stopped on the other side of the tunnel out in the open, so that the other full wagon came to stand just outside the exit of it. A side-tipping car is engineered for the container to be tilted to the side while the wheels are stopped, be emptied of its contents, and then brought back into its upright position. The workers climbed down and arranged the coal and wood into an easily lit heap, but in such a way that the sleepers wouldn't be damaged by the fire. The driver then steamed ahead for another short stretch, stopped the engine, and then climbed down from the locomotive to walk back and join the others.

His mistrust had completely vanished. What he saw informed him that he was among the right people. The tunnel had been dug through a tall cliff, which shielded a fire from the river valley where the outlaws had been camped. The rafters, and everyone else who had come to Eagle Tail with Old Firehand, were sitting around it. Two sturdy sapling tree trunks had been cut and trimmed to forks, and rammed into the ground on either side of the fire, to hold a spit. A long, strong pole, which held enormous pieces of buffalo meat, was being rotated in the forks over the fire. All the men around the fire had risen to greet the workers when the train had come through the tunnel.

"Well then, do you believe me now that I'm no outlaw?" Droll asked the driver when the man sat down with those around the fire.

"Yes, sir," he nodded. "You're an honest fellow."

"And I'm a decent one as well! I'll prove that to you by inviting you all to dinner. We've shot a fat buffalo cow, and you're going to experience what it tastes like when prepared *a la prairie*. There is enough for everyone, and I hope that your workers will be finished soon, so that they can sit with us."

Within a short time the men were enjoying the juicy meal. Of course only a few found room directly beside the fire. Various groups had formed; the rafters, who saw themselves as the hosts, were looking after them. There was smaller game apart from the buffalo cow, so there was plenty to eat despite the large number of railroad workers.

Before the train had departed from Sheridan, when the engineer had issued orders to the overseer for an early departure, Charoy had also said to Watson:

"Old Firehand asked me to inform you that, should you want to know more about Mr Engel, your erstwhile companion, then you ought to turn to a German by the name of Mr Pampel, whom you'll meet among the rafters."

Whereupon Watson had asked:

"Has he met him? Does he know of him?"

"Most probably, otherwise Old Firehand wouldn't point you in his direction," Charoy had replied.

Watson recalled the engineer's message at that point and paid attention to catch possible German accents among the rafters in order to find the person in question. After a short while he had heard all of them speak; but there was none among them who didn't speak a genuine Yankee English. The overseer decided to make direct enquiries. He was one of the few who had found a spot near the fire. Next to him sat Aunty Droll and Humply-Bill. He turned to the latter:

"Sir, allow me to ask whether or not there is a German among you."

"There are several at that," Bill replied.

"Truly? Who, for example?"

"Well, first there's Old Firehand, who's German, and then I can name our rotund Aunty Droll here and over there Black Tom. Perhaps even young Fred, who's sitting across there, can be counted as a German."

"Hm, none of the people you mentioned seems to be the one I'm looking for."

"Oh? Who is it that you're searching?"

"Someone by the name of Mr Pampel."

"Pam...Pam...Pampel?" Bill exclaimed and broke into roaring laughter. "Heavens, what a name! Who can utter that one? Pam...

Pam...Pam...what was it again? I must hear that word one more time."

"Mr Pampel," the overseer repeated, whereby everyone joined in Humply-Bill's laughter.

The word went from one group to the next, and laughter followed, so that there remained not a single serious face in the entire camp. Not one? Oh, yes. Droll's mien had remained unchanged. He had grabbed himself a large piece of buffalo loin, cut huge bite-sized morsels from it, put them in his mouth one after the other, and chewed on them with such fervour and devotion as if he had heard neither the name nor the laughter. When the latter had abated at last, Bill's voice resounded again:

"No, sir, you must be ill-informed. There is no one by the name of Pampel among us."

"But Old Firehand gave me a message to that effect!" Watson replied.

"In that case you misunderstood the name or haven't memorized it correctly. I'm convinced that each one of us would rather have a bullet in his head, than ridicule a man like Old Firehand. Don't you think so, old Droll?"

Droll interrupted his chewing and replied:

"A bullet? Wouldn't dream of it!"

"Of course you can say that, because your name is Droll, and not Pampel. But if you were carrying that name, I'm convinced that you wouldn't want to mix with people."

"But I have mixed with people!"

He emphasized his remark in such a way that Bill looked at him sideways, and then asked:

"Does that mean you're not laughing about the name?"

"No. I won't do that, so as not to insult the comrade who is indeed among us and carries precisely that name."

"What? How? There really is a person by the name of Pampel among us?"

"Indeed."

"Devil! Who is it?"

"That would be me."

That's when Bill jumped up and called out:

"You, you yourself are Pam...Pam...Pam...!"

Laughter prevented him from continuing, and the others had just as little self-control and chimed in again. The merriment was significantly increased by Droll's still stern expression, and the fact that he was evidently engrossed in the delicious buffalo loin, and continued to chew as if he had not the slightest business with the laughter and its cause. But after he had swallowed the last mouthful he rose, looked around the circle and called out, so that everyone heard it:

"Mesh'shurs, the fun is now at an end. No one is to blame for his or her name, and anyone who thinks mine is ridiculous can tell me so in all earnest, and then take his knife and accompany me a little to the side into the dark. We'll see which one of us will be laughing then!"

Deep silence fell immediately.

"But Droll," Humply-Bill pleaded. "Who could have thought that this is your name? It is really too precious. We had no intention of insulting you, and I hope that you don't take offence at my words. Come, sit back down next to me!"

"Alright, I'll do that. I'm not angry, because I know the name really does sound pamplesque; but now that you know it is my real name, you'll have to let it rest."

"Of course! That goes without saying. But why have you kept it from us until now? Come to think of it, you really are a fellow who dislikes to talk of his earlier circumstances."

"Dislike? Who said that? I fondly remember the times of my past; there simply hasn't been an opportunity to talk about it."

"Then make up for it now. You know what everyone of us is and was. We've all declared brotherhood during the ride here, and therefore ought to know each other; but we know nothing, nearly nothing from or about you."

"Because there isn't much to know at all. Besides, you know my place of origin already."

"Yes, Langenleuba in the region of Altenburg. What did your father do? May we know?"

"Why not?" Droll smiled. "He was more, much more than the father of many other men. We have to wait until three o'clock for the outlaws to get here; that means there's enough time to list all of his honours and distinctions. He was a wedding-, christening-, and funeral-crier, bell ringer, verger, waiter, and gravedigger, scythe grinder, orchard guard and at the same time sergeant of the civilian guards. There you have it!"

The men looked at him searchingly, to ascertain whether he spoke in jest or in earnest.

"You can safely believe it!" he assured them. "He truly and verily was all of that, and anyone who knows the circumstances over there in the old country knows that my father was as poor as a church mouse, and yet was respected by every one of his fellow citizens. We were almost a dozen children and have endured hunger and worry in order to go through life honestly, and I might even be able to tell you later..."

"Stop, please!" overseer Watson interrupted him. "You're only paying attention to the wishes of the others, but not to the fact that I've asked about you. Old Firehand has given me your name..."

"Yes, he and a couple of others are the only ones who know my real name."

"He gave it to me, so that I might find out from you what became of your fellow countryman Engel," Watson continued.

"Engel? Which Engel do you mean?"

"The hunter and trapper who was up there at Silver-Lake."

"Is that the one you're talking about?" Droll sat up attentively. "Did you know him?"

"Like myself! Is he still alive?"

"No; he's dead."

"Do you know that for sure?"

"Indeed I do. Where did you meet him?"

"Up there at Silver-Lake. We had to spend and entire winter there, because we were snowed in ..."

"That means your name's Watson?" Droll interrupted him.

"Yes, sir; that's my name."

"Watson, Watson! What a coincidence! But no, there is no such thing as coincidence! It is God's will! Mister, I know you like the insides of my own pockets, and yet I've never seen you before."

"In that case someone has told you of me? Who was that?"

"The nephew of your comrade Engel. Look here! This boy's name is Fred Engel; he is the nephew of your friend from Silver-Lake and has come on a journey with me to find the murderer of his father."

"Was his father murdered?" Watson asked while he offered his hand to the boy in a greeting and gave him a friendly nod.

"Yes, and all because of a drawing, which..."

"A drawing again!" the overseer cut in. "Do you know the murderer? It can only be Red Brinkley!"

"Yes, it is him, sir. But...he was supposed to have murdered you as well!"

"Only wounded, sir, only wounded. He missed the heart when he stabbed me. But I would still have succumbed to the loss of blood, had not a saviour turned up, an Indian who bandaged my wound, and then brought me to other Indians who let me stay with them until I had recovered. He, my saviour, is the most famous Indian there is, and his name is...”

He didn't finish his sentence; he paused; he slowly rose and stared at the nearby boulder as if he had just seen an apparition. From there, Winnetou slowly approached. The Apache had been out reconnoitring, and returned at that moment.

“There he comes, there he comes, Winnetou the chief of the Apache!” the foreman cried. “He is here, he is here! What good fortune! Winnetou, Winnetou!”

He rushed at the chief, grabbed both of his hands and pulled them to his chest. The Apache looked into his face and a mild, friendly smile graced his countenance when he replied:

“My white brother Watson! I visited the warriors of the Timbabachi and learnt from them that you had completely healed and left for the Mississippi. Good Manitou must love you very much for having allowed this wound to mend, because it was worse than I admitted to you. Sit down and tell me how your days evolved since then!”

Suddenly, thoughts of the outlaws had become less important to the men, and the overseer's story took priority. Winnetou had astutely redirected attention from the actual reason for the presence of so many people, towards Watson, because his reconnoitring had convinced him that the place was secure and the men could safely talk about something other than the outlaws.

Of course everyone was eager to hear the story of the man whose life Winnetou had saved, and there was hardly a breath audible when Watson recounted his adventures as he had told them to Old Firehand and Charoy. When he concluded, he didn't hesitate a moment to ask:

“And you, Mr Droll, can you tell me what became of my comrade?”

“Yes, I can,” the rotund fellow replied. “He became a dead man.”

“Does that mean the colonel murdered him?”

“No, but he wounded him, just like you, and that's what the poor devil died of.”

“Speak, speak, sir!”

“That's quickly told; I don't need many words for that. When the colonel had lured you away from the camp, Engel started to reflect about the point that you as an unarmed man were practically useless to Red Brinkley. Why had he taken you along?

He must have had a specific purpose that had nothing to do with hunting game. The two of you hadn't trusted the colonel, and at that point Engel, who had become quite fond of you, became afraid for you. That fear didn't let go of him, so he got up and followed your tracks, which were quite clear. The worry doubled the speed of his steps, and after perhaps a quarter of an hour he had come so close that he could see you. He had just walked around the corner of some bushes when he spotted you; but what he saw made him dash back behind them. He was almost paralysed by shock as he looked through the foliage. Brinkley had stabbed you and was kneeling above you to satisfy himself that the wound had been fatal. Then he rose to his feet and remained standing for a while as if he were contemplating something. What was Engel to do? Attack the well-armed murderer without any weapons to avenge you? That would have been madness. Or should he wait until the colonel had left, and then walk over to you to see whether life remained? Not that either! You were dead for sure, otherwise the fellow would have helped it along with another stab; and besides, Red Brinkley would have encountered Engel's tracks, followed and killed him as well. No, if the scoundrel had murdered you, then Engel was next in line; therefore he recognized that fleeing immediately was the only thing to do. Engel turned away, hurried along his own tracks, and when the terrain was favourable he turned east. But he would soon enough receive proof that the murderer hadn't spent much time at the place of his deed, and instead had returned, found the trail and followed it. Engel had climbed up a hill, and when he looked back, he saw Brinkley coming after him. He was still down in the valley, but only a distance of ten minutes away at the most. There was prairie on the other side of the hills. Engel ran down there and continued running, always straight ahead as fast as he could. He only dared to stop and look back after about a quarter of an hour. He saw the pursuer much closer behind him than he had been earlier. The chase continued for probably another hour, until Engel saw bushes ahead; he thought he was safe; but the bushes were standing far apart with fat grass between them, which showed up his footprints with great clarity. The fugitive was actually a good runner; but the privations of the hard winter had nevertheless weakened him; the pursuer gradually closed the gap. That drove Engel to mobilize his last bit of energy. He saw water ahead. It was the Orfork of Grand River. He ran towards it but hadn't reached it when he heard a shot being fired behind him. He felt a knock against the right side of his torso as if from a powerful fist, ran on and into the water to swim to the other bank. That's when he saw to his left a brook empty its water into the river. He turned towards its mouth and swam into it for a stretch until he spotted some bushes that extended their branches down to the water. The curtain had been made even denser by a covering of washed-down grass that had become tangled in it. He slipped under it and remained standing there. He reached the bottom with his feet. You can imagine that his entire body was shaking from the distress."

"And from the exertion and fear!" Watson added. "Go on, please!"

"The colonel had reached the river as well; since he couldn't see Engel, and the river was only narrow, he believed that the other had swum across, so he also went into the water. But he could only do that with the greatest of caution because he had to prevent his weapon and ammunition from becoming wet. It therefore took a long time before he arrived on the other side, swimming on his back and holding the items above water."

"He would certainly have turned around," Humply-Bill said. "When he couldn't find a track on the other side, he had to assume that the fugitive was still on the near side of the river."

"Indeed," Droll nodded. "He first searched a stretch of the far bank, and then returned to search along the near bank; but there was no trail either, and that confused him. He went past Engel's hiding place twice but didn't see the man behind the bushy curtain. Engel listened for a very long time during which he neither saw nor heard the murderer again. Nevertheless, he stayed in the water until it had become dark; then he swam across and walked west the entire night to get as far away as possible."

"Wasn't he wounded?"

"Yes, a grazing shot on his upper body, under the arm. During his agitation, and in the cold of the water, he had hardly noticed it; but the wound began to burn during the march. He padded it as well as he could, until the morning when he found leaves to cool it, which he applied and renewed from time to time. He was deathly tired and felt a raging hunger, which he tried to still with roots; he ate them although he didn't know them. And so he dragged himself along until he reached a lonely camp towards evening. The inhabitants were hospitable and took him in. He was so weak that he was unable to tell them what he had experienced; he collapsed unconscious. When he woke up he lay in an old bed and didn't know how he had arrived there. Then they told him that he had been delirious for almost two weeks and had only uttered incoherently about murder, blood, escape and water. It was then that he told of his adventure and learnt that a cowboy had met a red-haired man who had enquired whether or not a stranger had arrived at the camp. The boy had once seen the red-haired fellow in Colorado Springs and knew that he was called Brinkley; he didn't think of him as someone who was trustworthy, and answered in the negative. And so Engel found out the name of the murderer, because he had assumed that the man had used a false name before. The wound healed up, and then the good people took him to Las Animas at the next opportunity."

"Not to Pueblo," Watson said. "Otherwise I might have found his trail again when I got there later. What did he do then?"

"He joined a trader's wagon train, which was travelling to Kansas City along the old Arkansas route, as a driver. When he received his pay there, he had the means to visit his brother. Upon arriving in Russelville he heard that his brother had moved away. But a neighbour handed Engel a letter, which his brother had deposited with him, and in it he read that he would find him in Benton, Arkansas."

"Ah, there! Benton is one of the few places I didn't get to!" Watson said. "But what about the drawing he had with him?"

"That had suffered in the waters of the Orfork, and Engel had to make a copy. Of course he recounted the misadventure to his brother, who gladly and willingly was going to undertake the ride with him. Unfortunately it soon became evident that the ordeal he had suffered wasn't as inconsequential as first thought. Engel began to cough and quickly became emaciated. The doctor said that he was suffering from galloping consumption[3], and eight weeks after arriving at his brother's home he was a corpse. The prolonged standing in the spring-thaw water had condemned him to death."

"That means the colonel has Engel's death on his conscience after all!"

"If only he had nothing else on it! There are several people among us who have an account to settle with the multiple murderer. But listen to what happened next! Engel, your companion's brother, that is, was a wealthy man who grew crops on his fields and

_____

[3] Tuberculosis

conducted some profitable businesses on the side. He had a family of two children, a boy and a girl, his wife of course, and a young dogsbody, a boy who also carried out a maid's chores where necessary. One day a stranger visited Engel and made a lucrative deal with him. Engel was delighted about it. The stranger passed himself off as a canal barge entrepreneur and said that he had made his fortune as a gold prospector. On that occasion, he mentioned that he had made the acquaintance of a hunter by the name of Engel, who had also been German. Of course the hunter in question was none other than Engel's brother, your comrade, and subsequently there was so much to talk about that the afternoon turned into evening whereby the stranger gave no indication he intended to depart. Of course he was asked to stay the night, which he accepted after some encouragement. Engel ultimately told of his brother's death and the cause for it, and went to fetch the drawing from the small cabinet on the wall. At last, everyone retired to their rooms to sleep. The family slept on the first floor, up one flight of stairs, in the rooms facing the back of the house, the young farmhand slept on the same floor, but on the other side in a small chamber. The guest had been assigned the bedroom facing the front of the house. Engel locked everything on the ground floor and, as was his custom, took the keys with him to his rooms. As it so happened, Fred had had his birthday a few days earlier and had received a two-year-old horse. He hadn't been asleep long when he woke up again. He realized that he had forgotten to feed his horse because the many tales of interesting adventures had distracted him. He got out of bed again and quietly left the bedroom so as not to wake the others. On the ground floor he pushed open the bolt on the back door and walked across the yard and into the stable. He didn't require a lantern. Besides, the kitchen where it was kept had been locked. He had to feed the horse in the dark, that's why it took longer than usual. He hadn't quite finished when he thought he had heard a scream. He walked out of the stable into the yard and saw light in the family's bedroom. It disappeared, but not long after reappeared in the chamber of the farmhand. A loud commotion ensued. Fred heard the boy scream and furniture break. He ran to the wall and climbed up the vine trellis to the window. When he looked inside he saw the farmhand defend himself against his assailant with a knife, but he wasn't strong enough and was soon lying on the floor; the stranger was kneeling over him and had a hold on the boy's throat with his left hand, and with the right held a revolver to his head. Two shots rang out. Fred wanted to scream but couldn't get a sound out. In his shock he let go of the trellis and fell onto the cobblestones in the yard. He hit his head and lost consciousness. When he came to he wondered what to do. The murderer was likely still in the house; hence he couldn't risk going inside. But he had to get help somehow. He jumped across the fence, and screamed at the top of his lungs, in an effort to chase the man away and deter him from harming his family; and then he ran towards the house of the nearest neighbour. The property was also situated a stretch outside the town. The people heard the calls for help, got up immediately and came out of the house. When they heard what had happened they fetched their weapons and followed Fred, who was running back home. They saw that the first floor was burning even before they got there. The stranger had lit a fire, and had then absconded. The flames had spread so fast that it was already impossible to get upstairs; the helpers saved most of the possessions downstairs. The small cupboard on the wall was open and empty. It was impossible to reach the dead; they were going to burn."

"Ghastly—horrible!" the men around the camp exclaimed when Aunty Droll paused. Fred Engel was sitting beside the campfire, covering his face with his hands, and weeping quietly.

"Yes, ghastly!" Droll nodded. "The incident caused a stir. Investigations were carried out in all directions, but in vain. The two brothers Engel had a sister in St. Louis. She was the wife of a wealthy riverboat owner. She offered ten thousand dollars reward for the capture of the robber, arsonist and murderer; but that didn't bring anything either. Then she had the idea to contact the private detective agency of Harris & Blother, and that yielded a successful result."

"Successful?" Watson asked. "The murderer is still at large! I take it of course that it is the colonel."

"Yes, he is still at large," Droll replied. "But he's as good as finished. I went to Benton to have a more thorough look around than others had..."

"You? Why you?"

"To earn the five thousand dollars."

"But the reward was ten thousand!"

"The bounty will be shared," Droll said. "One half goes to Harris & Blother, the other to the detective."

"Are you trying to tell us that you're a policeman, sir?"

"Hm! I think that I'm dealing with nothing but honest people here, and that there is none among you who will one day have the law hard on his heels. I'll therefore tell you what I've kept quiet thus far: I'm a detective for certain districts in the far West. I've already delivered many a man, who thought he was safe, to Mr Hemp[4], and intend to carry on that way. So, now you know it, and also know the reason why I don't usually talk about myself. The old Droll, laughed at by many hundreds over time, isn't so ridiculous after all, once you get to know him. But that doesn't belong here; I must talk about the murder."

While Aunty Droll's peculiar name had caused general hilarity before, everyone had by then changed their attitude and subsequently looked at him with different eyes. His admission, that he was a detective, had thrown an explanatory light on his entire personality and his acquired idiosyncrasies. He hid behind his droll demeanour in order to more certainly get his hands on those he wanted to catch.

"Right, then," he continued. "I introduced myself to Fred in particular and quizzed him. I learnt what had been told and talked about during the evening. The villain subsequently killed the inhabitants of the house in order to open the small cupboard on the wall and steal the drawing. He hadn't taken the risk of breaking it open while they were sleeping upstairs, because the noise would have woken them. Of course he wanted to make use of the map; thus I figured that he was heading for Silver-Lake. I had to go after him, and took Fred along. He had seen him and was able to identify him. I gained near certainty on the steamer already, when I saw the outlaws, and that certainty has been growing by the day. Hopefully the offender will fall into my hands today."

"Your hands?" old Missouri-Blenter asked. "Oho! What will you do with him?"

"I'll do whatever is best in the situation."

"To transport him to Benton?"

"Perhaps."

"Don't go imagining that! There are people here who have a far greater right to have him. Consider the account I alone have to square with him!"

"The same goes for me!" Watson said.

"And for the rest of the rafters also!" several voices came from the circle of men around the fire.

---

[4] This means 'hangman'; ropes were still made from hemp fibres.

"Don't work yourselves up, because we haven't got him yet!" Droll replied.

"We have him!" Blenter insisted.

"He'll definitely be the very first to climb aboard the train."

"That may be so; but I won't get to eat a buffalo loin if I haven't shot the buffalo first. Besides, I don't care who gets him. It's not necessary for me to drag him anywhere. If I furnish the proof of his demise, and that I contributed to it, the reward is as secure as my sleeping gown. I've talked enough for now and will get some sleep. Wake me when the time has come!"

He rose to find a secluded, dark spot. The others, however, weren't thinking about sleeping. What they had heard occupied their thoughts for some time, and then there was the expected clash with the outlaws, which was a subject the men couldn't discuss extensively enough.

Winnetou didn't join in the conversation. He leaned against the rock and had his eyes closed; but he wasn't asleep because he lifted his eyelids occasionally, and then a flash-like, sharp and searching glance shot out from under them.

It was around midnight when the twenty workers went to the engineer's house to surround it. Old Firehand went to visit Hartley. He lay in bed asleep, but next to it sat Charoy's Negro assistant with the revolver in his hand. He had taken over guarding the two outlaws since the wounded Yankee required sleep. Old Firehand saw that there was no need to be concerned about the two prisoners being secure. Satisfied, he returned to the engineer and informed him that the time had come for him to depart and walk towards the coming train.

"Therefore the dangerous hour has arrived," Charoy said. "Aren't you afraid, sir?"

"Afraid?" the hunter was astonished. "Would I have volunteered for this affair if I were afraid?"

"Or at least concerned?"

"I'm only concerned about one thing; that the colonel might escape."

"But it is possible, and even likely, that they'll shoot at you!"

"It's even more likely that they won't hit me. Don't worry about me, and instead keep a clear house here. It's possible, after all, that the colonel will send a few people up here to ensure everything is progressing as it should. In that case he'll prearrange a warning signal with them. Behave normally."

Then he called the two railroad workers, who were going to stand on the locomotive in place of the two outlaws, and went down to the railroad tracks, but along a detour, so that the spies were unable to spot them. The engineer had also ensured that the two workers were dressed like the two imprisoned outlaws.

It was completely dark; but the two workers were familiar with the tracks and walked on either side of the hunter. While they were walking in the direction of Carlyle, he again coached them on how to act during every possible situation. They reached the spot that had been agreed upon by telegraphic messages, and then sat down in the grass to wait for the arrival of the train. It wasn't quite three o'clock when it came and stopped next to them. It consisted of an engine and four large passenger coaches. Old Firehand went aboard and walked through all of them. They were empty. A large rock-filled strongbox had been placed in the first one. There was no conductor; only two people were on the train: the driver and the fireman, who doubled as brakeman. When Old Firehand left the wagons, he went to greet the two men and give them instructions. He hadn't quite finished when the fireman said:

"Sir, wait a moment! I don't think it will be necessary to continue explaining your orders. I have no mind to follow them."

"Oh? Why?"

"I'm a fireman and have to shovel the fuel into the boiler; I'm getting paid to do that; but I'm not employed to get myself shot."

"Who's saying anything about getting shot?"

"You aren't, of course, but I am all the more."

"No one will shoot."

"Alright, in that case they'll take to stabbing or bashing, and that's all the same to me. There's no difference to being shot, stabbed, strangled or bludgeoned to death. I don't want to leave my post by any of those means."

"But didn't your superiors order you to follow our instructions?"

"No; they can't do that. I'm a family man and do my duty. To tackle outlaws isn't part of my range of commitments. I was told to drive here and listen to what was requested of me. It is at my discretion to decide whether or not I'm going to do it, and I'm not going to do it."

"Is that your firm decision?"

"Yes."

"What about you, sir?" Old Firehand asked the driver, who had quietly listened to the conversation.

"I won't leave my machine," the decent, fearless man said.

"Nevertheless, it is my duty to inform you that you might suffer an injury or worse through any number of unforeseen circumstances."

"And you wouldn't, sir?"

"Indeed I might."

"Alright then! If you, the stranger, are risking this, then I, as a railroad officer am also permitted to risk it."

"Quite so! You're a brave man. The fireman may safely go to Sheridan and wait for our return there; I'll take his place."

"Alright, I'll leave and wish you success!" the fireman mumbled and left.

Old Firehand and the two workers from Sheridan climbed onto the machine, and the hunter completed the instructions to the driver; then he blackened his face with soot. Thus he looked just like a fireman in his grey linen suit. The train moved on.

The passenger cars were built according to the American plan, and were illuminated; the engine was a so-called tender locomotive with a partly enclosed cab surrounded by high weather walls made of strong steel. That was a fortunate circumstance, because those walls hid the men standing on the machine almost completely, and they were thick enough to deflect pistol or rifle bullets.

After a short while the train reached Sheridan and stopped. There was only the engineer on the platform; he exchanged the usual remarks with the driver, and then let the train continue.

In the meantime the two spies, whom Old Firehand had listened to on the top of the embankment, had arrived where the colonel and his outlaws were stationed. They reported that no one in Sheridan had any idea what was about to happen, and caused great joy with that. But then they took the colonel aside and informed him of their concerns, which they had voiced earlier to each other. He calmly listened to them, and then said:

"I already know what you're telling me. I wouldn't think of keeping all of these men—most of them are useless scoundrels— and I would even less come by the idea to give those I have no use for even a single dollar of the half million; they'll get nothing."

"Then they'll take it by force!"

"Let's wait and see! I have my plan."

"But they'll board the train!"

"Never mind! I know that they'll all crowd inside; I'll remain standing outside and wait until the chest is brought outside. Once the train has left, we'll see what happens."

"What about the two of us?"

"You'll stay with me. By sending you to Sheridan I've proved to you that I trust you. Now go to Woodward. He knows my plan and will tell you the names of those I want to keep with me."

They obeyed his request and joined the man in question, who would have held a rank akin to a lieutenant under the colonel. It was black all around them; later, when three o'clock drew near, they lit a fire next to the track. The outlaws didn't realize that the early morning hours had been chosen for their demise. It was still dark at three o'clock; but by the time the train would reach Eagle Tail, day would dawn, making aiming at a target easy.

It was a quarter past three when the waiting outlaws at last heard the rolling of the train, and shortly afterwards saw the piercing light of the engine. Old Firehand kept the hatch of the firebox closed, so that he and the other three people weren't clearly recognizable. Just a little less than one hundred metres away from the fire the driver applied the breaks, as if he had obeyed a sudden, forceful demand. The whistle blew, the wheels screeched and grated along the tracks; the train came to a halt.

Until that point the outlaws had had misgivings about the ability of the false clerk and his assistant to intimidate the driver and fireman; when they saw that the train stopped, they were jubilant and pushed towards the doors of the cars. Each one wanted to be the first to get aboard. But the colonel knew his priorities. He walked to the locomotive, cast a glance around the cab wall and asked:

"Is everything alright, boys?"

"It is!" one of the railroad workers, who held the revolver to the driver's chest, replied. "They had no choice but to obey. Look here, colonel! The slightest move and we'll pull the trigger."

Old Firehand shrank against the boiler as if he were afraid, and in front of him was the other worker with the revolver. The colonel was completely fooled. He said:

"Splendid! You've done your job well and will receive a little extra money. Stay up there until we're done; you can get down when I give the signal, so that these good people can drive on and won't die of fright."

He stepped away from the machine and walked back into the dark. He was convinced that he had seen his two outlaws, especially since the worker who had replied, had imitated the voice of the fake clerk. When Brinkley had gone, Old Firehand leaned forwards to cast a glance over the place. He saw no one standing outside, but there was a crowd inside the cars. He could hear that they were fighting about the money chest.

"Away, away!" the hunter ordered the driver. "And not slowly, but fast! The colonel seems to have climbed aboard also. We mustn't wait any longer, otherwise they'll jump down again."

The train began to move, without the driver sounding the customary whistle.

"Stop, stop!" they heard someone yell. "Shoot the dogs! Shoot, shoot!"

The words were audible, but the voice was unrecognizable. Hence, Old Firehand didn't know that the colonel had been shouting those commands.

The outlaws inside the passenger cars were aghast when they realized that the train had rolled on. They wanted to get out, to jump off, but that was already impossible at the speed the driver had achieved. Old Firehand had to stoke the fire. The flames illuminated him and his companions. The door at the front of the first car was pulled open, and Woodward stepped out on the platform. He saw the tender ahead and, over the top of it, the brightly lit face of the hunter, with the fake outlaws standing quite peacefully next to him.

"Old Firehand!" he roared so loudly that it was audible even over the rolling of the wheels and the huffing and puffing of the machine. "It's that dog! To hell with you!"

He pulled out his pistol and fired at the hunter. Firehand threw himself to the floor and wasn't hit. The next moment, the hunter rose, his revolver flashed up, and Woodward crashed back into the car, hit in the heart. Others became visible in the open door, but were immediately hit by Firehand's bullets. The two railroad workers from Sheridan also aimed their revolvers at the door and kept firing until they had succeeded in moving a corrugated iron sheet into the opening between the tender and the locomotive. The outlaws were thus welcome to keep shooting.

Meanwhile the train had continued to race ahead. The driver kept an attentive eye on the line lit by the engine light. Half an hour passed; dawn began to light the east. That's when the driver blew the whistle, not in short bursts, but in one long, seemingly endless roar. He was approaching the bridge and wanted to inform the men waiting there of the coming train.

The latter had long since taken up their positions. The troopers from Fort Wallace had arrived just before midnight; they were posted on both sides of the river, under the bridge, in order to arrest any outlaw who might get away up top. Winnetou, the rafters, and the hunters were stationed at the approach to the bridge. At the other end, on either side of the tunnel entrance, stood three quarters of the armed railroad workers; the rest of them were waiting at the exit of the tunnel. The overseer Watson was among the latter. He had taken on the dangerous task of uncoupling the locomotive from the train inside the tunnel. When he heard the roar of the steam whistle, he ordered his men:

"Light the fire!"

While the men obeyed and went to set ablaze the heap of wood and coal in front of the tunnel opening, Watson walked inside the tunnel to wait for the train by tightly hugging the wall.

The train had come across the bridge with diminished power and speed, and approached the tunnel. Old Firehand saw the people posted there and called to them:

"Light it behind us!"

Shortly thereafter the train stopped. The locomotive stood exactly where Watson had expected it.

"Wait one moment!"

As he said that, he crawled between the tender and the first passenger car, unhitched the coupling between the two, and then ran out of the tunnel. The locomotive followed immediately; the coaches remained standing, and the fires that were burning at both ends of the tunnel were being moved into the middle of the track, where swiftly added extra gravel and rocks protected the sleepers.

All of this happened much more quickly than can be recounted, even too fast for the outlaws inside the passenger cars to realize their predicament. They had already become unnerved during the speedy ride. They had found out that Old Firehand was on the locomotive, and therefore knew that their plan had been foiled; however, they were certain that they would regain their freedom once the train stopped, even if it were in a busy station. They were well armed and so numerous that no one would dare to stop them.

The train had come to a halt; that's what they had been waiting for. But when they looked out of the windows, only a subterranean blackness stared back at them. When they pushed out through the doors to alight, it was as if they were looking through a giant pipe at mighty, smoking fires on either end. Those at the front realized that the locomotive had disappeared, and in its stead lay a burning heap of wood and coal. That's when one of them came to the correct conclusion:

"A tunnel, a tunnel!" he cried out in panic; and the others echoed: "A tunnel, a tunnel! What are we going to do? We must get out!"

Those inside pushed and shoved, so that the ones standing in the doors and on the platforms were forced out and fell down; those who followed landed on top of those already on the ground, and so on. There was a chaotic mess of bodies, arms, legs, and of shouts, expletives and curses, and consequently there were many injuries. Some of the men reached for their weapons to rid themselves of those who were holding onto or lying on top of them.

In addition to the darkness, which was only scantily penetrated by the fires burning at either end of the tunnel, the thick, heavy smoke was driven into the tunnel by the morning breeze.

"By the devil! They want to suffocate us!" someone screeched. "Outside, outside!"

Ten, twenty, fifty, a hundred or more screaming voices repeated it, and with genuine mortal fear everyone drove, pushed and rammed towards the two exits. But the continually stacked, raging fires were ablaze with broad and tall flames that offered no space to get through. Anyone attempting to get out would have to jump through the inferno, whereby their clothes would certainly ignite. The men at the front of the throng realized it; they turned around and pushed back; the ones at the back urged forwards and didn't want to yield. Consequently a ghastly clash ensued between people who had a short time earlier been friends and of like mind in all their evil endeavours. The tunnel amplified the roaring and raging tenfold, so that outside it sounded like all the wild animals on Earth had been let loose inside.

Old Firehand had walked back around the cliff to reach the fire near the bridge.

"We don't have to do anything," one of the railroad workers said. "The beasts are killing each other. Listen to that, sir! No one could have come up with a better plan than yours."

"Yes, they've come to hard blows," he replied. "But they are human beings, and we must spare them. Clear the entrance for me!"

"Do you want to go inside perchance?"

"Yes."

"For God's sake, don't do that! They'll attack and strangle you, sir!"

"No, they'll be glad if I show them the way to safety."

He assisted in moving the fire aside, so that a gap opened up between it and the tunnel wall, through which one could leap.

Walking slowly would have been impossible. He made the jump and arrived inside the tunnel, facing the furious mob alone. He had probably never before in his life demonstrated his daring as clearly as at that moment; and likewise his confidence had never been as steadfast as there and then. He had often experienced the fascinating and paralysing effect the courage of one single man can have on mobs.

"Hello; silence!" his mighty voice resounded. It drowned out the screaming of a hundred voices, and all of them fell silent. "Listen to what I'm telling you!"

"Old Firehand!" the outlaws uttered, full of astonishment at his incomparable fearlessness.

"Yes, that's me," he replied. "And you've found out that where I am there is no resistance. If you don't want to suffocate, then leave your weapons here and come out, one at a time. I'll be outside the fire and issue the orders. Anyone who runs out without waiting for my call will be shot immediately. And anyone who keeps a weapon will also get a bullet. We are enough men, workers, hunters, rafters and soldiers to make good on my warning. Consider it well! Throw a cap or a hat out; that shall be the signal that you're prepared to obey. If you don't do that, then a hundred rifles will be aimed at the fires and no one will be let through."

Because of the smoke he had only been able to speak the last few words with great effort, and immediately afterwards he swiftly jumped back out through the gap, so as not to become the target for a bullet. The caution was advisable, but actually superfluous. The effect his arrival in the tunnel had had on the outlaws was such that none of them would have dared to lift a gun and aim at him.

Then he instructed the workers to aim their guns at the tunnel opening to drive the outlaws back should they try to break out en masse. The men outside could hear the debate going on inside. There was a confusion of loud voices. The circumstances didn't allow for a lengthy discussion because the smoke that filled the tunnel became more dense, and made breathing increasingly difficult. Confronted by a man like Old Firehand, the outlaws had lost their courage; they knew that he would enforce his warning. Death by suffocation was approaching, and they saw no other means of salvation than to surrender. A hat was thrown past the fire, out of the tunnel, and immediately afterwards the outlaws were informed by Old Firehand's shout that the first one of them was allowed to leave the tunnel. He jumped out and was directed to walk straight across the bridge without stopping, where the rafters and hunters welcomed him. In anticipation of the successful outcome of their plan, which had actually originated in Winnetou's mind, the men had brought along plenty of ropes, straps and the like, and when the first outlaw arrived he was immediately bound. His comrades, who came after him, were dealt with likewise. They were released from the tunnel at intervals that allowed for the securing of each individual before the next arrived. That happened so fast that all outlaws were in the power of the victors after a quarter of an hour. However, to everyone's vexation and chagrin, it turned out that Red Brinkley was missing. When the prisoners were questioned about it, they stated that he and about twenty others had not climbed into the carriages. The men carefully searched the tunnel and the passenger cars after the smoke had cleared; they didn't find him, and thus had to assume that the captives had spoken the truth.

Was it possible that he, of all men, the one they had wanted to capture the most, had escaped? No! The prisoners were left in the custody of the soldiers and railroad men, and then Old Firehand, Winnetou, the hunters and the rafters rode back to the place where the train had been stopped, in order to pick up the fugitive's trail. When they arrived there, Old Firehand sent four rafters to Sheridan to bring his own horse, his hunting outfit, as well as the two outlaws imprisoned in Charoy's house, to the tunnel. He did not intend to return to Sheridan, and instead wanted to immediately travel to Fort Wallace with his comrades, where the gang of outlaws was being sent, because they were under military guard there, and much more secure than anywhere else. Old Firehand also tasked the four messengers with informing the engineer about the outcome of the nightly adventure.

They found the spot where the outlaws had been camped while waiting for the train. Their horses had been tied up not far from it. After a lengthy search and careful scrutiny of the many hoof and footprints, they found that indeed about twenty men had escaped. They had taken just as many horses with them, and had chosen only the best; they had chased the others away in all directions.

"The colonel was smart," Old Firehand remarked. "It would have been a great burden for the small troop to take all the horses along, and the trail left behind would have been so clear that a child could have followed it. By chasing the leftover horses apart, he made our search more difficult, and gained a lot of time. And since he's certainly not taken the worst nags, he'll make good progress and will already have a head start that we will only with great effort be able to make up."

"My white brother might perhaps be mistaken," Winnetou replied. "This paleface will certainly not have left the region without investigating what happened to his people. If we follow his trail now we'll find that it leads to Eagle Tail."

"I'm convinced that my red brother is correct. The colonel rode away from here to spy on us. He'll now know where he stands and will at once have made off. But we've come here to search for him, and have lost valuable time."

"If we rush back there, then we might still be able to catch him!"

"No. My brother must consider that we cannot immediately follow him. We must go to Fort Wallace to make our statement. That will take all of today, so that we won't be able to follow the outlaws before tomorrow."

"That means they'll be an entire day ahead of us!"

"Yes; but we know where they're headed, and don't need to waste time by following their trail. We'll head to Silver-Lake directly."

"Does my brother think they will still want to go there?"

"Definitely."

"Even now that they've been defeated?"

"Yes, in spite of it."

"But they weren't successful here. Won't that change their plans?"

"Certainly not. They wanted to have money to make some purchases. But those are not absolutely necessary. They can live off the game they shoot. They have weapons and most likely also ammunition. And should they lack the latter, they can always acquire some by honest or dishonest means. I'm convinced that they're headed for Silver-Lake."

"Then let's follow their trail to at least find out where they rode from this spot."

Twenty riders leave enough hoof prints behind, and there were plenty of experienced eyes in the group that wouldn't have missed an even fainter trail. It led to the river, and then upstream along the bank; it was so clear that the men were able to ride at a gallop without losing sight of it.

The twenty outlaws had stopped near the bridge. One of them, probably the colonel, had sneaked up to the railroad track under cover of the trees and bushes, where he would undoubtedly have been a witness to the imprisonment of the entire gang. When he had returned they had ridden away.

The hunters and rafters followed the trail for another half an hour, and when they had ascertained the direction of the fugitives, they returned to the bridge. The colonel and his small group of outlaws were heading for Bush Creek, which was a near-certain indication that they intended to ride into Colorado and from there to Silver-Lake.

In the meantime the four rafters had returned from Sheridan. They had also brought along Hartley and Charoy, the engineer, who both wanted to go to Fort Wallace where their testimony was of importance. The railroad workers returned to Sheridan on foot; they took with them the surrendered weapons as their reward. There were more than enough carriages available for the transport of the outlaws. The construction train was still there, and so was the 'money train', which hadn't carried any money, of course. After the prisoners had been loaded up, the others also went aboard and the two trains moved out. The cavalry detachment rode back to Fort Wallace.

Word about the event had already spread around Fort Wallace, and the inhabitants were very curious to know the outcome. When the trains arrived everyone crowded around them, and the outlaws were greeted in a manner that gave them a taste of what they could expect later in the afternoon. Had there not been so many prisoners, and had their been escort less skilled in preventing it, they would have been lynched right there and then.

They had suffered great losses regardless, since about a quarter of them had been found dead inside the tunnel. To this day people in the region talk about the famous smoke-out of the outlaws in the tunnel at Eagle Tail, and the names of Old Firehand and Winnetou are always mentioned.

Long Davy   Fat Jemmy

6

Among Utah Indians

Where the Elk Mountains rise on the far side of Cumison River, four men were riding across a high plateau that was covered in short grass, but not a single bush or tree was evident as far as the eye could see. Although the people of the far West are used to seeing unusual figures, the four riders would have been conspicuous to anyone who came across them.

One of them, the noblest, by the looks of it, rode a magnificent black stallion of the type that was bred by certain Apache tribes. He was not too tall, nor was he very broad-shouldered, and yet he gave the impression of great strength and endurance. A full, dark-blond beard framed his sunburnt face. He wore leather leggings, a hunting shirt of the same material, as well as long boots that he had pulled up over his knees. On his head sat a broad-brimmed felt hat, with grizzly bear ears threaded all along the chinstrap. The broad belt, woven from thin leather strips, appeared as though it was filled with cartridges; it also contained two revolvers and a bowie knife. In addition there hung two pairs of screw-on horseshoes, as well as four almost circular, thickly woven reed and straw mats fitted with straps and buckles. They were undoubtedly meant to be fastened to a horse's hooves when it was a matter of confusing a possible pursuer. From the left shoulder to the right hip was draped a rolled-up lasso, and on his neck, suspended from a silken string that was decorated with hummingbird feathers, hung an ornate peace pipe. In his right hand he held a short rifle the mechanism of which seemed to be of a distinctly peculiar construction, and on his back, suspended on its strap across his other shoulder, hung a long, and very heavy, double-barrelled rifle of an exceedingly rare make, which used to be known as 'bear killer' in earlier times; it fired bullets of the largest calibre. That man was Old Shatterhand, the famous hunter, who owed his nom de guerre to the fact that he was able to overpower an enemy with nothing more than a punch from his fist.

Next to him rode a short, skinny and beardless fellow in a long, blue tailcoat with yellow, highly polished buttons. Atop his head sat a large Amazon hat with a giant feather that moved about. His trousers were too short, and his naked feet were clad in old, rough leather shoes with large, Mexican spurs. The short rider had an entire arsenal of weaponry hanging on and around himself; but anyone looking into his small, good-natured face gained the opinion that the mighty armoury had only the purpose of scaring possible enemies away. That short fellow was Mr Heliogabalus Morpheus Franke, ordinarily called Hobble-Frank by his friends, because he walked with a limp, which was the consequence of an old injury.

Behind Old Shatterhand and Hobble-Frank came two other riders. One of them was at least one hundred and ninety centimetres tall, but all the more skinny, and he sat on an old, short-legged mule that seemed to have hardly the strength to carry the rider. He wore leather trousers that had undoubtedly been tailored to fit a much shorter, yet more solid figure. His naked feet also sat in leather shoes, but those had so often been mended and repaired that they consisted of nothing but patches; one of them would surely be as heavy as two and a half or three kilograms. The man's torso was clad in a buffalo leather shirt, which left the chest uncovered because it had neither buttons, nor toggle and loop to do it up. Its sleeves hardly reached past the elbows. A cotton scarf was wound around his long neck, but the original colour of it was no longer recognizable. On his pointy head rested a hat that had once been a grey top hat many long years ago. Perhaps it had once crowned the head of a millionaire; but afterwards it had fallen ever lower and had finally ended up on the prairie and in the hands of its present owner. He had regarded the brim as superfluous and had therefore torn it off, except for a small remnant to use as a handle for taking the incredibly contorted and crumpled head covering off. Two revolvers and a scalping knife sat in a thick rope that served him as a belt, and on it hung several pouches that contained all the necessities a Westerner cannot easily do without. From his shoulders hung a rubber coat that defied description! The magnificent garment had shrunk and shrivelled up with the first rain already, so that it could never again fulfil its original purpose, and had to be worn like a Hussar pelisse. The man had placed one of those rifles with which a skilled hunter never misses across his endlessly long legs. His age was impossible to determine, and so was that of his mule. At most one could assume that both knew each other well and had already experienced many adventures together.

The fourth rider was sitting atop a very tall and big-boned nag. He was overly portly and so short that his legs only reached to about the middle of his horse's belly. Although the sun was shining down quite hotly, he wore a fur coat, which suffered from extreme baldness. If one collected all the remaining hair on it, one wouldn't have been able to cover a mouse with it. His Panama hat was far too large, and from under the naked fur coat peeked two giant cuffed boots. Since the sleeves of the coat were far too long, only the fat, rosy and good-natured face of the man was therefore visible. He was fitted out with a long rifle. No other weaponry was apparent because the fur coat covered everything.

Those two men were David Kroners and Jakob Pfefferkorn, known everywhere only as Long Davy and Fat Jemmy. They were inseparable, and no one had ever seen one without the other having been at least nearby. Jemmy was German and Davy was a Yankee, yet the latter had learnt so much of Jemmy's language during the many years of being together, that he had become sufficiently proficient in expressing himself in German. The riders' animals had become just as inseparable. They always stood next to each other; they grazed together, and when they were forced to endure the company of other mounts in some camp, they shifted away from them just a little bit, and nudged closer side by side to caress each other with snorting, sniffling and licking.

The four riders had obviously travelled a significant distance already, although it wasn't far past midday, and not only across grassland, because they and their mounts were covered with a fair amount of dust. Yet neither the men nor their animals displayed any signs of fatigue. If they were exhausted, then that was only evident in their taciturnity. Hobble-Frank, the rider next to Old Shatterhand, was the first to interrupt the silence when he asked the hunter in his native dialect:

"So, camp will be made at Elk-Fork tonight, will it? And exactly how much further is it to there?"

"We'll reach the river towards evening," Old Shatterhand replied.

"Evening? As late as that? *O wehe*[1]! Who is supposed to endure dat? We're sitting in the saddle since early in the morning. We'll have to shtop at least the once jusht for the horses to have a breather at least. Don't you think so?"

"Indeed. Let's wait until we've got the prairie behind us; there will be a stretch of forest with some running water."

"*Schoen*[2]! The horses will have water to drink and also find grass to eat. But what will we find? We ate the last buffalo meat yesterday, and today the bones. Since then neither a sparrow nor any other game has come before our rifles; I'm therefore very hungry and must have something to nibble on, otherwise I'll perish."

"Don't worry! I'll get us a roast."

"Yes, but wat? Dat old paddock here is so lonely; I think not even a beetle is running around on it. Where, then, is a decent westman[3] supposed to get a roast from?"

"I can already see it. Take my horse by its reins for now and slowly ride on with the others."

"Truly?" Frank asked while he looked around and shook his head. "You can see dat roast already? I'm unable to detect any such vision."

---

[1] Oh, my

[2] Nice

[3] Karl May uses a peculiar term for frontiersmen, hunters, trappers, and any other capable adventurers in his imagined Wild West. As there is no such term in the English language—*Westmann* ('westman')—I ordinarily use known terms in the translations, such as frontiersman, or Westerner. Hobble-Frank, however, insists on saying 'westman' (and he does so a couple of times, with Aunty Droll doing likewise just the once), which will be appreciated by those Karl May fans who are familiar with Karl May's German text, and in their youth have played not 'Cowboys and Indians' but 'Westmen and Indians'.

He took the reins of Old Shatterhand's horse and continued to ride along with Davy and Jemmy. The hunter, however, walked away from them to the side, where a large number of mounds were apparent in the grass. There was a colony of prairie dogs, as the American marmots were called because of their yapping voice. They are harmless, innocuous, but very inquisitive creatures that, oddly enough, like to live close to or with rattlesnakes and owls. When someone approaches, they stand upright to observe him, resulting in many droll poses and moves. If they become suspicious, they dive into their burrows at the speed of lightning and disappear from view. If a hunter is successful in securing a different kind of meal, then he will spurn the meat of the prairie dogs, not because it is unpalatable, but because he is prejudiced against it. If he wants to kill a prairie dog, regardless, then he mustn't try to sneak up secretly, because those creatures are too attentive for him to be successful at it. He must wake their inquisitiveness and attempt to keep their attention until he has come within shooting range. But he can only achieve this by attaining the most ridiculous poses and make the most comical movements. Thus the prairie dog becomes confused and doesn't know what to make of the approaching creature. Old Shatterhand knew that. He executed all manner of crisscross jumps, ducked, jumped up, whirled around, moved his arms like windmill blades as soon as he noticed that he had been discovered by the animals sitting on their mounds; he had only one aim: to get close.

Hobble-Frank, who rode next to Jemmy and Davy at that point, saw the behaviour and voiced his worries:

"*Herrjemerschnee*[4], what's got into him? Has he gone mad? He's behaving exactly as if he had been drinking some Bellamadonna!"

"You mean Belladonna," Jemmy corrected him.

"Be quiet!" the short fellow roused at him. "Belladonna makes no sense. It's Bellamadonna; me, who was born in Moritzburg, ought to know dat after all. Bellamadonna grows wild there in the forest and I've probably seen it shtanding there a thousand times. Listen! He's shooting."

Old Shatterhand had discharged a couple of shots so fast one after the other that they sounded almost like one shot. They watched as he ran up the incline a stretch and bent down twice to pick something up. He returned to his waiting companions with two prairie dogs he had killed, stashed them in the saddle bags,

---

[4] Oh, deary me

and then mounted up again. Hobble-Frank made a sceptical face and, while they were riding on, asked:

"Ish dat supposed to be our roast? In dat case I'll be thanking you most humbly!"

"Why?"

"I won't devour such stuff!"

"Have you ever tasted it?"

"Nee! I wouldn't dream of it!"

"In that case you cannot judge whether a prairie dog is palatable or not. Have you ever eaten a young goat perhaps?"

"A young kid?" Frank replied and at the same time clicked his tongue. "Of course I have eaten dat. You must know: dat is something so entirely delectable!"

"Truly?" Old Shatterhand smiled.

"Upon my honour! Dat's a delicacy second to none."

"And thousands laugh about it!"

"Yes; but those thousands are stupid. I'm telling you dat we Saxons are bright and know our delights like no other European nation. Put a young kid in the pot, a small clove of garlic and a few sprigs of Marjoram, then roast it nice and brown and crispy, that's a veritable feast for the ladies and gentlemen gods on the Olympus. I know so, because around Easter, when the little goats appear, the whole of Saxony only eats kid roast on Sun- and holy-days."

"Indeed! But tell me whether or not you've ever eaten *lapin*!"

"Lepang? What's dat?"

"Tame hare, or more precisely: rabbit."

"Rabbit? *Alabonneur*! Dat's an affluent matter altogether. During my time in and around Moritzburg there was always rabbit to be had during the parish fair. The meat is tender like butter and melts on your tongue."

"There are many who would laugh at you, if you told them."

"They wouldn't be right in the head. A rabbit dat eats the best and finest herb tips can only have the most obligingly tender meat; dat goes without saying. Or don't you believe it?"

"I believe it; but I also request that, in return, you treat my prairie dog without contempt. You'll see that it'll taste just like young kid and almost like rabbit."

"I've never heard dat said."

"In that case you've heard it for the first time today, and will also taste it. I tell you that…stop, aren't there riders approaching?"

He pointed south-west, where a number of figures were moving. They were still so far in the distance that it was impossible to say whether they were animals, perhaps buffaloes, or riders. The four hunters continued to ride slowly and kept an eye on the group. After a while they recognized them as riders, and a little later still, it was evident that they were wearing uniforms; they were soldiers.

They had originally been heading in a north-easterly direction; but when they saw the four riders they changed their course to approach at a gallop. There were twelve of them, led by a lieutenant. They stopped about thirty paces away. The officer scrutinized the four riders with a dark gaze, and then asked:

"Where to, boys?"

"*Alle Wetter*[5]!" Hobble-Frank grunted. "Shall we really let them address us with 'boys'? Can't dat fellow see that we belong to the better social classes?"

"What's there to whisper?" the lieutenant called out severely. "I want to know where you're from!"

Frank, Jemmy and Davy looked at Old Shatterhand, to ascertain what he was going to do or say. He calmly replied:

"From Leadville."

"And where are you headed?"

"To the Elk Mountains."

"That's a lie!"

Old Shatterhand drove his horse on until it stood next to that of the officer, and then asked in the same calm tone of voice:

"Do you have a reason for calling me a liar?"

"Yes!"

"Alright, what is it?"

"You're not from Leadville, but have come up from Indian Fort."

"You're mistaken."

"I'm not mistaken. I know you."

"Ah? And who are we?"

"I don't know the names; but you'll tell me immediately."

"What if we won't?"

"Then I'll take you along."

"And what happens if we refuse, sir?"

"In that case you'd have to bear the consequences. You know who and what we are, and what significance these uniforms have. I'll shoot anyone who reaches for a weapon."

---

[5] One of Karl May's 'westman' exclamations, it could be translated as 'goshamighty'.

"Really?" Old Shatterhand smiled. "Then try it, why don't you. Here, look!"

He held the rifle in his right hand, which he aimed at the officer like a pistol; at the same time he had pulled out one of his revolvers. Frank, Davy and Jemmy had the weapons in their hands just as swiftly.

"All devils!" the lieutenant called out and attempted to reach for his belt. "I..."

"Stop!" Old Shatterhand thundered at him and cut him short. "Hands off the belt, boy! All hands in the air or our barrels will flash!"

During serious encounters, which that wasn't, the advantage belonged to the one who had his weapon ready first. He'd order the other to put his hands in the air, in order to remove them as far as possible from any weapons in the belt or the pockets. If the other didn't obey immediately, then he was done for because he'd receive a bullet on the spot. The officer knew that, and so did his men. Swept away by the feeling of superiority and security, they had neglected to keep their weapons ready, and thus saw the barrels of eight rifles and revolvers aimed at them; they were convinced that they were dealing with villainous rabble, hence they immediately obeyed and stretched their hands in the air.

It was actually a bemusing picture, to see so many well-armed cavalry sit on their horses with their arms raised up high. A faint smile crossed Old Shatterhand's otherwise serious features when he continued:

"So! What do you think we'll do now, boy?"

"Go on, shoot!" the lieutenant replied. "But revenge will pursue you until it has caught up with you."

"Pshaw! What would that bring us if we wasted our good bullets on people who are so intimidated by supposedly pathetic tramps that they throw their arms heavenward? Not much fame, that's for sure! It was my intention to teach you a good lesson. You're still young and obviously need it. Always be as polite as possible, sir! A gentleman doesn't submit to being called 'boy' by the first person to come along. And furthermore, never accuse people of having told a lie if you cannot furnish evidence that they actually are liars; you could easily come up against the wrong people, as the present example demonstrates. And thirdly, if you encounter someone here in the Wild West, and you don't intend to treat them too kindly, then take the guns into your hands; it could otherwise easily happen that you would be forced to display the exact same schoolboy pose that you strike at present. You're mistaken about us. We're neither 'boys' nor liars. And now you can lower your arms again; we don't intend to puncture your hides!"

Old Shatterhand placed the revolver back into his belt and lowered the rifle; his three comrades followed his example. Subsequently the soldiers lowered their arms. Their officer in his embarrassment and exasperation uttered:

"Sir, how dare you play such a charade with us? You ought to know that I've got the power to punish you for it!"

"The power?" Old Shatterhand laughed. "The desire, yes, but not the power; I've proved that to you. Now I'd like to know how you'd go about serving us any kind of punishment. You'd embarrass yourself just like you've done before."

"Ah! Now it depends on who's the first to have the revolver in his hand..."

He didn't get any further. Again he had reached for his belt, but at that very moment felt himself lifted out of his saddle and flung through the air over to Old Shatterhand, who threw him across the front of the saddle on his own horse. The hunter put the tip of his swiftly drawn knife against the chest of the soldier, and again laughed:

"Go on, sir! You were saying? It now depends on who's the first to have the other across his saddle; wouldn't you agree? As soon as one of your men makes a move, my blade will drive into your heart! Try it, why don't you!"

The soldiers retained their stiff positions on the horses. They hadn't expected such physical strength, agility and speed; they were taken aback and so baffled that they forgot about their weapons, and that they were the ones who outnumbered the others.

"A thousand devils!" the officer called out, though he was careful not to move even one of his limbs. "What are you thinking? Let me go!"

"I'm only thinking about proving to you that you've really tackled the wrong people. We're not in the least afraid of the number of men you have in your group. Even if it were an entire squadron, we would still not be worried. Stand here and politely listen to what I'm going to tell you."

Shatterhand grabbed the officer by the scruff of his neck, lifted him from the horse with one hand, and then planted him next to it in the grass. Then he continued:

"Have you ever seen any of us?"

"No," the soldier replied while he drew a deep breath. He felt a wrath inside that he didn't dare to express. He felt extremely humiliated in front of his men and would have liked nothing more than to pull out the sabre and run it through the hunter's body, but he was convinced that he wouldn't succeed with such an attempt, and only fare badly again.

"You haven't?" Old Shatterhand remarked. "Yet I'm convinced that you know us. You will at least have heard our names. Has anyone ever told you about Hobble-Frank? Here he is right in front of you."

"I know neither the man nor his name," the officer snarled.

"But you've heard of Long Davy and Fat Jemmy, yes?"

"Yes. Are these two supposed to be them?"

"Indeed."

"Pshaw! I don't believe it!"

"Are you trying to call me a liar again? Leave that be, sir! Old Shatterhand can usually furnish evidence for every word he speaks."

"Old Shatt..." the officer called out as he retreated a step and stared at the hunter. The other half of the name remained stuck in his mouth.

His troopers reflexively made gestures of astonishment, or rather, admiration. Several of them gave a loud, involuntary "Ah!".

"Yes, Old Shatterhand," the hunter said. "Do you know that name?"

"I know it; we all know it only too well. And you...you...you're supposed to be him, sir?"

His face expressed his doubts while he scrutinized the rider. But then his gaze fell onto the short rifle with the peculiar, ball-shaped mechanism, and he immediately added with a drastically changed mien:

"Behold! Isn't that a Henry rifle, sir?"

"Indeed," Old Shatterhand nodded. "Do you know this kind of gun?"

"I have not seen one, but have heard it described in detail. The inventor was said to have been an eccentric, and had made only a few of those weapons because he feared that the Indians and buffaloes would soon be extinct if his repeating rifle found wide-spread distribution. The few pieces there were are lost, and only Old Shatterhand is supposed to still own one of them, the last one."

"That's correct, sir. Of the eleven or twelve Henry rifles, only mine is still in existence; the others have vanished in the Wild West together with their owners."

"That means you really...really are Old Shatterhand, the famous frontiersman who pushes the head of a bison bull down to the ground with only his hands and knocks down the strongest Indian with his bare fist?"

"I've already told you that's who I am. If you're still in doubt, then I'll gladly furnish the evidence. I not only give Indians, but occasionally also Whites a taste of my fist. Would you like to experience it?"

He bent down from the saddle towards the officer and swung back with the fist as if he were preparing to punch him. But the soldier recoiled and called out:

"No thank you, sir, thank you! I'd rather believe you in this case, without having that proof. I've only got one skull and don't know where I'd get another if this one were smashed asunder. Please forgive me for not having been too polite before! We've got good reasons for looking sharply at the faces of certain people. Won't you be so kind as to accompany us? My comrades would not only be overjoyed, but also regard it as an honour if it would please you to be our guest."

"Where to?"

"To Fort Mormon, where we're headed."

"Unfortunately I cannot accept your invitation because we must travel in the opposite direction to meet friends at a certain hour."

"I'm sorry to hear that. May I ask your destination, sir?"

"Initially to the Elk Mountains, as I've told you already; from there we intend to cross to the Book Mountains."

"Then I must warn you, sir," the officer said. He employed a respectful tone of voice, as if he were standing in front of a superior."

"Why? Of what or whom?"

"The redskins."

"Thank you! I don't have to fear the Indians. Besides, I wouldn't know what kind of threat would come at us from that side. The Indians are living in peace with the Whites especially at the present, and the Utah, who are the Indians you're referring to, haven't done anything in years that could engender any mistrust against them."

"That's correct; but that's precisely the reason they're all the more enraged. We know that they've raised their war hatchets, and we must therefore ride daily patrol from Fort Mormon as well as Fort Indian."

"Really? We know nothing of it."

"I can believe it because you've come from Colorado, where the news hasn't reached as yet. Your route leads you right through the middle of the Utah's range. I know that the name Old Shatterhand commands great respect among all red nations; but don't take the matter too lightly, sir! The Utah in particular have good cause to be outraged about the Whites."

"Why?"

"A company of white gold prospectors broke into a Utah camp to steal horses; it was during the night, but the Utah woke up and defended themselves whereby many of them were killed by the better-armed Whites. The latter escaped with the Indian horses and other items they had appropriated during that opportunity; but the Indians ventured out to pursue them in the morning. The robbers were caught and a battle ensued whereby again many lives were lost. We heard that sixty Indians were shot, and only six Whites escaped. Now the Utah are traipsing around to find those six, and at the same have time sent a delegation to Fort Union to ask for compensation, one horse for each stolen one, one thousand dollars in total for the stolen goods, and two horses plus a rifle for each Indian killed."

"I don't think that's too expensive. Have the Whites agreed to the claim?"

"No. The Whites wouldn't think of granting the Indians the right to make any such claims. The envoys returned empty handed and consequently raised the war hatchet. The Utah have mobilized en masse; but, unfortunately, we here in the territories don't have enough military presence to crush them all at once, and hence have looked around for allies. A number of officers went down to the Navajo, in order to obtain their help against the Utah, and they succeeded."

"And what did they offer the Navajo for their assistance?"

"Any booty they'd make."

Old Shatterhand's face turned dark when he heard that. He shook his head and said:

"So, first the Utah are attacked, robbed and many of them killed; then, when they demand punishment for the perpetrators, and compensation for their losses, they are turned away; and now that they are taking the matter into their own hands, the Whites are setting the Navajo on them and are rewarding the latter with the booty that will be taken from the victims! Is it any wonder that the Utah feel they've been pushed to the limit? Their embitterment is bound to be great, and woe to any White indeed who falls into their hands!"

"I only have to obey orders and have no right to make a judgment. I gave you this information to warn you, sir. My opinions mustn't be yours."

"I understand. Thank you for the warning. When you tell about our encounter in the Fort, then please also say that Old Shatterhand is not an enemy of the Indians and deeply regrets that a richly talented nation must perish because it is not granted the time to develop naturally according to the laws of human culture; but instead one demands of it that it turn from a nation of hunters into a modern union of states over night. One could murder a schoolboy with the exact same right because he has not yet attained the skills or knowledge to be a general or a professor of astronomy. Good bye, sir!"

Old Shatterhand turned his horse and rode away, followed by his three companions, without giving the soldiers a second glance. The latter watched the hunters ride away, and then continued their interrupted ride. Anger had led Shatterhand to his parting speech, which he well knew was pointless; he was all the more taciturn afterwards when he silently pondered the thought that it was of no use to enlighten 'brother John' about the fact that he had no greater right to exist than the Indian, who was being chased from place to place, refuge to refuge, until predictably, he ends his life unpitied, having been hounded to death.

Half an hour passed before Old Shatterhand roused from his brooding and focussed his attention on the horizon, which had taken on the shape of a dark, increasingly broad line. He pointed at it and said:

"There's the forest I mentioned earlier. Use the spurs on your horses; we'll be there in five minutes."

It must be mentioned that the manner of interaction between him and his three companions had developed to the point that when speaking in German he addressed them informally with 'du', while they addressed him with the formal 'sie'[6]; though of course when they conversed in English, it was always 'you'. Old Shatterhand's companions would not have permitted anyone but

[6] Also refer to the Translator's Notes in *Black Mustang*, as well as *From The Rio De La Plata To The Cordilleras-Book 1.*

him to address them in familiar terms; nevertheless, they had not thought it prudent to place themselves at the same elevated level.

The horses were put to the gallop, and soon the four riders reached a tall, dense spruce forest the edge of which was so tight that there seemed to be no way in on horseback. But Old Shatterhand knew what to do. He headed straight for one particular point, drove his horse through the thin undergrowth, and reached a path that was occasionally used by local Indians, and had thus been trodden to a width of approximately one metre. He dismounted to inspect the spot for new tracks; but when he didn't find any, he mounted up again and asked his companions to follow him.

Not the slightest breeze was evident inside the tucked away old growth forest, and except for the hoof beat of the horses, no other sound was audible. Old Shatterhand held his rifle ready in his right hand, and his keen gaze straight ahead in order to be the first to aim a weapon at an opponent in case of a hostile encounter. But he was convinced that there was no such danger at that point. If Indians roamed about the region on horseback, then they were in such large groups that they were certainly not going to use a path in a dense forest where they would be unable to survey their surroundings, and which made moving difficult. There were very few spots on that path where a rider would have been able to turn around. In case of hostilities, an entire host of mounted Indians would have been lost if attacked by only a few people on foot.

After some time the path opened up to a clearing, in the middle of which stood a mound of large boulders stacked on top of each other. They were overgrown with lichen, and bushes the roots of which had found the necessary nourishment inside the cracks. That's where Old Shatterhand stopped and said:

"This is the place where we can afford the horses some rest and roast our prairie dogs in the meantime. Water is also here, as you can see."

A small spring emerged from under the rocks; the water flow meandered across the clearing, and then lost itself in the forest. The riders dismounted, freed the horses to graze, and then went looking for dry wood to light a fire. Jemmy took it upon himself to skin and gut the prairie dogs, and Old Shatterhand left to reconnoitre the safety of the place.

The forest was only three quarters of an hour's walk in breadth with the Indian path cutting straight through it. The clearing was about in the middle of it.

It wasn't long before the meat was roasting over the fire and an agreeable aroma came wafting through the area. Then Old Shatterhand returned. He had quickly walked to the other edge of the forest, from where he had a sweeping view across the prairie. He hadn't been able to see anything suspicious, so he brought the news to his three companions that they didn't have to fear a surprise.

The roast was done after an hour and Old Shatterhand cut a serving for himself.

"Hm!" Hobble-Frank grunted. "Eating dog roast! If anyone at any time in the past had come by the idea to foretell me dat one day I'd devour man's best friend, I would have given them an answer dat would have made their hair stand on end. But as it is I'm hungry and must therefore try it."

"But it isn't dog," Jemmy reminded him. "You've heard that this marmot received its name in error only because of its voice."

"Dat doesn't cause any improvements on the matter; on the contrary, it makes it worse. Marmot roast! Dat doesn't bear thinking about! Man is occasionally destined to quite consistent things. Well, let's see."

He took a slice of breast and hesitantly tried it; but then his face lit up; he stuffed a larger piece of meat into his mouth, and, while chewing, declared:

"Truly not bad at all, by my honour! It really tastes almost like rabbit, if not as delicate as kid roast. Children, I think there won't be much left of those two dogs."

"We must keep some for the evening," Davy said. "We don't know whether we'll be able to shoot anything else today."

"I don't worry about later. If I'm tired and can fling myself into Orpheus' arms, then I'm happy for the time being."

"It's Morpheus," Jemmy corrected him.

"Be quiet at once! Don't you go putting an M in front of my Orpheus! I know him very precisely; in the village Klotsche near Moritzburg there is a singing club that was named 'Orpheus in the Upperworld'; those fellows were singing with such tellurian loveliness that the audience always fell into the most comfortable of slumbers. Hence the saying about falling into Orpheus' arms hails from dat-a-way, namely from Klotsche. Don't argue with me, and devour your prairie dog with taciturn care; it'll be much more tasty for you if you don't squabble with a man of my experience. You know I'm a decent fellow, but if someone comes at me with a Morpheus during my meal I'll become desperate and imported!"

Old Shatterhand gave Jemmy a signal to be quiet, so that the meal could be eaten without disturbances; however, he couldn't prevent another disturbance, which wasn't caused by the short, easily agitated Hobble-Frank.

The four men were mistaken, if they thought they were safe. Danger approached in the shape of two groups of riders, which were both nearing the forest.

One of the groups consisted of only two riders who came from the north and encountered the trail of Old Shatterhand and his comrades. They stopped and jumped from their horses to inspect the tracks. The way they went about it would have led to the assumption that they were not inexperienced Westerners. They were well armed; but their clothing had suffered. There were indications that they had experienced bad days recently. Their horses were well nourished and lively, but without saddles and bridles, and only fitted out with simple strap halters. That was the way Indians grazed their horses near their camps.

"What do you think about this trail, Knox?" one of them asked. "Are there redskins ahead of us?"

"No," the other replied confidently.

"Whites in this case! How did you arrive at that conclusion?"

"The horses are shod, and the men rode side by side, not in single file like Indians."

"And how many are there?"

"Only four. We've got nothing to fear, Hilton."

"Except if they're soldiers!"

"Pshaw! Not even then. Of course we can't risk visiting a fort; there are too many eyes and questions, and we would undoubtedly make a mistake and be found out. But four cavalry wouldn't get anything out of us. What reasons would they have to deduce that we belong to the Whites who attacked the Utah?"

"I think the same, of course; but the devil often has his fingers on the pie without anyone suspecting anything beforehand. We're in a miserable situation. Chased by the Indians and wanted by the soldiers; we're wandering back and forth through the region of the Utah. It was stupid to believe the picture of the golden mountains, which the colonel and his outlaws painted."

"Stupid? Certainly not. To become rich quickly is a beautiful thing, and I have no doubts about it at all. The colonel and his troop will get here shortly, and then we don't have to worry any longer."

"But much can happen in the meantime."

"Certainly. That's why we must attempt to get out of this desperate situation. Once I apply myself, I usually find a way out, and one such way is opening up to us right now."

"What way would that be?"

"We must find Whites we can join. We'll be taken for hunters in their company and no one will even think of connecting us with the men who have forced the Utah to raise their war hatchets."

"And you think that we've got such men ahead of us?"

"I think so. They were heading for the forest. Let's follow them."

They rode along Old Shatterhand's trail towards the trees. Along the way they talked of their experiences and plans. Their conversation would have revealed that they were indeed allies of the colonel.

Red Brinkley had been endeavouring to increase the size of his troop, which had consisted of the twenty outlaws who had escaped from Eagle Tail. He had come to the conclusion that his gang would probably be decimated by the Indians in the mountains, and that twenty weren't enough. Hence during the ride through Colorado he had admitted into his group anyone who was inclined to join him. Of course they were desperate people whose morality required no investigation. Among them were Knox and Hilton, the two men who were riding towards the forest. The colonel's gang had soon become so large that it was bound to be conspicuous, and obtaining supplies became more difficult by the day. Consequently, the colonel had decided to split them up. He wanted to cross the Rocky Mountains in the region of La Veta[7] with half of the men, and the other half was supposed to turn to Morrison[8] and Georgetown[9], to traverse the mountains from there. Since Knox and Hilton were experienced men, they were supposed to lead the second party, which was a task they gladly took on. They had safely made it across the mountains and camped in the area of Breckenridge[10]. That's where disaster struck in the form of a hacendado's herd of horses that broke out and thundered past not far from the men's camp, causing their own horses to tear free and escape. In order to attain fresh

---

[7] Along a pass of the same name, and present on Stieler's Hand-Atlas.

[8] Founded in 1874, present on Stieler's Hand-Atlas.

[9] Founded in 1859, present on both the 1864 Johnson map, and Stieler's Hand-Atlas

[10] Founded in 1859, present on both the 1864 Johnson map, and Stieler's Hand-Atlas.

horses, the men then attacked a Utah camp, but were pursued and defeated by the Indians. Only six escaped. But the Indians were hard on the heels of the six men; four of them had been killed the previous day and only the two leaders, Knox and Hilton, had been lucky enough to escape the avenging missiles of the Indians.

That was the topic of their conversation as they approached the forest. When they arrived they soon found the Indian path and followed it. They reached the clearing right at the moment when the battle of words between Jemmy and Hobble-Frank concluded.

When they spotted the company sitting around the campfire, they stopped for a moment, but realized immediately that they didn't have to fear any hostilities from the men.

"Remember we're hunters, understood?" Knox whispered to Hilton.

"Yes," he replied. "But they'll ask us where we're from!"

"Then let me talk."

At that point Old Shatterhand saw the two arrivals. Anyone else would have been startled; but that was impossible for Old Shatterhand. He calmly took the Henry rifle into his hand and looked at them with serious expectation as they approached.

"Good day, gentlemen!" Knox greeted. "Is it perhaps permitted to rest up for a while in your company?"

"We welcome every honest man," Old Shatterhand replied while he sharply scrutinized the riders first, and then their horses.

"Hopefully you don't mistake us for the opposite!" Hilton said. He appeared to calmly withstand the penetrating gaze of the hunter.

"I only form an opinion about someone once I've gotten to know them."

"Alright, then permit us to give you the opportunity to do so!"

The two men dismounted and joined the others around the fire. They were undoubtedly hungry because they looked quite longingly at the roasts. Good-natured Jemmy handed Knox and Hilton a few morsels of meat for them to eat; he didn't have to repeat the invitation. Decorum called for the others to wait to ask questions; hence the time required for the two men to eat was spent in silence.

The other troop, mentioned earlier, was approaching the forest from the other side. It consisted of a host of around two hundred Indians. Although Old Shatterhand had been on the far side of the woods to reconnoitre, he had been unable to see them because at that time they had still been behind a wedge of forest that jutted out into the prairie. They also knew the region very well because they headed straight for the opening of the forest on the far side where the path, through which the Whites had reached the clearing from its other entrance, had formed.

The Indians were on the warpath, as was evidenced by the bright colours they had painted on their faces. Most of them were armed with guns, and only few with bows and arrows. A truly gigantic fellow, who was a chief because he wore an eagle feather in his mop of hair, rode in the lead. His age was impossible to gauge because his face was entirely covered with black, yellow and red stripes. When he reached the path he dismounted to inspect it. The Indians at the front of the train, which had come to a halt behind the chief, watched him with interest. One of their horses snorted. The chief lifted his hand as a warning gesture and the rider in question covered the nostrils of his animal. Since the chief thus demanded absolute silence, he was bound to have discovered something suspicious. He slowly walked along the path for a short stretch into the forest, step by step, stooped low down to the ground. When he returned, he whispered in the language of the Utah:

"A paleface was here a short while ago, for which time span the sun requires to travel one hand-width. The warriors of the Utah will hide under the trees with their horses. Ovuts-Avaht will go and find the paleface."

The chief was almost taller, broader, as well as stronger, than even Old Firehand, and on account of his stature and physical strength was called *Ovuts-Avaht*[11]. He sneaked back into the forest; when he returned after perhaps half an hour, none of his people were in sight. He quietly whistled and immediately his warriors came out from under the trees, where they left their horses behind. He gave a signal, upon which five or six sub-chiefs joined him.

"Six palefaces are camped by the rocks," he said. "Those are probably the six men who escaped yesterday." He therefore didn't know that another party had killed four more of the horse thieves. "They are eating meat and their horses are with them. My brothers follow me until the path ends; then they will separate; half will sneak to the left and the other half to the right, until the clearing is surrounded. Then I'll give the signal and the red warriors will

---

[11] Great Wolf

charge onto the place. The white dogs will be so afraid that they won't resist. We will catch them with our hands, and then take them to our village to tie them to the stakes. Five men will remain out here to guard the horses. Howgh!"

The last word is an expression of decisiveness and irrevocability, and means as much as *amen, basta,* or *agreed!* When an Indian speaks it, he considers the subject completely and exhaustively discussed and concluded.

With their chief in the lead, the Indians penetrated into the forest along the path, quietly, so quietly in fact that not the slightest sound was audible. When they had reached the spot where the path entered the clearing, they split up and moved to either side to surround the place. No rider would have been able to move through the undergrowth; but on foot it was possible for the agile Indians to do so.

The Whites had just finished their meal. Hobble-Frank put his bowie knife back into his belt, and then in English, so that the two strangers were able to understand him, said:

"We've eaten and the horses have had their rest; now we can continue on to reach our destination today before nightfall."

"Yes," Jemmy agreed. "But it will first be necessary that we get to know each other and find out where everyone is headed."

"That's right," Knox nodded. "May I therefore know what destination you intend to reach today?"

"We're riding into the Elk Mountains."

"So are we. That suits us splendidly. We might be able to ride together."

Old Shatterhand didn't say a word. He gave Jemmy a furtive signal to continue with the questions, because he wanted to speak only when he considered that the time was right.

"That's alright with me," the rotund fellow said. "But where are you headed once we get there?"

"That's still undecided. Perhaps across to the Green River, to find beaver."

"You won't find many there. If you want to catch beaver, then you'd have to go further north. Does that mean you're trappers, beaver hunters?"

"Yes. My name is Knox, and that of my companion is Hilton."

"But where are your beaver traps, Mr Knox, without which you won't catch anything?"

"Some thieves, perhaps Indians, stole them from us down by the San Juan River. We might find a camp where we can buy some. So, do you think that you'll allow us to join you up to the Elk Mountains initially?"

"I've got nothing against it, if my comrades agree."

"Splendid, sir! May we also know your names?"

"Why not? I'm called Fat Jemmy; my neighbour sitting to the right is…"

"Probably Long Davy?" Knox hastily interjected.

"Yes. You've guessed correctly!"

"Of course! You're known far and wide, and where Fat Jemmy is, one doesn't have to look far to find his Long Davy as well. And the short gentleman here to your left?"

"We call him Hobble-Frank; a splendid fellow, whom you'll get to know as well."

Frank gave Jemmy a warm, appreciative glance, and the latter continued:

"And the last name I have to mention will be even more familiar to you than mine. You've no doubt heard of Old Shatterhand, I should think."

"Old Shatterhand?" Knox exclaimed with joyful surprise. "Really? Is it true, sir that you're Old Shatterhand?"

"Why wouldn't it be true?" the hunter replied.

"Then allow me to tell you that I'm immensely pleased to make your acquaintance, sir!"

He extended his hand towards the hunter and gave Hilton a look that was supposed to tell him: "Be pleased about it because we're safe now. If we're in the company of this famous man, then we won't have anything else to worry about." However, Old Shatterhand pretended not to have seen the hand offered for a shake, and instead replied coldly:

"Are you really pleased? In that case it's a pity that I'm unable to share your joy."

"Why, sir?"

"Because you're the kind of people one cannot be pleased about at all."

"What do you mean?" Knox asked, taken aback by the hunter's frankness. "I assume that you're making a joke, sir."

"I'm serious. You're two swindlers and perhaps even much worse."

"Oho! Do you think that we'll tolerate such an insult?"

"Indeed I think you will, because what else are you going to do?"

"Do you know us, perchance?"

"No, that wouldn't be an honour for me."

"Sir, you're becoming increasingly rude. You don't insult someone you've just shared a meal with. Prove that we're swindlers!"

"To be sure, why not?" Old Shatterhand said with indifference.

"You'll find that impossible to do. You've just admitted that you don't know us. You've never seen us. How do you propose to prove that you've spoken the truth?"

"Pshaw, don't make such a useless effort, and for God's sake don't think Old Shatterhand is dumb enough to let people of your ilk pull the wool over his eyes! The first moment I saw you I knew who and what you are. So, you've had your traps set down by the San Juan River, have you? When was that?"

"Four days ago."

"And you've come here directly from there?"

"Yes."

"That would be from the south and is a lie. You arrived here shortly after us; therefore we ought to have seen you on the open prairie. However, the forest juts out a lot further towards the north, and you were behind that wedge when I checked the surroundings one last time just before we entered the path. You've come from the north."

"But, sir, I've told you the truth. You didn't see us."

"Me? Not see you? If I had such bad eyes, then I would have been lost a thousand times already. No, don't try to fool me! And now: where are your saddles?"

"They were also stolen."

"And the tack?"

"That, too."

"Mister, do you think I'm a stupid boy?" Old Shatterhand gave a disdainful laugh. "Have you put the saddles and the tack into the water with the traps, so that everything could be stolen at the same time? What kind of hunter takes the bridle off his horse? And where did you get the Indian halters from?"

"We traded them from an Indian."

"And the horses as well?"

"No," Knox replied. He realized that he could not possibly tell a lie about that as well; it would have been much too big and brazen.

"So, the Utah Indians are trading in halters! I didn't know that. Where did you get your horses from?"

"We bought them in Fort Dodge."

"That far from here? Yet I'd like to bet that these animals have been out on the pasture for weeks. A horse that's carried a rider from Fort Dodge to here looks much different. And why aren't your horses shod?"

"You'd have to ask the dealer, who sold them to us, about that."

"Nonsense! Dealer! These animals weren't bought."

"What else?"

"Stolen."

"Sir!" Knox exclaimed and reached for his knife. Hilton also put his hand on his belt.

"Leave the knives where they are or I'll knock you down like chunks of wood!" Old Shatterhand warned. "Do you really think I can't see that these horses have Indian training?"

"How can you know that? You didn't see us ride! You've only seen us sit on them on the short stretch from the path to the rocks here. And that's not enough time to make such an assessment."

"But I can see that they avoid our animals, that they keep together. These horses have been stolen from the Utah, and you belong to the people who attacked those poor Indians."

Knox didn't know what else to say. He was no match for the acumen of the hunter, and he reacted just like most people of his type would in similar situations: he sought his only remaining refuge behind rudeness.

"Sir, I've heard much of you, and thought you were someone completely different," he said. "You're talking as if you were dreaming. Anyone who puts up claims like yours must be quite mad. Our horses and Indian training! I would laugh myself silly if it weren't so vexing. I realize that we don't fit together and will move on, so that I'm not forced to listen to more of your phantasies."

He and Hilton rose. But Old Shatterhand also stood up, put his hand on Knox' arm and ordered:

"You'll stay!"

"Stay, sir? Is that supposed to be an order?"

"Indeed."

"Do you think you can do with us as you please? "

"Yes. I'll deliver you to the Utah for punishment."

"Ah, really? That would be even madder than the Indian training!"

He said it in a mocking tone of voice, but his lips were quivering as he spoke and it was obvious that he didn't have the confidence he tried so hard to display.

"But it will be just as correct as the horses' training," the hunter replied. "The horses belong to the Utah, which is evident by...all devils, what's that?"

While he had been speaking of the horses, he had been looking at them and in the process noticed something that attracted his entire attention. In fact, they stretched their noses into the air, turned in all directions, sucked in the air, and then ran towards the edge of the clearing with joyful whinnies.

"Yes, what's that then?" Jemmy also exclaimed. "There are Indians nearby!"

Old Shatterhand's sure eyes captured the danger with one single glance. He replied:

"We're surrounded, no doubt by Utah who have been betrayed by the horses and are now forced to rush in."

"What will we do in this case?" Davy asked. "Defend ourselves?"

"We'll first show them that we have nothing to do with these murderers and robbers. That's the main thing. Down with them!"

He punched Knox in the temple, so that the man collapsed like a block of wood, and then Hilton received the same whack before he was able to evade it.

"And now onto the rocks, quickly," Old Shatterhand ordered. "We have cover up there, but not down here. And then we'll have to wait and see what develops."

The rock mounds were not easy to climb; but in such situations a person's capabilities double or increase even more; the four hunters had disappeared behind corners, edges and bushes, where they crouched down within three, four or five seconds. Since the horses' first neighing hardly one minute had elapsed. The chief had wanted to give the signal for an immediate attack, but didn't when he saw that one of the palefaces knocked two others to the ground. He had no explanation for it and hesitated; thus the four men gained the time to retreat onto the rocks.

At that point Great Wolf asked himself what he ought to do in the given circumstances. He had missed the opportunity to catch the Whites unaware. They were up top, and protected from bullets and arrows from below; on the other hand, they were able to rule the entire clearing from the top of the rocks and send their bullets in all directions. Two hundred Indians against four or at the most six Whites! Victory for the former was assured. But how were they going to achieve that? Storm the rocks perchance? It was to be expected that many Indians would fall. If need be the Indian is brave, daring, even reckless; but if he can achieve his goal without having to risk his life, then he wouldn't think of spilling his own blood. The chief whistled again and called his sub-chiefs together for a powwow.

The outcome of it was evident soon after. From the edge of the clearing resounded a loud voice. Since the open area was at the most fifty paces across and the distance between the rocks in the middle and the spot from which the voice came only half of that, twenty-five paces, the four men could thus hear every word clearly. It was the chief who was standing next to a tree, calling across:

"The palefaces are surrounded by many red warriors, they can come down!"

It was so naive that he didn't receive an answer. The chief repeated his demand twice more; but when he didn't receive a response to that, either, he added:

"If the white men won't obey, we'll kill them."

Old Shatterhand replied to that:

"What harm did we inflict on the red warriors for them to surround us with the intention of attacking us?"

"You're the dogs who killed our men and stole our horses."

"You're mistaken. Only two of the robbers are here; they joined us a short while ago, and when I suspected that they are the enemies of the Utah, I knocked them down. They aren't dead; they'll soon wake up again. If you want them, come and get them."

"You want to lure us across to kill us!"

"No."

"I don't believe you."

"Who are you? What is your name?"

"I am Ovuts-Avaht, the chief of the Utah."

"I know you. Great Wolf is strong in body and spirit. He is the war chief of the Yampa Utah, who are courageous and just, and will not punish the innocent for the sins of the guilty."

"You talk like a woman. You're whimpering for your life. You call yourself innocent out of fear of death. I disdain you. What's your name? It will be that of an old, blind dog."

"Isn't Great Wolf blind instead? He doesn't seem to see our horses. Did they perhaps belong to the Utah? There is a mule among them. Was that stolen from their herd? Why does Great Wolf think we're horse thieves? Look at my black stallion! Have the Utah ever owned such a horse? It is of the kind that is only bred for Winnetou, the chief of the Apache, and his friends. Shouldn't therefore Great Wolf realize that I am a friend of the famous Apache? Is he permitted to accuse me of fear and cowardice in this case? The warriors of the Utah will hear whether my name is that of a dog or not. The palefaces call me Old Shatterhand; in the language of the Utah, however, I'm called *Pokai-Mu*[12]."

The chief didn't immediately reply and the ensuing silence lasted for several minutes, which was a sure sign that the name of the hunter had made an impression. Only then did Great Wolf speak again:

"The paleface passes himself off for Old Shatterhand; but we don't believe his assurances. He knows that the great, white hunter is highly respected by all red men and is taking his name to fool us and to escape death. We recognize from his behaviour that the name doesn't belong to him."

"Why?" the hunter asked.

"Old Shatterhand knows no fear; but this time fear took your courage away, and you're afraid to show yourself to us."

"If that were true, then the warriors of the Utah would be even more afraid. I'm not exposing myself because you're many, many armed men; but they, and you with them, are hiding from only four men. Who's more afraid, you or I? Besides, I'll prove to you that I know no fear. You shall see me."

He stepped out of his hiding spot, climbed onto the highest point of the rocks, slowly looked around and stood up there as carefree as if there weren't a single bullet that could hit him.

"Ing Pokai-Mu, ing Pokai-Mu, howgh!" several voices arose. "He is Hand-That-Kills, he is Pokai-Mu, certainly!"

Those remarks came from men who knew him because they had seen him. He remained standing, without fear, and then called to the chief:

"Did you hear the testimony of your warriors? Do you now believe that I really am Old Shatterhand?"

"I believe it. Your courage is great. Our bullets reach much, much further than to where you're standing. How easily could one of our guns go off!"

"That won't happen, because the warriors of the Utah are brave heroes, not murderers. And if you killed me, then my death would be avenged severely."

"We fear no revenge!"

---

[12] Hand-That-Kills

"It would catch and devour you whether or not you're afraid of it. I've fulfilled Great Wolf's wish and showed myself to him. Why is he staying hidden? Is he still afraid or does he think I am a treacherous murderer out to kill him?"

"The chief of the Utah is not worried. I know that Old Shatterhand only reaches for a weapon if he is attacked, and will show myself."

He stepped out from behind the tree, so that his tall figure was in full view.

"Is Old Shatterhand satisfied now?" he asked.

"No."

"What else does he demand?"

"I wish to talk to you up close, to find out your wishes in a more comfortable manner. Walk closer, to about half the distance; I'll climb down from the rocks and walk towards you. Then we'll sit down as befits worthy warriors and chiefs, to hold a powwow."

"Won't you rather come to us?"

"No; each shall honour the other by approaching the same distance."

"Then I would sit on the open clearing together with you, and be exposed to the guns of your people, without protection."

"I give you my word that nothing will happen to you. They'll only shoot if your warriors send me a bullet. You, of course, would be lost then."

"If Old Shatterhand gives his word, then one can trust it; it is just as sacred to him as the holiest oath. I'll come. What weapons will the great hunter carry?"

"I'll put all my weapons here and leave them behind; you, however, can do as you please."

"Great Wolf won't disgrace himself by exhibiting less courage and trust. Come down!"

The chief placed his weapons in the grass where he stood, and then waited for Old Shatterhand.

"You're risking too much," Jemmy warned him. "Are you really convinced that you ought to do that?"

"Yes. Had the chief first stepped back to confer with his men, or to give them an order or a signal, then I would have become suspicious without a doubt. But he didn't do that, and so I must trust him."

"And what shall we do in the meantime?"

"Nothing. Aim your guns at him, but in a way that is not noticeable from below, and shoot him immediately if I'm attacked."

He climbed down, and then both men walked slowly towards each other. When they met, Old Shatterhand offered his hand to the chief and said:

"I've not seen Great Wolf before, but have often heard that he is the wisest in counsel, and the most courageous in battle. I'm therefore pleased to see his face now, and to be able to welcome him as a friend."

The Indian ignored the White's hand, scrutinized the hunter's figure and face with a sharp gaze, and then replied, while he pointed to the ground:

"Let's sit down! The warriors of the Utah were forced to raise their war hatchets against the Whites, and therefore I cannot welcome any White as a friend."

He sat down and Old Shatterhand took his place opposite him. The fire had gone out; next to the ash lay Knox and Hilton, who were either still unconscious, or dead, since they didn't move. Old Shatterhand's mustang had smelt the Indians even before he had heard the voice of the chief and moved close to the rocks amid nervous snorts. Davy's old mule had a nose that was just as sensitive, and it followed the example of the mustang. Frank and Jemmy's horses thought they had best do likewise, so the four animals were standing hard against the rocks. Their bearing and conduct indicated that they recognized the danger their masters were facing.

Neither of the two men sitting opposite each another seemed to want to be the first to talk. Old Shatterhand waited and looked at the ground as indifferently as if nothing could happen to him. The Indian, however, was unable to keep his probing gaze away from the White. The thickly applied paint concealed the expression on his face; but his lips were pulled wide and the corners of his mouth pointed downwards, which indicated that he didn't see his mental image of the much-discussed hunter confirmed by Old Shatterhand's exterior. That was obvious when, at last, he made the almost ironic remark:

"Old Shatterhand's reputation is large; but his physique hasn't grown with it."

Old Shatterhand's height was above average, yet not that of a giant. He had undoubtedly lived as a veritable Goliath in the Indian's imagination. The hunter smiled and replied:

"What has my figure to do with my reputation? Shall I perhaps say to the chief of the Utah: 'The physique of Great Wolf is large, but his reputation and his courage haven't grown to match his stature'?"

"That would be an insult," the Indian said with flashing eyes. "I would immediately leave you and give the order for the battle to begin!"

"Then why do you permit yourself to make such a remark about my physique? Although your words cannot insult Old Shatterhand, they nevertheless contain a contemptuous remark that I mustn't tolerate. I'm a chief of at least equal standing to you; I will speak politely to you and demand the same courtesy from you. I need to tell you this before we begin our talk, otherwise it would not lead to a positive outcome."

He owed it to his three companions and himself to admonish the Indian. The more determined he conducted himself, the greater the impression he made. The direction his situation would take hinged on the effect he was able to achieve at that point.

"There is only one outcome, and no other," Great Wolf explained.

"Which one?"

"Your death."

"That would be murder, because we've not harmed you."

"You are in the company of the murderers whom we've been following!"

"Do you believe that I was with them when they attacked you that night?"

"No. Old Shatterhand is no horse thief; he would have prevented them from carrying it out."

"Alright, and why do you treat me as an enemy regardless?"

"You've been riding with them."

"No, that's not true. Send one of your warriors back on our trail. He will soon see that the two men have arrived here after us, and have then found our tracks."

"That doesn't change anything. The palefaces have attacked us during a time of great peace, stole our horses and killed many of our warriors. Our wrath was great, but our circumspection was no smaller. We sent wise men to demand the punishment of the guilty and compensation for our losses; they were laughed at and turned away. That's why we've raised the war hatchets and swore that every White, who falls into our hands, will be killed until our revenge has been completed. We must keep our oath, and you are a White."

"But I'm a White who is not guilty!"

"Were my dead warriors guilty of a misdeed perchance? Do you demand that we should be more merciful than our enemies and murderers were?"

"I bemoan what has happened. Great Wolf knows that I am a friend of the red men."

"I know it; nevertheless, you must die. If the unjust palefaces, who didn't consider our complaints, find out that they have caused the demise of many upright people, even Old Shatterhand's, through their behaviour, then they'll learn a lesson and act more reasonably in future."

That sounded dangerous. The Indian spoke in all earnest and the conclusion he drew wasn't at all illogical. Nevertheless, Old Shatterhand replied:

"Great Wolf only considers his oath, but not its consequences. If you kill us, then a cry of shock and indignation will resound across the mountains and prairies, and thousands of palefaces will move against you to avenge our deaths. The retributions are going to be all the more severe because we've always been friends of the red men."

"Not you alone? You are also speaking of your companions? Who are these palefaces?"

"One is called Hobble-Frank, and you probably don't know him; but you've often heard the names of the other two; they are Fat Jemmy and Long Davy."

"I know them. One is never seen without the other, and I've never heard it said that they are enemies of the Indians. And that's why especially their deaths will teach the unjust chiefs of the Whites how unwise it was of them to turn our envoys away. Your fate is decided, but it will be honourable. You are brave and famous men, and shall suffer the most torturous death that we can offer you. You'll endure it without batting an eyelid, and the news of it will travel across all lands. Consequently your fame will become even more glorious than it already is, and you will reach great esteem in the Eternal Hunting Grounds. I hope you realize how considerate this is, and that you will be grateful to us!"

Old Shatterhand was not at all delighted about the prospects offered to him. But he didn't let on and replied:

"Your intention is noble and I praise you for it; but those who will avenge us won't be grateful to you."

"I laugh about them; they may come!"

"Do you think that you'll defeat them, that there will be only a few?"

"Ovuts-Avaht is not in the habit of counting his enemies. And aren't you aware of how numerous we will be by then? We will combine with the warriors of the Weavers, the Uinta, Yampa,

Sampitche, Pah-Vant, Wiminutsh Elk, Capote, Pais, Tashe, Muatshe, and the Tabequatshe. All those tribes belong to the nation of the Utah; they will crush the white Warriors."

"Then go East and count the Whites! And then consider the ones who will be leading them! You'll create avengers of whom a single one counts as much as many, many Utah."

"Who would that be?"

"I'll name only one, namely Old Firehand."

"He is a hero; he is among palefaces what a grizzly bear is among prairie dogs," the chief admitted. "But he would also be the only one; you cannot name a second one."

"Oh, yes, I could name many more; but I'll only mention one other, Winnetou, whom you undoubtedly know."

"There's no one who doesn't know him, but if he were here, he'd also have to die; he is our enemy."

"No; he risks his life for his red brothers, and would also die for them."

"Be quiet about it! He is the chief of the Apache. The Whites feel they are too weak to oppose us; they have sent for the Navajo to incite them against us."

"Do you already know that?"

"The eyes of Great Wolf are sharp and no sound escapes his ears. Don't the Navajo belong to the nation of the Apache? Should we not regard Winnetou as our enemy in that case? Woe to him if he falls into our hands!"

"And woe to you then! I warn you. Not only would the warriors of the Whites be against you then, but also many thousands of Mescalero, Llanero, Xicarilla, Taracone, Navajo, Tshiriguami, Pilanenjo, Lipan, Copper, Gila and Mimbrenjo, who all belong to the nation of the Apache. They would move against you, and the Whites need not do anything but calmly watch how the Utah and the Apache destroy each other. Do you really want to give your pale enemies such joy?"

The chief stared at the ground and, after a while, replied:

"You spoke the truth; but the palefaces are crowding us from all sides; they are overwhelming us, and the red man is condemned to die a slow, painful death of suffocation. Isn't it preferable for him to direct the battle in a way that will allow him to die quickly, and to be annihilated more swiftly? The view that you're opening for me into the future cannot stop me, and it only reinforces my belief that the war hatchet is to be used without mercy or consideration. Don't go to any trouble; what I've said is final."

"That you want to let us die at the stake?"

"Yes. Are you surrendering to your fate, which I've indicated before?"

"Yes," Old Shatterhand replied with such calm that the Indian hastily said:

"Then surrender your weapons!"

"Of course we won't do that!"

"But you just said that you want to surrender!" the chief was bewildered.

"Indeed, to the fate that you have pronounced with your own words. But what did you say? That you will kill every paleface that falls into your hands. Isn't that correct?"

"Yes, those were my words," the Indian nodded, anticipating Old Shatterhand's reply to that.

"Good, then kill us once we've fallen into your hands, which hasn't happened yet."

"Uff! Do you think you can escape us?"

"Indeed."

"That's impossible. Do you know how many warriors I have with me? There are two hundred!"

"Is that all? Perhaps you've heard it said that even greater mobs have tried in vain to capture or even hold onto me."

"But two hundred against only four of you! There is no gap through which you could slip!"

"In that case we'll make one!"

"You would be killed trying!"

"Possibly! But how many of your warriors would you lose in the process? I figure that each of my companions can kill twenty of your warriors, and I personally will certainly shoot more than fifty before you get your hands on me."

He said it with such confidence that the Indian looked at him with astonishment. Then the latter produced a coarse laugh, and said, while he made a dismissive hand gesture:

"The thoughts in your head are mixed up. You're a daring hunter, but how could you kill fifty warriors?"

"With ease. Have you not heard what kinds of weapons I have?"

"You're supposed to have a gun from which one can shoot without having to reload a single time; but that's an impossibility. I don't believe it."

"Shall I show it to you?"

"Yes, show it!" the chief called out, utterly electrified at the thought of being able to see the rifle to which so many legends were attached.

"Alright I'll have it handed to me and bring it to you."

He rose and walked back to the rocks to fetch the rifle. In the prevailing circumstances he had to seek to intimidate and shock the Indians above all, despite their greater number, and the rifle was ideally suited for that purpose. He was aware of the many kinds of tales that were circulating among the Indians. They considered it to be a magic rifle, which Great Manitou had given to the hunter to make him invincible. Jemmy passed it down to him from the top of the rocks; Shatterhand returned to the chief, held it up to him and said:

"Here is the rifle; take it and have a look at it!"

The chief already stretched out his hands for it; but he pulled it back and asked:

"Is anyone else apart from you permitted to touch it? If it really is a magic rifle, then it will bring danger to anyone, except its owner, as soon as they touch it."

Old Shatterhand couldn't otherwise but to exploit that advantageous opinion. If he and his companions were forced to surrender to the Indians, then he would be forced to hand over all of his weapons. And in that case it was vitally important to at least be able to keep that rifle. Although Old Shatterhand didn't want to speak an outright lie, he nevertheless replied:

"I'm not permitted to reveal its secrets. Take it and try it yourself!"

He held the rifle in his right hand and, while he made that remark, placed the thumb onto the cartridge sphere to rotate it forwards with a small, imperceptible movement, so that the shot was bound to discharge at the slightest touch to the sphere. His keen eyes detected a number of warriors who had left their protected positions out of curiosity and had gathered at the edge of the clearing. That group formed such a good target that even a bullet not accurately aimed would have to hit one of them.

It all depended on whether the chief was going to grab the rifle, or not. He was probably less superstitious than the other Indians, but he still didn't quite trust the matter. "Should I? Or should I not?" Those two questions were evident in his eager gaze that was directed at the weapon. Old Shatterhand held it out to him with both hands, so that the barrel was in fact directed at the group of warriors in question. The curiosity of the chief was greater, after all, than his apprehension; he grabbed it. Old Shatterhand played it into the Indian's hand in such a way that he had to touch the sphere with it. The shot discharged immediately. And from over yonder, where the Indians were standing, came a scream, whereupon Great Wolf dropped the rifle with a start. One of the warriors called across that he was wounded.

"Was it me who has wounded him?" the chief asked, taken aback.

"Who else?" Old Shatterhand replied. "What happened was only a warning. The matter will become serious with the next touch of the gun. I permit you to hold it again, but I warn you; the bullet would now..."

"No, no!" the Indian called out while he defensively lifted both hands. "It truly is a magic rifle and only meant for you. If any one else grabs the weapon, it will go off and he will hit his own friends, or perhaps even himself. I don't want it; I don't want it!"

"That's very smart of you," Old Shatterhand said in a serious tone of voice. "Be glad that it only went off the once. You've received a small lesson; things would turn out differently the next time. I'll show you how often it discharges. Look at the small maple tree over there on the creek. It is only two fingers thick and shall receive ten holes that will be at a distance of the width of your thumb from each other."

He lifted the rifle, put it to his shoulder, aimed at the maple tree, and then pulled the trigger one—three—seven—ten times. Afterwards he said:

"Go there and look! I could shoot many, many more times, but this is enough to demonstrate to you that I could hit fifty of your warriors in the heart within a minute, if I wanted to."

The chief went across the clearing to the little tree. Old Shatterhand saw that he was measuring the holes with his thumb. Several Indians came out of their hiding place, driven by curiosity, and joined him. The hunter used the opportunity to swiftly push new cartridges into the eccentrically moving sphere.

"Uff, uff, uff!" he heard them exclaim. If the Indians regarded the fact that he had been able to fire so many shots without reloading as a miracle already, then they were doubly astonished to see that not one of the bullets had missed, and that they had instead all punched through the thin trunk exactly the width of a thumb apart. The chief returned, sat down again and with a hand signal requested the hunter to follow his example. He stared at the ground for a long while, and then said:

"I can see that you're one of the Great Spirit's favourites. I have heard of this rifle, but couldn't believe it. Now I know that they told me the truth."

"Then be careful and consider well what you're doing! You want to catch and kill us. Try it; I have nothing against it. When you then count the warriors who have been hit by my bullets, there will arise the lament of the women and children for the fallen men in your village; but you mustn't blame me for it."

"Do you think we'll submit to being hit? You must surrender to us, without the need for a shot to be fired. You're surrounded and have nothing to eat. We'll place you under siege until hunger forces you to lay down your arms."

"You can wait a long time for that. We've got water to drink and enough meat to eat. Our animals are standing there, four horses the meat of which would last us for many weeks. But it won't come to that, because we'll break through. I'll walk ahead with my magic rifle in my hand and will send bullet upon bullet at your warriors. You've witnessed how well I can aim."

"We will stand behind the trees!"

"Do you think this will protect you from my magic rifle? Beware! You would be the first I'd aim at. I'm a friend of the red men, and it would therefore pain me much if I had to kill so many of you. You've already suffered heavy losses, and when the battle with the white soldiers and the Navajo begins, then many, many more of your men will fall. Hence you ought not also force us, your friends, to send death among you."

Those serious words didn't fail to make the required impression. The chief stared at the ground for a long time while sitting immobile like a statue. At last, and with a tone of regret in his voice, he uttered:

"If we hadn't sworn to kill all palefaces, then we would let you move out; but an oath must be fulfilled."

"No. One can take an oath back."

"But only if the great powwow allows it."

"Then hold a powwow!"

"How can you tell me that? I'm the only chief here; who am I supposed to hold a powwow with?"

At that point Old Shatterhand had the chief exactly where he wanted him to be. If he was talking of holding a powwow, then the greatest danger had already passed. The hunter was familiar with the habits of the Indians. He had won the intended success and knew that the smartest thing to do would be not to pursue it further immediately. Hence he remained silent and waited for what else Great Wolf was going to say.

The chief scanned the clearing. He undoubtedly thought about whether or not it might be possible after all to overpower the four Whites in that place despite the dangerous magic rifle, and only when the brooding lasted a little bit too long, did Old Shatterhand say, while he prepared to get up off the floor:

"The chief of the Utah has heard everything I can tell him; there is nothing further to be discussed, and I'll therefore return to my comrades. Great Wolf may do as he pleases."

"Wait!" the Indian hastily replied. "Would you think of us as cowardly if we won't fight you here?"

"No. A chief must not only be brave and courageous, but he must also be smart and cautious. No chief will sacrifice his people uselessly. I've only ever attacked an enemy when I was certain of victory. Everyone knows that Great Wolf is a brave warrior; but if you were to permit half of your warriors to be killed here by four Whites, then there would be talk around all the campfires that you had acted foolishly, and that you are no longer capable of leading the Utah warriors into battle. Consider that the Whites and the Navajo are already on their way to move against you, and that you need your warriors to defeat those enemies. It would therefore be the greatest stupidity if you caused them to be shot uselessly here."

"You are correct," the Indian replied with a deep sigh over having to comply with the demands of only four men when he had two hundred warriors to pit against them. "I cannot rescind the oath on my own; I must let the assembly of the elders give it back to me. Hence you will travel with us as our prisoners to find out what the powwow will decide about you."

"What if we refuse to do this?"

"Then we'll be forced to begin the battle with you, and shower you with bullets."

"Not a single one will hit us. The rocks will serve us as cover, and because they have enough openings and cracks, we can get a good aim at you in any direction. Every one of our bullets will take its victim."

"In that case we'll wait until it is dark and you can't see anything. Then we'll sneak up to the rocks to heap firewood around them, which we'll light. In the morning, when the sun rises, we'll see wether you've suffocated or are still alive."

He said that in a very confident tone of voice; but Old Shatterhand smiled and replied:

"That's not as simple as you seem to think. As soon as it has become dark, we'll come down from the rocks. Each one of us will occupy one side and then woe to any red warrior who would dare to come near! He would be shot. You can see that we have the advantage in all cases; but especially because I love the red men and dislike killing even one of them, I'm prepared to forego that advantage. I am your friend, and you shall not remain in the dismal situation you're in at present. I'll talk to my companions. Perhaps they're prepared to ride with you. The only question is: what stipulations do you make? Someone can only be a prisoner if he has been captured. If you want to catch us, then you may safely try; I've got nothing against it; but that would result in precisely the battle you want to avoid."

"Uff!" the chief hastily uttered. "Your words hit their target just as true as your bullets do. Old Shatterhand is not only a hero in battle, but also a master of speech."

"I do not speak simply for my benefit, but also for yours. Why should we be enemies? You've raised the war hatchets against the soldiers and the Navajo; wouldn't it be of great benefit to you, if Old Shatterhand were your ally, and not your enemy?"

The chief was smart enough to recognize that the hunter was correct. But his oath tied his hands. Hence he explained:

"I must regard you as enemies until the assembly has spoken. If you don't agree, then the weapons must speak."

"I agree; I'll talk to my comrades, and I think that they'll be prepared to ride with you, but not as prisoners."

"As what else?"

"As companions."

"Does that mean you do not want to surrender your weapons or let us tie you up?"

"No, under no circumstances!"

"Uff! Then hear my last word on this. If you don't agree to it, we'll put a siege around you despite your magic gun. You will now depart to our village with us; you'll keep your guns, your horses, and you won't be tied up. We will pretend to live in peace with you; but in exchange you will swear that you will accept the decision of the council without resistance. I have spoken. Howgh!"

The last word was proof that he wasn't going to relent any further, under any circumstances; but Old Shatterhand was completely satisfied with the outcome of the negotiation. If the Indians were to attack them in earnest at that point, then it would be impossible for the four hunters to get away from them unscathed. It was very fortunate that they had such respect for the magic rifle; thanks to that, they had reached the best outcome possible at that point. That respect was bound to influence the decision of the council of the elders as well. Hence Old Shatterhand replied:

"Great Wolf shall recognize that I am his friend. I won't even confer with my comrades first, but give you my word right now, in their name as well. We will submit to the decision without resistance."

"Then take your calumet and swear that you will act accordingly."

Old Shatterhand untied his peace pipe from the cord, put a little tobacco into the bowl and lit it with the aid of punks. Then he blew the smoke towards the sky, the ground, into the four compass directions, and then said:

"I promise that we won't think of resistance!"

"Howgh!" the chief nodded. "Now it is good."

"No, because you must also seal your promise," Old Shatterhand said while he held the pipe up to the Indian.

Great Wolf had perhaps secretly counted on being spared it, in which case he wouldn't have felt bound by his promise, and once the Whites had come down from their rocks, he would have acted at his discretion. However, he obliged without hesitation, took the pipe, also blew the smoke in all directions, and then said:

"The four Whites will not be harmed until the council of the elders has decided their fate. Howgh!"

Then he returned the calumet to Old Shatterhand and walked over to Knox and Hilton, who were still lying on the ground where Old Shatterhand had knocked them down.

"My promise doesn't extend to them," he said. "They belong to the murderers, because we've recognized the horses they rode as ours. Their punishment will be severe. They may count themselves lucky if your hand has taken their souls from them. They seem to be dead."

"No," Old Shatterhand replied, whose keen eyes hadn't missed how each had lifted his head cautiously during the negotiations to look around. "They aren't dead; they aren't even unconscious anymore; they only play dead because they believe we'll leave them lying here."

"In that case the dogs will get up, otherwise I'll squash them with my foot!" the chief called out and served each one a powerful kick, so that Knox as well as Hilton gave up pretending to be unconscious; they rose. Their fear was so great that they didn't even think of fleeing or putting up a fight.

"You are the last ones to have escaped my warriors," the chief said fiercely. "Now Manitou has given you into my power, and you'll howl at the stake for your murderous deeds, so that all the palefaces in the mountains will hear it."

The chief spoke very good English and both men understood every word he said.

"Murderous deeds?" Knox asked in an attempt at saving himself by lying. "We know nothing of it. Whom were we supposed to have killed?"

"Silence, dog! We know you. And these palefaces here, who have fallen into our hands because of you, also know what you've done!"

Knox was a cunning fellow. He saw Old Shatterhand stand next to the Indian without an injury or other damage. The Indians hadn't dared to lay a hand on the famous man. Someone under his protection was undoubtedly just as safe from the Indians as he; hence the murderer came by a thought, which he considered to be the only salvation. Old Shatterhand was a White; he therefore had to take the sides of the Whites against the Indians. At least that's how Knox was thinking, hence he replied:

"Of course they're bound to know what we did, because we've been riding with them and have been with them for weeks."

"Don't lie!"

"I speak the truth. Ask Old Shatterhand, who will explain and prove to you that we cannot be the ones you think we are."

"Don't be mistaken," Old Shatterhand explained. "If you think that I will speak a lie, so that you can avoid due punishment, then I'll have to tell you that it wouldn't occur to me to lower myself to your level. You know what I think of you; I told you so and my opinion hasn't changed."

He turned away from the two men.

"But, sir," Knox called out. "You don't want to leave us in this dangerous situation, perchance, do you? Our lives are at stake!"

"Indeed, and so were the lives of those you've killed. You deserve to die, and I've got no reason to counter the idea that everyone receives his own just reward."

"Tarnation! If you talk to us like that, then I'll know what to do. If you refuse to save us, well, you shall perish with us!" He turned away from Old Shatterhand and to the chief, and then continued: "Why aren't you catching those four as well? They have been a part of the horse theft and have also shot at the Utah; most of your people died especially because of their bullets!"

That was an audacity second to none. Old Shatterhand made a movement as if he wanted to jump at the outrageous man, but thought better of it and remained standing where he was. Nevertheless, the punishment immediately followed the deed; and it was some punishment! The chief's eyes lit up; they literally sprayed flashes of lightning, when he thundered at Knox:

"Coward! You don't have the courage to carry your guilt alone, and attempt to throw it onto others, against whom you're a stinking toad. Hence your punishment won't start at the stake, but here and now already. I will take your scalp, and you shall live and see it hang on my belt. *Nani witsh, nani witsh!*"

Those words meant 'my knife, my knife'. He called them out to the Indians standing at the edge of the clearing.

"For God's sake!" Knox cried out. "Scalping alive, no, no!"

He made a jump, to flee, but the chief was just as fast and leapt after him, and grabbed him by the neck; one squeeze of his strong hand, and Knox hung from it, limp like a rag. An Indian came running up to bring the knife to the chief. He took it, tossed the half-choked man onto the ground, knelt on top of him, executed three swift cuts, yanked at the hair, which evoked a ghastly scream from the man lying under him, and rose with the bloody scalp in his left hand. Knox didn't move; he had fallen unconscious again; his skull was a horrid sight.

"This must happen to every dog who mauls the red men, and then seeks to destroy the guiltless!" Great Wolf called out while he put the scalp into his belt.

Hilton had watched horrified to what had happened to his companion. The shock rendered him almost incapable of moving; he slowly sank to his knees next to the scalped man and remained sitting there without saying a word.

The chief gave a signal upon which the warriors came onto the clearing; soon it was crowded with them. Hilton and Knox were tied up with straps.

As soon as Great Wolf had mentioned scalping, Old Shatterhand had climbed up onto the rocks, because he didn't wish to become a witness to the gruesome scene, and instead preferred to tell his companions what result he had achieved.

"That's bad," Jemmy said. "Couldn't you get us out of it completely?"

"No; that was impossible."

"Perhaps letting the battle begin would have been better!"

"Certainly not. It would definitely have cost our lives."

"Oho! We would have put up a fight. And considering the fear the redskins have of your rifle, we wouldn't have had cause to despair. They would certainly not have dared to get too close to us."

"That's more than likely; however, they would have starved us out. Although I've spoken about eating our horses, I'd rather die of hunger than kill my black stallion."

"You wouldn't have had to do that. To kill our horses would have been the redskins' first action as soon as the hostilities commenced."

"And that would have robbed us of the best means to escape."

"Never mind the horses! We would have saved ourselves. Two hundred men around the clearing! The Indians would therefore not stand closely together or even rows deep. We would have sneaked down and away from the rocks as soon as it became dark, four people towards one single point. We might perhaps have come upon a gap and escaped through it; but we would definitely not have encountered more than one or two Indians—two shots or two stabs, and we would have broken through."

"And then what? You're imagining the affair altogether differently than it would have developed. The Indians would light fires all around the place and thus immediately discover our attempt at breaking out. And even if we were successful with breaking through their cordon, then we would not get far before we had them on our trail. We would have to kill several of them, and with that lose the slightest prospect of mercy."

"Dat's indeed correct," Hobble-Frank agreed. "I don't quite know how a certain Fat Jemmy Pfefferkorn can come by the idea of wanting to be smarter than our Old Shatterhand. You always and forever want to be the goose egg dat wants to be more clever than the hen. Old Shatterhand did his best, and for dat I'll give him top marks number one and a little star beside it, and I definitely believe that Davy is of the very same opinion."

"That goes without saying," Long Davy replied. "A battle would have led to our inevitable demise."

"But for what purpose are we going with them?" Jemmy asked. "It is to be expected that the assembly of the old men will also treat us as enemies."

"I wouldn't suggest they do dat," Frank retorted. "I also have a word to contribute to dat shtory. No one will easily get me onto one of them stakes of torture. I'll resist with everything I've got."

"You're not allowed to do that. They swore on it. We must calmly endure everything."

"Who said dat then? Don't you realize, you pathetic soap-boiler, dat the oath in question has its peculiar parables? It truly doesn't take a gastronomical mirror telescope to realize dat our famous Old Shatterhand has left open a most delightful backdoor. Obadja don't write a thing about wat we are compelled to endure. As you've heard, dat means we're not to entertain the notion of putting up a fight. Alright, we'll comply with dat. Let them decide wat they want, we won't bash about with iron steam cranes that weigh a thousand tons; but cunning, cunning, cunning, dat's the real MacKay; dat's not resistance. If the prompter condemns us to death, then we'll disappear through any ol' trapdoor and reappear on the far side of the royal theatre with concentrated grandifloria."

"You mean grandezza," Jemmy corrected.

"Are you talking 'cross my moustache again?" the short fellow roused at him. "If only you wouldn't shpeak! I ought to know how I have to behave in a convexation lexicon! Grandezza! Gran is an apothecary's weight of twelve pounds, and dezza, dezza, dat's nothing at all, undershtood? But grand means great and floria means to be in flor, in luck, in bloom. Therefore, if we rise up in grandifloria, anyone sufficiently comfortable will know wat I meant and indicated with dat. But letting flowers speak to you is futile; you have no comprehension of nice figures of speech, and you couldn't care less or give a damn about anything of sublime height. I'm your loyal bosom friend; but when I see you shtanding here before me like dat, in protocol as personified as you're round, then the tears of melancholy well up into my eyelashes and I feel like chiming in with dead Caesar: 'You, too, my son, swim in the middle of the pond!' Therefore better yourself, Jemmy, better yourself as long as you still can! You embitter my life. And after I have closed my eyes at one point in the future, and have disappeared from the nobler existence, having been cheated of my better life by the servile impertinence of the pupil dat you are, then you will look up to my ghosts with regret and will wring your hands to the bone from grief and heartache about having been at variance with me so chronologically often!"

He hadn't spoken in jest at all; the prevailing situation of the four men in general wasn't conducive to making jokes. The short, peculiar person was very, very serious. Jemmy wanted to give him a reply that likely sounded ironic, but Old Shatterhand gave him a signal not to, and then said:

"Frank understood me. I have refrained from resistance, but not cunning. However, I would rather not be forced to a hair-splitting interpretation of my promise. I hope that other, and more honest means will be at our disposal later. For the moment we'll have to deal with the present."

"And the most urgent question is, whether or not we can trust the redskins. Will Great Wolf keep his promise?" Long Davy said.

"Most certainly. A chief has never broken an oath he made while smoking the calumet. Until the time of the powwow we can safely trust the Utah in our sleep. Let's climb down and mount up. The Indians are preparing to leave."

Knox and Hilton had been tied onto their horses. The former, who was still unconscious, was lying lengthwise on the horse with his arms tied around its neck. The Utah disappeared one after the other behind the first bend of the path. The chief was the last one; he was waiting for the Whites, in order to join them. That was a positive sign, because it was exactly the opposite of the expected hostile treatment. The hunters had believed that the Indians were going to take them into their midst and closely guard them. But at that moment they could assume that Great Wolf had no misgivings, but fully trusted Old Shatterhand's promise.

By the time the chief and the four Whites had covered the narrow Indian trail, and had arrived at the edge of the forest, the Indians had already led their horses out from under the trees and mounted up. The train moved out. The four Whites remained at the back of the troop, together with the chief, while the head was formed by a number of Indians who had taken Knox and Hilton between them. That was preferable to Old Shatterhand, because the Indians rode single file, which made the train so long that those at the back couldn't hear the wailing of the scalped man, who had regained consciousness in the meantime.

Since the open prairie lay ahead of them again, they could see right up to the Elk Mountains; the plain stretched far enough to reach their foothills. Old Shatterhand didn't need to ask the chief because he was able to deduce that the destination of the day's ride lay between those mountains. No one spoke. Even the Whites observed silence towards each other, because any and all talk would have been useless. They had to wait until they reached the camp of the Utah; they could only then make a decision and devise a rescue plan.

The Indians seemed to be in a great hurry; they mostly rode at a trot and didn't show the least consideration towards the two fettered prisoners of whom one had a life-threatening wound. The severing of the scalp from the skull is a very dangerous injury. Although one encounters a White occasionally who was scalped and has escaped, they are extremely rare exceptions; because a very strong constitution is required, in addition to many other things, to survive such a trauma.

The mountains seemed to move ever closer as the riders advanced. Towards evening they reached the first foothills. The Indians steered into a long, narrow transverse valley with forested walls. Later the train moved through several more side valleys, constantly climbing uphill, yet despite the darkness that had fallen in the meantime, the Indians found their way as easily as if it were daylight.

The moon rose later and illuminated the mountain sides that were densely studded with trees between which the riders quietly and constantly moved ahead. They seemed to arrive in the vicinity of their destination towards midnight, because the chief directed some of his men to ride ahead in order to announce the arrival of the warriors. The messengers silently rode away to carry out the order.

After a while the troop arrived at a fairly broad watercourse the tall banks of which kept getting broader as the troop rode along them, until they were no longer recognizable as such despite the bright moon shine. Further along, the forest, which had at first reached almost down to the water on both sides, retreated and opened up to a grassy plain where the men saw the campfires burning in the distance.

"Uff!" The chief spoke for the first time on the entire ride. "There are the tents of my tribe where your fate will be decided."

"Still today?" Old Shatterhand enquired.

"No. My warriors need rest, and your death throes will last longer and give us greater joy, if you've slept first to regain your strength."

"That's not bad!" Jemmy remarked in German, so that the Indian couldn't understand him. "Our death throes! He's acting as if there was no escaping from the stakes for us. What do you have to say to this old Frank?"

"Nothing for the moment," the short Saxon replied. "I'll be talking later, when the congressional time has arrived. No one dies before his demise and I'm not really in the mood for being the exception to dat historical rule. I'll only make the remark dat I don't feel like dying jusht yet. Let's therefore wait and watch the affair. But if I am supposed to be prematurely assembled before my grandfathers with brute force, then I'll defend my hide, and know precisely dat later, around my future tombstone, many widows and orphans will be wailing for those I've expedited into the Elise beforehand."

"You mean into the Elysium?" Jemmy asked.

"Don't talk silly! We're talking German, and Elise is genuine Germanic. I'm a good Christian and want nothing to do with dat Roman Elysium. It surprises me every time dat only those people who have not the slightest sense act the smartest! But it's always been dat way, the larger the potatoes the soapier they are!"

He would have further voiced his vexation about the correction he had suffered, had he found the time. But there wasn't any, because the moment of the welcome had arrived. The population of the village had set out to greet the returning warriors. They came running in great numbers, the men and boys ahead, behind them the women and girls, and all were shouting and hollering, so that it sounded as if the horde consisted of wild animals.

Old Shatterhand had expected to find an ordinary tent camp, but was surprised to see that he had been mistaken. The large number of fires evidenced that many more warriors were present than the tents could have accommodated. The inhabitants of various other Utah villages had gathered on that place to discuss the revenge march against the Whites. The messengers, who had been sent ahead by Great Wolf, had informed the people in the camp that the chief was bringing six palefaces, and the Indians were expressing their delight in a way only native peoples are capable of. They brandished their weapons and yelled at the top of their lungs while shouting the ghastliest threats.

When the troop reached the camp, Old Shatterhand saw that it consisted of buffalo hide tents and hastily erected tree branch huts that formed a circle inside of which the train stopped; everyone dismounted. The two prisoners were untied from their horses and flung to the ground. The horrible moaning of maimed Knox was completely drowned out by the howling of the Indians. The Indians led the hunters to the two outlaws. The warriors formed a broad circle around them, and then the women and girls stepped forwards to hold their screeching dance around the prisoners.

That was one of the biggest insults in existence. Letting women dance around prisoners was a declaration that they were deemed gutless, as well as dishonourable. Those who tolerate it would be regarded as standing lower than a dog. The hunters still had their weapons. Old Shatterhand called a few words to his comrades, whereupon they knelt down and took aim. He fired a shot from his bear killer the bang of which was audible above the howling, and then took aim with his rifle to the cheek. Deep silence fell immediately.

"What is this?" he called loudly enough for everyone to hear it. "Were we forced to ride with you, or did we come of our own accord? How can the red men treat us as prisoners? I've smoked the pipe of counsel with Great Wolf and have agreed for the warriors of the Utah to discuss whether or not we ought to be treated as friends or foes. That powwow has not yet been held. And even if the Utah wish to see us as their enemies, it does not mean that we are their prisoners. And even if we were their captives, we would still not tolerate that you let women and girls dance around us like around cowardly coyotes. We are only four warriors and the men of the Utah count in the hundreds; nevertheless, I ask: who among you dares to insult Old Shatterhand? He may step forward and fight with me, if he doesn't want me to think that he's a coward! Beware! You've seen my rifle and know how it shoots. As soon as the women even think of beginning their dance of insults again we will let our rifles speak, and this place will turn red from the blood of those who are disloyal enough to disrespect the pipe of counsel, which is sacred to all warriors!"

Those remarks made a great impression. The fact that the hunter dared to issue threats to such a superior force didn't seem an entirely crazy undertaking to the Indians; they were impressed. They knew that his words weren't simply empty rhetoric, but that he would turn them into reality. The women and girls retreated, without having received an order to do so. The men whispered a few semi-audible remarks, whereby the terms 'Old Shatterhand' and 'rifle of death' were heard. Several feather-adorned warriors joined Great Wolf and talked with him; then the chief approached the group of Whites, who still held their guns aimed at the Indians and, in the language of the Utah, which Old Shatterhand had also used, he said:

"The chief of the Yampa-Utah is not disloyal; he respects the calumet of counsel and knows what he has promised. Tomorrow morning we will decide about the fate of the four palefaces, and until that time they will stay in a tent I will assign them now. The two others, however, are murderers and have nothing to do with my promise; they will die as they lived—dripping with blood. Howgh! Does Old Shatterhand agree with my words?"

"Yes," the hunter replied. "But I demand that our horses stay in the vicinity of our tent."

"I will also allow that, although I don't understand the reason for Old Shatterhand to voice that wish. Does he think he can flee, perchance? I tell him that several rings of warriors will surround the tent, so that he cannot possibly escape."

"I have promised to await the result of your powwow; you do not need to post guards. However, I have no objections if you still want to do this."

"Then come!"

When the four hunters followed the chief, the Indians formed an alley and gave Old Shatterhand shy, reverential looks when he walked through it. The tent that was assigned to the Whites was one of the largest. Several lances were planted in the ground on either side of the entry, and the eagle feathers that adorned them led to the assumption that the tent was actually Great Wolf's abode.

A broad mat, which was folded back, formed the door. Not five paces away there was a campfire burning, which illuminated the interior. The hunters entered, put their guns away and sat down. The chief left, but after a relatively short time several Indians arrived who took up positions at a discrete distance around the tent, so that none of its sides was left unguarded.

After a few minutes a young woman entered. She placed two vessels in front of the Whites, and then left without having said anything. One of the containers was an old pot with water and the other a large steel pot that contained several pieces of meat.

"Oho!" Hobble-Frank smirked. "Dat's probably our supper. A pot of water, dat's noble! The fellows are showing off. We're supposed to throw our hands up in astonishment about their civilizational kitchen utensils. And buffalo meat, at least eight pounds! They wouldn't have rubbed it with rat poison, would they?"

"Rat poison!" Fat Jemmy laughed. "Where would the Utah obtain such stuff? Besides, the meat is from an elk, not a buffalo."

"Are you smarter than me again? Never mind wat I say, you always throw a spanner in my works. Dat won't ever get none the better. But I won't argue with you today, and inshtead only throw an extemporaneous glance at you from which you can glean how endlessly much my personality feels elevated above your pigment stature."

"Pygmy stature," Jemmy corrected.

"Won't you just shut up for a dozen six-eight measures!" the short fellow roused at him. "Do not cause my gall to inflate pneumatically, but rather devote the kind of admiration to me dat I have to demand with complete justification on account of my extraordinary life shtory! I can only make myself popular enough under those conditions, in order to grant the blessings of my undeniable culinary artistry to this roast."

"Yes, get roasting," Old Shatterhand nodded, to deflect the vexation of the short fellow.

"That's more easily said than done. But where do I take onions and bay leaves from? Besides, I don't know yet whether I'm allowed to take the pot outside and put it onto the fire."

"Try it."

"Yes, try it! If the fellows aren't going to tolerate it and send me a bullet in the stomach, then it won't matter to me whether dat meat grew under the hide of an elk or a buffalo. There's no fear as long as one is in the right frame of mind; *feni, fidi, fidshi*—I'll go outside!"

He carried the pot with the meat to the fire and busied himself with it in the capacity of cook, without being bothered by the guards. The others stayed back in the tent and observed the bustling Indian life through the open entrance.

The moon provided a light that was almost as bright as day. Its sheen fell onto a nearby dark, wooded mountain massif where a brightly glistening silver ribbon meandered down, a small river or large creek, which emptied into a sizeable, almost lake-like body of water. The exit of the basin formed the stream along the banks of which Great Wolf's troop had arrived in the camp. There seemed to be no bushes or trees in the vicinity; the surroundings of the lake were flat and open.

Indian warriors sat around each fire and watched their wives busy themselves with roasting meat over the flames. Occasionally, one or several of them got up and slowly ambled past the tent to take a look at the Whites. There was no sign of either Knox or Hilton, and it was a foregone conclusion that their prevailing situation was not at all as agreeable as that of Old Shatterhand and his companions.

After about an hour Hobble-Frank returned to the tent with the steaming pot; he put it down in front of his comrades and self-confidently said:

"Here you have your wonderful thing. I'm curious to see the look on your faces. Although the spices are missing, my inborn talents have easily made up for it."

"In what way?" Jemmy asked while he poked his diminutive nose over the pot. The meat was not only boiling, but also smoking, and not just a little; within a few moments the tent was filled with an acrid, burning smell.

"By such simple means that the result is a true miracle," the short fellow replied. "I've once read dat the ash from the firewood not only replaces the salt we're missing here, but also takes away the *haut gout* whiff of the meat, which is fairly indecently on the nose. Our roast was endowed with a very dissident mustiness, and I have therefore reached for dat mentioned remedy and broiled it in the wooden ash. That was easy because we have a wood fire. Never mind that the fire reached into the pot a little, because especially dat will be of a certain crackling effect, so my ingenious kitchen sense tells me. It will send any tender and palatable person into ecstasies at the dining table."

"Oh, my! Elk roast in wood ash! Are you quite sane?"

"Don't talk such apple salad! I'm always sane. You ought to know dat by now. The ash is a chemical opponent of all the alchemistic impurities. Enjoy the elk roast with the matching common sense; then it will agree with you and endow your constitution with those physical and mental powers without which a human being would be completely devoured by the despicable microbial organisms."

"But, you said yourself that the flames got into your pot," Jemmy shook his head. "The meat burned; it is spoilt."

"Don't talk, chew!" Frank roused at him. "It is very unhealthy to sing or shpeak during a meal, because the wrong gullet passage will open up and the food will end up in the spleen instead of in the stomach."

"Yes, let those chew who can! Here, look! Is this still meat?"

He skewered a piece on his knife, and held it up under Hobble's nose. The meat was charred black with a coating of fatty ash.

"Of course it is meat. What else it is supposed to be?" Frank retorted.

"But it's as black as Chinese ink!"

"Then take a bite! You'll immediately experience your miracle!"

"I believe it. And the ash?"

"Will be cleaned away and wiped off."

"You'll have to demonstrate that to me first!"

"With royal nonchalance!"

He fingered a piece out of the pot and rubbed it back and forth along the tent hide until the ash stuck to it.

"That's how you do it," he continued. "But you're always lacking the necessary dexterity and presence of mind. And now you shall see how delicate this will taste when I bite a corner off and squash it on my tongue. Dat..."

He suddenly fell quiet after he bit into the meat. Then he released his teeth, parted them and kept his mouth wide open, dumbfounded, while he looked at his companions one after the other.

"Well then, bite, why don't you?" Jemmy encouraged him.

"Bite...how? Wat the devil...dat's cracking and crackling just like...like...well, like a roasted scrubbing brush. Who would have thought?"

"That was to be expected. I think the old pot is more tender than the meat. Now you'll have to devour the creation of your culinary sense yourself!"

"Oho! No one is going to say you're forced to go hungry on my account. How about we bash it somewhat?"

"Try it!" Old Shatterhand laughed. "Let me see whether the entire lot is spoilt."

"Alright, there might still be a piece that hasn't entirely solidified its character yet. Let me search; I'll wipe the ash off!"

Fortunately there were some pieces that were still passably edible and of enough quantity to suffice for four people; but Frank had become fairly taciturn; he retreated into a dark corner and pretended to be asleep. Yet he heard every word that was spoken, and also saw what was happening outside in the camp.

Knox and Hilton were going to die at the stakes in the morning, and it was possible that the other Whites would suffer a similar fate. That provided cause for the Indians to have a large feast, for which they needed to make preparations early. Hence they retired after the late evening meal and went to sleep; the fires died down except for two, the one near the tent occupied by Old Shatterhand and his three companions, and one where Knox and Hilton were lying with their guards. A triple circle of Indians had formed outside the hunters' tent, and outside the village numerous guards had been positioned. Escape would have been difficult and dangerous, if not impossible.

So as not to have the Indians observe him all night long, Old Shatterhand had lowered the mat on the tent entrance. The Whites were therefore lying in the dark, yet trying in vain to get some sleep.

"What will have become of us by this time tomorrow night?" Long Davy said. "Perhaps the redskins will have expedited us into the Eternal Hunting Grounds."

"At least one, two or three of us," Jemmy replied.

"Why is that?" Old Shatterhand asked.

"I think they won't dare to tackle you."

"Only the three of you in that case? Hm! What are you thinking of me? We belong together, and none of us must think he can exclude himself from the fate of the others. If you're destined to die, then I wouldn't think of accepting an offer of being spared; we'd fight to the last man."

"But you've promised not to resist."

"Indeed, and I'll keep that promise to the letter. However, I've not promised that I won't flee. I would at least make an attempt to get away, and if someone stands in our way, then it will be their own fault if we do away with them. Besides, I'm worried about something completely different because I suspect that the Indians will decide not to kill us outright."

"And to release us instead?"

"Not that, either. Their rancour towards the Whites is so great and, I must admit, so just that they simply will not release palefaces once they've captured them. But our names have a good reputation with them; in addition, they fear my rifle so much that they don't even dare to touch it. I think it is not only possible, but also probable that they'll make an exception with us. This means they won't just let us go, but make us fight for our lives and freedom."

"Tarnation! That would be wonderful, and as straightforward as if they'd simply murder us because they'd pose the conditions so that we'd have to die."

"Indeed. But we still mustn't lose courage. The White has learnt from the Indian; he possesses just as much cunning and agility as the other, and with regard to perseverance he is superior to the Indian. We've all had that experience and it won't disappoint us. If I were to sum it up, I'd say that in an open hand-to-hand battle three Whites would take on four Indians, if the weapons were the same and their physical strength equal. The belligerent pride of the Indians will prevent them from pitting us against too great a number of opponents. And if they did so, regardless, we would cause them to withdraw with ridicule."

"But the pershpective you're showing us here is not delightful at all," said Hobble-Frank, who had been silent since the roast incident. "Those fellows will make the story as sour as possible for us, of course. But, you, with your physical strength and elephant power, you can laugh, indeed; you punch, whack and knock your way through; but we, the other three hapless chanterelles, will have enjoyed the last delights of existence today."

"In the shape of your elk roast?" Jemmy asked.

"Are you trying to nettle me again? I was under the impression dat our situation is such dat you might desist from annoying your best friend and brother in arms to death before his last ascension. Don't go fragmenting my intellectual capacity! I've got to direct all of my thoughts sharply onto our salvation. Or do you think perchance dat it is enormously noble-minded and heroic to slowly do away with a person by pathological mockery four hours before he's destined for his hippologic face?"

"The face would be Hippocratic, not hippologic," Jemmy said. He had been unable to refrain from making that correction, and Hobble worked himself up so much that he burst out:

"Listen, dat's shtrong; you're really getting too much for me. I can only crush you with Heinrich Heine's words in *The Singer's Curse*:

Thou dev'lish tyrant of a day,
Atrocious towards God, man, and beast,
That sought'st so hellishly thy prey
Thy time upon the Earth hath ceased,
The police I hasten to exhort
To summon thee to district court.

There—now you know my opinion. Take it to heart and mull it over in your mind, over and under, until you've arrived at the rueful insight!"

"But dear old Frank, I didn't mean it in a nasty way; as a friend it is my duty to make you aware of your errors. I won't let you embarrass yourself."

"Oh? Can I—I—I, that being me, Hobble-Frank from Moritzburg, can I really and truly make a mistake and embarrass myself?"

"Just like any other human being. Especially the rhyme you just used is evidence for that. Firstly, there is no talk of either the police or a district court; secondly, the poem is not from Heine, it is from Buerger, and thirdly, the title is *The Wild Hunter*, not *The Singer's Curse*."

"Oh, oh; upon my soul! The things you know or think you know! If you dare to approach me in this manner, then I can't do anything else but tell you that my literature history isn't made of tin, but shtands higher than any other. With your twisting of facts and impossibilities you intend to make dat wild hunter out of me; but you won't succeed. You can talk as you please henceforth, I won't say anything else, and instead wrap myself into deepest contempt of you. Someone who can confuse Heine and Buerger, and here in an Indian wigwam at that, has had all of his stars extinguished. I've always extended to you my entire, rich and exponential inner life; but I've been terribly mistaken in you. Your deceitfulness turns my diaphragm inside out; but I was born a Christian and educated academically, and will therefore forgive you. But our friendship is *perdue* and your cold temperament may never again sun itself in the rays of my spirit. Adieu, Jemmy, for all eternity! At this very moment your planet disappears in night and horror. *Requiriescat in panem!*"

He stretched out and closed his eyes. From the other side came something that sounded like a faint, suppressed laugh; he ignored it. The others didn't continue the conversation; deep silence ensued, which was punctured only by the occasional crackling of the fire.

Sleep gradually sank onto everyone's tired eyelids. They opened their eyes again only when loud shouts arose outside the tent, and someone lifted the mat hanging over the door opening. An Indian looked inside and said:

"The palefaces may rise and come with me."

They rose to their feet, took their weapons and followed him. The fire had gone out, and the sun was coming up from the eastern horizon. It threw its young rays onto the mountain massif mentioned earlier, so that the watercourse descending from it glittered like liquid gold, and the surface of the lake shone like a polished metal disc. The men could see much further than they had been able during the evening before. The plain, which held the lake in the western part, was approximately three kilometres long, half as wide and surrounded by forest. The camp was situated in the southern part and consisted of around one hundred tents and huts. The horses were grazing along the lake shore; those of the four hunters were near their tent; the Indians had therefore heeded Old Shatterhand's request.

In front of and between the huts and tents stood or moved red figures who had all donned their war adornments to celebrate the death of the two captured murderers. When the four whites were led past, the Indians politely moved aside and scrutinized their statures with an expression on their faces that was more probing and examining than it was hostile.

"What's wrong with these fellows?" Frank asked. "They're peeking at me just like one would look at a horse if one wants to buy it."

"They're checking our physiques," Old Shatterhand replied. "It's an indication that I've guessed correctly. They already know our probable fate. We'll have to fight for our lives."

"Splendid! Mine won't be too cheap. Jemmy, are you afraid?"

His vexation towards the rotund fellow had disappeared into thin air; it was evident from the tone of his question that he was thinking more about his friend than himself.

"I'm not afraid, but worried nonetheless, which goes without saying. Fear would only be to our detriment. It is now a matter of remaining as collected and calm as possible."

Two stakes had been driven into the ground outside the camp; five feather-decorated warriors stood nearby, Great Wolf among them. He approached the Whites a few paces and explained:

"I have sent for the palefaces, so that they may witness how the red warriors punish their enemies. The murderers will be brought at once, to die on the stakes."

"We don't wish to see this," Old Shatterhand replied.

"Are you cowards who are horrified at the sight of blood flowing? In that case we would be forced to treat you as such, and won't need to keep the promise I made to you."

"We are Christians. We kill our enemies fast, should we be forced to do so; but we don't torture them."

"You're now here with us and have to submit to our custom. If you don't want to do that, then you're insulting us and will be punished by being put to death."

Old Shatterhand realized that the chief was serious, and that he would have placed himself and his companions in grave danger if he had refused to attend the execution. Hence he reluctantly agreed:

"Alright, we'll stay."

"Then sit down with us! If you obey you'll be destined to die honourably."

He sat down in the grass, facing the stakes. The other chiefs did likewise, and the Whites were required to follow suit. Great Wolf gave a loud shout, and he received an answer in the form of a general howl of triumph. That was the signal for the horrid spectacle to begin.

The warriors approached and formed a half circle around the stakes, inside of which the chiefs and the Whites were sitting. After that came the women and children; they took their places oposite the men and formed another arc, so that the circle was closed.

Then they brought Knox and Hilton, who were fettered tightly, so that they couldn't walk and had to be carried. The straps cut into their flesh so deeply that Hilton groaned. Knox was quiet; he suffered from wound fever and had only just stopped hallucinating. He looked dreadful. Both were tied to the stakes in an upright position with wet straps that were going to contract while drying and inflict the worst pain upon the victims of a cruel justice.

Knox' eyes were closed and his head hung heavy down to his chest; he was unconscious and didn't know what was happening to him. Hilton looked around with fearful gazes. When he saw the four hunters, he called to them:

"Save me, save me, gentlemen. You're no heathens. Did you come here to watch us die a terrible death and take pleasure in our torture?"

"No," Old Shatterhand replied. "We're here under duress, and are unable to do anything for you."

"You can, you can, if you want to. The redskins will listen to you."

"No. You alone are to blame for your fate. If you have the courage to sin, then you must also have the courage to bear the punishment."

"I'm innocent. I've shot no Indian. Knox did it."

"Don't lie! Wanting to put the blame on him alone is impudent cowardice. You had better repent your deeds, so that you'll find forgiveness in the hereafter!"

"But I don't want to die; I don't want to die! Help, help, help!"

He yelled loudly, so that it echoed across the entire plain, and in the process yanked at his fetters until the blood spurted from his flesh. That's when Great Wolf rose to his feet and gave a hand signal that he wished to speak. Everyone looked at him. In the short, powerful, and yet spirited ways of an Indian orator, he told what had happened, and depicted the treacherous conduct of the palefaces, with whom they had been living in peace, as an unprovoked attack. The words made a deep impression on the Indians, so that they began to rattle their weapons. Then he explained that the two murderers were condemned to die at the stake, and that the execution was to begin. When he concluded and sat down, Hilton once again raised his voice to persuade Old Shatterhand to plead on their behalf.

"Alright, I'll try it," the hunter said. "Although I cannot avert death, I might be able to make it quick and less torturous."

He turned to the chiefs, but hadn't opened his mouth to say anything when Great Wolf angrily roused at him:

"You know that I speak the language of the palefaces and that I have therefore understood what you've promised to the dog over there. Haven't I done enough by giving you such agreeable conditions? Will you speak against our judgment and make my warriors so angry that I cannot protect you from them? Therefore be silent and don't say one word! You have enough to think about yourself and shouldn't worry about others. If you take sides with these murderers, then you put yourself on the same level as them and will suffer the same fate."

"My religion demands that I plead for them," Shatterhand said. It was the only excuse he was permitted to offer.

"Whose religion do we have to comply with, yours or ours? Did your religion command these dogs to attack us, steal our horses and kill our warriors although we were living in peace? No! This means that your religion will not influence the punishment of the perpetrators, either."

The chief turned away and gave a hand signal upon which around a dozen warriors stepped out from the crowd. He then addressed Old Shatterhand again and explained:

"Here stand the family members of those who have been murdered. They have the right to begin the punishment."

"What will it consist of?" the hunter asked.

"It will consist of diverse tortures. The knives will be thrown at them first."

When Indians tie an enemy to the stake to die, they endeavour to extend the torture for as long as possible. The inflicted wounds will be only minor at first, and then gradually increase in severity. The Indians usually begin by throwing the knives, which is led by someone indicating various limbs and body parts that are to be hit by the knives or where the weapons will remain stuck. The target areas are chosen for the least amount of bleeding, so that the tortured person doesn't die prematurely of blood loss.

"The right thumb!" Great Wolf ordered.

The arms of the prisoners had been tied to the stakes in a manner that left only the hands free. The Indians, who had stepped forwards, formed two groups: one for Hilton and the other for Knox. The first of them was standing about twelve paces away from the stakes, with all others behind him in a row. He took his knife into his right hand, between the first three fingers, lifted it, aimed, threw and hit the thumb. Hilton gave a cry of pain. Knox was hit as well, but he was unconscious and didn't come to.

"The index finger," the chief ordered.

In that way he indicated the fingers to be targeted, one after the other, and the warriors truly hit them with astonishing precision. Hilton had at first produced individual cries, but then taken to emitting a continuous howling. Knox only woke up when his left hand had become the target. He stared around the place absentmindedly, closed his blood-shot eyes again and produced an utterly inhuman wailing. He had seen what was happening to him; the fever took a hold of him again, and both, the delirium and the mortal fear, forced sounds out of him that ought not have been possible for a human voice.

The execution continued amid the uninterrupted screaming and yelling of the two. The knives hit the back of the hands, the wrists, the muscles of the lower and upper arms, and the same sequence was followed on the legs. That lasted for around a quarter of an hour and was the mild beginning of what was supposed to last for hours. Old Shatterhand and his three companions had turned away. They found it impossible to watch the proceedings. They had no choice and were forced to endure the screaming.

Indians are trained to endure physical pain from earliest childhood. They reach a stage whereby they can tolerate the greatest tortures without batting an eyelid. It may even be that their nerves are less sensitive than those of the Whites. If an Indian is captured and put to the stake to die, he suffers the inflicted pain with a smile, loudly sings his death dirge, and interrupts it only occasionally to mock and ridicule his torturers. To see a wailing man on the stake is an impossibility among the Indians. Anyone who complains about pain will be despised, and the louder the laments, the greater the contempt. It has happened that tortured Whites, who were supposed to die, were released because they demonstrated with their unmanly bawling that they were weaklings, that they weren't to be feared, and that killing them would be a disgrace for any warrior.

It wasn't difficult to imagine the impression that Knox and Hilton's crying made. The Indians turned away and gave shouts of disgust and disdain. When the family members of the Utah who had been murdered had received their satisfaction, and others were called upon to step forwards and continue the torture with other means, not one warrior volunteered. No one wanted to touch such 'dogs, coyotes, and toads'. Then one of the chiefs rose and said:

"These people are not worthy of being touched by a brave warrior; my red brothers can clearly see this. Let's leave them to the women. The soul of someone who dies by the hand of a woman will attain the shape of a woman in the Eternal Hunting Grounds and must work for all eternity. I have spoken."

His suggestion was agreed upon after a short deliberation. The wives and mothers of the murdered Utah were called; they received knives to inflict light cuts to the two doomed prisoners, also in the sequence determined by Great Wolf.

A civilized European would find it hard to believe that a woman could go as far as to participate in such cruelty. However, the redskins aren't civilized, and in this case revenge for the multiple murder banished any notion of mercy. The women, mostly old females, began their work. The howling and wailing of the two Whites recommenced, but it became unbearable even for red ears. Great Wolf interrupted the process and said:

"These weaklings are not even worth being women after their deaths. No red man will suggest that we let them go, because their guilt is too great, they must die; but they shall enter the Eternal Hunting Grounds as coyotes, which will be hunted and chased endlessly. Let the dogs have them. I have spoken."

They held a powwow the outcome of which Old Shatterhand foresaw and expected with horror. He dared to bring another plea, but was rebuffed so sternly that he was glad he hadn't come away any the worse for it. The decision was made according to Great Wolf's proposal. Several Indians left the circle to fetch the dogs. The chief turned to the Whites:

"The dogs of the Utah are trained to attack Whites; the animals ordinarily won't hurt them; but once they're set onto them, they'll charge. However, they will then butcher any White nearby. I will therefore have you taken to a tent and guarded until the animals are tied up again."

Upon his order, the four Whites were led into a nearby tent where several Indians guarded them. The hunters felt as if the fangs of the beasts were meant for them. The two murderers deserved to die; but to be torn apart by dogs was a ghastly end.

There had been a good ten minutes of silence outside, which was only occasionally interrupted by Hilton's whimpering. He was still unaware of his fate. Then the men in the tent heard loud, frantic barks that turned into bloodthirsty howling; two human voices screeched in most desperate mortal fear; then silence fell again.

"Listen!" Jemmy said. "I can hear bones cracking. I believe the Indians let the dogs eat the two men."

"That's possible, but I don't believe it," Old Shatterhand replied. "The cracking only lives in your imagination. Mine is also unusually vivid. It was fortunate for us that we didn't have to witness the scene!"

The Indians came to release the four Whites from the tent and take them back to the place of the execution. Further inside the camp they saw four or five Indians who were leading the dogs on strong straps back to their places. The dogs probably got the scent of the Whites; one of the animals was impossible to drag away; it looked around and saw the four hunters. It tore free with one mighty tug and raced towards the men. A general cry of shock came from the crowd; the dog was large and strong, so that it seemed impossible for a human being to tackle it. And yet none of the Indians wanted to shoot at the animal because it was valuable. Jemmy lifted his gun and aimed.

"Stop, don't shoot," Old Shatterhand ordered. "The Indians could take offence at the death of the magnificent dog, and by the same token, I also want to show them what the fist of a white hunter can accomplish."

He had spoken hastily. Everything was happening much faster than it can be told or described, because the dog had covered the entire distance in truly panther-like leaps within less than ten seconds. Old Shatterhand took a couple of fast steps towards the animal while holding his arms low.

"You're lost!" Great Wolf called to him.

"Wait and see!" the hunter replied.

The dog had reached him. The animal's tooth-studded jaws were agape, and it jumped at its opponent with a raptor-like snarl. Shatterhand kept his eyes firmly on those of the dog; when it took the jump and was already airborne, aiming for his throat, he swiftly lunged forwards and at the beast while he quickly opened his arms—there was a mighty collision between dog and human. Old Shatterhand clenched his arms across the neck of the animal and pressed the dog's head so strongly to his chest that it was unable to bite. Another forceful squeeze, and the dog ran out of air; its scratching legs went limp. The hunter pulled the dog's head away from him with a swift movement of the left hand, administered a blow with his right fist onto its snout, and then he flung it to the ground.

"There it lies," he called out while he turned to the chief. "Let someone tie it up, so that it cannot do any further harm when it wakes up."

"Uff, uff, uff!" the astonished Indians exclaimed. None of them would have dared to do that; they didn't deem it to be possible. Great Wolf gave the order to take the animal away, and then walked over to Old Shatterhand and said with admiration:

"My white brother is a hero. He knocked the dog to the ground, instead of letting it pull him down and butcher him. The feet of no red man would have stood so solidly, and the chest of no other person would have withstood the collision; their ribs would have been crushed. Why did Old Shatterhand not let the other man shoot?"

"Because I didn't want to deprive you of this magnificent animal."

"What carelessness! What if it had torn you apart?"

"Pshaw! Old Shatterhand won't be torn apart by any dog! What will the warriors of the Utah do next?"

"They will hold counsel about you, because the time for it has arrived. Will the palefaces not want to beg us to take pity on them?"

"Pity? Are you mad? You had better ask me whether or not I'm inclined to take pity on you!"

With a gaze of astonishment, as well as admiration, the chief led Shatterhand to the side, where the four Whites were to sit outside the circle of the Indians, so as not to be able to listen to the discussion. Then he went back to his original seat.

The hunters looked at the two stakes, of course. There the torn apart bodies and limbs of the murderers were hanging from the straps that the dogs had tattered; a truly ghastly image.

The decisive powwow began, which was held entirely in Indian fashion. First Great Wolf spoke for a long while; then the other chiefs followed, one by one. Afterwards Great Wolf began anew, as did the other chiefs; the ordinary warriors were not permitted to say anything. They were standing in a circle, listening respectfully. Indians are usually taciturn; but during powwows they talk gladly, and much. There are natives who have attained significant fame because of their skills as orators.

The meeting of the elders took the most part of two hours, which was a long time for those whose destiny depended on it; then a general and loudly called 'howgh!' announced the conclusion to the gathering. The Indians fetched the Whites; they had to step inside the circle to hear what had been decided about their fate. Great Wolf rose to his feet to announce it:

"The four palefaces have already heard why we have raised the war hatchets; I will not repeat it. We have sworn to kill all Whites who fall into our hands, and I ought not make an exception of you. You've followed me here, for us to hold counsel about you, and have promised me not to resist. We know that you are friends of the red men, and that's why you will not share the fate of other palefaces that we'll catch. They will be put to the stake at once; but you shall be permitted to fight for your lives."

He made a pause, which Old Shatterhand utilized to ask:

"With whom? The four of us against all of you? Good, I agree. My rifle of death will send many of you into the Eternal Hunting Grounds!"

He lifted his rifle. The chief was only barely able to conceal his fright; he swiftly made a defensive gesture and replied:

"Old Shatterhand is mistaken. Each of you will have one opponent with whom he'll have to fight, and the victor has the right to kill the vanquished."

"I agree. But who has the right to choose our opponents, we or you?"

"We will choose. I will have a request proclaimed for volunteers to come forwards."

"And how, or with what kinds of weapons shall the fights be conducted?"

"Those who volunteer will determine that."

"Ah! You will therefore not heed our wishes?"

"No."

"That is unfair."

"No, it is fair. You must consider that we have the advantage over you, and can therefore also demand an advantage."

"The advantage? How so?"

"So many against so few."

"Pshaw! What are your weapons against my rifle of death! Only those who are afraid demand an advantage over others."

"Are afraid?" Great Wolf asked with a glint in his eyes. "Do you wish to insult me? Are you insinuating that we are afraid?"

"I didn't speak about you specifically, but in general. If a slow runner has to run with a fast runner in a competition, he usually demands a head start. Because you place us at a disadvantage, you gave me just cause to believe that you think we're the better warriors. And if I were the chief of the Utah, I wouldn't do that."

Great Wolf stared at the ground for some time. He couldn't say that Old Shatterhand was wrong, but had to be careful not to agree with him; and in the end he said:

"We've already shown enough leniency towards you, so that you can't demand any more. Whether or not we're afraid of you will become clear during the fight."

"Good; but I demand honest conditions."

"What do you mean?"

"You say that the victor has the right to kill the vanquished. What if I overpower one of your warriors and kill him, will I then be able to leave this place freely and safely?"

"Yes."

"And no one will harm me?"

"No, because you won't win. None of you will win."

"I understand you. You will make a choice from among your warriors, and determine the means of the fight, in such a way that we will be defeated. Don't be mistaken! The outcome can easily differ from the one you envisage."

"I know the outcome so precisely that I pose one more condition, namely that those who are victorious will receive all the property of the vanquished."

"That condition is very necessary, otherwise no one would volunteer to fight us."

"Beware!" the chief roused at the hunter. "You only get to say whether you agree or not."

"And what if we don't?"

"Then you're breaking your promise, because you said that you wouldn't resist."

"I keep my promise, but want your word that you regard the one of us who is going to emerge from the fight as the victor, as a friend."

"I promise you."

"Shall we smoke the pipe of peace on it?"

"Don't you believe me?" Great Wolf retorted.

Old Shatterhand realized that he couldn't afford to be too harsh in his conduct, if he didn't want to lose the advantages he had gained earlier; hence he said:

"Alright, I believe you. Ask your warriors for volunteers!"

When the chief did, a great movement went through the Indians; they rushed and surged along in confusion, asked questions and hollered over the top of each other. Old Shatterhand said to his companions:

"Unfortunately I couldn't overstretch the bow, otherwise it would have snapped. I'm not at all satisfied with the stipulations."

"We cannot otherwise but be content with them, since we can't get any better ones," Long Davy said.

"Indeed, as far as I am concerned I'm not worried. The Indians are so scared of me that I'm curious to see whether they'll find a volunteer to fight me."

"Most certainly."

"Who?"

"Great Wolf in person. Since no one else will come forward, he's forced to salvage the honour of his tribe. He's an enormous fellow, a veritable elephant."

"Pah! I'm not afraid of him. But you! They'll choose the most dangerous opponents for you fellows, and will choose a method of combat at which they'll assume you're no good. For example: no opponent of mine will agree to a fist fight."

"Let's wait and see," Jemmy said. "All worry and fear is useless at this point. Let's keep our muscles taut and the eyes open!"

"And the mind bright and clear," Hobble-Frank added. "I personally am as calm as a milestone in the gutter. I don't know why, but it's really true that I'm not afraid. These Utah will make the acquaintance with a fellow from Moritzburg in Saxony today. I'll fight until the sparks fly to Greenland."

The Indians restored order among themselves. The circle formed again, and Great Wolf brought along three warriors whom he introduced as those who had volunteered.

"Then indicate the pairing now," Old Shatterhand bade him.

The chief pushed the first of them in front of Long Davy and said:

"Here stands *Pagu-Angare*[13], who will swim with this paleface for his life."

The choice was well made for the Indians. It was obvious that the water wouldn't readily float long, skinny Davy. The Indian, on the other hand, was a fellow with round hips, broad, fleshy chest and strong arm and leg muscles. He was definitely the best

[13] Red Fish

swimmer of the tribe. If his name hadn't hinted at it, then the disparaging gaze he gave Davy would have revealed it.

Then the chief placed a tall, very broad-shouldered person with bulging muscles in front of short Fat Jemmy and said:

"This warrior is *Namboh-Avaht*[14], who will wrestle with the fat paleface. They'll be tied together back to back. Each will receive a knife into his right hand, and the one who'll get the other under him first, is permitted to stab him."

Big Foot wore his name with full justification. He had enormous feet with which he would probably stand on the ground so solidly that short Fat Jemmy could have run away from fright already.

Then there was the third, bony fellow, almost one hundred and eighty centimetres tall, lanky, but with a barrel chest and endlessly long arms and legs. The chief placed him in front of Hobble-Frank and said:

"And here stands *To-Ok-Tey*[15], who is prepared to run with this paleface for his life."

Poor Hobble-Frank! While Running Stag took two steps with his seven-mile legs, Hobble had to make ten! Indeed, the redskins had been extremely mindful of their advantage.

"And who'll fight me?" Old Shatterhand asked.

"I will," Great Wolf proudly said while he stretched his tall frame even taller. "You believed that we're scared; I'll show you that you were mistaken."

"I like that," the White replied politely. "I've always chosen my opponents from the ranks of chiefs."

"You'll be defeated!"

"Old Shatterhand won't be defeated!"

"Neither will Ovuts-Avaht! There is no one who could say that he has overpowered me!"

"I will say that today already!"

"And I will become master of your life!"

"Let's not fight with words, but with the rifle!"

Old Shatterhand said it with a slightly ironic tone in his voice; he knew that the chief wasn't going to agree to it. And indeed, he hastily said:

"I won't have anything to do with your rifle of death. Knife and tomahawk shall decide between us."

"I'm also satisfied with that."

---

[14] Big Foot
[15] Running Stag

"Then you'll be a corpse very shortly and I will own all of your property, including your horse!"

"I believe that my horse spurs your desire; but the magic rifle is even more valuable. What will you do with it?"

"I don't want it, and no one else has any longing for it. It is too dangerous because those who touch it will hit their best friends. We will bury it deep in the ground where it may rust and rot away."

"In that case, may the one who touches it in the process of burying it be very careful, otherwise he'll bring great misfortune upon the entire tribe of the Utah. And now say in which order the individual fights will take place."

"First there will be the swimming duel. But I know that the Christians like to observe secret rites before their deaths. I will give you the time you palefaces call one hour."

The Indians had obviously only formed the circle around the Whites again to observe how scared they would be about their assigned opponents. But they didn't see anything of the sort and scattered again. No one seemed to bother about the hunters at that point; but they knew very well that they were being observed sharply. They sat together and spoke about their chances in the forthcoming duels. Danger was looming closest for Long Davy because he was the first who had to fight. He didn't make a desperate, but nevertheless very serious face.

"Red Fish!" he muttered. "Of course that scoundrel only got his name because he is an excellent swimmer."

"What about you?" Old Shatterhand asked. "I might have seen you swim a couple of times, but only during a bath or across fords. How well can you truly swim?"

"Not very well."

"Oh, my!"

"Yes, oh my! It's not my fault that my corpus only consists of heavy bones. And I believe that my bones are even heavier than those of anyone else."

"That means there's no counting on speed. What about stamina?"

"Stamina? Pah! As long as you want. I've got enough strength; but I'm lacking speed. I'll probably have to relinquish my scalp."

"That's not a foregone conclusion at this stage. I haven't lost confidence yet. Have you ever swum on your back?"

"Yes, and it seems to be easier that way."

"Indeed, past experience has shown that skinny and unskilled people swim better on their backs than on their bellies. Therefore lay on your back; put your head as deeply into the water as possible and your legs as close to the surface as possible; push out rhythmically and strong with your feet, and only draw breath when you fold your arms under your back during the stroke."

"Alright! But that won't do any good, because Red Fish will beat me anyway."

"Perhaps not, if my trick will work."

"What trick?"

"You must swim with the current, and he against it."

"Oh, how would that be accomplished? Is there a current at all?"

"I suspect there is. If it is missing, then you'd be lost, of course."

"We still don't know where the swimming will take place."

"Over yonder on the lake, of course, which is actually only a pond. It is oblong; five hundred paces long, and three hundred wide, approximately, as far as I can guess from here. The mountain stream flows into it from a steep waterfall, and it seems that it does so along the left shore. That results in a current along that particular edge, three quarters around the lake to the exit of it. Leave it to me. If it is at all possible, then I'll work it so that you will beat your opponent with this current."

"That would indeed be a merry occasion, sir! And I put the case that I'll win, should I stab the fellow then?"

"Do you feel like it?"

"He will definitely not spare me, be it only for the sake of my few possessions."

"That's correct. And even aside from the fact that we're Christians, to show mercy is in our own best interest."

"Splendid! But what will you do if he defeats me and comes at me with his knife? I'm not allowed to defend myself!"

"In that case I'll force them to wait long enough until all the duels are finished."

"Alright, that's a comfort even in the worst case, and I'm relieved. But, Jemmy, how about you?"

"I'm in no better situation than you," the rotund fellow replied. "My opponent's name is Big Foot. Do you know what that means?"

"Well?"

"He stands so squarely on his feet that no one will bring him down. I am two heads shorter than he, and am supposed to accomplish that? And the man has muscles like a hippopotamus. What's my fat against that?"

"Don't panic, my dear Jemmy," Old Shatterhand comforted him. "I'm in the same situation. The chief is significantly taller and broader than I am, but he'll be lacking agility, and I'd also like to claim that I've got more muscle strength than he's got."

"Yes, your physical power is a phenomenon, an exception. But I'm pitted against Big Foot! I'll resist for as long as I can, but I'll be defeated nevertheless. Indeed, if only there were such a trick available in this case, too!"

"But dat trick ish here already!" Hobble-Frank piped up. "If I were dealing with dat Florian, then I wouldn't be afraid at all."

"You? But you're even weaker than I am!"

"In body, yes, but not in shpirit. And one has to win in shpirit. Do you undershtand?"

"What am I to do with my spirit against such a muscleman?"

"There you go! Dat's how you are! Everything and always, you always know everything better than me; but when life and scalp are at stake you sit there like a fly in buttermilk. You flap about with hands and feet and still can't get out of it."

"Then out with it if you've got a good idea!"

"Idea! What kind of talk is that now? I don't need an idea; I'm always clever even without ideas. Just think yourself into your situation properly! The two of you shtand tightly back to back, and you both get tied together above your belly, just like the nice star sign of the Siamese twins up there in the milky way. Each holds a knife in his right hand, and then the knightly fencing will begin. The one who succeeds in getting the other beneath him has won. But how does one get his opponent to be in dat position? Only by getting him to lose his footing, which can happen by kicking him into the calves from behind or hooking one's foot around his in an attempt at pulling it away from under him. Am I right or not?"

"Yes. Continue."

"Gently does it! Dat has to happen with deliberation and without haste. If the experiment succeeds, then the opponent somersaults onto his nose and one gets to lie on top of him, but unfortunately with the back on his back, whereby one could easily lose one's European equilibrium oneself. Actually, you ought to be tied together face to face. At this point in time I cannot fathom what kind of ruse the redskins have connected to the back to front state of affairs; but I know this much: that double-cross will only be to your benefit."

"In what way? Why don't you get to the point already!" Jemmy pushed.

"*Herrjemerschnee*, I've been talking an entire quarter of an hour thus far! Listen here! Big Foot will kick you from behind in order to pull one of your legs out from under you and get you off balance. Dat won't hurt you none, because with the confessionable strength in your calves you'll only feel his kicks fourteen months down the track. Now you'll wait for the one moment when he's kicking again and therefore only shtands on one leg. That's when you'll bow forwards with all the strength you've got, and lift him onto your back, quickly cut the rope in two, and fling him over your head with a fast flip and onto the ground. But then onto him immediately, grab the fellow by the throat and put dat knife onto his heart. Have you undershtood me you old snow-plough?"

Old Shatterhand extended his hand to Hobble and said:

"Frank, you're not a bad fellow after all. I couldn't have figured that one out any better. This instruction is excellent and must lead to the desired outcome."

Frank's honest face gleamed from delight while he shook the hand offered to him and said:

"Don't mention it, dearest field marshal! I'm not becoming too conceited about something dat's so perfectly natural. My merits and asters are blooming elsewhere. It's merely more evidence dat unreasonable people oftentimes mistake a diamond for a boulder. Hence I think..."

"Pebble, not boulder," Jemmy cut in. "Heavens would that be a diamond, the size of a boulder!"

"Would you care to shut up already, you old, incorrigible brawler! I'm saving your life with my shpiritual superiority and, as thanks, you're tossing my unpolished boulder at my head! Dat's a nice fellow who's got such moody whims! Have you ever found a diamond?"

"No."

"Then don't talk about such things!"

"Did you ever find one?"

"Yes. The glazier in Moritzburg had lost his and I picked it up in the laneway. I was a young person at the time and received a gift for my honesty that was incredibly valuable. The glazier was also the local shopkeeper at the same time and gave me a clay pipe for two pfennig and half a packet of tobacco for three. I've never forgotten it, and you can therefore see dat I am very capable of speaking about diamonds. If you don't shtop rubbing me the wrong way soon, then it could easily happen dat I annul our friendship, and then you'll find out whether or not you'll make it through the world without me. Here is neither the time nor the place for arguments and spats. We all stand before the last light of our lives and have the sacred duty to support each other in word and deed, instead of becoming vexed. We are facing being terminated in an hour from now, so why would we want to damage our precious health even more and shorten our lives by being rude to each other? I would have thought dat right now would at last be the time to come to your senses."

"That's completely correct," Old Shatterhand agreed. "Let's think only about the duels we're facing. Jemmy will do his bit; I can see that his heart has become somewhat lighter. But what will you do, dear Frank?"

"Dear Frank!" the short fellow replied. "Dat sounds so nicely acoustic! It truly ish a completely different matter when one socializes with learned gentlemen! What will I do? Well, I'll run, what else?"

"I know that well, but you'll fall back!"

"I know dat well!"

"You need to take three steps, while he takes one!"

"I'm 'fraid so!"

"There's the question of the route you'll have to run, and whether or not you'll hold out. What about your breathing?"

"Dat's very excellent. I've got lungs like a bumble bee and hum and buzz all day, without getting short of breath. I can run, too. I've had to learn dat as a royal Saxon forestry warden."

"But you're no match for such a long-legged Indian!"

"Hm! Dat remains to be seen!"

"His name is 'Running Stag'; it means that speed is his main attribute."

"I'm beastly indifferent to what he's called, as long as I get to the finish line ahead of him."

"But precisely that's what you won't do."

"Oho! Why not?"

"As I've already said, and you agreed. Compare your legs with his!"

"Ah, so, the legs! And you think it depends on the legs?"

"Of course! What else would matter in a race for life or death?"

"The legs, too, of course, but they're not the main thing, by a long shot. It's mainly the head that decides."

"But that doesn't run along!"

"Of course it runs along. Or am I supposed to let my legs skip ahead and make the rest of my corpus wait for their return? Dat could be a dangerous affair. If they don't find their way back to me, I could be left sitting on the spot until I can grow new ones, and that's only supposed to happen with crabs. Nee, the head has to go along, 'cause it's got most of the work to do."

"I don't understand you!" Old Shatterhand called out, astonished about the short fellow's calmness.

"Me neither, at least not yet. At this particular moment I only know that one single good idea is better than a hundred leaps that run past the objective."

"Does that mean you have an idea?"

"Not yet. But I think if I've been able to give Jemmy some good advice, then I won't abandon myself, either. I don't know where the running will be done. Once that's decided, then I'll no doubt find an inspirational angle. Don't get your worries up on my account! Some inner tenor voice tells me that I won't yet turn my back on the world here. I was born to much more greatness, and such world historical personalities never die before having fulfilled their duties, not to mention having enjoyed the gentle delights of civilization."

At that point Great Wolf returned with the other chiefs, to request the Whites accompany them to the lake. The area was already swarming with people of every age, men, women and children, because the swimming contest was to be decided there.

When they arrived at the shore, Old Shatterhand saw that he hadn't been mistaken; there was a significant current. The lake had a roughly elliptical shape. The mountain stream entered the lake at its upper reaches and the current it caused first flowed past the long left hand side, all the way down to and past the other narrow end, towards the exit, which wasn't far at all from the stream's entry point. The current therefore followed the shore for almost three quarters of the lake's circumference. It would probably save Long Davy, if he were able to utilize it.

The women, girls and boys dispersed far along the lake shore. The warriors congregated around the lower narrow end, because that's where the duel was to begin. Everyone's attention was directed at the two combatants. Red Fish looked across the water with pride and self-confidence, like someone who was completely sure of himself. Even Davy seemed to be calm, but he frequently swallowed; his Adam's apple was constantly moving. For those who knew him, it was a sign of inner agitation.

At last, Great Wolf turned to Old Shatterhand:

"Do you think we ought to begin?"

"Yes, but we still don't know the details of the conditions," the hunter replied.

"You shall hear them. The two men will go into the water here right in front of me. When I give the signal by clapping my hands the race begins. The men will swim once around the lake, and have to stay one man's length away from the banks at all times. The one who cuts across to shorten the distance will be the vanquished. The one who returns here first, stabs the other one."

"Good! But to which side will they push off? To the right or to the left?"

"Left. They will then return to here from the right."

"Will they swim next to one another?"

"Of course!"

"My comrade on the right hand side of Red Fish, which means the warrior will be on my friend's left hand side?"

"No, the other way around."

"Why?"

"Because the one who swims on the left hand side is closer to the shore, and has therefore a longer way to travel."

"It is wrong and unjust to let them both swim in the same direction. You dislike cheating and will admit that it would be correct if they went in different directions. One of them swims along the right shore from here, and the other along the left; they meet and cross at the upper end of the lake, and then return along their opposite sides."

"You're correct," the chief said. "But which one of them will go to the right and which one to the left?"

"In order to be fair here as well, they will draw lots to decide. See here, I'll pluck two blades of grass and the two swimmers will choose. The one who draws the longer blade will swim to the left, the one who draws the shorter, to the right."

"Good, that's how it shall be. Howgh."

When the chief said his final remark, Davy's luck was sealed, because there would be no change possible to that decision. Old Shatterhand had plucked two blades of grass, but both of equal length. He first approached Red Fish and let him choose; then he gave Davy the remaining blade, but a moment earlier snipped off a small bit. The blades were compared; Davy had the shorter one and was forced to push off to the right. His opponent showed not the slightest vexation about it; he seemed to be unaware of the disadvantage. But Davy's face had lit up all the more. He scanned the water surface and whispered to Old Shatterhand:

"I don't know how I managed to get the shorter grass blade; but it'll save me because I'm hoping to return first. The current is strong and will give him much trouble."

He took his clothing off and waded into the shallow water. Red Fish did likewise. The chief clapped his hands—one jump and both men reached deeper water where they paddled away from each other, the Indian along the left shore and the White along the right.

"Davy, hold out!" Hobble-Frank called after his friend.

There was no noticeable difference between the swimmers, initially. The Indian used slow, but wide and powerful strokes like someone who felt at home in the water. He looked only straight ahead and was careful not to look around at the White because he would have lost time, although only a small amount. Davy swam more nervously and irregularly. He was not an accomplished swimmer and had to find the correct rhythm first. When it didn't eventuate, he turned onto his back, and immediately felt the improvement. The lake's current, as it pushed towards the exit from the left, was of very little significance at that point, but it helped Davy to advance nevertheless, so that he didn't fall back against the Indian.

At that point the Indian realized that he had been assigned the more difficult part. He needed to swim the entire length of the lake right up to the entrance of the mountain stream, and with each stroke he swam he was able to feel that the current increased in strength. He still relied on his capabilities, but soon it was evident that he was forced to greater exertion. He kicked out so powerfully that he lifted out of the water up to half of his chest with each stroke.

On Davy's side, the current weakened ever more, but it still had a favourable direction for him. In addition, he had also gradually found his rhythm. He was working more uniformly and deliberately. He observed the effect of each stroke and quickly learnt to avoid the wrong movements. Hence his speed doubled, and soon he was ahead of Red Fish, which caused the Indian to work even harder, instead of preserving his strength for the later, more difficult passage.

Davy approached the exit of the lake. The current intensified again; it wanted to grab him, pull him out of his lane, and out of the lake. He fought hard and lost some ground against the Indian. That was the moment on which everything hinged.

His companions were standing on the shore and watched him with great tension.

"The Indian is catching up to him again," Jemmy fearfully said. "He'll lose."

"If he keeps working like that for another six feet or so, he'll have overcome the exit surge and will be safe."

"Yes, indeed," Frank agreed. "He seems to realize dat. Look at him push and stomp! There, that's it, he's getting ahead; he's past it. Hallelujah, *vivat*, hooray!"

Long Davy had succeeded in overcoming the drag of the current, and entered calmer water. He soon finished his half circuit along the right shore, while the Indian was still going along the left. Davy turned around inside the narrow upper end of the lake towards the entry of the mountain stream

The Indian saw that and paddled madly to save his life; but each and every stroke, no matter how much power the man put into it, advanced him not half a metre, while Davy achieved twice the stroke length. Then the latter reached the inflow of the stream. The water grabbed him and swept him along. He had the last third of his way to go, while the Indian had hardly covered his first. They raced past each other.

"Hooray!" Davy couldn't help himself. The Indian replied with a furious hollering that was audible at quite some distance.

At that point Davy no longer needed to exert himself, on the contrary, swimming had become a delight for him. Only light paddle strokes were required for him to move in the prescribed direction. As the current gradually weakened towards the other end, he had to use more force again, but it was as easy for him as if he had done nothing his entire life except swim. He reached the predetermined spot on the lake shore and climbed ashore. When he turned around he saw that Red Fish had only just reached the outflow and had to battle the current once more.

A short, but bone-chilling chorus of cries erupted from the Indian crowd; thus they acknowledged that Red Fish had lost and was doomed to die. Davy, however, hastily slipped into his clothes again, and then ran to greet his comrades as if he had woken up with the gift of his reclaimed life.

"Who would have thought!" he said while he shook Old Shatterhand's hands. "I've conquered the best swimmer of the Utah!"

"With a blade of grass!" the hunter smiled and replied.

"How did you do that?"

"I'll tell you later. It was a little slight of hand, which can't be called cheating because it was a matter of saving your life without causing harm to the Indians."

"That's how it is!" Frank agreed. He was overjoyed at his friend's victory. "Your life didn't even hang on a piece of straw, it hung on only a blade of grass. Dat ish the same when it comes to a foot race. The legs alone won't do it by a long shot. Who knows what blade of grass will deliver my salvation. Indeed, one has to have a bit of oomph in one's legs, but even more in one's head. Look at dat, here comes the unlucky fish!"

The Indian approached from the right, more than five minutes after the White. He climbed ashore and sat down, facing the water. None of the other Indians looked at him; none moved; they waited for Davy to deliver the mortal stab.

At that point a squaw approached, leading a child on each hand. She joined him. He embraced one of the children with his right arm and the other with his left, and then quietly pushed them away, held his wife's hand, and then signalled her to move away. Then he looked around for Davy and called to him:

"*Nani witsh, ne pokai*[16]!"

Tears almost welled up in noble-minded Davy's eyes. He grabbed the wife with the children and pushed them towards Red Fish again, and then said in half English, half Utah, in which he wasn't quite fluent:

"Not *witsh*—not *pokai*!"

Then he turned away and returned to his friends. The Utah had seen and heard it. The chief asked:

"Why don't you kill him?"

"Because I'm a Christian. I'll spare his life."

"But if he had been victorious, he would have stabbed you!"

"But he didn't win, and therefore was unable to do so. He may live."

"But you'll take his property? His weapons, his horses, his wife and also his children?"

"Wouldn't think of it! I'm not a thief. He may keep what he owns."

"Uff, I don't understand you! He would have been smarter."

The other Indians didn't seem to understand Davy, either. The gazes they gave him clearly expressed how astonished they were about his conduct. None of them would have abandoned their claim, not even if one hundred human lives had depended on it. Red Fish sneaked away. He could not comprehend, either, why the White didn't stab and scalp him. He was ashamed for having been beaten, and thought he had best get out of sight.

---

[16] Your knife, kill me

However, there was some gratitude. The wife of Red Fish approached Long Davy and took his hand; she also lifted her children's hands up to him and stammered a few semi audible words, the meaning of which Davy may not have been able to understand, but he sensed it anyway.

Then Namboh-Avaht approached the chief and asked whether he ought to begin the duel with his paleface. Great Wolf nodded, and ordered everyone to the spot in question. That was situated near the two torture stakes. As was customary, the Indians formed a large circle, to the centre of which the chief led Big Foot. Old Shatterhand accompanied Fat Jemmy. The reason he did so was to ensure that there would be no underhanded tricks used against Jemmy.

The two combatants bared their upper bodies, and then stood back to back. Jemmy's head reached not quite to the Indian's shoulder. The chief tied them together with a lasso. The strap went over Big Foot's hips, but across the White's chest. By coincidence, and to the latter's advantage, the ends of the lasso reached just far enough for the chief to tie a hitch over Fat Jemmy's chest.

"Now you don't have to cut the strap, you only have to pull the hitch open," Old Shatterhand said to him in German.

Then each one received a knife to hold in the right hand, and the act could begin. Since the chief stepped back, Old Shatterhand did likewise.

"Shtand solid, Jemmy, and don't let him throw you!" Hobble-Frank called to his friend. "You know dat if he stabs you I'll be a widower and an orphan for all eternity, and you really wouldn't want to do dat to me. Just let him push, and then flip him over!"

The Indian also received encouraging shouts from various sides. He replied:

"My name is not Red Fish. I will squash the short, broad toad that hangs on my back in a few moments."

Jemmy didn't say anything. He was quiet and looked serious, but actually presented a droll figure behind the large frame of the Indian. As a precaution he had his face turned slightly sideways to observe the Indian's feet. It wasn't his intention, and also not in his interest, to be the one to begin the fight; he wanted to leave that to the Indian.

Big Foot stood motionless for a long time; he wanted to surprise his opponent with a sudden attack; but he didn't succeed. When he seemingly unintentionally shifted his foot backwards, to trip Jemmy, the German kicked him in the other weight-bearing leg so forcefully that the Indian almost fell.

But then followed attack upon attack. The Indian was stronger, but the White more cautious and circumspect. The former gradually worked himself up about the ineffectiveness of his efforts; but the more aggravated he grew, and the more furious he kicked back with his feet, the calmer the latter became. The fight seemed to drag on; it became boring since not the slightest advantage of one over the other was evident. However, the end was to come all the more swiftly, namely through a prearranged underhandedness of the Indian.

All Big Foot had intended to do with his action thus far was to lull his opponent into a false sense of security. The White was supposed to think that there was not going to be any other kind of attack forthcoming. At that point the Indian grabbed the lasso, sharply tightened it, so that he received room to move, and then turned around...but not entirely.

Had he been able to make good on his intentions, he would have turned around to face the White and simply push him to the ground; but Jemmy was a smart customer and very alert. Hobble-Frank, too, had caught on to the redskin's treachery and hastily called out to his rotund friend:

"Throw him; he's turning 'round!"

"I know!" Jemmy replied.

At the same moment he said that, and while the redskin had only turned halfway, and was therefore off balance, he swiftly bent forwards, lifted his opponent up by doing so, and pulled the hitch open. The lasso gave way. Big Foot somersaulted over Jemmy's head with arms flailing through the air, and landed on the ground whereby he lost his knife. As fast as lightning Jemmy knelt on top of him, grabbed the Indian's throat with his left and with his right placed his knife onto the heart region.

Perhaps Big Foot had from the start intended to defend himself no matter what, but the somersault had taken him by surprise. The White's eyes glowed at him so threateningly, and from such a short distance away, that he thought he had best lie still. Jemmy then looked at the chief and asked:

"Do you agree that he's lost?"

"No," the chief replied and stepped closer.

"Why not?" Old Shatterhand immediately enquired and also walked into the circle.

"He's not vanquished."

"I claim the opposite: he is defeated."

"That is not true, because the lasso is open."

"Big Foot alone is to blame for that, because he turned around and busted open the strap."

"No one saw that. Let him go! He is not defeated, and the fight has to begin again."

"No, Jemmy, don't let him go!" the hunter ordered. "As soon as I give the command, or as soon as he moves, you stab him!"

That's when the chief proudly rose tall and asked:

"Who's the one to give orders here, you or I?"

"You and I, the both of us."

"Who says that?"

"I say so. You are the chief of your people and I'm the leader of mine. You and I, the two of us, have entered into a contract about the conditions of the fights. The one who disregards those conditions has broken the contract and is a liar and a cheat."

"You...you risk talking to me like that, in front of so many red warriors?"

"That's not a risk. I speak the truth and demand loyalty and honesty. If I'm not permitted to speak any longer, so be it, the rifle of death will speak."

He had held the rifle with its butt resting on the ground thus far; at that point he lifted it demonstratively.

"Then say, what do you wish to do?" the chief replied, significantly more subdued.

"Do you agree that the two were supposed to fight standing back to back?"

"Yes."

"Big Foot, however, lifted the lasso and turned around. Is that correct? You must have seen it!"

"Yes," the chief admitted hesitantly.

"Furthermore, the one who was going to end up lying under the other was to die. Do you remember that condition?"

"I know it."

"Alright, who is lying on the bottom?"

"Big Foot."

"And who is therefore the vanquished?"

"He..." the chief was forced to admit, since Old Shatterhand held the barrel up, so that the muzzle almost touched the Indian's chest.

"Do you have anything to say to the contrary?"

With these words the chief received such a large, overpowering gaze from the eyes of the hunter that he felt small despite his tall stature and gave the expected reply:

"No; the vanquished belongs to the victor. Tell the White that he may stab Big Foot."

"I don't need to tell him that, because he knows it already; but he won't do it."

"Will he also spare him perchance?"

"We'll decide upon that later. Until that time, let's tie Big Foot up with the same lasso from which he wanted to release himself."

"Why tie him up? He won't escape you."

"Will you guarantee me that?"

"Yes."

"With what?"

"With my entire property."

"That suffices. He may go where he wishes, but shall return to the winner of this contest after the next two duels."

Jemmy rose and put his clothes back on. Big Foot also jumped up and made his way through the circle of the red spectators, who didn't know whether or not they ought to demonstrate disdain.

It was unlikely that any of the Utah had ever come across a White before who had treated them in the manner Old Shatterhand was dealing with them and their chief, while virtually being held captive. The hunter was in the Utah's power, and yet they didn't darc to refuse his requests. That was the influence of his mighty personality, and the effect of the nimbus with which legend and myth had surrounded him.

The chief was undoubtedly furious that two of his warriors had already been overpowered, despite the fact that they had seemed to be far, far superior to their opponents. When he spotted Hobble-Frank his mood improved immediately. The short fellow could not possibly be capable of running faster than Running Stag. The Indians' victory was assured at least in that case.

He signalled Running Stag to approach, led him to Old Shatterhand and said:

"This warrior possesses the speed of the wind, and has not been beaten by any other runner. Wouldn't you rather suggest to your comrade to surrender without a fight?"

"No."

"He would die swiftly, without having brought shame upon himself."

"Isn't surrender without a fight the biggest shame there is? Didn't you think Red Fish was invincible, and didn't Big Foot say that he was going to crush his opponent, the toad, within a few moments? Do you believe that Running Stag will be luckier than those two, who began so proudly, and then ended up sneaking away so quietly and modestly afterwards?"

"Uff!" Running Stag called out. "I race deer!"

Old Shatterhand had a closer look at him at that point. Indeed, the Indian had the physique of a good runner, and his legs were certainly suited to cover great distances without tiring. But the amount of brain didn't seem to match the length of his legs. He had a veritable monkey face, yet there was no evidence of those animals' intelligence.

Hobble-Frank had also joined them and had a closer look at Running Stag.

"What do you think of him?" Old Shatterhand asked him in German.

"He's the dull-witted boy from Meissen incarnate, as he stares at the fat rings but can't find the broth," Hobble replied.

"Do you think you can tackle him?"

"Hm! As far as his legs are concerned, he'll get the better of me three times over; but when it comes to his head, I hope to at least not be worse than him. Let's first try to find out where we're supposed to run. Perhaps I'll run better and faster with my head than he with his legs."

Old Shatterhand turned to the chief again:

"Have you decided yet where the race is going to be held?"

"Yes. Come, I'll show you."

Old Shatterhand and Hobble-Frank followed him out of the circle of Indians; Running Stag stayed back; he already knew the halfway mark and the finish line. The chief pointed south and said:

"Do you see the tree that stands halfway between here and the forest?"

"Yes."

"They have to run to that tree, as well as around it three times. The one who returns here first is the victor."

Hobble-Frank measured the distance with his eyes, as well as the terrain in the far distance to the south, and then said in English:

"But I hope that there will be honesty between the two parties!"

"Are you trying to say that you believe us capable of dishonesty?" the chief sharply asked.

"Yes."

"Shall I knock you down?"

"Try it! The bullet from my revolver would be faster than your fist. Didn't Big Foot turn around during the earlier bout, although it was prohibited? Was that honest?"

"It wasn't dishonest, but a cunning feint."

"Ah! And such a feint is supposed to be permitted?"

The chief mulled it over. If he said yes, then he'd justify Big Foot's conduct, and there would perhaps also be a reason for Running Stag to utilize subterfuge. Those particular Whites were accomplishing far more than he had believed them to be capable of. Perhaps the short fellow was also a good runner; in this case it was advisable to keep an escape route open for his red opponent. Hence the chief replied:

"Being cunning is not cheating. Why should it be disallowed?"

"Would a feint in that case also excuse the combatant from adhering to the conditions?"

"No, because they must strictly be followed."

"Then I agree and am ready to begin the race. Where do we start?"

"I will plant a spear in the ground where the start and finish line is."

He left to fetch a spear; and the Whites were alone for a while.

"You've obviously got an idea, haven't you?" Old Shatterhand asked Hobble-Frank.

"Yes. Can you tell?"

"Indeed, because you're quietly and merrily chuckling to yourself."

"As a matter of fact, it does amuse me. The chief intended to harm me with his cunning, and inshtead has done me the greatest service."

"Why?"

"You shall hear it in a moment. What kind of tree would dat be over yonder, around which we're supposed to dance three times?"

"It seems to be a beech."

"And look a little further to your left; there shtands another tree, but almost twice as far away. What kind ish dat?"

"A spruce."

"Splendid. Where are we supposed to run to?"

"To the beech."

"But I'll run straight to the spruce inshtead."

"Are you mad?"

"Nee. I run with my head to the beech, you see, but with my feet towards the spruce, although dat's twice as far to go."

"But for what purpose?"

"You'll see it in due course, and then be overjoyed. I believe dat I'm not mistaken in my expectations. If I take a peek at Running Stag's frontal countenance, then an error does not at all seem possible to me."

"Be careful, Frank! It concerns your life."

"Ha, if it only concerned my life, then I wouldn't have to exert myself at all. Should I be beaten, I'd go on living, regardless. Big Foot has to die, and you'll also get the chief to ground; I might then be exchanged for those two. Dat means I'm not worried about losing my life, at all; but we're dealing with my honour and reputation. Would I want the history books of the fourth quarter of the nineteenth century to tell that I, Hobble-Frank from Moritzburg, have been outrun by dat Indian Merino face? I won't have dat said of me."

"But then at least explain your intentions to me. Perhaps I can give you some good advice!"

"Thank you most humbly! I've already given myself dat advice and will also exploit my inventions myself. Just tell me one thing: what does 'spruce' mean in the Utah language?"

"*Ovomb.*"

"Ovomb? Peculiar name! And what would this short sentence mean: to that spruce?"

"*Intsh ovomb.*"

"Dat's even shorter with only two words. I won't forget them."

"What's intsh ovomb got to do with your plan?"

"It's the guiding star for my marathon. But quiet now; the chief returns!"

Great Wolf rejoined them. He placed a lance in the soft ground and explained that the race to the death would start immediately.

"And what will we be wearing?" Hobble-Frank asked.

"Whatever you wish."

Frank took off all pieces of clothing down to his trousers; Running Stag wore only a loincloth. He gazed at his opponent with a face that was supposed to express disdain, and instead was the image of divine denseness.

"Frank, make an effort!" Jemmy urged him. "Remember that Davy and I won!"

"Don't cry!" the short fellow comforted him. "And if you still don't know whether I've got legs or not, then you'll be seeing them protrude very shortly."

At that point the chief clapped his hands. Running Stag raced away with a piercing yell, short Frank after him. The inhabitants of the entire camp were assembled again, to watch the contest. According to their opinion, the winner had already become apparent three or four seconds after the start. Running Stag was a long stretch ahead of his opponent and gained more on him with each leap. The Indians were jubilant. It would have been madness to say that the White was still able to catch or even overtake the redskin.

It was truly marvellous to see how short Frank stretched his legs. He moved them so fast they were but a blur, and yet it seemed, at least to an attentive observer, as if he were not exerting himself to the fullest, and that he could have run even faster, if he wanted to.

Then, a stir went through the ranks of the Indian spectators; they emitted the occasional shout of derision, of glee; they laughed and truly believed to have every reason for it. And this is why:

The beech grew out in the middle of the prairie, perhaps three quarters of a kilometre away, and one was able to reach it in a straight line from the camp. To the left of it, but at least another half a kilometre further away, stood the spruce in question. When the two runners were at a great enough distance from the camp, it became obvious that short Hobble was heading for the spruce, not the beech. He ran as fast as his short legs would go. Of course, that was so ridiculous that the Indians' hilarity could be forgiven.

"Your companion misunderstood me," the chief called to Old Shatterhand.

"No."

"But he's running for the spruce!"

"Indeed."

"That means Running Stag will win twice as fast!"

"No."

"No?" Great Wolf was astonished.

"It is a feint, and you personally have permitted him to apply it."

"Uff, uff! Indeed," he uttered. "Uff, uff!" shouted the other Indians as well when the chief explained to them what Old Shatterhand had said. Their laughter fell silent, and the suspense doubled; no, it grew tenfold.

Running Stag had reached the beech within a short time. He needed to circle it three times. After he went around for the first time, while looking back, he saw his opponent move in an entirely different direction, about three hundred paces away from him. He stood still, dumbfounded and utterly astonished, and stared at the short man from Moritzburg.

Those in the camp could see that Frank stretched out his arm and pointed to the distant spruce; but they couldn't hear what he said.

"Intsh ovomb, intsh ovomb!" he called out to Running Stag.

The Indian gave some thought to whether or not he had heard correctly. His cognitive capabilities didn't reach any further than to the explanation that he had misunderstood the chief, and that the spruce, not the beech, was to be the halfway mark of the race. His short opponent was already much, much further along the track; he couldn't afford to have any misgivings or doubt; it was a matter of life or death! The Indian left the beech and rushed along, towards the spruce. A few moments later he sped past his opponent at some distance and, without looking around once, towards his second destination.

That caused some mighty tumult among the Indians. They howled and made a noise as if everyone's life was at stake. The Whites' joy was all the greater, and especially that of Fat Jemmy, as they watched Hobble's stroke of genius succeed so splendidly.

Frank turned and ran towards the beech as soon as Running Stag had gone past him. When he got there he circled the tree three, four, five times, and then hurried away to complete his run. He covered about four fifths of the stretch at a sharp trot before he paused to look back at the spruce. There in the distance was Running Stag, completely motionless. Of course hands, arms and face were unrecognizable, but it was clear to see that he stood as rigid as a pillar. He was utterly confused as his mind wasn't keen enough to guess how gloriously he had been tricked.

Hobble-Frank felt great satisfaction and covered the rest of the way at a leisurely pace. The Indians welcomed him with dark looks; but he was beastly indifferent to it, walked up to the chief, gave him a pat on the shoulder and asked:

"Well, old chum, who won?"

"The one who met the conditions," the Indian replied wrathfully.

"That's me!"

"You?"

"Yes, wasn't I at the beech?"

"I saw it."

"And the first to return here?"

"Yes."

"And didn't I go around the tree five times instead of only three times?"

"Why twice more?"

"Purely out of love for Running Stag. When he had gone around it once, he ran away, and I've made up for the missing rounds, so that the beech has no reason to complain about him."

"Why did he leave the beech to run to the spruce?"

"I wanted to ask him; but he ran past me so fast that I had no opportunity to do so. He might tell you when he gets back."

"Why did you run towards the spruce first?"

"Because I believed it was a pine tree. However, Old Shatterhand had called the tree a spruce, and so I wanted to know who was right."

"Why did you turn around, instead of going all the way there?"

"Because Running Stag went there. I can find out just as well from him later who was right, Old Shatterhand or I."

Frank spoke in the calmest tone of voice imaginable. The chief was seething internally. He virtually hissed his question:

"Have you perhaps cheated Running Stag?"

"Cheated? Shall I knock you down?" the short fellow roused at the chief in feigned anger, while he used the chief's earlier remark.

"Or did you use a feint?"

"Feint? What purpose would that have served?"

"To send Running Stag to the spruce."

"That would be a bad subterfuge, and I'd have to be ashamed of it. A human being running for his life won't let anyone send him to an even further destination once he's reached his goal. If he did that, then he'd have no brain and those he belongs to would have to be the ones to be ashamed for not having educated and trained him properly. Only a fool would let someone like him enter a fight for life or death with a White. I cannot comprehend you, nor understand your assumption since you would insult your own honour by doing so."

The chief reached into his belt and clenched his hand around the grip of his knife. He would have liked to immediately stab the courageous as well as cautious short fellow; but Hobble's remarks did not really furnish a justification for such a deed, he was forced to swallow his wrath.

Hobble-Frank joined his comrades who congratulated him with quiet, but all the more sincere joy.

"I've also won, are you satisfied with me now?" he asked Jemmy with regard to the reminder his friend had given him to take along.

"Of course! That was really smart of you. It was a veritable masterpiece."

"Truly? Then duly enter this in your memory, page one hundred and thirty six, and open that passage each time you're beset by the urge to doubt my superiority! There comes Running Stag, sneaking, not running. He seems to have a guilty conscience and is slinking off to the side, as if he's supposed to get a hiding. Take a look at his face! And I was supposed to have matched wits with such a Confucius! Yes, yes, it's not the legs dat do it, not even in a race, but mostly the head!"

Running Stag seemed to want to disappear from sight; but the chief called him over and snapped at him:

"Who won?"

"The paleface," he fearfully replied.

"Why did you run to the spruce?"

"The paleface lied to me. He said the spruce was the halfway mark."

"And you believed it? I told you which tree it was!"

Old Shatterhand translated and informed Hobble-Frank that he had been called a liar. Hence the wily short fellow turned to the chief and defended himself:

"I was supposed to have lied? I was supposed to have told Running Stag that the spruce was the mark? That's not true. I saw him stand beside the beech; he looked at me in astonishment and seemed to be beside himself with worry and fear about what I was up to. I felt pity for the poor fellow and called to him: 'intsh ovomb!' I told him therefore that I wanted to go to the spruce. I'm unable to fathom why he ran there in my place; perhaps he doesn't know himself. I've spoken. Howgh!"

Old Shatterhand couldn't help but laugh inwardly at the fact that the short jack-of-all-trades had used the Indian expression. However, the chief worked himself up even more. He called out:

"Yes, you've spoken and are finished; but I'm not finished with you yet, and will have a word with you when the time has come afterwards. But I must keep my word. The life, the scalp and the property of Running Stag are yours."

"No, no!" Hobble-Frank turned him down. "I don't want anything. You can keep him; he'll be very useful to you, especially when a race for life or death is to be run with a paleface."

A faint, but angry murmur went through the ranks of the Indians, and the chief hissed at him:

"You may keep spitting venomous remarks; but you'll whimper for mercy later, so that it will resonate to Heaven. Each individual limb of your body shall die separately, and your soul shall flee from you piece by piece, so that your dying will last for many moons."

"What can you do to me? I'm the victor and am therefore free."

"There is still one of you who hasn't won, yet, Old Shatterhand. Wait a few more moments and he'll be lying in the dust before me, pleading for his life. I will give it to him in exchange for yours, and then you'll be my property."

"Don't be mistaken!" Old Shatterhand warned him. "I'm not yet lying in front of you. And even if you'd achieve what no one else has, namely to overpower me, then I would never exchange my life for that of another."

"Wait until the fight! You're uninjured at this point; but your pride will bend and your mind change under the tortures that await you, so that you'd offer me the lives of a thousand others, if you had them! Everyone come with me; we'll go to the last, greatest, and deciding fight!"

The Indians followed the chief in a confused bunch; the Whites slowly walked behind.

"Have I said too much, perchance?" Hobble-Frank asked with some concern.

"No," Old Shatterhand replied. "It is quite good that their own warrior pride has to bend for once, and on account of a short fellow like you at that. Of course, if the chief kills me, then you'd all be lost as well, because they would immediately attack you. But they cannot be trusted even in the most likely case that I emerge as the victor. For some obscure reason I'm convinced that these Indians won't let us move out peacefully. They opted for individual fights because they were firmly convinced that we would all be killed. Since that effort was for naught, they'll think of something else. The main thing is that we impress them. It has kept them at bay thus far, and will be of further use to us. That's why I'm delighted that you've spoken so fearlessly to Great Wolf, you, the short fellow to the Goliath. Although he's worked himself into a state, he's also experienced that even the shortest among us feels not a trace of fear. It is now a matter of making him look small in front of his people. I'll see to that by pitting myself against him. It seems to me that they intend to keep us here as hostages. We'll have to thwart their plans because we wouldn't be safe for a single moment."

During the hunter's explanation they had arrived at the circle formed by tents and huts. The preparations for the impending and interesting duel were being made in its centre.

A strong post to which two lassos were fastened rose from a heap of heavy boulders. Everyone from the camp, men and women, were standing around the place to witness the spectacle. Old Shatterhand paid attention to the fact that all warriors were fully armed, which only strengthened his suspicions. He decided to do something about it and walked into the middle of the circle, where the chief already stood. He had the bearing of someone who was certain of victory. He pointed to the two lassos and said:

"You can see these ropes. Do you know what they're for?"

"I can imagine," the hunter said. "We're supposed to be tied up during the fight."

"You've guessed correctly. One end of the lasso is tied to the post; the other will be tied around the body."

"Why?"

"So that we can only move in this circle and cannot get away from each other."

"As far as I'm concerned this measure is superfluous because I wouldn't think of running away from you. I know the actual reason. You credit me with more speed and agility than strength and intend to prevent me from utilizing those advantages. So be it; I couldn't care less! What weapons did you say we will use to fight?"

"Each of us will get a knife in the left hand, and a tomahawk in the right. We'll fight with those until one of us is dead."

It was obvious that the chief had chosen this means of combat because he believed he was better at it than the White. However, Shatterhand calmly replied:

"I agree."

"Agree? With being killed? It is certain that I'll defeat you."

"Let's wait and see!"

"Test your strength and try to imitate this!"

He walked to one of the heavy rocks and lifted it up. He possessed incredible physical strength, and none of his Indians could have matched him. Old Shatterhand bent down to lift up the same rock, however, he didn't succeed in lifting it a hand width off the ground, despite all apparent exertion. The Indians around the circle emitted their satisfied 'uff!' exclamations. But the short Saxon said to Fat Jemmy:

"He's only foxing to lure the chief into a false sense of security. I know precisely that he can lift dat rock above his head and also toss it ten paces away. Let's see, and wait for the perplexity. Then the redskin will get a big surprise."

The chief, however, was of the opposite opinion. He had wanted to discourage the White with his test of strength and was convinced that he had been successful with it. Hence he said with forbearance in his voice:

"You can see what to expect. The palefaces usually pray if they face death. I permit you to speak to your Manitou before the fight begins."

"That's not necessary," Old Shatterhand said. "I'll speak with him when my soul goes to him. You're a strong man, and I hope that you'll only rely upon yourself during this fight!"

"I will do that. Who's supposed to help me?"

"Your warriors. It seems they think it is possible that I might overpower you. Why are they armed as if they were going to war?"

"Are your companions unarmed perchance?"

"No. But we will move all of our weapons into our tent. That's customary among palefaces. The pride of a brave white warrior doesn't permit any circumstances to arouse the suspicion of treachery. Do you want me to believe that you, too, are brave?"

"Are you trying to insult me?" the Indian angrily snapped. "I don't need the help of anyone else. My warriors will put all of their weapons into the tents, if your friends do likewise."

"Good! You'll see that we'll do it immediately. I'll only keep my knife."

He handed his guns to Hobble-Frank; Davy and Jemmy did likewise. Then the hunter said in German:

"You'll carry our weapons into the tent, and pretend to deposit them there, but then you'll push them outside under the back wall, when no one observes you. Don't return here. The Indians will only have eyes for the fight, and not pay attention to you. Then you also crawl out the back of the tent and get our horses ready to depart."

"What are you talking to this man for?" the chief roused at Shatterhand. "Why are you talking in a language that we don't understand?"

"Because that's the language we customarily speak."

"What did you tell him?"

"That he is to take our things into the tent, and then guard them."

"Why guard? Do you think we'll rob you?"

"No; but I can't leave my magic rifle unattended because there could easily be a mishap. You know that it'll go off and hit the red men as soon as someone touches it who is not supposed to."

"Yes, I've seen it. Have it guarded for the time being. Once I've killed you, I'll either bury it deeply, or have it thrown in the lake to make it harmless."

On the order of the chief, all the Indian warriors gave their weapons to the women, who were going to take them to the tents. Hobble-Frank also left. The chief undressed except for his leggings, so as not to be restricted by the garments. Old Shatterhand did not follow his example. After his victory, the waste of time necessary to dress again might easily become fatal. The women hastily returned, so as not to miss anything. Everyone's attention was focussed on the centre of the circle, and no one paid any mind to the short Saxon.

"Now you've got what you wanted," Great Wolf said. "Can we begin?"

"One more question beforehand. What will happen to my companions if you kill me?"

"They will be our prisoners."

"But they've fought for and won their freedom and can therefore go where they like."

"They will. But first they'll stay here as our hostages."

"That's against the agreement; but I don't think it is necessary to lose another word over it. And what will happen if I kill you?"

"That won't happen!" the redskin proudly proclaimed.

"But we must assume that it could be a possibility."

"Very well! If you overpower me, then you're all free."

"And no one will try to hold us back?"

"No one!"

"In that case I'm satisfied, and we can begin."

"Yes, let's begin. I'll have someone tie us up. Here you have a tomahawk."

Two war hatchets had been kept. The chief, who also had his knife, of course, took one of the axes and handed it to Old Shatterhand. The hunter took it, looked at it, and then flung it away in a tall arc outside the circle.

"What are you doing?" the chief was astonished.

"I threw the tomahawk away because it was useless. I can see that yours is of excellent craftsmanship; the other, however, would have disintegrated in my hand with the first blow already."

"Do you think I've given it to you for treacherous reasons?"

"I think that it would have done me more harm than good, nothing else!"

Of course, he knew very well that the Indians had given him such a bad weapon intentionally. Despite the thick paint that covered the chief's face, it was obvious that a sneer pulled it into wrinkles, when he said:

"You're permitted to throw the hatchet away; but you won't receive a replacement."

"That's not necessary. I'll fight with my knife, on which I can rely."

"Uff! Are you mad? The first hit by my tomahawk will kill you. I've got that, as well as my knife, and you're not as strong as I am."

"In that case you believed my joke was meant seriously before. I didn't want to intimidate you. But now you may judge for yourself as to which one of us is the stronger."

He bent down to a boulder that was much heavier than the one Great Wolf had thrown, lifted it up to belt level first before he hoisted it above his head, where he kept it steady for a while, and then flung it away nine or ten paces where it came to rest.

"Do likewise!" he called out to the redskin.

"Uff, uff, uff!" the voices came from the surrounding crowd. The chief didn't immediately reply. He looked at the rock, then at the hunter, at the rock, and then the hunter again; he was more than just surprised, and spoke only after a long while:

"Do you think you can scare me? Don't think that! I will kill you and take your scalp, even if the fight should last until the evening!"

"It won't last long, on the contrary, it will be over in a few minutes," Old Shatterhand replied and smiled. "So, you want to take my scalp?"

"Yes, because the hair of the vanquished belongs to the victor. Tie us up!"

The order was directed at the two Indians who were standing ready nearby. They tied the lassos around the hips of both the chief and Old Shatterhand, and then stepped back into the crowd. Tied to the post in that manner, the two combatants were able to move only within a circle the radius of which equalled the length of each man's lasso at full stretch from the post. The two men stood oppositely, so that the lassos formed a straight line, and thus spanned the diameter of the round space. The Indian held the tomahawk in his right hand and the knife in his left; Old Shatterhand held only the knife in his right hand.

Great Wolf had probably imagined the fight would unfold so that one would chase the other around the circle until they had wound the ropes tight enough for him to have an opportunity at a sure strike with the hatchet or stab with the knife. He had been forced to realize that his strength wasn't superior to that of his opponent; but the weapons were uneven, and he was convinced that he was going to be victorious, especially since the White held the knife completely wrong, in his opinion. The blade of Old Shatterhand's knife pointed up, not down; it was therefore impossible for him to execute a strike from above. The Indian secretly laughed about it and closely observed his opponent, so that he wouldn't miss any movements.

The hunter also kept a close eye on him. He had no intention of letting the chief chase him around the circle; he didn't want to attack, and instead waited for the other to charge, in which case the first clash would decide the fight immediately. It depended solely on how Great Wolf was going to use his tomahawk; if he used it in his hand, Shatterhand had nothing to worry about; but if he threw it, then the utmost attention and caution was required. The two combatants weren't standing far enough apart to easily evade a throw.

Fortunately, the chief had not planned to throw the hatchet. If he didn't hit, then it would be out of his hands and he couldn't retrieve it.

And so they stood in the ring for five, ten minutes, and neither of them moved forwards. The Indian spectators already issued shouts of encouragement or even disappointment. Great Wolf mockingly requested his opponent to begin; he called insults across to him. Old Shatterhand said nothing; his answer consisted in sitting down and calmly making himself as comfortable as if he were in the most peaceful company. But his muscles and tendons were ready to spring into the fastest and most powerful action required.

The chief regarded such conduct as an expression of contempt, as an insult, yet it was nothing more than a ruse of war, which was designed to seduce him into a careless move. It fully served its purpose. He believed he would be able to deal with a sitting opponent much more easily, and that he had to quickly make use of that opportunity. He emitted a loud war cry and lunged at Old Shatterhand with the tomahawk raised for the deadly blow. The spectators imagined they could see his strike successfully completed; many lips already opened to rejoice when the White shot up from the ground, slightly to the side, and the knife, intentionally held upside down, did its duty. The chief's strike missed and his fist fell straight into the raised knife blade, so that he dropped the hatchet. He received Old Shatterhand's punch against his left arm, whereby he lost his own knife from his other hand, too. Then the White slammed the handle of his bowie knife with an almost invisibly fast strike against the heart region of the chief's chest with such force that the Indian crashed to the ground like an empty sack and remained lying there. Old Shatterhand raised his knife and called out:

"Who is the victor?"

There was not one voice that gave a reply. Even those who had thought there was a possibility their chief could be defeated were surprised at the speed and manner in which it had happened. The people stood transfixed.

"It was he who said that the scalp of the vanquished belongs to the victor," Old Shatterhand continued. "His hair is therefore my property; but I don't want it. I'm a Christian and a friend of the red men, and I spare his life. Perhaps I've broken one of his ribs; but he is not dead. My red brothers may examine him; but I'll go to my tent."

He untied himself and left. No one prevented him from doing so, and neither did anyone prevent Davy and Jemmy from accompanying him. Everyone wanted to first know in what condition Great Wolf was, hence they all crowded around him. Consequently the hunters reached their tent completely unobserved. Behind it were their weapons, and there also stood Hobble-Frank ready with the horses.

"Mount up quickly and let's get away!" Old Shatterhand said. "We can talk later."

They leapt into the saddles and rode away, slowly at first, using the tents and huts as cover. But then the guards, who were posted outside the camp during the day as well, spotted them. They erupted in war cries and shot at them. Hence the Whites spurred their horses into gallop. When they looked around they saw that the hollering and shooting of the guards had made the others attentive. The Indians literally surged out between the tents and sent a satanic howling after the escapees, which was repeated manyfold by the mountain echoes.

The hunters galloped across the plain in a straight line towards the spot where the mountain creek emptied into the lake. Old Shatterhand was familiar with the region and therefore knew that the valley of the stream offered the fastest route of escape. He was convinced that the Utah were going to pursue them immediately; therefore he had to head for terrain in which it was as difficult as possible for the Indians to keep on their trail.

Hobble-Frank

m611

Old Shatterhand

7

An Indian Battle

It was on the same morning that a troop of riders moved upstream along the same mountain creek that the Utah had followed with their prisoners the evening before. Old Firehand and Aunty Droll rode in the lead. Behind them came Humply-Bill and Gunstick-Uncle with the English lord; in short, the troop consisted of all the Whites who had experienced the adventure at Eagle Tail, and who had afterwards departed for the Elk Mountains on their route to Silver-Lake. Mr Butler, the engineer, and his daughter Ellen had joined them in Denver[1]. He had travelled there

---

[1] Formal railroad operations between Kansas City and Denver began on 1 September, 1870, at which time Butler and his daughter would have been able to safely take the train to Denver as the events at Eagle Tail were at least two weeks in the past; Butler's farm wasn't far from Kinsley, from where he would have been able to connect with the Kansas Pacific Railway.

directly from his brother's farm because he had no intentions of exposing his child to the dangers of another encounter with the outlaws. The girl, who didn't want to separate from her father at all, and who accompanied him into the wilderness out of love for him, sat in a kind of sedan that was carried by two small but tireless Indian ponies.

Winnetou had ridden ahead as their scout, because of his exceptional skill. By coincidence, the route that he and Old Firehand had traced out had led the troop to the forest and across the clearing on which Old Shatterhand and his companions had encountered the Utah. The two men were astute and experienced enough to read the tracks; they saw that Indians had taken Whites captive, and had immediately been prepared to follow the trail to perhaps bring assistance.

They had no idea that the Utah had raised their war hatchets. Winnetou as well as Old Firehand were under the impression that they were at peace with that tribe, and both were convinced that they'd receive a friendly welcome and would be permitted to put in a good word for the captive Whites.

The riders didn't know where exactly the Indians had made their camp; but they knew the lake, and since its surroundings were splendidly suited for an encampment, they believed they would find the Utah there. Despite the presumption of a friendly attitude it would have been against the custom of the West to approach them without observing them beforehand. Hence Winnetou had ridden ahead to reconnoitre. Just when the troop had reached the spot where the banks of the watercourse widened to form the plain, the Apache returned. He rode in gallop and waved from afar already for them to stop. That was not a good sign, when Winnetou rejoined them, Old Firehand asked him:

"My brother wants to warn us. Has he seen the Utah?"

"I saw them and their camp."

"And Winnetou wasn't allowed to approach them?"

"No, because they have raised the hatchet of war."

"How did you recognize that?"

"By the colours they painted on their faces, and also by the numbers that have gathered. The red warriors gather in such large groups only during war and during the big hunts. And since this is not the time of year for the buffalo migrations, it can only be the war hatchet that caused so many to gather here."

"How many are there?"

"Winnetou couldn't see exactly. There were probably three hundred at the lake, and there would have been a few more in the tents, as well."

"At the lake? So many? What is going on there? Perhaps a large fish catch?"

"No. During a fish catch the people move forwards; but they stood still and quietly looked into the water."

"All devils! Could that mean there's an execution in the process? Would they have thrown the Whites in the water to drown them?"

Old Firehand's assumption wasn't altogether wrong because the Apache had observed the Utah at the time of the swim between Long Davy and Red Fish. Winnetou replied as confidently as if he had been standing at the lake and observed everything:

"No, they don't want to drown them; but there is a swimming race for life or death."

"Do you have reasons to suspect that?"

"Yes. Winnetou knows the customs of his red brothers, and Old Firehand is also familiar with them well enough to agree with me. The Utah are wearing war paint and are therefore regarding the Whites among them as enemies. They mean to kill them. But the red man doesn't let his enemy die fast, he tortures him to death slowly. He does not throw him in the water to drown him quickly; instead he assigns a superior opponent to the White with whom he has to swim for life or death. And since the Indian opponent will be the better swimmer than the paleface, the White is lost unconditionally. They let him swim only to extend the duration of his dying, and his mortal fear."

"That's correct, and I share your opinion. We've counted the tracks of four Whites, and then two more; that's six altogether. The Utah won't let them swim all at the same time, but let each fight for his life in a different manner. We must hurry to save them."

"If my white brother is going to do that, then he'll only hurry to get himself killed."

"Alright, I must risk it. I'm counting on the fact that I've never shown animosity towards the Utah."

"You mustn't rely on that. Once they've raised the war hatchets against the Whites, they'll treat their best friend as an enemy if he's a paleface; they wouldn't spare you, either."

"But the chiefs would protect me!"

"No. The Utah aren't loyal and honest, and no chief of this nation has the kind of influence on his warriors that could save you. We mustn't reveal ourselves."

"But you ought to be able to approach them!"

"No, because I don't know whether or not they've sharpened the axe against other red nations as well."

"But then those six Whites are hopelessly lost!'

"My brother shouldn't believe that. I have two reasons that speak against it."

"Alright, firstly?"

"Firstly, I've already said that the prisoners of the red men are only permitted to die slowly; it is still early in the morning, and we have therefore time to observe the camp. Perhaps we'll find out more than we know now, and then we can more easily make a decision."

"And secondly?"

The Apache had an exceedingly knowing expression when he replied:

"There is a man among the palefaces who won't let his companions or himself be killed that simply."

"Who?"

"Old Shatterhand."

"What?" the hunter called out. "Old Shatterhand, the man you intend to meet up there at Silver-Lake? Would he already be here?"

"Old Shatterhand is as punctual as the sun or a star in the sky."

"Did you see him?"

"No."

"Then how can you say that he's here?"

"I have known it since yesterday."

"And you didn't tell me?"

"Silence is often better than talk. Had I said whose gun had spoken at the clearing yesterday, you would not have remained calm, and would instead have pushed on much more hastily."

"His gun spoke? How do you know?"

"When we searched the tree line and the grass of the clearing for tracks, I found a small tree with bullet holes. Those bullets came from Old Shatterhand's magic rifle; I know it precisely. He wanted to scare the red men, and now they're afraid of his firearm."

"If only you would have shown me the small tree! Hm! If Old Shatterhand is among those Whites, then we need not be too worried. I know him; I know what he is capable of and what respect the Indians have for him. What shall we do? What do you suggest?"

"My friends will now follow me and ride single file, so that the Utah cannot count how many riders we are, should they encounter our trail. Howgh!"

He turned his horse to the right and rode on without asking whether or not Old Firehand agreed, and without ascertaining whether the others followed him.

As mentioned, the banks of the small river widened to turn initially into shallow, and then increasingly taller ridges that framed the plain of the lake. The meadowland was treeless, but the hilly ridges were covered in forest, which came down to the base of them, and then formed an open hem of bushes. While seeking protection and cover behind those bushes and under the trees, Winnetou followed the ridge on the right side of the lake. It formed the northern boundary of the plain and joined the mountain massif in the west where the stream fed the lake.

That way the Whites rode around the plain from its eastern to its western point, where they arrived at the watercourse under the trees, several hundred paces away from the lake; and from between the trunks they were able to observe the camp. They dismounted. However, they didn't tie their horses up, but instead kept the reins of their mounts in their hands while Winnetou went to inspect the surroundings. He soon returned and reported that he hadn't found anything suspicious. No Utah had ventured into the area that day. Only then did the men tie the horses to trees and sit down in the soft moss. The spot was ideally suited to secretly and comfortably watch the camp.

They saw the Utah crowd stand south of it. Then they spotted two men, who separated from the crowd and ran south as fast as they could. Old Firehand pulled out his telescope, looked through it, and then called out:

"A race for life or death between an Indian and a White! The Indian is already much further ahead and will win. The White is a very short fellow."

He gave the scope to the Apache, who looked through it. As soon as he had one look at the White he jumped up:

"Uff! That's Hobble-Frank! The little hero must run for his life and cannot possibly overtake his red opponent."

"The same Hobble-Frank you told us about?" Old Firehand asked. "We mustn't remain idle; we must make a decision!"

"Not yet," the Apache said. "There's no danger so far. Old Shatterhand is with him."

The trees stood so closely together that they couldn't overlook the entire terrain of the race. The two runners had disappeared out of view to their right; they were waiting for their return run and were convinced that the Indian would come back into view first. But they were astonished to see the short fellow returning, instead of the tall Indian, and walking along as if he were on a stroll.

"Frank is ahead!" Old Firehand said. "How is that possible?"

"With a feint," Winnetou replied. "He won, and we'll find out how he did it. Listen to the angry howls of the Utah! They are returning to the camp. And look, there stand four palefaces: I know them."

"I know them, too," Aunty Droll exclaimed. "Old Shatterhand, Long Davy, Fat Jemmy, and short Hobble-Frank."

Those names caused a general stir. Some of the men in the group were personally acquainted with one or several of those Droll had named; the others had heard enough about them to wake their keenest interest. The remarks went back and forth, until Winnetou said to Old Firehand:

"Does my brother see now that I was right? Our friends still have their weapons; they can therefore not be in great danger."

"For the moment, yes; but that can change very quickly. I suggest we openly ride up to them."

"If my brother wants to go there, then he can do that; but I'll stay here," the Apache replied in a very determined tone of voice. "Old Shatterhand knows the circumstances and knows what he's doing; but we don't know it and would perhaps interfere with the execution of his plan. Stay here, I'll advance as far as possible to find out what is happening."

He kept the telescope in his hand and disappeared between the trees. Half an hour passed after which he returned and reported:

"There was a duel in the middle of the camp. The Utah were crowding together so much that I couldn't see the combatants; but I saw Hobble-Frank. He secretly and cautiously led their horses behind the tent and saddled them up. The Whites want to get away."

"And secretly? Fleeing?" Old Firehand asked. "In that case we'll take up positions here along their route, as they can't go in any other direction, and welcome them into our group, or even ride towards them."

"We'll do neither," the Apache shook his head.

"My suggestions seem to meet with my red brother's disagreement today!"

"Old Firehand mustn't be vexed, but think about it. What will the Indians do when the Whites flee?"

"They'll pursue them."

"And if one pursues four or six men, then how many warriors does one need to do that?"

"Oh, about twenty to thirty."

"Good! We'll easily overpower them. But if we make ourselves known to the Utah, then the entire tribe will come after us, and then much blood will be spilt."

"You're right, Winnetou. But we cannot render the Indians blind. They'll soon recognize that there is a greater number of riders, from our tracks."

"They will only look at the trail ahead of them, but not the one that's behind them."

"Ah, are you saying that we'll be following them?"

"Yes."

"Without letting Old Shatterhand see us?"

"We will talk with him, but only you and I. Listen! What is that?"

From the plain came a horrid howling noise. The men under the trees saw four riders gallop out of the camp immediately following the hubbub. They were the Whites who were headed towards the upper end of the lake with the intention of reaching the creek, and then following it upstream.

"There they come," Winnetou said. "Old Firehand may follow me. But my other white brothers must pull the horses deeper inside the woods and wait there until we return. Take our horses as well."

He grabbed Old Firehand by the hand and pulled him away. The two men moved along the tall bank of the creek, under the cover of the trees, to a spot from which they could see the camp without being noticed. That's where they stopped.

Old Shatterhand quickly drew near. He and his companions kept close to the water, which meant they were riding below the bank, while the Apache and Old Firehand were standing above. When the four men had drawn level, they heard a voice from above:

"Uff! My white brothers may stop here."

The four riders reined in their horses and looked up.

"Winnetou, Winnetou!" they called out all together.

"Yes, it is Winnetou, the chief of the Apache," he replied. "And here stands another friend of my white brothers."

He pulled the tall hunter out from behind a tree.

"Old Firehand!" Old Shatterhand rejoiced. "You, here, you! I must come up there to greet you! Or you come down!"

Despite the danger he was in, he wanted to jump off the horse.

"Wait, stay there!" Old Firehand stopped him. "I cannot come down, either."

"Why not?"

"The Utah who are following you mustn't know anything about our presence."

"Ah! Are you on your own?"

"No. We're around forty hunters, rafters and other Westerners. You'll find good old friends with us. Now is not the time for chatting. Where are you headed at this point?"

"In the direction of Silver-Lake."

"That's where we're also going. Ride on. As soon as your pursuers have gone past, we'll come up behind them, and then we can whip them."

"That's good!" Old Shatterhand exclaimed. "What a joy and what luck to meet you here! And even if we are unable to hold long speeches, I must nevertheless quickly tell you what has transpired. Can you see the camp from up there?"

"Yes."

"Then keep a lookout, so that we won't be surprised. I'll tell you what's necessary."

The joy of the men about the meeting was certainly great; but the circumstances forbade voicing it and wasting time by doing so. They exchanged the briefest reciprocal reports, which the astute, experienced men could easily mentally complete. When that was done, Winnetou asked Old Shatterhand:

"Does my white brother remember the deep canyon the palefaces call Night Canyon?"

"Yes; I've been there with you several times."

"You'll easily reach it from here in five hours. It opens up in the middle to a round area the walls of which no one can scale; they seem to reach up to the sky. Does Old Shatterhand remember that place as well?"

"Very well."

"My white brother will ride to that spot. Once you've crossed that round area, you can barricade yourself on the other side. The canyon is so narrow there that two riders can hardly pass each other. You wouldn't even need your companions because you alone could easily keep several hundred Utah in check with your magic rifle. When they get there they'll be unable to move either forwards or backwards because we will be right behind them. They will have only one choice, and that's either to be shot down to the last man, or to surrender."

"Good, we'll follow that advice. But tell me one thing above all: why are you riding to Silver-Lake with such a large troop?"

"I'll tell you," Old Firehand replied. "There is a very rich silver mine up there, but it is in such a dry region that it would be impossible to mine it if we couldn't get water there. That's why I had the idea to divert the water from Silver-Lake. If we're successful, we'll take millions of dollars out of that mine. There is an engineer accompanying us who will first examine the technical aspects of it and, should luck be on our side, carry out the work."

An indefinable smile crossed Old Shatterhand's face when he said:

"A mine? Who discovered it?"

"I was among them who found it."

"Hm! Divert the lake to the mine and you'll make twice the deal."

"Why?"

"There are riches lying on the bottom of it against which your silver vein will be rather paltry."

"Ah! You mean the treasure in Silver-Lake?"

"Indeed."

"What do you know about it?"

"More than you think. You'll hear details about it later, when we have more time than is at our disposal right now. But you also know of the treasure. Who told you about it?"

"It was…ah, about that later as well. Get going! I can see Indians coming out of the camp."

"Heading here?"

"Yes, on horseback."

"How many?"

"Five."

"Pshaw! They're nothing to worry about; but you mustn't let them see you. They're the trackers who are supposed to keep an eye on us; the major horde will definitely follow soon. Let's move out! We'll see you in Night Canyon!"

He tapped his heels against the sides of his horse and rode away with his three companions. Old Firehand and Winnetou crouched low to observe the five Utah. They approached and rode past while keeping a sharp eye ahead and on the ground without realizing what dangerous people were nearby.

Then the two men returned to the others. Their friends had retreated into the forest and were close to where the mountain creek emptied into the lake. Old Firehand was just about to inform them of what he had discussed with Old Shatterhand when his gaze fell upon several Utah women who were approaching the lake; they carried the implements necessary to do some fishing. He pointed them out to Winnetou and said:

"If we could hear what these squaws are saying, then we might find out more about the intentions of the warriors."

"Winnetou will try when they have come close enough," the Apache replied.

Indeed, the women approached sufficiently near. They wanted to fish in the creek's outlet, not in the lake. They set their lines, sat down next to each other under the bushes along the bank, and then chatted with each other. They didn't seem to bother about observing the customary silence when fishing. Winnetou slithered up to them like a snake and lay down behind the bushes. It was entertaining for the others to observe them, as well as him. He lay there for about a quarter of an hour, and then returned to report:

"If these squaws don't learn to shut up, they'll never catch a trout. They've told me everything I wanted to know."

"And what was that?" the others asked him.

"The five warriors who rode past us are supposed to make Old Shatterhand's trail more distinct, and fifty others will follow within a short time, led by Great Wolf."

"Is he not injured?"

"Only slightly. Old Shatterhand's knife disabled his right hand, and the punch against the chest cut his air off. That came back, and the hand doesn't prevent him from leading the pursuit. Old Shatterhand is supposed to be shot dead, so that he cannot reveal the Utah's intentions to the Navajo. The former will scatter throughout the region today to hunt and gather meat because they'll break camp tomorrow."

"Where will they move it?"

"The women and children move to the old people in the mountains, where they're safe; the warriors, however, will follow Great Wolf to travel to the meeting place of all the Utah tribes."

"Where is that?"

"The squaws didn't seem to know it. I couldn't find out any more than that; but it's enough for what we're planning."

"That means we can't do anything until Great Wolf and his troop have gone past. The fact that he's taking fifty-five men along shows how much respect he has for Old Shatterhand. Such a large number against four Whites!"

"Old Shatterhand is my friend and pupil," Winnetou proudly said. "He is not afraid of fifty-five warriors."

The group then settled down to lie in wait, until Great Wolf and his warriors moved out about an hour later. They rode past without casting a single glance under the trees. They presented an exceedingly warlike image. All were armed with guns. The chief wore a bandage on his right hand, and had painted his face even thicker than in the morning. From his shoulders hung the feather-adorned war coat down to his horse's croup; however, his head was no longer decorated with eagle feathers. He had been beaten and was only going to wear that insignia again when he had satisfied his revenge. His men rode the best horses available in the camp.

Ten minutes later, daring Winnetou followed them on his own, and the others departed after another ten minutes. Of course there was no such thing as a real path. The riders followed the creek upstream. During the spring its high melt waters had eaten out the banks. Loose rocks and tree trunks were lying everywhere, hence the riders made only slow progress, especially since the sedan was difficult to transport across such obstacles. The terrain improved once they left the mountain slope behind them. The steep climb was overcome, and the shallower the gradient of the creek became, the less damage the water had created in its surroundings.

The trail the men were following couldn't have been any more distinct. Since Old Shatterhand had found such splendid allies, he didn't think it was necessary to render his tracks unreadable. The five Utah following him had ridden so as to leave easily visible hoof prints behind intentionally, and because Great Wolf knew nothing about the enemies behind him, he didn't give any thought to caution.

The route to Night Canyon led the men to the narrowest passage in the Elk Mountain range, where they went across. When they arrived at the top they left the creek, and then rode right through old growth forest without understorey. The widely spaced tree trunks combined their crowns to such a dense leaf cover that only occasionally a ray of sunshine managed to get through. The soft floor consisted of decaying plant matter, which clearly displayed the deeply cut tracks.

A few times Old Firehand and the group came so close to the Apache ahead that they were able to spot him. His bearing was one of nonchalance. He knew that the Utah would hardly direct their attention behind them.

Old Firehand and his group of men had departed from the lake at ten o'clock that morning. Up to one o'clock in the afternoon they had been riding almost exclusively through forest; later they entered grassland interspersed with stands of bushes, which was just to their liking. Had the prairie been open, they would have had to keep a greater distance to the Utah ahead. The grassland often dipped away to form a valley, only to rise again on the other side; then the riders came through forest again, but not for a long time because after a few minutes they already reached the other side of it. The Apache was waiting there for them. He answered the question of why he didn't continue on by pointing ahead.

An entirely unique vista opened up to the Whites. They had left the region of the Elk Mountains behind and were approaching that of the Grand River with its canyons. To the right, the left, as well as straight ahead of the riders there were three black rock plates that tilted downwards and towards each other like gigantic blackboards. They were so steep, and their surface so smooth that the riders could not possibly remain in the saddle. To look down onto the deep bottom was almost intimidating, yet the men needed to get down there. Water ran down on either side, where the giant boards met, but there was no tree or bush, not even a blade of grass for it to nourish. The two watercourses combined at the bottom to disappear into a crack in a cliff wall that seemed to be no wider than a ruler.

"That's Night Canyon," Old Firehand explained to the others while he pointed to the crack. "It received its name because it's so deep and narrow that the sun cannot penetrate to the bottom, and it is therefore almost as dark as night down there in the middle of the day; hence the name Night Canyon. It's a fairly dusky ride even at noon. And look, down there!"

He pointed into the depth, where the water disappeared in the crack. There were distant figures moving along the bottom; they seemed too small to even reach to the observers' knees. Those figures were the Utah who just then disappeared into the crack.

The canyon in question had been torn into a towering stone wall, above which a broad, expansive plain stretched away to the distant misty mountain giants that enclosed it. Aunty Droll looked into the abyss and said to Black Tom:

"Det's where we're supposed to descend? Only a roofer would accomplish det! It's nothing less than dangerous, if det's necessary! Sit yerself down here and let me give you a shove, then you'll be able to toboggan all the way down."

"And yet we'll have to go down," Old Firehand said. "Dismount and lead your horses by short reins. We must indeed descend, but by utilizing a technique that's used to get down mountainsides in snow. Since we have no means of arresting a slide, we can only prevent it by zigzagging our way down. Back and forth, from side to side, all the way to the bottom."

The men followed his suggestion and it turned out to be good advice. The ponies were freed from the sedan and Ellen also walked. Trying to get down in a straight line would not have been accomplished without accidents. The descent required more than half an hour. It was indeed fortunate that the Utah were so ignorant! Had they noticed their pursuers, and taken up positions in the rock opening, it would have been easy for them to shoot one after the other during the slow descent, without any danger to themselves.

At last the troop arrived at the bottom and made ready to enter the canyon, which was only wide enough to accommodate two riders abreast beside the water. Winnetou, of course, rode in the lead. Behind him came Old Firehand with Castlepool riding at his side. Then came the hunters; and after them, the rafters who flanked the engineer, Butler, and his daughter. The troop had increased in numbers after the events at Eagle Tail because Watson, the overseer, and several other workers had joined them.

They weren't permitted to talk because sounds carried further inside the canyon than outside in the open. The hoof beat of the horses could betray them; hence Winnetou had dismounted and gone ahead of his companions on his soft moccasins while one of the rafters led his horse.

It was like a ride through the underworld. Ahead and behind them the narrow slot, beneath their feet the austere, stone-littered rock surface and the dark, eerie water; and to the right and left of the riders the sheer cliff walls so tall they obscured the sky and seemed to meet at the top. The further the men advanced, the colder and heavier the air became, and daylight turned into dusk.

And the canyon was long—endlessly long! Occasionally it widened somewhat, so that it afforded room for five or six riders across; then the walls closed in again so tightly that some would have liked to scream out for fear of being crushed. Even the horses were uneasy; they snorted fearfully and urged forwards quickly to find relief from the tightness.

A quarter of an hour went past, and another; a bang as if ten canons at once had been fired caused everyone to stop at once.

"For God's sake what was that?" Butler, the engineer asked. "Are the rocks caving in perhaps?"

"A rifle shot," Old Firehand replied. "The moment has arrived. One man for three horses each stays back here; the others move forwards. Dismount!"

In no time at all more than thirty men, each with a rifle in his hands, were ready to follow him. After a few paces they already saw Winnetou from behind as he stood to take aim with his silver rifle.

"Drop your weapons or my magic rifle will speak!" they heard a mighty voice, but were unable to determine where it came from, whether from the top, or from the ground.

"Down with your weapons!" the order was repeated in the language of the Utah, and with such a booming voice that the few syllables were transformed into a mighty roll of thunder inside Night Canyon.

Then three shots were discharged in quick succession. It was evident that they came from the same barrel. It had to be Old Shatterhand's Henry rifle, the report of which had indeed attained the volume of a canon shot inside the canyon. Immediately afterwards Winnetou's silver rifle flashed up as he fired it. Those hit screamed, and then followed a howling as if the multitudes from hell had been let loose.

Old Firehand had reached the Apache and was able to see what and who was ahead of him. The canyon opened up for a short stretch and formed a room that could best be described as a rocky chamber. Its circular shape was large enough to accommodate perhaps a hundred riders. The water flowed along its left edge. Dusk ruled in there also; yet the host of Utah was clearly visible.

The five warriors who had been sent ahead had committed a grave mistake. They had stopped in there, to wait for those who followed later. Had they not done that, then the four Whites posted in the exit of the canyon on the other side would have been forced to address them, and the Utah could then have fled back to warn the others. But since they had waited for them to catch up, they were all surrounded. On the other side stood Old Shatterhand with his Henry rifle aimed, and next to him knelt

Hobble-Frank, so that Davy and Jemmy were able to shoot over him. The Indians had not dropped their weapons immediately upon Shatterhand's request, and therefore he and Winnetou had fired the shots. Five dead Utah lay on the ground. The others were unable to even think of resistance; they had enough to do with trying to regain control of their horses, which had become spooked on account of the extreme echo of the shots.

"Throw the weapons away, or I'll shoot again!" Old Shatterhand's voice echoed through the canyon once more.

And from the other side came the command:

"And here stands Old Firehand. Surrender if you want to stay alive!"

And next to him the Apache called out:

"Do you know Winnetou, the chief of the Apache? The one who lifts his gun against him will lose his scalp. Howgh!"

If the Utah had been of the opinion that the enemy was only ahead of them, then they were mistaken and realized at that point that their retreat was also blocked. Behind them stood the mighty figure of Old Firehand and the proud, slim figure of the famous Apache chief. Next to them in the water, because there was no other room, stood Aunty Droll with his gun aimed, and between those three there were diverse gun barrels poking out.

None of the Utah dared to lift his gun again. They stared ahead and backwards, and didn't know what they ought to do. To resist would have been fatal, they realized that; but to simply surrender quickly and without any negotiations went against their grain. That's when Droll jumped out of the water, walked up to the chief, held the barrel of his gun against the Indian's chest and snapped at him:

"Toss the gun away or I'll pull the trigger!"

Great Wolf stared at the fat, peculiar figure, as if he'd seen a ghost; the fingers of his uninjured left hand opened and the gun fell to the ground.

"The tomahawk, too, and the knife!"

The chief reached into his belt, pulled out the two weapons and threw them away.

"Untie your lasso!"

Great Wolf also obeyed that order. Droll took the lasso and tied the feet of the chief together under the horse's belly. Then he took the animal by its reins, led it aside and called out to Gunstick-Uncle, who was standing behind Old Firehand:

"Come here, Uncle, and tie his hands together!"

Uncle came along stiff-legged and solemnly replied:

"I'll take the belt around behind; His hands securely there to bind."

He leapt up onto Great Wolf's horse and sat behind him, turned his words into deeds, and then jumped down again. It was as if the chief had no comprehension of what was happening to him; he looked as if he were dreaming. His example worked. The others also surrendered to their fate; they were disarmed and tied up like their chief, and that went extremely fast since all the Whites were involved and paid attention only to the task at hand.

Hobble-Frank would have loved to greet Winnetou; Davy and Jemmy had precisely the same desire; but they couldn't afford to pander to such matters of the heart, and were instead forced to keep the realization of it for later. It was above all a matter of getting out of the canyon. Hence the ride was continued immediately after the last Indian had been tied up and the captured weapons collected from the ground. The hunters rode ahead; then came the Indians, and the rafters formed the tail end.

Winnetou and Old Firehand rode in the lead together with Old Shatterhand. They had quietly shaken hands, which was the only form of greeting they felt was necessary for the time being. Immediately in front of the prisoners rode two people who were much closer to each other than they realized, namely Aunty Droll and Hobble-Frank. Neither said a word to the other. After a while Droll pulled his feet out of the stirrups, climbed onto his horse's back while it was moving, and then sat down in the saddle again back to front.

"Good Heavens! What's that supposed to mean?" Frank asked. "Are you performing a comedy, sir? Have you played the clown in a circus once?"

"No, mister," Aunty replied. "But I'm in the habit of celebrating the holy days as they fall."

"What do you mean?"

"I'm sitting back to front, because it could otherwise turn out back to front for us. Remember that we've got fifty Indians riding behind us; that leaves a great many possibilities for something to occur that we haven't even considered. I'll keep an eye on them in this pose and the revolver in my hand to give them a pill, if that's necessary. If you're smart you'll do likewise!"

"Hm! What you're saying is quite correct. My horse won't mind; I'll turn around, too."

A few seconds later he also sat in the saddle back to front, so that he was able to supervise the captives. Thus there was no getting around it, the two droll riders could not do otherwise than look at each other quite often; in the process of it, their gazes gradually became friendlier; they obviously felt quite partial to each other's company. That went on for a while, without either of them speaking a word, until Hobble-Frank felt the urge to break the silence, at last. He said:

"Don't be offended if I ask your name. I've seen you before, just the way you sit next to me."

"Where was that?"

"In my imagination."

"Heavens! Who would have thought that I dwell in your imagination! How much rent do I have to pay, and what about giving notice?"

"As you please; but today the imaginary image vanishes into thin air, because I made your personal acquaintance. If you are the one I think you are, then I've heard many a funny tale about you."

"Alright, who do you think I am?"

"Aunty Droll."

"And where did you hear about that aunt?"

"In various places I've been to with Old Shatterhand and Winnetou."

"What? You rode with those famous men?"

"Yes, we were up north in the national park and also down south in the Estacado."

"Tarnation and thunder! Methinks you must be Hobble-Frank, yes?"

"Yes. Do you know me?"

"Of course! The Apache has spoken about you on many occasions. It was today, in fact when we were lying behind the Utah camp that he called you the little hero."

"The—little—hero!" Frank repeated while a blissful smile appeared on his face. "The—little—hero! I must write that down! Your guess about who I am is correct; but have I guessed correctly, too?"

"Indeed you have."

"You're Aunty Droll?"

"That's me alright."

"Truly? I'm delighted about that!"

"What made you assume that I'm the aunt in question?"

"Your clothing gave you away, and also your conduct. I've heard it told many times that Aunty Droll is an exceptionally plucky gentlewoman, and when I saw how you dealt with the chief of the Utah before, I immediately thought: 'That's Aunty Droll, and no one else'!"

"I feel honoured! Hence we're two fellows who do their duty. But what's even more important for me is that I've heard you're Old Shatterhand's fellow countryman; are you?"

"That's right."

"You're German?"

"Yes."

"Where from?"

"Right from the middle. I'm a Saxon, you see."

"You don't say! And what sort of Saxon? From which of the counties: Koenigreich? Altenburg? Koburg-Gotha? Meiningen-Hildburghausen?"

"Koenigreich, Koenigreich! But, you know these names so well. Are you German, too, perchance?"

"Of course!"

"Where from?" excited Frank echoed the other's question.

"Also from Saxony, namely from Saxe-Altenburg."

"*Herrjemerschnee*!" Hobble reverted to his homeland dialect. "A Saxon, too, and one from Altenburg no less? Ish dat at all possible? From the city Altenburg, or the country?"

"From Langenleuba, not the capital city."

"Langen...leuba?" Frank asked and his jaw dropped. "Langen-leuba-Niederhain?"

"Indeed! Do ye know it?"

"Why shouldn't I? I've got relatives there, very close relatives, and have been to the country fair twice with them as a youngster. You know, the fairs in Altenburg are legendary! The people continually bake cakes for two whole weeks. And when the fair is done and over with, it restarts in the next village. Hence everyone only refers to dat custom as the Altenburgian country feast."

"Det's correct!" Droll nodded. "We have it and flaunt it. But ye have family there, ye said? What's the name of those people and where are they from?"

"Oh, they're very close family. Here's the shtory: my father had a godfather whose dearly departed daughter-in-law remarried in Langenleuba. She died later, but her stepson had a son-in-law, and that's the one I'm talking about."

"So! What was he?"

"Anything you care to name. He was a capable fellow and a dab hand at just about everything. One moment he was a waiter, the next a verger, then a sergeant of the civilian guards, and at other times a wedding crier..."

"Stop!" Droll interrupted him, reached over and grabbed his arm. "What was his name?"

"I can't remember his first name; but his family name was Pampel. I only ever called him Uncle Pampel."

"What? Pampel? Am I hearing things?" Droll exclaimed. "Did he have children?"

"A whole bunch!"

"Do you know their names?"

"Nee, I've forgotten. But I still remember the oldest one, because I was very fond of the fellow. His name was Bastel."

"Bastel, Sebastian, det ish?"

"Indeed, because in Altenburg dialect Sebastian is colloquially referred to as Bastel. I believe his middle name was Melchior; dat's a very common name in dat region."

"Right, quite right! Det's correct and fits precisely! Sebastian Melchior Pampel! Do ye know what became of him?"

"Nee, unfortunately not."

"Then have a close look at me, here, look at me!"

"Why?"

"Because Bastel turned into me."

"You...you?" Hobble asked.

"Yes—me! I was Bastel, and I still know very well who came to the country fair with us; det was cousin Frank from Moritzburg, who later became a forestry warden."

"Dat's me, me in person! Cousin, we're finding each other again here in the middle of the wilderness as kinsmen and people related by tribe! Who would have thought dat was possible? Come here, brother, I must squeeze you to my bosom!"

"Yes, me, too. Here ye've got me!"

He reached across and the other did likewise. The embrace was accomplished despite the difficulties associated with sitting back to front on their horses.

The dour looking Indians definitely had no idea what they were supposed to make of the two riders; but the two cousins paid no mind to the painted faces; they rode side by side, holding hands with their backs facing the front, and talked about the blessed time of youth. They would probably have continued endlessly had not the train come to a halt. They had reached the end of Night Canyon, which opened up to become much larger and wider.

Although the sun was standing so deep already that its rays could no longer reach to the bottom of it, there was light, nevertheless, and clear, moving air. The riders gave a deep sigh of relief when they reached the open space. They didn't enter it, of course, until they had a careful look around to ensure no hostile creature was nearby.

The wide canyon was perhaps two hundred paces wide and accommodated a small, narrow rivulet along its bottom, which was shallow and easily crossed. There was grass and scrub, as well as a few trees along the water.

The Indians were taken off their horses, and then sat on the ground with their feet tied together again. The moment of extensive greetings had arrived, and the men made thorough use of it. Those among them who had only just met quickly got acquainted, and it didn't take long for most of them to address each other informally, with the exception of Old Firehand, Old Shatterhand, Winnetou, Lord Castlepool, and the engineer, Butler, of course.

Old Firehand's troop carried enough provisions, so everyone first consumed a meal. Then the fate of the Indians was to be decided. But there were several opinions. Winnetou, Old Firehand and Old Shatterhand were prepared to let them go; but the others demanded harsh punishment. Castlepool said:

"I don't think they're culpable up to the time when the duels ended; but then they were obligated to grant you free departure. Instead of doing this, they pursued you with the intention of killing you, and I don't doubt they would have done so, had they found an opportunity."

"That's very probable," Old Shatterhand replied. "But they didn't get the chance to make good on it, and have therefore not committed murder."

"Alright! In that case the intentions are punishable."

"How do you want to punish intentions?"

"Hm! That of course is difficult."

"Surely not by putting them to death?"

"No."

"With imprisonment, gaol, penitentiary?"

"Pshaw! Give them a thorough thrashing!"

"That would be the worst we could do, because there is no greater insult to an Indian than being whipped. They'd pursue us across the entire continent."

"Then impose a monetary fine!"

"Do they have money?"

"No, but horses and weapons."

"Do you think we ought to take those things from them? That would be cruel. They would die of starvation or fall into the hands of their enemies without horses or weapons."

"I don't understand you, sir! The more lenient you are with these people, the more ungrateful they become. You, especially, ought to have a much less tolerant notion, since it is you they have wronged in the first place."

"And precisely because they've ill-treated Frank, Davy, Jemmy and me, it ought to be the four of us who decide the Indians' fate."

"Do as you like!" Castlepool said and turned away indignantly. But he immediately turned around again and said:

"Shall we bet?"

"About what?"

"That those fellows will repay you with malice if you treat them with kindness?"

"No."

"I place ten dollars!"

"I don't."

"I place twenty against ten!"

"And I don't bet at all."

"Never?"

"Correct."

"Pity, what a shame! I've not been able to place one bet during the entire long ride from Osage-Nook to here. After everything I've heard about you, I must regard you as a genuine gentleman, and now you tell me that you never place a bet. I repeat: do as you like!"

He had worked himself up and become almost angry. It had been easy for him to adjust to life in the far West, but he couldn't get comfortable with the fact that no one wanted to have a bet with him.

Old Shatterhand's remark, that Frank, Jemmy, Davy and he alone had the right to decide the fate of the Indians hadn't been without effect, and after a lengthy debate, the men agreed that those four ought to come to a decision. However, they were to ensure that the Indians ceased all hostilities against the Whites. Hence a firm agreement was to be made with them. To that end it was necessary not to negotiate with the chief alone; his warriors needed to hear what he said and promised. Perhaps he would then keep his promises, out of consideration for the good reputation of his honour.

A large circle was formed that consisted of all Whites and Indians. Two rafters were posted as guards up and down either side of the canyon in order to report the approach of an enemy immediately. Great Wolf was sitting in front of Winnetou and Old Shatterhand. He didn't look at them, perhaps he was embarrassed, and perhaps his stubbornness prevented him.

"What does Great Wolf think we'll do with him now?" Old Shatterhand asked in the language of the Utah.

The chief didn't reply.

"The chief of the Utah is afraid; that's why he's not answering."

The Indian lifted his gaze, and stared at the hunter with a wrathful expression. He said:

"The paleface is a liar if he claims that I'm afraid!"

"Then give me an answer! Besides, you're the last one who should talk of lies, since it was you who lied."

"That's not true!"

"It is true. When we were still in your camp I asked you whether or not we'd be free to go once I had been victorious. What did you reply to me?"

"That you could go."

"Was that not a lie?"

"No, because you went."

"But you've pursued us!"

"No."

"Are you denying it?"

"Yes, I'm denying it."

"For what purpose did you leave the camp in that case?"

"To travel to the meeting place of the Utah, not to pursue you."

"Then why did you send five warriors along our trail?"

"I didn't do that. We've raised the war hatchet and once that's happened, one has to be careful. When I promised your freedom, in case you overpowered me, I didn't know in which direction you were going to leave. We've let you go and have kept our word. But you've attacked us, have taken everything from us, and killed five of our warriors. Their corpses are still lying in the narrow canyon."

"You know only too well what I'm to think of your words. Why did your guards shoot at us when we rode away?"

"They didn't know what I had promised you."

"Why did every one of your people chime into the war cries? They knew your promise very well."

"The war cries weren't meant for you, they were meant for the guards to stop shooting. You are interpreting our helpful action negatively."

"You know how to defend yourself cunningly; but you won't succeed in proving your innocence. I want to find out whether your warriors have the courage to be more honest than you."

Shatterhand asked why they had ridden away from the camp, and they gave answers that corresponded with the chief's claim that they hadn't harboured any hostile intentions towards the palefaces.

"These warriors do not want to give the lie to you," he turned back to Great Wolf. "But I've got incontrovertible proof. We sneaked around your camp and have eavesdropped on your people. We know that you wanted to kill us."

"You're only guessing!"

"No, we heard it. We also know that you'll break camp tomorrow morning, and that all warriors will follow to the meeting place of the Utah; the women and children, however, will travel to the old people in the mountains. Is that true?"

"Yes."

"That means the other part we heard is also true. We're convinced that you wanted to kill us. What kind of punishment do you think you'll receive for that?"

The Indian didn't reply to that.

"We hadn't harmed you, and you took us captive to kill us. And then you wanted to murder us here; you would have deserved death several times over. But we are Christians. We want to forgive you. You shall have your freedom and your weapons, and in return you must promise us that you will not ever harm any of us who sit here."

"Does your tongue speak or your heart?" the chief asked while he gave Old Shatterhand an incredulously searching, sharply penetrating look.

"My tongue never says anything different than my heart. Are you ready to give me your promise?"

"Yes."

"That all of us sitting here, red and white men, will be brothers henceforth?"

"Yes."

"And that we will and must support each other through all plight and danger?"

"Yes."

"Are you prepared to swear to it with the pipe of peace?"

"I am."

He had replied swiftly and without thinking about it; that led to
the conclusion that he was serious with his promise. Because of
the thick paint on his face, the expression on it was impossible to
determine.

"In that case the pipe may do the rounds," Old Shatterhand
continued. "I will say the words and you'll have to repeat them."

"Say them and I'll repeat them!"

The chief's readiness seemed to be a good sign, and the well-
meaning hunter was sincerely pleased about it, but couldn't help
issuing one more warning:

"I hope you're sincere this time. I've always been a friend of the
red men; I take into consideration that the Utah have been
attacked recently. If that weren't the case, you wouldn't get away
so cheaply. But if you prove disloyal once again, you'll pay with
your life. I assure you of that, and will keep my word!"

The chief stared at the ground and didn't look at Old
Shatterhand once. The hunter took the calumet from his neck and
filled the bowl with tobacco. After he lit it, he removed the chief's
fetters. Great Wolf was required to stand up, blow the smoke in
all six directions, and say the following in the process:

"I am Great Wolf, chief of the Yampa Utah; I speak for myself
and for my warriors here. I am speaking to the palefaces I see
here, to Old Firehand, Old Shatterhand, and also to Winnetou,
the famous chief of the Apache. All of these warriors and white
men are our friends and brothers. They shall be like us, and we
shall be like them. They shall never suffer any harm from us, and
we would rather die than to cause them to say that they deem us
to be their enemies! This is my oath. I have spoken. Howgh!'

He sat down again. At that point the other Indians were also
freed from their fetters, and the pipe went from mouth to mouth
until all had smoked it. Even young Ellen Butler had to do her six
puffs; she wasn't to be exempt, for her own sake.

Thereupon the weapons were returned to the Indians. There
was no risk involved in doing so, if they could be trusted with their
promises. Nevertheless, the Whites were as cautious as possible
and every one of them held his hand close to his revolver. The
chief fetched his horse, and then said to Old Shatterhand:

"Has my brother set us free entirely?"

"Entirely."

"Are we allowed to ride away?"

"Yes, where you wish."

"We will return to our camp."

"Ah! But you wanted to travel to the meeting place of the Utah! Now you're admitting that you only rode out because of us."

"No. You wasted our time; we'd get there too late. We'll turn back."

"Through the crack in the cliff?"

"Yes. Fare well!"

They shook hands and the chief mounted up. Then he rode back into Night Canyon without looking around for anyone else. His warriors followed him, after each of them gave a friendly farewell greeting.

"The fellow is a scoundrel nevertheless!" old Missouri-Blenter said. "If his paint weren't so thick on his face, then one would be able to recognize the deceit on it. A bullet through his skull would have been best."

Winnetou heard his remarks and replied:

"My brother may be right; but it is better to do good than evil. We'll stay here for the night, and I will now follow the Utah to observe them."

He disappeared in the rocky slot on foot, not on horseback, because he was able to better execute his intentions.

As a matter of fact, everyone felt much more comfortable and relieved than they did before. What could they have done with the Utah? Kill them? Impossible! Drag them around as prisoners? Just as impossible! They were thus obligated to uphold peace and friendship, and the Whites were rid of them. That was better than anything else.

Day gave way to night, especially since darkness came earlier in the canyon than outside of it. Several of the men went to find wood for the campfire. Old Firehand rode south down the canyon and Old Shatterhand went north up the canyon to reconnoitre. They had to be careful. Both covered a significant stretch and turned back when they hadn't discovered anything suspicious.

It was obvious that no one had been through there and lit a campfire for a long time, because despite the fact that there was no forest to speak of, there was enough firewood about. The spring flood had brought down and deposited much debris. No one was more delighted about the fire than Castlepool, because he found a splendid opportunity to develop his culinary skills with the aid of his roasting rack. The men still had provisions of meat, canned food, flour and more, which had been brought along from Denver. He was able to bake and roast to his heart's content.

Later on, Winnetou returned. Despite the almost complete darkness inside Night Canyon, the Apache had effortlessly found his way with his trained eyes. He reported that the Utah had collected their dead, and had then continued on their way. He had followed them to the other side of the crack and observed them climbing the steep rock face before they disappeared over the top into the forest.

Nevertheless, the men posted a guard deep inside the slot, to foil any attack from that side. Two other guards were standing a hundred paces each above and below the camp inside the main canyon; that way the men had provided for complete security.

Of course there was a great amount of story telling to do and it was past midnight when everyone retired. Old Firehand inspected the guards to satisfy himself that they were alert, and reminded the others of their shifts. Then the fire was extinguished and it turned quiet and dark in the canyon.

Yes, Winnetou had seen correctly; the Utah disappeared over the canyon edge into the forest, but they stopped, and didn't ride through it. The transport of the corpses was not difficult because the Whites had also returned the horses of their dead companions. The chief ordered the dead warriors to be taken down. He walked outside the forest, looked down into the crack in the cliff and said:

"They will have observed us. I'm sure there's one of the white dogs down there who wants to see whether or not we're really returning to camp."

"Aren't we doing that?" one of his people asked. He had undoubtedly distinguished himself with bravery or other skills that he dared to ask such a question.

"Do you have as little brain as the jackal of the prairie?" Great Wolf snapped at him. "We must take revenge on these pale toads."

"But they're now our friends and brothers!"

"No."

"We've smoked the pipe of peace with them!"

"Whose pipe was it?"

"Old Shatterhand's."

"Alright, in that case the promise is valid for him, but not for us. He was dumb enough not to use my pipe! Don't you realize that?"

"Great Wolf is always right," the man replied as he agreed with his chief's logic completely. His explanation was certainly bound to satisfy any warrior of the Utah.

"The souls of the palefaces will be in the Eternal Hunting Grounds by the morning, so that they can serve us there later on," the chief continued.

"Do you want to attack them?"

"Yes."

"We don't have enough men, and we cannot return through the crack because they'll have it guarded."

"Then we'll take another route and fetch as many warriors as we need. Aren't there enough camped over yonder in the *P'a-mow*[2]? And isn't there a path straight across the canyon that the palefaces don't seem to know? The corpses and their horses remain here, with two guards. The others ride north with me."

His orders were executed. The forest was narrow, but it formed a strip that was an hour's ride long, inside of which the Utah galloped along until the elevation slowly dipped away towards a gulch that led straight through the rocks. Through that rock chasm, Great Wolf reached the main canyon where the Whites were camped, but about five kilometres beyond them. Directly opposite, another opening cut into the walls of the main canyon, but it wasn't as narrow as the one where the clash between the Whites and the Indians had taken place earlier in the day. That's where Great Wolf and his warriors were headed. He seemed to know the way precisely because he didn't lose his way once despite the darkness and led his horse as confidently as if he were on a wide, German military road.

The gorge carried no water and gradually rose. Soon the Indians reached the watershed of the wide rocky plain, which was deeply cut by the maze of canyons. It was light up there; the moon was glowing in the night sky. The troop galloped across the plain, and after half an hour the landscape dipped away slightly into a broad, gentle depression. The protective cliffs remained standing to the left and the right, gaining in height as the ground fell away between them. Then lush canopies came into view under which many fires were burning. It was an actual forest, in the middle of a plain scoured smooth by storms and parched rock hard by the sun.

The forest owed its existence to a depression in the ground. The storms howled over the top of it without affecting the trees, and the rain was able to collect and form a kind of lake with the water softening the ground and making it fertile for the roots. That was the P'a-mow, and Great Wolf was riding straight towards it.

---

[2] Forest of the Water

He wouldn't have required the moonlight to find his way around, that's how many fires were burning there. It was a lively camp, to be precise: it was a war camp. There was no tent, no hut. The many red warriors were lying around the fires either on their blankets or on the bare ground; between them were just as many horses lying, standing or grazing. That was the place where the hosts of all the Utah tribes were to assemble for their war expedition.

When Great Wolf arrived at the nearest fire, he stopped, dismounted, signalled his people to wait there, and then called the name Nanap Neav to the nearest member of a group of warriors sitting at the fire. Those two words mean 'old chief'; therefore the one with this name was the supreme chief of all Utah tribes. The warrior rose and led Great Wolf to the lake where a large fire was burning separately from all the others. Four Indians sat there, each adorned with the feather of the eagle. One of them attracted special attention. He hadn't painted his face; it was crisscrossed by countless, deep wrinkles. His white hair hung long down his back. The man was bound to be at least eighty years old, and yet he sat there as straight, proud and powerful as if he counted fifty winters less. He looked sharply at the arrival without saying a word of greeting; the others remained silent as well. Great Wolf sat down, didn't speak and only stared at the ground. That's how they spent quite a while; then at last the old man said:

"The tree sheds its leaves in autumn; but if it loses them beforehand, then it must be chopped down because it is useless. Three days ago he still wore them. Where are they today?"

The question pertained to the eagle feathers, which Great Wolf no longer wore; it contained a damning accusation for any courageous warrior.

"The decoration will be in place again by the morning, and the scalps of thirty palefaces will hang on my belt!" Great Wolf replied.

"Has Great Wolf been overpowered by palefaces, so that he is no longer permitted to wear the insignia of his courage and honour?"

"Only by one paleface, but by the one whose fist is heaver than the hands of a hundred white men combined."

"That could only be Old Shatterhand."

"It is him."

"Uff!" the old man let out. "Uff!" the others chimed in. Then he asked:

"Does that mean Great Wolf saw the famous White?"

"Him and many others as well, Old Firehand, Winnetou, the long and the fat hunter, a troop of around fifty men. I've come here to bring you their scalps."

An Indian was supposed to be able to hide his emotions; it was expected of elders and chiefs in particular; but what the leaders heard at that point rattled their self-control, and they broke out in exclamations of joy, surprise and astonishment. The expression on the face of the old man became taut, so that only few wrinkles remained visible.

"Great Wolf may tell us!" he requested.

The chief obeyed. His report didn't correspond to the truth; he made every effort to make himself look good, and embellished his actions. The others sat motionless and listened to the chief with the utmost attention. When he concluded, the oldest of them asked:

"And what will Great Wolf do now?"

"You will give me another fifty warriors with whom I'll attack those dogs. Their scalps must hang on our belts before dawn."

The old man's wrinkles reappeared; his brows furrowed and his aquiline nose seemed to have grown twice as thin and sharp.

"Before dawn?" he asked. "Are those the words of a red warrior? The palefaces have attacked us, robbed us and killed our men. And now they're moving against us with great force to spill our blood, and have even sent for the Navajo. They're out to annihilate us, and now that the Great Spirit has given their greatest and most famous men into our hands, they're to die quickly and painlessly like a child in its mother's arms? What are my red brothers saying to the words of Great Wolf?"

"The Whites must die on the stakes," one of the other chiefs replied.

"We must catch them alive," the second said.

"The more famous they are the greater their tortures must be," the third added.

"My brothers have spoken well," the old man praised them. "We will catch those dogs alive."

"The old chief may wish to consider what kind of men are among them!" Great Wolf warned. "Old Shatterhand pushes the head of a buffalo to the ground, and Old Firehand has no less strength. Their weapons contain all the evil spirits there are. And Winnetou is a great warrior..."

"But an Apache!" the old man angrily interjected. "Have you forgotten that the Navajo belong to the Apache? He is our mortal enemy and shall be tortured more than the palefaces. I know what kinds of powers and skills those palefaces have been given, but we have enough warriors to smother them. You have the first claim to revenge and shall be the leader. I'll give you three hundred warriors, and you'll bring the palefaces alive."

"Am I permitted to have the scalps of Old Firehand, Old Shatterhand and Winnetou, once they've been tied to the stakes?"

"They belong to you, but only if none of the Whites are going to be killed beforehand. The premature death of any one of them will cheat us of the delight of seeing their torture. You already have fifty warriors with you; it means that there will be seven red men to each of the Whites. If you sneak up well, then you ought to be successful in surrounding them and tying them up before they're even awake. Take enough ropes with you! Now come; I'll choose the warriors who will accompany you. Those who have to stay back will be aggrieved about it, but they will sit closest to the stakes."

The chiefs rose and went on their walk around the camp from one fire to the next to hand pick the warriors. Soon three hundred men were together, as well as another fifty to guard their horses since they couldn't be taken right up to the camp of the Whites. Great Wolf explained to the warriors what it was all about, described the situation precisely, and detailed his plan of attack. Then the Indians mounted up and started out on the ride that was supposed to be fatal for the Whites. The names of Old Firehand, Old Shatterhand and Winnetou reverberated in everyone's ears. Such great fame awaited them for having caught heroes like those, and for having put them to the stake!

Great Wolf rode back along the exact same route on which he had arrived, but only to the intersection with the main canyon. There, they dismounted and left their horses under the protection of the additional fifty warriors. With the given superiority in numbers, the undertaking could almost be said to be harmless. Nevertheless, the success of it wasn't guaranteed, namely because of the horses. Great Wolf knew only too well that the horses of the Whites easily detected the scent of an Indian sneaking up. It was to be expected that the animals would reveal the presence of a mob of three hundred Indians through great nervousness and loud snorting. How were they going to remedy that? While the chief was pondering the question, he spoke it out loud, so that everyone could hear it. One of the warriors bent down, pulled out a plant, held it up to him, and then said:

"Here is a reliable solution to confuse the odour."

The chief recognized the plant from its aroma. It was sage. The far West is home to large stretches of ground covered by the plant, which can be many square kilometres in size. In that canyon, too, where the sun reached the bottom, there were masses of those plants. The advice was good and it was acted upon immediately. The Indians rubbed their hands and clothes with the sage. That produced a strong odour with which they hoped to fool the Whites' horses. Besides, Great Wolf noticed that the faint breeze in the canyon moved up towards them, in their favour.

They had armed themselves with only knives, considering their numeric superiority, not with guns. It was a matter of catching the Whites unawares, and to crowd them enough, so that no fight would break out.

The Indians continued on their five-kilometre march on foot. They were initially able to do so quite fast, but when they had covered about two thirds of the way, they had to be more careful.

At that point the chief came by the thought that the Whites might have pitched their camp in some other place as a measure of precaution; it put him into an almost feverish unrest. Further and further they progressed, silently and snake-like. Six hundred Indian feet, and yet there was not the slightest sound audible; no pebble was moved from its place, no twig cracked. There—Great Wolf, who was in the lead, stopped and stood still. He saw the guard-fire burning. It was the time when Old Firehand checked the guards. In daylight, Great Wolf had seen them being posted, one above and one below the camp. Those guards were still in place; they had to be rendered harmless first.

He quietly ordered the warriors behind him to stop, and only two to follow him. The three lay down on the ground and crawled ahead. Soon they were near the post above the camp; the guard gazed after Old Firehand, who had just left to return to the camp, and turned his back towards the three Indians. Suddenly two hands clamped shut around his neck and four others grabbed him by his arms and legs. He couldn't breathe and subsequently lost consciousness; when he came to again, he was tied up and had a gag stuck in his mouth, which prevented him from screaming. Next to him sat two Indians, one of them held a knife to his chest. He was able to recognize that much, although the moonlight did not reach down to the bottom of the canyon where he was lying.

In the meantime, the chief had ordered another two warriors to join him. They had to go after the guard posted below the camp, and thus move past the camp. Since that was situated on the nearside of the watercourse, it was advisable for the Indians to move along on the other side of it. Great Wolf and the two other warriors waded across and crawled on, which was not too dangerous. He assumed that both posts had been placed a similar distance from the camp each, so he was able to calculate the approximate distance to cover. The water had a slightly phosphorescent sheen, and the splashing could reveal them, hence they crawled an additional stretch further downstream, crossed back, lay on the ground again and crawled back up the canyon on hands and feet. It wasn't long before they saw the guard post; he was standing six paces ahead of them, the face turned sideways. Another short minute, one jump, a quiet, short struggle, and he, too, was overpowered. The two warriors stayed with him, and Great Wolf returned across the watercourse alone to lead the main attack.

The Whites' horses were standing in two groups between the camp and the two posts. Up to that point they had remained calm; but the Indians couldn't assume that would also be the case later. If the Utah moved past them close-by, the animals would become suspicious despite the sage scent. Hence Great Wolf thought it advisable to have the entire troop also cross to the far side of the watercourse first. That took place with truly masterly silence. Once on the other side, they all lay down to crawl the distance of a hundred paces, until they were opposite the camp. The greatest difficulty consisted in the overcoming of the tight space in which so many people had to move about, and in complete silence at that. When the warriors were lying side by side, opposite the Whites and the horses, the latter began to get nervous after all. The Indians had to act swiftly. It was impossible to cross the water without making a sound.

"Forwards!" Great Wolf gave the order; although his voice was suppressed, it was still audible to his warriors.

The small river was swiftly crossed. None of the Whites were still awake; they were all in the first phase of their sleep. The scene that followed is impossible to describe. The palefaces were lying so close together that the three hundred Indians didn't have room to move. Five or six of them jumped onto one White at the time, pulled him off the ground and flung him to the warriors behind them, and then immediately grabbed the second, third and fourth, and so forth. It happened so fast that the sleeping Whites were in the Indians' power before they were entirely awake.

And completely contrary to Indian custom, accompanying an attack with their war howls, the Utah worked almost silently, and only raised their piercing yells when the Whites made use of their own voices. The noise carried far into the distance and reverberated in multiple echoes from the canyon walls.

In the process of the melee there was a confusion of bodies, arms and legs, which were indistinguishable from one another in the darkness. Only three groups were somewhat recognizable; they weren't far apart from each other and positioned hard against the cliff walls. At the centre of them were Old Firehand, Old Shatterhand and Winnetou, respectively. The three men weren't as easily caught as the others on account of their greater presence of mind. They had jumped up and sought cover with their backs against the cliff wall. They defended themselves with knives and revolvers against the superior might of the enemies, who weren't allowed to use their own knives because the Whites had to be caught alive. The three men were bound to be defeated despite their famous skills, agility and physical strength. They were so densely crowded by the Indians that it became impossible for them to even move their arms to resist, and were at last crushed to the ground and tied up like their comrades. A spine-chilling Indian howling announced that the attack had been successful.

Great Wolf ordered a fire to be lit. When the flames illuminated the battleground it was evident that more than twenty Indians had been wounded or even killed by the three hunters alone.

"These dogs will have to endure a tenfold torture for this!" the chief ranted. "We'll cut their hide from their bodies in strips. They will all die a ghastly death, and not one of them will see the stars of the coming night! Take the dead, the horses, as well as the weapons of the palefaces. We must return to our camp."

"Who will touch the magic rifle of the white hunter?" one of the Utah warriors asked. "It goes off by itself and kills the one who touches it, together with many others."

"We'll leave it lying where it is and put a mound of rocks on top of it, so that no red man will be able to touch it. Where is it?"

They went looking for it, but in vain; it had vanished. When Great Wolf asked Old Shatterhand about it, the hunter didn't give him an answer. When he had woken up in the middle of the battle confusion, and had jumped up, someone had yanked the rifle out of his hands and tossed it away. The chief ordered torches to be lit to illuminate the clear water of the stream. It was shallow enough to recognize every pebble on its bottom, but the rifle wasn't there.

During the day, the Yampa Utah had seen Old Shatterhand hold the rifle and couldn't explain its disappearance. Perhaps it was lying in the narrow cleft. The Indians inspected it for a fair stretch, with the aid of torches, of course, but also in vain. Consequently, those Indians who had still doubted the supernatural traits of Old Shatterhand's rifle then also gave credence to that view. The magic rifle could possibly make use of its incomprehensible powers while the Indians stayed there, hence Great Wolf, who also became spooked, said:

"Tie the prisoners onto their horses, and then let's get away from here! An evil spirit made the rifle. We mustn't stay here long enough for it to send us its bullets."

The warriors immediately obeyed his order, and by the time the troop left the campsite, not much more than an hour had passed since they had set out from their camp.

"Not one of them will see the stars of the coming night," the chief had said. He believed that all of the Whites had fallen into his hands, and yet that wasn't the case.

As mentioned, Old Firehand had also posted a third guard inside Night Canyon, in order to prevent a possible attack from the returning Yampa Utah. That post was—Aunty Droll, who was supposed to be relieved after two hours. Hobble-Frank had joined him voluntarily, to chat about their dear homeland. They sat together in deep darkness, with all of their weapons, conversed in whispers and occasionally listened back into the narrow rift for any sound or noise. They didn't feel tired at all, and there was so much to tell that they weren't going to run out of topics soon.

Suddenly they heard a noise from the opening, which was entirely suited to attract their attention.

"Listen!" Frank whispered to his cousin. "Did you hear dat?"

"Yes, I've heard it," Aunty replied just as quietly. "What was det?"

"Several of our people must have risen."

"Nee, det's not it. There must be many, many people. Det's a foot-scuffling of at least two hundred..."

He interrupted himself aghast, because those who were being attacked had awakened and raised their voices.

"Thunder and knife, dat's a battle!" Hobble-Frank jumped up. "Methinks we're mostly being ambushed!"

"Yes, det we are!" Droll agreed. "And by red scoundrels, if det's necessary!"

The very next moment proved their assumption correct, because the victory howls of the Indians arose.

"May God be with us; dat's really them!" Frank called out. "Upon them! Come, let's get out there quickly!"

He grabbed Droll's arm, to pull him along; but the hunter, known for his craftiness, held him back, and, shivering from tension, said:

"Stay here! Let's not rush out there! If Indians undertake an attack by night, then there are so many that one has to be as careful as possible. Let's first take a peek at the situation. We'll know what to do afterwards. We must lie down and crawl."

They did that. On hands and feet they pushed forwards to the exit of the narrow canyon. And despite the darkness they recognized that their comrades were lost. The might of the Indians was too great. The battle raged to one side of them. The sounds of the shots discharged by Old Firehand, Old Shatterhand and Winnetou cracked, but not for long; then the victory cries came from the hundreds of Indian voices. Right in front of the opening was some vacant space.

"Quickly follow me across the water!" Droll whispered to his cousin.

He crawled as quickly and carefully as possible along the ground. Frank followed him. In the process of doing so, Hobble put his hand on a long metal object; it was a rifle with a spherical cartridge magazine.

"Old Shatterhand's Henry rifle!" the recognition flashed through his mind. He grabbed the firearm and took it along. The two cousins safely reached the watercourse, and then the other bank. On the far side, Droll grabbed Hobble-Frank's hand and pulled him away, downstream, in a southerly direction. The escape succeeded because it was dark, and because the yelling of the Indians drowned out their footsteps. But soon the space between the river and the canyon wall grew so narrow that Droll suggested:

"We must get back to the left side. There might be more space."

They waded across. Fortunately they were already far below the point where the guard post had been standing. They walked, or rather ran along, occasionally into the cliff wall, at other times stumbling across rocks that lay in their way, until they could no longer hear the hollering of the Indians; that's when Hobble-Frank held his companion back and reproached him:

"Hold on there and shtand shtill, you overwrought zealot! Why did you actually run and miserably seduce me into running away with you? Dat ish against all duty and comradeship! Have you no shred of ambition in your body?"

"Ambition?" Droll replied. He was almost breathless on account of his rotund figure. "I have plenty of det in my body, but if ye want to keep det ambition, then ye must above all first aim at saving det body. Hence I ran away."

"But dat was actually not permitted!"

"So? Why would det not have been permitted?"

"Because it was our duty to save our comrades."

"So? And how did ye want to save them?"

"We should have lunged at the redskins to knock them asunder and stab them all."

"Hee hee hee! Knock them asunder and stab them!" Droll laughed in his peculiar manner. "And would have achieved nothing but getting caught as well."

"Caught? Do you think our friends were only captured, not shot, stabbed and pummelled?"

"Nee, they weren't murdered; that's for certain. I know det precisely."

"Dat could have a calming effect on me!"

"Good! Calm down in det case. Did you hear any shots?"

"Yes."

"And who was it det's been shooting? The Indians perchance?"

"Nee, because dat were revolvers I heard."

"Alright! The Indians didn't use their guns at all; they were only intent on catching the palefaces alive, in order to torture them all the more later. Hence I've skedaddled. Now the two of us are safe and can do more for our friends than had we been caught with them."

"You're right, cousin, you're absolutely right! There's a mighty weight just lifted off my chest. I wouldn't want for anyone to say that world-famous Hobble-Frank turned tail and ran while his comrades were in mortal danger! Over my dead body! I'd much rather throw myself into the thickest fray and thrash about me like a raging Hufeland. It is absolutely ghastly. Who in his quiet, peaceful temperament could have guessed dat something like this would happen! I'm utterly beside myself!"

"I'm also deeply shaken and shocked; but I refuse to be bewildered. One cannot declare men like Winnetou, Firehand and Shatterhand as lost before they are lost in reality. And they're not even alone, they're in the company of fellows with hair on their teeth. So, let's quietly wait and see!"

"That's easier said than done. What kind of Indians were they?"

"Utah, of course. Great Wolf didn't return to his camp. He knew that other Utah were nearby and went to fetch them."

"The scoundrel! And he smoked the peace pipe with us beforehand! From which direction could he have come?"

"If I knew that, then I'd be smarter than I am now. He definitely won't stay at our campsite, but instead have the prisoners moved some place else. And since we don't know in which direction he'll turn, we mustn't remain shtanding here; we must get away, much further away, until we've found a place where we can hide well."

"And then?"

"Then? Well, we'll wait until daylight; then we'll inshpect the tracks and run after the Indians until we know what we can do for our friends. Now come, let's get away from here!"

He grabbed Frank's arm again and touched the rifle in the process.

"What?" he asked. "You've got two guns?"

"Yes. When we left the slot and crawled towards the water, I found Old Shatterhand's Henry rifle."

"Det's good; det's splendid. Det can be of great use to us. But do you know how to shoot with it?"

"Of course! I've been with Old Shatterhand long enough to know his rifle as well as he does. But we had better move along now! If the redskins get the idea to ride downstream, then they'll catch up with us and we're done for. I, however, must take care of my dear life, so dat I can sacrifice it for the rescue of my friends. Woe to the Indians, and woe to the entire Wild West, if anyone even touches a single hair on them! I'm a good person; I'm two souls and one thought, so to shpeak; but when I become violent, I'm capable of tipping out the entire formidable world history together with the bath water. You'll get to know me yet. I'm a Saxon. Do you undershtand me? We Saxons have always been strategically amusing folk, and have dished out the mightiest thrashings in all diatonic squabbles and wars."

"Or been at the receiving end of it!" Droll retorted while he pulled his cousin along.

"Silence!" Frank replied. "You Altenburgians are only cheese Saxons; but we along the River Elbe are the genuine ones. As long as human lips have been capable of speaking about cultural events, Moritzburg and Perne have always been the Symplegadean centres of all Kalospinthechromokrenean greatness and decency. Napoleon was defeated near Leipzig, and in Raecknitz near Dresden Moreau was relieved of his only two legs; and along the River Weisseritz lies the plantation of boldness and bravery, which I consume within my bosom, and so I wouldn't suggest that the redskins push me to the wrath of the Berserkers. I'm astringent in my fury and incapable in my anger. Tomorrow, tomorrow I'll have a good talking to you, tomorrow when the first ray of the first sun plunges into the bloody realm *dos a dos* and back to back with the last sheen of darkness!"

He shook his fist menacingly behind him. He had never before in his life been as agitated and furious as at that moment; it was evident not only from his words, but also from how he stormed ahead despite the darkness, as if it were a matter of overtaking the enemies, who were really behind him.

And yet the direction the two men had taken was the correct one, and the most suited for them to get to the Indians, as they were going to find out later to their great amazement. In order for the Indians not to catch up with them, they walked as fast as permissible in the prevailing darkness. With the water on their right hand side, and the vertical canyon wall to their left, they kept going south, until the canyon described a bend towards the east after they had been travelling for about an hour. They were astonished to see the moon appear above the bend. Through a side canyon on their right hand side an unencumbered view had opened up for them. Droll stopped and said:

"Stop! We must consider where we ought to turn, hither or thither."

"There's no doubt about it," Frank said. "We must turn into the side canyon."

"Why?"

"Because we can assume with absolute consecration dat the redskins will remain in the main canyon. If we hide in the side canyon, then they'll travel past us, and in the morning we can dog their heels with obligatory hypnology. Don't you think so?"

"Hm, the thought isn't bad at all, especially since the moon is standing straight above the side canyon and is lighting our way."

"Yes, Luna beams comfort into my heart and kisses away the rushing streams of tears from my soul dat has dried up from utter vexation. Let's follow her sweet beam! Perhaps the trusted sheen will lead us to a place where we can hide well, which is the main thing in our imponderable situation."

They jumped across the watercourse and entered the side canyon, where there was no water flowing at the moment, yet there were enough signs to indicate that the entire base of the narrow valley formed a river bed during other seasons. The direction they were following at that point led them precisely west. They had to penetrate deeply into the narrow gulch, so as not to be detected by the Indians. They had followed it for about half an hour when they stopped because of a pleasant surprise. The rock wall on their right hand side suddenly came to an end, and formed a sharp corner with a north-running wall. And ahead of them lay— not open terrain, but forest—a real forest that someone new to the area would not have expected to find there. The canopies arched so densely above the scant undergrowth that the moonlight was able to penetrate only in a few places. They had come to the Forest of the Water where the Utah had pitched their war camp.

The depression it filled lay in a precise north-south direction, parallel with the main canyon that wasn't more than half an hour away. Between it and the forest there were two connecting trails, two side-valleys, a northern one, which Great Wolf had used, and a southern one through which Droll and Frank had come. The two side valleys, which ran from east to west, the main canyon and the forest together formed a rectangle that consisted of the tall endlessly long rock ashlar into which the waters had carved their vertical and almost one hundred metre deep courses.

"A forest, a real forest with real trees and bushes, as if it had been planted by a royal Saxon forestry warden!" Frank said. "We couldn't possibly find anything better, because dat here will give us a hide spot right out of a picture book. Don't you think so?"

"Nee," Aunty Droll replied. "Det forest seems suspicious or almost fearsome to me. I don't trust it."

"Why and wherefore then? Do you think that bears have pitched their nightly domicile there?"

"Not so much det. Bears aren't fearsome at all, but there are other creatures, who are just as dangerous."

"What kind?"

"Indians."

"That would be dumb; that would indeed be dumb!"

"I would be very pleased if I were mistaken, but my thoughts will likely be correct."

"Won't you be so kind and give me a logical perturbation of these thoughts?"

The two men stood at the cliff corner in the shadow and kept their eyes keenly trained on the moonlit forest edge. Droll asked:

"Who would more likely know that there is a forest here, we or the red fellows?"

"The Indians."

"And would they also know, as well as we do, that a forest is the best hiding place?"

"Naturally."

"Haven't I already explained to you det I suspect Indians to be nearby?"

"Yes, because that's where Great Wolf went to fetch help."

"And where would these people be stashed away? In the barren, naked canyon or in the comfortable forest?"

"In the latter."

"Good, therefore we'll have to be very careful here. I'm convinced det we have reason to be ever so circumspect."

"Do you think we ought to give the forest a miss?"

"Nee, but we must pay attention. Can you perhaps see anything suspicious?"

"Nee, nothing at all."

"Me neither. Let's try it in that case. Quickly across, and then duck under the bushes and listen out for anything that moves. Let's go!"

They ran across the open, moonlit expanse. When they arrived at the trees they crouched low to listen. They heard nothing; not one leaf moved; but Droll sucked the air in through his nose, and then quietly asked:

"Frank, get a whiff o' det! It smells of smoke. Don't ye think so?"

"Yes," his cousin replied. "But the smell is almost undetectable. Dat's only half an inkling of a quarter trace of smoke."

"Because it's from quite a distance. We'll have to inspect the matter and sneak closer."

They took each other by the hand and walked on, slowly and quietly. It was dark under the canopy, and they had to rely more on their sense of touch rather than vision. The further they went, the more noticeable the smoke became; of course, they advanced only slowly. Hobble-Frank might have had second thoughts about their undertaking after all, because he whispered:

"Hadn't we better leave the smoke be smoke? We're quite needlessly getting ourselves into a dangerous situation dat might not compress me at all."

"Of course it's dangerous," Droll replied. "But we must risk it. Perhaps we can rescue our friends."

"Here?"

"Yes. If Great Wolf doesn't stay at our campsite, then he'll come straight here."

"Dat would be splendid!"

"Splendid? Not so hasty, it could cost our lives!"

"No harm done if we can save our comrades. I wouldn't think of turning around now."

"Quite so, cousin; ye're a decent fellow. But cunning is better than force. Let's be careful, very careful!"

They sneaked on, until they were forced to stop because they saw the sheen of a fire. They could also detect indefinable sounds, like distant human voices. The forest seemed to spread more to their right. They followed in that direction and soon saw more fires.

"A large, large camp," Droll whispered. "Dat would be the Utah warriors who are combining for an attack against the Navajo. There must be hundreds here."

"Dat won't hurt. We must get closer. I want to know wat's going to happen to Old Shatterhand and the others. I must..."

He was cut short because vociferous, jubilant howling arose ahead of them.

"Ah! Now they're bringing the prisoners," Droll said. "Great Wolf is coming from the north, and we've arrived from the south. We'll have to find out at all costs what they're going to do with them."

Up to that point they had advanced by walking upright; at that point they were forced to lie on the ground and crawl. After a short while they reached the seemingly sky-high rock wall that formed the eastern boundary of the forest. They sneaked along it side by side. The fires were on their left hand side, and soon they spotted the small lake on the shore of which the fire of the chiefs was burning.

"A pond, or a lake!" Droll said. "I thought as much. Where there is forest, there must also be water. We can't continue in this direction because the water extends to the rock. We've got to head over yonder to our left."

They were at the southern end of the lake; the fire around which the chiefs had been sitting was burning at its western bank. Hobble and Droll crawled along the water's edge until they reached a tall tree with branches low enough for them to reach with their hands. At that moment the Indians threw more wood onto the campfire; the resulting tall flames illuminated the captured palefaces who were brought along.

"Now we've got to pay close attention," Droll said. "Can you climb, cousin?"

"Like a squirrel!"

"Then up into the tree. We have a nicer and much more open view from up there."

They pulled themselves up and kept climbing until they sat hidden in the foliage, so that not even the most keen-eyed Indian would have been able to spot them.

The prisoners had been forced to walk; hence their feet weren't tied. They were led to the fire where the chiefs, including Great Wolf, had sat back down again. The latter pulled out the eagle feathers, which he had concealed in his belt, and placed them back into his mop of hair. He was the victor and therefore entitled to wear his insignia again. He looked at the Whites with the expression of a hungry panther, but he refrained from saying anything at that point, since the oldest chief had the right to speak first.

Nanap Neav's gaze flew from one White to the next, until it rested on Winnetou.

"Who are you?" he asked the Apache. "Do you have a name, and what is the name of the mangy dog you call father?"

"Only a blind worm that lives off scum doesn't know who I am. I am Winnetou, the chief of the Apache."

"You are no chief, no warrior, you are the carrion of a dead rat!" the old chief mocked him. "These palefaces shall all die a death of honour at the stake; you, however, we will throw into the water here, so that the frogs and crabs will devour you."

"Nanap Neav is an old man. He has seen many summers and winters and had great experiences; but he doesn't seem to have learnt that Winnetou does not submit to being mocked without exacting revenge for it. The chief of the Apache is ready to suffer any torture, but he won't be insulted by a Utah."

"What would you do to me?" the old man laughed. "Your limbs are fettered."

"Nanap Neav ought to consider that it is easy for a free, armed man to be rude to a shackled prisoner! But it is not dignified. A proud warrior refuses to say such words, and if Nanap Neav does not want to take heed, he shall bear the consequences."

"What consequences? Has your nose ever taken in the odour of the stinking jackal that even vultures ignore? You are such a jackal. The stink that you..."

He didn't get any further. A cry of shock arose from the mouths of the Utah nearby. Winnetou jumped at the old man's chest with a mighty leap, so that the Utah chief toppled to the ground, whereupon the Apache dealt him several kicks and blows with his heels against the chest and head, and then returned to his place.

Deep silence fell for a moment after the outcry, so that the loud voice of the Apache was audible:

"Winnetou warned him. Nanap Neav didn't listen and will never again insult an Apache."

The other chiefs had jumped up to examine the old man. The right side of his skull, as well as part of his chest had been kicked in. He was dead. The red warriors crowded around the group, holding the knives and giving Winnetou bloodthirsty looks. One would have thought that the Apache's deed might have provoked the Utah to erupt into raging fury; but not so. Their wrath remained silent, especially since Great Wolf lifted his hand with a repelling gesture and ordered:

"Back! The Apache killed the old chief in order to die quickly and without torture. He thought you would attack him and kill him swiftly. But he figured wrongly. He shall die a death the likes of which no other human being has ever suffered. We will confer about it. Move the chief away in his blanket, so that the eyes of these white dogs cannot feast on his corpse! They shall all be sacrificed at his grave. We will bury Old Shatterhand and Old Firehand alive with him."

"You won't live long enough to be able to bury me!" Old Shatterhand replied.

"Silence, dog, don't speak unless you're asked! How will you know the days I still have to live?"

"I know them. You won't live one more day, because tomorrow at the same time your soul will have left your body!"

"Are your eyes so keen that you can see into the future? I'll have them cut out!"

"It doesn't require keen eyes to know when you'll die. Have you ever heard that Old Shatterhand has spoken an untruth?"

"All palefaces are liars, and you're also a paleface."

"The redskins lie; and you're the proof. We were four Whites and fought with four Indians for our life. We were permitted to kill our opponents, and then be free, if we were victorious. We won and spared you. Nevertheless, you didn't want to let us go. You pursued us and fell into our hands. We could have killed you. You deserved it; and still we didn't do it because we're Christians.

We smoked the peace pipe with you and you promised to be our friends and brothers until death. We released you, and out of gratitude you attacked us and dragged us here. Who is lying, you or we? But do you remember what I said to you before we parted when evening drew near in the canyon?"

"Great Wolf is a proud warrior; he never takes notice of a paleface's words."

"In that case I'll remind you of them. I warned you and told you that breaking your promise one more time will be your death sentence. You've broken your promise and will therefore die."

"When?" Great Wolf grinned.

"Tomorrow."

"By whose hand?"

"By my hand."

"You have a hole in your head through which your brain is draining away!"

"I've said it, and so it will be. Your life was in my hands twice; I spared you, and you still lied to me. It won't happen a third time. The red men shall experience that Old Shatterhand might be lenient, but he also knows how to punish."

"Dog, you won't punish anyone ever again. You'll be surrounded and tightly guarded during the night. But we will now hold a powwow about you, and as soon as day breaks your tortures, which will last several days, will begin."

The prisoners were taken to a small clearing inside the forest where a fire was burning; an Indian sat next to it to maintain it. The Utah also tied the prisoners' feet together, and then laid the men on the ground. Twelve armed warriors were posted around the clearing under the trees, to guard the place. Escape was impossible, or at least it seemed so.

Droll and Frank had seen everything clearly from their lofty vantage point. Their tree stood perhaps one hundred and fifty paces away from the chiefs' fire, so that they had also been able to understand the majority of what had been spoken there. At that point it was imperative to find out where the prisoners had been taken, and to get near that spot.

Just as the two men climbed down from the tree, the captured weapons and other property were being brought to the chiefs, and placed near the fire. Because the items weren't given much attention, Hobble and Droll deduced that the Indians would decide about their distribution the next day, which was a detail that served to put Droll's mind at ease quite a bit.

Only the leaders were still sitting around the fire by the lake shore. There had to be a reason why all other warriors were drawn to another spot. Frank and Droll would soon enough find out what that was. There were peculiar lamenting sounds emerging from somewhere. For some time they heard a solo voice, and a while later an entire chorus chimed in. That went without interruptions, softer at times, and then louder again.

"Do ye know what det ish?" Droll asked his cousin from Moritzburg.

"Ish dat supposed to be the funeral aria for the old chief?"

"Yes. The Utah sing their dirges even before the corpse is cold."

"Dat's important for us because the fellows will hardly hear anything else during their noisy laments. We must find our friends at all costs."

"And what will we do when we've found them? We can't take them away!"

"Dat's not necessary, because they'll be able to walk of their own accord. The main thing is dat we untie them or cut the straps. If the place where they're kept isn't far from the fire of the chiefs, where their weapons are, then we've won dat game. What good fortune about the darkness under the trees. The fires are not a hindrance, on the contrary, they're very useful since we can easily recognize the silhouettes of the redskins and get out of their way."

"Det's quite correct. Down on the ground once more, and then away! I'll crawl ahead."

"Why you?"

"Because I've been in the West longer than you, and am better at sneaking up."

"Ah, you don't say! What big ideas you have! I'm experienced in all counterpoint affairs of the western existence. The incredible discomfort, with which I comprehend even the most difficult subject as mere child's play, has honed my perceptive faculty to such a terpsichore, dat there cannot be anything at all from which I don't emerge as a master immediately. But because you're my beloved kinsman, I'll let you go first. But pay close attention! If anyone wants to stab you from the front, just say so and I'll assist you from the back. I won't abandon you!"

The short Saxon demonstrated that he had indeed attended a splendid school while in Old Shatterhand's company. He did a good job. Although he had two rifles to carry, he moved along nimbly and silently. Aunty Droll in the lead had the more difficult task, of course, which consisted of utilizing every suitable object for cover.

They passed by the chiefs at a distance of perhaps fifty paces and turned to the fire nearest to them. Fortunately, it was the one where the prisoners were lying. Droll told himself that they weren't to be found in a dark spot. Surely but slowly, and steadily, they drew nearer, which couldn't be accomplished without at least some risks. It happened several times that an Indian scurried past them. Frank had to swiftly throw himself sideways at one point to avoid the foot of an Indian who rushed past. The back-and-forth stopped after a while. Those who had taken on the duty of singing the dirge sat around the corpse, and the others had stretched out to sleep for a while.

And so the two Saxons arrived behind the guards who surrounded the clearing where the prisoners were held. Droll lay behind one tree, and Hobble behind the next. The man who was responsible for maintaining the fire had left it for a while to chime in with those who were singing their laments, and several of the twelve guards had done the same. The flame had died down and threw only insufficient light. The figures of the prisoners were hardly visible. Droll crawled a few paces to his right, then to his left, but didn't encounter a guard. When he returned to Frank, he whispered to him:

"The moment seems to be favourable. Can you see Old Shatterhand?"

"Yes. He's the nearest."

"Crawl up to him and lay beside him as long and stiff as if you were tied up!"

"What about you?"

"I'll work my way over to Old Firehand and Winnetou, who are lying over yonder."

"That's dangerous!"

"Not more than here. Imagine Old Shatterhand's joy when he gets his rifle back! Be quick!"

Hobble-Frank had to cover only a short distance of perhaps eight paces. Just then the last flames died down so low that it seemed the fire was going to go out completely; it grew so dark that the figures of the prisoners became indistinguishable from one another. One of the guards went to stack more firewood on it; but before he could do so, Frank and Droll had used the opportunity; they were already in place.

Frank was lying next to Old Shatterhand. He stretched out his legs as if he were tied up, pushed the Henry rifle across to his neighbour, and then pulled his arms tightly against his sides, so that the guard would think they were tied to his body.

"Frank, you?" Old Shatterhand asked quietly, but not at all in surprise. "Where is Droll?"

"He's lying over yonder beside Firehand and Winnetou."

"Thank God you've found the trail and arrived before dawn!"

"Did you know we were going to come?"

"Of course! When the Indians lit the fire I saw that you weren't among the captives."

"We could still have been inside Night Canyon and captured!"

"Pshaw! The redskins were looking for my gun. I was afraid they'd find you in there; but they returned without you, and my rifle had vanished; that told me everything. I was so sure you wouldn't abandon us that I've warned Great Wolf he'd die."

"That's bold!"

"Dear Frank, the world belongs to the bold!"

"Yes, the bold and Hobble-Frank. Didn't I do disputably well? We've executed our comradely duties and obligations at pizzicato level, haven't we?"

"That was exceptional conduct, exceptional!"

"Yes, you'd have gone bust without us!"

"Not entirely. You know I'll only throw up the sponge when the game is truly lost. But in this case there are not only enough cards, but also trumps to be played. If you had not come, we would have had to help ourselves in other ways. Here, look!"

Frank looked over to him and saw that the hunter showed him his liberated right arm.

"I've already freed that hand," Shatterhand continued. "And I would have had the other untied in a quarter of an hour, too. I've got a small penknife in my secret pocket, which would have gone from person to person, so that we would have had our fetters cut within a very short time. Then up swiftly and run across to get the weapons that lie beside the chiefs…"

"You know dat already?"

"I would have to be a bad Westerner if that had escaped me. There would be no salvation for us without the weapons; I therefore paid very close attention to where they were being taken right from the beginning. But I must know how you got here above all. Did you follow the redskins?"

"Nee, not dat; we've left much earlier than they did."

"To observe and follow them?"

"Not dat either. We've skedaddled entirely inflexibly, always down the canyon until we got to a side valley into which we were able to compromise ourselves. We had planned to find the trail of the redskins later, when it got light again, in order to see what we could do for you."

"Ah! In that case you don't actually deserve credit for finding this forest?

"Nee, we don't actually deserve the forest; but since coincidence has thrown it in our direction, you won't think badly of us for having taken the liberty afterwards to extend the required New Year's visit to you."

"You're becoming ironic."

"Not entirely; I only wish to have stated herewith dat assimilating through the forest and the redskins was no simple feat."

"I know well how to appreciate that, old Frank. You've risked your lives for us, and we'll never forget that. You can depend on that. But take your gun closer to you! It can easily be spotted. And give me your knife, so that I can free my neighbour; he'll pass it along."

"And afterwards, when the fetters are off, what will we do then? First to the weapons, and then run to the horses, and then away?"

"No; we'll stay."

"All devils! Are you saying that in all serious earnest? Stay here! Do you call dat being rescued?"

"Yes."

"Thank you! Dat's how these fellows will make a remarkable deal because when the dear sun appears early in the morning it will shine upon two prisoners more than there were before midnight."

"We won't be imprisoned. Running to the weapons, and then to the horses would have to happen so fast that it would cause an absolute chaos. No one would find his gun and knife in such a short time, or even his other property. The Indians would be all over us before we would be able to reach the horses. And who knows whether they are still saddled. No, we must immediately take cover behind our shields."

"Shields? I'm no knight Kunibold of Eulenschnabel; I have neither armour nor shield. And should you be using dat word in a hectometric meaning, I'm asking for obedient clarification about what I ought to make of your shields."

"The chiefs."

"Ah, there you go, dat's you all over! Of course dat's a magnificent idea!"

"Not magnificent, just very obvious. We get a hold of the chiefs and are then assured that nothing will happen to us. Quiet now. The fire is burning low again, so the guards will probably not notice when we move our arms."

He cut the fetters away from around his feet, and then did likewise on his neighbour, who then handed the knife on. Droll's blade was already making the rounds. Then Old Shatterhand's order, that everyone was to rush over to the chiefs as soon as he had extinguished the fire, went quietly from mouth to mouth.

"Extinguish the fire?" Frank grunted. "How are you going to do dat?"

"Pay attention and you'll see! It must be extinguished, otherwise the guards' bullets will hit us."

Everyone lay ready. The Indian responsible for maintaining the fire was sitting next to it again. Old Shatterhand waited until the man was about to stack more firewood on it, whereby the flame would be subdued for a short while. That's when he jumped up and lurched at him, punched him in the head and tossed him on the fire. By rolling the unconscious man back and forth three or four times, he extinguished the fire. He had acted so swiftly that it was pitch dark before the guards realized what was happening. They emitted their alarm cries too late because the liberated prisoners already pushed through the forest towards the lake. Old Shatterhand was ahead of everyone else; behind him came Winnetou and Old Firehand.

The chiefs were still sitting around the fire, holding their powwow. It was a most welcome task for them, to think up and discuss the most horrible tortures by which the Whites and the Apache were supposed to die. By the time they heard the calls of the guards, they already saw the figures of the freed men approach—a few seconds later they were flung to the ground, disarmed and tied up.

The Whites picked up the rifles that were lying nearby without asking whether each had grabbed his own. When the guards appeared between the trees, they saw their leaders lying on the ground and several Whites kneeling beside them with their knives ready to stab the chiefs immediately. The others stood behind that group with their rifles aimed. The warriors recoiled with a fright, only to emit their howls of fury, which called all the others to the scene.

Old Shatterhand couldn't afford to let the situation develop into an attack. He loudly proclaimed that the chiefs were going to die as soon as anyone attempted to free them. He demanded that the warriors retreat, after which he would then negotiate with the chiefs in a peaceful manner.

It was a decisive moment, a moment upon which their lives depended, and not just that of a few, but that of many. The Indians were standing under the protection of the trees; the Whites were brightly illuminated by the fire, but there was no doubt that they would plunge their knives into the hearts of their chiefs at the first shot.

"Stay there!" Great Wolf called to his people. "I'll talk to the palefaces."

"We won't negotiate with you," Old Shatterhand said to him. "The others may speak."

"Why not with me?"

"Because your mouth is full of lies."

"I'll speak the truth."

"You've promised that the whole time without making good on it. You've instructed me before to only speak when I was asked to. I'm no longer your prisoner; on the contrary, you're mine, and I'm giving you the exact same order. If you speak without being requested to do so, the knife will plunge into your heart without mercy." Old Shatterhand then turned to the oldest of the chiefs and asked:

"What's your name?"

"*Kunpui*[3] is my name. Free me and I'll talk to you!"

"You will be free, but only after we've talked and you've agreed to our demands."

"What do you demand? Freedom?"

"No, because we've got that already and won't let you take it again. First of all call five of your noblest warriors over to join us!"

"What are they to do here?"

"You'll hear that later. Call them, quickly, otherwise our knives above you will become impatient!"

"I must first think about which ones to choose."

He said that only to gain some time to mull over whether or not it was really necessary to obey Old Shatterhand's orders. The hunter didn't mind because the Whites had the opportunity to also retrieve their other possessions during the ensuing pause. Of course they weren't completely satisfied because there was none

---

[3] Heart of Fire

among them who wasn't missing at least one item. At last Heart of Fire gave the names of five warriors, and they were requested to join the men at the fire, but leave their weapons behind. They sat down to wait for what was going to happen. They expected to hear what the Whites demanded from them, but first they heard something else. While the chiefs had been struck down and tied up, Old Shatterhand had in the meantime dropped his rifle on the ground. When he picked it up again, Great Wolf saw it and screamed in utter terror:

"The magic rifle, the magic rifle! It has returned; the bad spirits have brought it to him through the air! Don't touch it; don't touch him, either, otherwise it will cost your life!"

Old Shatterhand told Great Wolf to be quiet and turned to Heart of Fire:

"Our demands are as follows: We're still missing many things that you've taken from us; you'll return them to us. At daybreak we'll ride away and will take the chiefs with us, including these five men, as hostages. As soon as we're satisfied that we're no longer under threat from you, we'll free these people and allow them to return here."

"Uff! That's asking too much," Heart of Fire replied. "We can't allow that. No brave red warrior will be inclined to go with the white men as a hostage."

"Why? What is worse, being a hostage who will be released, or a prisoner who was careless enough to be caught? Surely the latter. You imprisoned us, and yet it has damaged neither our fame nor our honour; on the contrary, both have gained in significance because we've demonstrated to you that we don't despair even when captured and bound by such a superior number. It will be no disgrace for you to ride with us for a day, and then be allowed to return unharmed."

"It is a disgrace, a great disgrace. You were in our hands; the stakes were supposed to be erected at daybreak, and now we're the ones who are tied up, and you are the one making the rules!"

"Will the situation improve by your refusal to submit to my demands? Will a fight breaking out, during which you who sit here will certainly be killed, and many others on top of it, lessen the disgrace? The chiefs and these five noble warriors will die from our first bullets and our guns will then swiftly keep on devouring the others. Just think about my magic rifle!"

The last caution seemed to work especially well, because Heart of Fire asked:

"Where will we have to accompany you? To which region will you ride?"

"I could speak a lie out of caution," Old Shatterhand said. "But I detest it. We're going into the Book Mountains, up to Silver-Lake. If you're honest, we'll keep you with us for one day. I'll give you a quarter of an hour to consider it. If you acquiesce to our will, then nothing will happen to you; if you refuse, however, then our guns will begin to speak as soon as the indicated time is up. I have spoken!"

He had emphasized the last three words, which left no doubt that no amount of remonstration would sway him from his demands. Heart of Fire hung his head. It was entirely outrageous that those few Whites, who had been threatened with the cruellest form of death only a short while earlier, were in a position to make such demands. At that moment his attention was diverted to the trees, because he heard a muffled voice:

"*Mai ive!*"

Those two words meant: 'look here!'. They had not been called out aloud, but had been spoken almost as a whisper; they might have been meant for anyone else but the chief, their utterance a mere coincidence of no significance to the Whites; nevertheless, Old Shatterhand, Old Firehand and Winnetou immediately looked to the spot in question. What they saw there was of utmost interest to them. Two Indians, who held a blanket between them like a curtain suspended at two corners, were standing there. They raised or lowered that curtain in fast, but predetermined intervals. Visible behind them was the sheen of a fire. Those two Indians were talking to Heart of Fire.

Indians have a sign language that differs between tribes. At night they utilize such means as burning arrows. During the day they light a fire and, to collect the smoke, lay hides or blankets over the top of it. As often as the cover is taken away, or lifted, a smoke cloud that forms the signal rises up. It is a kind of telegraphic message transfer, similar to our own, because the intervals between the individual smoke clouds have a specific meaning, like our dots and dashes. However, tribes do not adhere to the same signals for long; on the contrary, they replace them often, so that the deciphering of the sign language is made as difficult as possible for strangers.

If the two Indians were of the opinion that no one noticed their actions, then they were mistaken. As soon as they began to move the blanket, Winnetou walked a few steps to the side, so that he came to stand precisely behind Heart of Fire, for whom the signs were meant. The two Indians were standing in a straight line between the chief and the fire; while they lifted and dropped the blanket alternatively, they let the fire appear, and then disappear from his view, namely in longer and shorter intervals of which each had a particular meaning.

Old Firehand and Old Shatterhand immediately knew what it was all about, but pretended not to notice; they left the deciphering of the signals to Winnetou. As a native red man, he was even more skilled at it.

The transmission of the signals lasted for probably five minutes. During that time Heart of Fire didn't avert his eyes once from the spot where the two Indians were standing. Then they parted and walked away from each other; they had concluded their message and probably didn't even consider that their opponents had observed them. Heart of Fire noticed only then that Winnetou was standing behind him. That was conspicuous to him; he was worried and turned around quickly, to see where the Apache was looking. But Winnetou had been smart enough to turn away immediately, and to pretend that the moonlight glimmer on the lake surface occupied his entire attention. Heart of Fire was relieved. Winnetou, however, slowly walked over to Old Shatterhand and Old Firehand. Together they walked another stretch further, and then Firehand asked angrily:

"Those two redskins were talking to the chief. Did my brother see and understand their words?"

"I saw them, but was unable to decipher every single one," the Apache replied. "Nevertheless, I understood the meaning of the message, because by reasoning I was able to complete what I didn't understand."

"Alright, what did they say?"

"The two Indians were two young chiefs of the Sampitshe Utah, whose warriors are also among those assembled here. They encouraged Heart of Fire to ride with us without a care."

"Then they are being honest? That would surprise me very much."

"They are not honest. If we want to travel to Silver-Lake from here, then our route takes us first across the Grand River and into the *Teywipah*[4]. Many warriors of the Tash, Capote, and Wiminutsh Utah are camped there in preparation for the attack

---

[4] Elk Valley

against the Navajo, and to wait for the Utah who are assembled
here. We're bound to encounter those, and will be crushed, so
they think, and the hostages will be freed. Several messengers are
being sent to them right now to inform them. And so that we
won't be able to escape at all, the Utah here will break their forest
camp and follow us, as soon as we've left. We're supposed to be
caught between the two Utah forces and be hopelessly lost."

"Tarnation! The plan isn't bad at all. What does my red brother
say to this?"

"I agree that it has been well thought out; but it has one big
flaw."

"What flaw?"

"The fact that I've espied it. We are aware of it and now know
what we have to do."

"But we must get into the Elk Valley if we don't want to make a
detour of at least four days."

"We won't have to make a detour, but will ride to that valley, yet
still not fall into the hands of the Utah."

"Is that possible?"

"Yes. Ask my brother Old Shatterhand. I've been in the Elk Valley
with him. We were alone; a large mob of wandering Elk Utah had
been chasing us. We escaped them because we found a mountain
trail that perhaps no one has walked on before or since. It is quite
risky; but if one has to choose between death or the trail, the
choice is not in doubt."

"Good, let's ride that route. And what will we do with the
hostages?"

"We won't release them until we have the dangerous Elk Valley
behind us."

"And will we free Great Wolf as well?" Old Shatterhand asked.

"Do you want to kill him?" Winnetou asked.

"He deserves it. Down below in the canyon, when I spared him,
I told him that it would cost his life if he betrayed us again. In
spite of that he broke his promise once more, and I'm of the
opinion that we cannot let that go unpunished. It's not about us
alone. If he isn't punished, then we'll reinforce his opinion that
promises towards Whites need not be kept, and the example of
such a chief influences all other Indians."

"My brother is right. I don't like killing a person; but Great Wolf
has betrayed your group several times and deserves to die several
times over. If we let him live, then that will be interpreted as a
weakness. However, if we punish him, then his warriors will

experience that they can't break a promise given to us without being punished for it, and will henceforth no longer dare to act so disloyally. But we don't have to mention anything about that yet."

The quarter of an hour had passed, and Old Shatterhand asked Heart of Fire:

"The time is up. What did the chief of the Utah decide?"

"Before I can say that, I must know precisely where you intend to drag the hostages," the chief replied.

"We won't drag them; they'll ride with us. They might be fettered, but we won't cause them pain. We'll travel to the Teywipah."

"And then?"

"Up into the mountains to Silver-Lake."

"And that's how far the hostages must ride with you? The Navajo dogs might already be up there; they would kill our warriors."

"We don't want to take them along that far; they will accompany us to the Elk Valley. If nothing bad has happened to us by the time we get there, we'll assume that you've kept your word, and will let them go."

"Is that true?"

"Yes."

"Will you smoke the peace pipe on it with us?"

"Only with you alone; that suffices, because you speak and smoke in the name of the others."

"Then take your calumet and light it."

"We had better take yours."

"Why? Is your pipe not as good as ours? Or is yours only capable of creating clouds of untruth?"

"The other way round would be correct. My calumet always speaks the truth; but the smoke of the red men is untrustworthy."

That was a severe insult; hence Heart of Fire called out with the glint of anger in his eyes:

"Were I not bound I would kill you. How dare you say that our calumet lies!"

"Because I'm justified in saying that. Great Wolf's smoke has lied to us repeatedly, and you have become guilty of the same shameful deed by having given him warriors to catch us. No, we'll only smoke from your calumet. If you don't want to do that, then we'll assume that you're not honest with us. Decide fast! We don't feel like wasting more words."

"Then untie me, so that I can use the pipe!"

"That's not necessary. You're a hostage and must remain tied up until we free you in Elk Valley. I will handle your pipe and hold it to your lips."

Heart of Fire preferred not to reply any longer. He was forced to tolerate the insults since his life was at stake. Old Shatterhand took the pipe from the chief's neck, filled its bowl and lit it. Then he blew the smoke up, down and into the four cardinal directions, and then briefly explained that he was going to keep the promise made between him and Heart of Fire if the Utah refrained from any and all hostilities. Heart of Fire was lifted upright and turned around to face all four directions. At the same time he had to draw the six puffs from the pipe and give the reciprocal promise on his and his warriors' behalf. The ceremony was thus concluded.

Then the Utah were forced to return the remainder of the missing items to the Whites. They obliged since they figured they'd get them back very soon. Immediately afterwards the horses of the Whites as well as those of the hostages were brought. That was just when dawn broke. The Whites thought they had best make haste with their departure. They needed to apply utmost caution and couldn't afford to show the least weakness that might have afforded the Indians an advantage.

The five chosen warriors and the chiefs were tied onto their horses; then two Whites per hostage, one on either side to hold the Indian in the middle, kept their revolvers ready to shoot immediately, in case the Utah would object to the leading away of the hostages. The train moved out towards the side canyon from where Hobble-Frank and Aunty Droll had come sneaking into the camp. The Indians kept calm; only the dark gazes they gave the Whites revealed that the outcome of the adventure was less than satisfactory for them. No one was more proud than the two Saxons, whose smart intervention brought about the successful outcome, or at least the speed with which it had been achieved. They rode behind the prisoners, side by side. After they had left the camp, Droll produced his peculiar wily, yet funny chuckle and said:

"Hee hee hee, what a joy for my old soul! Oh my, won't the Indians be vexed det they have to let us ride away! Don't you think so, cousin?"

"Of course!" Frank nodded. "Dat was a stroke of genius better than anything in a book. And do you know who were the main matadors?"

"Well?"

"You and I, the two of us. They'd still be lying in chains and shackles, just like Prometheus, who's forced to eat only eagle liver all year round."

"Oh, you know, Frank, methinks they would have found their own way out of it, too. People like Winnetou, Shatterhand and Firehand don't submit easily to being tied to torture stakes. They've often been in much worse situations and are still alive today."

"Although I believe dat, too, it would nevertheless have been more difficult for them. It might not have been impossible, but also not dat easy to make a contrapuntal exit from this bedevilled trap. I'm not at all conceited about it, but it still is an uplifting feeling when one can say that, aside from outstanding intellectual gifts, one also possesses an expansion of ones mental capacity that even the fastest horse wouldn't be able to catch. Some day after I've retired, and am in good ink, I shall write my memoirandums, which all famous men do. After dat, the world will recognize all the more for what kinds of hallucinations one single human shpirit owns its competent capabilities. You're also one such highly gifted and honourable Earthly inhabitant, and we'll be able to remind ourselves with the pride of our imitated self-confidence that we're not only fellow countrymen, but also configured cousins and kinsmen."

The train had arrived at the side valley. The men didn't turn left, to return to the main canyon, but instead headed to the right, to follow the extension of the side arm. Winnetou, who knew the route best of all, rode in the lead as usual. Behind him came the hunters, and then the rafters, who flanked the prisoners riding in their midst. After them came the sedan, in which Ellen sat; her father rode next to her, and several rafters again formed the tail end.

Ellen had shown extreme courage during the past two days; fortunately the Indians hadn't treated her as harshly as the adult prisoners. After the men had freed themselves, and her, from their ties, and had then run to the chiefs to apprehend them, she had remained hidden on her own near the fire that Old Shatterhand had extinguished. What luck that the Indians hadn't come by the idea to find her and use her to force the release of the hostages!

The narrow canyon continued at an even steeper incline than the short stretch Droll and Hobble had climbed up the night before, and after perhaps an hour it terminated in a wide, open rocky plateau, which seemed to be bounded by the dark masses of the Rocky Mountains. Up there Winnetou turned to the others and said:

"My brothers know that the Utah will follow us. We shall now ride at a gallop, to put as much distance as possible between them and us."

Consequently the riders used the spurs on the horses and drove them on as fast as consideration for the sedan and the ponies that carried it permitted. Later the speedy ride was interrupted for a very welcome reason. They had spotted a herd of pronghorn antelopes and were successful in surrounding and killing two. That resulted in sufficient provisions for the day.

The mountains seemed to draw increasingly closer. The high plateau appeared to meet the foothills; yet that was not the case at all because the valley of the Grand River was in between. Towards noon, when the sun's rays burned down so hot that it bothered animals and humans alike, the troop reached a narrow spot on the rocky plain where the ground fell away.

"This is the beginning of the canyon that will take us to the river," Winnetou explained as he followed the descending slope. It appeared as though a giant had applied a plane to slice a gradually deepening track into the hard rock. Initially the walls to either side were hardly noticeable, then they grew as tall as a man, then as a house, and they kept on increasing in height until they seemed to meet at the top. Down inside the narrow space it became dark and cool. Water seeped from the walls, collected on the bottom and soon became foot deep, so that the thirsty horses were able to drink. However, the canyon had a peculiar feature: it didn't show the slightest bend. It had been eaten into the rock in a straight line, so that a narrow strip of light was visible long before the riders reached the end; it grew wider the closer they came to the gap. That was the exit, the end of the close to one hundred metre deep cut.

When the riders arrived at the opening, they were presented with an almost overpowering view. They had arrived in the valley of the Grand River. It was perhaps eight hundred metres wide. The river streamed along the middle and left a strip of grass on either side, which was bounded by vertically ascending canyon walls. The valley ran north to south, as straight as if drawn by a ruler, and neither side showed even the narrowest crack or the smallest protrusion. Above it stood the glowing sun, which caused the grass to almost wither despite the depth of the canyon.

Not a single crack? But yes! Directly opposite the riders on the right bank of the river there was a fairly broad cut from which a stream of considerable size flowed. Winnetou pointed to it and said:

"We must follow that creek upstream; it leads to Elk Valley."

"But how do we get across?" Butler asked, as he was concerned about his daughter. "The river isn't a raging torrent, but it seems to be deep."

"Above the creek inflow is a ford. It is so shallow at this time of the year that the water won't touch the sedan. My brothers will follow me!"

They rode across the grass to the ford. Once across the river, the riders also had to cross the creek in order to get to its right bank because it was broader and more comfortable to travel than the left. Winnetou drove his horse into the water, and the others followed him. He was right; the water didn't reach to his feet at all. Nevertheless, when he approached the far bank he suddenly stopped and gave a half loud shout, as if he had noticed danger.

"What's the matter?" Old Shatterhand, who rode behind him, asked. "Has the river bed changed?"

"No; but men rode past over there."

He pointed to the bank. Old Shatterhand drove his horse on for a few more paces, and then also saw the trail. It was broad, as if many riders had made it; the grass had not yet recovered.

"That's important!" Old Firehand said. He had joined the two. "Let's investigate this trail; the others have to remain in the water for the time being."

The three rode onto the bank entirely, dismounted and looked at the tracks with expert eyes.

"They were palefaces," Winnetou said.

"Yes," Old Shatterhand agreed. "Indians would have ridden single file and would not have created such a broad, conspicuous trail. I would even say that these people aren't genuine Westerners. An experienced hunter is far more cautious. I'm guessing that the troop numbers between thirty and forty people."

"I agree," Old Firehand said. "But Whites, here, under the present circumstances! They must be greenhorns, careless people who are in a hurry to get up into the mountains."

"Hm!" Old Shatterhand grunted. "I think I can guess whom we're dealing with."

"Alright, whom?"

"Red Brinkley with his gang."

"Tarnation! It is possible. The outlaws could well be here, according to my calculations. And that tallies with what you've found out from Knox and Hilton. We have the trail..."

Winnetou interrupted him. He had walked to the creek. While he pointed into the shallow margin, he said:

"My brothers come here. It was the red-haired colonel."

The others joined him and looked into the water. The bottom was plainly visible in the crystal clear water. The men recognized a series of imprints that led from one bank to the other alongside the trail made by the riders where they had crossed the creek.

"Before the riders crossed one of them dismounted to check the depth of the water," the chief explained. "They were stupid people because anyone with open eyes can see that the water won't reach above their legs. And how did the person inspect the creek? My brothers may tell me."

"With a pickaxe, holding the handle. That's clearly evident from the imprint," Old Firehand replied.

"Yes, with a pickaxe. These men don't want to hunt, they want to dig. It was the red-haired colonel."

"I agree; yet we still have to consider the possibility that it was someone else."

"In that case they could only have been gold prospectors," Old Shatterhand said. "And I disagree with that."

"For what reasons?"

"Firstly, gold prospectors are experienced people, and not as careless as this, and secondly, with the tracks of forty horses, we can assume that there are ten packhorses; that leaves thirty riders; gold prospectors don't wander around mountains and canyons in such significant numbers. No, it is Red Brinkley with his men. I'd like to swear on it."

"I have no doubts, either. But where did they go? They turned right over there, therefore no longer followed the Grand River downstream, and instead headed up the creek to Elk Valley. They're riding straight into the arms of the Utah."

"That's a fate they've created for themselves. We can't change it."

"Oho!" Old Firehand called out. "We must change it."

"Must? Why? Have they deserved it?"

"No. But we must have the map, the drawing, which the colonel stole. If we don't get the drawing, we'll never know where the treasures of Silver-Lake lie."

"That is true. Do you want to ride after these scoundrels to warn them?"

"Not to warn them, no, but to bring them down ourselves."

"That is impossible. Consider their head start!"

Old Firehand bent down to inspect the grass again, and then said with a tone of disappointment:

"Unfortunately! They've been through here five hours ago. How far is it to Elk Valley?"

"We won't reach it before nightfall."

"Then I must give up on my idea. They'll be in the hands of the Indians even before we've covered half of the way. What about the messengers that were to be sent to that valley by the Yampa Utah? They left the camp before we departed, and we haven't seen any of their tracks."

"Those men walked, they didn't ride," Winnetou explained. "The route is much shorter on foot, since a moccasin can get across places where horses and riders would break their necks. My brothers mustn't think about the colonel, but about the fact that we must wipe out these tracks."

"Why wipe out?"

"We know that the Yampa Utah are following us. We will deviate from the path they think we are following. We must make an effort to fool them, if we want to escape. They must think the trail of the colonel, which goes directly to Elk Valley, is ours; then they'll follow them and won't even think of the possibility that we've turned off the path and eluded them. Hence they mustn't find out that there were riders here before us. My two white brothers know how to extinguish tracks. Hobble-Frank, Droll, Humply-Bill and Gunstick-Uncle have also learnt how to do it, as have Watson and Black Tom. Would these men please lift the grass and water it from their hats, because the sun will straighten it once it's wet. This has to happen on a stretch that reaches as far as we can see it from here. When the Yampa Utah arrive, the grass will be tall again and only trampled where we've been riding."

That was a splendid plan. The men Winnetou had named came over and carried it out while the others finished crossing the ford with all the horses, and then went straight across the creek as well. The hunters backtracked the colonel's trail for a good one hundred paces, sprinkled the grass with water and raised it by dragging their blankets along the ground while slowly walking backwards. The sun had to do the rest, and there was no doubt that it would do so. If someone, who hadn't been witness to the procedure, came along only half an hour later, he was bound to assume that only the trail of Old Firehand and his companions lay ahead. Those of the group who had wiped out the tracks then crossed the creek as well and mounted up again.

The Indian captives had watched in silence. None of them had spoken since the group's departure. What they had just witnessed seemed suspicious to them. Why did the palefaces wipe out the strangers' tracks? Heart of Fire could no longer keep quiet; he turned to Old Firehand:

"Who are the men that rode here before?"

"Riders," the hunter gave the brief reply.

"Where did they go?"

"How should I know?"

"Why did you wipe out their tracks?"

"Because of your warriors."

"Because of them? What business of theirs is this trail?"

"They're not supposed to see it."

"They won't see it at all, because the trail is here, and my warriors are camped in the Forest of the Water."

"They are not camped there, on the contrary, they're coming after us."

"Don't believe that!"

"I not only believe it, but also know it."

"You're mistaken. For what purpose would my warriors follow you?"

"In order to get us between you and those Utah who are camped in Elk Valley."

It was obvious that Heart of Fire was aghast. But he quickly regained control and said:

"Did my white brother dream this? I know nothing of what you're saying."

"Don't lie! We saw the signals that the two young chiefs gave you with their blanket. We understood them just as well as you and know that you have lied to us with the calumet."

"Uff! My words were without falsehood!"

"We'll see. Woe to you if the Yampa Utah are following us! I've got nothing further to say to you. We must continue."

The interrupted ride continued upstream along the creek. The trail they followed was broad; therefore they also had to ride in a broad formation, so that it was impossible for the pursuers to recognize that there were two trails in front of them. The Indians had been quiet before, but at that point they also hung their heads. They knew they had been found out, and realized that their lives weren't worth a tinker's cuss. They would have liked to get away, but there was no question of escaping; their ties were secure, and the Whites surrounded them so tightly that it was impossible for them to break through.

The men followed the creek, which gradually led them uphill along many bends and turns. The valley grew broader, and further uphill, it was studded with trees and bushes. At last it branched out into several side valleys from where small watercourses came to form the creek that originated there. Winnetou followed the discharge of the strongest spring. Its valley was fairly broad for about a quarter of an hour, and then suddenly formed a narrow rock passage behind which it widened into a lush, verdant meadow. When the men had passed through the narrows, the Apache stopped and said:

"This is a splendid place to rest and eat. Our horses are tired and hungry, and we also require rest. My brothers may dismount and roast the antelopes."

"But then the Utah will catch up to us!" Old Firehand said.

"What harm does that cause? They shall see that we know their plans. They can't lay a finger on us because if we place even one man at the narrows, he'll see them approach from afar and notify us. They can't storm this place and must retreat."

"But we'll waste much time here!"

"We won't lose even a minute. If we eat and drink, then our strength will increase, which we might need later. And if we feed our horses grass and give them water, then they can run faster later. I've chosen this place. My brother may do as I asked of him."

The Apache was correct, and the others also agreed that they ought to rest in that spot. They posted a guard where the rock walls locked off the valley. The prisoners were tied to trees; the horses were left to graze, and soon two fires were burning, above which the game was being roasted. A short while later the hunters were enjoying the meal. The Indians received their portions, and even water from Castlepool's beaker.

The English lord was in a splendid mood. He had come to America to have adventures, and he had found more than he had thought possible. He had pulled out his book, in order to tally the sums he owed to Bill and Uncle.

"Shall we make a bet?" he asked the former.

"What bet?"

"That I'm already in debt to you for a thousand dollars, or even more?"

"I told you I don't bet."

"That's a crying shame! I would have won this bet."

"That's fine with me. Besides, you'll probably have to make more entries today, sir, because it is quite possible that we'll experience something."

"Delightful! Let it come, as long as we survive it. See, it's already begun!"

The guard post had given a half loud whistle. He waved. The leaders rushed up to him. When they looked through the narrows, hidden behind the rocks, they saw the Utah come up the valley; they were still around a thousand paces away.

On the valley side of the rock narrows grew bushes. Old Shatterhand quickly posted the best marksmen there and ordered them to shoot as soon as he fired the first shot, but they were to shoot only the horses, not the riders.

The Indians quickly advanced but kept their eyes on the tracks. They believed the Whites were happy for having escaped, and were so sure of themselves that they didn't even send a scout ahead. Then a shot cracked; ten, twenty followed, and more, many more. The horses that were hit collapsed or reared and ran back, throwing their riders and creating chaos in the train. There was bone-chilling howling, and then the Indians disappeared; the place was empty.

"So!" Old Shatterhand said. "Now they know that we're on our guard and know their intentions. But we'll have to depart since they could be sneaking up on us from the side. Let's go!"

The troop mounted up and moved out within a few minutes. It was safe to assume that the Indians would push forwards only slowly, with the greatest of caution.

They rode up the meadow, across the ridge of the mountain, and then reached a labyrinth of canyons and valleys that seemed to come from all directions only to head towards one and the same point. The spot in question was the entrance to a broad, desolate, endlessly long rock ravine in which not a single blade of grass seemed to find nourishment. Boulders of every shape and size lay on top of each other in tall piles, or strewn all over. It looked as if a gigantic, natural tunnel had collapsed in prehistoric times.

It was difficult to find a continuous trail in the rubble. Occasionally a displaced rock or one that had been marked by a horse's hoof showed that the outlaws had ridden through there. Winnetou pointed ahead and said:

"In another two hours' ride from here, this confusion of stones will dip towards the large, green Elk Valley. We, however, will ride to the side here. Old Shatterhand and Old Firehand may dismount, give the horses to someone to lead, and then walk behind us to wipe out any possible tracks, so that the Yampa Utah don't notice that we've changed direction here!"

He turned left into the rubble. The two hunters obeyed his directive and only mounted their horses again when the group was far enough from the trail. The Apache proved that he possessed an incomparable sense of direction. It seemed as if no one would be able to find a way through the jumble; years had passed since Winnetou had been there last, and yet he recognized every rock, boulder, incline, or bend, so that he wasn't uncertain for even one moment about the direction he had to take.

The incline was very steep, until they reached a broad, desolate high plateau. They crossed it at a gallop. The sun had already disappeared behind the Rocky Mountains when they reached the end of the plateau, or rather came close to it, because the Apache stopped, pointed ahead and explained:

"Another five hundred paces further, and the rock falls as straight as a drop of water into the depth; on the other side it does just the same; in between, however, lies Elk Valley with good water and much forest. It only has one known entry, namely the one from which we've deviated; and only one exit, which leads to Silver-Lake. Old Shatterhand and I are the only people who know an additional access. We found it by chance when we were in danger. I will show it to you."

He approached the edge of the plateau. Boulder rubble lay there side by side, like a parapet, seemingly preventing a fall into the ghastly depth. The Apache disappeared from sight between two such pieces of rubble, and the others followed individually.

Oddly, there was a path. On the right hand side yawned the deep valley, where they were headed; but the path led to the left into the rock, and was so steep that the riders preferred to dismount and lead the horses. The immense, almost two-kilometre long and very broad rock colossus had sustained a crack, from the top to the bottom in various angles. Rubble and rocks had then rolled into it and formed a solid floor that could be trusted.

The horses were in no danger of sliding and falling since the bottom didn't consist of a smooth rock surface but of fairly solid gravel, which prevented slipping. The lower they moved the darker it became. Old Firehand had put Ellen on his horse and walked next to it, holding and supporting the girl. It seemed as though they had been climbing down into the deep for hours, until the steep passage suddenly stopped, the floor levelled out, and the rock crack became so wide that it formed a large hall without a roof. Winnetou stopped there and said:

"We're almost in the valley. We'll stay here until darkness permits us to get past the Utah. Move the horses to the back where they can drink, and apply gags to the prisoners, so that they can't make a noise!"

The Indians had also been forced to climb down the crack; hence the Whites had untied their feet. At that point the hunters tied them up again and also covered their mouths to prevent them from calling out. Shadowy twilight ruled the room, but the men's eyes were accustomed to the dark, almost like those of cats, and the hunters easily found their way around. At the back of the cleft the moisture from the rock walls collected in a small pond from which a small runnel flowed away; they couldn't see where to at that point.

Winnetou took several of the hunters along to show them the lay of the place. What they saw created no small amount of astonishment. At the front, where the hall narrowed again, there was an exit so tight that two men could hardly walk side by side. That corridor also sloped downwards, but it wasn't very long. After a few bends the men stood in front of a dense, natural curtain of climbing plants under which the water trickle vanished. Winnetou pushed the curtain aside a little, and the men could see forest, tree after tree in front of them, tall and powerful with such dense foliage that the last light of the day was unable to penetrate their crowns.

The Apache stepped outside to reconnoitre. When he returned he reported:

"To the right of us, north, therefore up the valley, there are many fires burning under the trees; that's where the Utah are camped. It is dark further down in the valley. That's where we have to go. Perhaps there are no Utah in that area. They would at most have posted two or three warriors at the exit of Elk Valley; they are easily rendered harmless, and we could leave the valley without exposing ourselves to too much danger—if the red-haired colonel does not occupy that spot. We must definitely find out what has happened to him. Hence I'll sneak to the fires to spy as soon as it has become dark. We can't move out before that's happened; until that time we must remain completely quiet."

He led the men back inside, to show them the rest of the place. That was necessary because everyone had to know where he was, and where there was a way out, in case of an emergency.

The prisoners were well fettered; however, each of them had a special guard assigned to them. If the Whites had been able to undo their ties the night before, then the Indians might easily do that as well.

Winnetou had been of the opinion that he alone should reconnoitre, but neither Old Shatterhand nor Old Firehand agreed with that. The undertaking would be so dangerous in that place that an individual scout could easily be prevented from returning, so the others wouldn't know what happened to him, nor how to help him. Therefore the two hunters wanted to go with him.

After they had waited for almost two hours, the three men departed. They sneaked out into the forest, and there stood still at first, to listen for any sound that would tell them whether or not someone was nearby. There was nothing to hear or even see. The fires were burning quite a distance away; there were many, and from their number the men deduced that an unusually large number of Utah were camped there.

The three sneaked forwards, from tree to tree, Winnetou ahead. The closer they came to the fires, the easier their task became because, looking towards the flames, they were able to see every object in front of them.

They moved along the left edge of the valley. The fires were situated more towards its centre. Perhaps the Indians didn't trust the cliff wall. The debris evidenced that, occasionally, pieces of rock crumbled away into the depth, smashed trees, and became deeply embedded in the ground. The three men advanced fairly quickly. They were parallel with the nearest fires. To the left of them, even further back, there was a very bright, tall fire, separate from all others. Around it sat five chiefs, their status indicated by the eagle feathers that adorned their hair.

At that moment one of them rose. He had cast off the war coat. His naked upper body was thickly painted with a bright yellow colour.

"*T'ab-Wagahre*[5]," Winnetou whispered. "He is the chief of the Capote Utah and possesses the strength of a bear. Look at his body! What thick, strong muscles, and what a broad chest!"

The Utah signalled to another chief, who rose as well. He was taller than the first, and no less powerful.

"That's *Tsu-In-Kuts*[6]," Old Shatterhand explained. "He carries that name because he once killed four buffaloes with four arrows."

---

[5] Yellow Sun
[6] Four Buffaloes

The two chiefs exchanged a few words with each other, and then left the fire. Perhaps they intended to inspect their guards. They avoided the other fires, and therefore drew nearer to the cliff wall.

"Ah!" Old Shatterhand said. "They'll pass by here quite closely. What do you think, Firehand? Shall we take them?"

"Alive?"

"Of course!"

"That would be a stroke of genius! Quickly, to ground; you'll take the first, I'll take the second!"

The two Utah came closer. One walked behind the other. Unexpectedly to figures rose next to them—two mighty punches, and the two Indians collapsed to the ground.

"Good!" Old Firehand whispered. "We've got them. Now quickly into our hide spot with them!"

Each hunter hoisted his captive over his shoulder. Winnetou received the instruction to wait, and then the men hurried away towards the rock hall. They delivered the two new prisoners, had them bound and gagged, and then returned to Winnetou, but not before issuing the order that none of the companions were to leave the hiding place before the three scouts had returned, no matter what happened.

Winnetou was still standing on the same spot. There was less of a need to eavesdrop on the other three chiefs, than there was to find out where Red Brinkley and his gang were. In order to reach that objective, the three daring men needed to sneak around the entire camp. They continued to walk along the cliff wall, leaving the fires behind to their left.

They were able to see quite well to that side; it was dark in front of them, and they had to be very careful. Where the eye couldn't penetrate, the touch of the hand was required. As usual, Winnetou sneaked ahead. He suddenly stopped and emitted an almost overly loud, and shocked: "Uff!" The other two also stopped and listened in anticipation. When Winnetou remained silent, Old Shatterhand quietly asked:

"What is it?"

"A human being," the Apache replied.

"Where?"

"Here, with me, in front of me, in my hand."

"Hold onto him! Don't let him scream!"

"He cannot scream; he is dead."

"Did you strangle him?"

"No. He was already dead; he's hanging on a stake."

"Oh dear Lord! At a torture stake?"

"Yes. His scalp is missing, and his body is full of wounds. He is cold, and my hands are wet from the blood."

They touched their way around the place and within ten minutes found near enough to twenty terribly mutilated corpses, which were tied to stakes and trees.

"Horrible!" Old Shatterhand groaned. "I believed we could still save these people, at least from such tortures! Indians usually wait until the next day; but they haven't wasted any time here."

"And the plan, the drawing!" Old Firehand said. "That's lost now."

"Not yet. We have captured the two chiefs. Maybe we can exchange them against the drawing."

"If it still exists and hasn't been destroyed!"

"Destroyed? Hardly! These Indians have learnt to appreciate the importance of such pieces of paper. They would much sooner destroy anything but a paper found on a White, especially if it is something hand-written, instead of printed. Don't worry about it yet. Besides, I've just realized why they killed these fellows so quickly here."

"Why?"

"To make room for us. Our arrival has been announced to them. We've not arrived yet; consequently they're expecting us tomorrow morning for sure, and if we're not here by then, they'll send out scouts."

"The messengers, who were sent here, have arrived, but not yet the Yampa Utah," Winnetou said.

"No, they're not here yet. It would probably have taken hours before they dared to pass the spot where we rested, and then follow us into the rock gorge. Perhaps they'll wait to come here since the last part of the way is so bad that the night...listen! Truly, they're coming, they're here!"

Above the spot where the three hunters were standing, there erupted a sudden, loud and joyful hullabaloo, which was replied to from the lower part of the camp. The Yampa Utah had arrived despite the dark of night as they were obviously familiar with the bad path. The hollering and yelling was so loud that one would be tempted to cover one's ears. Those around the campfires pulled burning logs from the flames to use as torches and ran towards the arrivals. The forest became illuminated and alive, so that the three hunters were in great danger of being discovered.

"We must get away," Old Firehand said. "But where? The place is full of people ahead of us, as well as behind us."

"Up into the trees," Old Shatterhand replied. "We can wait inside the dense foliage until the excitement has died down."

"Good, let's climb! Ah, Winnetou is already up there!"

Indeed, the Apache hadn't needed any encouragement. He'd pulled himself up and hid in the canopy. The other two followed his example by each climbing a tree nearby. There is no disgrace in hiding from such superior might.

The three men saw the Yampa and their allies arrive in the sheen of the fires and torches. They climbed down from their horses, which were taken away, and then asked about the arrival and capture of Winnetou and the Whites. The question was received with the greatest of bewilderment. The Yampa didn't want to believe that the group, whose trail they had followed, hadn't arrived. Questions were asked back and forth; a hundred speculations were voiced, but the truth remained a riddle.

It was of utmost importance for the other Utah to hear that Old Firehand, Old Shatterhand and Winnetou were nearby. The three men were able to gauge their reputation among those Indians from the immense effect the news had on them.

When the Yampa learnt that more than twenty whites had been tortured to death, they believed them to be those they were looking for and demanded to see them. They came along with torches to have a look, and thus afforded the three men hidden in the canopy a sight that was twice as ghastly in the uncertain, flickering illumination. The Yampa recognized that the corpses weren't the right ones, and took their anger out on them in an indescribable manner. Fortunately the scene was not of a long duration; it received an entirely unexpected ending.

To be precise, from the lower end of the valley came a long-drawn scream, which no one, who has ever heard it, will ever be able to forget, namely the death scream of a human being.

"Uff!" one of the chiefs standing under the trees said aghast. "What was that? Yellow Sun and Four Buffaloes are down there!"

There was a second, similar scream, and then the cracking of several shots.

"The Navajo, the Navajo!" the chief yelled. "Winnetou, Shatterhand and Firehand went to fetch them to exact revenge. Upon them, warriors, upon the dogs! Destroy them! Leave the horses where they are and fight on foot from behind the trees!"

The Indians ran about in great confusion for a moment. They went to grab their weapons and they tossed wood onto the fires to gain the necessary light for fighting. They shouted and hollered;

the forest reverberated from the war cries. Shots were fired; the noise came increasingly closer. Unfamiliar, dark figures rushed from tree to tree where their guns flashed upon discharge.

The Utah replied, first individually, here and there, and then combined into defensive groups. There was no actual, general battleground, unless one called the entire valley that; instead, individual battles developed around each fire.

Indeed, those were the Navajo; they had wanted to take the Utah unawares, but failed to silently kill the guards, who had been standing at the valley exit. The death screams of those had sounded the alarm, and it was thus a matter of fighting man against man, since they could not bring about a decision by surprise, to force victory by courage and superior numbers.

The Red Indians prefer to attack towards morning, when sleep, at least in those realms, is the deepest. It was difficult to assess why the Navajo had diverted from that rule. Perhaps they believed they could invade unnoticed, and then hurriedly shoot the enemies illuminated by the fires. When that had failed, their bravery hadn't allowed them to retreat; they advanced regardless and were forced to fight and sustain great losses.

It turned out that the Utah were in the majority; besides, they were more familiar with the terrain than the attackers, so the Navajo were pushed back gradually, although they fought bravely. There were battles fought across distances and at close quarters, with firearms, as well as with the knife or tomahawk. It was a very suspenseful scene for the three spectators, savages against savages in a most savage manner! There were two Indians involved in a battle amid the most brutal howling; in another spot several others butchered each other in demonic silence. Where one combatant fell, the victor was upon him immediately to take his scalp, only to lose his own the next moment, perhaps.

Of the three chiefs who had still been sitting around their fire, two were also fighting, so as to encourage their warriors by their example. The third leaned against a tree near the fire, sharply observed the course of the battle, and shouted his orders to his left and right. He was the general, so to speak, where all the strings of defence joined. Even when the Navajo were pushed increasingly further back, he remained standing where he was and didn't follow the advancement. He proudly intended to remain loyal to his spot, and left the pursuit of the enemies to the other chiefs.

The battle gradually drifted further and further away. The time had come for the three involuntary witnesses to get to safety. The way to their asylum was open. Later, if the battle took a reverse direction, or if the Utah returned as the victors, it would probably be impossible to get back to the hiding place unnoticed.

Winnetou climbed down from the tree. The others noticed it despite the darkness, and descended also. The Utah chief still stood against his tree. The din of the battle came from a considerable distance.

"Let's get back now!" Winnetou said. "The bonfires will be lit later, and then it will be too late for us."

"Shall we take this chief along?" Old Shatterhand asked.

"Yes. We'll easily catch him, because he's on his own. I will sneak up to..."

He cut himself short. And what he saw was eminently worthy of causing him great astonishment, and of making his words stick in his throat. To be precise: out of the dark, and as quick as a flash, jumped a short, skinny, limping fellow, who swung back his gun and with its butt knocked the chief to ground with a well-aimed strike. Then he grabbed the redskin by the scruff of his neck and swiftly dragged him away, into the dark. In the process of it, the three hunters heard the muffled, but nevertheless audible words:

"Wat Old Shatterhand and Old Firehand can do, dat can be done and mostly undershtood by us Saxons, too!"

"That's Hobble-Frank!" Old Shatterhand was astonished.

"Yes, Frank!" Old Firehand agreed. "The fellow is crazy! We must go after him immediately, so that he won't commit a stupidity!"

"Crazy? Certainly not! He's a comical little fellow; that's true; but his heart is exactly where it needs to be, and he's not careless at all. I've given him a good schooling and can say that I'm pleased with him. Nevertheless, let's follow him, because we're headed in the same direction."

They rushed away, after Hobble, into the dark. They had almost reached the entrance to their hiding place; a shot cracked just ahead of them.

"An Indian came upon him. Quickly on..." Old Shatterhand was about to say more, but didn't, because there was the laughing voice of Hobble:

"Numbskull, pay attention to where you aim! If you want to hit me, then you mustn't shoot at the moon! Here's your reward, and now good night!"

There was a cracking sound, as if made by a heavy punch, and then it was quiet again. The three men pushed on and came upon Hobble.

"Back!" he called out. "We shoot and stab here!"

"Stop, don't shoot!" Old Shatterhand warned. "What are you searching for out here?"

"Searching for? Nothing and naught at all. I don't have to search because I've already snatched a double foundling. You can thank God dat you've opened your mouth! If I hadn't recognized your conglomerate voice, by my soul, I would have shot you through and through. I've got two bullets in my shooting iron, which truly is no reason for jollity on account of my presence of mind and consubstantiality. I must warn you in all seriousness not to throw yourself at danger, and at me so blindly in the first and second instance, because thirdly, you might just be assembled to your forefathers and patriarchs at the speed of wind!"

Despite the grave situation, the two white hunters couldn't help laughing about the tirade. There was no enemy nearby for the moment, thus Old Shatterhand had no qualms about enquiring:

"But who gave you permission to leave the hiding place?"

"Permission? No one has to permit me anything. I'm my own master and fee tail owner. Solely the concern about you has caused me to don my cuirass. As soon as you had left, a brouhaha broke loose as if the Cimbri had invaded the Teutons. Dat in itself would have been bearable, because my nerves have been rubbed with tar and train oil. But when the shooting started afterwards I got worried and concerned about you. My childish nature is emotionally attached to your vital existence with fatherly devotion, and I cannot possibly tolerate it quietly when you're being cheated of your beautiful life by the redskins. Dat's why I grabbed my gun and sneaked away without any of the others noticing anything in dat Egyptian darkness. There was shooting to my left; you had wanted to go right; therefore I also turned to my right. And there shtood the chief against the tree like a marinated tailor's dummy. Dat vexed me, therefore I served him a vertical whack, so dat he came to ground horizontally. Of course I wanted to secure him successively and dragged him away; but he was a little too heavy for me after all, and I sat down on his corpus juris for a while to rest. Then came sneaking along one of them Francs-Tireurs and saw me against the light. He aimed his shooting iron; I knocked it aside and his bullet flew into the Milky Way. I, however, placed myself in such conjunction with him, with the aid of my rifle butt, that he buckled down next to the chief. Now both the fellows are lying there, without any and all sense and comprehension, and don't know what to think. What's the world coming to?"

"Be glad nothing worse happened! Had you come any earlier, then you would have been lost!"

"Don't you worry none! Hobble-Frank never arrives before he has victory in both hands. What will happen to these fellows now? I can't deal with them on my own."

"We'll help you. Let's get inside, quickly! The shooting has stopped down there, and it is to be expected that the Utah are returning."

The two unconscious Indians were brought into the hiding place, and bound and gagged just like the others. Then Winnetou and Old Firehand took up their positions beside the curtain of climbing plants to observe the events outside.

Indeed, the Utah returned as the victors. They lit twice as many fires, and with the burning pieces of wood they searched the forest for the dead and wounded. The Navajo had taken theirs with them, as was the Indian custom.

With each dead fellow warrior the Utah found, they raised a howl of lament and fury. The Indians collected the corpses, in order to bury them honourably. They were missing several people, who had undoubtedly been captured. The three chiefs, who went missing without leaving a trace behind, were thought to be among them. When that discovery was made the forest reverberated from the roar of the angry warriors. The remaining two leaders called together the most decorated of them for a powwow, during which loud, angry speeches were held.

That gave Winnetou the idea to sneak up and perhaps find out what the Utah were going to decide. It wasn't difficult for him. The Utah were convinced that they were alone in that place, and considered any caution as superfluous. The repelled Navajo were certainly not going to return; the Utah placed guards at the valley exit as a precaution. Of course they didn't realize that there were even more dangerous enemies than the Navajo right in the middle of the valley. Hence Winnetou heard everything that was being discussed.

They wanted to bury the dead during the night, but save the dirges for later. Their priority was to free the captured chiefs. That was even more important than to await the arrival of Winnetou and his white companions. Since the group was headed to Silver-Lake, the Utah were going to capture them anyway.

Because of their chiefs, the Indians had to break camp as soon as possible in order to free them. Hence preparations were required, so that they could start out on their pursuit ride at dawn.

At that point Winnetou slowly and cautiously retreated. When he arrived in the vicinity of their hiding place, he spotted several horses. The animals had become spooked during the fighting and had separated from the others; there were five. The Apache realized that their new captives had to be transported as well, three chiefs and a warrior. There were horses needed for that. No one was nearby. The animals didn't shy away when he approached them because he was an Indian. He grabbed one by the halter and led it into the hiding spot. Old Firehand was sitting behind the curtain and took it from him. Three more were moved inside in that manner; they snorted a little, but Winnetou soon calmed them down.

No one was bored inside the hiding spot. There was much to tell, to hear and—to overhear. Hobble-Frank had sat down beside his friend and kinsman, in complete darkness, of course. Before he met Droll, he was inseparable from Jemmy, the two being one heart and one soul, so to speak; but since he found the Alten-burgian Saxon, things had changed. Droll didn't aspire to be a learned scholar and let his short cousin speak without ever correcting him; that tied Hobble to him with a powerful force. Besides, Droll, the experienced Westerner, had a fair amount of respect for the short Saxon; he appreciated his good traits fully, and was mightily pleased about Hobble's act of heroism. The fact that Frank had first knocked the chief down, and then the other Indian, had not been the work of recklessness, but of reflection and presence of mind. The deed found general acknowledgment, and everyone had expressed their praise except one, namely Castlepool. At that point he made up for the omission. He was sitting beside short Hobble and asked:

"Frank, shall we bet?"

"I don't bet," Hobble replied.

"Why not?"

"I don't have any money for that."

"I'll lend it to you."

"*Borgen macht Sorgen*[7], as we say in Saxony. Besides, it is neither Christian nor contributionally social to lend money to a poor person only to weasel it off him again through a bet. You've

---

[7] Borrowing is worrying

come to the wrong person. I keep my money, even if I don't have any."

"But you might perhaps win!"

"Wouldn't think of it! I don't feel like getting rich with betting. There's no blessing in it. I've got my fundamental maxims and contrasts, and I absolutely refuse to confuse them."

"That's a pity. I planned on losing on purpose this one time, as a kind of reward for your heroic deed."

"Every heroic deed rewards itself deep within and on its own. One carries the accusative recognition in one's own and holiest localities of the heart. *Dem Verdienste seine Krone, und den andern nich die Bohne*[8]! And besides, methinks rewarding lords and heroes by means of a bet is a multiplied custom to say the least. May those give who want to give, and in fact direct, with the hand into the mouth, not indirect through a false bet. Dat's custom in all elevated-culture nations and dat's why it's no different within the vicinity of my own personality."

"In that case you wouldn't be offended if I gave you a present?"

"I would very much! Hobble-Frank won't have anything given to him; he's got far too majestic ambitions for dat; but a memento, which the conscientious Frenchman calls a souvenir and cataplasm, dat may well be given to me, without having to worry about composing the lyra strings of my nature into ill-humoured secondary sounds."

"Alright, in that case you'll have a—memento. I hope that it will please you. I have two and can spare one."

He placed one of his splendid rifles into Hobble-Frank's hands. But Frank pushed it back and said:

"Listen, milord, dat's where the joke ends! Don't attack me where I can become pernicious! I smile gladly and sincerely, but I can also pull canon faces, if someone steps too close to my unguarded interference. A little joke is good and also readily digestible for the benefit of one's health; but I won't tolerate having my leg pulled; because I think much too highly and diagonally of myself!"

"But I'm not making a joke; I'm completely serious!"

"Wat? You really want to release this rifle from your property?"

"Yes," the Englishman replied.

"And make it a gift to me as a *bona immobilia*?"

"That's how it is."

---

[8] To the merit its crown, to the others the frown

"Then hand it over, quickly hand it over, before you change your mind! Delusion is short, like Jemmy, but remorse is long, like Davy, sings Freiligrath. This rifle be my property, my irrefutable and concentrated property! I feel like I'm opening my Christmas presents today! I'm beside myself with joy! I'm utterly complexed and overawed! Milord, should you ever need a good friend, who'll stick by you through thick and thin, then you only have to whistle and I'll immediately be *a present*! How shall I thank you? Do you want to shake hands, or let me give you a lucrative kiss, or an interim embrace on behalf of the whole world?"

"A handshake will suffice."

"Good! *Tu l'a voulu*, Anton. Here's my hand. Shake; squeeze it as long as it pleases you. I'll have it at your daily service henceforth, as often as I don't require it myself, because gratitude is a virtue, and you'll find it with me. Droll, kinsman from Altenburg, did you hear wat today's good fortune has bestowed upon me with all due respect?"

"Yes," Droll replied. "If you were anyone else, I'd envy you, but because you're my friend and cousin, I'm pleased for you from the bottom of my heart. Congratulations!"

"Thank you, I wish you the same! Hooray, dat will be some shooting from now on! I will put my millennium in its place with this rifle, without advocate or protocol. Here, milord, is my hand once again; shake it; keep shaking it; I'll gladly tolerate it. You Englishmen are quite splendid fellows; and if necessary, then I'll state it writing with my handwritten signature. Count me among your most intimate house and family friends from here on in. As soon as I get to Newskij Prospect in London I'll visit you. You don't have to be embarrassed; I'm modesty personified and make do with anything."

He was ever so happy about the gift and carried on for a while with his idiosyncratic soliloquy, which greatly amused the others.

Fortunately it was so dark that he couldn't see the faces of his companions.

Because the men expected to experience significant exertions the next day, lots were drawn to set guard duties. Everyone tried to sleep, but no one succeeded in doing so for a long time. They only fell asleep after midnight, but were woken up again at dawn because the departure of the Indians took place amid excessive noise.

When silence fell in the valley, the Apache slipped outside to ascertain whether or not it was safe yet to leave the hiding place.

He brought positive news. Not a single Utah was left in the valley. The group was able to leave the hiding spot, which had provided enough space, but had been uncomfortable because of the horses.

As a precautionary measure they first posted a guard each at the entry and exit points of the valley, and then went about to inspect it. They found a mass grave. It consisted of a rock pile erected above the corpses. There were also several dead horses; stray bullets had hit them. The Indians had left them behind unused; the Whites were smarter. Their trail to Silver-Lake led them through desolate regions, especially since the group had to avoid getting too close to the Utah, and those areas were devoid of any plant and animal life. It wasn't easy to find enough food there. The dead horses were quite opportune. A Westerner isn't choosy; he satiates his hunger with the meat of a horse if he has nothing better. When he is a guest of the Indians, he is often served fattened dog during a feast! The men carved out the best pieces, distributed them, and lit several fires where everyone was able to roast his ration to preserve it.

That wasn't a loss of time because they couldn't follow the Indians immediately. It was also wiser to prepare readily consumable portions at that point, rather than waste precious time with it later on. Of course their own horses were left to graze and drink water to replenish their energy for the upcoming ride.

After the Utah had left, the prisoners were freed from their gags. They could therefore breathe freely and speak. Yellow Sun was the first to utilize the opportunity. He lay still for a long time, but had observed the Whites' preparations, and gave each one a scrutinizing, dark gaze. At that point he turned to Old Shatterhand:

"Which one among you has knocked me to the ground? How dare you take us prisoner and tie us up; we have not harmed you!"

"Do you know who we are?" the hunter replied.

"I know Winnetou, the Apache, and know that Old Shatterhand and Old Firehand are with him."

"I am Old Shatterhand, and it was my fist that knocked you to the ground."

"Why?"

"To render you harmless."

"Are you saying that I intended to harm you?"

"Yes."

"That's a lie!"

"Don't bother trying to fool me! I know everything. We were supposed to be killed here, although we've smoked the pipe of peace with the Utah. The Yampa sent you messengers yesterday, and then came here, too. Every untruth you utter is spoken in vain. We know where we stand and don't believe a single word you say."

The chief turned his head and fell silent. In his stead the ordinary warrior, who had been knocked down by Hobble-Frank outside the hideaway spoke up:

"Are the palefaces enemies of the Utah?"

"We're friends of all red men; but we will defend ourselves if we are treated with hostility by them."

"The Utah have raised the war hatchets against the palefaces. You are famous warriors and don't fear them. But do you also know that the Navajo are moving against them, to help the palefaces?"

"Yes."

"The Navajo are Apache, and the most famous chief of that nation, Winnetou, is your friend and companion; he is among you. I see him standing there with the horses. Why do you knock down a warrior of the Navajo and tie his arms and legs?"

"Are you referring to yourself?"

"Yes. I'm a Navajo."

"Why aren't you painted with the colours of your tribe?"

"To get revenge."

"And why were you still here when your other warriors had already retreated?"

"Because of my revenge. My brother was fighting at my side and was killed by a chief of the Utah dogs. I took his body to safety, so that they couldn't take his scalp, and then returned to avenge his death, although my warriors had already withdrawn. I sneaked past the enemies without being spotted. A chief had bludgeoned my brother to death; a chief was going to give his scalp in return. I knew that one of them had remained in the valley, and I wanted to find him. That's when I saw two men in my way, a dead one and a live one. The latter saw me, too; I was revealed and wanted to shoot him; he was faster than I and knocked me down. When I woke up I lay in darkness and was fettered. Call Winnetou to join us! He doesn't know me; but if I'm permitted to speak with him, then I can prove that I'm a Navajo, not a Utah. After I had handed my brother to my comrades, I wiped the war paint from my face, so that the Utah wouldn't recognize me as an enemy."

"I believe you; you're a Navajo and shall be free."

At that moment Yellow Sun interjected:

"He is a Utah, one of my warriors, a coward who wants to save himself with a lie!"

"Shut up!" Old Shatterhand ordered him. "If he really were one of your warriors, then you wouldn't betray him. The fact that you want to ruin him proves that he spoke the truth. You're a chief, but your soul is that of a despicable coward!"

"Don't insult me," the other barked. "I have the power to destroy all of you. If you take our fetters of we'll forgive you. But if you don't do that, then a thousand indescribable tortures await you!"

"I laugh at your threat, you're at our mercy and we'll do anything we like with you. The quieter you surrender to your fate, the more bearable it will be. We're Christians and don't enjoy causing pain to our enemies."

While he spoke he untied the young Navajo. The Indian jumped up, stretched and flexed his limbs, and then said:

"Give these dogs into my hands, so that I can take their scalps! The more lenient you are with them, the more they will deceive you."

"You'll not have one part of them," Old Shatterhand replied. "You might be travelling with us; but if you dare to even touch a hair on them, then I'll kill you with my own two hands. They can only be of use to us alive; their demise, on the other hand, will be detrimental to us."

"Of what use will they be?" the Indian said with contempt. "These dogs are good for nothing."

"I don't have to explain that to you. If you wish to get back to your tribe safely, then you'll have to comply with our will."

The expression on the Navajo's face clearly showed that he disliked having to give up on his intentions; but he had to resign himself to it. To make a concession of sorts, Old Shatterhand assigned him to guard the imprisoned Utah and promised him the scalp of any of them who dared to make an attempt at escaping. That assuaged the man, and was a smart arrangement at the same time, because there couldn't be a more attentive and tireless guard than the Navajo who was so greedy for the scalps of the prisoners.

Afterwards, they had to give priority to inspecting the dead outlaws. They were a sight the description of which is best omitted. The men had died amid enormous torture. The hunters standing beside the corpses had seen and experienced much during their lifetime; but they couldn't fend off a shudder when they saw the mutilated bodies and disfigured limbs. The outlaws had reaped what they had sowed. The colonel had fared the worst. He was hanging on the stake upside down. He was naked, just like all of his comrades; the redskins had distributed the clothes among themselves, and hadn't left the smallest shred of fabric behind on the scene.

"What a pity!" Old Firehand said. "If only we had been able to come here earlier to prevent the killing of these people!"

"Pshaw!" old Missouri-Blenter said. "You don't feel sorry for these fellows, do you? And even if we had arrived in time, and you would have been able to save them, the colonel would have had to die anyway. My knife would have said a word or two to him."

"I didn't mean it this way, because I'm not sorry about their demise, although I wish it could have been less cruel. But the paper, the piece of paper, the drawing that the colonel carried on him! I wanted to have it; we needed it! And now it's gone; lost for good."

"Perhaps we'll find it. We will definitely encounter the Utah again, and then it will somehow be possible to get at his suit, which we can then examine."

"Hardly! We don't even know what he wore last; the garments wouldn't have remained together as a suit, they were distributed among several Indians. How are we going to piece them back together? The drawing is lost, and the old chief Ikhatshi-Tatli, who gave Engel the document to copy, is dead; there won't be a second one."

"You forget that the chief had a grandson and a great-grandson," Watson, the erstwhile overseer, cut in. "Although they weren't present at the time, the old man's hut is their home nevertheless. Perhaps they're still up there. It goes without saying that they know the secret. They can certainly be persuaded, whether by hook or by crook is all the same, to tell us."

"An Indian won't be forced to divulge something like that, especially not if it's about gold and silver; he'd rather die than help the loathsome White to get his hands on such wealth."

"That begs the question whether or not they'll count us among the loathsome ones. The two bears might be friendly towards Whites."

"Bears?" Old Firehand exclaimed. "Tarnation! How could I have overlooked that? Of course! Great Bear and Little Bear! Why didn't I think of the two Tonkawa; they were on board the steamer with us! Nintropan-Hauey and Nintropan-Homosh!"

"Father and son Nintropan live at Silver-Lake," Winnetou confirmed. "I know them; they are my friends and have always been friendly towards the palefaces."

"Indeed they do, which means there's hope they'll supply us with the required information. Unfortunately there is a battle about to rage up there, and the Utah will be between us and the lake. We might not get through."

"We don't need to get through the Utah to reach the lake; because I know a trail that no Utah and no White has walked on. It is very cumbersome, but if we move out soon, we will arrive at the Lake before them, and even before the Navajo."

"Then let's make haste. We've got no other task here than to bury these Whites; we can't simply leave them hanging here. It won't take long if we place them side by side and cover them with rocks. We'll be on our way immediately after that. I hope for the best, especially since we've got so many hostages with which we can force the Utah to accept a peace proposal."

Fred Engel At Silver-Lake

8

At Silver-Lake

A scene of enormous proportions opened up before the eyes of the Whites when they approached their destination after an arduous ride of several days. They were moving up a slowly ascending canyon with sides of mighty, soaring rock masses, and with a gloss of colour that nearly blinded the observer. Colossal rock pyramids, one standing next to the other, or forming a staggered backdrop, were reaching skywards in individually coloured layers and storeys. Some of those pyramids formed straight, vertical walls, others rocky castles or fantastic citadels with their many pillars and protruding edges, needles and crags. The sun stood at an angle high above the magnificent formations and gave them an indescribably rich colouration. Some of the rock layers shimmered in the brightest blue, others in deep golden red; between them lay stratums that gleamed in yellow, olive-green and fiery copper, while a saturated blue shadow rested inside the grooves. But the splendour, which almost caused the eyes of the onlookers to overflow, was dead; it was lacking life and movement. There was no drop of water between the rocks; no blade of grass found nourishment in the deep bottom, not one twig was sprouting from the barren walls, not one leaf, the green of which would have soothed the eye, was evident.

However, the clearly visible traces along the rocks on both sides evidenced that there had to be water at certain times. The dry canyon would then have formed the bed of a river that emptied its broad, deep, raging floods into the Colorado. At such times, the gorge would be impassable for any human foot, and even the most daring Westerner or Indian would hardly risk his life in a swaying, fragile canoe on the rushing waves.

The bottom of the canyon correspondingly consisted of a deep layer of rounded pebbles packed with sand. In consequence, the trail was very arduous because the round stones gave way under the hooves of the horses and tired the animals, so that the group had to stop from time to time to let them rest.

Old Firehand, Old Shatterhand and Winnetou were riding ahead. Firehand gave the surroundings conspicuous attention. IIe was obviously searching for something that was of importance to him. Where two mighty pillars were leaning away from each other, and leaving a gap at the bottom, he stopped his horse, gave the spot a probing look, and then said:

"This must be the place where I came out after I had found the vein. I don't think I'm mistaken."

"And you want to go in there?" Old Shatterhand asked.

"Yes. And you'll come along."

"Is the cleft that long? It seems to be quite short."

"Let's see. It is possible that I'm mistaken."

He wanted to dismount and inspect the opening; but the Apache steered his horse towards the narrow gap between the rocks. Quietly and confidently, as was his manner, he said:

"My brothers follow me, because the trail that commences here will cut off a large stretch of the route. Besides, it is much more comfortable for the horses than the gravel bottom of the canyon."

"Do you know this cleft?" Old Firehand sounded surprised.

"Winnetou knows all the mountains, valleys, gorges and clefts precisely; you know that he never errs."

"That's true. But it is odd that you know especially this place, and can say that it is the beginning of a trail. Do you know the region it leads into?"

"Yes. This crack will become narrower first; then it widens very much, not simply to become another canyon, but to turn into a flat rocky plateau, like a giant table, which gradually rises."

"That's correct, indeed! I'm therefore at the right spot. That plateau rises for several hundred feet. And what comes after it? Do you know?"

"The upper edge of the plateau falls away with a sheer drop, into a large, round basin from where a narrow, serpentine path leads up into the broad, beautiful valley of Silver-Lake."

"That's also correct. Have you been in that basin?"

"Yes."

"Have you perhaps come across anything peculiar?"

"No. There is absolutely nothing, no water, no grass, and no animal. No beetle or ant crawls across the eternally dry rock."

"In that case I'll prove to you that there is something to be found after all, and it is much more precious than water and grass."

"Do you mean the silver vein you've discovered?"

"Yes. There is not only silver, but also gold. The mountain valley is my reason for having undertaken the long ride. Let's go and turn off here!"

They rode inside the gap, individually, one behind the other, because there was not enough room for two to ride abreast. But soon the space between the rock walls began to widen; the gigantic pillars opened up and there lay before the riders a mighty, smooth, triangularly shaped rock plateau, which gradually rose between the receding walls on either side, and at its furthest reaches ended in a straight line against the bright sky.

That's where their ride took them. It looked as though the horses had to climb a huge roof, but the slope was not significant enough to pose great difficulties. The group needed probably an hour to arrive up top, from where the rocky high plateau stretched away west for several kilometres. In the foreground, however, they saw the deep, sunken basin of which Old Firehand and Winnetou had spoken. From their vantage point they spotted the dark streak that led south out of the basin; it was the narrow cleft that would take them to Silver-Lake.

They began their descent into the depth. The downslope was so steep that they had to dismount. There were also dangerous passages. The prisoners were untied and taken from their horses, so that they could walk. The young Navajo stayed close behind them and didn't leave them out of his sight. After the arrival at the bottom, they had to mount up and be fettered again.

At that point Old Firehand wished to show his find to the comrades; but the Utah weren't to know about it. Hence they were taken a stretch into the exit opening, under the guard of several rafters and the Navajo. The others hadn't even mounted up. The news that they were at their long-awaited destination, the site of the discovery, caused general excitement.

The basin-shaped depression had a diameter of almost two kilometres. Its floor consisted of deep sand, mixed with smooth pebbles of varying sizes but no larger than a man's fist. At that point, the knowledge of two men became important, namely that of Old Firehand, who had to indicate the vein, and that of Butler, the engineer, whose task it was to assess the technical requirements for making the exploitation of the find possible. The latter cast a scrutinizing gaze all around, and then said:

"It is possible that we could encounter a rich bonanza. If there really is precious metal here, then we can expect it to be present in great quantities. This immense depression was washed out of the surrounding rock during a centuries-long process. The water flowed in here from the south through the rocky narrows, and because it couldn't go any further, it formed a whirlpool that gradually removed the rock and ground it to gravel and sand. We're standing on the sediment that gradually built up. It is bound to contain the washed-down metals, which were heavier than the rest of the debris and thus sank the deepest and are lying beneath the sand. If we dig down for a few cubits we'll soon find out whether our trip was successful or in vain."

"We won't need to dig. Wouldn't it suffice to show that the shores of the erstwhile water hole contain the sought-after metal?" Old Firehand asked.

"Indeed. If there is gold and silver in the walls, then the floor of this basin is certainly also impregnated by the metals."

"Then come! I'll furnish such proof."

He walked straight to a spot that he seemed to know well. The others followed; they were in the grip of great tension.

"Cousin, my heart is missing a few beats," Hobble-Frank confessed to his Altenburg kinsman. "If we happen to find silver here, or even gold, then I'll fill all my pockets and go back home to Saxony. I'll build myself a so-called villa next to the lovely banks of the River Elbe, and stick my head out of the window all day long just to show people wat a noble and splendid fellow I've turned out to be."

"And I'll buy a farmstead with twenty horses and eighty cows and produce nothing but Quaercher and goats cheese," Droll replied. "Det's what actually matters the most in the dukedom of Altenburg."

"What if we don't find anything?"

"Well, if there is nothing to be found, then there's nothing we can do. But methinks we'll be lucky, because it is self-evident det there has to be silver somewhere near Silver-Lake."

His confidence wouldn't be disappointed. Old Firehand had arrived at a spot along the rock wall that was undercut and crumbling. He pulled out a loose rock, another, and several more, and opened a crack behind them. It had formed naturally, but had been widened mechanically, which was clearly evident. Old Firehand reached inside and said:

"I've taken some of what is lying in here with me and had it assessed. Now let's see if Butler's assessment is the same."

When he pulled back his hand, he held in it a white, brown-tarnished, and wire-like structure that he handed to the engineer. As soon as Butler looked at it, he exclaimed:

"Heavens! That's pure, solid silver! And that's what's been in this crevice originally?"

"Yes, the entire fissure was full of it. It seems to run deep into the rock, and be very rich in metal."

"This means I can almost guarantee extremely rich yields here. There will definitely be more such clefts and cracks that contain pure metal."

"And even solid veins with ore, as I'll show you right now," Old Firehand smiled.

He pulled out a second, much larger object and gave it to the engineer. It was a big piece of ore, twice as large as a fist. Butler studied it attentively, only to call out:

"Of course a chemical analysis would be much more precise; but I'd like to swear that we're dealing here with horn silver, meaning chlorargyrite, or cerargyrite!"

"That's correct. The chemical test results show that it is horn silver."

"How great is the percentage?"

"Seventy-five percent silver."

"What a find! And indeed, in Utah one finds chiefly horn silver. Where is the vein in question?"

"Further back in the basin, on the other side. I've covered it thickly with gravel, but will show it to you. And now, what's this?"

He pulled several hazelnut-sized grains out of the crack.

"Nuggets, gold!" the engineer was excited. "Also from here?"

"Yes. We were hiding here once and couldn't get away because the Indians were waiting in ambush. We had no water and I dug down into the sand to see whether the ground contained moisture. There was no water, but I found several of these nuggets."

"Which means there are also gold deposits here, just like I said before! Old Firehand, here lie millions of dollars worth of metals, and the one who discovered it is a wealthy man!"

"Only the one who discovered it? You shall all share in it. I'm the one who discovered it, Mr Butler is the engineer, and the others will help to exploit it. I've invited you along for that purpose. We'll set down the conditions of our cooperation and determine each person's share later."

Those remarks caused general jubilation that wouldn't abate. Then Old Firehand showed the others the ore vein, which was quite significant. It was to be expected that it wasn't the only one. Most of the men would have loved to begin searching right there and then, but Old Shatterhand stopped them and warned:

"Not so hastily, gentlemen! We've got other matters to think of first. We're not up here alone."

"But we've arrived here ahead of the Indians," Castlepool said. Although he didn't lay claim to any of the precious metal finds, he nevertheless was just as pleased as the others about it.

"Ahead of them, yes, but not by very much. The Navajo who's with us knows the withdrawal route of his fellow warriors precisely. He calculated that they'll arrive at the lake only a few hours after us, and the Utah will definitely be right behind them. We've got no time to lose and must prepare for it."

"That's true," Old Firehand agreed. "But I would still like to know whether the exploitation of the metals here will cause us great difficulties or not. Mr Butler will probably only require a few minutes to be able to tell us. Mr Butler, would you be able to give us an answer, please?"

Mr Butler searched the surroundings with a long gaze, and then said:

"We need water above all. Where's the nearest source?"

"Silver-Lake."

"How far is it from here?"

"We'll be there in two hours."

"Is it situated at a higher level than this valley?"

"Significantly so."

"In that case the required gradient is available. The question is: will there be a possibility of diverting it to here?"

"Yes, through the narrow cleft, which is the only access between this basin and the vicinity of the lake."

"That's important, because I can thus assume the supply won't encounter insurmountable obstacles. But we'll need pipelines, metal ones later; the first lot can be made of timber. Is that available around here?"

"Masses of it. Silver-Lake is entirely surrounded by forest."

"That's splendid! We might not necessarily have to fit the entire stretch with pipes. We could build a reservoir at an elevated position. The water could be left to flow freely from the lake to the reservoir. From there it would have to be fed into pipes, so that we achieve the necessary pressure."

"Ah, because of the water jets?"

"Yes. Of course we'll be careful not to work the rock with pickaxe and shovel. We'll water-blast it, and use explosives only where the jets are ineffective. The same goes for the floor that contains metal; it will be treated with water."

"But then we'd have to have an outflow, otherwise the basin will fill up and we won't be able to work."

"Yes, the outflow! There isn't one here, and yet it will have to be created. A pump or a paternoster will do initially to lift the water across the heights from which we've come. From there it will run down the crack and into the canyon. I'll give some thought to the matter of how to accomplish this, while we ride up to the lake. Of course we'll require machinery that we don't have; but that should not create any difficulties. All of that could be organized within one month. There are only two issues that alarm me somewhat."

"Which ones?"

"Firstly the Indians. Shall we gradually be slaughtered by them?"

"We don't have to worry about that. Old Shatterhand, Winnetou and I are on very friendly terms with the tribes in question, so that we can easily come to a friendly agreement with them."

"Good! But the land? Who owns it?"

"The Timbabachi. Winnetou's influence will sway them to sell it to us."

"And will the government acknowledge that purchase?"

"I'd like to see the man who will dispute my rights to it! That issue doesn't cause me any pains whatsoever."

"That satisfies my concerns. The main thing is the water supply to this valley, and I'll inform myself about it during the ride. Let's go!"

The men covered the small crack that Old Firehand had opened, as well as the ore vein; and then everyone mounted up to continue the interrupted ride.

The prisoners and their guards had been waiting in the rock cleft, which was a sort of hollow ravine: a gutter that wound its way upwards. Water had at some time in the distant past eaten a gulch into the rock and thus created a trail uphill that was between two and five metres wide. It, too, was entirely devoid of vegetation. The water flow had completely dried up and perhaps carried a little water only in spring, which wasn't capable of bringing forth plant life.

The two hours were almost up when the erstwhile stream bed suddenly widened to form a place that contained a pool of water, framed by cliffs. There was grass for the first time after a long ride. The horses had suffered considerably because of the heat, the lack of water and the bad trail. They didn't want to obey the reins any longer, and instead wanted to eat. Hence the riders dismounted to let them have their will. They sat together in individual groups and conversed about the future riches they'd soon own. Enemy Indians weren't suspected to be nearby; the group only wanted to rest for a short while, hence no one considered it necessary to post guards.

The engineer had given the track on the way up his undivided attention; at that point he expressed his findings:

"I'm very satisfied so far. The hollow ravine affords more than enough room for not only a water pipe, but also the transport of any equipment we require. If our demands are met like this henceforth, then I must say that nature is accommodating us in a very friendly manner."

"Listen!" Hobble-Frank said and elbowed Droll in the ribs. "Did you hear dat? My villa could become reality."

"And so could my farmstead! Well, rejoice Altenburg, when the most famous of your sons drives up with a twenty cubits-long money bag! Cousin, come here, I must kiss you!"

"Not yet!" Frank warded him off. "The riches are still lying in the lap of time secreted in the confernal future tense, and as cautious people we must beware dat my villa and your farmstead could vanish into a substantial nothing. As the born Saxon and learned crafty devil dat I am, I don't doubt in the least that my hopes will absolve themselves into the most beautiful fulfilment, but it is still too early for kisses. I'm..."

He was cut short, because the engineer called out in a worried tone of voice:

"Ellen! Where is Ellen? I don't see her!"

The girl had not only encountered the first grass in two days, but also spotted a few flowers, and had rushed along to pluck them for her father. The moisture of the nearby lake penetrated as far as that spot; that's why the vegetation began where the group had paused. It became lusher the further up it grew, and covered the entire continuation of the hollow ravine that led up to the lake. Ellen had walked on without a care. She continued to pluck flowers until she came to a bend. Then she remembered that she ought not be walking so far away from the others. She had just attempted to turn around when three men came walking around the bend, three armed Indians. The girl was paralysed with fear, wanted to call for help, but was unable to utter a sound. Indians have presence of mind by education; they act fast and decisively in any situation. As soon as the three men spotted the girl, two of them lunged forwards to grab her. One put his hand over her mouth; the other held his knife up to her and warned in broken English:

"Quiet, or dead!"

The third hastily sneaked forwards and investigated to whom the white girl belonged, because it was obvious she wasn't on her own. He returned after two minutes and whispered a few words to his companions. Ellen couldn't understand them. Then they dragged her away. She didn't dare to make a sound.

After a short while the hollow rock alley was at an end; it opened up onto a shallow mountain ridge the lower reaches of which were studded with bushes that merged into a forest. Ellen was pulled between the bushes, and then towards the trees, where a number of Indians were sitting. Their weapons were lying next to them on the ground; they grabbed them and jumped up as soon as they saw their comrades arrive with the girl.

Ellen didn't understand a word of what they were saying; but she saw their gazes threateningly directed at her and thus believed she was in grave danger. That's when she remembered the totem that Little Bear had given her on the boat. He had said that the writing would protect her from any hostility. "His shadow is my shadow, and his blood is my blood; he is my older brother," was its content. She pulled out the cord on which she had the totem secured around her neck, untied it and gave it to the Indian she thought was the most dangerous on account of his grim face.

"Nintropan-Homosh," she said as she handed it to him because she had repeatedly heard that Little Bear was named thus in his own language.

The Indian unfolded the piece of leather, looked at the figures, emitted a shout of surprise and gave the totem to the one next to him. It went from hand to hand. The faces became friendlier, and the one who had addressed Ellen before, asked:

"Who gave you?"

"Nintropan-Homosh," she replied.

"Young chief?"

"Yes," she nodded.

"Where?"

"On the boat."

"Large fire canoe?"

"Yes."

"On Arkansas?"

"Yes."

"Correct. Nintropan-Homosh was on Arkansas. Who—men—there?"

He pointed back to the hollow ravine.

"Winnetou, Old Firehand, Old Shatterhand."

"Uff!" he called out, and "uff!" called the others also. He wanted to ask more questions; but there was a rustle in the bushes and the Whites with the three hunters in the lead rushed out from between them to surround the Indians immediately. Winnetou had discovered their tracks and the men had immediately followed them. The Indians didn't make any attempt at resisting because they knew they weren't going to be harmed. The one who had sneaked back into the ravine to investigate the group had obviously not noticed Winnetou; he knew him from earlier times and recognized him then.

"The great chief of the Apache!" he called out. "This white girl possesses the totem of Little Bear and is therefore our friend. We took her with us because we didn't know whether the men who belonged to her were our friends or foes."

The Indians wore blue and yellow paint on their faces; that caused Winnetou to ask:

"Are you warriors of the Timbabachi?"

"Yes."

"Which chief is leading you?"

"*Tshia-Nitsas¹.*"

The man was obviously famous on account of his keen hearing.

"Where is he?" Winnetou asked further.

"At the lake."

"How many warriors are here?"

"One hundred."

"Are other tribes here as well?"

"No. Another two hundred Navajo warriors will join us here, to fight against the Utah. We want to move north with them to also fetch the Utah scalps."

"Beware that they don't take yours. Have you posted guards?"

"Why? We're not expecting any enemies."

"There are more enemies approaching than you'd like. Is Great Bear at the lake?"

"Yes, and Little Bear as well."

"Lead us to them!"

Just then the rafters with the horses and the prisoners exited from the hollow ravine, because the hunters had followed Ellen on foot. Everyone mounted up and the Timbabachi rode ahead to lead them. No one was more relieved about the outcome of the brief adventure than the engineer, who had suffered great fear for the safety of his daughter.

The trail led all the way up the mountain ridge, and then along it for a stretch under the trees. Then the ground dipped away on the other side, and soon shimmering water came into view.

"Silver-Lake," Old Shatterhand said while he turned around to the companions behind him. "We've reached our destination at last."

"But we'll probably not find much peace," Old Firehand said. "We might just get to smell the smoke of a lot of gunpowder."

Before long they were able to overlook the entire scenery, and it was truly magnificent.

Towering rock bastions, gleaming in all colours like those in the canyon, enclosed a valley that was perhaps a two hours' ride long and half as wide. Behind those bastions more and new mountain giants rose, one lifting its head above the other. But those mountains and rocks weren't bare. Inside the countless clefts that crisscrossed them grew trees and bushes; the lower down the denser the forest, which extended to the lake shore and left only a small strip of grass along the water. There were several huts on

---

¹ Long Ear

the grass strip near which a number of canoes had been tied up on the shore.

In the middle of the lake lay a green island with a peculiar adobe building. It seemed to originate from a time before the present Indians had pushed the ancient inhabitants out. The island was circular with a diameter of perhaps one hundred paces. The old building was entirely overgrown with flowering climbers; the rest of the island had been cultivated like a garden and planted out with flowers and shrubs.

The forest mirrored its canopy in the water of the lake, and the mountain tops threw their shadows over the alpine mere. Yet it was neither green, nor blue or dark coloured at all; its gleam was of a silvery grey. Not a breath of air disturbed the water. If it were possible at all, then one could have been forgiven for thinking that it was a bowl full of quicksilver.

Indians were sitting or lying around and inside the huts; they were the one hundred Timbabachi. The arrival of the Whites caused a bit of a stir among them; but since their companions rode in the lead, they quickly calmed down.

The arrivals hadn't quite reached the huts when two men came out of the building on the island. The Apache cupped his hands around his mouth and called across the water:

"Nintropan-Hauey! Winnetou has arrived!"

There was a reply shout; then the people on the shore observed the two men climb into a canoe that was moored at the island, and paddle across to shore. They were father and son Nintropan. Their astonishment at seeing so many familiar faces was certainly great, but they didn't reveal it with a single expression on their face. When Great Bear had climbed from the canoe, he shook Winnetou's hand and said:

"The great chief of the Apache is everywhere, and where he goes he gladdens peoples' hearts. I also greet old Shatterhand, whom I know, and Old Firehand, who was on the boat with me!"

When he spotted Aunty Droll, a smile flew across his face after all; he remembered the encounter with the droll fellow on board the paddle steamer and shook Aunty's hand while he said:

"My white brother is a brave man; he has killed the panther, and I welcome him."

And so he went from man to man, to shake hands with each one. His son was still too young; he wasn't yet permitted to put himself on an even par with the famous warriors and hunters, but it was no offence to talk to Ellen. After he had tied up the canoe, he approached her as she climbed from the sedan. During his journeys he might have observed how ladies and gentlemen greet each other, and thought it advisable to demonstrate that he hadn't forgotten it. Hence he took the hat from his head, waved it a little, bowed and said in broken English:

"Little Bear didn't think it would be possible to see the white miss again. What is the destination of her journey?"

"We don't want to travel any further than to Silver-Lake," she replied.

A red flush of joy went across his face, and he couldn't suppress an expression of astonishment.

"Will the miss stay here for a while?" he asked.

"I'll be here for some time," she replied.

"Then I ask for the permission to be with her all the time. She shall get to know all the plants and flowers. We will fish on the lake and hunt in the forest; but I must always be near her because there are wild animals and hostile people around. Will she permit me that?"

"Gladly. I will feel much safer in your company, than I would on my own, and I am pleased that you are here."

She offered her hand to him, and truly, he lifted it up to his lips and executed another bow like a genuine gentleman!

The Timbabachi led the horses of the new arrivals into the forest, where theirs were already grazing. Their chief had thus far proudly remained in his hut and at that point slowly emerged, fairly annoyed about the fact that no one had taken notice of him. He was a gloomy fellow with long legs and arms, which gave him a look not unlike that of an orangutan. He hadn't been any less astonished than his warriors about the sudden arrival of so many Whites but considered it worthy of his dignity not to show it, and instead to take their presence as a matter of fact. Hence he remained standing at a distance and looked past them across to the mountains as if he didn't have the slightest business with the visitors. But he hadn't figured on Aunty Droll, because the Saxon walked up to him and said:

"Why won't Long Ear join us? Doesn't he want to greet the famous warriors of the palefaces?"

The chief muttered something unintelligible in his language, but was barking up the wrong tree, because Droll gave him a pat on the shoulder like a good, old acquaintance, and said:

"Speak English, old boy! I've not learnt your dialect."

Long Ear muttered some gibberish again, and so Droll continued:
"Don't pretend! I know you speak a passable English."
"No!" the chief lied.
"No? Do you know me?"
"No!"
"You've not seen me before?"
"No!"
"Hm! Try to remember! You must remember me."
"No!"
"We've met down south at Fort Defiance!"
"No!"
"Shut up with your 'no'! I can prove to you that I'm right. We were three Whites and eleven Indians. We were playing cards a little and drinking a little. The Indians, however, drank a little more than the Whites, and in the end no longer knew their own names or where they were. They slept all afternoon, and then the entire night. Can you remember now, old fellow?"
  "No!"
"That's fine! But you are giving me answers, nevertheless; that's proof you understand me, hence I'll carry on talking. We Whites also went to lie down in the weatherboard shed with the Indians, because there was no other space available. When we woke up the Indians had gone. Do you know where to?"
  "No!
"However, my gun and my bullet pouch had also disappeared together with the Indians. I had the initials A.D. engraved on the barrel. Oddly enough those initials are on the barrel of yours. Do you know perhaps how they got there?"
  "No!"
"And my bullet pouch was embroidered with pearls, and also fitted with an A.D. I wore it on my belt, just like you wear yours. And I notice with sincere delight the same letters on it. Do you know how my initials came to be on your pouch?"
  "No!"
"I, on the other hand, know all the better how my rifle got into your hand and my bullet pouch on your belt. A chief only wears things he captured; he disdains stolen goods. Let me relieve you of them."
  In an instant Droll snatched the rifle from the Indian's hand, the bullet pouch from his belt, and then turned away from him. But the Indian came after him as fast as a flash and demanded in fairly good English:

"Give it back!"

"No!" was Droll's answer.

"This gun is mine!"

"No!"

"And the pouch as well!"

"No!"

"You are a thief!"

"No!"

"Give it back, or I'll force you!"

"No!"

At that point the Indian pulled out his knife. Those who didn't know Droll believed that there was going to be a fight; but he burst into merry laughter and said:

"Now I'm supposed to be the thief of my own things! Would anyone think this could be possible? But let's not argue. You're Long Ear, I know you. Your ears aren't the only unusually long things on you. Respect the truth and you'll keep what you've got; I've long since replaced the lost things. Let's try again: Do you know me?"

"Yes!" the Indian replied against all expectations.

"You and I were at Fort Defiance?"

"Yes!"

"You were drunk?"

"Yes!"

"And then you absconded with my rifle and my bullet pouch?"

"Yes!"

"Good, in that case you shall have both; here. And here is my hand, too. Let's be friends; but you must speak English, and you mustn't pilfer things. Understood?"

He shook the Indian's hand and returned the stolen objects. The Indian took them without batting an eyelid, but said in the friendliest tone of voice:

"My white brother is my friend. He knows what's fair, because he found the things with me and returned them to me. He is a friend of the red men, and I love him!"

"Yes, my bosom friend, I love you, too. You'll soon recognize the truth of my words; because had we not come here, you'd probably lose your scalps."

"Our scalps? Who is supposed to take them?"

"The Utah."

"Oh, they're not coming here; they've been beaten by the Navajo, and we'll soon follow them to fetch many Utah scalps."

"You're mistaken!"

"But we can see chiefs and warriors of the Utah as prisoners among you. Therefore they must have been defeated!"

"We've caught them on our own account. The Navajo have been beaten miserably and have fled; the Utah are riding after them and will perhaps arrive at Silver-Lake as soon as today."

"Uff!" Long Ear exclaimed whereby his mouth remained agape.

Even his subordinates emitted shouts of shock.

"Is this possible?" Great Bear asked. "Does the white aunt speak the truth?"

"Yes," Winnetou replied. Among the group of hunters, he knew the region of Silver-Lake best, and therefore spoke. "We will inform you of everything, but only after having ensured that we cannot be surprised by the enemy. We must expect the Utah to arrive at any moment. Fifty Timbabachi warriors must ride down into the gorge immediately; Humply-Bill and Gunstick-Uncle will accompany them."

"I'll go, too!" Hobble-Frank volunteered.

"Me, too!" Droll added.

"Good, you'll also ride with the Timbabachi," Winnetou said. "You'll go to the spot where the canyon becomes very narrow and take up positions behind the cliffs. There are enough protrusions and gaps where you'll be protected. The Utah will be chasing the Navajo unrelentingly, in order to reach Silver-Lake at the same time. You will assist our friends, and as soon as you see the enemy approach send a messenger, and we will join you. Let your horses drink enough; ensure that you'll drink enough water as well because there is none down in the canyon. Great Bear will give you some food."

There was enough meat. It was hanging on ropes tied from tree to tree, in order to dry. There was plenty of drinking water. Several creeks flowed down from the mountains and fed the lake. The horses had gathered beside one of them and were satiating their thirst.

Soon fifty men were ready to depart with the four Whites. Little Bear asked his father for permission to join them, and it was granted to him immediately. He knew the lake and the gorge better than any of the Timbabachi; his presence could be of great benefit to them.

The mountain valley of Silver-Lake stretched north to south, was completely inaccessible from its east and west sides, and could be reached from the north only through the gorge, as well as the hollow ravine through which the Whites had arrived, while the lake emptied its waters into a gully to the south, and thus afforded access from that direction.

There was no enemy expected from the south; on the contrary, more friendly Navajo were to come from there. No precautionary measures were needed in that direction; they were only called for in the north.

Someone inspecting the surroundings of Silver-Lake in that part of the valley would soon gain the opinion that the lake once had its exit towards the north, not the south. There was no doubt that the outflow once went through the gorge. But there was a fairly wide, dam-like elevation between the two, which had obviously not always been there. It hadn't come into existence on its own, hence it must have been man-made. But the hands that had once toiled to build it had long ago turned to dust, because the dam carried trees the age of which was certainly in excess of one hundred and fifty years. Why had the dam been erected? Did there still exist people who could answer that question?

The group of warriors sent out by Winnetou rode away across the dam, behind which the gorge began. It was hardly five metres wide in that spot, quite shallow at first, and only gradually cut further into the ground. The lower down the gorge the riders progressed, the wider it became. Vegetation seemed to exist only near the lake, at least on that side of it. A short stretch behind the dam there were no trees and bushes, and soon there was no grass, either.

The troop had been riding for only ten minutes when the walls of the gorge already reached a height of more than thirty metres; another quarter of an hour further on, and they seemed to reach into the sky. The riders already encountered the round river gravel, which made riding so difficult. Three quarters of an hour after the riders had departed from the lake, the canyon suddenly opened up to twice the width of the gorge. Its walls were not only jagged up top, but also at the bottom. It looked as if the rocks were standing on pillars, which formed arcades where the men could hide.

"We are to stop here," Little Bear said. He had ridden ahead of the Whites. "There are enough holes and caves where we can hide."

"And we'll take the horses back a stretch, so that they can't be spotted from here, where a fight can easily break out," Droll said.

His directive would be beneficial and was therefore carried out. The fifty-five men hid inside the hollows along both sides of the gorge. The Whites kept Little Bear in their company because he would be able to give them the necessary information about the locality. He enquired about the events of the past days as sensibly and earnestly as an adult warrior, and found it difficult to believe that the Navajo had been driven back. He gave the Whites enthusiastic praise:

"My white brothers have acted like courageous yet circumspect men," he said. "The Navajo, on the other hand, were blind and deaf. They ought to have been victorious because the Utah hadn't expected them so soon. If they had sneaked into the valley quietly, and then attacked the Utah, they could have completely destroyed them; but they cried out and shot their guns much too early and thus had to relinquish their scalps. Now the Utah have an advantage over them, and if the fight draws up as far as Silver-Lake, then..."

"Then we'll also have something to say about it," Droll cut in.

"Indeed, we will have a word with them," Frank also said. "I wouldn't mind testing the rifle Castlepool gave me for the first time against those fellows. Say, what's the situation: does the canyon have other accesses?"

"No. There is only one other, the ravine through which you reached the dry basin, and the Utah don't know about it."

"But the Navajo?"

"Only few of them know it, and they won't think of using it because the way is..."

He stopped mid-sentence to listen. His keen hearing had detected a sound. The others also heard it. It sounded like the stumbling of a tired horse on the gravel. After a while a single rider came into view, a Navajo, whose horse was hardly capable of walking any further. The man seemed to be wounded because his clothes were stained with blood, yet he tirelessly worked with hands and feet to urge his nag to keep going.

The young bear left his hiding spot and stepped outside. As soon as the Navajo spotted him, he stopped his horse and rejoiced:

"Uff! My young brother! Have the expected Navajo warriors arrived yet?"

"Not yet."

"Then we're lost!"

"How can a warrior of the Navajo give up?"

"The Great Spirit has left us and turned to the dogs of the Utah. We attacked them in Elk Valley to strangle them; but our chiefs lost their minds, and we were beaten. We fled, and the Utah followed us. They were stronger; yet we would have held out, but a new troop joined them this morning. They are now four times as strong as we are; they came after us with a great push."

"Uff! Does that mean you're annihilated?"

"Almost. The battle is raging ten rifle shots from here. I was sent to fetch help from the lake, because we thought the other Navajo had arrived in the meantime. Now our people are lost."

"Not yet. Dismount and rest here! We'll bring help."

The man was astonished when he saw fifty Timbabachi and four Whites emerge from the rock hollows! The latter had not been able to follow the report of the Navajo because they weren't fluent in that language; Little Bear translated. When they heard what had transpired, Droll said:

"If that's the case, then the Navajo must retreat immediately. Someone quickly ride down to them and tell them that we're waiting for them here. And a second rider must get back to the lake, to fetch our comrades and the rest of the Timbabachi."

"What are you thinking?" Hobble-Frank contradicted him. "If the Navajo follow this plan they will be lost."

"Why?" Droll was astonished. "Do you think I'm not a westman?"

"Even the best westman can have a bad idea once in a while. The Navajo are facing such a superior force that they'll be annihilated as soon as they turn to flee because the Utah will then simply ride them down. They must stay there at all costs; they must hold out until the battle is brought to a standstill. And we're going to make sure this will happen."

"Well said, Frank, you're right!" Humply-Bill agreed.

And Gunstick-Uncle opined:

"Yes, yes below must they yet stay, 'Till we drive the Utah far away!"

"Good!" Hobble nodded. He was pleased about the praise he'd received. "One of the Timbabachi warriors will quickly return to the lake to fetch help; three stay here with the horses, so that they won't do anything stupid, and the rest of us will run as fast as we can to bring help to the Navajo. Let's go!"

His directives were immediately followed. With daring Little Bear in the lead, the four Whites and the Timbabachi ran further down the canyon as fast as the bad ground allowed. They hadn't gone very far when they heard a shot, and then another. Since friend and foe were mainly equipped with bows and arrows, there were no gun salvos. However, only a short while later they heard the cries of the combatants, and then they saw them.

Indeed, the Navajo were in a bad situation. Their horses were almost all shot dead; the only cover they found was behind the cadavers, because the walls of the canyon in that spot were smooth, without any protrusions or indentations, giving no opportunity to hide. The Navajo seemed to be running out of arrows because they did not shoot carelessly, but only when they were sure to hit a target. Some of their most daring warriors ran around to collect the arrows of the Utah, to send them back. The enemy were so numerous that they filled the width of the canyon several rows deep. They were fighting on foot, for they had left their horses behind so they wouldn't be shot. That was very fortunate for the Navajo. Had the Utah mounted up to storm them, none of the Navajo would have survived.

At that moment the battle cries ceased for a short while. The combatants had spotted the arrival of the helpers. The four Whites remained standing openly in the middle of the canyon as soon as they knew the Utah were within range of their guns, lifted their guns, aimed and pulled the triggers. The howls from the ranks of the Utah proved that the bullets had hit their targets. Another four shots—more howling. The Timbabachi crouched low and crawled forwards in order to shoot as well.

Humply-Bill suggested that the four Whites not shoot simultaneously, because the pause created during reloading was too long. Two were to load, and two were to shoot; that's how they were to proceed, and the others agreed.

It was soon evident what four skilled marksmen with good guns were capable of. Every bullet hit its man. Those of the Utah who owned guns aimed at the Whites, and no longer at the Navajo. The latter thus gained some breathing space.

Little Bear was down on one knee to one side of the hunters; it was a real pleasure to see how he used his gun. Shot upon shot struck where he sent it. The Utah retreated. Only those who owned guns remained; but their bullets didn't carry far enough, and they didn't dare come any closer. Hobble-Frank called to Little Bear:

"The five of us will stay where we are. The Navajo must retreat behind us. Tell them!"

The son of the chief obeyed Hobble's request and the Indians jumped up and ran back to settle in behind the Whites. They were a sad sight. It only then became evident how much they had suffered. They counted sixty men at most, and not even half of them still had horses. Fortunately they were able to retreat unhindered because the Timbabachi held their positions, lying on the ground, and kept the Utah at bay. It was a disgrace for the latter that they didn't risk a fast, general advance; but then a number of them would have fallen; Indians try to avoid that at all times. They prefer to attack when there is no risk to their own men.

The Timbabachi then ran back as well, after which the Whites and Little Bear also retreated a stretch. The Utah didn't prevent them from doing so. They were simply following while saving their arrows and continuing the battle only with their few guns. Thus the defending party retreated stretch by stretch, while the attackers followed at the same interval until the former reached the spot where the hunters and Timbabachi had been hiding earlier on. The Whites suggested that everyone hurry into the holes and hollows; Little Bear translated—a sudden, general retreat, and those who had been so badly harassed earlier had disappeared from sight. They were safe because the jagged walls offered cover against every projectile while the Utah were unable to hide. And as soon as the expected help arrived, they could safely face the next stage of the battle.

And that help was already underway.

Winnetou had informed Great Bear in broad strokes what had happened. The Tonkawa looked very worried and said:

"I've warned the Navajo. I advised them to wait until all of their warriors were assembled. But they believed that the Utah hadn't combined yet, and wanted to annihilate the individual mobs one after the other. And now they've suffered the fate they wanted their enemy to suffer."

"Oh, no!" Old Shatterhand said. "I don't think they've been annihilated yet."

"Don't you? I think differently. I know the meeting places of the Utah. If the Navajo have to flee backwards from Elk Valley, then they'll have to pass by several of those places and can easily be locked in on all sides. And even if they're successful in escaping into the mountains, then the number of Utah will increase at each meeting place and it can easily happen that we'll get to see a thousand of their warriors here at Silver-Lake. It is doubtful that the Navajo will reach it under these circumstances."

"What about you? Will the Utah treat you as their enemy?"

"Yes."

"In that case you're in grave danger."

"No."

"Probably because the Timbabachi are here and you're also expecting more Navajo?"

"No; I'll rely neither on one nor the other, but on me alone."

"I don't understand."

"I am not afraid of a thousand Utah."

"You'll have to explain."

"I only have to lift my hand, and they're lost. One single, short moment will kill them all."

"Hm! All?"

"You don't believe it? Yes, you cannot comprehend something like that. You palefaces are very smart men, but none of you would come by such an idea."

He had said it with a proud tone of voice. Old Shatterhand cast a glance across the entire lake, as well as along the mountains, and then replied, while a faint smile twitched around his lips:

"But neither are you the one who thought of it."

"No. Who told you that?"

"I did. As Whites and Christians we wouldn't conceive of such an idea because we abhor mass murder; but we're still smart enough to look into your souls."

"Do you think you know why I don't fear a thousand enemies?"

"Yes."

"Tell me!"

"Shall I reveal your secret in the process?"

"You won't reveal it, because you cannot possibly guess correctly. It is a secret that only two people still know: my son and I."

"And I!"

"No! Prove it!"

"Good! You can kill a thousand Utah within a few moments?"

"Yes."

"If they are in the gorge?"

"Yes."

"That cannot happen with knives, guns or any other weapons."

"No. And it is precisely the means by which it will happen that are impossible for you to imagine."

"Oh, but yes! Namely by the force of nature. By means of air, therefore storm? No. By fire? Not that either. It has to be by water!"

"Your thoughts are good and smart; but you won't get any further!"

"Let's see! Where do you have enough water to kill so many people? In the lake. Will these people walk into the lake? No.

Therefore the lake must go to the people; it must suddenly discharge its flood into the gorge. How will that be possible? There is a tall, strong dam between the two! The dam was not in existence in very old times; it was built, and has been fitted with a mechanism by which it can suddenly be opened, so that the dry gorge is immediately transformed into a raging river. Have I guessed it?"

Despite the calm that an Indian, but especially a chief, must uphold in any situation, Great Bear jumped up and called out:

"Sir, are you all-knowing?"

"No, but I think about things."

"You've guessed correctly; truly, you've uncovered it! But how did I become the owner of this secret?"

"By inheritance."

"And how will the dam be opened?"

"If you permit me to investigate, I'll answer that question fairly soon as well."

"No, I cannot allow that. But can you also guess why the dam has been erected?"

"Yes."

"Well?"

"For two reasons. Firstly, for defence. The conquerors of the southern regions all came from the north. This large gorge was a preferred route of the conquerors. The dam was built to block it, and to be able to suddenly release the water."

"And the second reason?"

"The treasure."

"The treasure? What do you know of it?" the chief asked while he took a step back.

"Nothing; but I can guess well. I can see the lake, its shores, its surroundings and think about it. The lake was not in existence before the dam was built; there was a deep valley through which the creeks that still run here flowed into the gorge they had carved over eons. A rich nation lived here; the people fought against the persistent conquerors for a long time; at last they recognized that they had to give in, to flee, perhaps only on a temporary basis. They buried their precious possessions, their sacred vessels, here in the valley and erected the dam, so that a large lake was created. Its water became the invincible, silent guardian of the treasure."

"Be quiet, quiet, otherwise you'll reveal everything, everything!" Great Bear exclaimed aghast. "Let's not talk about the treasure, but about the dam. Yes, I can open it; I can drown a thousand and more Utah once they're in the gorge. Shall I do that when they come?"

"For God's sake, no! There are other means to defeat them."

"Which ones? Weapons?"

"Yes, and then there are the hostages who are lying in the grass here. They are the most famous chiefs of the Utah. Their people will agree to many of our conditions in order to save their leaders. That's why we have caught and brought them here."

"That means we'll have to put the prisoners somewhere safe."

"Do you have a suitable place?"

"Yes; let them eat and drink; then we'll take them there."

The prisoners' hands were untied; they received meat and water, and were then tied up again. Afterwards they were brought to the Island with the aid of some of the Timbabachi and the canoes that were lying on the shore. Old Firehand, Shatterhand and Winnetou also went across. They were curious to see the interior of the building.

It consisted of one storey above the ground; a wall divided it into two rooms. In one of them was the fireplace, and the other represented the living room. It was furnished exceedingly sparsely and consisted of a hammock and a primitive bed, nothing else.

"And this is where the prisoners are supposed to stay?" Old Shatterhand asked.

"No, because they wouldn't be secure enough here. There is a much better place."

He pushed the bed, a layer of solid timber battens covered with reed mats and blankets, aside. It had served as the cover for a square opening that was thus revealed. A notched tree trunk served as a ladder that led down into a lower room. The Tonkawa descended; Old Shatterhand followed him, and the others then let the prisoners down one after the other.

Sufficient light fell through the opening into the cellar-like space, so that Old Shatterhand could easily acquaint himself with it. The room was larger than the one with the hammock and the bed; the additional space lay under the garden. The other side was locked off with a wall of adobe that had neither a door nor other opening. When the hunter knocked on it, he heard a shallow but hollow sound. There was another space behind the wall, which was situated under the room with the fireplace. And yet there was no access from there down below.

The Utah were lowered and laid next to each other. Old Shatterhand was worried that they wouldn't have enough air. When he made a remark to that effect, Great Bear replied:

"They can breathe freely. The ceiling contains openings that lead outside via hollow bricks installed in the wall of the house. The old inhabitants of this region knew what they were doing."

Old Shatterhand stomped on the ground a few times with some force, as if involuntarily, yet on purpose. The floor of the cellar also sounded hollow. The island had undoubtedly been built as a hollow construction before the lake was created, and clad in a waterproof clay and rock coating. Was the treasure secreted down there, on the bottom of the lake?

There was no time for any further, inconspicuous inspections because the last of the prisoners had been placed, and the Tonkawa climbed back up. Old Shatterhand was forced to follow him. Large pieces of dried and smoked meat hung from poles under the roof. They loaded some of it into the canoes and took it ashore to be eaten. Just when they returned there, the messenger, who had been sent back from the gorge to fetch help, arrived on a frothing horse. Neither the Timbabachi nor Great Bear had believed the enemy was that close. They all grabbed their weapons and rushed to the horses.

Ellen had to stay back, of course, but not without protection. Since no one else wanted to be excluded from the ride, it was her father who remained with her. Great Bear advised him to paddle to the island, because they would be safest there since no one was left behind at the lake. Although there was no immediate cause for concern, caution was always advisable in such cases. He climbed into a canoe with her, took his weapons along, and pushed off just when the others rode away.

The men drove their horses much harder than the riders who had left earlier. They galloped at a helter skelter pace and covered the same distance that the fifty-five men ahead of them had taken three quarters of an hour to traverse, in only one quarter of an hour. They encountered the horses of the others. Shots rang out ahead of them. They dismounted, left their animals behind as well, separated to the left and right as quickly as possible and reached the jagged rock section where their friends were hiding, without the Utah spotting them.

Of course the embattled men were overjoyed about the quick arrival of help. Humply-Bill reported what had happened, and Hobble-Frank was not just a little proud about the praise that came his way because of it.

The Utah still believed that they were dealing only with those they had seen. They seemed to have come to the conclusion that they should have put an end to the battle much sooner by a swift advance, and they intended to make up for the lapse. Those among the defenders of the gorge who were posted inside the hollows and holes at the front noticed that the Utah were massing together, and let their comrades know. Everyone prepared for their welcome.

Suddenly a howling arose as if the proverbial savage hordes had been let loose, and the Utah advanced. After salvos from both walls of the gorge, which lasted not even two minutes, they retreated while leaving scores of dead and wounded behind. Old Shatterhand had been standing behind a pillar and fired several shots, but had aimed to only wound the men and render them unable to fight, not to kill them. When the Utah retreated, he saw the Timbabachi rush out to scalp the fallen; their chief was with them.

"Stop!" Shatterhand called out with his booming voice. "Leave these people be."

"Why? Their scalps belong to us!" Long Ear replied.

He pulled out his knife and bent down to take the scalp off one of the wounded. The next moment Old Shatterhand stood next to him, held the revolver to his head, and threatened:

"Make one cut and I'll shoot you!"

Long Ear might have had the guts to steal a rifle and a bullet pouch, but he didn't have enough of it to submit to being shot. He rose and with friendly pretence said:

"What objection could you possibly have? The Utah would also scalp us."

"If I were among them they'd leave that be. I don't tolerate it, at least not with those who are still alive."

"Alright, they can keep their scalps; but I'll take those of the dead."

"What gives you the right?"

"I don't understand you!" the redskin was taken aback. "A defeated enemy must be scalped!"

"Here lie many. Was it you who defeated them all?"

"No. I've hit one."

"Which one?"

"I don't know."

"Is he dead?"

"I don't know that, either. He kept running."

"Then show me the dead Utah who has the bullet from your gun in his body; you may scalp him, but no other!"

The chief grunted and retreated into his hiding-hole, and his men followed his example. At that point a hullabaloo arose further down, where the repelled Utah had gathered again. Because the hunter had been standing between the Timbabachi, they hadn't been able to see him clearly before; since the Timbabachi had moved away from him he was standing out in the open and the Utah were able to recognize him. The hunter heard them shout:

"Old Shatterhand! The magic gun, the magic rifle!"

They were unable to comprehend how the man could possibly be at that location. His presence made a truly disheartening impression on them. He on the other hand displayed all the more courage. He slowly walked towards them, and when he was within earshot, he called to them:

"Come and collect your dead and wounded! We give them to you."

One of the leaders stepped forwards and replied:

"You will shoot at us!"

"No."

"Are you speaking the truth?"

"Old Shatterhand never lies."

He turned around and went back to his cover.

As treacherous as those Indians were, they didn't believe that particular paleface to be capable of betrayal. In addition to that, Indians regard the abandonment of their dead or wounded as a great disgrace. Hence the Utah sent two of their warriors at first, to tentatively test the situation; they slowly approached and picked up a wounded man to carry him away. They returned and took a second one away. When no hostile action was forthcoming, they gained full trust and several more came. Old Shatterhand stepped out from behind his cover again; they received a fright and wanted to run away. But he called to them:

"Stay! Nothing will happen to you."

They stood still apprehensively; he went up to them and asked:

"How many chiefs are with you now?"

"Four."

"Who among them is the noblest?"

"*Nanap Varrenton*[2]."

"Tell him that I want to talk to him! He shall approach half the way, and I'll approach the other half; we'll meet in the middle. We'll leave the weapons behind."

_____

[2] Old Thunder

They went to deliver the message, and then returned with the answer:

"He will come and bring the other three chiefs as well."

"I'll bring only two comrades, whom he probably knows. As soon as you've completed your task, they may come."

Soon the four chiefs approached from one end, and Old Shatterhand, together with Old Firehand and Winnetou from the other. They met in the middle, exchanged a greeting with a serious nod, and then sat down on the ground opposite one another. Pride forbade the Utah to speak immediately. It was impossible to see their expressions because of the thickly applied paint, but their gazes evidenced the astonishment to see the other two famous men next to Old Shatterhand. And so the members of both parties looked at each other for a long while, until the oldest of the Utah, Old Thunder, lost his patience after all, and decided to speak. He rose, stretched into a dignified pose and began:

"When the wide Earth still belonged to the sons of Great Manitou, and there were no palefaces among us, then..."

"Then you were able to hold speeches as long as you wanted," Old Shatterhand cut in. "The palefaces, however, prefer to be brief, and we shall do precisely that."

Once an Indian begins a palaver about something, there will be no end to it. Their powwow might have taken hours, had not Old Shatterhand curtailed the introduction there and then. The old chief gave him a half surprised, half angry look, sat down again and said:

"Old Thunder is a famous chief. He counts many more years than Old Shatterhand and is not used to tolerating being interrupted by young men. If the palefaces intended to insult me, they needn't have called me to meet them. I have spoken. Howgh!"

"I had no intentions of insulting you. A man can count many years, and yet be much less experienced than a younger one. You wanted to speak of the times before the palefaces; but we intend to speak about the present day. And if it was I who called you to come here, then I will have to be the one who speaks first to tell you what I want from you. I have also spoken. Howgh!"

That was a sharp rebuke. By doing that, he indicated to the Indians that he was the one to speak and make demands. They remained silent, hence Shatterhand continued:

"You've said my name, and therefore know me. Do you also know the two warriors sitting next to me?"

"Yes. They are Old Firehand, and Winnetou the chief of the Apache."

"In that case you will also know that we've always been friends of the red men. No Indian can say that we've opposed him without having been insulted first; indeed, we've often abstained from revenge, and instead forgave where we ought to have exacted punishment. Why are you pursuing us?"

"Because you're the friends of our enemies."

"That is not true. Great Wolf took us captive although we hadn't engaged in any hostilities against him. He repeatedly tried to kill us, and broke his promises repeatedly. In order to save our lives we had to defend ourselves against the Utah."

"Didn't Winnetou knock down and kill the old chief in the Forest of the Water, and didn't you take the other chiefs and a number of warriors with you?"

"Again to save our lives."

"And now you're with the Navajo and the Timbabachi, who are our enemies!"

"By coincidence. We were headed up to Silver-Lake and met them along the way. We heard that there was going to be a battle between you and them, and made haste to bring about peace."

"We want revenge, not peace, and from your hands least of all."

"Whether or not you'll accept it is your affair; we saw it as our duty to offer it to you."

"We're the victors!"

"Until a short while ago, but not anymore. You've been gravely insulted, we know that; but it is unjust of you to take revenge on innocent people. Our lives have repeatedly hung in the balance. Had it been up to you we would have long ago died at the stakes, like the other palefaces in Elk Valley."

"What would you know about it?"

"Everything. We buried their corpses."

"Were you there?"

"Yes. We were among you. We heard what the Utah spoke, and saw what they did. We were standing under the trees when the Navajo came, and saw that you drove them out."

"That is impossible; that is not true."

"You know that I don't lie. Ask the chiefs of the Utah, who were there, too."

"Where shall we ask them? They have disappeared."

"Where to?"

"How should we know?"

"Did the Navajo kill them?"

"No. At first we believed so, but we didn't find their corpses. Then we believed they had been taken prisoners; but we were right behind the Navajo and didn't see a single prisoner among them, while many of them have fallen into our hands. The chiefs of the Utah are not with the Navajo."

"But they cannot have disappeared!"

"The Great Spirit has taken them."

"No. The Great Spirit doesn't want to know about such disloyal and treacherous men. He has given them into our hands."

"Into your hands?"

"Yes, into the power of the palefaces whom you wanted to destroy."

"Your tongue is false; you only speak such words to force us into peace."

"Yes, I will and shall force you into peace, but I speak the truth. When we were among you in Elk Valley, we took the three chiefs captive."

"Without their warriors noticing it?"

"No one was able to see or hear it. We knocked them down without leaving them a chance to utter even a single word. Am I not called Old Shatterhand?"

"It is not true. Someone would have seen you."

"There is a hiding place in Elk Valley, which only we know. I will prove to you that I speak the truth. What is this?"

He pulled a narrow strap, studded with cylindrically cut buttons from the shells of venus clams from his pocket, and held it up to the chief.

"Uff!" Old Thunder was aghast. "The wampum of Yellow Sun! I know it precisely."

"And this here?"

Shatterhand produced a second strap.

"The wampum of Four Buffaloes! I know it as well."

"And this third wampum?"

When he showed the chief the third wampum, the words almost got stuck in the old man's throat. Old Thunder's reflexive gesture was one of horror as he stammered in disjointed phrases:

"No warrior gives away his wampum; it is sacred to him above anything else. Anyone who has someone else's wampum has either killed him or taken him prisoner. Are the three chiefs still alive?"

"Yes."

"Where are they?"

"In our power, safely locked away."

"At Silver-Lake?"

"You're asking too many questions. Consider who else is with them! They're all chiefs, as well as brave warriors who will undoubtedly be chiefs one day."

"What will you do with them?"

"A life for a life, blood for blood! Agree to peace with the Navajo and the Timbabachi, and we will hand the prisoners over!"

"We have also made prisoners. We'll exchange them, man against man."

"Do you think I'm a boy who doesn't know that a chief is exchanged against at least thirty warriors? Consider my offer, and take into account that it is better to secure the release of these chiefs, rather than to kill another one or two hundred enemies."

"And you don't take the booty into account?"

"Booty? Pshaw! There is no question of booty; you won't make any since you won't be victorious again. We—fifty white hunters—are now facing you. We were the prisoners of the Utah, and still laughed at them; they had to let us go, and even give us their chiefs. We did that while we were fettered as your prisoners. Just imagine what we can achieve now that we're free and unencumbered! I am telling you: if you don't agree to peace with us, then only a few of you will ever see their home wigwams again!"

It was obvious that the hunter's depiction didn't fail to make an impression on the old chief. He stared at the ground with a grim look. Old Shatterhand continued in order to enhance the impact of his remarks:

"Your chiefs tried to kill us; they fell into our hands and we not only had the right, but also the duty to kill them to render them harmless. We didn't do that, because we mean well to them and to you. If we advise you now to accept peace, then this is just as well-meant because we know that we will defeat you. Decide, before it is too late."

At that point Old Firehand rose, stretched his tall figure in a gesture of boredom, and then said:

"Pshaw! Why all the words, we have weapons! Old Thunder shall tell us quickly whether or not he wants war or peace. We then know where we stand and will give him what he deserves: life or death!"

That brought about a swift reaction; at least an answer was immediately forthcoming:

"We cannot decide so fast."

"Why not? Are you men or squaws?"

"We're not women, we're warriors. But we have to first talk to our people."

"If you really are chiefs, then this will not be necessary. I can see that you wish to gain some time to think of a new treachery no doubt, as is your custom; but no amount of intelligence will assist you against our fists."

"Old Firehand ought to speak as calmly as we give our answers. To have boiling blood doesn't befit a man. We will go and consider what is to be done."

"Then consider that it will be night in half an hour!"

"We can also tell you at night what we have decided. The one who wants to speak, you or us, may fire a shot, and then call out. The other party will answer. Howgh!"

He rose, nodded faintly, and then left; the others followed his example.

"Now we're just as smart as before!" Old Firehand sounded irate.

"My brother spoke too angrily," Winnetou said in his mild calmness. "He should have let Old Shatterhand continue to speak. Old Thunder had already become pensive and was about to listen to reason."

Firehand seemed to realize the validity of the reproach, because he didn't reply. When they returned to the others, Long Ear welcomed them with the question:

"There were four Utah. Why did you only go with three men?"

"Because we were enough men," Old Firehand replied gruffly.

"There were other men here, too. I am also a chief; I had a right to participate in the powwow, just like you."

"There was enough nonsense spoken; we didn't need a fourth for that."

Long Ear fell silent; but had his face not been smeared with paint, then it would have been obvious how vexed he was. He was in a bad mood anyway. He had been embarrassed by Droll, without being able to give expression to his rancour. And to add to it, Old Shatterhand had then badly insulted him in front of all of his warriors by preventing the scalping. The chief was a coward, who didn't have the courage for direct confrontation; but the anger, which he didn't show openly, was embedded all the more solidly inside of him.

Dusk came, and then night fell. Although the men didn't expect the Utah to risk an attack, they nevertheless implemented precautionary measures to foil a possible strike. They needed to place guards. Long Ear volunteered for that task with his warriors, and no one could deny him that. But so as not to be remiss in his duty, Old Shatterhand assigned the Timbabachi chief and the selected warriors their places and impressed upon them the importance of not moving any further ahead.

Together with the chief there were five men who formed a line straight across the gorge. Long Ear was on the outermost post on the right hand wing. Old Shatterhand lay on the ground and crawled forwards to perhaps eavesdrop on the Utah. Within a short time he succeeded in doing so, even though they had posted three guards; they didn't notice him. He even dared to crawl past them, and then saw that the enemy Indians were camped where the gorge abruptly widened, lying closely next to and behind each other right across the bottom of the canyon. He was satisfied and returned.

Long Ear had witnessed that the hunter had gone reconnoitring. He was annoyed that they hadn't entrusted him with that. He, the chief of a red tribe, would definitely be much more skilled than such a paleface. The rancour kept gnawing on him. He wanted to be able to show the Whites that he was an important person, who wasn't going to be ignored. What if the Utah were hatching a plan and he was able to espy it? The thought didn't let go of him, and at last he decided to put it into reality. He crawled forwards, on and on. But it wasn't as easy as he had imagined, because the gravel wasn't solid; it moved under his limbs. Hence he was forced to direct most of his attention underneath, rather than ahead. Again a pebble rolled away from under his foot— something dark appeared in front of him; two powerful hands clamped shut around his neck like iron claws; two other hands held his arms against his body; he couldn't breathe and lost consciousness.

When he came to again, he was lying between two men who held the tips of their knives on his naked chest. His limbs were fettered, and in his mouth was a gag. He made a movement that the third one who sat at his head noticed. The man whispered, while he put his hand on Long Ear's head:

"We have recognized Long Ear. I am Old Thunder. If Long Ear is smart, then nothing will happen to him; but if he is stupid, then he'll taste the knives he can feel on his chest. He can indicate by a nod whether or not he heard my words!"

The captured chief gave the required signal. He was lying between life and death, and it went without saying that he chose life. A great satisfaction overcame him when he realized that it had become possible for him to take revenge on the proud, conceited Whites for the slights and insults he had suffered at their hands.

"Long Ear may also indicate whether he will only speak quietly when I remove the gag from his mouth," the other continued.

The prisoner nodded again, and immediately the others removed his gag, but Old Thunder warned:

"If you speak one loud word, you will die. However, if you become my ally, then we will forgive you for everything, and you will partake in our booty. Answer me!"

Booty! That word conjured up an idea, a great, precious idea in the mind of the Timbabachi. He had overheard a conversation between Great Bear and Little Bear, a conversation that still echoed in his ears, word for word. Booty! Yes, there was to be booty the likes of which had never been doled out after a battle! From that moment onwards, he was devoted to the Utah and their endeavour with heart and soul.

"I hate and despise those Whites," he replied. "If you help me, then we'll destroy them."

"As well as father and son Nintropan?"

"Yes. But my warriors shall be spared!"

"I promise you. But why were you my enemy before?"

"Because I didn't know then what I know now. The palefaces have insulted me so much that I must have their blood."

"You shall have your revenge. I will soon see whether you are honest, or want to cheat me."

"I am loyal to you and will prove it better and more completely than you could possibly imagine."

"Then tell me first whether it is true that the palefaces have taken our chiefs captive!"

"It is true. I have seen them."

"Then these dogs are in league with the bad spirits, otherwise they wouldn't have accomplished what would be impossible for anyone else! Where are the chiefs of the Utah?"

"In the house on the island in the lake."

"Who is guarding them?"

"One paleface and a girl, who is his daughter."

"Is that true? One man and a girl are holding so many brave and famous warriors? You're lying!"

"I speak the truth. You must consider that the prisoners are bound."

"In that case I'll believe it. That's on the island. But how many warriors are on the shore?"

"None."

"Have you lost your mind?"

"None! The Whites and my Timbabachi were up there, no one else. And all of them rode to the gorge to fight you."

"What carelessness! And I'm supposed to think that's the truth?"

"It's not carelessness; these dogs truly think you're harmless since it seems impossible to them that you could get to the lake without their knowledge."

"Is that possible at all?"

"Yes. And that in particularly will let me prove to you that I'm honest towards you."

"Uff! The route up this gorge is not the only one? There is another?"

"Yes. I'll lead you, if you wish."

"Where is the path?"

"A stretch further back from here there is a narrow gap between two rock pillars through which one reaches an elevation, and then a deep mountain basin; from there a hollow ravine leads to the lake. I rode that path with Great Bear."

"And there really are no warriors at the lake?"

"Not if the two hundred expected Navajo haven't arrived in the meantime."

"They haven't arrived yet, otherwise they would have rushed down here into the gorge to fight us. How long will we require to get to the lake along the other route?"

"Three hours."

"That's a long time!"

"But the reward is great; many enemies will fall into your hands; you will free your chiefs and warriors and..."

He hesitated.

"And—keep talking!"

"And besides you'll find a booty like there has never been before."

"A booty? With the Navajo? You mean their horses and their weapons? Because there won't be anything else to be found on them."

"I'm not talking about the Navajo, but about father and son Nintropan and their Silver-Lake, on the bottom of which immense treasures are stored, gold, silver and precious stones in large quantities."

"Who told you that?"

"No one. I overheard it when the two were talking. One night, when I was lying under the trees in the dark, they came along and remained standing nearby without realizing that I was there. That's when they spoke of the enormous treasures."

"How did they get into the lake?"

"A nation of people, who lived here a long time ago but were driven out, stored them there."

"The things will have perished in the meantime. And how would we be able to raise them if they are lying on the bottom of the lake? We would have to empty the lake."

"No. Where the lake is today there was a dry valley once. Those people built a tower. Its tip is the island. From that tower they built a sturdy hollow corridor, a duct, across the valley bottom to end where the gorge starts now. Then they erected a strong broad dam, so that the water could no longer run to the north. The water rose and the valley became a lake, and the tip of the tower the island. Since it filled up, its water has been flowing away to the south. The exit of the duct, however, is hidden with rocks."

"And this is all supposed to be true?"

"Completely true. I went to see for myself, and when I secretly removed the rocks, I found the corridor. At the entrance are torches. They are necessary to illuminate the duct. It leads along the bottom of the lake to the island, the tower. The treasures are stored in the base of it. The duct also serves the purpose of draining the lake water to destroy possible enemies in the gorge. One opens a part of the duct; the water enters, rushes down into the gorge, and everything in it must drown."

"Uff! That would be just what we need. What if we could drown the palefaces?"

"I cannot allow that because my Timbabachi would then also drown."

"That is true. But if everything really is as you say, then the Whites are lost anyway. We'll see if you're honest. Will you lead us to the lake now?"

"Yes, I'm very pleased to do it. But what part of the treasures will I get?"

"I'll decide that as soon as I'm convinced that you've told me the truth. I'll untie you now and have a horse brought to you. But you'll die at the slightest attempt to escape."

The chief gave his orders with a hushed voice. Soon all the Utah were sitting in the saddle and riding back down the canyon very cautiously, so as not to make a noise. They reached the spot in the canyon where the Whites had turned off towards the rocky basin, and followed the same route.

The ride was even more arduous during the night than it had been for the hunters during the day; but the Indians had veritable cats' eyes, and their horses easily found their way, too. They rode up the sloping plain, down into the basin on the other side, and then through the hollow ravine, along precisely the same trail that the Whites had ridden. The last half of the ride was made easier because the moon had risen. As the path wasn't deeply cut, it was fairly well illuminated.

Exactly as Long Ear had estimated, three hours had elapsed when the Utah arrived where the first trees stood. They stopped and sent several scouts ahead to investigate whether they could move further up. They hadn't gone five minutes when a shot cracked, and shortly thereafter another one. Before long they returned, carrying one of theirs. He was dead.

"The palefaces are no longer in the gorge," they reported. "They are posted at the entrance to the lake and have shot at us. A bullet hit our brother in the heart. He was careless enough to stand up in the moonshine."

The news awoke Old Thunder's distrust. He believed Long Ear had cheated him; he thought that he was in league with the Whites and had received the task of getting himself caught on purpose to deliver the Utah to their guns. Long Ear successfully allayed Old Thunder's suspicion. He proved that he could not possibly have had such intentions, and then added:

"The palefaces didn't feel safe in the darkness of the gorge since they're much weaker in numbers than your group. They have gone back to the lake where they believe you can't attack them. The entrance to the valley is so narrow that they can easily defend it against you; therefore it is not possible for you to force it, especially not at night; but you can get at them from behind."

"How is that possible?"

"Through the corridor I mentioned. The access to it is not far from here. We open it by removing the rocks, and climb inside. Once we've lit the torches, we can easily walk along it; that's how we'll reach the tower, and then we'll climb up inside, to exit on the island. There are always a few canoes in which we can paddle to the shore. Then we'll be at the rear of the enemy and will easily overpower them, especially since my Timbabachi will join you, as soon as I order them to do so."

"Good! Half of the Utah remain here, and the other half will follow us into the corridor. Show it to us!"

The Utah had dismounted. Long Ear led half of them away to the side until they reached the spot where the gorge began. A pile of rocks was leaning against the cliff.

"We must remove these rocks," the Timbabachi said. "Then you'll see the opening."

The pile was taken down, and there was a dark hole about two and a quarter metres wide and about one and a half metres high. The chiefs entered, and when they felt their way along they found an entire supply of torches made from elk or buffalo tallow. The Indians lit them with the aid of punks. After they had distributed them they advanced into the duct.

The air inside was musty but there was no moisture. The masonry had to be incredibly strong, and in addition it had to have been covered thickly with compacted clay in order to withstand the force of the lake water for such a long time.

So as not to be exposed to the stale air for too long, which was made worse through the smoke of the torches, they walked as fast as possible, until, after a seemingly endless amount of time, they arrived in a wide hall where many packets wrapped in mats were stacked against the wall.

"This must be the bottom of the tower that forms the island," Long Ear said. "Perhaps the packets contain the treasures of which I told you. Shall we have a look?"

"Yes," Old Thunder replied. "But we won't spend too much time here because we must hurry to get to the island. We'll have more time for it later."

When they removed the wrapping from one of the packets, they saw glittering in the sheen of the torches the figure of a golden idol. The statue alone represented a fortune. A civilized person might have become drunk from excitement; the Indians remained cold. They spread the mat over the idol again and prepared to climb up.

Small steps of sorts had been built from masonry, which led upwards; they afforded room for only one person; hence the Indians had to line up in a single file.

Long Ear climbed ahead with a torch. He hadn't reached the topmost step of the stairs leading out of the bottom room when he heard a scream below him and many cries of fear that followed. He stood still and looked back. What he saw was eminently suited to fill him with horror. From the corridor, where many more Utah had been waiting, a wall of water came pushing in as broad and tall as the cavity. The torches cast their flickering light onto the dark, gurgling flood, which was already up to half a man's height in the treasure room, and it rose with terrifying speed. The warriors in the corridor were lost; the water had engulfed them immediately. And those who were still standing on the steps were lost also. They pushed forwards; every one of them wanted to save himself upwards; one tore the other from the steps. They tossed the torches away in order to defend themselves with both hands. Consequently none succeeded in gaining a foothold. All the while the flood rose so fast that it already reached up to their necks one minute after the first scream had resounded. It lifted the men up; they swam; they fought against death and against each other—in vain.

Only five or six were up high enough to possibly escape. Old Thunder was among them; Long Ear held the only torch left burning. A narrow opening led through the ceiling into the next storey, from where identical steps led further up.

"Give me the light, and let me go ahead!" the Utah chief ordered.

He reached for the torch, but Long Ear refused to give it to him. A short scuffle ensued, which lasted long enough for the water to catch up to them. It was welling up from the opening into that chamber already. The room was much, much narrower than the one below. As a result, the flood rose with a tenfold speed up the walls.

Long Ear was younger and stronger than Old Thunder. He tore free and with a powerful push threw him to the floor. But then the other Utah closed in on him. He had no weapons and only one hand free to fend them off. One of them already aimed his gun to shoot him; he called out:

"Stop, or I'll toss the torch into the water, and then you're lost! You won't be able to see where you have to climb and the water will catch you."

That helped. They realized that they could only save themselves if they had light to see. The water had already risen to their hips.

"Then keep the torch and climb ahead, you dog!" Old Thunder replied. "But you'll pay for it later!"

The Timbabachi already stood on the steps and rushed along. Again he came through a narrow opening onto the next level. The old Utah chief had been serious with his threat. Long Ear knew that. He figured that the only means for him not having to worry was for the Utah to die in the flood. Therefore he remained standing above the opening after he had climbed through, and looked back. Old Thunder's head appeared behind him.

"You called me a dog and want to take revenge on me," he barked at him. "You are a dog yourself, and shall die like a dog. Get back into the water!"

Long Ear kicked him in the face, so that the old man fell back and disappeared in the opening. A moment later the head of the next Utah popped up; he also received a kick and fell back. And so fared the third; no one else came after him, because the water had reached all others and washed them off the steps; it surged up through the opening; the Timbabachi chief was on his own; only he was left.

He climbed on and up a few more levels, and the water followed him with almost the same speed. Then he detected better air. The space to climb had become very tight; there were no more stairs, but a notched piece of timber was leaning against the wall. He already placed the tip of his foot in the slot to climb up when he heard a voice above him:

"Stop, stay down, or I'll shoot you! The Utah wanted to destroy us; and now it is they who are lost altogether, and you shall die as the last one of them!"

Long Ear recognized the voice of Great Bear.

"I'm not Utah! Don't shoot!" he replied amid great fear.

"Who are you?"

"Your friend, the chief of the Timbabachi."

"Ah, Long Ear! You deserve to die all the more, because you're a defector, a traitor."

"No, no! You're mistaken!"

"I'm not mistaken. Somehow you've uncovered my secret and revealed it to the Utah. Now you shall drown like they've drowned."

"I've not revealed anything!" panic-stricken Long Ear insisted because the water had already climbed to his knees.

"Don't lie!"

"Let me up! I've always been your friend!"

"No, you'll stay down there!"

At that point the Timbabachi heard another voice, namely that of Old Firehand:

"Let him come up! What's happened is already dreadful enough. He'll confess his sins."

"Yes, I'll confess; I'll tell you everything, everything!" Long Ear assured them because the water reached to his hips.

"Good, I'll spare you and hope that you'll be grateful to me for it."

"My gratitude will have no boundaries. Tell me what you want, and I'll do it!"

"I'll keep you to your word. Now come up!"

The Timbabachi threw the torch into the water, so that he was able to climb better, and then went up. He arrived in the room that contained the hearth. A fire was burning outside the door and in its sheen he saw Great Bear, Old Firehand and Old Shatterhand. He collapsed from exhaustion and the fear he had suffered, but quickly struggled to his feet again to run outside, and called out:

"Away, away, outside, otherwise the water will come before we can save ourselves!"

"Stay here!" Great Bear replied. "You've nothing more to fear from the water because it cannot rise higher inside the island than its level outside. You're safe and will now tell us how you got away from your post and ended up here."

After Old Shatterhand had concluded his daring reconnoitring mission in the canyon, he had returned to his companions. They and the Timbabachi lay quietly in their hiding places, because everyone's attention needed to be focussed towards the outside, since the Utah were well capable of sneaking up on them.

An hour might have elapsed when Old Shatterhand thought it was time to check on the guards again. He sneaked outside and first headed to the spot where he had left Long Ear behind; it was empty. He went to the nearest guard post to ask about their chief, and found out that he had sneaked away.

"Where to?"

"To the Utah. He's not returned yet."

"When did he leave?"

"Almost an hour ago."

"That means he must have met with misfortune; I'll go and investigate."

He hunter lay down and crawled to where he had spotted the enemy guards earlier; they were gone. He sneaked further along. He couldn't see a single Utah where their camp had spanned the entire width of the canyon before. Old Shatterhand kept searching amid extreme caution. He neither saw nor heard a Utah, nor found the Timbabachi chief. That was more than worrying. He returned to fetch Winnetou and Old Firehand in order for them to participate in the search. Their efforts were in vain. The three men penetrated a significant stretch down the canyon without encountering the enemy, and returned with the report that the Utah had disappeared. That in itself would not have been entirely incomprehensible or even worrisome, had not Long Ear vanished with them.

"They've caught him," Great Bear said. "He risked too much. That's the end of him."

"And perhaps of us," Old Shatterhand said.

"Why of us?"

"It is conspicuous to me that they've left. That has to have a very particular reason. The fact that the Timbabachi chief fell into their hands, can not in itself be the cause of their unexpected departure; rather, I think there must be a completely different explanation, which is connected to the chief."

"What reason could that be?"

"Hm! I don't trust Long Ear. I've never liked him."

"I wouldn't know why we ought to mistrust him. He has never been hostile towards me."

"That may be so; nevertheless, he's not a man I would want to have to rely on. Does he know this locality well?"

"Yes."

"Is he also aware of the trail that leads to the lake via the rock basin?"

"He knows it because he accompanied me there."

"Then I know enough. We must get away immediately, to get to the lake."

"Why?"

"Because he's revealed that path to the Utah."

"I don't believe he would be capable of doing this!"

"And I wouldn't put it past him. I may be right or wrong; he may have spoken of his own volition or was forced to divulge it. None of this matters; I'm convinced that the Utah left an hour ago and will be at the lake in two hours."

"I think so, too," Old Firehand agreed.

"Long Ear does not have a good face," Winnetou said. "My brothers may quickly come to the lake, otherwise the Utah will be there before us and will take Butler and his daughter captive."

Because the three men shared the same opinion, Great Bear lost some of his confidence and didn't object to an immediate departure. After mounting up, the group rode back up the gorge as well as they were able in the darkness.

It took them a good hour before they reached the entrance to the lake valley. They occupied it, but posted only Whites since the

Timbabachi could no longer be trusted entirely because they had lost their chief.

Butler was no longer on the island. He and his daughter had been sitting inside the building; below them lay the prisoners who were talking to each other. Their voices were audible as a dull murmur; it sounded so ghostly that Ellen became anxious and asked her father to leave the island and return to the shore with her. He fulfilled her wish and paddled across. When night fell he lit a fire, yet was careful enough not to sit beside it, but rather retreated into the shadows with Ellen, where they were able to overlook the illuminated place without being noticed. It was eerie for both, to be alone like that in a deserted and dangerous place; hence they were pleased when the Whites and the Timbabachi returned.

The Utah were expected to get there an hour later, and it therefore sufficed for half the rafters to be posted at the access point. The other Whites sat around the fire; the Timbabachi lit a second one, gathered around it and talked about the disappearance of their chief; the battle-weary Navajo lit a third. The Timbabachi were convinced that Long Ears had fallen into the hands of the Utah against his will. The Whites had wisely withheld from them the fact that they suspected him of treachery.

Since their arrival at the lake, Watson, the erstwhile overseer, had had no opportunity to talk to Great Bear, and the Tonkawa hadn't paid any attention to him. But while they were sitting around the fire, the White said to the Indian:

"My red brother hasn't spoken to me yet. He may look at me and tell me whether he remembers having seen me once before."

Great Bear gave Watson a searching glance, and then replied:

"My white brother wears his beard longer today than he did earlier; but I recognize him."

"Alright, who am I?"

"You are one of the palefaces who spent an entire winter up here. Ikhatshi-Tatli, Great Father, was still alive at the time, but he was ill and they cared for him until he died."

"Yes, we nursed him, and he was grateful for it. Great Bear has heard before that he gave us a gift."

"I know it," the Indian nodded, but in a way that indicated he disliked being reminded of it.

"It was a secret he entrusted us, a secret about a treasure that's hidden here."

"Yes; but Great Father was wrong in speaking of that secret. He had grown old and feeble, and his gratitude prevented him from remembering that he had sworn eternal silence. He was permitted to speak of the secrets, which are passed on to his descendants, only to them. The objects he spoke of were not his property; it wasn't his place to give away anything. On the contrary, it was his duty to remain silent towards palefaces in particular."

"Does that mean I'm not entitled to speak of the matter?"

"I cannot forbid you to do so."

"We had a drawing of it."

"That is useless to you because if you follow it you won't find anything. I've moved the objects somewhere else."

"And I'm not allowed to know where?"

"No."

"Then you're less grateful than your grandfather!"

"I am doing my duty, but will never forget that you were present when he died. Yet you must foreswear the exploitation of that secret; I will gladly fulfil any other wish you have."

"Are you serious?" Old Firehand hastily asked.

"Yes. My words are always meant the way I say them."

"In that case I will express a wish in place of our comrade."

"Do so! I will readily oblige if it is within my power."

"Who owns the land on which we are at present?"

"It is mine. I have acquired it from the Timbabachi, and will one day leave it to my son Little Bear."

"Do you have evidence of ownership?"

"Yes. A promise is valid among the red men; but the white men demand a piece of paper with black letters. I have had one such document made up and signed by the white chiefs. There is also a large seal affixed to it. The land at Silver-Lake, as far as the mountains gird it, is my property. I can do with it as I wish."

"And who owns the rock basin through which we've come here today?"

"It belongs to the Timbabachi. The white chiefs have surveyed the entire region and drawn it; then the white chief in Washington has signed the drawing to say that it is the property of the Timbabachi."

"Therefore they can sell, lease or give away parts of it as they like."

"Yes, and no one has the right to object."

"Then I will tell you that I wish to buy the rock basin from them."

"Do it!"

"Do you agree?"

"Yes. I cannot forbid them to sell, or you to buy."

"That's not what I meant, rather, I wish to know whether you like or dislike having us Whites as your neighbours."

"You all? Not only you alone? Do you all want to live in the basin?"

"Indeed. And I also wish to buy the stretch of land that contains the hollow ravine, right up to your boundary."

The face of Great Bear took on a wily expression when he asked:

"Why would you want to live in a place where there is no water, and where not a single blade of grass is growing? Whites only buy land that yields a profit for them. I can guess your thoughts. It is the rock that has value for you."

"That's correct. But only if we can get water there."

"Take it from the lake!"

"That's what I wanted to ask from you."

"You shall have as much as you need."

"May I construct a pipeline?"

"Yes."

"You'll sell the rights to me and I'll pay for it?"

"If the purchase is required, then I have nothing against it. You're free to determine the price, but I'll make it a gift to you. You've done me a great service; we would have fallen into the hands of the Utah without you; I will fulfil all of your wishes. The man who spoke with me before wanted to have the treasures of the secret; I'm not at liberty to grant that; instead, I will help you to exploit the treasures of the rock basin. You can hear that I'm guessing what it is all about. I will be pleased if your hopes become realized."

"I like dat," Hobble-Frank whispered to his cousin. "We've already got the water, so to speak; if the gold will flow as readily as this, we may soon be able to play Crassus."

"Ye mean Croesus, no? He was considered to have been det particular king who was so stinking rich."

"Don't you start on me, too, like Fat Jemmy, who always fell into the wrong counterpoint! Crassus is the correct modulation. If you want to remain my friend and kinsman, then...listen!"

They heard a whistle from the valley entrance. It was the signal that had been prearranged with the rafters. The Whites jumped up and rushed towards the gap. The Indians stayed at the fire. When the hunters arrived they were informed that the sound of hoof beats had emanated from the ravine. The men were soon prepared. They were lying under and behind the trees, tensely anticipating what was going to unfold.

In front of them lay the aforementioned bushes. The spaces between them were sufficiently lit by the moon. Hobble-Frank and Aunty Droll were lying next to each other. Ahead of them lay a fairly open stretch of ground that they attentively observed.

"There," Frank whispered. "Did you see something move over there, to the left of dat bush?"

"Yes. I saw three dark shapes. Det must be Indians."

"Good! They shall find out immediately dat I am now the proud owner of a fine rifle."

He aimed. At the same time one of the Indians rose to swiftly run across the open space. He was clearly recognizable in the light of the moon. Frank's shot cracked, and the Indian collapsed, hit in the chest. His two comrades rushed up to him to take him to safety; a rafter shot at them, but missed; they disappeared from view with the dead man.

Some time passed, no one heard or saw anything else. That was suspicious. Hence Winnetou crawled forwards, to search the area further along. After about a quarter of an hour he returned to where he had left Old Firehand, Old Shatterhand and Great Bear waiting for him. He reported:

"The warriors of the Utah have split up. Half of them remained with the horses where the trail comes out of the rock basin; the others have gone to their right where the gorge begins. They have opened up a hole, and are now walking into it."

"A hole?" Great Bear was aghast. "That means they know the submerged corridor, and my secret has been betrayed. No one else apart from Long Ear could have done that. How did he find out? Come with me! I must see if it is true."

He rushed away, along the top of the dam, and the three hunters followed him. They hid among the trees and saw the light-coloured entrance to the gorge lying below them. The pile of rocks had been removed, and by the sheen of the moon they were able to recognize the Utah who were entering the corridor.

"Yes, they know my secret," Great Bear said. "They want to get to the island to get at us from the rear, and they want to have my treasure. But they won't succeed. I must quickly go to the island. Old Firehand and Old Shatterhand will accompany me, but Winnetou must stay here; I must show him something."

He led the Apache a few paces further along to a spot where the dam fell away vertically into the lake. There lay a large boulder that weighed several hundred kilograms. It rested on a footing of small rocks that had been placed in a peculiar formation. Great Bear pointed to one of the rocks and said:

"As soon as Winnetou sees that I've lit a fire on the island, he will push this rock away, which will cause this huge boulder to roll into the water. My red brother must jump away immediately and not panic if he hears loud cracking."

"Why is the boulder supposed to roll into the water?" Winnetou asked.

"You'll see that later. There is no time to explain now; I must get away. Fast!"

He ran away, and the two hunters followed him. When he got to the fire in front of the hut, he pulled out a burning piece of wood and climbed into one of the canoes. While he ensured the flames didn't die, Firehand and Shatterhand grabbed the paddles; they pushed off the shore and steered towards the island. When they got there Great Bear hastily jumped out and rushed into the building. He moved the dry wood, which had been stacked on the fireplace, outside and lit it.

"My brothers listen!" he said and pointed to the area where he had left Winnetou behind.

From the distance they heard a short, hollow roll, and then the splash caused by the boulder. Soon after followed a cracking and crashing as if a house had collapsed.

"It is done!" Great Bear exclaimed and took a deep breath. "The Utah are lost. Come inside!"

He went back inside, into the room with the fireplace. It was placed on a movable support because the Indian pushed it aside without any great effort. An opening became visible and Great Bear listened down into it.

"They are inside; down there; I can hear them come up," he said. "Now quickly, the water inside!"

He ran outside, behind the building; the two hunters were unable to see what he was doing there; but when he returned he pointed to a nearby spot on the lake and explained:

"Can you see that the water is moving there? It is forming a whirlpool, a funnel; it is being pulled down into the corridor I've opened."

"Heavens! The Utah will drown miserably!" Old Shatterhand exclaimed.

"Yes, all of them! Not one will escape."

"Dreadful! Was that unavoidable?"

"Yes. None shall escape to tell what he's seen down there."

"But you've destroyed your own building!"

"Yes, it is destroyed and can never be restored. The treasures are lost for the people; no mortal will be able to lift them now, because the island will fill with water to the top. Come inside!"

The two Whites were gripped by a cold dread. The rising waters pushed the musty air up; they could feel it escape from the opening in the floor. That meant death for more than one hundred people.

"But our prisoners, the ones in the next room!" Old Shatterhand said. "They will also drown!"

"No. The wall will withstand the pressure for a while. But then we'll have to get them out, of course. Listen!"

They heard a sound from below, and then they saw an Indian with a torch. It was Long Ear. Great Bear wanted to let him drown as well, but upon Old Firehand's urging, he desisted from that cruelty. At the same time as the Timbabachi climbed to safety, the water inside the island became level with the one outside. The funnel-shaped whirlpool had disappeared.

Long Ear sat down next to the fire; it was impossible for him to stand. Great Bear sat down beside him, pulled out his revolver, and menacingly said:

"Now the chief of the Timbabachi may tell us how he and the Utah came to be in the corridor. If you lie, then I'll shoot a bullet into your head. Did you know the secret of the island?"

"Yes," Long Ear confessed.

"Who told you?"

"It was you."

"That is not true!"

"It is true. I was sitting over yonder under the live oak, when you came along with your son. You paused close to me and spoke of the island, of its treasures and of the duct from which the water can be drained into the canyon. Do you remember?"

"Yes, it is so. We were standing there and spoke of it. We believed we were alone."

"I understood from what you said that the corridor begins where the pile of rocks lay. The next morning you went to hunt a stag, and I used the opportunity to remove the rocks. I walked into the duct, saw the torches and knew enough. Then I piled the rocks up again."

"And today you went to the Utah to reveal the secret!"

"No. I wanted to spy on them, but they caught me. I only spoke of the corridor and the island to save myself."

"That was cowardly. Had Old Shatterhand not noticed that you were missing, you would have been successful with your treachery, and our souls would be entering the Eternal Hunting Grounds tomorrow already. Did you see what lies at the bottom of the island?"

"Yes."

"And did you open the packets?"

"Only one"

"What was in it?"

"A god, made from pure gold."

"No human eye will ever see it again, not even yours. What do you think you deserve?"

The Timbabachi remained silent.

"Death, tenfold death! But you once were my friend and comrade, and these palefaces don't wish that I kill you. You shall live, but only if you do what I demand from you."

"What do you demand?"

"I want your solemn vow, your most sacred oath, that you will not ever tell anyone about the island and what it contains."

"I'm prepared to swear it."

"Not now, later. In addition I demand that you do as Old Firehand wishes. He wants to buy the rock basin from you, to live there. You will sell the place to him, as well as the trail that leads from there to Silver-Lake."

"We don't need the basin because it is useless, no horse finds grazing in there."

"How much do you ask for it?"

"I must first talk to the other Timbabachi about it."

"They will ask you what they ought to demand, and you shall determine the price. And I will tell you now what that will be. Old Firehand will give you twenty rifles and twenty pounds of powder, ten blankets, fifty knives and thirty pounds of tobacco. That is adequate payment. Will you agree to it?"

"I agree, and I will ensure that the others will also agree."

"You will have to accompany Old Firehand and a number of witnesses to the nearest chiefs of the palefaces, so that the purchase will be made valid there. You will receive an additional present for doing that, large or small, a lot or a little, as you deserve, or as Old Firehand deems appropriate. You can see that I look after your interests; but I hope that you let me forget your betrayal. Now call a few of your warriors across to move the Utah prisoners to the shore, so that they won't drown as well!"

Long Ear obeyed the request, and it was high time that the prisoners were brought to safety. When the last of them was placed outside the building on the ground, there was a cracking and gurgling; the water had collapsed the thin wall and filled that chamber as well. Had they waited ten more minutes, the Utah chiefs would have drowned as well.

They were moved to the shore in the canoes, and entrusted into the care of the Timbabachi. Long Ear wasn't permitted to join them, as he was considered too untrustworthy after all. He was made to accompany the hunters to the valley entrance, where the Whites were still attentively guarding it from their posts because the Utah were standing opposite them and hadn't retreated yet.

The enemy warriors didn't now where they stood. Most of those who were supposed to go to the island had already entered the submerged corridor when it suddenly collapsed because it had been crushed from above with a huge rock and clay mass. That same mass had crushed many of the intruders and blocked the duct so completely and tightly, that the lake water could not escape. And that had been Great Bear's intentions. The water wasn't supposed to drain into the gorge but enter the hidden chambers of the island.

The few Utah at the end of the group, those who hadn't been buried, had fled back out of the duct in panic, and had returned to the others to tell them what had happened. They didn't know whether or not everyone in the corridor was lost, or whether those who hadn't directly been under the collapse had made it to the island. If the latter was the case, then they were going to attack the Whites from the rear. They waited for that to happen minute after minute, but time passed and the night turned to dawn without their hopes being fulfilled. At that point it became clear that all of them had become a victim of the catastrophe.

Day broke and still the Utah were in the same place with their horses. So as not to be taken unawares by the palefaces, they had posted several guards. Then Old Shatterhand came into view from under the trees. He called to them that he wanted to speak to their leader. The Indian in question was convinced that the hunter had no treacherous intentions, and approached him. When they met, Old Shatterhand said:

"Do you know that we are holding several of your chiefs and warriors hostages?"

"I know it. They are the most famous of our men," the man grimly replied.

"And do you know what happened to your warriors who entered the submerged corridor?"

"No."

"The duct collapsed and the water rushed in; they all drowned. Only Long Ear has escaped. The expected two hundred Navajo have also just arrived. We are far superior to you in numbers, but we do not wish to spill your blood, and instead wish to offer peace to you. The hostages do not believe us that so many of your warriors have lost their lives in the lake. One of you is going to have to tell them, to convince them. If they don't agree to peace, they must die within the hour, and we will chase and pursue you until you collapse. Be smart and come with me! I will lead you to the chiefs. Talk to them, and then you can return here."

The man stared at the ground for a while, and then said:

"Old Shatterhand knows no treachery. You will keep your word and let me return here. I trust you and go with you."

He informed his warriors of his intention, took off his weapons, and then followed the hunter to the lake. Life had become much more busy there, because the Navajo had really arrived. They were eager to avenge the defeat their fellow warriors had suffered, and it had taken the mediators more than the usual persuasiveness to sway their inclination towards peace.

The hostages were freed from their ties; they were sitting together under sufficient guard when Old Shatterhand brought their comrade. He sat down with them, and then Long Ear was sent to join them, and to explain exactly how the catastrophe had unfolded. No one else became involved in their meeting; they were forced to recognize at last that there was no assistance forthcoming from the outside.

Their discussion took a long while; then Long Ear reported that they had decided to accept the peace offer. Consequently, a ceremonious powwow ensued with the leaders of the Whites and those of the Indians; it lasted for several hours, and many speeches were made until the peace pipe made its rounds at last.

The result was an 'everlasting' peace between all parties; none of the sides were obliged to pay restitution; the prisoners were freed, and everyone, the Utah, the Navajo and the Timbabachi, pledged friendship to the palefaces, who were going to work in the rock basin, and to foster that friendship.

Thereupon everyone went on a large hunt that lasted until the evening, and brought home much game. Of course the evening meal consisted of roasts, of which the Indians managed to eat seemingly impossible amounts. The festivities lasted until the early morning hours. The rising sun watched as the heroes of the peace pact wrapped their blankets around themselves to sleep.

As far as the drawing was concerned, which Red Brinkley had stolen, it had disappeared; it would have been useless at that point anyway.

The Whites found the duty of treating Great Wolf with friendliness exceedingly difficult. He was the one who had trespassed the most against them; he carried the responsibility of everything that had happened; but even he was forgiven.

Of course the entire next day was used to rest and sleep. The hour of separation came the following morning. The Utah moved north, and the Navajo south. The Timbabachi also returned to their home wigwams. Long Ear promised to hold a powwow about the sale of the rock basin, and then to report the results. He returned by the third day and informed everyone that the meeting had taken place, and the price determined by Great Bear had been agreed to. It was then a matter of sealing and validating the purchase with the appropriate authorities.

The diggings were thus secured, and work could begin, which would be very soon. It created much enthusiasm and the men raved about it and expressed their hopes, with which only one person didn't concur—Castlepool. He had hired Humply-Bill and Gunstick-Uncle to take him to Frisco; neither had any inclination to honour their promise, under the circumstances. Castlepool's notebook contained sizeable amounts in both their names. If they accompanied the Englishman, then they could expect to be paid honoraries and gratuities for many more adventures between Silver-Lake and San Francisco. However, they stood to gain much more from the placer that Old Firehand was in the process of purchasing. Hence they wanted to stay, and the Englishman was understanding enough not to take offence. Besides, it would be a while before the work in the rock basin got under way. Lord Castlepool had plenty of time to traipse around the mountains with his two guides in pursuit of adventures.

Old Firehand rode to Fillmore City with Great Bear and Long Ear, where the purchase was put in order. The town was also a suitable place to order the necessary machines and tools. Aunty Droll had accompanied them in order to make a notarized statement that Red Brinkley was dead, in front of witnesses. He intended to claim the bounty that he had been after for so long.

A beautiful fraternal relationship had developed between Ellen and Little Bear. He was keeping her company every day, and if he was late occasionally, then she missed him to no end.

At last, after almost one and a half months, the message came that the machines were ready to be picked up. A group of men left to do that, and Castlepool used the good opportunity to join the company and thus reach inhabited places where he would easily find other guides.

When the troop reached Fillmore City it caused a stir. The residents had guessed that there was a large mining enterprise in the making and went to great efforts to find out more. But the prospectors maintained their silence because it wasn't in their interest to attract all manner of adventurous rabble.

Then, when everything was in place at the lake, the engineer began to develop his operation. The water pipe was installed, and then the bottom sand of the basin was tackled first.

Flour and other provisions had been brought up in sufficient quantities to stock the food store. Three people were out hunting every day, in rotation, and supplied the meat, while the others worked in the placer. Ellen's activities frequently also extended to the meal preparations, and her presence became a genuine comfort for the tough men.

The hopes pinned on the placer were confirmed. The sand was rich in gold and led to the expectation that the yield from the solid rock would be just as rich. The gold dust and the nuggets accumulated day by day; every evening the proceeds were weighed and assessed, and when the result was positive, as it always was, then Droll would merrily whisper to his cousin:

"If it keeps going the way it is, then I'll be able to purchase det farmstead pretty soon. Business is booming."

To which Hobble-Frank would reply as usual:

"And my villa is almost complete, at least in my head. Dat's going to be a composing construction by the beautiful banks of the River Elbe, and the name I'll give it will be even more composing. I have spoken. Howgh!"

The End

About The Translator

Some time in my early twenties, I left Switzerland for a new life in New Zealand. I chose to acquire New Zealand citizenship and am proud to be able to call myself a Kiwi. In 1988, together with my Australian husband, David, I moved to Tasmania and have lived on Australia's island state ever since.

My passion about the rare and threatened Tasmanian fauna and flora inspired a series of illustrated children's adventure novels set in picturesque Tasmanian wilderness, titled *The Green Heart Books*, with: *Kangaroo Dog, Bluegum Christmas, Tazzie Devil Double Trouble, Quoll Quandary, Golden Wings* and *Bat Whispers*; my own Bernese Mountain Dog, Bertie, inspired *Swiss Tradition In Black And White*, a compact work about the history of this Swiss icon, the breed's development and how to care for a magnificent and loving friend.

The remote and exotic island of Tasmania has also provided the inspiration for *Wafters, Frazzlers & Black Unicorns*, a collection of Tasmanian fairy-tales set in a Tasmanian garden, which tell of Peachblossom's adventures while fighting the evil deeds of the two-headed troll.

Birds In Tasmania, by David Irwin, is a photo book of birds captured within the natural landscapes of our Tasmanian home in the south-eastern corner of the island. The album with its unusual images is a continuation of our combined endeavours to document the diversity and uniqueness of Australia's island state.

In 2004 I began the translation of the Karl May novel "Holy Night!". Four years later, in 2008, I became the first author/ translator to have translated and produced the entire unabridged Winnetou trilogy from Karl May's last authorized version of 1909; it is the first publishing of the unabridged trilogy as a homogeneous work by a single translator in English; my translations and my research of the work created by the enigmatic German author of the nineteenth century are now available from Verlag Reinhard Marheinecke.

More Karl May Translations By Marlies Bugmann

Savage to Saint, The Karl May Story (Biography)
Including:
Winnetou (1878) (Travel Fiction)
A Blizzard (Travel Fiction)
The Rose Of Shiraz (Travel Fiction)
The Fable Of Sitara (Philosophical)

Inn-Nu-Woh to Merhameh (Travel Fiction) - Companion to
Savage To Saint, The Karl May Story

Winnetou I (Travel Fiction)
Winnetou II (Travel Fiction)
Winnetou III (Travel Fiction)

Winnetou—Book 4 (Travel Fiction)

"Holy Night!", A Winnetou Story (Travel Fiction)

Old Surehand—Book 1, A Winnetou Story (Travel Fiction)
Old Surehand—Book 2, A Winnetou Story (Travel Fiction)

From The Rio De La Plata To The Cordilleras—Book 1 / 2
(Travel Fiction)

Old Shatterhand—Genesis, A Winnetou Story Collection
(Travel Fiction)

*Karl May: The Inca's Legacy, (An Adventure In South
America)* (Adventure Novel)

Karl May: Black Mustang, An Adventure With Winnetou
(Adventure Novel)

Other Books
By Marlies Bugmann

Swiss Tradition in Black and White
History and breed information about the Bernese Mountain
Dog.

Noldi Mister Capricorn
Guetnachtgschichtli us Auschtralie zum Vorläse.

The Green Heart Books
The adventures of the children at Sassafras Creek Valley and
their unique Tasmanian animals:
Kangaroo Dog
Bluegum Christmas
Tazzie Devil Double Trouble
Quoll Quandary
Golden Wings
Bat Whispers

Wafters, Frazzlers & Black Unicorns
Magical and impossible adventures with a two-headed troll in
a Tasmanian garden

My Sketch Book
My Sketch Book 2
A selection of more than one hundred and sixty drawings,
sketches and studies of various subjects and objects;
illustrations for my own and other authors' books.

Birds In Tasmania by David Irwin
A full colour photograph album capturing Tasmania's rich
bird life, featuring the photography of David Irwin.

All books available through http://www.tasmanianartist.com

Appendix

URLs to online documentation used in chapters 'Victory In Vienna', 'Old Shatterhand's 'Magic' Rifle', 'Research', and 'On Butler's Farm', as given in the relevant footnotes, are listed in this appendix with additional source information. All links are listed on the following website: http://australianfriendsofkarlmay.yolasite.com, follow 'Silver-Lake Maps' in the navigation panel. All URLs were last called up in February 2012. The author/translator assumes no responsibility for the contents of any external websites.

Victory In Vienna
Page lix – footnote 1
http://www.karl-may-gesellschaft.de/kmg/seklit/jbkmg/1970/47.htm
Documentation of fragments of Karl May's speech in Vienna, 1912

Old Satterhand's 'Magic' Rifle
Page lxii – footnote 1
http://lewisandclarkjournals.unl.edu/index.html
The Journals of the Lewis & Clark Expedition – see also Karl May & Josiah Gregg, free PDF from http://australianfriendsofkarlmay.yolasite.com

Page lxix – Videos and information to rifles on Rifle Poster (as well as the Girandoni Air Rifle as used by Lewis & Clark)
http://youtu.be/-pqFyKh-rUI
Video: Girandoni air rifle as used by Lewis and Clark. A National Firearms Museum Treasure Gun
http://youtu.be/Jopg6DdEQZw
Video: Colt 1839 revolving percussion rifle. A National Firearms Museum Treasure Gun
http://www.youtube.com/watch?v=wOZL-zVY5wY
Video: Samuel Hawken Plains Rifle. A National Firearms Museum Treasure Gun
http://www.nramuseum.com/the-museum/the-galleries/a-nation-asunder/case-37-arms-for-the-union-union-rifles,-a-northern-arms-factory/us-new-haven-arms-co-henry-lever-action-repeating-rifle.aspx
Images and info on Henry Leaver Action Repeating Rifle

Page lxiii – footnote 2
http://www.kancoll.org/books/gregg/
Commerce Of The Prairies, Josiah Gregg, 1844, 1845 – see also Karl May & Josiah Gregg, PDF download from my website.

Page lxvi – footnote 3
http://www.varsityrendezvous.com/pdf/HawkenRifle.pdf
PDF download: *History of the Hawken Rifle*, text by Varsity
Scout Blackfoot Fort Mountain Man Rendezvous

Page lxvi – footnote 3
http://en.wikipedia.org/wiki/Hawken_rifle
Wikipedia article on Hawken Rifle

Research
Page lxxxi – footnote 1
http://www.karl-may-
gesellschaft.de/kmg/seklit/biographie/747.htm (p759/year 1889)
*Chronologische Übersicht und Zusammenfassung: Der Mensch
und sein Werk*
Online edition of '*Hermann Wohlgschaft, Grosse Karl May
Biographie*'

Page lxxxiii – footnote 2
http://books.google.com.au/books?id=0zFOAAAAYAAJ&dq=%2
2zw%C3%B6lf+sprachen%22&source=gbs_navlinks_s
*Twelve Languages from south-western North America (Pueblo-
und Apache-Dialect; Tonto, Tonkawa, Digger, Utah): a
Dictionary by Albert S Gatschet*, published in 1876

Page lxxxviii – footnote 3
http://www.karl-may-
gesellschaft.de/kmg/seklit/jbkmg/1997/292.htm
Wolfgang Hammer, '*Der Schatz im Silbersee*' – eine
Strukturanalyse

Page lxxxix – footnote 4
http://www.wild-west-reporter.com/wp-
content/uploads/2010/03/A5-Flyer-KMSG-2010.pdf
(http://www.wild-west-reporter.com/osterreich/)
Wild-West-Reporter, News vom Kalkberg, (Oesterreich / Gfoehl /
2010) advertisement for open air play, PDF download

Page xci – footnote 5
http://www.discoveroakley.com/city-of-oakley/history-oakley
History of Oakley

Page xci – footnote 6
http://forums.ghosttowns.com/showthread.php?16740-
Sheridan-Kansas
History of Ghost Towns and Historical Sites

Page xci – footnote 7
http://www.kansasmemory.org/item/214196/page/1
Antique map depicting Wallace County before Logan County was
split from it.

Page xci – footnote 8
http://www.kans.com/bfrahm/sheridan.htm
Personal website of Bruce Frahm and Janice Frahm, A Tale of the
Ghost Town of Sheridan

Page xciv – footnote 9
http://www.karl-may-
gesellschaft.de/kmg/seklit/jbkmg/1991/324.htm
Andreas Graf, *"Habe gedacht, Alles Schwindel"*, Balduin
Möllhausen und Karl May–Beispiele literarischer Adaption und
Variation (Jahrbuch der Karl-May-Gesellschaft 1991)

Page xciv – footnote 10
http://www.lexikus.de/Reisen-in-die-Felsengebirge-
Nordamerikas--Band-1
Volume 1: *Tagebuch einer Reise vom Mississippi nach den
Kuesten der Suedsee*, by Moellhausen

Page xciv – footnote 10
http://www.lexikus.de/Reisen-in-die-Felsengebirge-
Nordamerikas--Band-2
Volume 2: *Reisen in die Felsengebirge Nordamerikas bis zum
Hochplateau von Neu-Mexiko*, by Moellhausen

Page xcv – footnote 11
http://www.kancoll.org/khq/1948/48_3_mollhaus.htm
*The Pictorial Record of the Old West: VI. Heinrich Balduin
Möllhausen* by Robert Taft August, 1948 (Vol. 16, No. 3), pages
225 to 244

Page cii – footnote 13
http://www.maproom.org/00/09/present.php?m=0083
Stielers Hand-Atlas Sheet 1

Page ciii – footnote 13
http://www.maproom.org/00/09/present.php?m=0086
Stielers Hand-Atlas Sheet 4

Page ciii – footnote 14
http://quod.lib.umich.edu/m/moa/AFK4383.0002.001?rgn=ma
in;view=fulltext
*Reports of explorations and surveys, to ascertain the most
practicable and economical route for a railroad from the
Mississippi River to the Pacific Ocean*: United States. War Dept.,
Henry, Joseph, 1797-1878., Baird, Spencer Fullerton, 1823-1887.,
United States. Army.

Page civ – footnote 15
http://digitool.library.colostate.edu/webclient/DeliveryManager
?pid=80825
PDF download of *Renaming of the Grand River, Colo. Hearing
before the Committee on Interstate and Foreign Commerce of
the House of Representatives, Sixty-sixth Congress, third session
on H.J. Res. 460, February 8, 1921*

Page civ – footnote 16
http://www.gregmetcalf.com/stallions.html
Chapter 24, PDF download, name variant of upper Colorado, p. 488

Page cv – footnote 17
http://www.karl-may-
gesellschaft.de/kmg/seklit/biographie/747.htm
*Chronologische Übersicht und Zusammenfassung: Der Mensch
und sein Werk* (Hermann Wohlgschaft, Grosse Karl May
Biographie)

Page cvi – footnote 18
http://go.owu.edu/~jbkrygie/krygier_html/envision.html
*Envisioning the American West: Maps, the Representational
Barrage of 19th Century Expedition Reports, and the Production
of Scientific Knowledge* J.B. Krygier Published in 1997 in
Cartography and GIS 24:1, pp. 27-50. (3a. Egloffstein's
Illustrations: "*A Curious Schizophrenia*")

Page cvii – footnote 19
http://www.geographicus-
archive.com/P/AntiqueMap/Southwest-johnson-1864
Antique map showing inscription 'Silver Lake Desert'

Page cvii – footnote 20
http://www.karl-may-
gesellschaft.de/kmg/seklit/jbkmg/1997/361.
htm#a34, (page 377, footnote 34), Eckehard Koch, "... *den Roten
gehörte alles Land; es ist ihnen von uns genommen worden ...*"
Zum zeitgeschichtlichen Hintergrund von Mays 'Schatz im
Silbersee'

Page cviii – footnote 21
http://balsam-hill-cabin.com/php/book/ch1.php
*Salt Lake City, Big Cottonwood Canyon, and William Stuart
Brighton*, by Rod Morris of Balsam Hill Cabin

Page cviii – footnote 22
http://americantalesandtrails.com/history/brighton-jewel-of-
the-wasatch-mountains-of-utah
Brighton – Jewel of the Wasatch Mountains of Utah, By: Jaromy
Jessop

Page cviii – footnote 23
http://www.nevadaobserver.com/Reading%20Room%20Docum
ents/stenhouse_2.htm
The Nevada Observer, June 1, 2010, Nevada's Online State News
Journal

Page cxii – footnote 24
http://quod.lib.umich.edu/m/moa/AFK4383.0002.001/72
Illustration of cliffs along 'Grand River' (today's Gunnison River),
from Making Of America (MOA) digital library. *Reports of
explorations and surveys, to ascertain the most practicable and
economical route for a railroad from the Mississippi River to the
Pacific Ocean*: Author: United States. War Dept.

Page cxii – footnote 24
http://www.karl-may-
gesellschaft.de/kmg/primlit/jugend/silbers/reprint/zeitung/288.gif
Illustration to Karl May's '*Der Schatz Im Silbersee*', depicting the
arrival in the dry canyon below Silver-Lake.
(Also see image on my website.)

Page cxvi – footnote 25
http://americanindian.net/StatesUV.html
Online text of *The Indian Tribes of North America* by John R.
Swanton, 1953

Page cxvi – footnote 25
http://www.karl-may-
gesellschaft.de/kmg/seklit/jbkmg/1997/361.htm#8 (page 365,
footnote 8)
Eckehard Koch, "... *den Roten gehörte alles Land; es ist ihnen
von uns genommen worden* ..." Zum zeitgeschichtlichen
Hintergrund von Mays 'Schatz im Silbersee'

Page cxvi – footnote 25
http://www.karl-may-gesellschaft.de/kmg/seklit/m-
kmg/093/bilder/m093s026.gif
Page/Link 26 of http://www.karl-may-
gesellschaft.de/kmg/seklit/m-kmg/093/, Mitteilungen Der Karl-
May-Gesellschaft #93, Sep 1992, References to various sources
used by Karl May.

Page cxvi – footnote 25
http://scholarship.rice.edu/jsp/xml/1911/27279/1/aa00374.tei.h
tml
Personal narrative of explorations and incidents in Texas, New
Mexico, California, Sonora, and Chihuahua, volume 2: Connected
with the United States and Mexican Boundary Commission,
during the years 1850, '51, '52 and '53, by John Russel Bartlett
(digital version)

Page cxvii – footnote 26
http://www.davidrumsey.com/luna/servlet/detail/RUMSEY~8~
1~33 527~1171013:Vereinigte-Staaten-von-Nord-
America?sort=Pub_List_No_InitialSort%2CPub_Date%2CPub_
List_No%2CSeries_No&qvq=q:Sohr;sort:Pub_List_No_InitialS
ort%2CPub_Date%2CPub_List_No%2Cseries_No;lc:RUMSEY~
8~1&mi=82&trs=134
David Rumsey Historical Map Collection, North America,
German atlas of 1855 by C. Flemming, in Glogau (also called
Sohr-Berghaus Hand-Atlas), placing Timbabachi south of Grand
and Green Rivers confluence.

Page cxvii – footnote 28
http://www.geographicus.com/P/AntiqueMap/CaliforniaUtah
NewMexicoArizona-johnson-1863
Geographicus Fine Antique Maps, 1863 Johnson Map placing
Timbabachi south of Grand and Green Rivers confluence.

Page cxxii – footnote 30
http://www.cchscolorado.com
Comanche Crossing Historical Society, ...where the first
continuous chain of rails from the Atlantic Ocean to the Pacific
Ocean was joined August 15, 1870

Page cxxii – footnote 31
http://en.wikipedia.org/wiki/Kansas_Territory
Wikipedia article about Kansas Territory

Page cxxii – footnote 32
http://utahrails.net/up/kansas-pacific.php
Kansas-Pacific Railroad history copyright 2000-2011 by Don
Strack

Chapter 4, *On Butler's Farm*
Page 148 – footnote 5
http://www.karl-may-
gesellschaft.de/kmg/seklit/jbkmg/1997/361.htm#a4
Eckehard Koch, "... *den Roten gehörte alles Land; es ist ihnen
von uns genommen worden ...", Zum zeitgeschichtlichen
Hintergrund von Mays 'Schatz im Silbersee'*, page 362

Page 148 – footnote 5
http://history.lawrence.com/project/community/thesis/chap4.h
tml
Small Town Germans: The Germans of Lawrence, Kansas, from
1854 to 1918

---

endnote

Because Indonesia represents the largest Karl May fan community outside of Europe, and the numbers of the Indonesian language Karl May books have thus far created a surprisingly long list, I've included it here, as supplied by Pandu Ganesa, to illustrate how the 'narrow genre' of Karl May's unique work is continuing to spread at an almost constant rate.

Karl May books in Indonesian language

Published by Noordhoff-Kolff NV in the 1950s
1. *Raja Minyak* (*The Oil Prince*) (1 & 2)
2. *Disudut-sudut Balkan* (*In The Gorges Of The Balkans*) (1 & 2)
3. *Winnetou Gugur* (*Winnetou's Death* [*Winnetou III*]) (1 & 2)
4. *Wasiat Winnetou* (*The Testament Of Winnetou* [*Winnetou IV*]) (1 & 2)

Published by Pustaka Dua Tiga in the 1960s:
1. *Winnetou I* (in 6 volumes of very small trim sizes)
2. *Winnetou II* (in 5 volumes of very small trim sizes).

Published by Pradnyaparamita, between 1961 and 1980
1. *Kepala Suku Apache* (*Winnetou I*)

2. *Pemburu Binantang Berbulu Tebal di Rio Pecos* (*Winnetou II*)
3. *Rahasia Bison Putih* (*The Son of the Bear Hunter part I and II*)
4. *Llano Estacado* (*Old Surehand I*)
5. *Gunung Setan di Rocky Mountains* (*Old Surehand II/III*)
6. *Putra-putra Suku Mimbrenjo* (*Satan and Ischariot I*)
7. *Old Shatterhand Sebagai Detektif* (*Satan and Ischariot II/III*)
8. *Harta Terpendam Dalam Danau Perak* (*Treasure of the Silver Lake*)
9. *Raja Minyak* (*Oil Prince*)
10. *Mustang Hitam* (*Black Mustang*)
11. *Surat Wasiat Inca* (*The Legacy of the Inca*)
12. *Winnetou Gugur* (*Winnetou III*)
13. *Wasiat Winnetou* (*Winnetou IV*)
14. *Harta Karun Winnetou* (*Weihnacht!*)
15. *Menuju Daerah Silver Lion I*
16. *Kara Ben Nemsi* (*Through the Desert*)
17. *Di Kurdistan*
18. *Dari Bagdad Ke Stambul*
19. *Di Pelosok-pelosok Balkan*
20. *Kafilah Budak Belian* (*The Caravan of Slaves*)
21. *Menjelajah Negeri Skiptar*
22. *Kara Nirwan Khan di Albania* (*The Schut*)
23. *Puri Rodriganda* (*Waldroschen I*)
24. *Piramida Bangsa Aztek* (*Waldroschen II*)
25. *Hantu Pegunungan Baru* (*Buschgespenst*)
The titles are derived from the Dutch titles (translated to either English or German where given).

Karl May novels published in Bahasa Indonesia in the twenty-first century based on the original 19th century text by Karl May:
Note: The publisher's name, Pustaka Primatama, Jakarta, Indonesia, is the imprint (or publishing brand name) of the Indonesian Karl May Society Paguyuban Karl May Indonesia (PKMI).

1. 2002 *Dan Damai di Bumi!* (*And Peace on Earth!*), Kepustakaan Populer Gramedia (KPG), Jakarta
2. 2003 *Winnetou I: Kepala Suku Apache* (*The Chief of the Apache*), Pustaka Primatama
3. 2004 *Winnetou II: Si Pencari Jejak* (*The Scout*), Pustaka Primatama
4. 2004 *Winnetou III: Winnetou Gugur* (*Winnetou's Death*), Pustaka Primatama
5. 2005 *Kara Ben Nemsi I: Menjelajah Gurun* (*Through the Desert*), Pustaka Primatama
6. 2005 *Kara Ben Nemsi II: Penyembah Setan* (*Devil Worshipper*), Pustaka Primatama

7. 2005 *Kara Ben Nemsi III*: *Petualangan di Kurdistan* (*Through Wild Kurdistan*), Pustaka Primatama
8. 2006 *Anak Pemburu Beruang* (*The Son of the Bear Hunter*), Pustaka Primatama
9. 2006 *Hantu Llano Estacado* (*The Ghost of Llano Estacado*), Pustaka Primatama
10. 2007 *Winnetou IV*: *Ahli Waris Winnetou* (*The Heirs of Winnetou*), Pustaka Primatama
11. 2008 *Old Surehand I*: *Oase di Llano Estacado* (*The Oasis in Llano Estacado*), Pustaka Primatama
12. 2009 *Kara Ben Nemsi IV*: *Kafilah Maut* (*The Caravan of Death*), Pustaka Primatama
13. 2009 *Kara Ben Nemsi V*: *Dari Bagdad ke Stambul* (*From Bagdad to Stambul*), Pustaka Primatama
13. 2009 *Harta di Danau Perak* (*Treasure of the Silver Lake*), Pustaka Primatama
14. 2009 *Raja Minyak* (*The Oil Prince*), Pustaka Primatama
15. 2009 *Mustang Hitam* (*Black Mustang*), Pustaka Primatama
16. 2010 *Old Surehand II*: *Di Jefferson City* (*In Jefferson City*), Pustaka Primatama
17. 2010 *Pusaka Inca* (*The Legacy of the Inca*), Pustaka Primatama
18. 2010 *Di Pelosok Negeri Asing* (*On Foreign Trails*), Pustaka Primatama

Non-fiction works
1. 2010 *Otobiografi* (*My Life and my Aspirations*), Pustaka Primatama

Collection of short stories:
1. 2004 Collection of stories: *Desert and Prairie I* (*The Oil Inferno, Inn-nu-woh* and others), Pustaka Primatama

Books for children with colour illustrations published by Kepustakaan Populer Gramedia, KPG (2002)
1. *Winnetou I*
2. *Winnetou II*
3. *Anak Pemburu Beruang* (*The Son of the Bear Hunter*)
4. *Harta di Danau Perak* (*Treasure of the Silver Lake*)
5. *Si Raja Minyak* (*The Oil Prince*)
6. *Malam Natal di Rocky Mountains* (*Weihnacht!*)

Comics in colour, 2006
Winnetou I and *Winnetou II* in 5 volumes, published by Gaya Favorit Press, in cooperation with PKMI

Nomics (novel and comic combined), 2007
3 volumes of unfinished interpretation of *Winnetou I, Mizan Dar!*
Publisher, in cooperation with PKMI.
1. *Beginning of the Adventure*
2. *Teacher of the Apache*
3. *The Kiowa*

Comic in black and white
1. 2009 *Api Maut vol 1* (*Death Fire, Oil Fire*), Pustaka Primatama
2. 200x *Api Maut vol 2* (in progress)
3. 2009 *Pasir Maut vol 1* (*Er Raml El Helakh 1*), Pustaka Primatama
4. 2009 *Pasir Maut vol 2* (*Er Raml El Helakh 2*), Pustaka Primatama
5. 200x *Pasir Maut vol 3* (in progress)

Expected to be published in 2011
1. *Winnetou dan Cerita-cerita Lainnya* (*Winnetou and other Stories*): a compilation of 25 short stories, in the Wild West, Middle East, and Far-Away Countries.
2. *Weihnacht!*

Novels in the process of being translated, as well as at editing stage, by Pustaka Primatama
1. *At the Pacific Ocean*
2. *Kara Ben Nemsi VII: In the Gorges of the Balkans*
3. *Old Surehand III: Di Gunung Setan* (*At Devil's Head*)

Novels available as free e-books:
1. *Puri Rodriganda* (*Waldroschen I*)
2. *Piramida Bangsa Aztek* (*Waldroschen II*)
3. *Hantu Pegunungan Baru* (*Buschgespenst*)
from http://id.karlmay.wikia.com/wiki/E-Book